DORA THE DUCHESS;

OR,

LOVERS' TRIALS!

A MYSTERY OF THE HIGHWAY,

BY

CAPTAIN THE HONOURABLE G. V. BELTONE.

LONDON: H. VICKERS, STRAND, AND ALL BOOKSELLERS.

MDCCCLXI.

DORA THE DUCHESS;

OR,

LOVERS TRIALS!,

A TALE OF THE HIGHWAY,

BY

CAPTAIN THE HONOURABLE G. V. BELTONE.

CHAPTER I.

OLD TYBURN GATE—THE INNOCENT HEART—A FIGHT FOR A LIFE—THE COACH AND THE DEATH CART—THE ESCAPE IN THE SNOW—DORA'S RESCUE—THE SPY AND THE REFUGE.

ON the 28th day of October, 1760, in the midst of such a snowstorm as London

had rarely witnessed so early in the season, there was brought out to die at Tyburn, with all the fearful formalities of the law, and amid such a mass of spectators as never scarcely before had assembled at an execution, one of the most beautiful young creatures the light of day ever shone upon.

The culprit—she was called the culprit, although in reality as innocent as an angel, was a girl of about 18 years of age, and of

No. 1.—DORA.

such wondrous beauty that tears started to the eyes of all who looked upon her on the progress to death.

King George the Second was lying dead at the Palace of Kensington. On the table close to the head of the bed on which he had breathed his last there were several papers and documents. One ran as follows:—

"There are too many doubts of the guilt of the girl, and my Lord Kingston is an unscrupulous man, therefore her execution will—"

There the writing left off abruptly: it was in the hand of the king—who shall doubt but that the following words would have been "not take place"—but death had stilled that hand for ever, and the writing, which as that of a living king, would have had the power of life, belonged to a dead one, and had no vitality.

And so this young girl so young, so fair, with such a freshness of beauty in her eyes, and on her brow, that no guilt could live in her sweet presence, was brought out to die.

To die by the hands of the common executioner.

To bid adieu to the world on that day of storm at old Tyburn-gate, and thousands of people were there assembled, not exactly to be pleased to see the last moments of one whom all must have deeply pitied, but to hope that even at the last hour mercy, as it would have been called, but justice as it would really have been, might intervene to save her.

But there was the terrible instrument of death. There was the fearful machinery by which a heroic soul was to be sent to its account long, long before Heaven itself would have demanded it.

The mob increased each moment, and as the head of the ghastly procession that brought the condemned one to death emerged from among the houses at the top of the Oxford-road, there arose such a cry from the densely packed assemblage, that the officers were alarmed, and closed more compactly around the victim.

There was one man who had mounted on the top of some scaffolding of a house that was undergoing repair close at hand, and he, with violent gestures, beckoned the cavalcade to come on more quickly.

Suddenly the attention of the mob was drawn towards this man. He was tall, bulky, and ferocious looking, and he had the deep indentation of an old sword cut over his right brow.

With one voice then the mob shouted out—

"Turnbull! Turnbull! It is the villain, Turnbull, the false witness!"

This man tried to escape when he heard his name thus mentioned, and he ran along the scaffolding where a thousand hands were ready to seize him. He cried and shrieked for mercy, but he was soon down, and tossed from hand to hand until against a doorway he was thrown, apparently bereft of life.

All this was done in less than a minute of time, but it was wonderful to see how that slight act of violence had inflamed the feelings of the crowd.

There were shouts, cries, screams, and yells from hundreds of throats, and by the time the procession of death got freely clear of the houses in the Oxford-road, and confronted the scaffold, the officers who accompanied it on horseback began to see that there was danger.

One of the body was instantly detached, and at a gallop went back down the Oxford-road for assistance.

It was too late!

The horse that drew the cart in which was the condemned girl—in which was, with a refinement of cruelty that was common enough a hundred years ago, the coffin which was to hold her lifeless remains—in which was the Reverend ordinary of Newgate—that horse grew restive, and would not advance another step.

It was in vain that the officers struck the creature about the head and face with the flats of their hangers—it was in vain that one actually wounded it. The horse would not move a step.

And now from among the straw which was at the bottom of the cart there rose up a man.

A man he was of small stature—of thin, spare, foxy aspect—he wore a red nightcap on his head.

The mob knew him in a moment. He had hidden till then—he had not intended to make his appearance until the last moment, when his services would be required.

He was the executioner!

But the restiveness of the horse had forced him to some action, and so he rose up, and the people saw that he said something, and that he pointed to the dreadul beam which towered above all their heads at Tyburn-gate.

Such a shout of rage then arose from the populace as was perfectly appaling to hear, and the executioner cowered before it.

There was immediately a rush towards the fatal cart.

Then officers, people, horses, all became in a few moments mingled together in one scene of inextricable confusion.

The officers fought fiercely, and beat down upon the heads of the people with their hangers, and then, standing up in the middle of the cart appeared the young girl who had been brought out to die.

So young, so fair, such a gentle, dear, kind English girl she looked. Her beautiful hair hung in wavy masses far below her waist. The plain grey dress she wore—close around her delicate throat and right down to her small hands, set off her faultless figure to great advantage.

And now, in the middle of all this wild turmoil and uproar, she raised her hands as if in an attitude of prayer, and while the snow fell upon her beautiful hair—while it melted into tears upon her fair face, she cried aloud—

"I am innocent! oh, I am innocent! Henry! Henry! save me! oh, save me!"

There was a hackney coach drawn up at the corner of the Edgware-road. It was one of those coaches the top of which could open at pleasure—and even as the young girl spoke those imploring words, her eyes fell upon that coach.

She uttered a cry of joy;

"Henry! my Henry!"

The top of the coach had been thrust open, and half kneeling on the roof—half holding to the open portion of the vehicle, was a young man. He was pale as death itself. A blood stained military undress was about him; but there was a fire in his eyes which made them look like two stars at that distance.

And the voice of this young man rose high like a note of music above all the jarring sounds of the conflict.

"Now! now!" he cried! "Dora! Dora! my Dora! Saved! saved! she is innocent."

"Innocent?" shouted the mob, as if with one breath.

The man who was on the coach box began to urge his horses forward in the direction of the cart containing the condemned.

At the same moment, far down the Oxford-road, there appeared, approaching, a troop of mounted men.

The cart was itself so wedged into the mob, that even had the horse which drew it, been willing to advance, it could not have moved a step.

"Henry! Henry! Save me! oh, save me!" cried the condemned girl.

"I come! I come!" he shouted.

The mob almost lifted forward the hackney coach and its two horses. Strong stalwart men put their shoulders to the wheels—others almost lifted the very horses off their feet—a lane was made from the coach to the cart of the condemned, as if by magic.

And now the young girl stretched out her arms, and the people could see that the flush of hope was on the fair face.

But the troop of horse was coming up the Oxford-road at a gallop.

It was a race! The cart was the goal of both parties.

"Henry! Henry! my Henry!" She cried again, and she stretched her arms still further over the side of the cart, as if she would have flown from it.

The executioner hid deep down among the straw now.

The party of horse had reached the outskirts of the crowd, and had began to trample their way through the people. A fierce contest was about to commence—some of the horsemen were already torn from their saddles. Of the party of officers who had accompanied the procession from Newgate to Tyburn, but one or two were to be seen in the midst of the mob fighting for life.

"Now! Now! my Dora!" shouted the young hero, on the roof of the coach.

The vehicle had reached the cart.

There was a cry of joy, and in a moment the condemned girl was lifted from the cart to the coach.

"Saved! saved!" cried the young man with the pale face and blood stained apparel, "Saved! May God bless you all!"

The cheer that came from ten thousand voices was tremendous.

Then the young girl herself stood up in the coach so that all could see her, and for one moment she pressed her hands upon her heart—then she placed them both upon her lips, and kissed them, and threw them, so to speak, towards the mob, while tears of grateful feeling coursed each other down her cheeks.

And the vast crowd knew that she was thanking them. They felt she was, in most expressive pantomime, telling them all that she thanked them—that she left a kiss for a life upon every cheek, because they had believed in her innocence, and saved her.

And tears then started to the eyes of strong, rough men, and there were cries and shouts of "God bless you! Off at once! They shan't harm a hair of your pretty head! We will die for you! Off and away! Bless your pretty eyes!"

Then the top of the coach was closed up—it turned and made its way through the crowd to the left hand side of the Oxford-road.

The mob opened like the waves of the sea, before some swiftly careering ship, as the coach wheeled on, and closed behind as quickly as the heaving waters close upon the tracks of the deep sea.

The fight between the party of horse that had been brought up the Oxford-road, was now at its height.

Each horseman was in the centre of a little throng, with which he had to do battle for his life.

But there were some of the men who were wise enough to abandon such a contest, and they dropped their sabres and sheathed them, and let the people do what they would, and in such cases, man and horse were only swayed to and fro in the deep surges of the crowd.

A hundred hands had seized on the cart, and it was torn plank from plank.

The clergyman was carefully hoisted over the heads of the people to a place of safety.

The executioneer was seized upon, and with cries of delight the mob moved off with him towards the scaffold.

He shrieked for mercy, and it was not until he grew so hoarse with his own shouts, that he was still from sheer exhaustion, and those who had charge of him, reached the scaffold with him.

The intention evidently was to hang him then and there at once; but the party of horse had done already a good deal of mischief to the crowd, and as the young girl had been rescued, many of the people began to make their escape down the side streets, and into the park.

A rope was placed around the neck of the hangman, and he was hoisted up to the cross beam, and then the rope broke, and down he fell.

From that moment the mob began to disperse quickly. The snow fell in huge flakes, and the sky darkened each moment. Another troop of horse began to show themselves up Park-lane.

And now a sort of panic took possession of all the crowd still on the spot, and they fled in all directions.

When the second troop of horse came up to Tyburn-gate, the authorities had the ground all to themselves.

But there was no execution.

The coach in which was Dora the condemned, and the pale young man she had named Henry, had rapidly disappeared down a narrow street, about a hundred paces above Bond-street.

She was saved!

But there were two other persons in that coach as well as Henry, the pale young man, and the fair Dora.

One of those persons was Doctor Langford, a celebrated physician of that time—the other was a little child.

The doctor had kept out of sight during the whole of the tumult, and the only remark he had made, when Dora was brought into the coach was "Thank God!"

The little girl who was about two years old, clung with frantic fondness around the neck of Dora.

The pale young man in the blood-stained uniform folded his arms around them both, as in a voice of intense affection he cried—

"My Dora! my own, dear Dora! my wife! You are saved! you are saved!"

"Dear Henry! And our dear little Mina here. Oh, I never, never forgot you both for one moment."

"Nor we you, dear Dora! nor we you."

"But your wound, Henry, your wound? Oh, Doctor Langford, how could you let him come?"

"My dear lady," said the doctor, "It was with one exception the most dangerous thing for him in the world to come out on such a day as this, with such a half healed wound as he has in his breast."

"Then why—oh why?—"

"Nay, hear me out! I said with one exception. That would have been had he staid at home, for he was rapidly contracting a fever that would have killed—a fever of the heart and mind, which I could have done nothing for."

"Ah, how much have we to thank you for!"

"Do not say anything about that yet, until at least you are in entire safety. I will speak to my man if you please."

The Doctor opened, a short distance, one of the front windows of the coach.

"Thomas! Thomas! where are we now?"

"We are in Soho, sir!"

"Is any one following?"

"Oh dear no, sir!"

"Then go as quickly as you can, and yet not by the most frequented way, to the 'Savoy.'"

"Yes, sir!"

The Doctor closed the window, and turning to Henry Dacres, who was an ensign in a regiment that was then quartered in the Tower, he said—

"I hardly know what to advise you both to do. The enemy you have in the Duke of Kingston, is so great, that I fear me, he will never pause unless he can ensure your destruction. You see that your wound is altogether owing to him, and he has very nearly succeeded in bringing to death your fair and gentle wife, on the false charge of setting fire to his house."

"He is, indeed, our enemy," said Henry Dacres, "but yet we will not abandon hope."

"No!" said Dora. "Nor will I consent to allow him, because he is so false and wicked, to trample over us. I am the daughter of his brother, and he knows well that I am Duchess of Kingston in my own right, for the patent of nobility, so carries the title—he would fain destroy me, but I am noble.

"You are, Dora the Duchess," said the young officer.

"I am, and well does my Lord Kingston know it. For the sake, this title, I will yet strive for my right. I may lose my life in so striving; but yet I am a Duchess in my own right."

"I can scarcely blame you," replied the Doctor, "but yet I fear that the power and the unscrupulous will of the Duke of Kingston will be too much for you—particularly as he is in possession, no doubt, of all the evidence of your birth.

"Dora! Dora!" said the young husband faintly at this moment, "Do not be alarmed!"

"Ah, he faints!" said Doctor Langford. "I feared as much."

The excitement of the morning had been too much for this young man, who had been severely wounded by a pistol bullet in the chest, and had only risen from a sick bed to help in the rescue of Dora.

And now that she saw how pale—how death like he looked, all Dora's tenderest fears were awakend, and she cried aloud—

"Oh, if I could die for you! If I could only die for you, dear, dear Henry!"

The coach stopped.

"Hush!" said the Doctor, "Hush! we are safe now, I hope. This is 'The Savoy.'"

CHAPTER II.

THE OLD HOUSE IN THE SAVOY—THE TWO BRAVOS—A PROTECTOR OF THE HELPLESS—THE COMBAT IN THE SNOW—A VOICE FROM THE DEAD—AN ALARM.

THE "Savoy," close to the Strand, is an odd old out-of-the-way place now; but a hundred years ago it was more odd, strange and out-of-the-way, than it is at present.

It was there, at the door of one of the most ancient houses of the place, that Doctor Langford's man, Thomas, stopped the coach.

The young officer was quite insensible, and it needed all the assurances of Doctor Langford to convince her that he was not dead.

Alas! that fainting of Henry Dacres was a sad thing, for it took up so much of the attention of all in the coach, that they failed to see that a man, who had been crouched behind it, got down just as it turned into the "Savoy," and dodged it for the remainder of the way to the actual door of the house at which it stopped.

Dora stepped out of the coach first and opened the house with a key, which she took from one of the pockets of Henry, her husband.

The Doctor was supporting the fainting, wounded man.

As quickly as possible, then, they conveyed him into the house, and the little child followed, crying and sobbing.

Then the door was closed, and the coach driven away.

And then the man who had been behind the coach, and hiding, and spying, and watching all that had taken place, crept out from the doorway in which he had shrunk, and going up to the door of the house in which the Doctor, and Dora and her husband had found themselves at home, he made a mark upon it with a piece of red chalk, which he took from his pocket.

Then a diabolical smile came over his face as he said,—

"I have you now—I think I have you now. All's well! all's safe! Ha! I have you now!"

Then this man ran off at a rapid pace into the Strand, and so towards Charing Cross.

And the snow still came down swiftly upon London, and the day was near to its close, and the shrinking and shivering passengers in the streets wrapped their coat collars about their necks and flitted along like so many spectres.

Among those passengers that so made their way through the streets of London, seeking their homes as soon as they could possibly do so, there was one who, more spectral-like than all the rest, paused for a moment or two at the corner of the Savoy, and let the snow beat upon him, and lay upon him until it would have been difficult soon, enveloped in a large cloak such as at that period was called a Roquelaire, to have decided upon what he was.

Then, with a deep sigh, this man made his way down the narrow turning that led to the "Savoy."

His actions, as he went, were strange and unusual: he would clasp his hands at one moment with a gesture of despair; then he would elevate them above his head as though calling down upon the heads of unknown foes the vengeance of Heaven. Then again, he would appear involved in the most intense grief, and would walk along for a short space bowed down, and oppressed.

But still this man kept the Roquelarie closely about him, and from the manner in which he wore that, and the manner likewise in which he had pulled his hat down over his brows, it was pretty evident he had some object in concealing his identity as much as possible.

The cloak that he wore was of a dark hue, and had no trimming on it whatever. The collar was of a dull red colour, and seemed to be made of some kind of plush or coarse velvet. His hat was low in the crown, and looped up in front, or rather, indeed, the side than the front, with a piece of faded silk cord.

This man wore horseman's boots, reaching to the knees, upon which there were faded silver-lacquered spurs.

Just about six inches of it, showing beneath the Roquelarie, appeared the scabbard of a sword, and take the appearance of this personage for all in all, he had the look of one of those disbanded captains as the military adventurers of the period usually called themselves.

Down the narrow turning, then, from the Strand into the Savoy, this man took his way. He did not go towards the house which was in the occupation of Dora and her husband, but he evidently knew it, for he stationed himself exactly opposite to it.

And there, hidden, or at all events, partially hidden by the angle of a wall connected with the chapel of the Savoy, this mysterious man paused, and, heedless of the fast falling snow, gazed at the house opposite to him.

Then again, he made some of those strange actions with his hands, which betrayed that deep feeling was at work in the heart of this man, and then he was about to turn from the spot, when he suddenly shrunk back, and crouched even yet more closely to the wall.

Two men came with quick steps down the narrow street from the Strand.

These two men were enveloped in overcoats, and had short hangers by their sides, and by the swaggering way in which they walked, evidently belonged to the class "bully" of the then London life.

They both passed close to the angle of the wall, where the mysterious stranger, half hidden by the snow, and much favoured by the rapidly approaching gloom of the evening so far as concealment was concerned, was waiting.

"Are you sure, Bendig," said one of those men, "that this was the place?"

"Oh, quite—quite," said the other. "Didn't I tell you I got up behind the coach?"

"To be sure you did; but you are such a coward, and must have been in such a fright all the time, that I don't put much faith in your being right."

"Stuff—stuff! I tell you I am well acquainted with Turnbull; and is he not in the service of the Duke?"

"The Duke of Kingston?"

"Hush! no names, if you please. There is no occasion to use the Duke's name, so don't, I beg, because if Master Turnbull should turn out to be really hurt past all service, his grace may take me on."

"You?"

"Yes; and why not. And why not?"

"Well, Bendig, on second thoughts, I, too, say why not. You could possibly be a greater rogue than Turnbull was or is."

"And who are you, if you come to that? Who are you, I should like to know! You are a common cut-throat—you know you are; and for a couple of gold pieces you would—"

"Ah! that puts me in mind. I won't stir an inch further in this matter without I have something in advance."

"Something in advance? What for?"

"Who knows? It may not succeed!"

"Not succeed? Why, I tell you there is no danger at all—there is nothing to fail. The house is in the hands of a sick man. A woman—almost a girl, though she is his wife, and a child. As for the Doctor, he is nobody; and, indeed, he is in all likelihood gone by this time."

"Very well—very well; but I will have something in advance!"

"A pest take you. There, then!"

"What is it?"

"A guinea."

"Good?"

"Now, do you think that I would impose upon a friend? Come, come, now I tell you what has to be done. We must make our way into the house, and I advise that we wring the neck of the child. Give that young husband who is so bad another cut with a hanger. It will be quite a mercy to put him out of his pain, and take off Dora Dacres to the Duke.

"Well," said the other ruffian, carelessly, "I don't deny but you lay it all out well."

"Don't I?"

"But if the Doctor is there?"

"Then he should not be there; and I say, we must have no witnesses."

"Very well. But what does the great, rich Duke of Kingston want with this young wife—this Dora Dacres?"

"I don't know—I won't know; but he wanted her hanged; and I do know one thing."

"What?"

"That he will pay us handsomely if we give her up to him."

"Well, that is all we have to look to."

"Not quite," said the mysterious stranger, as he glided out from his place of concealment, and his bright sword, as he drew it from its scabbard, flashed in the dim ray from an oil lamp that had been lighted at the corner of the street.

"Not quite."

The mysterious stranger passed the two ruffians, and placed his back against the door of Dora's house.

The first impulse of the two men was evidently for flight, but when they saw there was but one person opposed to them, the man who had been named Bendig by his comrade, called out :

"At him! at him! Will, give him a taste of your hanger."

"That will I."

Both the ruffians assailed the Stranger, but one of them, in a moment, with a cry, fell on his back, pierced through the heart.

The other immediately fled.

That was Bendig.

But the avenger was on his heels. Bendig cried aloud for help as he struggled through the snow to make his way up to the Strand, where he hoped that some one would come to his aid; but the mysterious stranger overtook him before he could reach so far.

"Villain!" he said, "you would have murdered the helpless and the innocent. Take your reward."

With a scream of pain the fellow fell forward on his knees, and then he turned and faced his pursuer, who had withdrawn his arm and hand in which he held the sword, to deal another thrust at the villain.

"Mercy! oh, as you hope for mercy, have some on me—some on me!"

The Stranger stayed his hand.

"I could kill you with those words in your mouth," he said; "I could send you to judgment with such a cry, Ambrose Bendig."

"Ah, good sir, you know me!"

"I do!"

"And—and—who, may I ask—who—"

"Who I am!"

"Yes, I should like to—to—know."

"Beware!" said the Stranger, in a deep, solemn tone; and he stooped a little, and let the cloak fall from the lower part of his face, and raised the hat from off his eyes and brow.

Bendig had one fair, clear look at his face, and that look seemed sufficient to turn him to stone with terror. He uttered one shriek, and fell flat upon his face in the snow.

"Beware!" said the Stranger again, and he walked right over the prostrate form of Bendig, and made his way to the Strand."

When some passengers, attracted by the noise, ran down the narrow street, and picked up Bendig, they found him at his last gasp.

He tried to speak.

"The dead—the dead!" he said, "they —they—come back—back again—the dead Duke—the—the—dead—ah!"

He breathed his last, and fell a lifeless mass in the arms of the Watch."

"The noise of the conflict that had taken place immediately opposite their door in the "Savoy," could not fail to reach the ears of Dora and the Doctor, as they were both, with deep anxiety, seeking to restore Henry Dacres to consciousness.

Dora sprung to the window.

"There is danger! there is danger!" she cried. "I have been tracked to this well concealed house. Oh sir, there is danger!"

The Doctor thought that Dora's fears were but too well founded, when he heard loud voices, and the clash of swords.

It was difficult to see what was taking place below, owing to the rapidly gathering darkness of the night, but yet they could just perceive the three figures, and that one was left lying on the snow, whilst the two others, one evidently in pursuit, fled towards the Strand.

"It is but some sudden brawl, I fancy," said Doctor Langford, with which we need have nothing to do."

"Thank Heaven!"

The young wife turned again to Henry Dacres, and recommenced bathing his brow with vinegar in a sponge.

"He moves," said Doctor Langford. "He opens his eyes—he will speak!"

"Henry! my Henry!"

"Ah!"

"You are better now. The faintness has passed away?"

"It will," said the Doctor, "but he must take this. Take it freely."

In a small cup the Doctor held out a draught to Henry, who took it with pleasure, and the colour slowly came back to his cheeks. With it came, too, a full recollection of all that had occurred, and he held out his arms as he cried,—

"You are saved—you are saved! my own dear, dear Dora!"

"I am," said Dora, but we have all passed through a dreadful day."

"Think not of it," said the Doctor, "It might have been a great deal worse. But you promised to tell me more at large how it was that you incurred the hatred of the Duke of Kingston so that he has evidently tried to kill you both."

"I will! I will!" said Dora. "You shall know all, dear and kind friend as you are. We will keep nothing from you."

One heavy blow with the knocker on the street door at this moment interrupted Dora in what she was about to say, and spread alarm in all their hearts.

CHAPTER III.

THE PARDON—A MURDERED COURIER— THE DUKE OF KINGSTON AT HOME—THE GREEK GIRL — A MYSTERY OF ST. JAMES'S.

BEFORE we proceed to give that explanation of the mysterious condition of Dora and her young husband, which she was so willing to give to the worthy Doctor Langford, it becomes necessary that we should step back a few paces in our story to speak of other personages.

When His Majesty, King George the Second expired at Kensington Palace, his successor, George the Third, was at Windsor.

The page, who was principally with the King in his last moments, had heard him say that he would send a pardon in favor of Dora Dacres, who was lying in Newgate under sentence of death.

Death decreed to her on the completely unsupported testimony of the Duke of Kingston, to the effect that she had been found concealed in his house, in St. James's, and had come there with the object of setting it on fire, and had, in fact, commenced to do so.

This page then, when the King was no more, had gone at once to my Lord Kingston, and told him of the King's motives with regard the condemned young girl.

He had paid no attention to the case, and had not the least idea that there was any special designs on the part of the Duke of Kingston against the prisoner.

The Duke took good care that no such designs should appear to the page, but suggested that a messenger should be sent to Windsor, to state as much, and that the signature then of the new king would no doubt be obtained, and would answer all the purposes.

The page offered at once to go himself, and it was on the evening before the day fixed for the judicial murder of Dora that, well mounted on a good horse from the Royal Stables, at the King's Mews, the page started for Windsor.

He was quite successful in his mission. The young king generously gave his signature, and the letter, addressed to the Sheriffs of London was placed in the hands of a King's messenger, of the name of Henson, to proceed to London with it.

This messenger started from Windsor at eight o'clock on the evening of the day preceding that fixed for the execution.

He never reached his destination, but was found dead at the foot of a little bridge that crossed a stream on the roadway, about five miles out of Windsor.

It was two hours after the death of the King's Messenger that a horseman, covered with mud, and his horse showing great signs of fatigue, made his way into St. James's Street, and thence into one of the streets leading towards the Park of St. James's.

This horseman was no other than the Duke of Kingston.

Alighting at the door of his town own house, he made his way into the hall, desiring the servants to see to his horse, and take it to the stables.

Then throwing off the cloak he wore, and letting it fall to the ground, the Duke took his way to his own private room, and at once locked himself in.

"So," he said, as he took a pair of pistols from his pocket and placed them on the table before him, "So, that is all well—no pardon will reach Newgate in favour of Dora. Ah! here it is—let me see—ah! indeed—full and complete enough. It would, indeed, have saved her, and what a world of popularity the young King would have got, too, by this act—I am sorry to baulk his Majesty of all that, but it is much more necessary to me that Dora Dacres should die than that the young King should be popular."

There was a bright fire burning in the grate, and the Duke of Kingston approached it with the packet he had taken from the murdered Courier in his hand, when he suddenly paused, on hearing the sharp tones of a bell.

"Ah! that is Margaret," he said, "what can she want at such a time, or, rather, it is his bell—his—Surlina's. I wonder if that strange compound of craft and mysticism is really faithful to me? I have my doubts—I have my doubts."

The Duke now opened a bureau in one corner of the room, and thrust carelessly into it the pardon of Dora. Then he went very slowly and cautiously to the room door, and saw that the little blind eye was over the keyhole, so that no one could be spying upon him. Being then quite satisfied on that head, he went to a portion of the wall on which hung a full length portrait of King Charles the First, and running his hand down the side of the frame, which seemed to form part of the solid panelling of the room, he touched a spring, and the whole picture moved back upon concealed hinges.

The space behind it was perfectly blank, and quite dark, but the Duke did not hesitate a moment in passing on.

The portrait was restored to its proper position, and some spring on an opposite wall, about four feet in advance, opened a similar panel in another room.

In that room there was a dull blue looking light.

"What is it?" said the Duke. "You rung, you Surlina. What would you? Are you not safe here? This house, which is my property, and adjoins my own—this house, which is ever To Let, and yet which is never let, owing to the obstacles I throw in the way, is a secure asylum for you and for Margaret, I fancy. Why do you summon me now?"

"Because," said a voice, "all is not well."

At the same moment there emerged from a distant portion of the large apartment, a man who had all the appearance of extreme age, but whose voice was vigorous.

"All not well? "What has happened?"

"Something will happen. It is more than strange, but the girl has fallen into one of her trances of her own accord, and she says strange things."

"What things?"

"You shall hear."

"But it is her revelations as you well know, that have urged me on so far, that to-morrow morning the only obstacle to my certain safety will be removed."

"Dora?"

"Yes—she will die to-morrow."

"Hush!"

"Ah! she comes."

A door was suddenly opened at the further extremity of the apartment, and by the dim blue light, to which the eyes of the Duke were getting accustomed, he saw approaching a figure, clad in a long white garment, similar to the beautiful draperies which are handed down to us as classical on Grecian statues.

It was of a pearly whiteness the long trailing dress, and the soft blue with which it was trimmed seemed to have been borrowed from the skies of Greece.

A fillet of white flowers was around the head of this girl, for in truth she was little more, since seventeen summers had not yet passed over the young head.

She advanced into the room slowly, and with a strange action, like one walking in sleep, and by the aspect of her eyes it would seem, indeed, that such was the case, for they were fixed and motionless.

At times this young creature, who was very beautiful, uttered low moaning sounds, as if some great distress sat heavy at her heart.

A superstitious fear came over the Duke.

"I thought," he said, "that she—that—that she never fell into this state unless by the power of your will to make her."

"Yes, at times—and then she will say strange things."

"What things?"

"You can question her. Is she not your slave? Am I not your slave? Both slaves to you, O Great Chief of a great nation! What are we but dust? What are we in the eyes of you, Great Lord that you are?"

The young girl, in her beautiful classic costume, moved slowly forward, still in the same jerking fashion with which she had entered the room, and still she moaned and seemed inclined to weep.

The Duke stepped back as she advanced, and fear sat upon his face.

"Speak, Margaret, speak," he said.

"Call her Neoni—it is her native name. The spirit of the Greek girl is great now."

"Neoni," said the Duke.

"I am here," she said.

Her voice was deep, low, and sweet, and as she spoke, she paused, and seemed to feel about her, as she slowly moved her arms like one in the dark.

"Speak now to her," said Surlina, "and she will reveal that which you wish to know. She is in that trance in which things hidden are revealed. Speak to her, great noble, and she will answer you."

"Neoni!"

"I listen."

"You have guided me to the possession of that rank, and to the possession of those fair estates which I never thought to call my own. Tell me, will all yet go well, or is disaster to come over me, for I seem to have a presentiment of its coming."

"All will go well but one thing."

"Ah, there will be one disaster, then?"

The Greek girl only sighed deeply.

"Speak! say more to me," exclaimed the Duke, "I would be warned, not alarmed. You speak of disaster. I would have you define it. What is it? where is it? When is it to come to me, and in what shape?"

The Greek girl was still silent, with the exception of the low moans that came from her breast.

Then the aged man who answered to the name of Surlina, stepped a pace forward and spoke.

"My Lord Duke, you must most specially question her, or she cannot, or will not answer."

"Then be it so. Neoni, tell me, shall I succeed in procuring the death, to-morrow morning, of that girl who so threateningly stands in my path—of Dora Dacres.

"No," said the Greek girl.

"No, say you? no! why, she is at her last hour of peril. I have accused her—she has been hastily tried, condemned, and is to die."

"No," said the Greek girl.

"Then all will be to do again. But once again, I say, tell me, will he die who had the audacity to scorn my advice, and to wed with her when I told him she was my enemy—I mean Henry Dacres."

"No!"

The Duke fell back a pace or two.

"You prophecy evil to me. Did I not set the bravo, Turnbull, on him, and did he not fall mortally wounded? Oh, that I could discover his whereabouts, I would soon disprove your words with my own sword."

The Greek girl sighed deeply, and it would appear as if tears were about to come from her eyes, but she did not weep.

"It is enough" said Surlina, "she will say no more now. Question her not further, my Lord Duke, but let her be."

"Well, well, be it so! You, Surlina, tell me, how goes your projects?"

"Well, I am making diamonds for you, but I want more gold."

"Take this purse Control your wants as much as may be, Surlina, or your diamonds, when you produce them, will cost me more than their market value."

"No, no! when from my crucible below there shall come forth the sparkling gems, each one shall be worth the crown jewels of a nation. I am the only chemist who has discovered all the science of the Arabian and Egyptian Philosophers. I must succeed."

"Well, well, be it so. You do not find me impatient."

"I do not. Hush! let her go!"

The beautiful Greek girl, with a slow movement turned and left the room, passing through a doorway into another apartment of the house, and moaning slightly as she went.

The door closed after her.

"Now, my Lord Duke," said Surlina, "let me remind you of all your promises."

"I do not forget them, Surlina. I will make Neoni my duchess as soon as you produce to me the diamonds which you say you science can make. By that act I shall at once repair all the ill that I have done her. But the other obstacle must be removed."

"It shall!"

"That I will leave to you, then. How fares it with her now?"

"Come, my Lord Duke, it is fit that you should see your present duchess. She still raves for freedom, but is as far off it as ever. The time will come, though, when she will be free."

"Ah, you will betray the confidence I place in you, and let her go?"

"Yes, into her grave."

"I comprehend you. Lead on, I will see her, or I will listen to her. She is proud and haughty, but her pride has had a fall. Lead on, Surlina, I will follow you!"

The old man led the way, and the Duke of Kingston followed him up several staircases, and finally through a dismal suite of rooms, into which no light was allowed to penetrate; and the small hand lamp that Surlina carried only cast a melancholy radius of light around it.

They finally arrived at a door which had hanging over it some heavy folds of cloth. The old man removed them, and opened the door by the aid of a key which he had with him.

The moment the door was opened, there came a wailing cry from some one within, and upon her knees, making frantic gestures with her hands—gestures of an imploring character for mercy, there advanced as far as a chain, which was around her would permit, a poor-looking, emaciated woman.

Her voice was low from weakness and long suffering.

"Oh, have mercy upon me!" she said. "Pray release me, and I will say nothing—will disclose nothing. Indeed and in truth I will be as silent as the grave. Am I not your wife—your duchess? Oh, say that you will take my solemn promise, and let me free!"

"Ha, ha!" laughed the Duke.

"You have come to think, now, Edward, to have some mercy on me. Your heart has at length repented, and you have begun to pity me. Oh, Heaven send you some gentleness—some remorse. I will promise—on my knees I will promise to say nothing—to tell no one, if you will let me free. Oh, in mercy think of the horror of the long long days and nights in this place."

"Ha, ha!" laughed the Duke.

"All alone—all alone, too! no friend—no voice to cheer me! My child, too,—my little one! Oh, tell me, where is he? Edward! Edward! have some mercy upon me!"

"Ha, ha!" again laughed the Duke.

He turned from the door.

The wretched creature who was there, with straw for her furniture, and a chain only to caress her, uttered a wild and terrible cry.

Surlina closed and locked the door again.

"You see," he said, "that she still lives."

"She does. She would have destroyed me. It is now a year and a half since that girl, who lays claim to my title and estates, called upon that wife of mine, and so impressed her with the truth of her story, that she was about to go at once and lay the case before the King; but I stopped her, and since then, for my own safety's sake I have made her a prisoner, and given her to your care, Surlina."

"Yes," replied the Greek, "and you will not deny that I have taken good care of her. It was one week before the circumstance you mention that I promised myself I would take care of her."

"I do not comprehend you, Surlina?"

"It needs not, my Lord Duke, that you should do so. There is much in the world that I do not comprehend, but be assured that if you keep faith with me, I will with you."

"I will, indeed!"

"Let us repeat it!"

"Most willingly. So soon as you produce to me artificial diamonds which will stand the test of real ones, I will make your daughter, Neoni, my wife, and Duchess of Kingston."

"Agreed! and as soon as you are ready to perform the promise your present wife and Duchess, whom we have just seen, shall die."

"It is agreed! It is agreed!"

The Duke of Kingston passed through the secret doors in the panels to his own house adjoining. The moment he was alone he turned, with a look of mingled ferocity and cunning in the direction of the gloomy residence he had just quitted, and in a low, deriding voice, he said,—

"Indeed! so you think I will make the girl who has already sunk so low as to become my mistress, the Duchess of Kingston. No, no! a thousand times no. Make for me by your art, for you are a rare chemist, Master Surlina, the diamonds you say are within your power, and then I shall know what to do. I will at once, then, rid myself of you; and the fair Neoni may still be the secret companion of my hours of leisure. Ha, ha! make her a Duchess, indeed! Ha, ha!

The Duke of Kingston would perhaps have started could he only have seen the look of terrible hate and ferocity with which the old Greek, Surlina, regarded that portion of the panel of the wall through which he had just passed.

It seemed almost as if his eyes could pierce through the woodwork, and strike daggers into the heart of the Duke.

"Fool! fool!" he muttered, "I do but play with you, that my vengeance may be more complete. You have disgraced my innocent-minded child, my own Neoni, under promise that she should be your duchess, and you shall yet keep your word, and then you shall die. I do but play with you awhile—I do but play with you, and your real present Duchess, who lingers a prisoner in this house, pays but the penalty of her hardness of heart. She was appealed to by my Neoni, and the story of her wrongs found no pity. I will have revenge on all! revenge on all. Neoni! Neoni! my child, where are you? Ah, I can hear you weeping, my bright-eyed maid of the many islands; but you shall yet triumph over the betrayer. The time is coming, my Neoni—my own Neoni!"

CHAPTER V.

THE DREADFUL VISITOR—A MURDER AT THE OLD HOUSE IN THE "SAVOY"—— DORA'S COURAGE—THE HIDDEN CUPBOARD AND THE SWORD—THE ABDUCTION OF MINA—A CRY FOR HELP—THE FIGHT ON THE STAIRS.

A LOUD, single, heavy knock had come upon the street door of that house in the "Savoy," which was in the occupation of Dora and her young wounded husband. It caused the hearts of all in that house to beat violently with alarm. So amenable as Dora was still to the law which she had escaped from, she felt that she might, at any moment, be sought for to her destruction.

The one, single, heavy knock came again!

Dora had been upon the point of making some explanations to Doctor Langford. She had felt that to him, of all men, was due an account of those circumstances which had produced the present combination of events: feeling, as she did, that to his skill she owed the life of her dear Henry, she could not hesitate to impart to him all that he could wish to know.

But it was this summons to the door, at once so startling and so singular, for no visitors ever found their way to that house, which stopped the revelations.

The colour moved from the face of Dora as she listened for a repetition of the knock.

Yes; it came again!

Not impatiently, but loudly and imperatively, as if the person, be he whom he might, had determined, by perseverance, to obtain attention.

"I will go," said Dora.

"No, no!" cried Henry Dacres, in a voice of emotion. "No, no! I seem to feel that there is danger."

"Ah! he speaks again, and he is better," said Dora, while she clasped her hands, and a joyous light shone forth from her eyes.

"He is much better," said Doctor Langford, "and I hope will soon entirely recover. Stay here, and I will see who it is that so pertinaciously demands admission to the house."

"No," said Henry, faintly, "it is not fit that our honoured friend and guest should go to the door. I think if I were roused up, I should feel strong enough to do so."

"By no means," said the physician, as he laid his hand upon the breast of the young officer. "By no means—I will go!"

Was it that little Mina, the dear and gentle child of this young and persecuted couple, had some presentiment of danger, that she clung so closely to her mother's breast, and with eyes of alarm regarded the door through which the good physician had passed?

"Hush, hush! dear one," said Dora. "All is well—well—"

Dora could hardly be considered to be speaking to little Mina: her thoughts and attention were with Doctor Langford, and she was listening intently to catch any sounds from the lower part of the house.

We will follow the doctor.

It was very strange that, as he went down the stairs there came over his mind the memory of one very dear to him, whom he had lost in early life.

It would not have taken much to convince him that he was not alone on those stairs, but that the pure spirit of one whom he had loved and lost accompanied him step by step as he went.

He reached the gloomy hall—he reached the door—to fling it open carelessly enough was the work of a moment.

"Who knocks here?" he asked, "and what is the errand?"

"Death for a life!" said a voice.

There was a half stifled cry, and the flash of a sword, and the physician fell in the hall of that silent and gloomy house bathed in blood.

A tall, meagre-looking man stepped over the fallen physician, and then, turning, with a long reach of his arm, he closed the door.

"Mine! mine!" he said. "She shall be mine, or she shall rue this night. I care not for consequences. I will not consider them. I am madly, wildly in love with this fair creature, and she must and shall be mine. From the moment that she met my gaze, when Henry Dacres told me she was his, I have known no peace. I must and will call her my own! She is to me more than life itself. I will remove all that oppose my progress; and then, when helpless and despairing, I will make her my own."

Step by step, with something of a stealthy as well as a heavy tread, this man now made his way along the hall and up the stairs.

Dora had heard the faint cry of the physician, as the sword plunged into his breast, and she stood with the door of the room in which were her two treasures, open partially, while she, with bated breath, listened intently.

She heard the footstep approaching, and her heart told her there was danger.

The footstep then ceased for a moment. The man who was approaching, had paused to affix to the upper part of his face one of those half masks which were used at masquerades, then a fashionable kind of entertainment.

It was but a moment he so paused, but that moment was enough for action on the part of Dora

She felt that the danger was great, and that the kind-hearted physician must have met with some mischance, or he would speedily have returned to her.

"Husband—Henry! Dearest Henry, there is danger." she whispered hurriedly. "I know—I feel that there is danger."

The wounded officer made an effort to raise himself to his feet.

"My sword—my sword! he said. "I—I—will defend—de—fend—you."

With a deep sigh he sunk back on to the old chair, with its mass of cushions—where he had been resting. He was too weak—by far too weak for action. What should she do? Oh, what could she do? To whom could she look for help? Where could she fly for protection?

For a few moments the brain of poor Dora was a whirl of disconnected thoughts and terrors. Then as if by inspiration a sudden idea occurred to her. She would save him—him, her husband, from probable death, if it were a foe who approached.

There was in one corner of the old-fashioned room a deep recess, which by the assistance of old panelled doors, had been long ago, made into a cupboard. It was the action of a moment now to open those doors, and to wheel the chair on which Henry Dacres sat, with him still on it, into the old recess. He was too weak to speak—she gave him one long, sweet kiss upon the pale brow, and then she closed the doors.

Little Mina began to cry and sob.

"Hush, oh, hush, dear one," said Dora. "Mina will not speak till her mamma tells her—Mina will not speak!"

"Oh, no, no, no!"

The child clung to her arm, and kept a convulsive clutch of her clothing; but Dora disengaged the little hands—she had work to do.

"Hush! hush!" she said. "Hush, darling! Mina, must not speak."

In one corner of the room was the sword and belt of Henry Dacres. Dora possessed herself of the weapon in a moment, and drew it from the scabbard. She clasped her left arm over the fair head of her child, and stood on the defensive in that room—looking pale, but resolute, with the drawn sword, advanced and pointing towards the door.

The terrified child, now, had no power to speak, or to cry out, for the aspect of Dora was so full of alarm, that the little creature dreaded, by the sound of its own voice, to invoke the possibility of some fearful sight.

Then the ascending footsteps of the man who was approaching paused at the door of the room, and there came one deep hollow knock upon the panel.

Dora did not speak: she scarcely dared even to breathe.

The knock was repeated, and this time it was accompanied by the grating sound of the turning of the handle of the ancient latch. The meagre light that was in the room but dimly made objects visible, and when the door was swung open and a tall figure appeared upon the threshold, Dora could not distinguish if it were the figure of a stranger, or of one whom she could name.

It was in choking accents which sufficiently betrayed the terror that sat at her heart—terror not for herself, but for her wounded and helpless husband, that Dora spoke.

"Who—who—" she gasped, "Who and what are you?"

Then there was a dull clanking sound, and the tall figure dropped close to its feet the deadly sword with which he had assailed the good physician, and all but dropping to his knees—bending, at all events, so far forward, and so low down in his supplicatory posture, that Dora thought he knelt—this stranger who had with such violence found his way to the house, spoke.

"Dora, Dora, do you not know me? Is it possible you do not know me?"

Dora uttered a cry of terror.

"Ah, yes, you know me now. I can tell by that cry that you know me now. Dora! Dora! Dora!"

"Hence! away, villain! worse villain than tongue can tell."

"No, no; I am the victim of the heart. Dora, you do know me. I am named Van Esling. I am a captain, as you know now, in the regiment of Henry Dacres, and before he told you that he loved you, I told you that you were my heart's divinity—that I lived and breathed but for you—that day and night the thought of you was the one all-absorbing idea that chased all others from my mind—that without you I were but a stranded wretch upon a dismal shore, where all was barren. Dora! Dora! I love you! I ever loved you from the moment these fierce, thrilling eyes of mine—in which there seem now two separate fires—looked upon you. You, and you only, may save me—save me from myself and from a thousand evils. I love you! I love you! Dora, I love you!"

"The voice of this man rose higher and higher as he spoke, until, by the time he got to the end of the incoherent speech he uttered, his tones were frantic and wild, and he clasped his hands together as he added,

"Kill me! oh, kill me, if you will not pity me!"

"Villain!" exclaimed Dora. "I do, indeed, know you now."

"You know that I love you? you know that I adore you?"

"Ah! oh God! the masked foe!"

"Masked foe! what? what?"

Captain Van Esling tore from his face the half mask he had put on as he came up the stairs.

"Yes," added Dora, with a shudder and a cry of grief and agony, "Yes, my husband told me—Henry told me that the foe with whom he fought was masked, and you are the man!"

"I am! I am! but, angel of my life, was it not from love of you I killed him?"

"Killed him?"

"Yes, is he not dead?"

"Remorseless villain! if he were you should find that I was worthy of his love by spurning yours."

"No, no! oh, say not so. No, no! Dora, hear me. Hear that which I have to say to you, ere you decide to cast me from you, Dora, hear me—hear me!"

"I will not—I will not—your very voice is a horror and a reproach."

"You shall hear me!" cried Van Esling, with a shout of rage, as he picked up his sword and advanced two steps further into the room.

Dora did not flinch, but still maintained her position, with the glittering point of her husband's sword extended towards the breast of the intruder.

"You are armed," said Van Esling, "and you would fain have me believe that despair will give you strength to resist my presence here, but you shall hear me, and know well who and what you are. You are the daughter of the Duke of Kingston—of him, at least, who should be Duke of Kingston; but that his complicity with the Pretender to the throne of these realms would have attainted him of high treason, had he appeared, and the title of the Duke of Kingston would have become extinct, and the estates the property of the crown."

"Begone! Begone!" cried Dora. "I wish not to hear from you the story of my own wrongs."

"You shall hear. Your father has not then claimed the title. He fell, as you have heard, in some obscure conflict on the confines of the Meuse; and your uncle, the present Duke, who has been an Hanoverian Royalist, claimed, and has the title and estates, and disputes your legitimacy; but he has the proofs, I am assured, in his own possession, which would make you a duchess— A peeress in your own right—Dora, the Duchess—while he would then be but a private gentleman."

The point of the bright sword which Dora held still towards the breast of Van Esling, trembled in the small glistening light that fell upon it.

"Ah," added Van Esling, "you hear me now, and attend to me. Dora, Dora! I love you! There is no one who will love you as I do. Be mine, and I will wrest from the false Duke those proofs which will give you your birthright. Be mine, and you shall, indeed, and in truth, be Dora the Duchess."

"Never! never! Villain! assassin!"

"No, I am no assassin. He who was

your husband, but who now, no doubt, is with the dead, fought with me. It was a fair fight : he or I must fall. The chance of life was mine. You are alone in the world—be mine, and I will make you so high that you shall forget all the past that might bring a pang to your breast."

"Never ! never ! never ! "

"Oh, say not so ! say not so ! In the blaze of your rank, your wealth, and your power, you will cast so strong a shadow upon the past, that you will not see it. Be mine, and you shall be a Duchess ! "

"Hence, villain ! you do not even tempt me. Assassin, I loathe you ! "

A terrible expression came across the face of Van Esling, and a hateful fire shot from his eyes. He advanced another step.

At that moment there was a deep groan, and the sound, as of the fall of some heavy body, in the cupboard at the corner of the room where Dora had hidden her wounded husband.

CHAPTER VI.

THE CHILD'S DANGER — THE VILLAIN'S THREAT—A FIGHT FOR A LIFE—THE ESCAPE—PURSUIT AND THE SNOW DRIFT —STARLIGHT, THE GALLANT STEED—THE ESCAPE OF VAN ESLING—DORA'S DESPAIR —THE MYSTERIOUS GREY MAN.

THE little Mina uttered a scream of terror, and Dora's cheeks flushed for a moment with fear.

Van Esling recoiled a step, and hastily put his sword upon its guard.

"What is that ? what is that ? " he said, hoarsely, "what is that ? "

Nothing was so terrible to Dora as the idea that he should suppose her wounded Henry was at hand. From what he had said, it seemed that he was possessed with the idea that he had killed him, for it was from his hands that Henry had received the wound which still battled with his life. That Dora was alone—alone with that little one, now appeared to be the notion of Van Esling, and to keep him in that mind Dora would encounter any danger.

"It may be," she said, "that Heaven, in its mercy, will send some help to me. That may well shake your heart, and fill you with a thousand fears."

She thought that by these words she should possibly be approaching to a superstitious element in the villain's disposition ; and she was partially successful, for she saw the sword tremble for a moment in his grasp.

It was but for a moment, though.

"It is in vain," he said. "In vain you seek for help in another world when there is none in this. These old houses are full of sounds that have no fears for mortal hearts. Again I speak to you—to your heart and brain, Dora. I love you, and will save you."

He stepped forward again.

"Off ! off, villain ! " cried Dora. "One more step, and weak and unskilled in fence as I am, I will kill you."

"You are mad, girl ! I tell you you are mad ! "

The sword blades clashed together.

The little Mina, with a shriek of terror, forsook her mother, and strove to fly from the room, but as she passed, or tried to pass Van Esling, he caught her by the long flowing curls of her beautiful hair with his left hand, and in a voice of wild, half mad exultation, he cried out :

"A new thought ! a happier thought ! I have sought you, Dora, through love, through hate, through the heart's agony of slighted passion, through death I have sought you ; but the time has come when you shall seek me. This child—this little one, around whom is centred your heart strings, shall be the magnet that shall draw you to me. Ha, ha ! you will now seek me ! me, everywhere ! me, for ever ! and I will baffle you ! upon you will I inflict some portion of the pangs which I have suffered from despised love. I will take this little one as the hostage of your affections ; and when you are inclined to be mine—when you will make up your mind to love me, write a placard, on which shall appear the words, ' Dora will be a Duchess,' and place the placard on the base of the statue of the First Charles, at Charing Cross. Then, and not till then shall you look into the bright eyes of your child. Ha, ha, ha ! a rare thought ! a brave thought ! Mine—mine ! You will yet be mine, or this little one shall grow up to compensate me for the mother's loss. She is my hostage ! Follow—follow ! how you can and when you can ! through blood—through shrieks, fire, and despair you may follow me now, and pray to me, even as I have prayed to you."

He buried his hand deeply amidst the beautiful tresses of the shrieking child, and swung her from the floor up to his shoulder.

Dora screamed aloud, and rushed forward with the sword to assail the villain, but as often as she would have thrust the glittering sword into his breast, he interposed the child between them.

"Help ! help ! Oh, in mercy, help ! My child ! my own darling ! my little one ! Help—oh, God, help me—now ! "

"Ha, ha, ha ! " laughed the villain.

The little Mina shrieked aloud, and held out her fair arms towards her mother.

Alas those little arms only kept the poor mother farther off, for she dreaded to touch them with the sharp sword's point.

And Van Esling retreated step by step from the room.

He reached the door—he reached the landing—he reached the head of the stairs, and still waving his rapier in one hand, and holding the child in the other, he, step by step, began the descent to the hall below.

"Murder! murder!" cried Dora. "Help —oh, help! Van Esling, give me back my child, and I will forgive you all—all the past. Give me back my child!"

"Be mine!"

"Never!"

"Ha, ha, ha! Follow me now—follow me now, and for ever!"

"Better—oh, Heaven! better to die, than have my child thus torn from me!" cried Dora, as with a feeling of desperation, she now sprung half way down the stairs, and assailed the ruffian.

But Dora's despair would not make her such a master of fence as was this ruthless savage man, and only twice did the swords clash together before Dora found herself disarmed, and blood upon her hand.

Then, with screams and cries, she still pursued Van Esling, who, with terrific leap, cleared the last flight of stairs, and reached the hall.

He trampled over the prostrate body of the physician, and opened the outer door.

"Seek me to be mine," he yelled, "and you will get your child again, and be Dora the Duchess!"

Another moment he was in the open air, and sped towards the Strand.

But Dora was not to be detained from the pursuit by the heaped up snow, nor by the piercing cold.

"Help! help!" she cried. "Stop the villain! oh, stop him! Help—oh, help! he robs me of my child!'

The hour was not a very late one, but the inclemency of the season had thinned the streets, and but few passengers were about. Nevertheless, at these wild and frantic cries from Dora several persons ran towards the top of the narrow street that led from the Strand to the "Savoy."

At the corner of that street was a horse.

It was evidently towards that horse that Van Esling tried to make his way, and could he once have mounted, he would have defied pursuit.

"Ho! Starlight! Starlight!" he called out. "Ho, boy, here!"

The horse seemed to recognise the name of Starlight, but not the voice of Van Esling; and when he made a dart forward to mount it, the creature swerved, and then, as several people ran up the Strand, Van

Esling saw that it was too late to get on horseback, and that his capture was imminent.

Dora, too, was close at hand, and still kept up her cries for help.

With a terrible imprecation on his lips, Van Esling turned abruptly to the right, and ran along the frozen pavement, and dived down a dark court that was not above a hundred paces from the spot.

Dora was confused for a moment as to which way he had gone, and thought that he was on the other side of the horse, as it stood in the obscure light from the wretched oil lamp in the street.

"Help! oh, help me!" she cried. "Where is he? oh, who sees him?"

"That way—that way!" said several people. "He runs towards the City. The man with the child!"

"Yes—oh, yes! my child! my own little one. It is mine—mine!"

It was the impulse of a moment. Dora's hand was on the bridle of the horse, and she made a sidelong spring and sat on the saddle.

"On, on!" she cried. "I must overtake you now, villain, by the means which you provided for your own escape. I will overtake you."

The horse darted forward with a bound, and carried poor Dora in a few seconds far past the court down which Van Esling had plunged with the little Mina.

And Dora reached old Temple Bar, but neither child or Van Esling could she see. She became then convinced that by turning down some one of the numerous narrow streets or courts, the villain had escaped her, and that she was, indeed and in truth, robbed of one of her earthly treasures—her dear little Mina.

Oh! what a world of agony swept over the heart of poor Dora as she now checked the horse, and clasping her hands over her eyes, burst into tears.

What should she do? What could she do? What course adopt to discover where Van Esling was with her heart's treasure? Doubtless, there would be on the morrow a price put upon her own capture, for had she not, only by a hairbreadth, escaped death on the scaffold?

And how, then, dared she invoke the aid of the law to procure justice and restitution for her? Oh, how sad was her fate! How bitter did human life appear to the beautiful Dora at that moment.

Who could—who would help her?

The drifting snow began to fall again, and there she was, so full of grief that had the cold hand of winter grasped at her heart and stilled its beating for ever, she would have welcomed extinction.

Alas, poor Dora!

"Lost! lost!" she moaned. "All lost! all that I loved on earth torn from me!"

Even as Dora uttered these words, her heart smote her, and she felt that she was committing high treason against the affection of Henry, whom she had left, perhaps, to die of the heart's bitterest agony, alone—that agony which must have come over him on finding—on hearing that those whom he loved best on earth were in peril and he too weak to help them—too weak to be other than a heavy and useless burden on Dora at such a critical moment, when he would gladly have sacrificed all he held most dear to have been able to render her assistance, were it ever so slight.

"No, no!" she said, "I am not quite desolate. Henry—Henry! at least you will weep with me. You live still—you must live. Oh, Heaven! do not—do not leave me desolate.

The new fear now came over her, that upon her return to the "Savoy," she might find her husband no more, and it nearly broke her heart.

She turned the horse's head in the direction of the "Savoy" again, and the gallant creature carried her swiftly to the door of the old house.

The door was swinging open.

The snow was beating into the hall.

Dora uttered a sob of anguish, and then she recollected, and it felt strange that she should so recollect it at that moment when her mind was so full of other things, that Van Esling had called the horse Starlight.

As she dismounted she held the bridle in her hand for a moment, and uttered the name.

"Starlight! Starlight!"

The creature, with its head, made a caressing movement to the shoulder of Dora, and her heart warmed to this poor dumb thing, who seemed to feel for her.

She patted the horse's neck, as her tears fell fast.

Come! she said. "Come, you shall not endure the bitter cold without. Who knows but you may yet be a friend to the poor, desolate, wretched Dora? Come!"

Dora led the horse into the wide old hall, of the house, and the creature followed her with the docility of a dog.

All was still in that house.

Dora closed the door.

She pressed her hands upon her heart as she ascended the stairs. Then she paused a moment to listen. No, it was nothing. She had thought she heard a sound; but it was surely fancy.

And as she went, Dora strove, amid all the agony of apprehension she felt, to steel her pure, true heart for the worst.

"Heaven grant me strength and judgment," she moaned. "If Henry—if my poor dear Henry be no more, I must still live for my dear Mina's sake; and if—if I am never to look again into the bright eyes of my child, why surely—surely Heaven will leave me my Henry—my husband!"

It seemed to her too much to hope that both would be left to her.

It seemed, to her, so hard to despair that both would be lost to her.

And now Dora had reached the door of the room. It was open, and with a rush she crossed its threshold.

"Henry! Henry! if you live—if you can, speak to me. Do but utter one word—one sigh—to—tell me— Oh, God! I hear nothing—I hear nothing!"

"He lives!" said a deep-toned voice.

"Ah!"

"He lives! I am too late! I was too late. But the time will come. Hope—hope! Dora, Duchess of Kingston, hope still."

A dark figure, arrayed in a cloak of grey cloth, passed Dora, and left the room. The candle was burning low in the socket of the candlestick, and Henry Dacres was sitting in the chair which she had wheeled into the cupboard. The cupboard door was open, and he had his arms extended to clasp her to his heart, although he was too weak to rise and welcome her.

But who shall describe the agony of his look? What pen shall picture the world of suffering that looked out from every feature of his face? Hearing much, and fearing much more, the wounded young officer had endured all the pangs of feeling that those who were dearer to him than life itself were surrounded by many dangers.

But he looked into his Dora's eyes again—now he saw those features which had their reflex in his heart, and it was with a cry of joy that he so held out his arms to welcome his own, much-loved Dora.

"Safe, safe!" he cried. "Safe, and once again to this poor heart!"

Dora, with a gush of tears, clasped her arms about him. How could she tell him what had happened? How could she rend his heart with the news that their child—their only one—the dear, prattling, sharer of their love, was gone—gone, perhaps, for ever.

"Ah, my Dora, you weep! but surely all is well, now that I can look into your eyes again, my own, my joy, my hope, my Dora!"

The horse pawed the flooring of the hall below, and Dora started at the sound. It seemed to her to speak of danger.

D·

CHAPTER VII.

THE DYING OFFICER—A SUMMONS FROM THE SNOW—THE VOICE OF THE DEPARTED DUKE—A LIFE POTION—THE LAST SIGHT OF MINA—THE OLD SAVOY STAIRS.

DORA, with one arm clasped around her husband, and with her fair and gentle face averted from him for a moment, that she might give her whole attention to any sound that might come from the lower part of the house, felt certain now that she heard the horse in the hall below stamping on the old flooring with his iron shod hoofs.

Poor Henry Dacres who, in his wounded state, had but a dim perception of what had taken place, listened to those sounds with alarm.

"Dora—my Dora," he said, faintly,

No. 3.—DORA.

"what do I hear? who is it that in this, our only refuge, seeks to harm us?"

"Oh, no, no! I do not think—I do not think—I do not believe— Henry! Henry! may I leave you once again, only for a few short moments?"

"And all this is for my sake," sighed Henry. "Dora! Dora! what misfortune I have brought upon you! You so beautiful! you so dear, and good, and gentle! Ah, our child—our little one! I do not see her, and I could see her, weak as I am; and dim as is the light in this poor home! I do not hear her breathe, and I have heard it through many a sad and weary hour. She is safe, my Dora! she is well? Ah, you will tell me that she sleeps soundly with the smile of innocence upon her lips."

This was what Dora had shrunk from.

Henry Dacres had yet to be informed that the little Mina had been torn from home by the villain Van Esling, and fain would Dora have delayed the communication, if by so doing she might have changed or softened its import.

But that was not within the range of possibility; and now, turning to Henry, while she folded her trembling arms about him, and rested her head upon his breast, she spoke in a low, wailing tone, and each word seemed to come with a painful throb from the inmost recesses of her tortured heart.

"Henry! Henry! You will not blame me! You will not say that I should have given life itself before this thing could have happened, but—but— Oh, Henry—speak! have pity!"

"Good Heaven! what would you say? This suspense, Dora, is the poor heart's worst agony. What has happened? speak —oh, speak!"

"Mina!"

"Ah!"

"Our child—our little one stolen from us—forced from home—from your arms, and from mine—from all the fond affection. Oh, Henry! I cannot speak! my words choke me! The villain, Esling! He has our child! I fought for her! Oh, Henry, believe me that I defended her and you. Look, there is blood upon my hands!"

Henry uttered a terrible cry.

Dora understood that cry, and she answered it aloud.

"No, no! It is my blood—not Mina's! See—see! the wound! The villain struck at me with his sword. Nay, pale not, Henry, I do not feel the hurt. There's so much keener a pang at my heart; but it is not Mina's blood!"

The young wounded officer was weak as a child. Just rescued from death when the life blood had nearly been drained from his veins, he had lingered for some weeks, hovering on the confines only of existence, and it was only that else he must have expired from the agony of waiting and watching that Doctor Langford had permitted him to be present in the coach on the occasion of the rescue of Dora from the hands of the executioner.

But now the reaction of the stimulants which the physician had been compelled to give him to enable him to face the execution, together with the agony of soul which the news of the abduction of Mina inflicted upon him seemed as if they had at once beckoned the hand of death to lay its icy fingers on his heart.

"Dora—my own Dora!" he spoke gently and faintly. "My dear, good, fond, gentle Dora, you—you will not weep for me when I am gone, because—because, dear, the time, you know, must come when, passing through this mortal life, so brief and so full of the storms of Fate, we shall all reach the eternity, which, sanctified by affection, will be to us the reward of our mortal love. Dora, my Dora! I am so faint, and I seem to see things that—that those only see who are closing the eyes of mortality to open those of the spirit."

Dora uttered a scream of agonised dismay.

"No, no! oh, stay with me! stay with me! Henry—my own Henry—my lover— my husband! father of our dear Mina, stay with me—stay!"

Fain was the young wounded soldier to stay with the darling of his heart.

He clung to her arms—he clung to her fair hair as it streamed about him. He held her close to his heart as though death would surely be unable to bear him from her, and his tears fell hot and fast, for it was, in good truth, hard to die so young, and to leave one behind him who so dearly loved him.

Those tears were not those of a coward spirit, afraid to die.

Ah, no! How gladly and cheerfully would he have suffered many deaths for the happiness of his own, much loved Dora.

And now, to that noble, courageous Dora, the world seemed passing away. If he whom she loved so well were really torn from her, what hope remained? What to her, at such a moment of apprehension, were titles—estates—the world's applause, and all the dignities and luxuries of mortal life?

Oh! how sad and useless a life would she then lead! What a waif—a stray upon the ocean of existence would she be!

Alas, poor Dora!

How fondly she clung to him now! with what frantic cries she called upon Heaven to "Let him live!" How she mingled her tears with his!

"Henry! Henry! my own treasure! Henry, I never yet have told you as I will tell you now how I love you. Stay with me! stay with me—your own dear Dora! You are not so pale! Oh, you will live yet— live, my own dear, dear love—my hope— my life. Henry! Henry! speak to me again! you can speak, dear. Let me hear your voice!"

"God!"

"Yes, yes, that is well! Trust—trust in Heaven! it looks down upon us now. Stronger—you are stronger, Henry!"

He spoke faintly.

"Mourn not for me, my Dora. I shall be permitted, perhaps—I will pray that I may be so, and my prayer will be granted to watch over you."

"Strive—strive, Henry—strive with me. Do not tell me that you feel death creeping over you!"

He shuddered.

"Help! help!"

Dora saw, or thought she saw by the dim light of the wretched candle that had burnt low down in the socket of the candlestick in the room, that the paleness had, if we may use the expression, deepened on his face. And yet there was a gentle smile there present, and she could see by the mild lustre of the eyes that he still lived.

"Help! oh, help!" she cried a second time. "Doctor Langford, where, oh, where are you now, with all your rare skill, to help us? He is dying—he is dying!"

"Dora! Dora!"

Henry Dacres spoke faintly.

"Yes, yes, you speak to me again, my Henry."

"The little one—our child!"

"Yes, our Mina!"

"Bring her—bring her! Let me give her perhaps the last kiss.

"Ah, he forgets!" cried Dora, as she clasped her hands despairingly. "He forgets that when he is gone, I am indeed alone. Ah! what sounds are those? what is that? more woe! more danger! Good heavens! what is that?"

"Dora! Dora! Dora!" cried a loud and mournful voice from the open street.

She started towards one of the windows of the apartment, in an attitude of intense listening.

"Dora! Dora! Dora!" cried the voice again.

"Yes, yes! that voice calls on me!" she said. "It should be a voice from the grave—from one who once loved me. It conjures up a thousand recollections of the happy days of infancy and girlhood, for that voice reminds me of my own father."

"Dora! Dora! Dora!" cried the voice again.

"I come!" said Dora. "That is not the voice of a foe. I hear! I come! What would you? I am here!"

She flung aside one of the old French casements of the window, and looked out into the night air.

Over the old houses of the Savoy she could see towards the river. The lights on the opposite shore sparkled in the frosty air. The snow reflected a strange radiance into the night atmosphere, and Dora saw a tall, dim-looking figure opposite to the house, attired in that same grey cloak which the mysterious person had worn who had passed her as she had returned to the house after her unsuccessful chase of Van Esling.

"I am here! I am here!" she cried. Oh, tell me who and what you are! If you can aid one who, sorely wounded, but now breathes between life and death, I will trust you, for your voice reminds me of my dead father."

The figure moved its arms above its head in the strange, reflected light from the snow, and then spoke in deep, earnest tones.

"The restorative—the life draught that the good physician intended to give to his patient when the hour of reaction and possibly of death should come, hangs by the mane of the horse. Quick! quick! if you would save your husband!"

"Yes—oh, yes! but you—oh, speak again! you who, to my fancy, have come from another world to help us. Tell me of my child—my Mina—shall I look upon that dear face again?"

"Behold!" said the figure, and it pointed with a long arm, that seemed to cut the night air like a bar of steel towards the river.

"Behold! you see yon star-like light that dances on the troubled waters? In the boat which carries it is the villain Esling, and your child!"

"Ah, I see! I see! help me! oh, help me!"

"I dare not! hope! hope, pray, and watch!"

The figure abruptly left the spot, and seemed to be making its way towards the river at some steps which then were much frequented, called "The Old Savoy Quay."

But Dora was not unmindful of her first duty, which was to verify, if possible, the strange words that had been uttered by that most strange and mysterious person who so much reminded her of her father, who had perished in one of those Jacobitical risings, in Scotland, in which so many of the nobility of both kingdoms were totally involved.

It will be remembered that Dora could not have any very accurate knowledgge in regard to what had happened to Doctor Langford, for when she had pursued Van Esling from the house, her mind and attention had been by far too much engrossed by the peril of the little Mina, to permit her even to take a glance on the floor of the hall of the house, where lay the assassinated physician.

The disappearance, then, of Doctor Langford was a complete mystery to her, Dora, for she did not believe for a moment that he would have willingly deserted Henry Dacres at a time which he had himself declared would be most critical to him.

Now, however, she was distinctly informed that he was gone, but that she should find the remedy which Henry's condition so urgently required, in charge of the horse, Starlight.

Who shall say but that the stamping the noble creature had made in the hall of the house was not some indication that it knew it had a part to play in the strange drama of real life which these pages will unfold to the reader?

Dora turned from the window, which she closed, and lifting the little light from the table, she held it with trembling hands, so that its best radiance—and poor, indeed, was the best—fell upon the face of Henry."

It was a terrible moment, that, for her. Perhaps the young, chivalrous spirit had fled! Perhaps the loving heart had ceased to beat!

"Henry! my Henry!"

He lived!

His lips moved slightly. No sound came from them, but she knew that it was to the sound of her name they strove to shape themselves.

"He lives! he lives yet!" she cried, "and all may yet be well!"

She left one kiss upon the pale face, and then she turned from the room, and down the antique staircase to the hall.

"The restorative!" she cried. "The potion of life! Can it be, then, as that man of mystery has said?"

Dora had taken the little light with her, and by its faint rays she saw the noble horse still in the hall.

The creature uttered a grateful sound at her approach, and when she got close enough it bestowed upon her the same kind of mute caress with its head that she had received before from it.

But now Dora was surprised to see, tied round the slender, arched neck of the horse, a silk handkerchief from the corner of which depended something, which, upon examination, she found to be a small green vial.

There was a label such as chemists attach to medicaments around the neck of the vial, and upon it, in strange letters, evidently not traced by a pen, nor with ordinary ink, for it looked more like blood, was the one word "All."

Dora comprehended what that meant. It was that Henry was to partake of the whole contents of the vial.

But now a dreadful fear came over her.

What if this were, after all, but some foul treachery on the part of Van Esling? What if the vial contained some potion that would at once sap the springs of life instead of revivifying the sinking heart.

Oh, terrible apprehension!

How could she verify or rid herself of this suspicion? But even as she held the small vial in her hand, the fearful thought that it might possibly contain a subtle poison, glided from her mind like some faintly remembered dream.

"No," she said. "No—I will not think it. And yet, were there enough of the few crimson drops contained within this little vessel on my own life I would try it ere it sought his—but I will not think it. I will trust to the inspirations of that voice which spoke to me in tones of the happy past."

Dora bestowed a gentle recognition on the horse, by passing her hand for a moment over its sleek arched neck, and she could see as she did so, that it was well equipped for the road. Long pistols, with rich silver mountings, were in the holsters of the saddle, and the horse carried a small round valise or travelling portmanteau, strapped behind the saddle.

These appointments of the gallant animal had escaped the observing of Dora when she had mounted it so hurriedly in pursuit of Van Esling.

It was but for a moment, however, that she suffered her eyes to stray over these equipments, and then, with a quick step, she sought the room above with hope fluttering at her heart that the contents of the small vial she held in her hand would bring new life to him, whose death, to her, would be a desolation, indeed.

"Hope! hope!" she cried. "Be cheered even by the thought of succour. Henry, you hear me—you see me yet—and all may still be well. The good physician, our kind friend, Dr. Langford, he is not with us, but his skill remains. We have the product of his years of study—there is life yet in this small vial—it is the restorative, Henry, that he spoke of. New pulses will yet beat in your heart, and we shall yet be happy because we shall be yet together."

He could not speak. The faint wan look upon his face was something terrible to gaze upon. The small amount of vitality his desperate wound had left him had been nearly spent as some prodigal might spend a fortune in the efforts of that fearful day.

But still he lived.

There was life, and there was the hope that ever clings to life.

And now, Dora, with trembling fingers, decanted the contents into a small tin cup, and held it to his blanched lips.

"Drink, Henry, drink!" she cried, "and should I see that it extinguishes, instead of re-illuming the flame of life, there may yet be left enough at the bottom of the cup for your Dora."

The large, wan, lustrious eyes were fixed upon her as he drank, and the pale colour faded from his cheeks, giving place to a faint hue of health.

Ah, yes—the potion was a truth! A potent life-giving elixir.

"He is saved! he is saved!" she cried. With a deep sigh, but a smile upon his lips, Henry sunk back in the old chair—a deep sleep came over him—but it was the sleep of life, and not that slumber of the tomb, which the heart of Dora had so sadly foreboded.

CHAPTER VIII.

THE MYSTERIOUS WARNING—THE HORSE AND THE BOAT—A FEARFUL PERIL— TURNBULL'S TRIUMPH—THE DEATH SHOT AND THE STAR-LIGHT IN THE BOAT.

DORA was content. Trouble upon trouble—woe upon woe was not to be her absolute portion in this world—and as she knelt by the side of that old chair, and watched the slow breathing of the slumbering Henry Dacres, a conviction crossed her mind that *his* present danger had passed away.

"He will live!" she said. "He will live! we may both suffer—suffer much—but he will live! and as the longest and weariest journey, with dear companionship, loses more than half its toil, we shall pass through life, and perchance share as many of its blessings as its cares."

But even then, as the terror of the present evil passed away, and as she felt that Henry was spared to her, Dora's thoughts soon became heavily oppressed with the loss of Mina.

Did she dream it? or was there a something said to her "By that mysterious man, who had stood amid the cold reflected snow-light and spoken to her, both of Henry and her child?"

Dora clasped her hands over her eyes, and for a moment, shut out her contemplation of the pale slumbering face of Henry.

Then her thoughts at once reverted to the words which had been uttered by the man of mystery, and to the strange action by which he had pointed to the river, indicating to her the undulating light which he had said was in the boat, containing her darling little one.

And now that Henry was safe—or comparatively safe—her thoughts flew to that light on the cold heaving tide of the river, and she seemed to see in it the sweet gentle eyes of the child that had been torn from her by the villain, Esling.

Dora rose softly from her kneeling posture at the feet of Henry, and repaired to the casement. Again she opened it sufficiently to allow her to look out upon the wintry sky, upon the old dilapidated houses upon the Savoy Quay, and upon the heaving river, where huge masses of ice had floated through the bridges, looking like snow islands from the far north.

"The light! the light!" she cried. "The light in the boat—I see it still! It stems the tide with difficulty—I hear the rush of the ebbing river! Mina—my Mina! my child! Can it be possible that that light, which to me is but a star in the distance, shines upon your dear face?"

Dora could not bear the thought. It was one of concentrated agony. She stretched out her arms, and tears streamed from her eyes—it seemed as if her heart could leap the distance, and alight in that boat which contained one of the treasures of her life.

"Henry! Henry!" she cried, as she turned from the casement. "You will pardon me—you will forgive me if I go? Nay, you will bid me forth, for it is to seek our Mina that I leave you. We are alone—alone—we have no friends—no strong arms to do battle for us—no fleet footsteps to run our errands of mercy or of love."

The deep sleep was still upon him, but it seemed as if the tones of Dora in some manner reached his heart, and he moved one of his hands gently, while a soft and tender smile played upon his face.

"Yes," she said, "I will go—you mean me to go, Henry. I will go, and surely Heaven will help me."

But Dora felt sad and sick at heart, for she knew not to what danger she was leaving him she loved.

All alone in that deserted house, so sorely wounded that the weakest foe who ever raised an arm in mischief might easily subdue him. No wonder that Dora felt she had left half her heart behind her as she went on an enterprise, the desperation of which she dared not think of.

She glanced around the apartment—she seemed as if a something could even yet be done, were she to linger for hours to add to the security of that room and of that house.

And yet, what could she do? It was but in the silence of the place—it was but in its presumed desertion that she could place her hope.

Dora clasped her arms once more around the slumbering form of Henry—she left but one trembling kiss upon her husband's cheek, and hurried from the place.

The horse was in the hall. And still in that strange fashion, which its Arab blood had taught it, it gave her tokens of recognition.

And what was Dora about to do? What plans of action had she? What scheme of procedure had she laid down for the pursuit of a boat upon the river, in which appeared a starlike light, that might or might not guide her to her child.

None—none.

If ever human heart threw itself upon

the wide waves of chance, Dora's did at that moment, as she issued from that house in the Savoy, into the deep snow that lay between her and the Thames.

The horse followed her.

She had intended to close the door upon the creature—there had been a pleasant but strange confidence in her mind in its capacity and will to act as guard to Henry in her absence.

But the horse trod quietly and daintily out of the house into the snow, and it was not until then, that reflected against the whitened earth she saw the exquisite beauty and symmetry of the creature.

But still she felt that she could not take it with her—and to abandon that living thing in the streets, perchance to a cold or cruel taskmaster, after it had shown affection towards her, she could not think of.

By coaxing and gentle pattings she tried to get the horse to return to the hall of the house.

If she returned first, it would do so, but when she stepped forth it followed her with its head upon her shoulder.

Dora was much perplexed.

She glanced towards the river.

The little light was gone.

Ah, no! it might still be there. It was from the casement she had seen it—some twenty feet above her present position, and it was, doubtless, merely hidden by the low-lying wooden houses on the river's bank.

Dora forgot everything in her desire again to see that starlike light—and she ran down the narrow tortuous way which led to the Savoy Quay.

With a graceful and easy action, the horse followed her, more than fetlock deep in snow.

There were some old slippery wooden steps, worn by age and long use, that led into the stream. The water looked as black as ink between its banks of snow, and was ebbing with a rushing sound. The boats were moored closely to the shore.

Far out in the stream a huge block of ice was sailing down with the tide, carrying with it some planks and timbers from some wharf or river craft, with which it had come in contact.

"The starlight! the starlight!" cried Dora. "I see it now again."

"Want a cast down stream?" said a gruff voice, as a man came straggling up the old wooden steps.

"Yes," cried Dora, "yes—yonder boat—it surely makes no progress? yet the light dances in the stream—take me there, I pray you, and I will give you—"

Dora came to an abrupt pause. She knew that she had not a coin or article of value about her.

"And what will you give me, my lass?" said the man,

"Indeed, indeed, I know not—but if for the love of mercy—of goodness—of charity you will take me to that boat—"

"Well!" said the man, "that's strange coin to pay a half-frozen out Thames waterman with—but if you would clap a couple of guineas in my fist, I should like to know who's to go up stream with the tide running like a mill-race. Look ye here, my lass! If you want to get to yon boat you must come down upon it—not up to it. Get round to the old Rose Wharf, by Mill Bank, that'll be just above it, I reckon."

"I thank you—I can only thank you."

There was at this moment a grating sound of the side of a boat against the old wooden steps, and as some one clumsily clambered up, a harsh voice cried out

"Holloa, there! Where can a man who's dead with cold and bruises, find something hot and strong, to put new life in him?"

Dora uttered a cry of alarm. Too well she knew that voice, and as the head and face of the new comer arose into view, she saw, as she expected, the brutal, bloated countenance of none other than Turnbull, who had been so anxious for her execution, and who was the especial bulley, bravo, and retainer of the Duke of Kingston.

Terror, more than the intense cold of that bleak river's bank, froze the faculties of Dora. She could but utter one more cry as she saw the hideous face, and that cry was echoed by Turnbull himself, as he held up a lantern, from the lens of which he had just dashed its covering, and sent a broad ray of light full upon Dora and the horse.

"By the fiends!" he cried, "but this is lucky! This is Dora Dacres! Ah, ah! I'm in high favor with the devil himself to-night. So—so my dainty morsel, Jack Ketch was too rough for you—but we shall see yet if the hempen cord, well greased as it was, will not make a necklace for a Duchess! Fiends and furies! I'm lucky. Your fortune's made, Turnbull—and all in a crack.

Dora shrunk back step by step among the snow, and for a few short moments she believed that all her hopes of freedom—all her dreams of yet being able to love, to cherish, and to protect those who were dear to her, had come to an end.

There was her terrible foe before her—there was the man who had been the principal in the hands of the unprincipled Duke of Kingston, in accomplishing the ruin—nearly the death of her husband, and her own destruction.

"Oh, Heaven!" she cried, "now save me! Now have some mercy upon me!"

She clasped her hands together and leant

upon the neck of the horse, which was between her and the villain Turnbull now, for as Dora had stepped back, the noble animal had seemed to feel that she needed some interposition between her and danger, and it had stepped forward a pace or two, and with its clear sparkling eyes, and proud arched neck looked, as though in dumb eloquence it would bid defiance to Turnbull.

"Mine, now!" cried Turnbull. "My turn now! Ha, ha! It was well to feign death when the mob at Tyburn flung me against the doorway! I feigned to be dead that I might live again — that I might live for such a moment as this, and it has come! it has come! Dora, you are my prisoner!"

He drew a heavy, short, square-looking horse pistol from the huge flap of his overcoat, and presented it at Dora, as with a laugh of derision, he said—

"What shall it be? Ha, ha! which shall it be? The bullet or the cord? Say the word—which shall it be? There is one who will give as much for the dead Dora Dacres as the living one."

"Help—oh, help me!" said Dora. "You —you, who cannot side with this ruffian."

It was the waterman that she appealed to, but he was intimidated by the aspect of Turnbull, and, with a cowardly aspect, slowly crept away.

"You see," said Turnbull, "you are mine. Come, now, you were ever a dainty and delicate piece of beauty! what do you say to making some terms, even with me, eh?"

"You mean," said Dora, "that there is some human feeling in your heart yet— some touch of compassion! You mean that Heaven has not fashioned any of its creatures, and left them destitute of pity?"

"Pity? pity? Ha, I don't know the word!"

"Ah, there is help yet!"

Dora had uttered this exclamation—something cold had touched her hands. They had slipped along the sleek neck of the horse until they touched the massive silver butt of one of the holster pistols attached to the saddle of the gallant Arabian.

One moment, and the despair of Dora was changed to courageous hope.

The pistol, with its long shining barrel, and its mountings was in her grasp. It was levelled over the saddle of the horse, and Turnbull saw that he had to encounter a danger for which he was most completely unprepared.

"Yes, yes!" cried Dora—"I feel now that I am not deserted—I feel that Heaven has aided me at this dread moment! I am free from you now."

"You are mad, girl! you are mad!" said Turnbull. But he spoke in very different tones now to those which had before come in taunting fashion from his lips. "You are mad, I say, if you think you can escape me. Put aside that weapon which you cannot know how to use."

"My husband is a soldier," she said, "and I do know how to use the weapon that Providence has placed at this moment within my grasp."

A paleness spread itself over the face of Turnbull, and the lantern trembled in his left hand. He could see with what clear and motionless aim the pistol was levelled at his head. He feared that one touch at the trigger, which would be sufficient to explode it, would be given, and that he should feel along with the report the deadly dash of a bullet in his lungs or heart.

"Forbear! forbear!" he said. "I will forego my purpose. Dora, you will not commit murder! We shall meet again. Let me pass, and I will go quietly from this place."

"No!"

"I swear it! I will not seek to injure you."

"Go, villain!"

"Ah, you are reasonable now."

"Go, go, villain! but it shall be the way you came."

"To the river?"

"Ay, to the river. Go at once, or I will fire—I will here count three, and then—"

"Hold! hold! The boat has gone adrift. Hold, a moment!"

"One!" said Dora.

"Hoi! a boat! a boat! Who has a boat on hire at the quay?"

"Two!"

"Ah, there they are! They have come at last down from the Strand to the old Savoy!"

Turnbull made a movement with the lantern as though he were encouraging some people to come down to the old quay by the same route that had brought Dora to the spot, and for the moment she was thrown off her guard, for finesse was not one of the characteristics of that pure and gentle being. She turned her gaze for one instant in the contrary direction to the river and Turnbull.

The villain then fired the short stumpy pistol he had in his right hand, full at Dora's head.

If the horse had not swerved at that instant, there might then and there have been an end, by murder, of Dora the Duchess; but as it was, the slight movement of the steed placed her head out of the line of fire, and the two bullets with which Turnbull's pistol had been charged, passed her fair cheek harmlessly.

Then, quick as thought, Dora comprehended all the treachery of the would-be assassin, and through the smoke from the discharge of his pistol, she fired the richly ornamented weapon she was possessed of.

There was a yelling cry, and Turnbull fell backwards down the wooden steps that led to the half-frozen river.

The horse had stood still as a statue while Dora had fired the pistol, and Dora, without then waiting for a prolonged contest, or to see what effect the shot had had, sprung lightly to the saddle of the horse, and turning its face towards the Strand, she galloped from the old Savoy Quay.

Dora was not forgetful of what the waterman had said in regard to the only way of reaching the boat in which was the little star-like light which she hoped shone upon the face and form of the little Mina; so she turned the horse's footsteps towards Charing Cross.

Fleetly and lightly the creature made its way through the deep snow, and Dora was about to turn into Whitehall, and had just cast a passing glance upon the statue of the First Charles, associated as it was with what Van Esling had said to her on the occasion of his tearing from her arms her child, when loud shouts came upon her ears, and she saw approaching her a party of horsemen.

For a moment Dora could not believe that these cries and shouts had any reference to her, but she was soon convinced that such was in reality the case, by the gestures of the horsemen, and by the glitter of arms with which they menaced her.

"Forward! forward, my men!" cried one. "I know the horse too well to doubt it. Forward! That is Hawk, the highwayman's horse, for a thousand pounds! There is not such another in the three kingdoms. Forward! forward!"

A couple of pistol shots rung in the night air, and poor Dora found herself in a position of the most passing danger.

What was she to do?

If taken by these men, of course they would see in a moment that she was not the owner of the horse they recognised, but might not some of them, if, as was most probable, they were mounted officers of the police, at once identify her as the condemned Dora Dacres?

Was she, after all, then, to be dragged to death, after the escapes she had had, and the many dangers she had run?

Oh, the thought was maddening. She felt for a moment as though her heart would break. Her thoughts flew back to the old Savoy—to that chamber in which slept her poor wounded Henry in that critical sleep which would be life or death to him—to her

little Mina, in the hands of the ruffian, Van Esling.

What was to become of those two helpless beings — husband wounded, and child a prisoner with its mother's worst foe, if she should die?

"Seize him! seize him!" cried a voice. "If he once gets a quarter of a mile the start of us, there is not a horse in England can reach him!"

"Ah!" cried Dora, with a joyous cry— "Help has come again—all is not lost!"

Those words, unconsciously spoken by one of the horsemen, had aroused her to a perception of where her only chance of safety lay.

In the speed of the horse—in the matchless fleetness of the gallant Arabian. There was safety yet.

Dora tightened her hold upon the rein of the noble creature.

"Now we have him!" cried the voice again of the leader of the party of officers, as no doubt in the imperfect night light he thought the veritable Captain Hawk, whom he had mentioned, was on the horse he had recognised. "Now for it! Three of you to the right of the statue, and three to the left. Now we have him!"

The officer divided this force in the manner indicated by their chief, and for the space of about a moment Dora felt that she was nearly surrounded by her foes, but she gave one touch to the neck of the steed, and raised a cry, half of personal alarm and half of encouragement to the animal, and, with one leap forward, the horse cleared the grasp made at its head by a couple of the officers.

"On—on!" cried Dora. "On! now for liberty—for life!"

The horse caught the contagion of her fears, and it darted forwards with a speed that set pursuit at defiance, and yet withal the motion was so easy that Dora had no difficulty in keeping her place in the saddle.

"Fire!" cried a loud voice.

The sharp sound of the pistols in the night air, clear and frosty as it was, immediately succeeded to the order, but neither Dora nor the horse were touched. The speed of the Arab steed rather increased than diminished, and although Dora, by a glance she cast now and then behind her could see that the officers were in full pursuit, she did not entertain the remotest apprehension of being overtaken.

"Oh, what a chance is this?" she said to herself, "that now, in such an extremity of my fortunes, I should light on a friend so fleet of foot as this noble horse. I am saved—I am saved!"

From Charing Cross, up the long thoroughfare that led to Hyde Park Corner—

dashing on through the heavy snow which the further they got out of the close region of houses, lay thicker and deeper on the highway, went Dora and the horse.

With shouts and cries the officers pursued her still.

They could have but one hope in that chase, where they went but three feet to the Arabian horse's four, and that was that by keeping up a clamour as they went, some mounted and armed men—for most men in those days travelled on horseback and well armed—might meet the flying horse and so bar its progress.

Moreover, spanning the high road at the very commencement of the then quite rural village of Knightsbridge was a turnpike gate, which had more than once proved a serious obstacle to the "Knights of the Road" when chased from London.

The officers had, perhaps a hope that the high barred gate, with its formidable row of spikes at the top, would prove an obstacle to the horse of which they were in chase.

And so it might, had that steed, which so gallantly carried the life of Dora, been of ordinary mettle.

The gate was in sight!

The shouts of the pursuers came still hoarsely on the night air.

There was a rushing sound—a shower of snowy particles, and the horse had cleared the gate with a good two feet to spare.

The pike keeper ran out in his nightcap with a shout, and then he cried out—

"By Jove! it's Starlight and the Captain. There is not another horse I know of could do that. Hurrah!"

From that time Dora lost both sight and sound of her pursuers; but she galloped on five miles further into the open country, and then, as the horse made its way through a hollow in the road, into which the snow had drifted to the depth of some three or four feet, Dora checked the creature's speed, and finally halted on the rise of a gentle slope, which was comparatively free from snow.

The night had nearly passed away now, and the first flash of the early dawn was beginning to make the tree tops look of that dull grey colour which their denuded branches wore in that cold, winter light.

Some birds twittered in the still air.

The Arabian steed pawed the frozen earth, and did not seem to be in the least distressed by its tremendous gallop of eight miles.

And there was Dora, alone on that solitary road, with all she loved now far from her—her heart in that old, dim house in the Savoy—her child she knew not where.

What was she to do?

The horse seemed resolved to put an end to all doubt upon that subject, for suddenly, without any impulse being given to it by Dora, it trotted to the roadside, and abruptly turned down a narrow lane—a lane so narrow, indeed, that its opening escaped Dora's observation altogether; and no doubt, in summer time, it was completely shadowed and shrouded by the luxuriant hedgerow and the tall trees that grew about its entrance.

It seemed to Dora as though the horse felt it had a destination down that lane, and partly from a doubt of her own powers to stay its progress and partly from curiosity to know whither it was going, Dora made no opposition to a trot of about a quarter of a mile along the narrow bridle path.

The horse then stopped at a low, moss-grown wall, and as the morning light now came more and more over the dim, wintry sky, Dora could see that there was a low, arched, Gothic door in the wall, and an iron ring in a niche, which, in all probability communicated with a bell.

That Starlight, the horse, found himself at home at this low, arched doorway in the dilapidated wall, or that it was some place at which he had been in the habit of stopping, was sufficiently evident; but whether it would be prudent on her, Dora's part, to seek shelter and rest there, even for an hour, was but a doubtful proposition.

Indeed, the circumstances surrounding Dora, at the present, were of the most perplexing character. Her anxiety to reach London again was most intense, but the question arose in her mind of when and in what way it would be safe to do so.

At all events, she felt that the sound and riot of the pursuit that had taken place of her and Starlight should subside before she could venture back even with the assistance of Starlight, considering that eight weary miles of snow laden streets lay between her and that dim old mansion where she hoped yet slept the object of her affections.

And poor Dora felt sick and faint at heart —want of rest and want of food, together with the re-action of the violent excitement she had passed through, would have told upon a stronger frame than hers; and now more than once, with a feeling of great exhaustion, she let her head sink low down upon the neck of Starlight, and tears that would not be controlled gushed from her eyes,

"Rest! rest!" she said, "but one hour's rest!" and she went on speaking as though addressing her wounded husband in the Savoy. "Rest! but one hour's rest, Henry —some little food—a crust of bread, if it be but that—and a draught of water—lest I faint by the way in returning to you—rest and peace until the turmoil of pursuit has died away. I shall be sooner with you— much sooner for the lapse of one short hour."

But where was she to rest.

Dared she place her hand upon that iron ring, and ask for food and shelter—perhaps in the very haunt of the Captain Hawk who had been named by the officers as the well-known highwayman and rider of the Arab steed.

No—no! she dared not—That would be to court danger—to bespeak attention—to ruin all!

Then for a moment Dora thought that death was near her—a fearful faintness crept about her heart—her eyes grew dim, and she sank lower still upon the neck of Starlight. It was but a question, to perish there amid the snows of that desolate region, or to hazard all by asking succour at that lone and mysterious abode. Dora, with almost the last effort of strength she could bring to her aid, rung the bell.

She heard the faint tingle for admission within the place, and then there came an upward flash of light from some candle or lantern from the other side of the wall.

A loud voice broke the stillness of the dim morning air.

"Captain? hilloa! It's you and Starlight—I thought I heard the well-known step on the frozen ground.

"Here!" said Dora.

The low arched door was flung open.

"You're hit at last," said the same voice, "there's a bullet in you, Captain, or you wouldn't speak in that tone. Gently, Starlight, gently."

The horse was evidently accustomed to enter by that low-arched doorway—and as evidently depended upon his rider to take care of his head in passing beneath the narrow arch, and it was well for Dora that at that moment she was by far too weak and faint to sit upright on the saddle. Her right arm was flung round the neck of the horse, and her face and head rested low amid its silken mane.

And so Dora passed unscathed into what, no doubt, in the soft summer time was a wildly luxuriant and beautiful garden—but now the snow lay in huge mounds upon the flowering shrubs, and Dora could but dimly see before her one of those gable-ended thickly-thatched cottages which are so frequently found away from high roads, and thickly embowered in vegetation.

The horse stopped abruptly, and it was rather instinctively than with any wish to do so that Dora alighted, and staggered a few paces forward towards the house.

She fell like one in a dream, and was scarcely roused even when the man who admitted her rushed forward, and grasping her by her mantle, exclaimed "Who, and what are you, that you come here on the Captain's horse? Have you slain him? And must I after all do vengeance on a woman? I have sworn it—the horse has brought you to your doom, for nothing but death would make him part with it."

CHAPTER IX.

THE FATE OF THE INNOCENT—DORA'S NEW FRIEND—CAPTAIN HAWK—THE HIGHWAYMAN AND A MYSTERY—DORA MAKES A RESOLVE—THE ROUTE TO LONDON.

HAD this man resolved upon the instant to take the life of Dora, she would have had no power of resistance. She could but sink down among the snow and hold up both hands imploringly, as, after disappearing in the cottage for a moment, he returned with a costly sword in his hand, and raised it threateningly above her head.

"Speak!" he said, "Speak! have you killed him? He always said it was prophesied he should die by the hands of a woman, and I have sworn that I would avenge him. Speak, I say, have you killed him?"

"I know not" said Dora faintly, "of whom you speak. The horse—the horse!"

"Ay, the horse, Starlight—it has brought you here. The creature knows the way on the darkest night that ever gloomed beneath the sky. Tell me, what have you done with the captain? Betrayed him, I fancy, in some fashion. Ah! I see, you cannot answer me, or will not. Then I must do my duty."

"In mercy slay me not. As you are a man, and I a weak, defenceless woman, spare my life. The man did not reply; but it seemed as though there were something in the tones of Dora which struck a tenderer chord in his heart than those which were attuned to violence and vengeance.

The morning light was still too dim to be available in the thorough recognition of form and feature; but lifting the lantern from the snow, which he had cast from him, this man, whose tones were rather those of one who wished to cheat himself into the performance of a duty he half revolted from, held the light close to Dora's face.

She felt that she was safe.

The rays of the lantern fell impartially upon his face as well as hers, and then a smile, such as probably had not mantled on her lips for many a day, was seen in the flashing light, and it was in a shrieking voice, she called out—

"Dottman—Dottman! I know you now—my father's friend, servant, and soldier. Joseph Dottman, I know you now. You cannot kill me—you would not—dare not—Oh, heaven, I thank thee!"

The faintness that Dora had baffled up to this moment, and which the strong sense of danger and the necessity for action had kept at bay now swept over her heart and brain with full force, and she was barely conscious of some one uttering cries and supplications, and of the feel of hot tears upon her cheek, as she was lifted from the snow, and carried into the cottage.

Then there came to Dora a short period of oblivion from care, and when she opened her eyes again, the strong aromatic perfume which had been used by some means for her restoration, was the first sensation that struck her senses.

"Ah!" cried the man she had named Dottman. "She lives! my dear old master's only child. I know her now—the daughter of the Lady Geraldine. Alas—alas! what misfortunes—what misery—what deaths! Dora—Dora, look up. I who have not seen you since a child, know you now. But whether this be all a dream, from which I shall awaken to find myself own man to a highwayman, or really looking into your face, Lady Dora, I know not."

"Dottman!" said Dora, gently, "And so you would have killed me?"

"No—no! a thousand times no—I never could have done it—though I did promise Captain Hawk that if any body came here on Starlight, I was to take for granted they had killed him, for you see the creature has been trained to gallop like the wind, heedless of bit or spur—of wind or weather—gate, fence, or obstruction—from Charing Cross to here."

"Gracious Heavens!" said Dora, "there is more than mortal accident in all this. Dottman, it is many a long year since I looked upon yon—do you recollect my poor father's escape from that little port in Devon—when accused of high treason, he sought safety with me in the frailest boat that ever sought an angry ocean?"

"Remember it?" cried Dottman. "I think of it often for a whole day, and dream of it for a whole night. I heard that the good Duke was dead?"

"Alas! yes."

"And you, Lady Dora—why you should be the Duchess?"

"I should be, Dottman—but there is one who calls himself the Duke, who would rather see me in my grave than let me assume that title, and yet he is my father's brother!"

"Ah, yes! I know that," said Dottman. "If the good Duke, your father, had been taken, he would have been found guilty of high treason, the title attainted, and the estates confiscated; but as he died abroad, your uncle, who stands well with the present Government, stepped forward, and denying that your poor father was ever really married to Lady Geradine your mother, got the title and estates. I thought both you and your father dead, and as your mother was no more, why there seemed an end of the matter. But now— Why surely you are Dora the Duchess."

Dora's eyes filled with tears.

"I am desolate, poor, friendless, and a hunted criminal."

"You—you?" cried Dottman. "Nay, it is not possible. The Duke, your uncle—the false Duke—"

"A traitor and a persecutor."

"The high nobility, who all knew your father—he had many friends."

"Fair weather friends! none will now look upon the desolate Dora; they no doubt crowd the gilded saloons of the present Duke of Kingston, while I might have died by the hands of the common hangman, and all I loved have perished with want."

Dottman was deeply affected. He clenched his hands—he paced the old, low-roofed cottage with hasty strides.

"Good Heaven!" he said. "But is there no one will help you. This very Captain Hawk—the owner of Starlight. Do you know the horse is worth a thousand pounds. He is a man bad and good by fits and starts, but he will help you. Perhaps you know him?"

"No, no! I heard his name first mentioned by the mounted officers of police, who in vain pursued me."

"In vain, of course, Lady Dora, if you were mounted on Starlight. But let me tell you. After my good lord, the Duke, your father, had escaped from England with you, I came to London, and then some busy body must have given notice to the authorities that I was his servant, and had helped him, so they clapped me up in the Compter in Giltspur Street, and there I lingered two years, expecting any morning to be taken out and be hanged. Well, you see, Lady Dora, those two years sharpened my wits and two old nails at the same time, with which I effected my escape. Well, you will blame me, but I couldn't help it, I took to the road; but a meddling fellow in a mail coach lodged a bullet in my chest. I have not felt quite strong enough for the heath and the highway ever since, and then I met with Captain Hawk, and I'm his man now. I look after Starlight, and here I stay and dream of my old master, and wonder how the world goes on with all its wickedness."

Dora sighed deeply.

"I, too, Dottman, have a tale to tell."

"To be sure—to be sure! Alas! alas!"

"Leaving my father dead in Germany, I came to England. He had told me that among the family papers in that great, rich house in St. James's, Kingston House, would be found the proofs of his marriage with my mother."

"Yes, Lady Dora; and you found them?"

"I was spurned from the threshold by my uncle's menials!"

"No!"

"It was so, Dottman. But I was not then quite desolate, for there was one who loved me—a young officer in the Guard of England."

"Thank Heaven for that," cried Dottmann. "But did he love you for your own sake, or because he thought you would be Duchess of Kingston?"

"For my own sake, and ah, so truly—so nobly—so with all his heart."

Dora could not now control her tears again, for her thoughts flew back to the old Savoy, and then she seemed to see in her mind's eye, that noble heart awaiting her return.

"You shall know all, Dottman," she added, speaking hysterically through her tears. "He loved me! we came over from Holland in the same vessel. He had been to the Hague on some mission for his colonel —he is now my husband!"

Dottman looked surprised.

"Yes, my dear, loving husband of now more than two years, and we have a little one—the dear—dear—"

Dora's sobs choked her utterance.

"Don't tell me any more about it," said Dottman. "I would rather not know a word of it, than it should distress you, Lady Dora."

"Yes yes, I would fain tell you all, because I know that you will feel for me."

"Feel—Feel? God knows I do that?"

"This young officer, then, was named Henry Dacres We were married, and it was not until the day before that I told him who and what I was."

"That was right, Lady Dora! then he loved you for your dear, pretty face, and all your soft, gentle, winning ways; as who would not? Well, what did he say to that?"

"He was surprised, and for a moment there came to his cheek a flush of pride in the thought that I, whom he loved so truly, was of such rank and birth; but when I told him all, and that my poor father had maintained a falling cause in England, and that he was no more, and I was poor—very poor, he clasped me to his heart, and told me that I was his duchess—his peeress, and that the true patent of nobility was in my own affections."

"He is a noble fellow, this husband of yours, Lady Dora, but for one thing."

"What would you say, Dottman? What would you object to him in?"

"Why, you are here, faint, weary, and having passed through very many dangers. Where is he?"

"Sorely wounded, almost to the death."

"Ah!"

"Yes, and the pain of his wound is as nothing to the agony he feels that he cannot aid me."

"That is well! he is a noble fellow. But you have not told me all."

"I have not. We consulted about the matters of my rank and fortunes As I say, I had been to my uncle's house. I had heard that he claimed the titles and estates, and that he had been recognised in both by the King in Council; but Henry Dacres could not believe that there was so much wickedness in mortal man as there is in that man who now calls himself the Duke of Kingston."

Dottman shook his head sadly, as though he would have said that you might have any amount of faith in the wickedness of mankind.

Dora continued.

"My Henry, unknown to me, went to the Duke of Kingston, who had only recently been appointed colonel of his regiment, and he tried to move his heart to justice to me—that heart which never knew pity nor remorse."

"And what happened?"

"Alas! alas! most dire misfortune."

"To be sure. That was sure to be."

"There was a man who was a Captain in the regiment. This captaincy was but a cloak for the fact that he was the bravo and assassin, who was ever ready to do the detestable bidding of the Duke of Kingston. That man was set upon my husband, to pick a quarrel with him, and a duel was arranged. It was to be with the weapons of gentlemen. The sword was to decide the issue, but at the place of meeting the villain arrived with some companions of his own, and my poor husband was at once shot through the breast, and left for dead upon the field.

"The cowardly rascal!"

"I there found him, and from that time to this he has been at the point of death— he is halting but on the confines of life."

"Come, Lady Dora! This won't do," said Dottman, who had placed some refreshments before Dora. You don't eat, and I can see that you get paler and paler each moment."

"I will! I will! I cannot be so selfish."

"Why, you don't call eating selfish, Lady Dora?"

"O, no, I was going to say that I won't be so selfish as to neglect my own health and strength, for if I were to do so, what would become of those who are now dependent upon me."

"That's right," said Dottman, as he brushed away a tear from his eyes. "But you have not told me all."

"I have not!"

"And above all, you have not told me the name of the rascal who wounded your husband."

"He is named Van Esling."

"Van Esling!"

"Yes, that is his name. Alas! I have cause to know it too well."

"It is strange that I seem as if I had heard the name before," said Dottman; "and yet I cannot remember when or where."

"I will tell you all," added Dora. "I felt quite convinced, from what my father had told me, that, concealed in a particular cabinet in the house inhabited by the Duke of Kingston, I should find some documents that would substantiate my claims, and prove my birth."

Dottman shook his head.

"You may depend, Lady Dora, he would destroy all such documents."

"It may be so, but I thought that I would make one effort to procure the evidence, and after much watching, I found the opportunity of concealing myself in the house."

"In Kingston House?"

"Yes, I glided in in the daytime, when

a number of people were passing in and out, and in the dead of the night I sought for the room that my father had mentioned to me. I found it, but there was no cabinet there. The room was changed and altered to a much more modern aspect than that which the description of my father had made it wear in my thoughts. I would then fain have left the house, and I had reached the hall, when the doors were flung open, and the Duke, my uncle, appeared, inflamed with wine, and with a slight wound that he had received in some brawl.

"Oh, what danger!"

"Yes, I fled from the house, but was pursued and captured, and to my surprise the charge brought against me was that I had made an attempt to set fire to Kingston House."

"You? you?"

"Even so. There came forward a man named Turnbull, who swore that he had for some hours watched me; that I had made three several attempts to burn down the mansion. I was tried and convicted, and taken out to die."

"You to die."

"Yes, oh, yes! But I was saved by my husband, and by Doctor Langford, a kind good physician, who pitied us, and to whom I owe, not only my life, but that of my husband."

Dottman was deeply affected, but when Dora further told him of those subsequent events, which had resulted in getting possession of the horse, Starlight, in such a strange way, and the abduction of the little Mina, he was lost in wonder at the extraordinary character of the incidents.

"Good Heavens!" he cried. "What if this Van Esling and Captain Hawk the Highwayman should turn out to be one and the same person?"

"It seems more than probable," replied Dora.

Scarce had these words passed her lips, than both she and Dottman started to their feet as they heard from without, in the faint light of the morning air, a loud and prolonged whistle, which evidently had the character of a signal of some kind.

"What is that? oh, who and what is that?" said Dora.

"The Captain," cried Dottman.

"He whom you have mentioned?"

"Yes, that is Captain Hawk's signal!"

"And perchance the villain Esling! I will see him—I will confront him."

"No, no!"

"Yes, a thousand times yes—I will—I must! my child—my Mina! I will demand her of him while I have life to speak."

"Hold! oh, hold!" said Dottman. "You know not the angry passions of the man

you would provoke. If Hawk and Esling be one and the same person, he is a man to whom human life is but a plaything."

The whistle sounded long, loud, and clear again.

"I will see him," cried Dora. "He dare not kill me! he dare not look into my face when I shall ask him for my child."

With a vehemence that would not be controlled, Dora snatched up the beautifully ornamented sword with which Dottman had been armed on her first appearance at the cottage, and rushed out into the snow-covered little garden.

It was in vain that Dottman called to her to pause, even for a moment.

She reached the low arched door in the wall, through which Starlight had conducted her so cleverly, and acting on the impulse of thoughts that would not be controlled, she flung it open, and with the glittering sword in her hand, she stood on the threshold.

The faint gleams of the morning light fell on her fair form—on the beautiful hair and on the light graceful figure of this masterpiece of nature, and her voice was loud and clear, as she cried—

"My child—my own, my beautiful child! my little one! Villain, of you I demand her!"

Travel worn and snow encumbered, his face pale and cadaverous, Van Esling stood some few paces from the door in the wall.

There was no longer now any doubt of his identity with the highwayman, Captain Hawk, who had been the owner of the beautiful Arabian horse.

There he was, seeking on foot since he lost that horse in the manner we have related, the haunt which he had established in that quiet, charming spot of floral beauty; but to see Dora there, and armed, and to hear her voice demanding of him her child, was so intense a surprise to him that, had it been his life she sought, she might easily, then and there, have driven the keen blade of the sword through his heart.

With his arms elevated above his head—with his lips painfully retracted, and with a glaring look of surprise and fear in his eyes, Van Esling regarded Dora.

"Villain!" she cried; "I demand of you my child!"

Van Esling staggered back in the snow. He bit his lip till the blood started, and then, with a cry, he shouted—

"I am mad! I am mad! I see those who are in my thoughts, but who are not really present to my eyes! This is not Dora."

"I am Dora," she cried—"and I demand of you my child!"

"No, no! it is, perchance, a dream! it

may be but a vision of the night! and if it be not, I am mad! mad!"

With wild looks, he rushed from the spot, and was soon lost to sight in the wilderness of trees and shrubs that made that place almost a wood in itself.

CHAPTER X.

DOTTMAN GIVES DORA PRACTICAL ADVICE —THE TRANSFORMATION—A KNIGHT OF THE ROAD—STARLIGHT'S NEW MASTER— THE DAWN OF DAY—DORA'S NEW EXIS- TENCE.

DORA would fain have followed the vil- lain, Van Esling. She would fain, with that keen, bright sword in her hand, have sought to extract from his very heart the in- formation of where he had hidden the little Mina, but she found her strength inadequate to the task.

A few faltering steps in the deep snow were all she could make.

Dottman alone, by springing forward, saved her from falling, and caught her on his arm.

"Help! oh, help!" she cried. "I must —I will follow him! The horse! bring me the horse! Starlight! Ho, Starlight!"

With a bound, the Arabian steed rushed from the garden, and was by her side.

"No, no!" said Dottman, "it would be madness! I saw that Van Esling, as you called him, and Captain Hawk were one and the same man, but it would be madness to pursue him. He would soon recover from the strange fright that has come over him, and would turn upon you, and recover the horse, and how, then, could you reach London, and the old Savoy?

It was this last argument which had all the desired effect upon Dora.

No prophesy of hurt to herself would have staid her in her pursuit of Van Esling; but the moment Dottman spoke of the old Savoy, she saw again her husband, Henry Dacres, waiting for her, perhaps dying and helpless, in that old cold house, and all alone.

She wrung her hands and wept.

You are right—you are right!" she said, while the tears run down her cheeks. "You are right, and have reflected for me when I could not for myself."

"And, besides, you see, Lady Dora," said Dottman, "he had not the little one with him!"

"No, no! he had not! Perhaps now my own dear Mina is with no one but God's angels."

Dora suffered Dottman to lead her back to the cottage, and Starlight walked gently into a small barn that was at one side of the garden, and which the creature was evidently accustomed to consider as its home in that place.

Dora seemed now, for a few moments, as if she would give herself up to despair. The terrible idea had taken possession of her that as Van Esling had not the little Mina with him, he had, perhaps, taken the child's life rather than be encumbered with the care of it.

Dottman did all he could to combat this most depressing and heart-rending suppo- sition, and after a time he partially suc- ceeded.

He represented to Dora that if such were the case, Van Esling would feel that he had placed a barrier between himself and Dora which nothing could surmount.

"And," added Dottman, "however you, Lady Dora, and I may feel how absurd any idea he may have that time will soften your heart towards him, may be, he would never, professing to love you, as he does, at once put an end to all his hopes by the murder of your child."

"It may be so," sighed Dora, sadly. "But what shall I do? what will become of us all now? I have no means even to live! Poor Henry, since his wound, has, of course, not appeared in his place in the regiment, and never can again. We are lost—lost and desolate!"

Dottman paced the apartment of the cot- tage in an uneasy fashion, as though he were in a deep tangle of thought about something.

Then abruptly pausing before Dora, he said, in a hesitating voice—

"Lady Dora, you have so many enemies, that I cannot but feel it will be terribly dangerous for you to go to London, in day- light, as you are."

"As I am?"

"Yes, and if you would take advice from one who loved your father, and was trusted by him—"

"Oh, yes—yes, I will, indeed, take your advice, Dottman. I know that it will be dictated for my good."

"Very well!" added Dottman. "Then what I would advise is just this. Above stairs, in this cottage, there are some dozen trunks and boxes full of all sorts of apparel that belonged to different passengers, who were on the top of different coaches that have been stopped by Captain Hawk. I would advise, then, that you go up stairs and look over them, and select some costume which will effectually disguise you from all eyes."

"It is a good thought, Dottman."

"I hope it is, dear Lady Dora. You see that you have much to fear."

I have, indeed—I have everything to fear from reeognition, since now there are so many who know me turned against me."

"To be sure there are, Lady Dora."

"Yes—there is the Duke of Kingston, falsely so called, and there are all his myrmidons who know me—there are the officials and the officers of the police—there is Van Esling, too, who I hope, when I cast my eyes upon him again, may not know me, in which case I might be able to follow him, and discover where he has hidden my dear Mina."

"Ah!" said Dottman, with animation, "all that is as true as gospel, and so I make bold to say that I would advise you to disguise yourself like some young cavalier—you will find abundance of material with which to do so above here, and then, mounted on Starlight, you might ride through a mob of your foes, and never be known."

"I must and will do it," said Dora. "The safety of myself is the safety of those dear to me."

Dora had made a resolve, and she was not the one to allow a long time to elapse between that state of mind and the carrying it out.

In the little low-roofed room of the cottage, which was just under the thatch, she found that Captain Hawk, *alias* Captain Van Esling, had collected an immense quantity of plunder, and while Dottman went to attend to Starlight, before whom he placed a plentiful meal of boiled rice, mingled with crushed oats, which the Arabian steed was particularly fond of, Dora made those changes in her aspect which enabled her to defy her foes, and which had important results which at that moment she was far indeed from contemplating.

In one of the trunks that were in the room above she found a quantity of apparel that seemed to have belonged to some young foreign officer, who from the size of the clothing could scarcely have been older than sixteen or seventeen years of age.

The apparel was costly in its make and fashion, and when Dora slowly descended the staircase of the cottage, and presented herself before Dottman, he could not restrain an exclamation of surprise and admiration at the great change which had been effected in her appearance.

There is a portrait, even now, at that estate belonging to the Earl of Essex, at Castlebury Park, near Watford, of Dora as she appeared in that very dress, which she found in the trunk that had no doubt been stolen by Captain Hawk from some coach or chaise.

That portrait is unknown where it now hangs, but it is quite a gem of art, and was painted from recollection by one of the first artists of that period, who merely chanced to see Dora, and was charmed by her aspect.

We must endeavour to give our readers some idea of how Dora looked when she was disguised according to the advice of Dottman.

She wore—to commence with the head—one of those wigs which at that period had only been retained in court presentations, but which, by the whiteness of the hair imparted such a delicate tint to the complexion—her hat was of a dark brown beaver, and there lay along its rim a long feather of jet black, at the extreme end of which was a tip of pure white.

The coat was of dark purple cloth, trimmed with silver braid. It was partially open, so as to show the scarlet silk of the waistcoat, which reached low down, and was trimmed likewise with silver lace, contrasting well with the pure white of the thick kid pantaloons, and the half boots of wrinkled cordovan leather, which reached to the knees.

Upon these boots were a pair of gold spurs.

A rich lace cravat was tucked into the vest, and the ruffles in the coat were very handsome.

Gloves of soft white beaver completed the costume, and Dora, as she stood in the little cottage, looked pre-eminently handsome.

Dottman made a low bow.

"Colonel Arod!" he said, "I am your most humble and devoted servant."

"Colonel who do you call me?" said Dora.

"Arod," replied Dottman, "that you know is the contrary way of spelling Dora—A—R—O—D."

"Well, then, let that be my name—but I don't know that I ought to be called Colonel!"

"You look like a prince," said Dottman.

Dora shook her head. Her heart was too heavy to smile.

"If by the aid of this disguise," she said, I shall be able to pass through London streets, and reach in safety the abode in the Savoy, where I have left my dear Henry, I shall be content with it."

"Oh!" said Dottman, "there can be no doubt of that—you will not be known; only still I would have you hide your face as much as possible."

"Indeed?"

"Yes, more than ever!"

"Alas! shall I be known then?"

"No, not as Dora Dacres—but one half the women will be so madly in love with you, that you will never get along the streets."

"Ah! Dottman, you jest with me, and my poor heart is too full to smile at you."

Not I, by Heaven!" said Dottman; "but allow me to hand you this sword, child. A better weapon you could not possibly have. The pistols that are in the holsters of Star-

light's saddle are of the very best, too, and here is a small cartouche box which Captain Hawk used to sling about Starlight's neck, and which contains thirty charges for the pistols."

"But you, Dottman?"

"What of me, Lady Dora?

"What are you to do? what is to become of you?"

Dottman's eyes glistened, and his hand trembled, as he held the sword.

"Do you think, dear mistress," he said, "that now the happy day has come that I look upon you once again, I am going to abandon you—no, no, no!"

"But—"

"Ah do not cast me off. I was faithful to my good lord, your dear father, and will

No 5.—DORA.

be faithful to you. There may occur a thousand occcasions when you will want a sure and faithful friend—one who will live but for you—one who would at any time die for you if it were necessary."

"Ah, how can I reply to you? How can I repay all this faithful and noble service?"

"By letting me be ever with you. By letting me follow you now and always. Who have I in all the world to love or to see to—but you?"

Dora held out her hand.

Tears gushed to her eyes.

"Dottman," she said, "my friend—"

"No, no—your servant!"

"It cannot be—you must be my friend. Take my hand as a friend, Dottman, and believe me, that to have found you, and to have you with me will be the first allevia-tion of all the sufferings I have gone through, for the past six terrible months."

Dottman took the little hand that was held out towards him, and kissed it tenderly.

He left a tear upon it.

"God send prosperity to Dora the Duchess," he said.

"Amen! Amen! to that prayer, Dott-man," she replied, "for if I am blessed and prosperous then will those whom I love be so. Come now! The horse! the horse! I see the morning light gets stronger, and I would fain ride at once to London."

"Ho! Starlight!" cried Dottman.

The Arab horse came out of the barn with a proud dancing step.

Dora, light as a bird, sprung into the saddle.

"Ah!" she cried, "I had forgotten—what are you to do, Dottman?"

"As how, Colonel?"

Dora could not help it—the first smile that had sat upon her fair face came across it at this moment.

"I mean, how are you to come with me, as you have no horse?"

"You will not go fast, and I will run on after you until I see one."

"See one, Dottman?"

"Yes, and then I will take it. You see, Colonel, that the world is not using us well just now, and has made war on us, so we must do the best we can, and help ourselves to what we want, and cannot do without."

"I am afraid, Dottman, that your old ex-periences upon the road are still strong upon you?"

"Well, it may be so—but here is the open door in the wall, and a canter across two fields, and a leap of one low hedge, will take you into the high road to London."

"That way?"

Dora pointed to a group of trees at some little distance off.

"Yes, Colonel, to the right of the trees. Don't be uneasy about me, I will soon be after you."

Dottman went back into the cottage for a moment. And then he called to Dora saying—

"There is a fine cloth cloak strapped to the back of the saddle—and the morning is raw."

"Thanks," said Dora, as she patted Star-light, and unfastening the cloak, wrapped it around her, where it not only served to keep out the raw cold morning air, but by covering up much of the rich and costly suit of apparel she wore, rendered her ap-pearance much less remarkable.

Dottman then shut the little door in the garden wall behind him, and as Starlight, at a pleasant walk, went through the snow,

he soon ran up and walked by the side of Dora, and the horse.

"Do you know, Colonel," he said, "I fancy that the villain, Van Esling, will be afraid even to show himself again at the 'Shadows'."

"The 'shadows'! what is that?"

"I forgot—I should have told you that was the name of the cottage.

"Oh! I understand."

"And a good name it is, too, for it, in the summer time, for there are so many trees about it that it is at all times of the day in complete shadow."

"Then you think he will not return there?"

"That is my notions, colonel; and if ever there was downright fright on the face of any one, it was on that of Van Esling when he saw you at the door in the wall, with the sword in your hand."

"He did look terribly scared."

"He was, too. He will think that you, have, by discovering the place of refuge which he has kept a secret so long, rendered it quite unfit for his purposes, and he will never come near it more."

"It may be so."

"And you see, Colonel, in that case it will do for you."

"For me?"

"To be sure, Colonel. In case of your being hard-pressed sometimes."

"Hard-pressed?"

"Yes. The officers may chase us."

"Why, Dottman, I do believe you fancy I am about to take to the road!"

"To be sure, Colonel."

"What? is it your idea that I am about to become a highwayman?"

"Yes, Colonel—and a very pretty pro-fession it is, too. Lord bless you, as times go, there is nothing at all to be compared to it. The moon is in a rack of clouds—there is, perhaps, a soft rain falling—the night air is full of the fragrance of flowers —your horse goes like the wind— Ah, some one comes! 'Stand!' you cry—'Stand and deliver!' Gold flows into your pockets —jewels flash in the moonlight as they are handed to you. Oh, what life is like the life on the road?"

"But Dottman—"

"And besides, what else, Colonel, are you to do? You must have the means, you see, of supporting and providing for all the wants of that dear fine fellow, Henry Dacres. You must have money with which to take care of yourself—you want money, by the aid of which you will hunt for your dear Mina—you have me too to look after. Oh, believe me, the road is the thing, and besides, you take only from the rich, and now and then, if you see deserving cases, you can give to the poor. You will be called the handsome highwayman. The ladies will come out on dark nights on the road you are good enough to frequent on purpose to be robbed by you."

"Dottman! Dottman! you are an enthusiast!"

"Not at all, Captain! Here's the road."

CHAPTER XI.

LIFE ON THE ROAD—AN ATTACK AND ITS CONSEQUENCES—THE PISTOL SHOT—A MYSTERY AND A PURSE OF GOLD—DORA RIDES HOMEWARD.

PROUDLY and gently the gallant Starlight cantered into the high road that led to London. A strange feeling of exultation came over the spirits of Dora, and she seemed, from that moment, to feel that, if hitherto she had suffered much in her intercourse with the world, the time had come when she had the power to act upon the defensive.

"Dottman! Dottman!" she cried—"for the sake of that dear heart that loves me so well, and now pines for me in the old Savoy, I will follow your advice, and henceforward I will be known and dreaded by all who have hitherto been the persecutors of Dora the Duchess."

"Bravo! bravo, Captain! Hurrah for the road!"

"Hurrah!" cried Dora.

The horse gave a bound of delight, as if the words had inspired him with fresh life and courage. The keen morning air was full of vitality, and for the first time for many a day, Dora felt that her spirits were rising, and that she had a task before her which would be plain and tangible, and which it required but courage and determination to carry out.

"Dottman! Dottman!" she cried—"am I not right in this thought that has come to me? With abundant means I can fight for my rights. With money I shall be able to pave the road with gold that may conduct me to my dear Mina—with money I can soothe the drooping health of my Henry."

"To be sure, Captain—to be sure! You must let me call you Captain, I think; it is better than Colonel, you see, and all the gentlemen of the road who were worth anything, that ever I knew, were called Captain."

"Captain, then, be it. But tell me now, Dottman, do you think I may venture to ride to London?"

"To be sure you may. But hark, Captain!"

"What is it?"

"Do you hear nothing?"

"I do now. The sound of carriage wheels."

Dottman laughed.

"Look you now, Captain Arod," he cried—"what's to hinder you now from taking to town with you the means that would bring warmth and comfort for many a long day to that old house in the Savoy you have mentioned?"

"Ah, I comprehend you!" said Dora.

For a moment there came over her face a deathlike paleness, and that was succeeded by a flush of colour that imparted a brilliancy to her eyes.

"So be it," she said—"so be it. I am on the road, and let the adventure that comes to hand be that which I shall feel bound to engage in—I will not shrink. I have suffered much! let me in turn take up arms in my own defence, and cry again, Dottman, hurrah! hurrah for the road!"

"That's it, Captain. We shall lead a jovial life now, I'll be bound!

"The sound that now approaches,
Is sure the wheels of coaches.
          Ha, ha, ha!
'Stand!' I cry—so bold;
'Your jewels, watch, and gold.'
          Ha, ha, ha!
That's a scream from some fair dame,
But to me it's all the same!
          Ha, ha, ha!
Now go your way in peace,
But remember Captain Fleece.
          Ha, ha, ha!"

"Peace, Dottman! the sounds approach!" cried Dora. "Are the pistols in good order?"

"Trust the life of a king on them if you like," replied Dottman. "Beautiful! beautiful! bravo! By Jove, that's the way!"

Dora had backed Starlight close to the hedge on one side of the road, and then, like some most picturesque and fair cavalier, she waited with a pistol in her right hand for the approach of the carriage, the grinding of the wheels of which upon the road came more distinctly to her ears each passing moment.

There was the crack of a postilion's whip, the tramp of horses feet, and then, at a turn in the road, there came into view a chariot, drawn by a pair of handsome grey horses, one of which was ridden by a postilion.

The postilion was a mere youth.

Dora put up her disengaged hand, and pulled half over her fair face, a silken mask, which she had found, and which she had attached to the hat she wore in such a way that she could slip it down like a visor whenever she chose.

The moment for action had come,

The carriage came on at a rapid rate.

Dottman hid himself completely behind a tree, but he was carefully ramming, at the same time, tightly down, the charges of a pair of pocket pistols, in case Dora should need any assistance.

Then, with her lips closed for a moment, with such tightness that the blood forsook them, Dora gave one touch to the bridle of Starlight, and with a leap, the creature was in the very middle of the road.

The horses of the carriage were not above thirty paces from that spot.

"Stand!" cried Dora, in a strong, high, clear voice. "Stand!"

The postilion drew the rein of the horse he rode rather instinctively than from any desire to do so, and the carriage swerved, owing to the other horse not obeying with the same quickness the impulse to stop, and was partially swung round towards the hedge.

"Stand!" shouted Dora again. "Another step, and your life is lost!"

"Murder!" cried the postilion, as he saw that Dora levelled a pistol at his head. "Oh, good Mr. Highwayman, don't shoot me! Lord bless you, I'm only a poor fellow!"

"Still! keep still, or your life!" added Dora.

Another touch to the rein of Starlight, who seemed quite at home in what was going on, and to understand all about it, brought the beautiful creature to the side of the carriage.

It was a mercy that Dora had sought the side of the carriage that she did, for the window was not down on that side, although it was at the other, and there sat a lady, so that a gentleman, who was in the vehicle, and who had let down the window on his side from some idea that the attack would take place there, was rather at a disadvantage.

"Your money and valuables, if you please," said Dora, in as manly a voice as she could assume.

The lady screamed.

The gentleman uttered some hasty words, and then reaching past the lady, he let down the other window violently.

Bang! went a pistol as he at once fired it with the full intent of lodging the bullet it had contained in the brains of Dora.

But the act of shifting his position, and the hurry of moving nearer to the other side of the chariot and open that window, disturbed his aim, and the bullet flew some six inches aside of Dora's face.

Another moment, and the barrel of Dora's pistol rested on the edge of the coach panel, as she said—

"Now, sir, your life as well as all that you have of value with you."

"No, no! Oh, do not murder him!" cried the lady.

"Confusion!" cried the gentleman.

Then Dora uttered a cry, and it was a wonder that, as her finger was upon the trigger of the pistol, it did not explode.

In the occupant of that carriage she had recognised the greatest enemy she had in all the world—the author of all her troubles —of everything that had brought misfortune upon her and upon those she loved.

It was the villanous Duke of Kingston himself who occupied that carriage, and who had been so near taking the life of Dora.

For one moment the strong desire to avenge herself, by taking his life at once, came over Dora, but it was only for a moment

Even that pause, short as it was, would, to her mind, full of high and noble feelings as it was, have converted the act into a murder.

She could not do it!

"Villain!" she said; "I know you, and your life is at my mercy. That I do not take it is because I am not, as you are, unscrupulous, murderous, and with the heart of an assassin."

"You know me!"

"I do—I do! but it is contamination to parley with you. Had you the revenues of your usurped dukedom with you, I would wrest from you every coin. Quick, sir! quick! I will not brook delay. False brother! base peer! ignoble wretch, who, with wickedness beyond all human villany, are not what you seem to be to the world. I demand of you money and all that may be money's worth about you."

The Duke of Kingston's eyes flamed with rage, and he turned white and cadaverous-looking with concentrated wrath.

"Oh, give him all—give him all!" cried the lady, in tones of affright.

"As for you, madam," said Dora, " I can only pity and scorn any one of your sex who can consort with such a man as the Duke of Kingston."

The lady began to sob.

"Sir," cried the Duke, "you are a strange highwayman, that take upon yourself to speak in such terms to me, a peer of the realm."

"Peace, villain—peace! I will not parley with you. You are in danger."

Dora raised the pistol, and held it now on a level with the eyes of the Duke of Kingston."

The lady screamed.

There was evident fear about the bad heart of that man of iniquities, and he was in vain endeavouring now to subdue the shaking of his hands.

"Take what you want, then," he said, "and let me be free of your presence."

He held out a pocket-book, which, from its bulky appearance, seemed to be well filled.

It was in his right hand that he so held it, and Dora did not see that his left was busy in a pocket of the chariot, where he had another pistol, the fellow to the one he had already fired at her, and which he thought he should be able to use with deadly effect the moment the highwayman, as he thought her, should turn away from the vehicle.

But my Lord Kingston was foiled in the perpetration of this little piece of treachery —for treachery it would have been, after Dora had spared his life when so fully in her power.

There was a sudden shadow cast into the coach, and from the other side an arm was projected through the window, and the voice of Dottman was heard.

"Oh dear no, my lord, that won't do at all."

Dottman had made his way up to that other side of the coach, and had heard and seen all that had passed, and now he pulled the Duke of Kingston's hand out of the pocket where was the other pistol, and so suddenly was this done, that the Duke had no time to let go of the stock of the weapon, and he brought it out of the pocket, but only to be dexterously snatched from his hand by Dottman, who, as he got hold of the barrel, dealt the Duke such a crack with the butt of it on the top of the head, that he half fell back, confused and stunned by the blow.

"He's a treacherous and dangerous fellow, captain," said Dottman. "Take the plunder and away!"

"I have it," said Dora.

"Not a bit!" cried Dottman, as he opened the door of the coach, and dexterously relieved the Duke of Kingston of his watch and a full purse, the gold in which shone through the silver network of which it was composed."

"Help! help!" cried the postboy at this moment.

He had heard the sound of horses' feet on the road.

"Ware hawks! ware hawks, captain!" cried Dottman. "The wood—the wood! make for the wood!"

"Hoi! help! hoi! thieves! highwaymen!" yelled out the postboy.

"Give that fellow a shot, captain," cried Dottman, "or shall I!"

Dora levelled the pistol she had in her hand over the postboy's head some two feet or so, and fired.

At the report he uttered a shout as if he had been actually shot, and fell off the horse.

The regular tramp of some approaching horsemen now came up the road from the direction of London.

Dottman again cried aloud to Dora to take to the wood which lay by the side of the road, but before she could do so the horsemen, who were two, were in sight.

Dora was irresolute what to do.

"Ride on—on country ways!" said Dottman. "Don't mind me. I will be close at hand. So soon as you come to a turn in the road and you are not seen, leap the hedge, and get into the copse by the road side. Starlight will lie down if you tap his knees with your glove."

Dora waved her hand to signify that she both heard and comprehended, and off she went at a sharp trot.

Dottman was through the hedge in a moment, and ran along in the same direction in a frozen ditch that was on the other side of it.

The two horsemen had seen that there was something amiss, and had clapped spurs to their horses and galloped up to the spot.

One of them was a tall, gentlemanly-looking man, dressed in a grey suit, and with a thick grey moustache and a black silk patch over one eye.

The other was in the puritanically plain suit of a quaker.

The horseman in the grey suit had a long straight sword hanging by his side.

To all appearance the Quaker was unarmed.

"What is all this?" cried the horseman in grey, as they reached the chariot.

"A gang of highwaymen, I fancy," said the Duke of Kingston. "I have been assailed and robbed, and but that I resisted, I might have been murdered. A pretty state the highway is in, when a peer of the realm cannot travel from Windsor to London without such an adventure as this.

"Good God!" said the horseman in grey, and he at once fell back as far out of sight of the Duke of Kingston as possible.

The quaker turned towards him, saying hurriedly,—

"Who is it?"

"The present Duke of Kingston," replied the horseman in grey.

"Ah!"

"Gentlemen! gentlemen," cried the Duke, "I beg of you to ride on, and either kill or capture my assailant."

"Go, on!" said the horseman in grey.

He made his horse, as he spoke, dart past the chariot at a bound.

The quaker was but a few moments behind him, and during that time he spoke to the Duke of Kingston.

"Friend," he said, "I know thee now, and I tell thee that thou art the most black-hearted villain that disgraces the roll of peers."

Before the Duke could make any reply to these words the quaker had galloped off after his companion

Both these men were well mounted, and Dora, as she rose to a little eminence in the road, where she could command a view, for some distance behind, saw that they were coming on at speed.

That Starlight would easily outrun them she did not doubt for a moment, and she began to feel the necessity, if she would avoid a contest with them, to put the beautiful Arabian to its speed, but she was surprised to see one of the horsemen making signs to her, and waving a white handkerchief in the air.

"Can those be signals of peace to me?" said Dora to herself.

"Hoi! hoi! captain!" called Dottman from the other side of the hedge. "You can manage them. One is only a broadbrim as you may see."

"I know not what to make of them," said Dora, "they are making signals to me!"

"Signals?"

"Yes—they wave a white handkerchief."

"Well, that's about the oddest thing to do when you see a highwayman ahead of you that ever I heard of. You have a charged pistol?"

"I have!"

"Keep it in your hand, Captain, then, and wait for them."

"I will—I will!"

Dora pursued the same course as that she had done in the case of the carriage, that is to say, she backed Starlight against the hedge on one side of the road, so as to leave it clear, and there awaited the arrival of her supposed foes.

The two horsemen rode up.

But if Dora had been surprised at the signal of peace which they made her with the white handkerchief, she was still more surprised at their conduct on reaching her.

The horseman with the grey apparel only slightly touched his hat by way of a salute, but the one who was dressed as a quaker, spoke to her—

"Friend highwayman," he said, "we have so little objection to thee for robbing the Duke of Kingston, that we beg to congratulate thee if thee hast got anything worth thy while, and make thee welcome to it, and bid thee good day."

Dora said not a word.

"Ah, friend, added the quaker, "it hath even now, verily ah, occurred to me that thou wilt think it is to save our own purses we say this to thee, so to prove to thee that such is not the case, there is mine, which is moderately well furnished, and my friend

here would give thee his too, but that I assure thee, friend, upon my honour he has already left it where he thinks it will be of service."

"Pass on," said Dora.

"We bid thee good day, friend. Thee look'st a gallant fellow, yea verily."

The grey horseman did not utter a word, only when Dora said "pass on" he gave a sudden start, as though he had heard a sound that was familiar and interesting to him. Then he shook his head, and Dora could hear a deep sigh come from his lips.

Another moment and they had both ridden onwards, and were soon lost to sight in a curve of the road, as it wound down the hill.

CHAPTER XII.

DOTTMAN FINDS A GALLANT STEED—THE OLD HOUSE IN THE SAVOY AND THE STRANGE VISITOR—STARLIGHT MAKES HIS TOILETTE—THE SOUTH WIND.

DOTTMAN made his way through the hedge.

"Hurrah! for the road!" he said, "It's quite refreshing all this, Captain, and has put new life into me."

"It is very strange," said Dora.

"Strange, Captain?"

"Yes—the conduct of those two horsemen. One of them uttered a sigh that seemed to find an echo in every corner of my heart."

"Well, Captain," said Dottman, "I won't say that it don't look strange, and yet, when you come to consider it, perhaps it is easily enough understood. You see that rascally uncle of yours, the present Duke of Kingston, is pretty well known as a bad fellow, and these two gentlemen were rather well pleased than not that he should be stopped on the highway."

"It may be so," said Dora, thoughtfully.

"That's it, you may depend, Captain," added Dottman.

"The quaker," said Dora, "has handed me a purse with money in it."

"Ah! he is dressed like a quaker, and looks and speaks like one as far as all that is concerned, but if he is a quaker I am a Hanoverian and a Dutchman. He is an officer!"

"An officer?"

"Bless you, yes, Captain! I know a cavalry officer by the way he sits his horse, as well as I know my own name. He is no quaker.

"What shall we do now, Dottman? My mind is getting so pained by anxiety to get to London, that it will soon amount to agony."

"There is a cross road about another half mile from here," said Dottman, that would take you to London in half-an-hour, but I could not keep up with you."

"I will not part with you, Dottman."

"Oh, don't mind me—you ride on, Captain, and I shall come in good time. My only care will be not to meet Captain Hawk."

"I cannot expose you to that danger," said Dora. "By parting company now we might both fall into some evil adventure. If you had but a horse, Dottman!"

"Hark! hark!"

"Ah!"

"I hear some one on the road."

"And I too!"

"Why, Captain, you are in luck's way to-day."

"No, no—not now! for I am content, and would fain get to the Savoy."

Before Dottman could make any further remark there came, at a swinging trot, along the road from the country a mounted man.

The costume of this person was the then common one of a gentleman who had come out to follow the hounds, and differed in no way from the present dress of the sort, except in the cut of the coat and waistcoat, and in the shape of the cravat.

The moment this person saw Dora, he rather increased than diminished the pace of his horse, and as he approached he fixed, by muscular contraction, in his eye a glass, and upon coming sufficiently near to speak, he said in affected accents—

Aw! Aw! sir—aw—can you be so good as to tell me aw—if you have seen the *dawgs?*"

"The what?" said Dora.

"The—a—aw—the dawgs!"

"Oh! the dogs."

"Yes—I came out to meet the hunt, and to follow the dawgs, but I don't see any dawgs! Ah! sink me—I don't see the dawgs!"

"Take my advice, sir," said Dottman, coming up at this moment from the concealment of a tree.

"Eh? what? Fellow, have you seen the dawgs?

"No—but I was going to say, sir, that you will never see them while you keep on horseback."

"Eh?"

"Certainly not. You see, sir, the dogs go on the ground, and you might overlook them on horseback, whereas on foot, you see you would be sure to see them, for even if you were not looking you would fall over them.

"Aw—aw—you are an impertinent fellow!"

Dora comprehended in a moment that Dottman intended by fair means or by foul to get possession of the handsome hunter which was ridden by the exquisite

The desirableness that Dottman should be mounted as soon as possible was quite evident to Dora, and she was quite prepared to assist him.

"Sir," she said, "I fully agree with what this man says, and you will oblige me personally, by dismounting."

"Eh—what?

Dora presented a pistol exactly opposite to the eyeglass of the fop, and as he looked straight down the barrel of it, there came an expression over his face of such abject fear that it partook of the ludicrous.

"Dismount, sir!" said Dora. "This is a hair trigger, and my hand is rather cold. A slight touch, you know, and an accident might happen."

"Murder!"

"Just so."

"My dear sir—aw—aw—weally now—aw—aw—I'm going, indeed I'm—don't! Oh take it away—don't now—aw—aw—I'm going to the *dawgs!*

The exquisite slipped back over the saddle, and so fairly off the horse into the road, in that highly orignal way of dismounting, and there he sat in the snow, with the eyeglass still fixed to his eye, and looking the picture of woeful discomfiture.

"Now, Dottman," said Dora, "off and away."

"All right, Captain! Woa—woa horse! That will do, all's right!"

"Ride fast," said Dora, "and show me the nearest way to"—

"Hush!" said Dottman.

"You are right—you are right—I am incautious! Sir, I bid you good-day."

"The *dawgs!*" gasped the fop.

"Oh, you will find them in time, and they will find you," said Dottman, "you have only got to sit there long enough."

Another moment, and at a rapid pace Dora and Dottman left that part of the road.

As Dottman had said, they soon came to a cross road, which they pursued so fleetly, that in a little over half an hour they were near to Tyburn Gate,

That place had some terrible and grateful recollections for Dora; but she did not pause, and she and Dottman started down the Oxford-road.

There were many glances cast upon Dora as she followed Dottman. Not only the elegance of her own costume, but the symmetry and beauty of the Arabian horse attracted the attention of many eyes.

But Dora's thoughts were all at that old house in the Savoy. As she neared it, she became each moment more and more anxious about the fate of her dear Henry, whom she had left in so precarious a condition.

And yet she had a kind of dread of approaching the house in daylight. Who could tell that some foe might not be hiding there to watch for her, and that she might encounter danger which she might not be able to resist.

"Dottman," she said, "I feel that I hardly dare seek the house in the Savoy yet."

"You may depend all is safe," said Dottman. "From what you have told me, I think I can reckon up your foes on my finger, and can say just now where they all are."

"If I could think so, Dottman."

"I fancy you may, Captain. First of all there is the Duke of Kingston."

"Ah, he we know is far off."

"Good! Then there is that scoundrel, Turnbull. I think you said you were sure you shot him?"

"Yes, yes—I saw him fall!"

"Good! he then is disposed of."

"He is a villain who well deserved his fate. It was but in self defence I used a weapon against his life."

"Then Captain, I can't see what there is to dread in making way at once to the old Savoy. Nobody will heed us you may depend, and by the look of the gathering clouds, I should say another storm, of some sort, was not far off—let us get housed, Captain—let us get housed. There may be more danger even in the streets of London than in a quick march into the Savoy."

"It must be done—it must be done," said Dora. "I could not endure the suspense of waiting until night-fall. Ah! the clouds thicken and seem about to descend upon the streets of the city. A premature darkness is over the sky—I do, indeed, think Dottman, we may venture now."

As Dora spoke, a deep gloom seemed to settle over London. One of those rapid changes of the weather incidental to our climate had begun.

It was the break-up of the frost, and the last streak shewed itself before the summer's sun imparted its own beauty to all things. A wind from the south-west was bringing up legions of clouds. For a few moments there was a dash of snow, and then it changed to sleet, the arrowy particles of which were intensely cold; but they soon subsided into rain, and the change in the season was complete.

The snow gradually thickened—rivulets began to run in the streets—and a sensible feeling of warmth began to pervade the atmosphere.

"Now or never," said Dottman, as they reined up their horses for a moment at the corner of a narrow street which led into Soho. "Now or never, captain! let us push on for the Savoy. This cloudy gloom is almost equal to twilight."

"Yes," said Dora "Now or never. Henry—Henry! how much would I give to know how it fares with thee!"

Dora still allowed Dottman to lead the way. Upon an answer to the inquiry he had assured her that he was well enough acquainted with the intricacies of London, and on this occasion he showed that this was no idle boast, for he led Dora rapidly by unfrequented streets down to the Strand.

The gay and elegant apparel in which Dora was attired would have suffered greatly from this deluge of rain and sleet; but Dottman had unbuckled the ample roquelarie, which was strapped at the back of the saddle, and in its folds Dora was not only well protected from the inclemency of the weather, but it, likewise, by concealing the remarkably rich dress she wore, aided more effectually in disguising her from any enemies she might meet.

A few moments more, and they were at the top of the narrow turning which led down to the Savoy.

The street seemed to be entirely deserted. Chance passengers had fled from the rapidly descending storm into deep doorways, and a more favourable opportunity for seeking, unobserved, that house where all the hopes and fears of Dora were centred, could scarcely have been found.

"Let us dismount," said Dottman, "and lead the horses—the descent is steep."

Dora did so at once, but there was no occasion for her to lead Starlight, inasmuch as the creature followed her as closely as it could with that remarkable affection which seemed, from the first moment it had known her, to have been engendered in its mind in regard to her.

The horse which Dottman had in so strange a way obtained possession of was not so docile as the Arab, but still no difficulties presented themselves in leading the creature by the bridle.

Skirting the houses closely, they soon turned into the Savoy, and with a beating heart Dora found herself once more upon the threshold of that abode in which she had endured such intense anxiety, and where she hardly dared to hope affairs would be found as she had left them, with the joy in addition of the recovery of Henry.

Dora, in her change of costume at Captain Hawk's cottage, had not been unmindful of the means of procuring admittance to her home again. She had an ancient key, which fitted the lock of the street door. She could not speak for a moment as she flung

that door open and again set foot in the large hall of the house.

Starlight followed her.

Aud Dottman, leading the hunter by the bridle, followed Starlight.

But Dora forgot all else now in her eagerness to ascertain the state of affairs in the first floor of that old mansion.

Starlight—Dottman—the hunter—her own change of costume, and the adventures she had gone through since last setting foot in that dwelling—all were forgotten in the one absorbing feeling that possessed her.

"Henry! Henry!" she cried, as she rushed up the staircase. "I am here! I am here! Speak to me if you have but a breath to do so. I am here—your own

No. 6.—DORA.

Dora! I return to you—I return to you! Speak—oh, speak!"

She reached that large and gloomy apartment! the door was closed, but Dora opened it in an instant, and well might she start for a moment in surprise upon the threshold to note the air of unusual comfort that reigned in the place.

A bright fire of wood blazed and crackled on the hearth, and although it was the only means by which light irradiated the apartment, Dora could see there were refreshments upon the table, and a flask of wine glittered in the rays from the fire-light.

"Henry—Henry!" she cried again.

"I am here," was the reply.

There was new health and strength in the sound of the voice, and at a glance Dora saw that all her fears had b̲een vain, and that, whatever had happened in the old mansion since she had left, had been of a beneficent character.

But Dora had forgotten her new and strange costume. The roquelaire had fallen from her shoulders, and she appeared before the eyes of the astonished Henry Dacres in that attire which has been already described to the reader.

"Ah, Henry," she said, "you look at me with strange eyes; but I am still your Dora. I have a world of strange things to tell you."

"What is is best," said her husband, with a faint smile, for he was still weak and powerless.

"Nay, I will tell you all. Most mysterious, most wonderful, and full of strange escapes and incidents have been the last few hours."

"And to me, too, my Dora," said Henry, "for as I slept I became half conscious that some one was about the room, yet was there such a weight upon my eyelids that I could not raise them to observe if it were friend or foe. The heavy hand of an opiate was upon my senses, but when it passed away, and I could look around me, I saw and felt the genial influence of this fire, which crackles so cheerily before us, and on the table were placed these unwonted viands, together with surely some of the rarest wine that ever warmed a frozen heart. I am weak and ill, and the unhealed wound is still deep in my breast, and yet am I wonderfully better."

"Heaven be thanked!"

"We have some friend, my Dora, who, in his eccentric goodness, will not be known, for here lies a purse likewise, in which there is gold."

Dora took the purse from the table, and as she looked at it, a strange feeling of recognition came over her.

"One moment, dear husband," she said. I must satisfy a doubt."

She ran to the door of the apartment.

"Dottman—Dottman!"

I am here," said her faithful follower from below.

Give me the purse that one of the two horsemen bestowed upon me on the road."

"Ah! Dora, Dora!" cried Henry, "who is that you call? We have too many foes to risk the making of new friends. False—false—all false!"

"Nay, Henry, this one is true, but you know not who and what your Dora is."

"Dora the Duchess!"

Ay, and something more. They will not let me be that which I should be. I have been hunted, persecuted, trodden down, and treated with contumely and scorn, but I have turned at bay, Henry, and for those dear to me I fight the world."

Dottman reached the door of the room, and handed to Dora the purse.

Her suspicions were correct. It was identical in shape, colour, and texture with the one which had been left upon the table in that apartment by the unknown friend who had visited Henry in her absence.

And then Dora recollected what had been said by the horseman in the garb of a quaker, viz: "That his friend in grey had no purse to give her, as he had already bestowed it where it was much needed."

"What could all this mean? What mysterious person was this, who hovered around her and about her, and put forth a protecting hand in moments of greatest peril?"

Dora could not answer these questions—they half terrified and wholly perplexed her; but a few words of fear that she had encountered serious dangers which happened to fall from Henry's lips, awakened a new idea in the mind of Dora, and she rejoiced that she had not told him of her dangers and adventures on the road, and her determination to continue them.

Weak and helpless as he was, and might be for many weeks to come, what agonies of apprehension would he not endure in the fancy that she was exposed to all the perils, dangers, and vississitudes of a life on the heath and on the highway.

There was gold now mysteriously placed in their hands—and he would have no means of calculating its diminution, and so would express no surprise at a more continued supply. What then, she thought, if she could keep from him all her dangers, while he shared but in the luxuries which her adventures might provide him with, and which, in his condition, were so much required.

All this passed through the mind of Dora in a moment, and she resolved to spare him many a pang, while she hoped to supply many a want.

There was but a dreamy idea upon the mind of Henry Dacres, concerning the loss of the little Mina—but in an agitating interview between him and Dora he became aware of all she knew upon that subject.

"I will seek her while I have life," said Dora, "and you will feel, Henry, while I am away from you, that I am searching for our lost one."

"Alas! alas! said Henry Dacres, "Why have not I strength to take this task upon myself while you remain here in peace? It is sad, my Dora, this reversion of our duties —but I am helpless as a child, I cannot aid you."

Dora, with every argument in her power, strove to reconcile him to a state of things for which there was no help, and as she had acquainted him with sufficient of what had happened to account for the appearance of Dottman, she now left him for a few moments, to arrange with the gallant and kind-hearted servitor, that he was not by any incautious word to let her husband know the pursuit to which she had engaged herself.

Dottman had not been idle in her absence —but had taken possession of two of the apartments in the lower part of the house, in one of which he had installed Starlight, and in the other the hunter.

"Quite right, Captain," said Dottman, when Dora had explained her wishes to him —you're quite right—why, the young officer would be fancying a thousand dangers where none existed."

"And you will now be with me, Dottman, on occasions of any peril, or it will be a consolation to me to leave you here to protect the better portion of my life, which I leave behind me in this house."

"Ay, ay! Captain—we'll see to all that, and as soon as night fairly comes I'll creep down to the river side; there's a hay and straw wharf not far from here, and I'll get up enough to make comfortable beds for our horses, as well as a sack or two of food. They've capital quarters here--there's Starlight been looking at himself in a mirror in his room. And as for the hunter, he's beginning to take to me as if he'd known me all his life."

"Ah!" said Dora, "if I could but find that little one who has been torn from me, I could almost begin to feel happy now."

"Never fear, Captain—never fear—we'll rout out this rascal, Van Esling! But something has been amiss here—there's blood in the hall!"

"Ah!" cried Dora, "how selfish are we in our own miseries and wants. The kind physician, Dr. Langford—where is he? Where can he be? I have a thought that the villain, Esling, has slain him, for he is not here."

"There's no one here," said Dottman, "I've been all over the lower part of the house. Hark! how the rain comes down— what a deluge! The road will be rather heavy, Captain, when we take to it again, but what a life it is—twenty lives in one— on the heath or on the shadowy highway, you feel greater than a king. Hurrah! indeed, for the road—no care—gold shining in your eyes and flashing from your purse— a good horse, and your pistols well loaded. Ah, ah! there's nothing like the road!

CHAPTER XIII.

DORA'S VISIT TO THE OLD KING'S MEWS— A COMBAT AND THE FLIGHT—THE FATE OF A VILLAIN—A PURSUIT ON THE THAMES.

IT was towards the dusk of evening on the day succeeding these events, that what appeared to be two horsemen might have been seen wending their way up the narrow street, which by a sharp declivity led from the Strand to the Old Savoy.

The most remarkable change had taken place in the aspect of the weather. The heaped up snow and the glassy particles of ice had disappeared from the thoroughfares —a soft south wind was careering through London, and the clear blue evening sky was flaked with fleecy clouds.

Torrents of rain had fallen in the night, which had washed away every particle of frost and snow, and the atmosphere felt pleasant, soft, and genial.

The foremost of these horsemen was mounted on an Arabian steed of great beauty, and even the ample roquelaire cloak in which the rider was shrouded, could not conceal the graceful outline of the youthful form.

Need we say that this was Dora, and that the steed was Starlight? and that the other horseman on the tall slender hunter, who wore a plain dark suit, and horseman's boots, was Dottman?

At first sight these two equestrian figures might have been taken for some great noble and his follower; and any one who noticed the beauty and symmetry of the horses, and had any idea of their great value, might well have supposed that some magnate of the land had issued from one of the princely dwellings still lingering about the Strand, and was about to take a night ride, possibly to Windsor, where the court was then staying.

Little rivulets of water were running down the sides of the way, and it was with evident sensations of pleasure that Starlight inhaled the soft and comparatively warm air which had succeeded the chilling breezes of the previously severe weather.

Dora turned her horse's head to the left, and for a few moments suffered the animal to splash through the soddened streets in silence.

Then she drew rein, and half turning on the saddle, spoke to Dottman.

"True friend," she said, "and faithful follower of my father and of myself, assure me again that your news is true?"

"As true, Captain," said Dottman, "as

that I heard what I cannot vouch for. I went to the Royal Mews where the regiment of the guard is stationed, and the sentry assured me that Captain Van Esling was on duty.

"It is very strange—I thought the villain would scarcely show himself."

It is as strange to me, as to you Captain, and I must confess, I fain would see him to identify him, if possible, with my old master, though in good faith it seems to me more like a romance than anything else, to think that they can be one and the same person.

"I see no cause to doubt it," said Dora, "but I will seek him, were he enshrined behind a thousand hearts that would keep him from me."

"Oh, beware—beware, Captain. I could bite my tongue out now for spite, that I told you he was there. Do not, I pray you, venture into the King's Mews; the gates may be closed against your retreat, and all may be lost."

"Nay," said Dora, "I must seek this villain who has stolen from me one of my earthly treasures. It is he who should shrink appalled from me, not I from him."

"He may take your life."

"And yet he affects to love me, Dottman; but have no fear of that. I have told you that in many a spare hour it was a pleasant sport of both my father's and Henry's to teach me many a trick of fence. I can handle back, sword and rapier well, and there is no weight of dire iniquity upon my arm to paralize my strength; but, tell me, oh, tell me one thing. Dottman—do you think, in this disguise, the villain will know me?"

Dottman was silent for a moment and then he spoke doubtingly.

"It is hard to say yes or no to that, Captain, but with the half mask upon your face he could not know you."

"I will chance all with the dear hope of wresting from that villain my Mina."

The Arabian steed then dashed forward, and a few moments brought both Dora and Dottman to the heavy gates of the old massive heap of buildings which was known up to about the year 1825, as the King's Mews, and where a regiment of the household brigade of guards was always quartered.

These irregular buildings comprised the vast space now occupied by Trafalgar Square. The National Gallery and the buildings in its rear.

"Aid me, Heaven," said Dora, "as my cause is just."

She drew rein within a few paces of the gate, and dismounting, she turned to Dottman, speaking in a low voice of deep emotion, as she flung her arm for a moment across the neck of Starlight.

"But that I have sworn," she said—"to myself—to my husband, and to the memory of my child, to seek and confront this villain, Esling, wherever he may be found, I might not hazard this visit. But I have faith in Heaven, and I do not think my time is come. Await me, Dottman; and if one hour should pass, and you should see me not, or hear not from me, hie thee back to that old house in the Savoy, and be to my Henry as faithful and true a friend—"

Emotion for a moment choked the utterance of Dora.

"Nay—nay, Captain!" cried Dottman. "What is my life compared to yours? Let me inquire for and confront this man—I, too, know him, if what we think be true of his identity."

"No, no!" said Dora—"one hour—remain one hour."

At that moment the clock of St. Martin's Church struck eight, and while the sounds yet lingered on the soft south wind, Dora flung her cloak more closely around her, and approached the sentinel on duty at the King's Mews.

If Dora had made the most elaborate attempt to disguise her voice, she would scarcely have succeeded to the extent that contending emotions changed its tone as she addressed the sentinel.

"I would speak with Captain Van Esling."

There was an indescribable air and manner about Dora which won an involuntary respect from the soldier. He did not carry arms or salute her, but it was in the tone with which he cried out "Visitor to Captain Esling, pass on!" that might be gathered the fact of his considering the visitor no ordinary personage.

Dora passed through the small door in the large gate.

An orderly sergeant came out of the guard-room.

"Captain Esling, would you see, sir?" he said.

"I would," replied Dora, "if he be in the mews. Tell him that Captain Arod calls on him."

"I believe, sir," said the Sergeant, "he is in his quarters, and if you will please to wait a moment, or if you do not mind walking with me, sir, you will find the captain within."

"I follow you," said Dora.

The sergeant led the way through a slant portion of the court-yard, and through an open doorway—where door there was none—and up an ancient flight of steps lighted by dim oil lamps at intervals, and so through a long and dreary looking corridor, from whence opened many doors, each one of which had a number painted on its panel. At one of these doors the sergeant paused, and tapped with his knuckles, but there was no reply.

"The captain should be in," said the sergeant as he placed his hand upon the latch of the door.

"Pardon me," said Dora, slowly, "I am an acquaintance, and may take a liberty— I thank you."

The manner of Dora was a dismissal, and the sergeant, with a military salute, marched down the long melancholy looking corridor again, and Dora opened the door gently, and glided into the room.

It was an apartment of some pretensions both as to size and to decoration, but it was only lit by two wax candles in lustres on the ample chimney-piece. A half decayed fire was in the grate, and although various indications of the habitation of an officer of the Royal Guard were present in the apartment, it was at that time unoccupied.

At its further extremity, however, there was a door standing partially open, possibly about the width that might have permitted any one to glide sideways into the inner room. A glare of light that overpowered the feeble illumination in the outer apartment came from this inner room; and although Dora could see no one, and not the faintest sound came to her ears, the impression was strong upon her that the man she sought was there!

And oh! with what eagerness she now leant forward to listen, in the fond but vain hope that some slight disturbance of the deep stillness that reigned in that place might proclaim to her the presence of her child.

Against all probability that Esling would bring the little one to such a place, Dora yet hoped to hear some sound that would assure her of the presence of her Mina.

No! all was still! still for a few anxious moments, and then there was a rustling sound as of some one rising from a chair or couch, and she heard a deep sigh!

Then a voice, in faint but anxious accents, spoke, rising higher with the vehemence of the feeling that gave it utterance.

"Oh, this passion is madness!" it cried, and will destroy me. "I who never yet had a love—a hope—or a fear in my heart for aught that lived, am now stricken as with a madness. She loathes me, and I will try to hate her. All she loves shall perish by my hand. She will not love me, but my name shall be familiar to her as her fate. Oh, this weary life of routine and duty! and but for the favour I hold with the Duke of Kingston, I had been dismissed the service with disgrace."

The door was flung open that communicated between the two apartments, and Van Esling, pale and sallow, as though he had risen from a sick couch, strode three steps into the outer room.

In his hand he held his regimental sword, the belt of which trailed on the floor. He was in full costume as an officer of the guard on duty; but it was the wan and colourless look of his face, and the terrible aspect of his eyes that, to Dora, were objects of attention.

"Oh, surely, surely," she thought, "the man who can suffer so much, cannot yet be destitute of all human feeling.

It was evident that he had not the slightest consciousness that any one was in those apartments but himself, for he still continued, although in a lower tone than before, to mutter disjointed sentences, expressive of the tumult of his mind.

But Dora had nerved herself for this terrible interview, and she was resolved that Van Esling should not escape it.

The mask was over her eyes.

The roquelaire that she had with her enveloped her form. Her voice, from mere excess of emotion, sounded strange and most unlike her ordinary tones.

She stepped forward, so that Captain Van Esling could not but see that there was some one in his path.

"Hold!" she cried. "Villain! worse villain than tongue can tell, I command you to reply to me!"

With a cry of surprise, Van Esling stepped back a pace, and he placed his hand upon the hilt of his sword.

The light in that outer room was so imperfect that he could only just see that there was, to all appearance, an armed and richly dressed man before him, who had spoken to him in terms he could brook from no one.

Recovering his first confusion, then, Van Esling loosened the sword blade in its scabbard, as he said,—

"Who and what are you—an assassin?"

"No. If that had been so, the fair earth would not have been encumbered with a Van Esling."

"Ah!"

He made a step forward, and Dora saw the flash of the light that came from the inner room playing upon the bright steel of his sword, as he half drew it.

In a moment the sword of Dora was in her hand, and, like a dazzling pencil of light, it seemed as if it had confused the eyes of Esling.

"In the name of Heaven," he cried, "tell me who and what you are, and what you want.

"I am the questioner, and the avenger."

"For whom? what would you question me of? who would you avenge?"

"Dora Dacres!"

"Ah!"

"Henry Dacres!"

"Confusion! in whom have they found a champion or an avenger?"

"In me! in me, villain! assassin and robber of the innocent! I ask you now for Dora's child. In the name of that young mother—in the name of the father whom you assailed as an assassin only could, I demand of you the restoration of the child."

"The—the child!"

"Ay, villain, you dare not look at me, although you well strive to trifle with the truth, and let your convict tongue perform the dastard office of evasion. Where is the child of Dora Dacres? on your answer hangs your life."

"My life!"

"Ay, your life! I am an avenger."

"It is strange—most strange!" said Van Esling, but there is a seeming echo in my breast which points to the fact that I ought to know you. Your voice sounds familiar to me."

"The child!" cried Dora. "Where is the child? For the time, Van Esling, your life will be spared if you restore the child."

"I know not what you mean!"

"False villain, you know too well."

"Tell me who you are," suddenly yelled Van Esling, in a real or affected torrent of rage, "in order that I may know that I shall not disgrace my sword by dyeing it in your heart's blood."

"Coward!"

"Coward! coward, say you?"

"Yes, base coward! You were good in fence when in the lone house in the Savoy you fought with the young mother, and bore from her her child. But now you tremble."

"Have at thee, then!" cried Van Esling. "You shall rue this boastful reproach, or all skill has deserted this right arm. I did go to that house in the Savoy, but it was not on the errand you would assert. I went to tell one who was there alone that she might still live in life and hope."

"Where is the child?" reiterated Dora.

Van Esling's only reply now was to dart forward and make a furious pass with his sword at Dora, which, had it been successful, would at once have consigned to death that young and fair spirit."

But Dora was upon her guard.

From the first moment of that interview she had not taken her own sweet eyes off the hateful orbs of Captain Van Esling, and she had seen by the slight flash and quiver of them the fell purpose of his soul.

Letting the ample roquelaire fall off her left shoulder, Dora gathered it by a rapid motion of her left hand into a dense mass around that hand and arm.

It was better than the best shield that ever armed warrior bore to battle; for, by a half turn, Dora at once and easily caught the blade of Van Esling's sword in the thick folds of the cloak, while she had her own sword arm at liberty.

By a sudden movement, then, Dora brought her sword forward so as to give point with it at the neck of Van Esling.

"Die, then, in your crimes and iniquities, villain!" she said.

The sword was well aimed at the throat of Van Esling, but his cravat turned the point aside slightly, and although it passed through the flesh at the side of his neck, the wound was but a superficial one.

Van Esling uttered a cry of rage.

"To the death! to the death, then!" he shouted. "Be it a combat to the death!"

Dora did not speak. She held her breath for the battle that was to ensue, and she saved her strength.

She saw the blood trickling down the gold lace in the front of Van Esling's apparel, but she could not tell if the wound she had given him was one that would disable him or not.

By the fury with which he now began the combat with her it would seem that such was not the case.

The swords clashed together, and for a few seconds seemed to be each instinct with life, and to be twining around each other like two serpents engaged in deadly conflict.

And now Dora felt that the many compliments—and at the time she had deemed them as such—which both her father and her husband had bestowed upon the skill she had acquired in the use of the rapier, were not mere idle words, of course.

She had no reason to apprehend that Captain Van Esling was not a master of the weapon, and yet each moment now she began to feel high confidence in the assurance that she could keep him at bay, and probably soon inflict upon him some new wound that would place him at her mercy.

"Die! die!" cried Esling. "Die, for your insolence, be you whom you may."

Dora would not speak; she had been taught that lesson, among others, never to utter one word during the actual continuance of a contest.

This silence on the part of his opponent now seemed to perplex and confound Van Esling, and he made desperate attempts to beat down Dora's guard, in order that he might end the combat by her death.

"Speak!" he cried—"Speak but a word, to tell me not to kill you."

Dora still fought warily and well, but still she spoke not a word.

Van Esling began to give way.

Step by step he retreated towards the

inner room from which he had so recently emerged, and Dora could see that he was, with his left hand, apparently feeling for the door which had partially closed of itself.

She thought that his object was to escape by some means, and she assumed more the offensive than she had done, and inflicted upon him another wound, although a slight one, on his sword arm.

Van Esling had now reached the door that separated the two apartments. He pushed it open with his left hand, and as Dora pressed him hard, taking a full step forward for every one of his backward, he could not shut her out of that inner room, which she thought, perhaps, he might wish to do.

Such was not, however, the plan of the treacherous Van Esling.

No sooner had he got fairly within that inner room, than he made so sudden and reckless an assault on Dora, that, for a moment, he beat down her sword blade, and the instant that he had sufficient freedom from that resistance to do so, he dashed round a table that was in the centre of the room so as to place it between himself and his assailant, before she could prevent him.

To throw down his sword, then, was to Van Esling the work of a moment, and from that table he lifted a pistol, and, with a shout of triumph, he pointed it full in the face of Dora.

"Die!" he said—"and in your death I shall feel that I am rid of another obstacle that has risen up between me and Dora."

He pulled the trigger, even as he spoke, and Dora felt as if a red hot iron had touched her right cheek.

The bullet had coursed by her so closely that, although the fair skin was not actually raised by it, there was a red streak where it had passed within a hair's breadth of the cheek of Dora.

She thought surely now that her career was at an end. The feeling and impression on her mind was that she was shot, and that so for ever poor Henry Dacres was abandoned, and her little one left to the mercy of that treacherous man.

Dora could not but utter a scream of anguish.

The bullet, too, had snapped asunder the piece of ribbon which confined the black silk mask she wore, and it fell to her feet.

"Oh, at last I may be avenged! Oh, surely Heaven will grant me that!" cried Dora.

Van Esling uttered a strange yell, for when the mask fell from her fair face, he at once saw and recognised the fair features of Dora.

She seemed, then, to feel that there was no time to go round the table that was between them—she felt that the moment she should take her eyes off his, that would be her last.

On to the table Dora sprung.

"Death! death!" she cried. "At last I will accuse you before the throne of Heaven."

Van Esling was almost wedged in between the table and the wall, for Dora, by dashing against it immediately after Esling had fired the pistol, had propelled it forward several feet.

He had cast down his sword, too, to the floor, so that he was unarmed.

All happened in a moment—quicker—far quicker than tongue can tell, or pen describe. There was a flash of the keen sword blade that was in Dora's hand, and then it was plunged into the breast of Van Esling.

Such was the vehemence of the thrust, in consequence of Dora falling forward on the table, and so, whether she meant or not to do so, adding her whole weight to the attack, that the sword struck against the wainscot wall of that old room, and then penetrated it to the depth of some six inches, and then the blade snapped in two, about a couple of inches below the hilt, which alone was left in Dora's hands.

Van Esling uttered a fearful scream.

He was pinned by the sword blade to the old wainscot wall, and could not, without such a world of agony that death were preferable, make even an effort to extricate himself.

We have said all this was the work of a moment: if it had not been so it would have been simply impossible.

Dora had had no time to reflect—she had thought that her time in which to act was in all possibility numbered by a few fleeting moments, for the idea that the bullet from Van Esling's pistol had reached her brain, had come strong upon her.

But now horror took possession of her.

It was for a few seconds now one of the most dreadful sights in that small chamber that probably the eyes of mortal ever looked upon.

There was Van Esling pinned by that red sword blade to the old wainscot wall, and such an expression of mortal agony in his eyes and face as was a terror to be remembered for a life.

There, too, was Dora, kneeling now upon the table, and with her body bent back as if to recede as far as possible from the spectacle before her.

The sword hilt was in her hand, and she saw how utterly impossible it was, even had she felt inclined, to render the least assistance to the fainting, screaming wretch before her.

Then she heard suddenly the rapid tread of feet from a distance.

"Surely the report of the pistol had spread an alarm in the barracks. There was help coming, not for her, but for him, Van Esling—and what would be her fate if she was found in such a position before him."

The feeling of self-preservation came strongly upon her.

"For myself," she said, "as well as for those who are dear to me, I must escape."

Dora sprung off the table—the first thing she saw close to her feet on the floor was the sword which Van Esling had thrown down when he made up his mind to trust to the pistol to rid him of his unknown and most dangerous foe.

Dora picked it up.

She had exchanged swords with Captain Van Esling, but what a terrible exchange it was for him!

The footsteps approached, and Dora could now heard the sound of voices.

CHAPTER XIV.

DORA'S ESCAPE FROM THE KING'S MEWS—
DOFFMAN TAKES A PLACE ON THE OX-
FORD MAIL.—A SURPRISE ON THE ROAD.

One glance around the small apartment in which she now was, convinced Dora that it was not there she need look for any traces of her lost child.

The apartment was merely such an one as would be in the temporary possession of an officer in a barrack.

At one end there was a small camp bed, and there did not seem to be any means of concealment in the room.

Van Esling uttered another terrible cry.

Probably he had made some effort to wrest himself free from the sword blade, and the anguish it had inflicted extorted that cry from him.

It seemed to reach the heart of Dora, for a perceptible shudder crossed her frame.

"I do pity you!" she said, "As heaven is my judge, I pity you—but on your own head be all this agony and all this horror! Not on mine—oh, not on mine!"

As she spoke Dora darted from the small room into that much larger apartment which adjoined it, and it was a relief to her to find that whoever had taken the alarm and were approaching that part of the Royal Mews, had not yet reached the door of that room.

The sound of footsteps, however, and of voices, convinced Dora that there were people immediately without the door.

She had not time to look about her in that large apartment for some place of concealment even if it really would have afforded any, but she took the precaution of extinguishing the light which was upon the chimney-piece, and then she had but just time to shrink into as small a space as possible behind the door, when it was flung open.

"Hilloa!" said a voice, "What's amiss here?"

"Captain Van Esling!" said another, are you in your rooms?"

"It certainly was a pistol shot!" said a third voice, as the three speakers made their way into the room.

"How dark!" added one.

"There is light in the inner chamber!" said another.

"Draw your swords, gentlemen, then!" said the first speaker, "Draw your swords, and follow me, for I have an impression on my mind that there is danger here."

They all three rushed with drawn swords across the large room.

Dora had just time to hear a simultaneous expression of horror from them all, and a fresh cry from the wretched Van Esling, when she dashed round the open door, and gained the long corridor which she had traversed with the sergeant.

If she would escape now she felt that there was not a moment to loose.

Her whole safety, she felt, now lay in her reaching the outer gate of the barracks before the three officers who had sought Van Esling's apartments should emerge from them.

If even the order was given, which doubtless it would be, to close the outer wicket, and let no one out of the barracks, she would be lost.

Full of this conviction, Dora was clear of the gallery, and down the ricketty flight of old steps leading to the barrack yard in a few seconds.

As she went she placed Van Esling's sword, which she had picked up, in the emptysheath she had by her side.

To run across the barrack yard she thought would be probably to arouse some suspicion, so she walked, although at a tolerably quick pace.

She had got about half way to the wicket in the great gates when she heard a loud voice, as if from some window, calling out—

"Guard! guard!"

She felt that there was indeed not a moment to be lost.

With a bound she was at the wicket gate. There were a couple of soldiers lounging close to it, and one of them stepped forward to open it.

They both saluted Dora, and she thought

it wisest to return the salute without uttering a word.

There was then the roll of a drum in the barracks, and the long wailing sound of a bugle.

"Why," cried one of the men "that means close the gates—it is a governor's call that."

Dora had just slipped outside.

"Sir," said one of the men, "you had better not go, there is something amiss.

"No," said Dora, "nothing!"

"The guard will close the wicket against all egress!" shouted the loud sharp voice of a sergeant, in his highest tones of command.

Dora was close to the sentinel on the outside of the gate when this order was

given, and he at once brought his musket to the charge, as he said—

"You must not go, sir!"

"I?" said Dora, "The order does not apply to me, my good fellow."

"I don't know"—

"But I do!" said a voice.

It was the voice of Dottman, who now suddenly put his foot behind the heels of the sentinel, and flung him to the ground.

"Mount! mount, Captain!" cried Dottman. "Mount, and be off! Bless you, but I know what that drum and bugle means—it is an alarm."

The horses were close at hand, and in a moment Dora was in the saddle."

"Off and away, Captain! Off and away," cried Dottman. Don't wait for me! off! off!"

"No!" said Dora! We fall together or escape together.

Dottman had found some little difficulty in mounting the hunter, owing to the creature swerving a little, just as his foot was in the stirrup.

Trivial as that incident was, it very nearly proved fatal to them both.

The barrack gate was flung open, and an officer with several soldiers rushed out.

"Seize him! seize that man in the roquelaire," cried the officer.

"All right!" shouted Dottman.

He was safe on the horse.

"Now!" said Dora.

She gave one slight touch to the neck of the Arabian, and off it went as fleet as the wind.

"Fire!" she heard some one cry.

The loud report of a musket—doubtless that of the sentinel, awakened the echoes of the night air; but the bullet flew wide of its mark. It hit the pedestal of the statue of Charles the First at Charing Cross, and the curious may to this day see the blackened, flattened piece of lead upon the old weather beaten stone.

"To the right, Captain!" cried Dottman.

"Yes!" said Dora.

"Not hit?"

"No, no!—and you?"

"Quite safe."

Dora guided the horse up the Haymarket, by the side of the Opera House, and as Dottman followed fast, they soon, through some of the narrow streets about Soho which still remain, reached the Oxford-road.

"To the left, Captain," said Dottman.

Dora obeyed his directions, and they neither of them halted until they had placed a good mile between them and the Royal Mews at Charing Cross.

Then it could scarcely be called a halt that they made, for they let the horses proceed at a brisk enough walk. Dottman riding close up to Dora, spoke in tones of emotion.

"Captain, I am full of curiosity to know what happened in the Barracks. I hope you have sustained no hurt."

"None, I think—none"—.

"Ah, you only think so!"

"Nay, I fancy I ought to feel certain of it, Dottman, and yet it has taken me some time to convince myself that I was not shot through the head."

"Good Heavens!"

"The villain, Esling, fired at me, and so closely, and so unexpectedly too, that I am lost in wonder that he did not kill me."

Dottman shook his head.

"Ah I was all the while against that most desperate expedition," he said, "and I would not, for my life's sake, endure the tortures of suspense again that I went through while you were in the old Barracks of the Kings Mew's.

"It is over now," said Dora, with a deep sigh, "and the danger has passed away. It has been guiltlessly incurred, and unless it may be said that in killing Esling"—

"What?" exclaimed Dottman, interrupting her in surprise. "Have you killed the villain?"

"I have!"

"Bravo, Captain! Why that's one good job done, and the best one of all, now that you are taking to the road. Why, do you know, Captain, that I thought nothing of any danger you might run compared to that of being hunted by Captain Hawk, *alias* Captain Van Esling; and he would have laid in wait for you, and tried for your life to a certainty."

"He will try for no one's life again."

"Bravo, Captain! But do tell me, Captain, all about it, or I shall expire with curiosity."

Dora told Dottman, in rather a sad tone, all that occurred in those rooms at the old mews, and how she had left Captain Van Esling in so terrible a predicament.

"Well," cried Dottman, I shall never forget all that while I live. Why, it is a most wonderful victory! I only wish one thing, though."

"What is that?"

"Why, that you had actually seen the rascal breathe his last."

"He surely cannot live!"

Dottman looked doubtful.

"If he were a respectable man, and an ornament to society," said Dottman, "of course he would die; but I have often noticed that the greater the rascal, the more chances he has. A respectable gentleman dies by a scratch, but men like Captain Esling seem like cats, to have nine lives."

"I do not want to have his death upon my hands," said Dora. "Oh, how much rather would I have heard from his lips, in life, some news of my lost darling.

"Cheer up, Captain—cheer up!" said Dottman—"I feel a presentiment that all will be well."

"Would that I could feel it. But where are we now, Dottman, and where are you leading me now?"

We have taken a cross turning," replied Dottman, "and shall soon reach the old Oxford Road, which runs through Wycombe."

"Have you any reason, Dottman, for seeking this road?"

"Well, Captain, I may say I have. If you would like a good booty to-night, and no doubt an adventure, which will be more amusing than dangerous, I can suggest one to you."

"My mind is in such a state of excitement," said Dora, that I fancy I shall readily enough fall in with anything you may propose."

"Good," said Dottman. "Now, in about a quarter of an hour from this time, the old Oxford mail will pass this way."

"Yes!"

"Well, Captain, if you don't mind letting me off my horse for a little time, I think of going with it as an outside passenger."

"You, Dottman?"

"Just so! but not far."

"Ah, you have some plan!"

"I have, and it is one that can very easily be carried out. I will take a place in the mail when it comes up—or rather on the mail, and I will take good care to get next to the guard, and I shall not be long there before I will manage to put his blunderbuss so completely out of order that when you stop the mail—"

"I stop the mail?"

"Certainly, Captain!"

"Why, it has four horses."

"Not a bit of matter. Indeed, the more horses the better."

"Why so, Dottman?"

"Because, you see, Captain, on the first alarm they are sure to get into a tangle, and pull all manner of ways."

"I see—I see!"

"To be sure, Captain. Well, I will take good care of the guard's blunderbuss, and that is all you have to fear. I'll be bound you will get a good booty from the inside of the mail."

"Be it so. Since I have taken to this life," said Dora, "I will make means for those who depend on me, or I will fall."

"All right, Captain. Now you shall not fall while I am with you. Take the bridle of my horse, and gallop on a couple of miles or so, till you come to a hill. You must go over it, and right down into the valley on the other side. Then you will find a flat bit of road of about a quarter of a mile long, and then another hill. At the foot of that other hill there is a little rivulet, that goes right over the road. You will see a narrow wooden bridge, and it is at that exact spot that I would advise you to cry 'Stand!' to the Oxford mail."

"I comprehend," said Dora.

"To be sure you do, Captain."

"But what shall I do with your horse, Dottman?"

"Tie the bridle to an old sycamore tree that is close to the little bridge, and I shall find him. The moment you stop the coach I will get down and be ready to help you."

"Be it so," said Dora.

Dottman now dismounted, and Dora took the bridle of the hunter."

"Off at once, Captain," cried Dottman, "or the mail will be too close upon your heels."

Dora gave Starlight a signal to proceed, and with the hunter by her side, she set off at a very quick pace down the road.

The air was soft and pleasant enough; but the road in places was very heavy, and the horses as they dashed onwards, splashed through many hollows, which were half full of melted snow.

Dora galloped the Arabian, and finding that the hunter, without a rider could keep up very well with it, she did not curb the speed of the gallant Starlight in the least.

The two miles of road were passed over in a very short period of time, indeed, and then Dora drew rein at the little wooden bridge, which Dottman had mentioned to her, as crosssng the rivulet over the road.

The spot was a romantic and beautiful one.

In the summer time, when the tall trees that now carried but their leafless branches in the air, were covered with foliage—that place must, indeed, have been one of rare beauty.

At the same time, too, it must have been one of profound shadow.

The little stream made a pleasant murmuring sound, as now that it was released from the hard frost which had held it for long in bondage, it took its way over the stones, and past the roots of the old trees.

And not another sound broke the stillness of the spot.

The sharp gallop of two miles had had the effect of somewhat calming the excitement of Dora's nerves, which had all seemed to be throbbing wildly after her desperate and terrible adventure in the King's Mews.

"Ah!" she said, "what would I not give for some peaceful spot—some pleasant little cottage home, where with all the gentle pursuit of a sylvan life, I could glide happily down the stream of time forgotten and unknown by all who would disturb my peace. With my Henry, and with my dear Mina, no hours would seem long and weary—no! Ha! what sound is that?"

The distant note of a horn came upon the night air with a pleasant sound.

It was the guard's horn of the Oxford mail.

The coach had reached a portion of the road where there was a remarkable echo, and the guard was accustomed there to blow his horn, in order that the passengers might be pleased with the sounds as they reflected from the face of a hill some miles off.

"They come! they come!" said Dora. "They come, and the period of action is at hand. Farewell, pleasant dreams of rural peace. I am compelled to be of the great world yet, and I will play my part."

The horn sounded again!

There was abundance of courage in the mind and heart of Dora, but the same high qualities which produced that abundance of courage brought with them an amount of sensitiveness that made her feel sensibly the possible dangers that were approaching.

And yet it was not for herself that she felt them. Ah, no! had she been alone in the wide world, there would have been no danger that would have cost her a moment's shudder to encounter.

But her thoughts were with her suffering Henry—with her perhaps still more suffering child; for who should say to what unknown perils and distresses the villain, Van Esling, might not have exposed the little Mina?

Alas, poor Dora!

So soon as her thoughts flew in that direction, there was a welling up of tears from her heart, and the great world about her seemed to be a thing of mist and sadness.

The horn sounded now a third time.

Dora stooped low upon her saddle and listened intently.

There was the sharp tramp of horses' feet and the grinding sound of carriage wheels.

"Ah," she cried, "They come! they come! Away with all vain regrets now. I must and will provide myself with the gold that only can enable me to wage war successfully with the cruel Duke who holds all that should be mine in his possession. They come—come—they come!"

Dora took up her post close to the rise of the road not far from the little bridge that spanned the rivulet, and there she waited for the adventure which would at once endow her with a celebrity as a knight of the road that would long be the theme of romantic exaggeration on that old Oxford Road.

Dottman had not been idle. He, too, had done his part in the night's work.

"Holloa!" he cried, as the mail coach reached the part of the road at which he had taken up his post in waiting for it. "Hilloa! hoi- hoi!"

The coachman slackened his speed.

"Have you got one inside place for Lord Clarendon de Montmorency Deville," asked Dottman, in a loud voice.

"Bless me," said the coachman, "How many are there of them."

"Only one!"

"What a curious long name," said the guard. "I think there's one inside place, Joe."

"Yes, to be sure," said the coachman. "Where is Lord—Lord— What's his name?"

"Oh, he will meet us a little further on, or at all events, on this side of Wycombe. I am one of his three valets, and will get up outside now. Pull up!"

"All's right!"

The Oxford Mail was pulled up, and the leading horses pawed the ground and champed their bits, while Dottman scrambled on to the roof, and slipped into a seat close beside the guard.

"That will do," he said.

"All right, Joe!" cried the guard.

The coachman gently laid his long four-in-hand whip over the sleek backs of his horses, and off went the Oxford Mail again at an easy trot of about nine miles an hour.

"It's a nice night," said Dottman to the guard.

"Very. Did you say your master kept three valets?"

"Oh, yes, and a barber besides."

"You don't mean it?"

"I do. He is so rich that he is the most unhappy man in the world."

"No!"

"Yes he is, because, you see, he don't know how much money he has got, and so he can't tell whether he is robbed or otherwise, and as he believes he is, it makes him miserable."

"Well, I wouldn't be him for a trifle."

"Hem!" added Dottman after a pause. "Did the Oxford Mail ever get stopped since you were guard to it?"

"Yes, once it did."

"Only once?"

"That was all, and it didn't last long, because I brought the gentleman to a stop himself in double quick time."

"What do you mean?"

"Why, I had my blunderbuss that you see here well loaded with twopennyworth of mixed nails and about a quarter of a pound of gunpowder. I let fly at him, and he was picked up all in bits the next day, and had to be taken away in a wheelbarrow."

"Hem!" said Dottman.

"It's true, only I don't feel at all offended if people don't believe it, because I admit it don't exactly sound like an every day sort of an affair."

As he spoke, the guard took his horn out of a long case of wicker work which it was kept in, and which hung by the side of his seat, and placing it to his lips, he began those long winding notes that had first reached the ears of Dora in the solitary spot where she was waiting.

Then as the guard paused and the echoes

died away on the night air, a rather portly man, who was on the coach top, said,—

"Mr. Guard, here is a lady who feels quite poorly, and it's all owing to your telling such horrid stories about shooting a highwayman."

"Dear me, yes," said a gentle voice. I'm all of a cold shiver. I dare say, now, people no more thought about putting other things into that wheelbarrow that carried the pieces of the dead highwayman, than nothing in the world."

"It's a very odd thing," said Dottman, "but my master, the Lord Clarendon de Montmorency Deville, has had a dream, and it was all on account of that that he would not take his place in the coach on this side of the further milestone."

"A dream!" cried all the "outsiders" in a breath.

"Yes, ladies and gentlemen, he dreamt that the Oxford Mail was stopped and robbed, and that the robber was—was—"

"Oh, what—what?" cried every one.

"Not of this world," said Dottman, in a deep, sepulchral tone of voice.

Several females, who were on the outside of the coach, now screamed in chorus.

"What the deuce," cried the coachman, "is all that? anybody fell off, eh?"

"No, no, Joe, all's right," said the guard.

"Is it all right? I tells you what, all of you, if you goes on a startling my leaders like that, we shall be upset. Woa, woa! easy, easy! chut, chut! easy does it!"

The leading horses had broke into an irregular kind of gallop, which the coachman had some difficulty in subduing into a trot again.

"Swords, daggers, bombshells, and pistols! what is the matter?" cried a loud voice from one of the inside passengers of the coach, as the window was let down quickly. "What is it, eh?"

"Now, captain, dear captain!" screamed a female voice, "Be merciful and don't kill anybody."

"Spikes, bayonets, and cannonades!" shouted the captain. "I heard screams! I was half asleep, ladies, but I heard screams! and if anybody requires his throat cut, or his brains scooped out, I am the man to do it. Ha!"

Two ladies who were in the inside of the coach screamed aloud.

A little elderly gentleman, who made the fourth inside passenger, but who was only going to Ealing tried to hide under the seat.

"What now?" roared the coachman again? "Is His Majesty's Mail to Oxford to go on or isn't it, I should like to know, eh?"

"I don't know what they are all about, Joe," said the guard, "but the passengers seem half crazy."

"Well, I never *druv* such a lot in all my born days! Chut, chut! Them leaders will be off as sure as horse shoes ain't muffins, if there's any more screeching and screaming!"

The guard blew his horn again. The horses were well accustomed to the sound, and he thought it would perhaps restore the passengers as well to their ordinary state of equanimity.

Dottman adroitly now, while the guard was standing up and leaning over the back of the coach, pulling away at his horn, flung up the pan of the blunderbuss, and let the priming fall out. He had in his pocket some half dozen little wax ends of candle, and one of those he jammed beneath the pan of the blunderbuss and shut it down upon it.

Dottman felt certain that the fire arm of the guard was now perfectly useless.

The Oxford mail had commenced the descent of one of the hills.

Dottman then cried out in a loud voice of some alarm—"Ladies and gentlemen, I never yet knew of a dream of my master, Lord Clarendon de Montmorency Deville, that didn't come true, and as I have a valuable gold watch, I am putting it into my boot, in case we should be stopped."

At these words there was quite a commotion both inside and outside the coach.

"Dear me!" said a female voice from inside, "I will put my purse and rings into the pocket of the coach door."

"Good gracious!" said the little old gentleman who had tried to get under the seat, "Will any one tell me where I can hide for safety this little leather case. It has got some jewels in it, and more than a hundred pounds in money. Oh, I'll put it under the cushion of the seat."

The guard blew his horn for the third time, and then he cried out—

"What's the use of a guard, ladies and gentlemen, if he don't blow the head off of any highwayman who stops his coach, eh? You forget my blunderbuss."

"I don't!" said Dottman.

"Carbines! scymetars! grenades! rockets and bombards!" cried the military gentleman from inside, "I feel a great conviction that I shall have to leave some one weltering in his gore on the road to-night. Don't be alarmed, ladies, when you hear the screams of some dying wretch!"

Dottman at this moment raised such an unearthly cry that the whole of the passengers were at once seized with a panic, and the coachman involuntarily pulled up his team.

"Good gracious!" said Dottman, "there! I saw a man on horseback come right up out of the ground, and there he is."

"Stand and deliver!" shouted Dora, at this moment, as she darted on Starlight right out into the centre of the road, and levelled a pistol at the head of the coachman.

"There had been some fleeting clouds close down to the horizon, but they had seemed to be chased by the rising moon, which now showed itself, and shed a strange supernatural looking light upon the scene.

There was the hill side—there was the little wooden bridge that spanned the rivulet—and there was the group of trees that cast a deep broad shadow over the road.

It was just on the verge of this shadow that Dora and Starlight were to be seen.

The outside passengers began to cry out in all sorts of tones of alarm.

Screams came from inside.

But strange to say the voice of the captain was not heard. Perhaps he was preparing some fearful fate for the highwayman, which was too terrible to talk of.

We shall see.

Dottman, the moment after he had uttered the last words which we have recorded as coming from his lips, let himself drop down from the top of the coach, and dashed away to the trees to get his horse. He found it all safe, and in another moment was by the side of Dora.

"There's an army of 'em!" said the coachman. "But I'm not a going to be stopped. Come up!"

"Don't, Joe! don't!" said the guard.

"What for?"

"I have 'em! Look out! Duck! duck!"

"What's a duck?"

"Duck your head, stupid!"

"Oh!"

"There you go!"

The guard levelled his blunderbuss, and while the outside passengers all fell down flat, right and left, like a pack of cards, to let the terrible discharge pass in harmlessness over their heads, the guard pulled the trigger.

Flop! came down the lock.

"A miss, by Jove!" said the guard!

"Coachman, your life!" cried Dora, and she pointed a pistol wide enough of the man, but it had the effect of alarming him, and he cried out—

"I have a wife—two wives, I mean, and one child, who is very bad—no, I mean one wife and two small children. Spare my life!"

Dottman dashed forward and seized the leading horses by the bits.

"Now, Captain!" said Dottman, "now is your time—I will take good care of the horses—now's your time!"

"Murder! murder!" cried one of the outside passengers, as Dora dashed up to the side of the coach.

"Oh!" she said, "do you particularly wish it?"

"Wish what? Oh, good Mr. Highwayman, be merciful!"

"I thought you said you wanted to be murdered. Don't let me hear that cry again, or I will make it a truth!"

"With a sudden dash now upon the edge of the window of the coach door Dora placed the barrel of a pistol, and in as deep a tone as she could assume she cried out—

"Your money or your life!"

The two ladies both screamed for a few moments in chorus, and then a very submissive voice said—

"I beg your pardon, Mr—a—a—highway gentleman, but I am a poor fellow, you see, and only travel for orders for buttons."

"Why, you are a captain!" said both the ladies.

"Oh, lord! oh, lord! said the little old gentlemen, "I thought, sir, you would eat up a single highwayman, horse and all!"

"Have mercy upon me, dear good sir," said the valiant pretended captain. "Indeed I am only traveller to Mr. Bumming, the Button Maker, in Covent Garden, I assure you, dear sir."

"Quick!" said Dora. "Your money, watches, and jewellery. Quick! I am apt to get impatient."

One of the ladies handed a small bead purse to Dora, with about two shillings in it.

The other declared she had nothing at all but a lap dog, which she offered at once.

The little old gentleman produced a handful of halfpence, and the gallant captain a dollar piece.

"Hark!" said Dora, suddenly.

There came a strange, wailing voice through the air.

Now in order that the reader may know the mystery of this voice at once, we will state that Dottman had whispered to Dora, just as he took hold of the horses heads, that he had information to give her about what booty she ought to get, and that he would alarm the passengers by giving it in a seeming supernatural manner.

Dottman, therefore, had folded up some paper into a tolerable imitation of a speaking trumpet, and through that he now hallowed in a very strange way to Dora.

"Captain Arod! Captain Arod! Captain Arod!"

"Speak!" cried Dora. "I listen, spirit."

"It's a ghost after all!" cried the guard, and he rolled off the top of the coach, and ran and hid himself in the hedge.

CHAPTER XV.

DORA SECURES A GOOD BOOTY—A PURSUIT —THE BANKS OF THE RIVER, AND THE FLOOD—A SURPRISE.

WHEN the passengers of the Oxford Mail heard this seeming supernatural voice addressing the highwayman, they almost swooned with fright, and not a sound, for a few moments, after the escape of the guard, disturbed the stillness of the night but those strange tones of Dottman.

"Speak again!" cried Dora. "What would you say to me, O familiar spirit?"

"In the pocket of the coach door is booty."

"Ah!"

"Beneath one of the cushions of the seat is booty."

"Thanks! thanks! Then the time has come at which to end the mortal career of those who have attempted to deceive me!"

A yell of dismay burst from the lips of the little old gentleman and the button-dealing captain together at these words, and one handed out to Dora a small leather case, and the other a canvas bag, which was of a goodly weight with gold.

The lady who had hidden her property in the pocket of the coach door, fainted at once, or pretended to do so.

The younger lady who was in the coach, however, dived her hand into that pocket, and brought out its contents, and handed them to Dora.

"That is all," she said—"unless you want my earrings—they are only garnets."

"Keep them, my dear," said Dora.

There was something mild and kind in the tone in which Dora uttered these words, and the young lady said, smilingly—

"You are like Claude Duval."

Dora laughed.

"And I am sure quite as handsome. He used to make any young lady who happened to be in a coach that he robbed, get out and dance a 'Minuet' with him. Will you let me see your face?"

Dora shook her head.

"No! You will not? Then you are ugly!"

"Am I?" said Dora.

She just lifted the silken mask a little way, upon which the young lady could see the sweet, regular features of Dora, and the cherry lips, and sparkling teeth. She clapped her hands as she cried—

"You don't know me, but my name is Bellair, and this is my aunt, and—"

"Take that, you impudent hussey!" exclaimed the aunt at this moment, whose faint had, in all probability, been a *feint*, and she dealt her rather pretty niece such a box on the ears, that, for a few moments, she was unable even to see the handsome highwayman.

Dora laughed, and turned from the coach door towards Dottman.

"Release!" she said. "Release the horses—it is done!"

"And so are you, my fine fellow!" cried a voice from one of the outside passengers, and at the same moment, a pistol was discharged at Dora.

Starlight reared suddenly now, and gave a snort of pain.

Dora felt confident the noble creature had been hit by the bullet.

"That was a foul shot," she said.

A man on the moment dropped from the roof of the coach, and made a run to get to the hedge, but Dora dashed after him, and Starlight caught him by the back of the neck in his teeth.

"Murder! murder! murder!"

"Oh, you are the same rascal," said Dora, who called murder before, and now I comprehend; it was because you wished to commit one. Hold him, Starlight! hold him!"

Dottman galloped up now, seeing Dora, as he thought, engaged in some conflict.

The coachman, then, seeing that his horses heads were free, laid the whip savagely into them, and the Oxford Mail went off at a most tremendous pace.

But Dora—or rather Starlight, had a prisoner.

"What and who is it?" said Dottman.

"A rascal, who tried to shoot me from outside, and who has, I fear, wounded Starlight, although I took nothing from him.

Dottman hastily dismounted, and Dora took the bridle of his horse. He then collared the man, as he cried—

"So, scoundrel, you must needs interfere in what don't concern you, eh? Go!"

The hedge was a blackthorn one. Dottman, with a strength that he could not, in cool blood, have mastered, flung this man right into the middle of it."

"On! on!" he then cried—"On, Captain! this little affair is over. I hope it has been profitable?"

"I think it has!"

Both Dottman and Dora now rode on towards London; but they had not gone above half a mile, when they heard a terrible clattering of horses feet behind them on the road.

"Hold!" said Dottma —"I don't seem half to like that, Captai'n

"What is it?"

"Why, from the noise, I should say it was a good strong troop of mounted men on the road, and far too many for us to have anything to do with."

"What shall we do, Dottman?"

"I think we had better be polite enough to leave them all the road to themselves. It is quite clear, that if Starlight has been touched by the pistol bullet that rascal fired at you, it is but a slight wound, for he would not carry himself as he does if he were hurt much."

"I see the wound. It is only a skin graze on the neck."

"All right, then. Let us leap the hedge —it is but low here, and on the other side we can see these people pass, be they who they may."

The road was wide enough to enable Dora and Dottman to back their horses some thirty or forty feet from the hedge, so that there was space for a rush before the leap.

Both the horses did it in good style.

Immediately on the other side of the hedge was a meadow, which, in consequence of the recent snows and frost, was, now that a general thaw had taken place and the season had altered its character, excessively soft and saturated with moisture.

It was well that the horses had to leap from the hard high road into that meadow oozing with water, instead of from it, and it was well, too, in consequence of the softness of the soil, they alighted noiselessly upon the winter grass.

The hedge was scarcely high enough to enable the horses to hide securely behind it from the observation of mounted men in the high road, but Dottman led his horse into a deep hollow or water way at the roots of the hedge trees and shrubs, and Dora followed his example with Starlight.

The moonlight that now streamed through the air was rather an advantage to them than otherwise, inasmuch as it was so low in the horizon that it cast long and dark shadows, being more perplexing even than darkness.

Under these circumstances there might be a reasonable hope that the horsemen, be they whom they might, who were coming with such a clatter along the road, would pass on their way.

But such was not the case.

A loud, sonorous voice called Halt, and very nearly opposite to that portion of the hedgerow over which Dottman and Dora had leaped their horses, a troop of men paused, some fifteen in number.

Somewhat to the consternation of Dottman, and likewise of Dora, they could both see, by the slant rays of the moon, that these men were in military costume, and in fact, they were a small party of light cavalry coming from Hounslow to Whitehall, and

who had chosen to take some cross roads to get to where they were.

A non-commissioned officer was in command of the party, and having encountered the Oxford Mail at the turning of a lane, the little old gentleman, who was an inside passenger, offered them at once a reward of fifty pounds if they would pursue and capture two most atrocious highwaymen, who had robbed him of a leather packed containing a thousand pounds worth of jewels.

It was upon this impulse, then, that the troop had made so tremendous a clatter in coming down the road after Dottman and Dora.

"I'm afraid we've come too far, comrades," said the sergeant, who had an idea of giving his men a guinea a-piece, and pocketing the remainder of the reward himself. "Trot back, some of you, and at the first gap in the hedge, or gate that you see, get into the meadows. The fellows have taken to the fields, I'll be bound."

This was a mode of proceeding at once dangerous and alarming to Dottman and Dora.

"It is over," said Dora. "We shall be captured."

"Not at all, captain! Bless your heart, those troop horses never get beyond a certain speed. We can distance them easily. It's heavy riding in the meadows, but that's as bad for them as it is for us, and we can take leaps that they can't touch by half way."

"Then you advise flight?"

"Instant flight, captain; for if once they hem us in, they'll get the better of us."

"I am ready."

Dottman took the lead, and stooping low in the saddle, a manœuvre which was imitated by Dora, he stepped his horse out of the water way in which they had taken refuge into the deep shadow of the hedgerow, which extended far and wide over the meadow.

They did not expect but that they would be seen at once by the troop of light cavalry, but such, indeed, was the case, for the sergeant and some ten of his men, who remained with him, raised a shout as they saw the two flying figures on horseback emerge from the deep shadow, and make their way across the saturated fields.

That shout was in reality the last they saw or heard of the troop of light horsemen from Hounslow, since there was not one of the troop horses that was capable of leaping the hedge.

Dottman took the lead by about a couple of horses' lengths, and Dora had to curb the speed of her beautiful Arabian, in order to keep it from passing the hunter ridden by her companion.

THE FLIGHT OF DORA AND DOTTMAN FROM THE KING'S MEWS.

By a glance backward, it was soon evident to them both that they were no longer pursued, and as nothing could very well be more distressing to the horses than a gallop across country, while the meadows, too, were in such a state, Dottman looked anxiously about him for some road or lane which would afford a harder surface, but this seemed difficult to find, and in fact they came upon the precincts of a farmhouse, with its outbuildings and orchards, which seemed to be directly in their way.

It was no part of the policy of Dora to allow herself to be seen by the occupants of any of the farms about the district, where probably she would carry on her operations as a

highwayman; and she came to rather an abrupt pause at a high fence, which was immediately in the way, and which Dottman seemed to be measuring with his eyes as though debating the propriety of attempting to leap it.

"No, captain," he said. "It is a trifle too high; and, besides, before we got through the farmyard, we might find another higher still. We must skirt it."

This was done, and to the surprise of Dora, when they got clear of this farm and its outbuildings, she saw a long white streak of something glistening in the moonlight, which, on second observation, convinced her must be the Thames, as there was no other stream near London of such width.

No. 8.—DORA.

"Why, Dottman," she cried, "we are at the banks of the river."

"Just so, captain, and do you know, I think our best plan, since you have, perhaps a considerable booty, will be to make our way as near as we can down the stream to Westminster.

"Yes," cried Dora, with animation, "and there is one spot on the river I fain would look upon again, since there was moored the boat which contained, I believe, the villain Van Esling and that dearest portion of my life, my child."

Dottman was so well acquainted with all the paths, lanes, and byeways of that neighbourhood, that he had no difficulty in leading Dora to the bank of that portion of the river which she presumed to be opposite to where the boat had been moored, which, in the middle of the snowstorm she had tried in vain to reach.

It had never occurred to Dora's imagination for a single moment that that boat could be still at its moorings, and her surprise was intense to see either it or a similar one occupying that same spot.

Yes, there was the boat! that boat which Dora had believed to contain the darling little Mina. The tears gushed to her eyes as she looked upon it, and she stretched out her hands with an imploring gesture as she cried aloud,—

"Oh, what is all the world to me compared with one glance of your dear eyes, my own dear, dear Mina?"

Dottman seemed to be upon the point of making some reply, when a strange, rushing sound came upon their ears.

A man ran past them at the moment with some oars and planks upon his shoulder.

"Take care of yourselves," he shouted. "The flood is coming!—the flood is coming!"

"What do you mean?" cried Dottman. "Are you mad?"

"Wait and see," added the man, as he disappeared in the darkness."

"Ah!" cried Dottman, "I do see!"

"What is it?" asked Dora anxiously.

"Look! oh, look!"

Dottman pointed to the right, and as he and Dora were upon some elevated ground, they could see for a considerable distance up the stream.

The sight which presented itself was at once strange and alarming.

The long frost had by the assistance of the tides which had from day to day forced the ice higher and higher, accumulated an enormous heaped up mass of frozen water above the small bridges of the river.

That vast mass had now given way before the change in the temperature, and aided by the reflux of one of the spring tides, it was coming down the stream like a cataract.

There was a heaving, rolling mass of water some fourteen or fifteen feet in height, which, with a terrible surging sound, like a mighty wave, was sweeping onwards, bringing with it huge heaps of ice, trunks of fallen trees, broken barges, and all the *debris* of the river's banks, which it had submerged and flooded.

For a few moments, then, neither Dottman nor Dora spoke a word, as they sat on their horses and watched this foaming, splashing mass come surging down the Thames.

Then there came a scream from the direction of the river.

Dora nearly echoed that scream, for she felt and knew that it came from the direction of that mysterious boat, which was still moored near to the centre of the river.

The moonlight fell strongly over that portion of the stream, and Dora saw some dark looking figure, in sombre drapery, rush from some cabin, or covered place on board, and after standing for a moment with gestures of distress and despair on the side of the boat nearest to the opposite bank, plunge into the stream and disappear

The rolling, surging, hissing mass of waters that was advancing like a wall of dark coloured foam down the Thames was not above one hundred yards from the boat.

By a kind of fascination, Dora's eyes were fixed upon the little vessel.

Then the cry she uttered alarmed Dottman for her safety or her sanity.

Dora has seen a sight which had forced that cry from her heart.

Projected from the opening to the little cabin of the boat had appeared two little arms and hands—the arms and hands of a child!

Did Dora know them? Did not her heart at once tell her they were the hands and arms of her own child—her Mina, who had been torn from her? Her darling little one, whose absence was the ever present agony of her heart! Ah, yes! Dora needed no second glance—she needed no reasoning upon such a subject.

"Mina! Mina! my child—my own lost dear one. I am here—I am here!"

Another moment, and Dora had leaped the beautiful Arabian horse right into the stream.

The creature obeyed the impulse which Dora had given it to the leap, without a moment's hesitation, and it swam gallantly.

But the flood was coming!

"Stay, oh, stay!" cried Doteman. "You seek death! to the shore again! Help! God have mercy now upon her!"

He paused an instant now, and then he added the words,

"And upon me, too, for I will live with her, or die with her."

As he spoke he leaped the hunter into the river.

The hunter was more reluctant than the Arabian steed had been, but still it swam well.

But what was all the swimming against that terrible flood that came on like some fearful living thing, with awful and unknown powers of destruction.

The line of the advancing wave must have met with some obstruction, or the varying depth of the river had some effect upon it, for when Dora sprung on horseback into the stream, she could see that the advancing wave was slant across the Thames.

It would reach the boat where still she could see those little hands held up imploringly, before it would reach her and the beautiful Arabian she rode.

Dora uttered another cry!

It might have been fancy, but she thought that cry was echoed by one on board the boat.

She thought she heard the word mother! That was, indeed, a terrible moment.

The flood caught the boat!

"Mina! Mina! Oh, Heaven save my child!" cried Dora.

The boat was in a moment dashed from its mooring. Yes—oh, Heaven, yes! Surely that was the wailing cry of her child that she now heard, even amid the hiss and the roar of the waters.

The boat was borne onwards like a floating straw by the flood, and then for a brief moment Dora felt as if she reached, on a plateau of foam, some strange place in which mountains of water rose up and held their place between the earth and sky.

That was only for a moment.

Then, with a rushing sound, as if all the cataracts in the world had united to roll over her, she was submerged by the flood.

CHAPTER XVI.

THE DUKE OF KINGSTON STRIVES TO RID HIMSELF OF A FOE — THE WOUNDED ASSASSIN — THE DARK MYSTERY OF KINGSTON HOUSE NEARS A CATASTROPHE.

THE Duke of Kingston—that false Duke, whose wickedness was the source of all the misfortunes of Dora and her father—sat alone in one of the magnificent apartments of Kingston House, St. James's, his head rested on his hand, and among all the magnificent objects that surrounded him, glittering, as they were, with gold and the most exquisite colouring, there was not one that had sufficient charms to arrest his attention for a moment.

Alone—alone—how truly alone was that man! and yet, in the eye of the world, what a great, successful noble he was.

With what envy, shivering and thinly clad pedestrians had, during the last inclement season, looken up at the blaze of light and warmth which came from the windows of Kingston House; how happy they thought the man who could command the wealth that was to be found within that palatial residence, and how little they suspected that this man of rank, wealth, and power, had his moments of depression, during which, all the world and its enjoyments seemed to slip from him, and he would have given everything he possessed for a quiet grave.

But these moments were not frequent in comparison with the remainder of his life— they rather sprung out of what may be called the exhaustion of his wickedness, and then he would howl and rave to himself until he thought of some new combination which should promise him temporary pleasure, if not permanent contentment.

"What is all this?" he muttered to himself—"what is all this that I hear whispered about the court, that no one saw the late earl, my brother, die? He is dead, he must be dead; and this daughter, who would claim the titles and dignities that I would peril my soul for, shall die likewise. She and her husband, and their brat shall all perish! And how strange it is that, although Van Esling assured me he must have killed Dacres—all that I can hear of him, is that he has disappeared, and my utmost vigilance can find no traces of his whereabouts."

The Duke sprung from his chair, and struck his breast with a savage energy.

"I shall have a world of care," he cried, "until I can feel certain they are all in their graves; and much I begin to fear, too, that I am the dupe of Surlina, the artful Greek, who pretends to the secrets of alchemy; but who looks upon me, whenever he thinks my eyes are off him, with glances of such hatred that I fear me for my life."

The Duke, in pacing the large apartment in which he was, had neared the door, and as he did so, a low tap at the outer side of it warned him that some one requested admittance.

Retreating hastily to a considerable distance, he buried his hand in the folds of his apparel about his breast, where he doubtless had concealed weapons, and then he cried hoarsely—"Come in—who knocks?"

A servant in gorgeous livery appeared at the door, and on a salver, presented a card to the Duke. The card bore the name of Major Bentinck, and in straggling writing beneath it, were the following words.

"Captain Van Esling lies dangerously wounded at the King's Mews, and much wishes to see his grace, the Duke of Kingston."

The Duke uttered an exclamation of surprise, and then turning to the servant who still lingered at the door, he said harshly—

"Where is the messenger who brought this card?"

"It was a soldier of the guard, your grace, who merely left it and then went his way."

"A carriage—a carriage! No—bring me a cloak. The night is calm—I will go on foot. The sword with the silver hilt, knave —this toy is not fit for a man to go abroad with."

As he spoke the Duke took from his belt one of those long slender steel rapiers so common at the court, and flung it on a couch close to one of the distant walls of the apartment. A valet, in plain dress then, who was summoned by the gorgeous footman, brought him a much more serviceable weapon, the hilt of which was of frosted silver, and the scabbard of which was covered with black velvet, clampt with the same metal.

"Begone!" said the Duke, imperiously, and the domestic left him alone.

"I will see Surlina for a moment," he said, "before I leave; there are more ways than one from this house to that which he occupies, but the one he knows shall be that alone with which I will make him acquainted —yes, I will see him a moment, for something seems to tell me the villain is treacherous."

As upon a former occasion the Duke of Kingston locked the door of this apartment, and took every precaution that no prying eyes should spy upon his conduct. He then pressed the spring in the frame of the full-length portrait of Charles the First, and the secret panel opened which communicated with the next house.

"Surlina! Surlina!" he cried, "I would speak with you."

"I am here!" said the Greek.

"You have no light—you were not wont to be so in love with darkness."

"I have a light in the laboratory, and the furnaces are well heated."

"Look you here!" added the Duke, as he stood at the entrance to the next house, through the second entrance, "Look you

here, Surlina—I have been unfortunate at play—I have lost to my Lord Cleaveland more than I can pay—you have amused me here some time with the prospect that by your art you could change to gold the baser metals. Have you done so? For gold I must have—and that in no small abundance."

"Patience!" said the Greek.

"Patience? Flames and fury! have I not had patience?"

"I serve you, my good Lord, in other ways."

"Ah! say you so?"

"Yes—and even should I fail in the great project—"

"Fail! Fail? Talk you to me of failing when you have half beggared me with your wants of some strange chemical and another —hark you, Surlina! I think you deceive me!"

"My Lord, I do not."

"It is well—it is well—I have a secret for you, which you must keep. A guest will be brought hither—one whom I believe is badly wounded—at least, so they say— and as a wounded man suffers much, and death, Surlina, is the end of all suffering— you comprehend me!"

"I do—you would have him killed!"

"Killed is a harsh word—you will play the part of his good physician—a composing draught—you understand, Surlina—so composing that the patient stirs not hand or foot until——well, well, I must not think of that—time enough—time enough! Be near at hand when I call to you—I shall be absent, perchance an hour."

The Duke hastily closed the panel, and then strode from the room and left the house.

In the intense darkness of the apartment in which he was, the Greek remained listening for a while, and when he felt quite certain that the Duke of Kingston had left the house, he burst into a strange paroxysm of rage—a paroxysm all the more intense that it was choked and silent, for he feared to awaken the dreary echoes of the house he inhabited.

He tossed his arms wildly above his head —he clenched his hands—he ground his teeth together, and sob after sob seemed to well up from the bottom of his heart.

"He thinks me sunk so low, he said, as to be his slave. The insidious assassin who is to murder at his pleasure! Vengeance— vengeance shall be mine—but it shall be on him—on him alone! Neoni—Neoni—oh, Neoni!

"I am here, father!" said a soft voice.

"Ah! my child—my bright-eyed daughter of the sunny islands—art thou here?"

"You called me, father!"

"Nay—did I so? I knew not that I

did—but your fair name is ever on my lips, as is your image is ever on my heart. The time will come—oh, the time will come, my Neoni, when this proud frankish noble shall do you justice."

"Alas! father, I am very sad. Know you the date and time?"

"Date? time?"

"Yes, father, it was this night twelve-months since that I appealed to the great duchess, who I then found was wife to this faithless noble, who, not with such allure-ments as win the vain and giddy to destruc-tion, sought me, but with the potent spell of some draught that lured me to repose. You know, father, I sought this Duchess, to lay my wrongs before her. I knew not what I asked. I had no thought that she could aid me, but she might have pitied me!"

"The very night—the very night!" gasped the Greek. "Twelvemonths since, I know it now, was it not engraven on my heart? How strange that other records should slur it out."

"Yes, father, twelve long weary months have passed away, and I am still what I am!"

"My child—my child!"

The Greek girl sobbed biterly.

"Hush! hush! I cannot bear those tears. Strike daggers to my heart, my Neoni, but do not kill me with those sobs. Has she not suffered?"

"Oh! I could pardon; vengeance is but another weary load to carry. 'Tis restitu-tion of my heart's innocence I ask for. Our race is ancient as the hills on which in olden times the fawn and dryad, and many a gentle wood nymph danced in beauty beneath the sunlight of our ancient clime, while the old gods of noble Greece looked down approving. Let this man make me his wife, and I shall die in peace."

"He shall! he shall! But meanwhile, retribution is the cry. Come with me, Neoni, we have one hour to ourselves. We will pay a visit."

"A visit! O, father!"

"Yes, my child. There is one whom we hold in bondage in this house in expiation of her pride. She spurned you, my child, with bitter words and cruel taunts. What is she now?"

"Alas, I pity her!"

"Hush! It is a word I may not hear. My heart is steel, adamant to all who have wronged you. Come, come, you will please me, my gentle Neoni—I who have loved you so fondly—have tended you and watched over you from early childhood. Since that time, with the old Greek war-cry on my lips, I fled with you from our burning village, attacked by the barbarian Turk. Come, you will please me, Neoni! We will visit this proud duchess—she lies on straw, and chains encompass her—we are her gaolers, Neoni, but we will, in imagination, restore her this night to her native rank."

"How mean you, father?"

"I mean that you should repeat to her, my child, word for word, the humble prayer you offered up to her when, in her pride, she only listened but to spurn the lonely Greek girl, who had fallen a victim to her husband's baseness."

"It will be but a mockery now, father."

"And I would mock her. Let her sue to us now, and sue in vain. She knows not but that she is merely the prisoner of the Duke on account of some matters con-nected with the descent of these barbarous English. But now she shall know that the arbitress of her destiny is the young Greek girl whose sorrow was of no account, and whose ruin was a jest."

Neoni would have shrunk from this pro-ject of her father, but she was too much accustomed to yield implicit obedience to his wishes to do so effectually, and she fol-lowed him up the dreary staircase which led to the wretched attic in which the un-happy Duchess of Kingston had been nearly twelvemonths a prisoner.

It was a terrible combination of circum-stances for her that she had made an impla-cable foe of her false-hearted husband, the Duke, and of Surlina, the Greek alchemist, within a few days.

Her threat to take up the cause of Dora at any sacrifice, from a conviction of its justice, had brought about one enmity.

Her scorn at what she considered the mere artful tale of one whose virtue she thought was a myth, had brought about the other.

And so the Duke had condemned her, and Surlina became her gaoler.

Unhappy Duchess!

The Greek and his fair daughter reached the door of the prison apartment of the wretched woman, and Surlina tapped in an accustomed manner on the panel.

In a faint, moaning voice, that would have risen to a scream had it had the power, the persecuted Duchess of Kingston spoke,—

"Is there no mercy yet? Am I still the sport of those who surely mean to destroy me? Is there no pity? Oh, what have I done? what have I done, that I should suffer thus? No light—no liberty—no cheerful sight or sound of the world which surely I have a right to enjoy. Mercy—mercy! have some mercy upon me!"

"She suffers," said Surlina, "and we, too, have suffered, my Neoni."

Neoni shuddered.

"Alas! alas!" she said. "It cannot surely be, father, that my wrongs are to be redressed by this sad infliction of another wrong on the Duchess of Kingston. She was proud and haughty to me, and spurned me from her, but I never hear that terrible voice of woe and misery, but I feel that I forgive."

"No, no!" said the Greek through his clenched teeth. "That may not be, for while this woman lives, my child, you are a thing of shame. When she is no more, you may have some justice done you, but that is not the present purpose. I would now have you again recollect what time this is!"

"Time father?"

"Yes, what anniversary it is? Again, my child, I would have you speak to this high, proud, haughty duchess, and tell her that the Duke has wronged you. Once before you have so spoken to her, and you had your answer. We will see what it shall be now!"

There was a something in the tone of her father as he uttered these words, that horrified Neoni. There was a bitterness—a concentrated scorn—a hate that made her young heart shrink within her with fear.

But she felt that it was no time to disobey, and she crept close to the panel of the room door.

"Madam! madam! madam!"

The Duchess uttered now a cry of hope. That hope which springs upward in the human heart had arisen in all its strength and beauty now, because she heard that the words which were addressed to her were spoken in the tones of a woman.

"Oh, speak to me—speak to me!" she cried, with all the power she could summon to give strength to her voice. "Speak to me—speak to me, for you are surely one who will pity me."

"Speak," said Surlina.

Neoni shuddered, but she obeyed. Her quick apprehension made her thoroughly comprehend what it was her father wanted her to do. She was to wring the heart of that proud Duchess by letting her know that the once humble supplicant whom she had scorned was now armed with power over her.

"Madam," she said again. "Duchess of Kingston, I come to you with an appeal. As one woman's heart may appeal to another's for a sympathy which may not be found in the breast of man, I appeal to you."

"Oh, what words are those?" moaned the Duchess. "What tones are those? I seem to have heard them in a dream."

"It was no dream," added Neoni. "You heard them twelve weary months since, when a young Greek girl appealed to you, and appealed in vain."

"Ah!"

"You remember now?"

"I do! I do!"

"Then I am here once more, and now once more I tell you, Duchess, that I have suffered foul and grievous wrong from the man you call your husband."

"I know it now," replied the Duchess, faintly. "I know it now. I feel it all now! Believe me, I know it now."

"Too late!" said Surlina, as he dealt the panel of the door a heavy blow. Too late, Duchess of Kingston — too late, I say! You are now the suppliant—she who was in that position, holds your life utterly in her hands. Too late! too late!"

"Oh, spare me! Oh, forgive me! I spoke out of the pride of my heart a year since! I now speak from its anguish and repentance! Oh, spare me, and have mercy upon me!"

Surlina struck the panel of the door again a heavy, startling blow, and laughed mockingly.

"You cannot," added the Duchess, "but have some spark of humanity yet unextinguished in your heart. You must feel that I have already suffered much—enough —more than enough to move your pity!"

"Ha, ha!"

The Duchess screamed and sobbed.

"Father! father! this is terrible!" said the fair Neoni."

"Yes," said the implacable Greek, with sarcastic vehemence—"it is almost as terrible as the destruction of the honour and the hopes in life of a young girl, the descendant of a race of warriors, whose fame, till now, had known no stain."

Neoni trembled.

Then Surlina struck upon the panel of the door a third time, and in a voice of ferocity he spoke.

"Duchess of Kingston, I will give you information. It is the will of the Duke, your husband, that you shall continue a prisoner in that gloomy chamber you now occupy. You alarmed him because you threatened some act that would interfere with his wealth and dignity; but he could hardly have held you captive so long without some assistance, and that assistance he could never have purchased. It must be the assistance of hate—of revenge!"

"Oh, mercy—mercy!"

"And so I am your gaoler—I, the father of the injured girl who was scorned by you, when in your pride of station and power. You now understand? Ha, ha! you are the the prisoner of the Duke's policy—of my revenge. Abandon hope, wretched woman, for you shall never see the light of day again in this life!"

The Duchess uttered another faint cry, and then all was still.

"Come, my child! come!" said Surlina. "That is done."

He had opened high up in the door a small square piece of the panel, and through it he thrust some coarse loaves of bread. They fell into the room with a sound that testified to their quality.

Neoni was in tears, but the look of Surlina was cold and stern as ever.

While these events were taking place at the house of the Duke of Kingston, he had taken his way, on foot, to the King's Mews, in consequence of the pressing application from the sorely wounded Van Esling.

The Duke grasped the hilt of his sword as he proceeded, and held his cloak tightly about him, and as the distance was but short, he soon found himself at the old gate of the barracks.

"What has happened to Captain Esling?" he asked abruptly of the sergeant of the Guard."

The Duke was known to the sergeant, and he replied with all respect.

"We fear, your grace, that he is murdered!"

"By whom?"

"That we cannot tell—but some one called to see him, and must have taken him at some great disadvantage, and he is now lying in his rooms fearfully wounded."

"This is strange! Conduct me to him!"

The Duke of Kingston then traversed that very gallery which Dora passed through on her route to the apartments in the occupation of Van Esling, and was soon in the anti-chamber where that fearful combat had taken place that had left Van Esling so dreadful a spectacle, pinned to the wall of the room by the broken sword blade.

Deep and horrible groans saluted the ears of the Duke as he entered the apartment, and by the light of several tall wax candles, he saw Van Esling lying on the bed, and several persons about him.

"His grace, the Duke of Kingston!" announced the sergeant who had slightly preceded the Duke, to show him the way.

At the sound of that name, Van Esling ceased his groans, and fixed his wild anxious looking eyes upon the face of his wicked patron.

"Death! death! death!" he said—"it has come at last!"

"Is it so?" said the Duke, with an inquiring look about him at the persons in the room.

Then one of them, who was the regimental surgeon, spoke.

"It will be impossible to tell as yet. If he be still alive in twenty-four hours from now, there will be hope."

"No, no, no!" said Van Esling—"you have done for me all you can, and I would now speak with the Duke of Kingston."

It was with evident pain and difficulty that he uttered these words, but the surgeon immediately replied to them.

"I warn you, Captain Esling," he said, "that the only thing that can give you a chance of life is quiet and repose."

"I must speak."

"Well, I have done my duty. The consequences be upon your own head."

The surgeon left the room, and the orderly sergeant, who had accompanied him, left with him. The Duke of Kingston was alone with his accomplice in crimes.

"What would you say to me?" he asked, in a low tone.

"Are we alone?"

"We are."

The Duke stepped towards the door, and closed it.

"Then I would tell your grace that the hand which has dealt me this mortal blow, was that of Dora, the daughter of the Duke, your brother."

"Ah! is that possible?"

"It is but too true. Alas, alas! In obedience to your wishes and your commands, I assailed her husband, and, I believe, killed him—but I had another motive."

"What other motive?"

"I loved her!"

"You—you loved her?"

"Ay, from the first moment that I looked upon her a passion, wild, insane—call it what you will, rushed into my heart, and I loved her with a frenzy that knew no bounds. I fancy it was a punishment to me that I should do so, but I could not battle with the passion, and it was driving me to madness!"

"This is, indeed, strange! You love? you who never yet exhibited a remorse or a human feeling? You the victim of a hopeless passion?"

"Yes—yes—oh, Heaven! yes—but listen—oh, listen to me while I can yet speak—the child! the child!

"What child?"

"Dora's child!"

"What of that? Speak to me of that? I did hear that there was a child!"

"I stole it from her—I feel faint—I know not if it be death that is coming over me—but let me tell you I took the child from her, not because I thought it would advance your interests, but because I thought that it was a kind of a hostage as between her and me— Oh, this deadly faintness—it lays a hold upon my heart."

For a few moments the Duke of Kingston

hought that this man who had been so useful a tool to him in the unscrupulous course he had pursued to get possession of the title and estates which should have belonged to his brother's daughter, Dora, was indeed at his last gasp. He knew not whether to be pleased or sorry that one who knew so much was passing away from the world.

But in a few moments Van Esling spoke again.

"Not yet!" he said, "not yet—the cold hand of death has relaxed its grip upon my heart, but before it tightens again I want to tell you where the child is."

"Ah, Dora's child?"

"Yes—yes—that child is another heir to the Dukedom of Kingston."

"Assuredly—and I will take good care of it. Tell me, Van Esling, where I can find it. Add that one more to the obligations I owe you."

"In a boat!"

"Yes—a boat?"

"On the river—a covered boat—one of those boats with a half deck—on the Surrey side, somewhere between the Old Savoy stairs and Westminster. All alone—all alone!"

Van Esling, now, with a deep sigh lapsed into insensibility

The Duke thought he was dead.

"Gone at last!" he said, "gone at last —but surely the information he has given me is enough. In a boat, with a half deck, moored on the Surrey side of the Thames, between the Old Savoy stairs and Westminster. That will do—that's well! Farewell, Captain Van Esling! you have been an useful villain to me in your time, and I would fain have retained you yet further in my service, but since you are gone, why so be it."

The Duke left the room, and as he passed out of the Royal Mews he said briefly—

"I fear that Captain Van Esling is dead —but I will spare no pains to find his murderer!"

CHAPTER XVII.

DORA ESCAPES DEATH IN THE RIVER— STARLIGHT SAVES A LIFE—THE WRECK OF THE BOAT—OLD LONDON BRIDGE.

WE left Dora in the most perilous position she could possibly occupy, and yet hope to escape with life.

At the moment that the wild raging flood of water rolled over, she gave herself up for lost.

It was only in a faint, choking voice, that she could call out—

"Henry! Henry! Farewell—farewell! we shall never meet again, but in Heaven!"

Then that impetuous flood—that waving wall of water swept over her. All was darkness for a few seconds—those seconds seemed to Dora an hour—she thought she had heard some person's voice cry out despairingly, as the flood enveloped her, and then, with a gasping sob of relief she was able to breathe again.

A thousand strange noises were in her ears, but she was on the surface of the flood.

Starlight had risen with his rider, and was gallantly swimming with the stream.

And an awful sight was that stream now, as it swept along with the speed of a torrent, carrying with it Dora and the noble Arabian, as though they had been accidental straws upon its surface.

For a few moments the waters surged and leaped so much over the eyes of Dora that she could see nothing, and it was only the consciousness that she breathed the open air that convinced her she was not again deep down amid the roaring flood.

But the horse swam well, and at length Dora was able to dash aside the waters from her face and eyes, and to see about her.

With a terrible swiftness she was being borne down the centre of the river.

Then she uttered a cry that was half of hope, half of despair, for some short distance in advance of her she saw the boat which undoubtedly contained her child still intact and whirling round and round as it was carried down the torrent.

"My Mina! my child! my life! oh, Heaven help me now!" she cried.

The Arabian steed appeared to comprehend that it was not to stem the torrent Dora wished him, but to make more speed along its foaming, roaring surface. The creature fought the waters with its fore feet, and Dora saw that they were nearing the boat.

But there were no little hands now held for her to see, as an assurance that the child still lived.

The boat might be swamped with water, and still be floating on that turbulent current, and the dear one whom she loved so fondly might be but a floating corpse in that half cabin from whence she had seen the mute, heart-breaking appeal for help!"

Dora cried out aloud in the agony of her heart, and her voice mingled with the roar and the rush of the water.

Past those old Savoy steps that she knew so well rushed the boat, and past them swam Starlight. Past the old Temple, and still onwards down the river went boat and prisoner, and Dora began then to feel that it would not be possible for any mortal

SURLINA AND NEONI PAY A VISIT TO THE DUCHESS OF KINGSTON.

horse to continue, by mere muscular force, such a pursuit.

Despair took possession of her.

Then she heard a terrible roaring sound, apparently in advance. A sound almost as terrible as had been the rush of the torrent, as it made its appearance from the upper part of the river.

A huge dark object, too, seemed to be coming nearer and nearer each moment towards her and the boat.

That was a delusion of the senses. It was the boat, and Dora and Starlight, who were each moment nearing that huge dark object, and the object itself was old London Bridge.

No. 9.—DORA.

The roar of waters that Dora heard was the stream tearing, and hissing, and foaming its way through the narrow arches of the old bridge.

Then she felt that all was lost, for the boat would surely be dashed to pieces against the piers of the bridge.

Dora for a moment lost all wish for life. She almost forgot her Henry in that old house in the Savoy in the soul-absorbing agony of seeing her child pass away to death in so terrible a fashion.

Then there was a rush and a crashing sound, and Dora and the horse seemed to be swept through one of the arches of the bridge as if by some invisible and mighty hand.

But the boat was gone.

The feeling that came over Dora can only now be described by the word desolation, and she looked about her for a few seconds like one who felt that she had no longer any concern with the great world about her, and all its jarring interests.

"Lost! Lost!" she cried, "Lost now for ever, and no hope remains!"

The strength of the torrent down the river had been a decreasing one from the first, since it was an artificial force arising from the accumulation of ice and water at the upper part of the stream, and by the time it had reached and struck against the piers and arches of old London Bridge, it was materially checked in its rushing career, and Dora found but little difficulty in getting Starlight now to stem the torrent, and preserve almost a stationery position in the stream.

But alas! the boat was gone—and what further errand now had she amid those troubled waters of the Thames? Common humanity and feeling now for the gallant creature which had carried her in safety through the perils of that night, urged her to seek the shore—her heart was heavy as with a thousand griefs—but still as the first burst of anguish passed away she felt she had something still to live for.

Still was there one who loved her, and who waited anxiously for her return—and that one so helpless, too, and dependent upon her, that it became criminal to despair while that human heart was still all her own. Then she thought of Dottman, and wondered where he could be, amid all the terrors and uncertainties of that time of danger and distress.

There was a long, irregular, roughly-paved jetty, that led down from a narrow lane right into the Thames, for the convenience of the wherries that plied for hire, and it was towards this now that Dora urged Starlight. She knew that she was a considerable distance from the river, and that this jetty and the lane connected with it must take her somewhere into the eastern part of the city, still it would be but a short gallop to the Savoy, and there she now longed to be, to divide her griefs with one whom she knew would, with deepest sympathy, share them with her.

But something was happening at London Bridge which would have sent a thrill of emotion, of delight, to the heart of Dora could she but have seen the occurrence.

Some dozen of stray passengers had collected upon the ancient structure to look down upon the surging, boiling waters of the Thames, as the flood lashed them into fury, and these persons had seen the boat which Dora so vainly pursued, and they had seen that there was some one on horseback battling with the surging waters.

But they had no means of connecting, either by fact or sympathy, the feelings and action of the rider of the horse with the boat, which whirled around in the eddying torrent to some two or three hundred yards ahead.

The boat struck against one of the piers of the bridge, and it seemed as if every timber that she was composed of must have been dislocated from its neighbour by that terrible crash. Then those people, who were gazing downwards, saw the horse and its rider carried whirling onwards beneath the arch of the bridge, but the boat remained wedged for a few minutes against the side of the arch, while the water whirled, foamed, and hissed past it in wild confusion.

A shout arose from the people on the bridge, for more than one, as they looked down upon that doomed boat, saw that there was some living thing on board of it.

Something evidently moved among its shattered timber, and then there was an excited cry among the people, as some one said,—

"It is a child! it is a child!"

"It is lost!" cried another. "The boat will go to pieces in a few moments."

Every eye was intently fixed upon the frail bark, from which shattered pieces of timber each moment floated away, so that it seemed as if piece by piece it would yield to the destructive flood until it disappeared before their eyes.

"I see it now," cried one of the men. "It's a child, holding on to the stanchions of the half deck. Who will save it?"

"Who can save it?" cried another.

Then one of the spectators, who had uttered not a word, but who, on the first assurance that there was some living being on board that frail vessel had ran hastly from the bridge, returned with a coil of rope.

He was a sailor, and what he proposed to do was with him a matter of small moment, as regarded the mere fact of his doing it.

"Hold on, mates!" he said, as he securely tied the coil of rope round his waist. Hold on cheerily, and let me down hand over hand. I shall be on board that craft in a moment."

The people understood him, and at that very time when Dora had reached the little jetty that led up to the narrow lane, and when Starlight was shaking the river froth from his mane, this sailor was swinging down from the parapet of the bridge to the wrecked boat below.

The people above raised a cheer, and he answered with a sailor's "Hilloa!"

They saw him grasp something in his left arm. They heard the cry of a child, and they knew that it was a living thing. A dozen eager hands were on the rope, and just as, with another crash, the boat parted into two pieces, and swung through the arch of the bridge, the sailor was clear of the wreck with the little lost Mina in his arms.

The rope was stout and good, and the ready arms that bore it upwards worked right willingly. A minute more, and over the parapet of London Bridge there were plenty of hands outstretched to help Mina and her gallant rescuer.

"Clear away, mates," cried the sailor, as he leaped on to the carriage way. "It seems to me I've saved the whole crew, for beyond this little one there wasn't another living thing on board the boat, and what's to be done with it now? I hardly know. May-hap some of you about here have got a few more of these sort, and don't mind letting this one make one at the mess-table. What say you, hearties? I'm but a seaman, and shall be off for the North Sea to-morrow. Who'll look after this little thing that's saved from the wreck?"

They were poor and struggling people who were upon that bridge, and the winter had been hard and trying. They shrunk from an additional burden, and the sailor stood alone, with the little Mina in his arms, and no one offered to relieve him of the burden.

"Oh, that's it," he said, "is it? You're a lubberly set of pirates, you are, with your cheers and brayos. Well, never mind! there's some shots in the locker yet, so come along, my little one. We'll go down to Gravesend. There lies the 'Lovely Polly,' four hundred tons burden, and bound for the whale fishery."

"Well," said one of the spectators, "you're a brave fellow, and I wish you every good luck. I think we ought all to help you, and there's a halfpenny."

There was something about the look of the sailor as this liberal offer was made which induced the donor of the halfpenny to get off the bridge as quickly as he could.

"Out of the way, you lubberly shore-going pirates," cried the sailor, "or it will be the worst for some of you. Come on, little 'un, it won't be much if you have share and share with me in the 'Lovely Polly.'"

The sailor departed with the little Mina, and at the moment he left London Bridge with the weak and exhausted child in his arms, Dora passed through Temple Bar on her route to that old home in the Savoy, to which, notwithstanding all that she had hitherto suffered, she never carried so heavy a heart as upon the present occasion.

"Alas!" she said, "even to befriend me seems to be fatal, for Dottman surely has perished in the flood, and now I have but one hope—but one aspiration in this world, and that is that Henry may recover his strength so that we may fly far from the dangers which surround him. I may yet, from these wild adventures on the road, secure sufficient for peace and serenity, far away from those who feel it to be their wicked interests to make war against all I love. The villain Esling is doubtless no more, but my uncle, the false Duke of Kingston, lives, and how can I alone now hope to overcome his malice?"

Dora had reached the corner of the narrow turning leading down to the Savoy, and then, as if at once, as a practical contradiction to her assertion that she had alone to seek and continue her adventures upon the road, rose up in the person of Dottman, who, like a sentinel, stood exactly at the corner of the street.

Dora looked upon him at the moment as she would have looked upon one rescued from present death.

"Ah, Dottman, my friend!" she cried, "how is it that I see you here, when I thought you were engulphed in that terrible torrent?"

"And you, too," said Dottman, in a voice of great emotion, as he placed his hand on Starlight's neck. "And you, too! I hardly dared to hope I should ever look into your eyes again."

"I am saved," said Dora, and that safety I owe to Starlight. But, oh! Dottman, the boat has sunk, and with it has perished that little one I would have given my own life to save."

"It's a battle, captain," said Dottman—"it's a battle! Life is but a battle, you know, and those who are gone are out of the strife."

"I fain would think so—but my heart is sad. You have been home, Dottman?"

"No—I dared not. What news could I carry? Suppose that young officer, Mr. Dacres, had been awake, and had been able to ask me where I left you—could I tell him, to the best of my belief, at the bottom of the Thames?"

"And could you have deserted him had I not arrived?"

"No, not that—not that. But I should have waited a long time. Ay, until all hope had fled, and then I should have gone to him, and I should have said——No, no, captain, we won't talk of those things now, that's all past and gone—so it don't matter what I should have said. But I've seen you shudder twice, and you're soaked with river water, as, indeed, I am myself for the matter of that—but here we are, at the door of the old house. Let me take Starlight. I have already so quietly, as not to be heard, put the hunter into one of the rooms below."

Dottman went rattling on in this disjointed kind of talk, for he was too delighted to see Dora back and in safety to feel very acutely on any other account ; but her heart was too full and heavy to permit her to answer him ; and as she ascended the staircase she asked herself over and over again how far she should be justified, considering the invalided state of her husband, in the suppression of some of the terrible truths she had to impart to him were she to tell him all.

"Time enough—time enough !" she said to herself. "I will not wring his heart. Let him recover, and there is not a thought —a wish—a hope, or an anguish that I will keep from him—but not now—not now !"

Henry Dacres was in a deep sleep, and there was a faint smile upon his face, as his light and gentle breathing betrayed how calm was that repose.

One small light was burning in the apartment, and the fire was low in the grate, but the air was warm and genial, and Dora, heedless of her saturated apparel sat down in silence, and clasped her hands over her face.

What a whirl of thoughts passed through her mind in the silence of that chamber ! Her thoughts flew back to that troublous period, when her father was a hunted fugitive, and when, in the midst of difficulty and of danger he had to fly for his life from that political wrath which ever assumes so deadly a character.

Then came his death—a death, however, which she was spared the contemplation of, since the news of it was only brought to her, and that in but an indistinct and unprecise fashion, except in so far as the actual fact went.

That she never doubted.

Then came her voyage to England from the Netherlands, and her meeting with Henry, and their mutual attachment.

How young she still was to have passed through such a life of troubles, cares, and disasters—and what, even, could she look forward to now, but to many perils as well, contingent upon that life on the road, which she had determined to lead, as from the unceasing hostility and machinations of of the Duke of Kingston, who could never be at peace until he could be assured that the grave had closed over that fair young being, who ought to be Dora the Duchess!

CHAPTER XVIII.

DORA GOES TO DR. LANGFORD'S HOUSE— THE PURSUIT — DORA FINDS A NEW FRIEND—HER RETURN TO THE SAVOY.

THERE was much that might be called hopeful in Dora's present circumstances, and yet there were some events which presented themselves to her mind as fraught with many dangers.

In regard to the life on the road, which she had embraced, she could not but feel that if it brought with it some advantages, it was full of perils. Not that, with her bold, active spirit, she would have feared the pronunciation of that word as applied to herself, but a growing terror begun to take possession of her that either she or Dottman might be dogged to that old house in the Savoy, where, in consequence of his helplessness from his wound, Henry Dacres must, of necessity, be the greatest sufferer.

The exploits she had already performed had supplied her already with a considerable sum of money, and it was not until now, when the excitement was over, that she began calmly to reflect upon the many dangers she had run through.

Then Dora, likewise, begun to accuse herself of a neglect which was, that she had, as yet, allowed herself to remain in ignorance of the fate of the kind physician, who had done so much for Henry, and had so mysteriously disappeared then from the Savoy.

It was mid-day, following that last night of adventures we have recorded, that Dora made up her mind to visit the physician. She thought her safest plan would be to attire herself in her own proper costume, but so plainly and unobtrusively, that she might mingle with the passengers in the streets of London without exciting observation.

Henry spoke to her feebly when he saw that she was about to leave the house.

"Dora, Dora!" he said, "I've had sad and troublous dreams about you—I seem as if I saw you in constant danger, while I was chained down by sickness, and powerless to help you."

"Nay, I beg of you," said Dora, "to think nothing of these disturbed visions of the night—all will be well now. My errand forth is not one of peril, but one of gratitude. It is to visit Dr. Langford, who was so kind to us, and who, I fear, has come to some sad hurt by that very kindness."

"I will not stay you a moment, then, Dora. Go forth with the blessing of your grateful Henry."

Dora crept down the ancient staircase of the old house, and summoned Dottman.

"I never know," she said, "I never seem to know now when I go forth whether I shall ever return again, and so—and so—Dottman, if I should not—"

Emotion choked the utterance of Dora, and Dottman hastily replied—

"I will go with you—I will go with you!"

"No, no! rather remain here, where my chief anxiety resides—and should I not return, you will remember your promise, never to desert him who is in suffering and dependence in this house."

"I never will," said Dottman, "while I have life!"

Dora left the house, and with a quick step, made her way into the Strand, and thence onward to a street near Cavendish Square, where Dr. Langford resided.

She was surprised to see that the house was closely shut, and it was with a sad presentiment of evil that she knocked for admittance.

An old woman answered the door, and in answer to her inquiry for the physician, exclaimed—

"Bless us, and save us all! don't you know he's dead?"

"Dead! alas, alas!"

"Well, you do seem to take on about it, I must say! Perhaps you were one of the poor folks he attended, and was so kind to?"

"He was, indeed, kind to me," said Dora. "What was the manner of his death?"

"Well, you'd better step in and see Mr. Pomeroy, his brother-in-law, who is master of the house now. He wants to see everybody who calls about the doctor, because, you must understand, he came home badly wounded one night, and couldn't speak, but just died off in a few hours, and nothing could save him."

"What is all this?" said a voice, as a man now emerged from one of the side parlours. Is it any one who can give information about the manner of the death of Dr. Langford?"

Dora shrunk back in some alarm, as well she might; for in this man she recognised one of the passengers of the Oxford Mail she had so recently stopped on the road.

It was the small elderly gentleman, who had offered so handsome a reward for the recovery of his jewels.

"Who are you?" he cried, "and where do you live? and when did you see the doctor last? We want to know all the particulars we can, that we may find out how he came by his death."

"I know nothing—I know nothing!" said Dora.

"And what brings you here, young woman?"

"The doctor was good enough to advise one who was sick, and who is very dear to me—but since he is no more, I can but pray for him, and still thank him in my heart."

As Dora thus replied to her questioner, she made a movement from the door, and was no less surprised than pleased to find that she was allowed to leave the house without any more inquiries being put to her. Dora had not, however, gone many paces before she fancied that she was being dogged by a man in a cloak, and made various endeavours to find out whether or not it was nothing more than imagination; for this purpose she turned down several streets—but upon nearing the Savoy, she again perceived the figure emerging from a street, and she had no longer any doubts as to his object."

And now Dora began to wish that she had sent some one else on this errand of inquiry, which seemed destined to turn out so disastrously for her, since she felt how incompetent she was to evade such a pursuit in the streets of London.

"What could she do? Was she to go direct to the Savoy, and so call down destruction upon the head of Henry, or was she to endeavour to take refuge elsewhere, and so baffle her pursuer?

A sudden thought then took possession of Dora, and with a boldness, that one so little skilled in the social arts of life could hardly have been deemed capable of, she determined upon adopting a mode of baffling her pursuer as ingenious as she hoped it would be effectual.

She watched the different doors as she passed them in the street in which she was, until she saw a plate with the name of "Hargrave" upon it.

Quite at a venture, then, Dora knocked at this door, and as she did so, she saw her pursuer slink into another doorway, and keep his eyes intently upon her.

The door was opened by a trim-looking servant girl.

"I wish to see Mr. Hargrave," said Dora—for she had made up her mind to test the kindness of human nature, and to ask this Mr. Hargrave, whoever he might be, to permit her, without question, to remain in his hall for a time, in order to baffle some one who pursued her.

It was an immense relief though to Dora, when the servant replied—

"There is no Mr. Hargrave here—it is Mrs. Hargrave."

"Then I will speak to your mistress!" said Dora.

There was something in Dora's manner

which at once interested the servant girl, and she said—

Certainly, ma'am, if you will walk into this room I will tell my mistress that a lady wishes to speak to her.

It was a great relief to poor Dora, after all the agitation she had experienced in her walk from Doctor Langford's house—to find herself seated in a small, but comfortably furnished room—half sitting room—half library, in which a cheerful fire was burning, and as Dora half unconsciously surveyed the different articles of furniture, while awaiting the appearance of Mrs. Hargrave, she could not refrain from indulging in a feeling of envy, when she contrasted the quiet serenity of that peaceful and well regulated household with her own unsettled life.

"Alas!" cried she. "Never shall I know happiness in this world—for if my Henry be restored to health, where, oh, where is my Mina, my beautiful child, Mina?"

As these thoughts chased each other through her mind, she clasped her hands over eyes and buried her face in the cushion of an easy chair upon which she was seated.

She had not, however, long to indulge in these sad meditations, for she heard the sound of footsteps approaching the apartment in which she was, and she made an effort to arouse herself, so as to be able, so far, to enlist the sympathies of this unknown friend, that she might permit her, Dora, to remain under the shelter of a roof until her pursuer should have given up all hopes of tracking her to the home in the Savoy.

The handle of the room door turned gently, and a lady in deep mourning entered, and Dora felt at once that she might hope for both sympathy and whatever assistance could be given in her present embarrasing circumstances.

"You wished to speak to me," said a soft voice.

"I do, madam! I wish to ask your permission to remain in your hall for some little time," said Dora.

"To remain in my hall?" said the lady. "I do not understand you."

Dora felt that the most ingenuous thing to do would be to tell Mrs. Hargrave as much as she felt she could tell her, without running the risk of endangering her husband and herself by mentioning the old house in the Savoy, so she said at once,

"I wish, madam, to remain secreted in this house for a short time, in order to baffle some one who has been dogging my footsteps. I knew no one in the neighbourhood, and seeing your name on the door, I resolved to throw myself upon the kindness of the inmates of this house, and I feel sure that I shall not ask in vain for a refuge."

Mrs. Hargrave, who had been listening with great interest to the sweet tones of Dora's voice, and perhaps read in her countenance an expression of truthfulness and candour, at once replied—

"Your request is a strange one—but I will ask no questions—I can see you have known trouble, and from the few words I overheard as I entered the room, I fear you have perhaps followed to the grave some favourite child—if so, I can, indeed, feel for and with you, for I too"—

As Mrs. Hargrave was about to finish the sentence, the servant girl knocked at the door of the apartment, and said that a man was in the hall, and wished to speak to her mistress.

As soon as poor Dora heard these words, she clasped her hands together and begged of her protectress—for such she felt she was willing to become—to hide her from him, for she felt a conviction that this man was the same who had followed her so perseveringly.

Mrs. Hargrave whispered—

"Fear not, dear child, I will myself see this man, who shall learn that my house is not to be invaded, and *my friends* to be thus intruded upon."

She then left the apartment.

In the hall was a man enveloped in a dark cloak, which he held tightly around him, while his hat was pulled down over his eyes to conceal his face as much as possible.

"I'm sorry to trouble you marm," said the man in a surly voice, as soon as Mrs. Hargrave made her appearance. "I'm sorry to trouble you, marm—but I wants to know the name of the young woman as came in here just now."

"And what business is that of yours?" said Mrs. Hargrave, in no way taken aback by the man's bold effrontery.

"Well, marm, I've had orders to watch her, as she's suspected of having killed, or of knowing who killed Dr. Langford—so perhaps, marm, it will save you trouble if you lets me speak to the young woman myself."

"I shall do no such thing," said Mrs. Hargrave, "and the sooner you get out of this house the better. If my friend knows anything about the matter of which you speak, let the proper authorities interfere; and once more I command you to leave this house before I summon those who will put you out."

The man turned to leave the house, for he never anticipated for a moment that he should see and speak to Dora, but he was not quite sure of the precise house into which she had entered, and had merely made these inquiries to make sure of his victim.

As soon as he had left the house, Mrs. Hargrave returned to Dora, and having communicated to her all that had taken place, advised her to remain where she was for some hours, and then to take her departure as soon as the dusk of evening would allow her to do so with safety.

In good truth, poor Dora was not unwilling to avail herself of her hostess's kind offer, for grief, anxiety, and want of food and rest had prostrated her both bodily and mentally, and after partaking of some slight refreshment, she was prevailed on to seek repose on a sofa, which was drawn up beside the fire.

And Dora slept.

The sleep into which Dora had fallen promised to be lasting, for it was a deep and dreamless slumber; but as time wore on, her kind hostess thought she should be awakened, as Dora had told her how anxious she was to return to her suffering husband.

Dora was soon equipped to take her way to the old house in the Savoy, hoping that, under cover of the night, to elude the prying eyes of her pursuer, if, indeed, he were not already tired of watching for her reappearance.

Taking leave, then, of kind Mrs. Hargrave, with many expressions of gratitude, Dora found herself once more in the dark and dismal streets of London; with joy and sorrow contending at her heart—joy at the thought that she should soon behold her beloved Henry; and sorrow to think that, in addition to her other griefs, she had that of knowing their kind friend Doctor Langford was indeed no more.

Slowly and sadly did poor Dora pursue her way, jostled occasionally by the busy wayfarers; and ever and anon, casting an anxious look about her to see if she were followed.

All, however, seemed to pass her without taking any notice, and poor Dora reached the house in the Savoy without any interruption.

But Dora saw not in an opposite doorway a man enveloped in a large cloak—the same man who had tracked her from the house of Doctor Langford.

As Dora ascended the staircase of the old house, she was met by Dottman, at sight of whom she exclaimed,—

"What news, Dottman? How is my Henry?"

"Much the same; but I have been anxious about you, and I fear this house will no longer afford us the security it has hitherto done."

"What mean you? oh, what mean you," cried Dora.

"I may be mistaken," said Dottman, "but I fancy, somehow, the house is watched. There is a man now in the doorway of a house opposite, and my mind misgives me. We must find some means of leaving this place, and that soon."

Dora for a few minutes seemed lost in thought, but then, turning to Dottman, she said,—

"I must go to Henry first, and then I will rejoin you and talk over our plans. I have often fancied that there must be some connection by a secret passage from this house to the next. We shall see—we shall see!"

Dora entered that gloomy apartment in which sat poor Henry Dacres, suffering both in body and mind.

Many times had he essayed to rise from his chair, that he might go forth and search for his Dora, whose long absence had filled both him and Dottman with alarm; but as often as he had done so, he had sunk down again exhausted, unable to make any exertion to shield that being whom he loved so tenderly, from harm.

"No, no!" he cried, "I may not follow her. Oh, cruel fate, that I should be thus deprived of the only consolation that remains to me—that of at least sharing her dangers."

As Dora flung herself on her knees beside her husband, she was alarmed at the alteration which those few hours of mental suffering had produced, and passing her hand caressingly over his clustering curls, as she said softly,—

"I am here, my Henry—safe and well! Will you not speak to your Dora?"

"Bless thee—bless thee! my darling," said Henry Dacres, as he pressed that fair young creature to his heart. Bless thee, my Dora; but promise me not to leave me again. The time will come, I feel assured, when my arm will be able to shield you, and together we will seek our child—our Mina."

"We will—we will!" said Dora; and then promising to return in a short time she left the apartment to arrange with Dottman the means of escape.

Our readers will remember that Dottman, on a former occasion, had made an examination of the lower part of the house, so that, if there had been any way of egress from it in that direction, he must have known it then and there; but no such means existed, and he and Dora then ascended to the upper portion of that old dilapidated house, in order to ascertain whether, if they were hunted to this their retreat, they could escape by the next house, as Dora had hoped.

And now it was that Dora felt the imminence of their situation. Perhaps while they were engaged in thus searching for the means of escape, Henry, in that lonely room would be far from them, unable to help himself, and perhaps unable to call for assistance, should any of their foes effect a noiseless entrance into that house. Turning, then, to Dottman, as these thoughts passed through her brain, she said,—

"Alone, Dottman, I would explore these rooms. I have no fears for myself—you stay here! who knows but that you may have to defend the life of my Henry."

"Well, be it so," said Dottman, "I will remain !"

CHAPTER XIX.

DORA DISCOVERS A SECRET PASSAGE— DORA BIDS FAREWELL TO STARLIGHT— THE ESCAPE—THE SKELETON.

As Dora mounted the staircase, a new hope sprung up in her heart, for she felt, she knew not why, that the means of escape were not far from her, and Oh, how she longed for the time—distant though it appeared to be—when her Henry would be able as he had said, to share with her the dangers and perils she was so willing to encounter for those dear to her.

And now Dora had reached the third storey of that old deserted house, and as she entered the first room on her right hand, she said to herself—

"Who knows but that some chance of escape may now present itself to me? I will first of all examine this room, and it will at least have the effect of withdrawing my mind from more painful thoughts.

With this idea, Dora, by the aid of a small oil lamp, which she carried in her hand, began a search in this room.

Alas! That search revealed nothing that could in any way tend to give her a hope of escape.

Each moment seemed fraught with alarm —lest she and her husband, and Dottman, should be tracked ere they could leave that house, and there as yet seemed no apparent means of leaving it but by the hall door.

"No, no!" she said, "there is no hope here !"

With these words she began slowly to descend the stairs again, and in doing so, a sudden draught extinguished the little lamp, and Dora was left in darkness.

The staircase now that she was descending, was so intensely dark that it naturally induced, as she went, a feeling of hesitation in her steps, and she stretched out her hands to the wall as she went, for fear that she should take a false step and

fall. In the intense darkness, too, the idea that she was in a complete void, and had nothing to guide her, came over her fancy.

The clutch she took of the wall, was quite a relief from that idea.

Suddenly the wall shook, and then gave way, and she fell forward; but a very few moments elapsed ere she began to recover from the shock she had sustained.

After a time, Dora determined, if possible to unravel the mystery of the sudden failure of the wall, and it was to that end she now directed her attention. By stretching out her arms in the direction in which the wall had given way, she could feel nothing, and therefore, that some sort of opening existed there was evident.

"Can it be a door?" she said.

This idea, once started in her mind, was sure to grow in strength and consistency, and the natural mode of ascertaining if such were really the case, by feeling carefully for the extent of the opening in the wall soon suggested itself.

By moving her hand backwards and forwards, Dora found that the opening was bounded by a smooth edge.

It was a door.

"Joy! joy!" said Dora. "We are saved —we are saved !"

Dora now retraced her steps as quickly as she could, in order to descend to the apartment where she had left her husband and Dottman, for she felt the necessity of expediting their escape as much as possible, especially as on entering the room, Dottman met her at the doorway, and said,—

"Quick—quick! there is no time to lose. We are watched, I feel certain. Have you discovered any means of reaching the next house ?"

"Yes, yes," said Dora.

"Bless these old houses," said Dottman, "they're always useful, and you never know what ins or outs and odd corners you find in them. It's one of the luckiest chances in the world, captain, that the old tumble-down place next door is empty, for we shall be able to make our way into it, and they will hardly think of following us there, if they see no visible connection between the two."

"I have a thousand fears now," said Dora. "Oh, hasten—hasten! but how shall we save the horses?"

"Why, I fancy the best plan will for me to see you and Mr. Dacres to a place of safety, and then what say you to me mounting one and leading the other by the bridle —a sudden dash out at the front door would, I think, puzzle our enemies to stop."

"It is the only plan, hazardous as it is— and it may succeed,"

Hardly had Dora uttered these words

DOTTMAN'S PLAN OF SAVING HENRY AND DORA.

when a tremendous knocking took place at the outer door of the house.

It was as if evil fortune had at once replied to her expressed hope and opinion by demonstrating how futile they were in the face of enemies upon the very threshold.

The knocking was evidently of that character which shewed that those who thus insisted upon admittance felt that they had the power to enforce it.

And now there was a sort of hurried confusion about the actions of both Dora and Dottman, that betrayed the anxiety they both felt for the issue of the proceedings even of the next few minutes. Dottman ran down stairs, but reappeared in a few

No. 10.—DORA.

moments, with a lantern, the light of which could be darkened by the use of a slide at any moment, and then he minutely inspected that mysterious opening in the wall, which Dora had providentially discovered.

"It's the very thing!" he said, "and in the very last place they will be likely to look for it—but we must not puzzle them too much—"

"What do you mean, Dottman?"

"Why, I mean that we ought to show them some other possible mode of escape, or they will never be satisfied until they have half pulled the house down—I have it—wait here a moment."

"No—no! not another moment—your

strength, Dottman, will suffice to convey Henry through this opening. There is life or death upon each passing instant."

The violent knocking was repeated, and then a loud voice from the street cried out—

"Open—open! Police—open! open!"

"Dottman, as he had uttered the few last words we have recorded, had darted down the stairs, and Dora was in agonies of apprehension until his return. He then had with him a rope, which he had brought from the lower part of the house, and dashing open a dim looking window upon the staircase, he fastened this rope to the topmost balustrade of the stairs, and flung the other end of it out of the window.

"There!" he said, " that will do—Heaven only knows where it goes to—but when they see it, it will lead them astray, and keep them amused for hours."

"Quick—oh, quick! Now for Henry!" said Dora.

"Instantly!"

At this moment, with a loud crash the street door was burst open, for the officers, from the first moment of their knocking had been working at it, never expecting to be quietly admitted from within.

"We are lost!" said Dora.

There was despair in her tones—but Dottman was not at all inclined to give in so easily. He rushed several steps down the staircase, and fired a pistol at random into the hall, while he cried out at the same time in a loud voice—

"Reserve your fire, my men, until they are coming up the stairs, and then shoot low!"

"A sort of panic took possession of the officers at these words, for they had no idea of attacking a well-defended garrison, when they thought they had only to make their way into an old house in the Savoy, and seize, perhaps, one or two persons.

The pause they made was all sufficient for Dottman's purpose. He only wanted a few moments to enable him to carry the wounded young officer through the opening in the wall.

Before the officers could at all recover from their panic, or make up their minds what to do, this was accomplished, and the mysterious panel was restored to its ordinary condition.

With what an immense feeling of relief Dora now drew breath within the precincts of the next house to that where she had encountered so many dangers.

But all was darkness, for Dottman feared even to remove the slide from off the face of his lantern, lest some wandering ray of light should make it's way through a chink, and so proclaim to their foes where they were.

Henry was full of fears for Dora, and could scarcely be kept from lamenting, in a voice too loud to be prudent, his inability to wield a sword in her defence.

"All will be well!" said Dottman. "But I don't mean to say that these old houses in the Savoy will suit us long—and my opinion is, the best thing we can do, so soon as the officers have left the coast clear, will be to make our way into the country, to that old cottage of Captain Hawk's; for if he be not absolutely killed, he must be too much hurt to interfere with our occupation of it."

"Anywhere—anywhere for safety!" said Dora. "Not for myself, but for Henry. There are those who seek his life as they seek mine, and they would sacrifice him on account of his affection and sympathy with me."

"Let us listen!" said Dottman.

"There was no difficulty in ascertaining the fact that the officers had made their way into the house, for they could hear them calling to each other, and rummaging and ransacking the rooms.

"Alas, alas!" said Henry Dacres, "when will all these terrors end? and when shall I get sufficiently strong to hold them at arm's length?"

They were all inexpressibly alarmed now to hear the officers beating on the panels with their hangers, in order to discover if there were any secret recesses in which the fugitives might be concealed.

Dottman then very cautiously removed the slide a short distance from the face of his lantern, and as Henry could just walk with the assistance of Dora, they made their way along a narrow passage, at the end of which a short flight of stairs led to some of the upper rooms of the house they were now in.

As they increased the distance from the actual wall separating the two houses, the sounds that each moment had spread such alarm in Dora's breast, decreased in intensity, and when a small apartment was reached, on a window-sill of which Henry could be seated, she almost began to think that the principal danger had passed away.

It was evident that the officers had not made any discovery in regard to the communication between the two houses, and Dora got as close to the window as it was prudent to do, in order that she might watch if they left the house.

In a few moments, to her intense grief, she saw the two horses brought out, and that they were led away by a man, who walked between them, holding a bridle in each hand.

"Farewell," said Dora, "my gallant steed. Farewell! I owe thee thanks, for saving me from many dangers. Alas! shall we ever meet again?"

A feeling of great depression came over Dora, and she would have shed tears, but she knew it would wring the heart of her Henry to see them.

All was still now in the house, and yet the little party, in whose fate we feel interested, felt convinced that the officers had not left it, and what to do appeared to be a proposition to which no rational answer could be returned.

"What will become of us?" said Dora, in a low tone to Dottman. "We are without food or firing, and if those men choose to keep watch and ward for but a few hours in the next house, we are lost."

"Well," said Dottman, "all are not lost who are in danger. They are tolerably quiet now, and evidently have no sort of idea of where we are; now I propose that we take a hunt through this house and see what sort of accommodation it may afford us. Who knows but we may find it not quite so desolate as it looks? It is not up "To let," and seems to have been deserted from some other cause than a change of tenants. The lantern will hold out for some hours longer, and if you stay with Mr. Dacres, I will soon bring a report of what the place is like."

"Do so—do so," said Dora. "It may be that I shall never have the power to thank you as I ought, but if in this world's great changes I should ever occupy a position different from the present, my heart would need to forget its best affections before I cease to remember how much I owe you."

Dottman made no reply, but the expressive manner in which he waved his arm sufficiently testified the effect these words of Dora had upon him.

He took his lantern and commenced the search in that house, which seemed a more ancient one still than the next door, and in a more ruinous condition.

From the recollection he had of the flight of stairs they had ascended after passing through the secret panel, Dottman considered that they were upon the uppermost floor of the house, and such he found to be the case, for, after opening two doors in the irregular and fantastically shaped building, he came upon the head of a tolerably wide staircase, which looked, in its lower depths, inexpressibly gloomy.

Descending this staircase, he entered a long wide corridor below, lighted on one side by tall windows, and the other was flanked by numerous doors.

The darkness was so intense that, at first, the rays of the lantern only served to dissipate the obscurity immediately around it, while the rest of the corridor beyond looked like the entrance to some yawning vault filled with gloom and shadows.

At the end of the corridor he came to a narrow staircase, and going cautiously down, and through another passage, he found himself in a small vestibule with two doors on either hand.

These doors were studded with large nails, and secured by bars of iron. Turning to the nearest, he quietly lifted the latch, and pushed it open.

The wind, as he did so, had nearly extinguished the lantern he carried, and in suddenly shading it with his hand, he let slip the ponderous door, which shut with a dull clang, and echoed far away through the lonely house.

Pausing to listen if he had drawn the attention of any one who might still be keeping guard in the next house, Dottman ascended again the little narrow staircase, but finding all was silent, he opened the door again, carefully shading the lantern with his coat.

Then gently closing the door behind him, he found himself in an apartment of medium pretensions as to size, and it was fitted up in an old-fashioned style of comfort—even luxury.

Hangings of rich faded silk shaded the windows—easy chairs and ottomans, covered with the same material, were the objects that met the eyes of Dottman as soon as he could take sufficient observation of what was contained in that apartment; and as his eyes grew accustomed to the gloom, a feeling of hopefulness took possession of him, as he said, half aloud—

"At least she will be at peace here until we can find means to reach the cottage."

Dottman was about to retrace his steps, when his eyes fell upon another door, which he had not observed before, but which evidently led into another apartment.

Notwithstanding his anxiety to place Dora and her husband in a more comfortable room than that in which he had left them, Dottman could not repress a feeling of intense curiosity to look into this apartment, even if it delayed him for a few moments from carrying the pleasing intelligence to Dora of his successful search.

He advanced, then, with less hesitation, to this second room than he had felt during his progress through that gloomy corridor and passage, and pushing open the door, he found that the apartment was furnished as a bedroom.

There were several chairs and a table drawn near to the bedside, on which lay a miscellaneous collection of objects—writing materials, books, &c.

There was a feeling in Dottman's mind that this room was occupied.

He turned his eyes towards the bed, and there was to be seen the outline of a human figure.

Terror—at what he knew not—took possession of Dottman; but he determined at once to put an end to all conjecture by making a noise so as to awake the sleeper; for this purpose he took a book from the table, and dropped it on the floor.

But there was no movement in the bed.

Dottman now approached the bed, and turned down a portion of the faded silk coverlet, and then—oh, horror of horrors! what a sight met his startled gaze!

There, lying surrounded by all that might have made life happy, lay the remains of a human form.

The object upon that bed was *a skeleton*.

For a few moments the cold perspiration stood upon the face of Dottman. He clasped his hands over his eyes to shut out the loathsome sight, and then feeling for the lantern, which, for a moment, he had placed upon the floor, he hurried from the apartment.

CHAPTER XX.

THE LITTLE MINA'S NEW FRIEND—THE HUT BY THE RIVER — THE THIEVE'S CONFERENCE—TURNBULL'S TRIUMPH—MINA'S ESCAPE.

IN a few minutes, Jack Stacy (for such was the name of the kind-hearted sailor, who had not only rescued the little Mina from a watery grave, but who had, at the same time, taken the determination to share with her his own limited means of subsistence), found himself almost alone with the helpless child, who now clung to him—that rough man—for protection from, she knew not what.

The child was still so far prostrated as to be unable to give utterance to words, but her head rested confidingly upon Jack's shoulder; and he carried her tenderly and carefully down to the river's side, where he was to take boat, in order to drop down to Gravesend, to embark in the "Lovely Polly."

Having made the little Mina as comfortable a bed as circumstances would permit, Jack sat down beside her, and seemed, for the first time, to realize the fact that he had now another to think of and to provide for.

"Well," said he, speaking to himself, "this a queer gift from Dame Fortune! Who would have thought now, that I should be sailing down the river with a little child as never never had mother or father! Poor little creature! she's very pretty!"

Here Jack touched, almost reverentially, one of the soft golden ringlets of the fair child.

"I wonder, now," continued Jack, "how she got into that there boat? She don't look like a child as would be left to take care of itself! I wonder what her name is?"

At this moment the child moved uneasily, and stretched out her hands, murmuring "mamma!"

"Ah! I thought as much—she's lost! and, I dare say, the poor mother is almost beside herself for grief. Well, well, I'll do what I can—that's not much. At all events, I won't leave her as those shore-going lubbers on the bridge would have done. She's not exactly the right sort of craft to go sailing over the Atlantic with an old seaman—but I'll see what can be done."

Hush! hush! In that boat—by that rough seaman's side, the fair child slumbers peacefully. God's blessing on its gentle slumbers! Will she dream of fairy kisses? Will busy, gorgeous fancy paint to that pure spirit a garden of the imagination full of sweets?

Hush! Dora, your little one sleeps—those fringed portals have closed upon the world and all its sorrows.

Those laughing orbs, that seem to have stolen their azure beauty from Heaven itself, are hidden.

The child still slept as the boat grated against the old wooden steps, which served for a landing place, and Jack gently lifted her in his arms, and carried her on shore.

Jack had not been idle as he was sitting by the side of that sleeping child; he had come, at last, to the conclusion that it would be much better to try and place the child with some poor family, who would take charge of her until his return.

For this purpose, Jack Stacy now made his way towards a group of huts which lay not far from the river's side.

Jack knocked with his knuckles upon the door of the first of these dim-looking tenements, and after waiting some moments, it was half opened by a man, whose appearance was anything but prepossessing, even in Jack's estimation.

"Who's there?" demanded a surly voice from within.

Jack contrived to get a look into the interior of the room which contained several persons, and which probably to any one, except a sailor, who was accustomed to the crowded and scanty accommodation of the forecastle of a ship, would have appeared a most wretched and inconvenient hovel.

Indeed, Jack himself recoiled a step, and would probably have gone further on to seek for that assistance which he required for the child, had not the sudden appearance of a woman near the door induced him to pause.

"Hark ye, mates," said Jack, "and you, my good woman! Here's a little bit of a female craft of a child, adrift—I picked her out of the river, but, you see, I sail in the 'Lovely Polly' with the tide, and, you see, it's coming down now like a mill-stream. Will you take care of the little 'un? and on the word of a sailor, when I come back, I'll come here, and pay off all scores—and here's a couple of guineas to begin with—they're all that's left of my shore-going money."

The woman was something of a virago in form and feature, and had opened her mouth to commence a torrent of abuse at Jack for presuming to think, for a moment, that there was the least particle of humanity to be found in that establishment—but the two guineas jinked one against another in Jack's hand, and the brute spirit of the hag bowed down before the only thing she had ever worshipped—gold.

"Bless the darling," she said, "we'll take care of her. Give me the little money—I mean the little dear. Two guineas did you say? Bless them, they shall want for nothing—that is, I mean the child shall want for nothing."

"All's right," said Jack. "That's off a fellow's mind, and so good bye, little 'un. Bless your heart, I'll come back and make a sailor of you yet."

"Ah!" said the hag, as she looked after Jack, "it will be off my mind, too, soon, for after I've looked at her clothes to see what they'll fetch, I'll fling her into the river again."

"Hilloa, Meg, what's the row?" cried one of the men, who was drinking in the hut. "What are you growling and grumbling there at the door for, and letting the fresh air in to spoil the nice smell of the tobacco smoke and the purl? I never could abide fresh air in my life."

"And what's that to you?" screamed the woman, an octave higher. "What's that to you, I say, Jack the cracksman, I should like to know. You'd best be jogging whilst you can, or you'll dance upon nothing some morning, and nobody to pay the piper."

The hag slipped back into the hut with the child, and banged the door shut with a vehemence that threatened to dislocate it from its hinges.

"There you go, Meg," said another of the men. "There you go, making a row, and waking up Turnbull. Didn't the doctor say he was to be kept quiet?"

"Yes, a pretty quiet," added the woman, "when you've been roaring and drinking here for the last six hours."

At the further extremity of this wretched room there hung, cutting off a corner into a triangular apartment by itself, the wretched old coverlet of a bed. It was one of those coverlets common in the country, composed of square pieces of chintz of various patterns sewn together, without regard to colour or symmetry.

This partial screen was flung over a rope fastened to two rough hooks on either wall, and now from behind it came hideous groans and moans as from one in great anguish, and the coverlet was shaken violently.

"Wretches! fiends!" moaned a voice. "You won't let me sleep in peace."

"No, that they won't," screamed Meg. "They won't let you die in peace, Mr. Turnbull."

"Die!" yelled Turnbull. "Who said die? I did not say die. Who dares to say die? I won't die in peace. I don't want to die in peace. It was sleep, I said. Wretches, don't talk of dying."

With a wasted hand he tore aside the patched coverlet, and haggard, ghastly, and with his eyes bloodshot, he glared into the room."

"Take it easy, Mr. Turnbull," said one of the men. "Nobody wants you to die, and the doctor says if so be as you don't go off the hooks in a few days more, the bullet won't be much of a detriment."

"What is it—what is it? what made the noise? what child is that?"

The little Mina, terrified at the company in which she found herself, began to cry, and the hag, with a view to pacify Turnbull, held her up towards the light, as she said—

"Don't you trouble yourself about her, Mr. Turnbull. The river keeps all secrets, and as soon as the ship that lies on and off goes down the stream—"

The woman had got thus far in her speech, when she was both interrupted and terrified by such an unearthly laugh from Turnbull, that she started back towards the door, and the thieves, who were carousing in the hut, sprung to their feet.

Turnbull yelled, and shrieked, and laughed like one possessed, and then, clapping his hands together, and straining half out of the wretched couch on which he lay, he found words to speak.

"Close the door—close the door! bolts—bars, and locks! a treasure—a treasure—we've found a treasure. A thousand pounds—two thousand pounds—three thousand pounds. Ha, ha, ha! ten thousand pounds—that child is worth it all."

He fell back exhausted on the wretched pallet, and it seemed at that moment an even struggle between life and death as a result of the wild frenzy that had taken possession of him.

The thieves who were in that haunt of crime carousing, and the hag, who was its mistress, all spoke at once.

"What child? who is she? what treasure? who will pay the money? Speak, Turnbull, speak again!"

Turnbull gasped for breath.

"Speak—speak!" cried all the thieves again.

"Oh, you beauty," screamed Meg. "Tell us all about it."

"Water—water," gasped Turnbull.

Meg held up her hands with surprise.

"It's the fust time he ever asked for such a thing in his life."

But the thieves saw that Turnbull was choking for water, and one supported him to a sitting posture, while another held a pitcher to his parched lips, a third had taken the candle from the neck of a bottle which had served for a candlestick, and held it so as to throw a strong light upon his face, while the hot grease fell drop by drop upon the wretched bedclothes.

The hag held poor little Mina, who was terrified into silence, by the arm, and they all waited for Turnbull to speak again.

"More! more!" he gasped.

The pitcher was again held to his lips, and he took a deep draught. Then glaring about him, he fixed his eyes upon Mina, and exultation shone in those fevered orbs as he said—

"It is she—her child—he will give ten thousand pounds."

"Who will? cried the thieves in chorus, and the hovel shook with the sound.

"The Duke!"

"What Duke?"

They crowded more closely about Turnbull, and the hot grease from the candle fell upon his hands.

He shook his head. "No, no, when I am well—when I get well—I—that is, you—no, no, not till I get well—not till I get well!"

A yell of disappointment and rage came from the men, but the hag cried out "hush!" and made some hideous faces at them, which seemed to imply that she would get the requisite information from the refractory Turnbull. The thieves paused for a moment, and drew back as if to give her a chance of achieving such a result, and she put on what she considered, no doubt, was a fascinating smile, but which was really such a malignant contortion of countenance, that the weakest observer would not be deceived by it for a moment.

"Dear Mr. Turnbull," she said, "I am quite sure you will tell me—we've always been such capital friends, and here am I, ready to nurse you—to tend you like a baby —of course you'll tell your own Meg, and if there's any money to be got, of course it shall all be brought in a nice little bag, and placed under your pillow till you get well again. Won't it, lads?"

"To be sure," said the thieves in chorus.

A malignant sneer came over Turnbull's face, and lifting up one of his haggard hands, while the fingers trembled in the light, he said,—

"I'll see you all— Well, never mind! but I wouldn't tell you if every drop of blood in my body was to be turned to melted lead, along with the hot bullet that that child's mother lodged in my breast. She's mine—mine—mine only. You've no right to her. I tell you she is mine; but I will pay you well. I will pay you well, for all that; but she is mine. A treasure—a treasure—ten thousand pounds, at least."

"Then if you won't tell us," cried one of the thieves, "you shall never have it."

"Never!" cried the others. "It's share and share alike here. You shall tell us."

"Who will make me?" screamed Turnbull. "Who will make me?"

One, more violent than the others, rushed at him, and grasped him by the throat. There was a fearful scuffle in the hovel, and the one light was dashed out. A chance blow levelled Meg to the floor, and the door swinging open, the little Mina rushed out into the darkness of the night, which had now come on in settled gloom, and made her way with all the speed that fear could impart to her movements, along the first path that presented itself.

The child did not scream nor cry out—it was too terrified for that, but reaching a low stile, which led into some meadows, the little creature crept beneath the two lowest bars, and crouched down into an inconceivably small space in the rectangular corner of a haystack, one half of which had been cut and carted away, so that Mina's position was as snug as a bird's nest, amid the sweet-smelling provender, which lay deep upon the ground and encompassed her by its two walls.

CHAPTER XXI.

DOTTMAN'S DISGUISE—THE OFFICERS IN THE SAVOY—THE MYSTERIOUS STRANGER—THE DEPARTURE.

WE left Dottman horrified at the spectacle which was presented to him in that lonely house adjoining the mansion in the Savoy where Dora and her husband had for a time found security from the persecutions of fate.

There was no living danger that Dottman would have refused to encounter, but he had a peculiar horror of anything connected with the dead, and the paleness of his countenance when he rejoined Dora and Henry Dacres sufficiently testified to the fact that he had seen or heard something which had awakened all his fears.

"Ah!" said Dora," I can well perceive you have heard or seen something which betokens danger to us."

"Not at all—not at all," replied Dottman; "but I only wish we were in peace and safely out of this house, for I would not pass a night in it for any reward that could be mentioned."

"What is it?" said Henry Dacres feebly. "Alas! it is not superstitious fears that we need dread. The beings of another world would be kinder to us than we have found those of this."

"Ask me no questions, I beg of you," said Dottman. "You know I would be the first to communicate to you any intelligence which concerned our common safety, but indeed this does not, and I can only beg of you to remain where you are, while I look further through the house, to see if I can find some disguise, by the aid of which I can sally forth into the street and gather intelligence of the movements of our enemies."

Dora could see that Dottman's hands trembled as he held the lantern, and she was so convinced that his nerves were much shaken by some object he had seen in the house, that she proposed to him to stay with Henry Dacres while she went on a further exploring expedition.

"Give me the lantern," she said, "and I will go through the rooms of this house, and probably I may find something that may suit your purpose."

"Now, shame on me if I let you do that," said Dottman.

"Nay, I am not easily terrified!"

"Which half means that I am! No, Captain Arod, you stay with Mr. Dacres, and I will continue my search of the house."

"What is that?" said Henry Dacres, faintly. "What name is that you use?"

"Oh! nothing—nothing!" said Dora, "it is not worth a thought."

"But why, Dora, does he call you Captain Arod?"

"Do you not see, Henry?" It is a transposition of my own name of Dora, and Dottman names me so for safety's sake, in case some lurking foe should ever overhear him speak to me."

"Yes—yes! I comprehend that," said Henry, "but my wound has made me weak, both of head and heart, and I feel as if much was going on of which I know nothing."

Dora was saved from the pain of a reply to these words, for she had as great a dread of informing Henry of all she had gone through as of the deception of keeping it from him, by the re-entrance of Dottman with a heap of clothing over his arm.

"Behold!" he said, "I have found what will disguise me most effectually—here is a lot of women's gear. which I can easily slip on over my clothes, and by stooping I think I can play the part very well."

It was found, upon examination, that these clothes which Dottman had found were plain and old, and of a fashion which might be worn by an elderly woman of the lower stratum of society.

With the assistance of Dora Dottman got on a much worn, faded, and ancient chequered pattern gown, a miserable shawl, helped to disguise him—and when he put on his head an old poke bonnet—such as even in those days of poke bonnets, had been out of fashion several years, it would have been difficult indeed in the twilight to have distinguished him from some elderly dame who might go out charing or nursing.

"That will do well," said Dottman, "I fancy."

"I think you are perfectly disguised," remarked Dora.

"Yes, Captain, I fancy I am—and down stairs, in one of the front rooms, there's an umbrella, that I think must have come out of Noah's Ark, it's so ancient and so heavy. I will take that with me, and he will be a bold man who will venture to think I am any other than what I picture to be."

"And what will you do, Dottman?"

"I want, you see, to make a reconnoitre, to find out whose watching the house next door, for I fancy they won't give up their pursuit quite so readily—and then I will see what can be done for the best."

"Heaven speed you, and guard you!" said Dora.

"Amen! to that prayer," ejaculated Henry.

"Be careful, Captain!" said Dottman, as he left the room, "and do not open the outer door to any one but me. When I come back I will knock three distinct raps, but not loudly."

"I will, indeed, be most careful," said Dora, "both for my own sake and for the sake of one dearer to me than myself."

Dottman crept down stairs and secured the ancient umbrella he had spoken of, and then crouching down so as to disguise at least twelve inches of his height, he went out into the Savoy, slamming the door behind him.

A man stood on the steps of the adjoining house, from which Dora and Henry had been compelled to make so rapid an escape; and when he saw the supposed old woman come out of the next door, he stepped down on the pavement as he said—

"Who lives in that house, my ancient dame?"

"What do you mean, imperance?" said Dottman. "Drat the man!"

"Well, don't be in a passion, old 'un. I only asked who lived in the house."

"Well, it's Mrs. Smith, if you must know—but it's a hard case that a poor old body like me can't go about her business without having improper proposals made to her in the street. Go along, do!"

The officer laughed, and called out to a companion, who was in hiding on the opposite side of the road, close to some railings,

"Here, Bonus!" he said, "here's an old lady waiting for you."

"Take that!" said Dottman, as he dealt the man a swinging blow with the umbrella, that was almost enough to take him off his feet. "Take that, jackanapes, and don't insult a lone female again. Where's my pattens? You've stole my pattens, you wretch! I'm sure I had my pattens in my hand—and where's my umbrella? Oh, it's here, to be sure. Bless us and save us, I shall miss my head next."

"Go along, you old witch!" said the officer, "and don't plague us with your nonsense—we're on business here."

"There's only two of them," said Dottman to himself, as he walked slowly off. "The others have left, I fancy, and these two are kept on the watch."

Dottman turned the corner which led up into the Strand, and thinking himself out of sight of the officers, he imprudently raised himself to his full height, and took six strides forward in anything but an old woman-like fashion.

From out a doorway then a tall figure emerged, completely enveloped in a gray cloak, and with a mask upon his face.

This figure grasped Dottman by the arm, and he, fancying it was another of the officers, immediately sunk low down, so as to assume again the character of an old woman.

The figure spoke in deep low tones, and with a curious articulation, as if it carried something in its mouth, for the purpose of disguising the voice.

"I know you," said the figure, "you are a friend to Dora Dacres."

"Ah!" cried Dottman, springing up to his full height again, and feeling for a pistol.

"Be not alarmed!" added the mysterious figure. "I too live for her, and for those whom she lives—I will aid you. What is it you purposed to do?"

"In the name of Heaven, tell me who you are!" said Dottman.

"No! but be content that I am a friend, who will fail you not!"

"But—but"—

"Cease these scruples. Has she not told you of a man in gray, who has already befriended her—but whom she knows not?"

"She has!"

"I am that man—trust me! What is it that you are about to do? For the enemies of Dora are in the old Savoy."

"You make me tremble," said Dottman, "but if you really are a friend to Dora, and know me, will you mention my name?"

"I will! It is Dottman. Sometime since a trooper and servant to the late Duke of Kingston."

"You do know me," said Dottman, "and I will trust you!"

"You do well. Credulity is a folly; but mistrust beyond a certain point becomes a crime. Tell me now how can I help you?"

"There are two officers in the Savoy, and they will impede Dora and her husband in leaving the house they inhabit there. I wish to take them to a place of greater safety on the Western road, and I thought by going into the Strand I might get a coach."

"That is well—but the officers?"

"I would have attacked them both—singly if possible, but together if necessary. I think I have a good sword which would enable me to give an account of them, and it would be a rare chance if they could use a weapon so well as I can."

"That is well; but two swords are surer than one. Secrecy and rapidity of action are elements in this transaction. Follow me! it cannot be, but we shall get a coach shortly."

There was an irresistible charm of manner about this stranger, mysterious and unknown to Dottman, as he was, which induced implicit confidence, and they now reached the Strand together, without the least apprehension of treachery being in Dottman's mind.

The mysterious stranger halted in the Strand, about twenty paces from the commencement of the street that leads down into the Savoy, and at the entrance to a narrow court.

In a few minutes a hackney coach came lumbering along from the city, and the driver seeing two figures upon the pavement, slackened his pace in the expectation of a fare.

"Stop!" said the mysterious man.

The coach drew up.

"Wait," he said.

The coachman seemed to understand that he was under the orders of some one accustomed to command, and then the mysterious man took Dottman by the arm again, and led him down towards the Savoy.

CAPTAIN VAN EELING LEAVING HIS ROOM TO SEEK MEDICAL AID.

"Re-enter the house," he said, "in your present disguise, and then, without fear, bring forth those who would escape. I will be at hand. Delay not for another hour. A further search may take place for the fugitives, which may be fatal.

Dottman was rather bewildered by all this, but he felt, at the same time, a sort of instinctive desire to obey the orders of this mysterious personage, and he made his way back again to the house at once.

"Here's old Mother Shipton," said the officer again to his companion. "Where have you been, old 'un, eh?"

Dottman affected to disdain an answer, and thumping the brass ferule of the um-

brella upon the pavement with energy, he made his way to the house where Dora and Henry Dacres were so anxiously expecting him.

He knocked three times, and then one of the officers said to the other,—

"I tell you what it is, Bonus, I don't half like the look of that old woman; and now I remember, somebody said the next house had been empty ever so long."

"I don't believe she's an old woman at all," said the other. "What an odd way of knocking, too. Keep your hanger in readiness, and mind we obey orders to capture or cut down whoever tries to leave this house."

No. 11.—DORA.

"Or the next one, I suppose, now. Perhaps we ought to have taken the old woman. A plague upon the old witch! she nearly broke my ribs with that old umbrella of hers."

Dora had heard the knocks, and she made her way rapidly to the street-door, which she opened for Dottman. The moment, then, he got into the passage and closed the door again, he spoke to her hastily.

"Quick—quick!" he said. "Lead Mr. Dacres down if you can. We must leave the Savoy at once, while there are but two officers without to interrupt us."

"Two?" said Dora. "How can we contend with two, when your arm or mine is requisite for the support of Henry?"

"There is a friend without. A man in grey, with a mask."

"What can this mean?" said Dora. "That mysterious man again! and yet I feel that he is friendly towards me, and will trust him, although my heart seems to whispers to me that he is a being not of this world."

"Good gracious! don't say that," said Dottman. "He has been talking to me for this five minutes, and has had hold of my arm twice, and knows my name, and all about me."

"It is very strange."

"Yes, and very alarming, too, and if he's a ghost, that may be the ghost of a hackney coach in the Strand that he stopped all of a sudden so short."

"A hackney coach? is there one in waiting?"

"Yes, captain. But never mind! ghost or no ghost, you and Mr. Henry must escape from the Savoy. I said I would use my own sword against the men who are waiting to capture you, and the grey apparition then said that his should not be wanting to help; but that in an hour it would be too late, and the hour is speeding away as fast as it can."

"I will bring Henry down directly. I will trust that mysterious man in grey with my life."

Dottman remained in the passage, and with his ear tolerably close to the street door, listened. He felt confident now that the two officers had come on to the doorstep of that house, for he could hear them conversing in low tones, and then one of them, as if to try the experiment, knocked three times with the handle of his hanger, against the door.

"Oh, no," said Dottman, "that won't do at all."

"What is that?" said Dora from the staircase, as she came down, assisting Henry."

"Our friends the officers," replied Dott-man, in a low tone. "Let the lantern down, Captain—let the lantern down."

"Yes, I will leave it on the stair."

"Do not come with Mr. Henry beyond the step, and all will be well."

It was an anxious moment for Dora, and Dottman, too, felt a degree of excitement with which he was not often visited, as he flung the door open, and with the sword in his hand, advanced on to the step.

"Surrender!" cried one of the officers.

"Cut him down," said the other. "A clip on the head with your hanger's the best thing."

"Not so fast," said Dottman, as he warded off an intended blow, and kept his antagonists for a moment at bay. "Not so fast, my fine fellows."

Both the officers attempted to close with him with those short cutlass-like swords which went by the name of hangers at that period, and with which the police, upon extraordinary occasions, were always armed.

Then, like a shadow, there darted from the opposite side of the way, where the iron railings enclosed the old chapel of the Savoy, a dim and dusky figure.

"Turn, villain!" said a voice, and one of the officers was struck sharply across the back with the flat of a sword. "Turn, villain, and fight or fly for your life."

"Oh, there's another of you, is there?" said the officer, as he attacked the newcomer with fury; but that battle was brief, for in a few seconds he fell with a cry and rolled into the road.

"It is done!" said the grey man, as he sheathed his sword.

Dottman had beaten down the guard of the other officer, and half stunned him by a blow on the head; and then, not wishing to take life unnecessarily, he flung him into the passage of the house and closed the door upon him.

When Dora and Dottman then looked around for the mysterious man in grey, who had been of such assistance to them, he was nowhere to be seen; and amid the silence of the night, they seemed to be the sole occupants of the Savoy, with the exception of the wounded officer, who lay half in the roadway and half on the pavement.

"Forward—forward," cried Dottman. "I fancy there's no time to lose.

The excitement of this little skirmish at the door seemed to have imparted, for the moment, fresh strength to Henry Dacres; and leaning upon Dora's arm, he walked with much greater ease than she had dared to expect.

"Oh, I shall be strong again! I shall be strong again!" he said, "and then my sword, likewise, Dora, will be wielded in your behalf."

Dottman led the way, and in less than five minutes they were in the Strand, where the coach, to his great relief, was still in waiting at the corner of the court.

Just as they reached its door, there came down, from the direction of the King's Mews, a throng of persons, some of whom were carrying links, and at their head marched a man with a sword.

"The Duke—the Duke!" said Dora. "It is the Duke of Kingston! they will not now leave a nook or crevice unsearched in the old Savoy."

"Quick! into the coach at once!" said Dottman.

"And you?" said Dora, as he closed the door upon her and Henry.

"I will ride with the coachman. Now, coachman, take the Western Road, and you will find this as good a night's work as you ever had.

The coach rumbled off, and for a moment the light of the links carried by the false Duke of Kington's party glared in at its windows.

CHAPTER XXII.

VAN ESLING RETURNS TO CONSCIOUSNESS —THE MIDNIGHT ROBBERS—VAN ESLING VISITS - SURLINA—AN UNEXPECTED INTERRUPTION.

THERE are injuries which, though appearing mortal to the human sufferer, are, in their actual results, by no means commensurate with their first appearances.

It is by no means the most deadly seeming shot on the battle-field which carries death on its swift wings.

The rapier may seem to pierce the heart, and yet, passing harmlessly many of the great organs of existence untouched, and the fainting sufferer, upon whose brow the dews of death have appeared to collect, may yet live to mingle with his fellow men, and be an actor on the great stage of existence.

So was it with Captain Van Esling, the creature of the wicked and unscrupulous Duke of Kingston.

When the Duke left him in that chamber in the barracks of the King's Mews, he fully believed that he had left behind him but the corpse of the ready tool who had always been ready to obey his orders without questioning their justice.

And even several persons, who visited the chamber after the departure of the Duke, believed that they looked upon the dead body of Van Esling.

But such was not the fact.

The wound was serious, but not mortal.

The conflict of his passions—rage, fear, and despair, combined with a deadly sickness, which the hurt had brought upon him, had produced a swoon, which so resembled death itself, that those who were prepared to expect such a catastrophe might well be excused for believing that they saw it before their eyes.

It was deep in the night when the senses of Van Esling returned to him, and then, indeed, after that long lapse of forgetfulness, he might well believe that he had passed through this mortal life, and trod the confines of another world.

The moon was high in the heavens—that moon which had lighted Dora upon her first enterprise on the road; and as it gleamed into his chamber, Van Esling mistook its unearthly light for the possible atmosphere of those realms of retribution, of which he might well consider himself a likely tenant.

"Mercy! mercy! mercy!" he said, three times, in an imploring voice.

But all was still around him. No mocking fiends came to add to the misery of his condition. No new tortures seemed to be devising for his wounded frame.

On the contrary, a feeling of ease and calmness began to spread over him.

He had received one of those marvellous sword-thrusts, of which there are numerous examples, and which seem as if they must be fatal, but owing to avoiding vital parts, really assume the character of a wound of trivial importance.

It could not be said that he did not feel his hurt, for when he attempted to move, there came a sensation of anguish through its course which elicited deep groans from him.

But yet he had not lain long enough for any serious diminution of his strength to take place, and the wound had bled but slightly.

"Help! help!" he gasped. "Why have they all deserted me?"

His brain was resuming its ordinary functions, and he began to understand where he was. His eyes fell upon familiar objects in the chamber, and he knew that he was still in the barracks of the old King's Mews.

That was a relief.

"Help! help!" he cried again. "Is it because a man is hurt that he is left to die in this fashion? Did I dream that the Duke of Kingston had been here, or was it real? Or, after all, is this whole occurrence but a fevered nightmare of the soul? Ah! No, no! my wound—that is a reality! The mind may breed visions, but a bodily hurt speaks of facts. She did come here—Dora, the peerless and the beautiful—she did come here, and fought with me! Surely my arm was paralysed, and I could not defend myself! Help—help! does no one hear me?"

A fearful thirst began to come over the wounded man. It was a symptom of the fever, which must necessarily attend the reperative efforts of nature.

"Water! water!" he gasped. "I burn for water! Why—oh, why is it they leave me thus? Heartless fiends! Help! help, I say! Water—water!"

He was at the end of that long gallery, far from any human ears. A light battling wind shook the casements of the old building, and no one heard him.

A dismal echo of his own cries made its way lightly to the corridor; but even if some wandering soldier or late-returning officer had heard the sound, superstitious fears might well have repelled any attempt to seek its solution in the chamber where it was believed lay the still warm body of a slaughtered man.

No one came to him.

Then he heard a clock strike.

It was St. Martin's Church—and amid the stillness of the night he counted the strokes.

One—two—three—four.

It was four o'clock. He had remained, then, for some hours in that state which was neither life nor death.

The cold moonbeams streamed into the apartment.

A dog howled in the distance, and a deadly fear crept over the heart of the man of many crimes.

He tried to scream, but his thirst stifled the sound, and then, as the moonbeams crept slowly onward, sending the broad, light, spectrum across a wall, he saw that there was abundance of water, almost within his reach, in a china pitcher, which stood upon a marble slab in the apartment.

"Water, or I die! water, or I die!" he said in a hoarse, choking whisper. "I must—I will reach it!"

Van Esling nerved himself for the utmost extremity of agony, when he should rise from the bed on which he was lying, but he was agreeably surprised to find that if he held his breath while he moved, the pain of his wound was but trifling.

That was a secret he discovered accidentally, and it enabled him to make his way to the pitcher of water, of which he took a deep draught.

He then found that, by breathing lightly and carefully, he could support himself well enough upon his feet, and it was with surprise that he found such to be the case, for well he recollected the fearful nature of the wound he had received.

"I am sadly hurt!" he said, but I am not killed; and since I have lived so long, it may be that my wound is not fatal, and yet it may be if I reach not the one man who, I believe in all London, can treat such a hurt as mine, that man is Surlina, the Greek alchemist. But how am I to reach him? how am I to reach him? Have I strength to proceed so far? even if carried, or in any vehicle that can be procured for me at this dead hour of the night."

Still Van Esling was wonderfully recruited by the water, which seemed to quench the fever in his veins; and as there were no possible means of making himself heard from where he was, he felt the necessity of arming himself with what strength he could, and making his way to the lower portion of the barracks.

How strange he felt, and how ghastly he looked, as with both his hands pressed upon his breast, and not daring to breathe but with short inspirations, he moved from that room, where, it was believed, he had received his death wound, and made his way across the outer apartment where he had first encountered Dora.

He walked better than could have been expected, but when he issued forth into the long gallery, where a dim oil lamp was burning, a thousand strange lights seemed to dance before his eyes, and he had to pause for a few moments to press his hands over them, and shut out the imaginary fires.

Slowly tottering onwards, then, he made his way along the gallery, and had traversed one half its length, when he heard footsteps ascending the stairs.

"Ah! there will be help now!" he said faintly.

The persons who were approaching, carried a light, for its beams mingled with the faint rays of the oil lamp, which was always kept burning the whole night long in that gallery.

Then, just as he was about to cry out, he heard voices, apparently in low and earnest conversation, and with a tone as if there were a fear of being overheard about them.

"It's little we'll get for our pains!" said one.

"I don't know that!" said another. "He may not be rich, but it'll be hard if there isn't something in his rooms worth the taking."

"It may be so."

"We can but try, for to-morrow it will be too late. Come on, comrade! if we get but a few gold pieces, they will set us up with something to drink at the old canteen for many a night to come."

Van Esling began now to understand that these were two soldiers of his own regiment, who were intent upon plundering his apartments, in the belief that he lay dead in them.

"You're quite sure he's gone off?" said one.

"What do you mean by gone off?"

"Why, dead, to be sure."

"Well, that's good. Didn't my Lord Kingston, as he passed out at the barrack gate, say that he was dead? and isn't that why he's left alone till to-morrow morning?"

"To be sure—to be sure! Come on—come on!"

The two men had a lantern, and without troubling themselves to look much before them, they reached the head of the stairs, when a broad beam from the lantern fell full upon the face and form of Captain Van Esling as he stood there with his hands pressed upon his breast, looking so wan and ghastly.

With yells of dismay the two soldiers, believing that they saw an apparition, fell headlong down the steep stairs, at the bottom of which one of them received so severe a blow on the head that he lay insensible, but the other, although badly bruised, fled across the barrack-yard, crying out in frantic tones,—

"A ghost! a ghost! the captain's ghost!"

Captain Van Esling could have exulted over this incident, but that his precarious physical condition occupied all his thoughts.

Step by step, like a child learning to walk, he crept down the staircase and reached the barrack-yard; but, instead of there finding the assistance he sought, the first person who saw him, who happened to be a drummer-boy, raised such a cry of fright, that he alarmed the guard at the gate, who began to fly in all directions.

Van Esling dared not cry out—he dared not gather breath sufficient so to do, for he had a conviction that even to make the attempt might be his death.

He spoke feebly:

"Help—help! I live—I live!"

But no one heeded him. He reached the gate—the guard had evaporated in all directions. The sentinel on duty flung down his musket and hid in his sentry-box. Looking then, indeed, like a spectre, Van Esling passed out of the barracks, and with a confused feeling about him, that he wanted a coach or some other conveyance to take him to the Duke of Kingston's house, he wandered like a man walking in a dream towards the Strand.

"Coach, your honour?" cried the driver of one of those old-fashioned hackney vehicles, with their two wretched horses, which used to ply in London streets.

"Yes, yes!"

"All right, your honour. Bless us! I see your honour's been out to dinner, and been a-enjoying of yourself."

Van Esling had reeled against the coach door.

"No, no," he said, "I am hurt—wounded. Take me to Kingston House—the Duke of Kingston's—you understand? Do you know it?"

"To be sure I do, your honour. All's right! Bless your honour, there isn't such an easy coach as this in all London, though I says it as perhaps oughtn't. It's as easy as a bed, and as light as a feather. We always puts fresh straw in it once a month."

It was with great difficulty that Van Esling got into the coach, and then the swaying of it to and fro brought him excruciating pains; but the distance was short, and Van Esling recollected that, after all, it was not to Kingston House he wished to go, but to the house adjoining, where he well knew that the Greek alchemist resided, although he was not sufficiently in the confi of his patron, the Duke, to know exactly what had become of the Duchess, nor was Van Esling quite aware of the short interview which had taken place between the Duke of Kingston and Surlina on his account.

Probably Van Esling would have approached that quarter of London with even more caution than he did, had he been aware of the proposition which the Duke had made to Surlina to destroy him should he find him alive at the King's Mews and think proper to bring him to Kingston House.

But still there was the vague suspicion on the mind of Van Esling that the Duke of Kingston was just the sort of man to rid himself in any way of those persons who were not likely to be further useful to him, but who, in consequence of having been useful once knew enough to be dangerous.

Within a few doors of Kingston House, Van Esling struck upon the glass windows in front of the coach as a signal to the driver to stop, for late as was the hour, he still had a dread of attracting observation.

The coach was pulled up, and with pain and difficulty Van Esling alighted.

He was in no humour to dispute the dictum of the driver that it was five miles from Charing Cross to St. James's, and a half guinea insured the prompt departure of the man, who was glad to place as large a space as possible between him and the customer who might possibly be struck with the idea of asking for change.

Van Esling tottered up the steps of that apparently empty house, in which Surlina carried on his pretended alchemical researches, and then he felt so faint, so sick and ill, that he grasped with both hands a huge brass knob that was in the centre of the door, and felt that but for it he should have fallen to the steps.

It was some moments before he could gather strength to raise the knocker and make a single application for admission.

If the Duke wished him ill, there was danger even in that, for he was a man of late hours or any hours—a man who turned night to day, and he might be familiar with the sound of the knocker of that door and sally out of his own house and see who demanded admittance to the more mysterious mansion next door.

And all in vain might Captain Van Esling have knocked at that gloomy mansion, for Surlina would have heard the demand for admission as though he heard it not; but it was the time of night when the Greek went prowling out for air and exercise, when London was wrapped in repose; and like a shadow, or some stealthy midnight assassin, he glided into the street, and up to the door within a few seconds of Van Esling's appeal for admission.

The keen eyes of the alchemist knew him in a moment.

"Van Esling!" he said in tones of surprise. "What could it mean that the Duke should say you were wounded unto death?"

At sight of Surlina, in whom he garnered up all his thoughts of existence, Van Esling uttered a faint cry, and then fell senseless on the door-step.

"What can all this mean?" muttered the Greek. "Is this man really hurt, or is this some subtle plan to entrap me to my destruction, and cheat me of my hopes of vengeance? No, no! there is blood upon him; and that wan look is of nature's own doing. I mistrust you, Van Esling, and know you for a villain; but it may be you can be of use to me, for there was a reason, or the Duke of Kingston would not have wished your death, and those to whom he wishes destruction, I will wish life and preservation."

He opened the door by the aid of a small key he carried with him, and half lifted, half dragged the insensible form of Van Esling into the hall.

"Neoni, Neoni, come and help me! I feel feeble to-night, and this man, although life is in him, has all the weight of death. Neoni—I say Neoni!"

"I am here, father!"

"A light, my child—a light!"

"In a few seconds Neoni appeared with a spirit lamp in her hand, for such were always burning in the laboratory of the alchemist.

"Set down the lamp, O my Neoni, on yonder slab, and help me, for here is one wounded nearly unto the death."

"Alas! alas!" said Neoni. "What accident is this?"

"I know not, but the Duke wishes this man dead, and so my utmost skill shall keep the flame of life within him. Yes, he lives! He has come by some strange hurt—what it is I know not, but he still lives. Hush! what is that?"

"It is the Duke," said Neoni.

"Surlina—Surlina!" cried the voice of the Duke from the upper part of the house.

The Greek passed his hand over the flame of the spirit lamp and put it out.

"Hush, my Neoni," he said, "not a word—I will go to him!"

CHAPTER XXIII.

THE PURSUIT—THE STRATAGEM—THE ATTACK—THE COACH WITHOUT HORSES—THE DUKE'S DISAPPOINTMENT.

THE proceeds of Dora's adventures on the road had been already considerable, and since those adventures had been undertaken solely for the purpose of providing herself with the means of surrounding her wounded husband with those comforts his situation required, she had been careful to take with her from that old house in the Savoy all the money of which she was possessed.

It was with a feeling of infinite relief that she felt the coach moving onwards in the direction of that suburban abode where she hoped there would be more peace and serenity than their London habitation had afforded them.

At first sight it will be considered, too, that Dora must feel a considerable diminution of anxiety in the prospect that there was of the speedy recovery of Henry Dacres; but such was not really the fact, for Dora had two anxieties, and the subsidence of one seemed but to bring the other with greater strength and power to her recollection.

Her thoughts reverted to her child, for although, to all appearance, the little Mina must have perished in that terrible flood on the Thames, yet there was something in the mind of Dora which ever seemed to contradict the assumption of Mina's death.

It was during that progress in the coach from the old Savoy that Dora communicated to her husband most fully and minutely the particulars of the visit of Van Esling to the Savoy, and how he had carried off Mina.

The agitation that this recital caused in the mind of Henry Dacres, warned Dora to reserve her further communications for a period of greater strength.

"Alas! alas!" cried Henry, "and all this has happened without my being able to raise an arm to prevent it."

"Let us hope still," said Dora.

"Yes, it is the last and only solace. The cup of bitterness and grief would kill us, Dora, were it not that it contained that one blessed infusion—hope—hope!"

The coach had by this time got pretty well clear of the town, for London had not at that period extended its arms so far into the country.

There were trees, and hedges, and garden walls on each side of the way, and Dora began to feel a sensation of great relief that she was leaving behind her the dangers of the city, and seeking a period of peace amid the leafy shades of the place to which they were hastening.

Dora was about to use some expressions indicative of this feeling to Henry Dacres, when Dottman tapped on the front glass of the coach to attract their attention.

Dora hastily let down the glass, for there was alarm in the hurried manner in which Dottman interrupted her conference with Henry.

"Is there danger?" she said.

"I scarcely know, but I've been listening for some time, and I'm confident that I hear the hurried beat of horses's feet upon the road."

Dora listened attentively, but she could hear nothing.

"Stop a moment," said Dottman to the driver. "It is well worth a few minute's pause if we ascertain whether we are pursued or not."

"Ah! I thought as much!" said the coachman with a sullen air. "I heard there was a gang of coiners down away by the Savoy, and you're the very people."

"Silence!" said Dottman. "Pull up, I tell you—we want to listen to other sounds than your nonsense."

"I will pull up for nobody; but I'll pull round and go to London again. I dare say there's no end of reward for the whole lot of you. Let go my reins, will you?"

"You bring danger on yourself, idiot," said Dottman.

A fierce struggle on the coach-box which deeply affected Dora, who, from within could render no assistance, and who had a terrible fear of these excitements having an injurious effect upon Henry in his weak state.

But Dora need have been under no apprehension whatever, for Dottman was far more than a match for the coachman, and although they both rolled off the coach-box together, Dottman was uppermost, and the driver, who had brought this calamity on himself by his own folly and obstinacy, lay half stunned in the road.

The hackney coach horses of those days had always a much greater inclination to stand still than to go on, so that the coach remained perfectly stationary during the brief struggle.

"Oh! Dora—what is this?" cried Henry, "Are our enemies upon us?"

"No—no! be calm—all is well!"

"Give me a sword—give me a sword. I have yet strength enough to defend you."

"No, Henry—no!"

"Yes, Dora, I have, indeed, and Heaven will grant me more!"

"Dottman, Dottman! speak to us!" cried Dora, from the coach window, "Where are you?"

"All right!" said Dottman, "we shall do much better without this mule-headed fellow, and, indeed, I was only wondering how to get quietly rid of him, when he settled the matter himself, as you heard."

"Is he dead? Oh, let me hope that our path is not stained by homicide!"

"Oh, no! he's perhaps stunned a little, for this bit of road is hard and flinty. I will put him in a place of safety."

The coachman's faculties were in such a state of confusion from the heavy fall he had had, that he evidently fancied himself asleep in a room he was in the habit of occupying over some stables, for he kept muttering—

"What a row the horses make—give 'em a handful more hay—is the place afire? Is the place afire?"

"A fool and his wits are soon parted," said Dottman, as he dragged him out of the carriage way, so that he could not be hurt by any passing vehicle or horseman.

Propping the coachman then up against a gate post, Dottman left him to recover as best he might, and mounting the coach-box himself, he said—

"Captain, Captain! we must make good speed, for I am more than ever convinced now that there are mounted men on the road, and I seem to feel that they are after us."

"Then we are lost!" said Dora.

"Nay — not so! perhaps I'm wrong. Hush! not a word—it is well we are rid of the coachman, for I can answer all questions without being contradicted. Do not speak, for here comes one of our pursuers."

Some horseman, who must have been exceedingly well mounted, came galloping along the road at a furious rate, and as he neared the coach, he reined up his steed, and said in a loud harsh voice—

"What coach is this and where are you going?"

"Bless your heart!" said Dottman, "I'm

only a going a little further on with Mr. and Mrs. Beagle—but I wish you'd come here before, for I thought we were a going to be stopped by highwaymen."

"Ah, indeed! said the horseman, "I wish you then a safe journey. Which way did the suspicious persons go?"

"There were three of them," said Dottman, "and they went townwards as fast as they could gallop."

"Thank you—you're a capital fellow, and give valuable information, "said the horseman.

As he spoke, he turned his horse's head and went back the way he had come.

The coach had reached the corner of a shady lane at this moment, and Dottman immediately drew up beneath some trees.

"It won't do, Captain!" he said, "It won't do, Mr. Henry—we shall be pursued and overtaken. That fellow has only gone back to bring up his party, because he was too great a coward to stop us alone."

"Then we shall be prisoners at once!" said Dora, "for there may be too many for us to cope with."

"I'm afraid so," replied Dottman, "and it may be that the Duke of Kingston leads the party; a little management, however, may baffle them yet."

"Tell me—oh, tell me what we can do?"

"Fight! we will fight!" said Henry. "A sword—a sword!"

"Nay, we will do much better!" said Dottman, "for we will lead them astray."

Dora could not conceive what Dottman was about as he spoke, for he appeared to be running round the horses in a singular manner, as though doing something to the harness.

And in the midst of all this Dora could distinctly hear the tramp of horses' feet at a brisk pace on the road.

"That will do," said Dottman suddenly.

What will do?" asked Dora, as she stepped out of the coach.

"Why, you see, captain," replied Dottman, "I've got the two horses out, and have cleared them of all but their head gear. If you and Mr. Henry can manage to ride on, however slowly, I think you may leave me safely to manage the rest."

"Henry!" said Dora, as she looked into the coach, "tell me, Henry, do you think you are strong enough, with assistance, to mount a horse?"

"Yes, yes! oh, yes! for you, Dora—to serve you—if you wish it! Tell me that it is for you, and I will do it."

Dora helped her husband from the vehicle, and Dottman almost lifted him on to one of the coach horses, and then assisted Dora to mount the other.

"It will not be the pleasantest riding in the world," he said, "but we cannot do better. Go on quietly, both of you, until I overtake you, which I hope to do soon. You cannot miss the road, for you have to turn neither to the right nor to the left; but if I should not rejoin you within another mile, turn into the first lane you come to on the left hand—or should you get so far that you see a little roadside inn, called the 'Bugle Horn,' stop at it, and I will seek you there."

"And you, Dottman?" said Dora, "we leave you in danger."

"I hardly think so."

"But what will you do?"

"Why, I have an idea of going on with the coach."

"On with the coach? I cannot understand you!"

"There is just time for me, then, to tell you that we're at the corner of a lane with a down hill road for about a mile. It would be no trouble to me in the world to pull the coach after me, as it would almost go of itself."

"Ah, I see!" said Dora, "you would mislead our pursuers."

"I hope so! but there is not a moment to lose! Here they come, and I want them to hear the grinding of the coach wheels in the lane."

"Oh, Dottman, how much we owe you!"

"Another time, captain—or no time will do for that. Off and away!"

"Come, Henry—come!" said Dora.

The two coach horses went off at an ambling sort of trot, which scarcely made any sound upon the road.

Dottman seized the coach pole, and turned the vehicle into the lane. It required, at first, some exertion of strength to get it on to the sloping road, but after that, as he had himself said, there was no difficulty whatever in letting it roll after him, and the principal thing he had to do was to keep it in the centre of the road.

Scarcely had Dottman started in this singular and novel manner, when a party of six mounted men arrived at the corner of the lane.

"Halt!" cried one.

"What is it?" shouted several of the others, as they brought their horses to a standstill.

"It is a good thing I have sharp ears, my lord," said the first speaker, or we should have overreached our game."

"What do you mean?" said the Duke of Kingston, for this party, was indeed, headed by himself."

"What do you mean, Mr. Bonus?"

"Listen, my lord duke—listen!"

"Ah, I hear!"

"To be sure."

DORA, DUCHESS OF KINGSTON.

"The grinding of carriage wheels down this dark lane."

"Exactly so," said the officer. "That's it! they have calculated upon us galloping straight on to the high road, while they go snugly down a bye one."

"Forward!" cried the Duke of Kingston. "Pursue them! pursue them! A hundred pounds for each of them, dead or alive! Forward, my men!"

Dottman, with the carriage, had got considerably in advance. The lane was pretty good and firm as a road, inasmuch as the considerable slope it was on kept it well drained; but Dottman knew he was approaching the bottom of the hill, where it

would be next thing to impossible for him to drag along so heavy and lumbering a vehicle.

He heard the horsemen turn into the lane, and was so far gratified at the success of his manœuvre.

"I will give them both a surprise, and an alarm," he said, "before I've done with them!"

Taking one of the pistols with which he was provided, from his breast pocket, he fired it past the side of the coach, and the report echoed far and near in the narrow roadway.

After this there could not be the shadow of a doubt on the mind of the Duke of

DORA.—No. 12.

Kingston and his party that they were on the right scent.

They raised a shout which, to some degree, had a tone of alarm about it, and Dottman was amused to perceive that the ardour of the pursuit visibly slackened.

"I will try the effect of another shot," he said. "They may perhaps give me and the old hackney coach up altogether."

The discharge of this second pistol evidently had an uncomfortable effect upon the nerves of the pursuers, for the loud clatter of the horses feet materially subsided.

Then Dottman heard the Duke of Kingston cry out—

"Fire! you who have pistols, fire upon them—it is in self defence now—fire, I say!"

The response to this was a volley of some four or five pistol shots.

Dottman was, however, so completely protected by the coach, that although he heard two or three of their bullets come crashing into its panels, none touched him.

"Very good!" said Dottman. "I think now, gentlemen, I will leave you your barren conquest, for here we are at the foot of the hill."

The coach came to a standstill, with its wheels rather deeply embedded in the much softer ground of the valley. Making his way then up a high bank by the roadside, he forced a passage through the hedge-row, and took to the fields.

Dottman was a little curious, however, to know how the Duke of Kingston and his party would attack an empty old hackney coach without horses, and he lingered on the other side of the hedge, to see the result of the encounter.

Gloomy, black, but still tolerably well defined in the night air was the coach, and when the Duke of Kingston and the officers who were with him, found it had come to a standstill, they drew rein and kept at a cautious distance from it.

"They will make a determined resistance," said the Duke, "because they know their criminality. Fire again, my men! I will take all the consequences, and hold you harmless to the authorities. A chance shot may spare us a world of trouble."

Another volley of pistol shots was fired at the hackney coach; but there it was, still silent and impassable, so that the Duke of Kingston and his party began to be more alarmed at this appearance of non-resistance than as if some activity in the way of defence had exhibited itself.

There was something mysterious and dangerous looking about the dim black object, from which no sound came, and several of the officers who had been most active in the pursuit, showed now a decided inclination to get into the rear.

The Duke of Kingston spoke in an angry voice.

"Follow me—follow me!" he said. "Who know's but our bullets may have had some effect?" This may be the silence of death."

"If your grace will wait a moment," said one of the men, "I will light a link."

"No don't do that!" cried another, "they will pick us off with their pistols like ninepins, if you do. I have a dark lantern."

"That will do!" said the Duke, "come on!"

The officers were rather ashamed of their pusillanimity, and they followed the Duke of Kingston up to the mysterious coach.

"Yield!" he cried, "all of you, if you are still in life—for resistance is madness!"

There was of course no reply.

"The lantern—where is the lantern?" added the Duke.

"Here!" said the officer, who had it.

The slide was removed from before the broad convex lens of the lantern, and then they all saw how they had been duped—by a coach without horses, driver or passengers.

The Duke of Kingston ground his teeth together with passion.

"Fooled, fooled! he said, "and by such a device as this."

The officers raised a shout of rage, and at this moment, when there was no enemy, felt themselves valorous enough for anything.

"That will do!" said Dottman to himself, as he struck across the fields in the direction which Dora and Henry Dacres had taken.

CHAPTER XXIV.

THE BUGLE HORN — DOTTMAN'S FORE-THOUGHT—THE PLOT OVERHEARD AND DEFEATED.

DORA was far more anxious concerning the strength of Henry in the midst of all this unwonted exertion than upon any other account, as they rode slowly from the corner of the lane where Dottman was executing his skilful plan for the deception of their pursuers.

"Tell me, Henry," she said, "that you feel none the worse for all this tumult?"

"I am better," he said, "better and stronger, for it seems to me as if I were doing something towards your safety."

"Thank Heaven for that!"

They had not ridden very far when they heard the sound of the firing, and they involuntarily checked their horses.

"What can that portend?" said Dora.

"Dottman is in danger!" ejaculated Henry. "It is my duty to go to his aid."

"No, no, Henry—depend upon him, and his courage, and his resources. Dottman is but carrying out the plan that he proposed. On—on, Henry! and trust that all will be well."

They rode on.

Again the sound of firearms came upon the night air, for they were not far enough off to have lost the echo of those pistol shots with which Dottman alarmed the Duke of Kingston's party, and with which they strove to destroy the supposed passengers in the hackney coach.

The agitation of Henry's spirits was very great, and it was with difficulty that Dora could calm him sufficiently to induce him to proceed with all the speed that their horses would accomplish.

That speed was as nothing compared to what Dora had been used to, when the gallant and beautiful Arabian horse, Starlight, was her own.

Henry Dacres then spoke in a low voice, which had the sound of much suffering about it—

"Dora! Dora!" he said, "I begin to fear I have overrated my own strength."

"Alas! alas!" cried Dora, at this confirmation of her worst fears. "What can we do?"

"Nay, do not be distressed, my own Dora! Your life is a thousand times more precious than mine! Ride on, dear one, and if I can, after a rest by the roadside, I will follow you."

"Cruel! cruel!" said Dora.

"Ah, do not say that! Do not kill my heart by saying that!"

"What can be more cruel, Henry, than for you to doubt my affection?"

"I will not—I do not doubt it."

"And yet you would propose that I should leave you?"

Henry was silent.

"No, Henry—no! We will live or die together. Your danger shall be my danger—your safety shall be my safety. If you cannot ride further, I will pause now with you, and we will wait."

"I see a light, Dora, somewhat in advance of us. If, now, it were from some friendly window in the lowliest cottage that ever nestled by the roadside, I would fancy it a place of security for a time."

"Yes, yes! It must be some cottage home! Try, my Henry—try if your strength will enable you to reach it. Think you it is possible?"

"Yes, yes—I will try!"

"For my sake!"

"Ah, yes, for your sake, Dora."

If any invocation could possibly have the effect of endowing Henry Dacres with fresh strength, this would certainly be the one, and he gathered together all the energy and vitality that remained to him to sit the horse and traverse the short distance between where they were and the cottage or other habitation from which there streamed a bright ray of light over the dim and silent roadway.

They soon came to a clump of trees, and then Dora saw that, hanging from one of them, there was the swinging sign of an inn.

Just below that swinging sign there was a lantern, from which the light they had observed had come.

By the rays of that lantern Dora saw that the sign was that of the "Bugle Horn."

"There is the house," she said, "that was mentioned to us by Dottman. We shall be safe here, surely!"

"Thank Heaven!" said Henry.

The tone in which he spoke betrayed great physical exhaustion, and Dora called out aloud—

"House! house! house!"

A man came to the door of the little inn.

"Hilloa! who calls 'house?'"

"I do," said Dora, "I do. We wish to wait here for a friend. This is the Bugle Horn?"

"Ah, it's the Bugle Horn fast enough!" replied the man! You are welcome! Who is your friend? Do we know him?"

Dora was afraid to mention the name of Dottman, for fear she should do mischief, and she replied—

"I do not think you do. But I shall thank you to help this gentleman from his horse, as he is far from well."

"Why, this is an odd freak!" said the man, as he assisted Henry to alight.

"What? what?" said Dora.

"There are no saddles on your horses, and they have yet the head gear of draught cattle."

Dora found it impossible to form any satisfactory answer to this remark, therefore she let it pass without a reply.

Henry Dacres leant heavily upon her arm now as they made their way into the Bugle Horn Inn, and it was with a sigh of relief that he sat down in the little sanded parlour to which he was shown with Dora by the man who had met them at the door of the hostelry,

They had heard this man call out to a boy by the name of Joe, to come and look after the horses; and when he made his way after them into the parlour, Dora could see that he had anything but the appearance of one she would like to trust.

"Have you any wine in the house?" she

said, for she thought that Henry might be restored by some such stimulant.

"Wine?" replied the man, "I should think not. What should we do with wine in such a place as this, where we don't get rid of our ale quite so quick as we would wish."

"What is wanted?" asked a woman, who now appeared at the door of the room.

"Wine!" laughed the man.

"Oh, we have no accommodation for such very fine folks!" said the woman, "and the sooner they go on their way the better."

"My good woman," said Dora, as she laid a guinea on the table, "we wish to wait here for some time, and are willing to pay you well."

The woman made a dart forward, and secured the guinea at once.

"Sweet young lady," she said, "you may wait here as long as you like. What can I get for the poor gentleman, who does look main poorly. There is some nice cordial now that I could let him have."

"Yes, yes!" said Dora, "bring what you think will be good for one who is weak and unwell."

"To be sure I will—to be sure. I said to myself, the moment I saw you, 'these,' said I, 'are real gentlefolks, and they ought to be attended to as such.' That's what I said to myself."

The woman left the room, and the moment she had done so, Dora felt confident she heard a whispered conference going on outside the door, between her and the man who had, in so surly a manner, first received them at the inn.

Dora had an irresistible desire to hear what they were saying, for isolated as she and Henry Dacres were, she was full of fears on his account.

"Rest still, Henry dearest," she said, "rest still for a moment."

"Yes, Dora—yes! You will not leave me?"

"No, no—oh, no!"

Dora darted lightly to the door, and put her ear close to its panels.

She heard the voice of the woman.

"Did you see? did you see? Why, the purse from which she took the guinea was quite full of gold?"

"Was it?"

"Ah, you were not looking!"

"I was not."

"Well, then, I tell you it was full of gold. There were more guineas there than were ever inside the old Bugle Horn before!"

"What then, missus?"

"Do you think I am going to let them go outside it again,"

"Oh, I see."

"To be sure you do. I will have that purse, or I will know the reason why. A sick man and a mere girl. Surely they won't be much trouble!"

"None at all," said the man.

"Come this way."

The voices died away as those two unscrupulous persons stepped from the door, and Dora was left in the most painful state of apprehension.

What could she do? What was to become of her and of Henry now?

Oh, how bitterly she accused herself of folly, in ever permitting herself to be separated from Dottman. It might be hours before he could reach that place, and what fearful dangers might she and Henry have to pass through in the interval.

And she was unarmed, too! What an omission was that! When she had changed her apparel, and no longer wore that suit of half military clothing with which she had performed her exploits upon the road, she had likewise laid aside the pistols which seemed actually to form a part of it.

She now flew to Henry's side—she clasped her arm about him.

"Henry! Henry!" she said, "you cannot rest here. We shall have to leave this place."

"Yes, Dora—yes, my Dora!"

"Do you feel at all equal to the task of walking any distance?"

"I will try. You take the pistols."

Dora could hardly refrain at these words from uttering a cry of joy.

"Pistols, Henry!" she said, "What pistols?"

"Your friend—our friend, Dottman, gave me the pair of small pistols before we left our old house in the Savoy."

"We are saved!"

"Saved, Dora?"

"Yes, you shall rest here now, my Henry, and let those who would disturb that rest beware!"

The pistols which Henry Dacres was so providentially possessed of were a small pair which Dottman had originally brought from the shadowy residence of Captain Hawk. Dora had seen them in Dottman's possession, but she had not been aware that he had handed them to Henry.

She now eagerly examined them, and to her great joy, found that they were both loaded.

"Yes—ah, yes!" she said, "we are, indeed, safe now. We have two lives in our hand. I will not shed blood carelessly even of those who would take our lives for the sake of the gold they have seen in my possession, but I will defend you, Henry."

At this moment Dora was certain she

heard more whispering at the door of the room, and it was in another moment opened.

The woman appeared with a small tray, on which were biscuits and some liquor in a glass.

"Bless the poor gentleman!" she said, "this will do him a world of good."

Dora would not have allowed Henry to taste of anything in that house on any consideration. For all she knew, there might be poison lurking in that pretended cordial, which was to "do him so much good."

"Thank you!" she said, "leave the tray."

"Hem!" said the woman, as she set the tray down on the table.

"Well," said Dora, "that will do."

"Pay to-day," said the woman, "and trust to-morrow, my dear. That is the rule of the Bugle Horn."

"I don't know what you mean."

"Then I will tell you. We give no trust, and everything has to be paid for at once."

"I have given you one guinea."

"That's for staying in the house. This cordial is another guinea."

There was an unmistakable air and tone and manner about this woman which betokened that she intended to bring affairs to a crisis with the guests chance had brought to the house.

Dora felt fully aware of the indiscretion she had committed in exhibiting so well filled a purse before the avaricious eyes of that person, and she resolved now that she felt strong enough to resist not to do so again.

"This is an attempted imposition," she said, "so gross and unwarrantable that I will not submit to it."

"You will not submit to it?" said the woman, with an air of defiance. "You cannot help yourself. Here, Samuel, come in! Come in and take charge of the sick gentleman—there's nothing to fear!"

"One moment," said Dora, as she rose and placed herself before Henry, "I loathe bloodshed, but self-defence is a sacred sentiment. Keep off, or take the consequences of your projected crime."

Dora held in her right hand, fully presented at the woman, one of those small pistols, to which, on that occasion, there can be no doubt she and Henry Dacres owed their lives, for there was evidently a look of murder in the eyes of that woman.

Whatever might have been her previous criminality, the sight of that well-filled purse of gold which Dora had so imprudently shown had evidently awakened so much cupidity in her breast, that no crime would have been thought too desperate or fearful, provided it ensured her possession of the glittering treasure.

But at the sight of the pistol she started back in alarm, and raised a cry of baffled avarice and rage.

The door of the apartment was opened half way at this moment, and the man who had been summoned, by the name of Samuel, stood upon the threshold.

This man carried a heavy bludgeon in his hand, one blow of which must needs have been instant death.

But he, too, when he saw that Dora was armed, shrunk back in conscious cowardice.

———

CHAPTER XXV.

DORA AND HER HUSBAND IN DANGER—ARRIVAL AT THE BUGLE HORN OF THE DUKE OF KINGSTON'S PARTY—DOTTMAN REJOINS HIS FRIENDS.

How this fearful adventure at the Bugle Horn would have ended, and whether Dora would indeed have had to take human life in defence of Henry or not must remain for ever a mystery, for at the moment that the woman was about to yell out some order to her companion in iniquity, there came upon not only her ears, but those of Dora, the sound of horses' feet in the road.

It was a peculiar combination of circumstances that these sounds should be equally alarming to both parties in the Bugle Horn.

Dora and Henry Dacres thought they might announce the arrival of the Duke of Kingston with the officers at his heels, for they were precluded from the supposition that it might be the arrival of Dottman, who, by some accident, might have procured a steed, inasmuch as the sounds announced unmistakably the approach of several mounted men.

To the woman of the Bugle Horn Inn, this arrival of unexpected guests brought with it great terrors; for, not knowing how great an object secrecy was to those persons whom she had attempted to rob and perchance to murder, she thought at once that they would proclaim what had happened, and solicit aid from the new comers.

"Hilloa, there!" cried a voice from the open roadway, "are you all asleep in the house, or is this no inn, after all."

"There," said Samuel, "we've done it now, *missus*."

The woman trembled violently.

"Oh, look over it," she said. "Oh, forgive it! It wasn't meant—it was only a little jest. Have mercy upon us!"

"Hilloa!" cried the voice from the road again.

Dora made no reply to the imploring words or gestures of the woman, for she was certain that she recognised in that voice from without that of one of the officers who had attempted to stop the progress of herself, Henry, and Dottman from the old house in the Savoy.

And thus Dora found herself between two dangers!

There was but the frail lattice of the inn window between her and her foes without.

There was but the fear of that presented pistol between her and those who had sought her life within.

What could she say?

What was she to do?

The woman staggered from the room. The man, Samuel, had already left the door. Another moment and Dora heard the key turned in the lock on the outer side.

Like a flash of light illumining the darkest night, there came a hope in Dora's mind.

Out of all this danger, what if safety should spring, and it might do so from the very circumstances which appeared at one time full of disaster and threatening with death.

From fear of a communication between her new guests, and her old ones, the mistress of the Bugle Horn Inn would do anything to keep them apart.

What bribe or call upon her sympathy would be so powerful as her own fears in such a cause?

And what could possibly be of greater assistance to Dora and Henry Dacres than these exertions which the landlady of the inn, for her own sake, would make, to deny the presence of any such persons beneath her roof.

Well content, then, was Dora to be locked into that apartment.

Well content was she to remain perfectly quiet and passive while the landlady concluded matters in her own fashion, and shewed her new guests into some other room of her little establishment

"I fear, Dora," said Henry, "that these new arrivals are our foes likewise."

"Yes, Henry," whispered Dora; "but the two dangers seem to neutralise each other. For the present I think we have but to be still, and we are safe.

Dora and Henry, then, could hear the tramp of feet in the little passage immediately outside the door of the little sanded parlour in which they were.

"Have you anybody in the house," cried a loud voice, "or have you had anyone within the last two hours?"

"No one," replied the landlady.

How she must have trembled at that moment with apprehension, for fear that Dora should make her presence known, and claim the aid of these new comers.

And how intensely astonished must she have been that such was not the case!

"Then we're at fault again," said the officer, who had been leading the party of the Duke of Kingston, and it seems to me that we are baffled for the present."

"Speak out, woman," said the Duke of Kingston, as he himself strode into the passage of the little inn. "There is a suspicious manner about you that I do not like. Tell me at once and truly, have any persons, either afoot or on horseback, passed this way?"

"Ah! you pursue them?" said the woman.

At this question the Duke of Kingston made a great mistake. If he had avowed his hostile intentions towards Dora and Henry, in all probability this woman would have made some pecuniary bargain for giving them up; but the Duke mistook her entirely, and assuming a manner which was quite different from that dictated by his angry passions, he replied—

"Oh, no! they are friends of mine, concerning whose safety I am most solicitous."

This decided the woman at once.

She shook her head.

"No," she said, "there has been no one here."

And yet, as she spoke, her surprise increased that Dora made no alarm indicative of her presence.

The Duke of Kingston strode out of the house, and when he reached the roadway, he gave vent, in various angry exclamations, to the rage that revelled in his heart.

"They've escaped me," he said. "They foil me when I seem to feel that I have them almost within my grasp; but I will yet hunt them to the death, for I shall know no peace and feel no safety beneath my coronet while Dora lives."

He mounted his horse, and turning then to the principal officer, who had led him on this chase, he endeavoured to suppress his passion so as to speak with calmness.

"You must have been mistaken," he said, "and we have been upon some wrong pursuit."

"Nay, your grace, that can hardly be," replied the officer. "One of my men saw the coach; and I think what happened in the lane above here ought to assure your grace we were on the right scent. They have escaped us cleverly, but we will scour the country for them, and if they are above ground I will find them."

"Be it so," said the Duke. "You know where to come to me. Your reward is certain if successful, and it shall be much larger than your most sanguine expectations point to."

The Duke of Kingston turned his horse's head towards London, and the officers, mounting again, trotted slowly in that direction. They could not but feel they had lost all clue to the fugitives, and that, at all events, they must give up the pursuit for the present, which presented itself to them in such tempting colours.

The Government had offered five hundred pounds for the apprehension of Dora since her escape on that terrible morning when she was taken out to die at Tyburn.

The Duke of Kingston had intimated that his liberality would reach a like amount.

No wonder, then, that some of the most active officers of the police were most anxious for the chase of one on whose head so heavy a sum was placed.

The situation of Dora and Henry was still most critical.

They had got rid of one danger, but the other still remained; and now that the designs of the mistress of the inn and her man Samuel had been thoroughly unmasked, it was to be suspected that they might attempt some other more desperate means of accomplishing the destruction of their guests.

But Dora was intent upon cheering Henry.

"Be comforted," she said, "be comforted, dear Henry—that worst foe we can ever have is gone."

"The Duke! yes, the Duke—the false and heartless Duke. I have heard all."

"Yes, Henry; and we are well armed now against those who would assail us in this house."

"Misfortune and villany haunt our footsteps," said Henry, mournfully. "What are we to do?"

Before Dora could reply, a sharp knocking came upon the door of the room.

"I speak to you," cried the woman from without. "I speak to you, within there! You can go when you like. Go in peace, so that you go at once."

"No," said Dora.

She was resolved, come what might, to wait the arrival of Dottman.

"Why do you say no? who bids you to stay? who wishes you to stay? Go at once, I say! Go at once! I do not want your gold!"

Dora did not speak in reply to this address, but she approached the door, as she had done on a former occasion, and listened intently. She heard a whispered conversation going on between the landlady and her man, Samuel, but it was conducted in so low a tone that she could only catch the words "as they come out, be certain of the rope!" There was quite suffi-in this fragmental sentence to make Dora feel assured some treachery was intended, and even if she had not had the powerful motive to remain where she was, she would have done so until circumstances altered sufficiently to make it much safer to leave the place.

Dottman had distinctly named that inn as the place beyond which they were not to go, and should they leave it they might never look upon his face again.

Dora felt quite certain she would not be able to guide Henry to that shadowy retreat where she had first met Dottman, while he was in the service of Van Esling, *alias* Captain Hawk.

The landlady now made another attempt to induce Dora to leave the inn.

She rapped at the door.

"Do you hear me? do you hear me?" she said, "if you value your own safety, go! for there will be those soon here who will not mind the loss of one life for such a purse of gold as that you have about you."

"No," said Dora again, "we will not leave."

"Then you are mad!"

It brought a fresh accession of alarm to both Henry and Dora now, to see that the miserable little light, which had been placed upon the table of the inn parlour, was upon the point of expiring.

Darkness might complicate their dangers, and could certainly not add to their defences."

It was with a pang, too, that Dora heard the woman say in a low tone—

"Fetch the gun, then."

Samuel probably would have had some reply to make to this suggestion, but whatever it was it became merged in the sound of a hasty footstep that strode into the passage of the inn.

"Hiloa!" cried a voice, "what cheer in the Bugle Horn to-night?"

It was the voice of Dottman.

Dora called out to him aloud—

"Dottman! Dottman! we are prisoners here, and our lives have been attempted. Help! help!"

"Ah, is it so?" cried Dottman.

There then immediately succeeded a tremendous scuffle in the passage of the inn. Screams from the landlady, and oaths from Samuel, lasted several seconds, and then all was still.

"Where are you?" cried Dottman, "where are you, captain?"

"Here! here!" replied Dora, "we are locked in."

Dottman was guided by the sound. The key was in the lock of the door, and quickly turning it, he dashed into the parlour to the rescue of Dora and Henry.

At that moment the light expired.

There was an oil lamp, however, in the passage of the inn, which sent some rays into the parlour.

"Thank heaven! thank heaven!" cried Dora, "you are in time to save us either from defeat or victory, and the latter must have been stained with blood."

"What on earth has happened?" said Dottman.

"I incautiously," replied Dora, "allowed the woman of this house to see a purse well filled with gold, and she and the man named Samuel, have sought to rob us, and to secure their safety by our death."

"What villany!"

"Where are they now, Dottman?"

"Why, they tried to get the better of me by throwing a rope with a noose over my head, and they have now both fled from the house."

"And the Duke—you escaped the Duke?"

"Oh, yes—famously! I left them all in the lane, having a pitched battle with the hackney coach."

"They have been here, Dottman."

"Here? Is that possible?"

"Yes— but they have given up the chase for the present, and from the sound of their horses' feet, I feel convinced they have gone towards town."

It was a singular conjunction of circumstances which left the fugitives in whom we have so strong an interest, completely masters of the old Bugle Inn.

The agitation of the scene which had been so recently gone through had first had the effect of rousing Henry to unwonted exertion, but the reaction of that excitement soon presented itself.

Pale, trembling, and haggard, he leant upon the arm of Dora, and could hardly be persuaded that, for the time, all danger was past.

"Dottman," he cried, this is a life we cannot lead. You, perhaps, or I might lead it, for we are men, but Dora must be saved from all these calamities, and from these dangers."

"All is well, Henry—all is well!" said Dora, "grieve not for my sake, but rather think that through all these dangers and oppressions, we are reaching a haven of safety, which will restore us to serenity and all to happiness."

Dottman had made his way with haste to the stable, for he was not a little anxious to leave the inn, standing as it was upon the high road, and exposed to many dangers as far as they were concerned, from casual travellers on the road.

He found the two coach horses in the stable yard, and what was of as much importance, he likewise found saddles with which to equip them, so that, in a few moments, Henry and Dora were enabled to quit the place, and most gladly did they turn their backs upon the old Bugle Inn, on the Western Road.

CHAPTER XXVI.

THE THREE FRIENDS PURSUE THEIR JOURNEY—THE MASKED MAN—THE ROBBERY—MORE MYSTERY—DORA'S DETERMINATION.

DORA felt a much greater relief when once more upon the road out of this habitation, which had promised to expose her to so many dangers, than she had felt even upon quitting the old house in the Savoy, attacked as it had been by the officers of police, eager for their prey.

"Dottman," she said, "have we far to go, and do you think, after all, that in seeking this cottage of Captain Hawk's we shall find safety?"

"Why, captain," said Dottman, "to answer the last question first, I have not a doubt about the safety of the place, for there are hiding nooks and corners in it that would defy all the officers in Christendom, unless they pulled it down brick by brick; and as for the distance, another mile and a half will take us to it."

As Dora had turned her head to address Dottman, she had become aware of a ruddy reflection in the sky over the tree tops, somewhere in the direction from which they were riding.

Henry Dacres had observed this colour in the sky likewise, and he said in a low, inquiring tone—

"There is a fire—there is a fire!"

"Yes," said Dottman, "and I think I can explain it. I took care, before we left the Bugle Horn, to fling the lighted lamp into one of the empty rooms, and I shouldn't wonder a bit if the old wooden structure will be burnt down."

Dora made no remark, but she could not but feel that such a retribution upon the owners of the old Bugle Inn was amply called for.

The party rode on in silence now for some time, Dora and Henry being somewhat in advance, while Dottman kept a wary eye upon the road some distance in the rear.

Dora was conversing in a low tone with Henry, when Dottman quickened his pace, and riding close up to them, he said,—

SURLINA STOPPED BY DOTTMAN.

"I can hear the sound of carriage wheels upon the road, but whether they bespeak danger to us or not, I cannot say; it would be best for you to ride on and leave me to encounter whoever is approaching, but do not, by any means, go past the group of poplars which you will come to on the right hand side of the road, for they stand at the corner of the narrow lane which leads to Captain Hawk's cottage."

"If there is danger," said Henry, "we ought to stay and share it."

"No, Mr. Dacres," said Dottman, "you would but increase it by staying; and let me beg that you will not make my position more dangerous by remaining."

DORA.—No. 13.

This was an unanswerable appeal, and Dora, laying her hand upon the bridle of Henry's horse, gently urged it forward.

Dottman purposely slackened his pace now, in order that, whoever was upon the road might come up to him; and it was not many minutes before there came, at a tolerable pace towards that part of the road, a low, heavy chaise, driven but by one person, but in which there seemed to be a horse of great strength and endurance.

It was a great surprise to Dottman to see, by the dim light that was upon the road, a mask upon this person's face; but narrowly as he looked at him, Dottman could not make up his mind that it was any one he had ever seen before.

To allow so suspicious and mysterious a personage pass him upon the road, at a pace which would soon bring him up to Dora and Henry Dacres, was what Dottman could not think of for a moment.

He had re-loaded his pistols since firing them off in the lane where he had had the strange adventure with the hackney coach without horses, and now, after letting this chaise and its mysterious occupant pass him for the space of about fifty yards, he put spurs to his horse, and galloping after the animal that drew it, he caught the chaise horse by the rein, and brought it to a standstill.

The mysterious occupant of the vehicle then called out in a voice, partly of anger and partly of entreaty—

"Hold! hold! stay me not! My errand is one of life or death!"

"And mine, too!" said Dottman. "I hold this road to-night against all comers, and must know whither you are bound."

"You want gold," said the mysterious stranger. "There is my purse—it is moderately well-filled—let me go in peace."

"I have not the slightest objection to the purse," said Dottman, "but still that don't satisfy me as to who you are, and whither you are proceeding."

"I am a physician."

"A strange physician."

"Strange or not, I tell you truth. I am on an errand which forces me to speed, for I must hasten back to one who lies sorely wounded."

"Back from where?"

The stranger was silent for a moment, and then he said—

"This can be but idle curiosity. But if to gratify it will free me from your importunity, I tell you I'm in search of a cottage called the Shadows."

"The Shadows!" exclaimed Dottman.

"Ah! you speak as if you knew the place."

"I do know it."

"Then for the value of the gold I have given to you, lead me to it, for I have there to make a search in the interests of one so badly hurt that he may never again, in life, cross its threshold."

"In the name of Heaven," said Dottman, "who are you, and of whom do you speak?"

The mysterious stranger at this moment partially rose up in the chaise, and cast something on the roadway, which looked like a small globule of glass.

A loud report immediately ensued, and a quantity of dense vapour began to rise from the ground.

Dottman's horse was terrified, and reared and plunged, so that he was compelled to let go the rein of the horse which drew the chaise.

The mysterious man in the mask took advantage of this moment's liberty, and urged the horse to a furious gallop.

It was some few seconds before Dottman could control his own steed sufficiently to bring it under the command of spur and rein, and by the time he had succeeded in doing so, the mysterious man and the chaise were sufficiently far off to render a chance shot at him almost an absurdity.

Dottman was excessively provoked, and perhaps a little bewildered, but so soon as he could, he galloped after this personage, who had played him so singular a trick.

For a few minutes he could hear the tramp of the horse and the rapid rush of the wheels of the vehicle, and then all was still, until the new sound came upon Dottman's ears occasioned by the feet of the horses ridden by Dora and Henry Dacres.

They had reached the group of poplars to which he had referred, and had come to a standstill, deeming it inexpedient to proceed beyond that point, since it had been mentioned by Dottman.

But horse, chase, and its mysterious masked occupant had disappeared so completely, that it would not have taken much trouble to have induced Dottman to believe he had been the victim of some waking dream.

"Did nothing pass?" he cried, as he reined in his panting horse.

"Nothing," said Dora.

"And you heard no sounds upon the road?"

"We heard a noise we thought was thunder, and then the hard galloping of your horse, but nothing more."

Dottman was silent for a moment, and then he said, in a low tone—

"It is nothing—it is nothing. Let us at once reach the Shadows. Come down the lane—follow me—this is the way. And yet, what am I to think? He said that this was his destination."

"You are perplexed and thoughtful, Dottman!" said Dora. "Let us know, I pray you, what has happened?"

"Yes—it is far better that I should, for you will then be upon your guard. I am perplexed, and know not what to make of an adventure I have had to-night."

Dottman then related the meeting he had had with the mysterious stranger in the chaise, and Dora's fears were at once awaked for the safety of Henry.

"Alas! alas!" she said, "we are hunted from place to place, and we shall know no rest. Was it the false and cruel Duke of Kingston?"

"Certainly not," replied Dottman, "the

figure was much smaller than his, and he never could have had the art of simulating so strange and uncommon a voice as that which came from the occupant of the chaise. The accents were decidedly foreign."

Dora, upon hearing this account, had unconsciously stopped her horse, and as her hand was on the bridle of the steed ridden by Henry, that paused likewise.

The lane was a very narrow one; in fact, it was but a kind of cutting through the fields here and there, certainly heavily timbered on either side, but in other places quite open to the meadows.

As they all three, then, stood for a moment irresolute, there came again upon their ears the grinding sound of carriage wheels.

"The chaise again!" cried Dottman in an eager whisper. "The chaise again!"

"It is in the lane," said Dora.

"It is—it is! and be that man whom he may, he seeks the cottage of Captain Hawk!"

"What shall we do, Dottman?"

"Prevent him yet, if there be any virtue in powder and ball."

"Nay, let me advise. It is fortunate that we have not reached the place. Will it not be better to allow him to go there, and find it, as he no doubt, expects, destitute of occupants, and then intercept him on his return."

"The very thing," said Dottman, "the very thing! It is far better—and if we were to search old England through, we should not find a better place than this for our purpose. Follow me."

They were in one of those shadowy portions of the lane where the trees of each side had grown to a great height, mingling their topmost branches, so that even at midday it was a shadowy twilight sort of spot. But Dora and Henry, after following Dottman for some few hundred paces, found that the trees on one side abruptly ceased, leaving the meadows easily accessible over the mere rudiments of a bank and hedgerow from the lane.

A few seconds more sufficed to carry them to the other side of the tall trees where they could remain in perfect obscurity, leaving the lane free, and yet it would be impossible for anyone to pass down it without being observed by them.

Not many seconds had they to wait, before the rapid sound of wheels convinced them that the chaise, with its mysterious occupant, was approaching, and Dora fixed her eyes with no small interest upon the last of the trees, in order that she might see emerge from its shadow the vehicle which contained the masked man.

There was so much of mystery about this whole occurrence that Dora found it impossible to establish in her own mind any sufficiently plausible mode of accounting for the affair.

Who could it be that, in so strange a manner, and at such an hour, too, should be seeking that very cottage among the trees which she and those who were near and dear to her sought as a place of refuge from the storms of fortune.

Who could it be that, with so much appearance of secresy, and with so many precautions against even letting his face be seen, was making his way to "The Shadows," as that verdantly enclosed little habitation was named?

Dora might well feel that conjecture was useless in the attempt to unravel the mystery, for the more thought she gave to it the more indistinct it seemed in the mists of the most inextricable confusion.

But she had not long now to wait for the approach of the mysterious man in the chaise.

The grinding sound of the wheels of the vehicle in the loose soil of the shadowy lane came more and more distinctly to the ears of the little party concealed behind the trees.

"He comes," said Dottman.

"This, then, is some new danger to my Dora," said Henry Dacres.

"No, no," replied Dora, "Do not think so, Henry. Danger to me now cannot come in the guise of one man."

"I should think not," said Dottman, briefly.

"Hush!" said Dora. "Look!"

The dim, shadowy outline of the horse and chaise emerged from among the trees. The pace at which the man was now urging the horse was not very great, but still it was sufficient to carry the vehicle out of the observation of Dora and her party amid the obscurity of the night.

Dora made her determination in a moment.

"Henry," she said, "dear, dear Henry, let me bespeak, beforehand, your consent to what I am about to ask you to let me do?"

"What is it, my own Dora?"

"Remain here with our friend Dottman while I follow that man."

Henry sighed.

"Nay," said Dottman, "why may not I go?"

"Because I go only to observe his movements, not to attack him. If there be any danger it is here, and not on the expedition I purpose. Let me go, and with the assurance, too, that I leave Henry in safety."

Dora dismounted as she spoke, and by

that Dottman and Henry saw that she considered it would be safest to go on foot.

This was an idea, though, that they both at once combatted.

"No, captain," said Dottman, for he still liked to name Dora Captain, since he had began to do so, and had got into such a habit of it. "No, Captain, do not, I beg of you, go on foot. Walk to the house if you like, so that the footsteps may not be heard, but you will feel much safer mounted."

Henry was equally urgent, and Dora gave way to their wishes as far as to mount the horse again.

The chaise had now either stopped, or it had got so far off that no sound of its wheels could be heard, so that Dora was anxious to start in pursuit of it at once.

The road was very soft, and the feet of the horse sunk deep into it, so that there was the least possible sound made by her advance.

Dottman had told her that the old garden wall of Captain Hawk, *alias* Van Esling's cottage was now not above a quarter of a mile from the place in the lane where they were, and Dora had a full expectation in her own mind of finding the chaise at that spot.

She was not disappointed.

Drawn up closely under the ivy covered garden wall of "The Shadows" was the chaise and horse.

The vehicle was empty.

It was here, then, that this mysterious man had come to make a visit to the cottage.

What could be his business there?

Dora withdrew to the other side of the lane where there was a clump of trees, among which she could remain in deep shadow.

She resolved to watch for the coming forth of the mysterious man with the mask.

Dora had not to wait very long, for in as nearly as she could guess about ten minutes there came slowly over the wall a dim figure.

It was the man with the mask.

He was muttering something to himself as he came over the wall.

Dora exerted her sense of hearing to the utmost to hear what he was saying.

"Yes," he said, "That is well! that is well! he has spoken the truth, and I have the gold and the jewels. What need I care how they have been come by? they will answer all my purpose."

The man had drawn the chaise so close under the wall of the old garden that he could easily drop into it from among the thick ivy which grew all over the ancient brickwork on both sides.

The chaise gave a heavy lurch upon its springs as he alighted in it.

"That is well! that is well!" he said, with a tone of satisfaction.

The voice in which he spoke was evidently foreign, and now that he could have no motive for attempting to disguise it in any way, Dora felt certain that it was this man's natural tones that she heard.

She felt certain, too, that, let her hear them where she might, at any other time or in any other place, she should know them again in a moment.

But what was to be done?

What had she achieved by watching this man, after all?

The mystery of who and what he was remained as profound as ever.

All that she had heard was that he had procured at the cottage what he came for, and that he had declared all was well.

Gold and jewels seemed to be the booty that he congratulated himself upon being possessed of.

What was Dora to do?

CHAPTER XXVII.

DORA COMES TO A DECISION—THE MASKED MAN CAPTURED—THE ELIXIR OF LIFE —DOTTMAN SECURES A RICH BOOTY.

FOR a few seconds Dora remained in the deep shadow of the clump of trees, where she had hidden herself and horse in a state of great incertitude as to what would be the best course to pursue in respect to this mysterious visitor to the cottage of Captain Hawk.

Whatever was to be her determination it would be necessary that it should be speedily carried out, for the strange being turned the head of the horse now in the direction of the high road again, and having accomplished all he purposed by his journey, was intent upon being off.

Dora then made a resolve.

"I will follow him," she said to herself, "and when sufficiently near to the trees where Dottman is watching, I will call upon him to stop him."

The chaise went down the lane now, towards its opening to the high road, very quickly.

Dora started in pursuit.

At the first sound of the horse's feet behind him, the mysterious driver of the chaise came to a standstill.

Dora did the same then.

In that strongly marked foreign voice that distinguished all this man said, he then called out—

"Hilloa! Hilloa! who is travelling in this out-of-the-way place? Speak! or I fire!"

Dora made no reply.

The stillness about the spot was something almost fearful. For a few moments it was completely unbroken, and then the stranger muttered to himself.

"I was probably mistaken, but I thought I heard the sound of horses' feet."

He drove on again.

Again Dora followed him.

This time the mysterious man made up his mind that there could be no mistake about the fact of some one dogging him in the shadowy lane, but he did not pause as before.

Dora heard the sharp slashing of a whip, and she felt conscious that the man in the chaise was attempting to ensure his safety by flight.

The horses tore along at a good pace with the light vehicle behind him.

It was useless now to attempt anything like care or concealment in the mode of following that man, and Dora urged the horse she rode to its utmost speed, which, however, was very far from good.

The distance, however, was very short to that part of the lane where Dottman and Henry would be waiting, and Dora thought that her voice would be heard.

"Stop him! Stop him!" she cried.

She had lost sight of the chaise, but almost immediately after she spoke, she heard two pistol shots fired, one after the other in very rapid succession.

Then there came a cry and a shout from some one, and it was evident that the occupant of the chaise had not been permitted to pass unmolested on his way.

Another moment and Dora came into sight of what seemed like a confused mass of something in the middle of the lane.

She then heard the voice of Dottman.

"Be it so," he said. "Fire again if you will, and my time will then come."

Something was then said by the occupant of the chaise in a tone of great anger, to which Dottman replied by a laugh.

Another moment and Dora was upon the spot.

The scene which then presented itself was exactly what her imagination would have pictured.

Dottman had heard the chaise rapidly advancing before Dora had cried out for him to stop it, and there is very little doubt but that he would have done so without any such inducement.

It was not, however, a very easy thing to accomplish to stop that chaise at the rate it was being driven.

Dottman, however, was not the man to accept such a state of things as an insurmountable difficulty.

Dashing out from among the trees, he called out in a loud stern voice—

"Drive on, and it is to destruction! You will find an obstruction on the road."

Instantaneously almost, the man who was driving the chaise, pulled the rein, and slackened his pace, and that was all Dottman wanted.

Another instant and he was at the head of the horse.

"Halt!" he cried. "Halt! resistance is as vain as it will be foolish!"

The only reply to this was the discharge of a pistol right, as it seemed, in the face of Dottman.

But that lane was by far too shadowy for any one to take aim with any certainty, and the bullet sped past Dottman's head certainly sufficiently close to be dangerous, but it did not strike him.

"Shot for shot!" said Dottman.

As he spoke he, too, fired, but it was more to let the occupant of the chaise see that he was provided with firearms, than with any intent to kill or wound him.

The bullet from Dottman's pistol, however, did just graze the neck of the man in the chaise, and for the moment gave him an impression that he was dangerously wounded.

It was then that Dottman backed the horse and the chaise in such a way to the side of the road that the wheels sunk deep into a ditch, and the mysterious man with the mask was conquered.

It took Dottman two glances in the darkness of that roadway, before he could make up his mind that it was, indeed, Dora who had arrived on the spot; then, however, he cried out—

"All's well—I have him!"

"Wherefore am I detained?" said the occupant of the chaise. "Wherefore am I stayed on my journey? Once already have I surrendered the gold I had about me, and now again I find myself a prey to robbers and assassins. Help—help! is there no one who will help me?"

"If you don't be quiet," said Dottman, "I will help you to silence in some manner that will be far from agreeable. What has he been about, captain?"

"He has wealth with him!" said Dora. "Gold and jewels by his own account."

"No, no!" cried the stranger, "it is not so."

"I heard you mention them with my own ears," repeated Dora.

"Ah, kind friends—kind friends! I see your mistake now! I am from the east, and spoke but the language of hyperbole. I did say that I had gold and jewels, but the gold and jewels I meant were not those which appeal to the imagination with visions of worldly wealth. I am a physic'an, and what I alluded to were some rare compounds which banish disease, and impart new youth, beauty, and vigour to the human frame. What are gold and jewels in comparison to one draught of the life-giving nectar, which carries with it youth, strength, and loveliness? That is what I alluded to, and I pray you not to deprive me of it."

"Did he go to the cottage?" whispered Dottman to Dora.

"He did."

"Not a likely place at which to get such a charming liquid which he mentions."

"He seeks to deceive us."

"Of course he does."

The stranger in the chaise had caught the latter part of this dialogue, and in almost imploring accents, he replied to it—

"I do not seek to deceive you—indeed, I do not. By a strange secret, I discovered there was hidden in the garden of an old cottage close at hand to this spot, the only vial that the world could boast of, containing the rare and precious compound. I have it with me. It is far more precious than gold or jewels, although I spoke of them in relation to it, as the visible elements of what the world thinks of value. If any one be sick or sorely wounded, or languishing with an unknown disease, one draught of this inspiring essence will restore them—or if youth in all its pride of health and strength would preserve itself, and bid defiance to the hand of time, I have within the one little vial the means of doing so. Ah, is not this vital essence more precious than gold or jewels?"

There was a real or affected rapture about the tones of this man which would have gone far to substantiate his words with minds of more credulous tendency than Dora's and Dottman's.

He went to the length even of producing from the breast of his apparel a small glass bottle, which he held up in the dim night light.

For one moment, then, and for one moment only, there came over the mind of Dora, the idea that if there really were any truth in the statement of the pretended physician, what joy it would be to give Henry a deep draught of the life-bestowing elixir—but she dismissed the delusion almost as quickly as it was formed, although it was with a sigh of regret that she did so.

Dottman then spoke—

"That's all very well," he said, "and since you possess so invaluable a treasure, you can't care much about anything else of value you may have with you."

"I have nothing. I have already been robbed on this road of my purse; but since you have had all this trouble, and wasted time which might have produced to you ample booty from some one else, I will bestow upon you both a draught of the life-giving essence.

"Thank you," said Dottman, "but I never take strange physic, and as we have a partiality for real gold and jewels, instead of imaginary ones in a small bottle, I will see how far your story tallies with the facts.

The stranger uttered a cry of dismay as Dottman, seeing something bulky about the breast of his apparel, suddenly drew from it a canvas bag, the weight of which sufficiently proclaimed its value.

"Lost—lost!" cried the stranger. "The dream has vanished—I am poor again."

"Take a drop of the essence, doctor," said Dottman, "and thank your stars that we let you go on your way in peace; and if I might advise you, I should say do not show yourself again in this part of the country. The air of this lane would be unwholesome to you, and you'll have to try the virtue of your wonderful elixir upon yourself, should you ever again hear the ring of a pistol shot beneath these old trees."

"Yet a moment," said Dora, "do not let him go. We know not who and what he is. Name yourself, man of mystery."

"My name is Surlina," said the stranger, moodily.

Little did Dora know, as she heard that name, how deeply interesting it was likely to become to her.

Little did she suspect that in this man she saw an inhabitant of the house of the Duke of Kingston, and one who, in fact, actually held the Duchess of that name a prisoner in the gloomy mansion adjoining Kingston House.

With the defective information Dora had, Surlina was but a name, as any other might have been; but to the reader it will bear a much more marked significance.

It will be remembered that the subtle Greek had now in his possession the fearfully wounded Van Esling, and it may be easily concluded that from him it was Surlina had obtained intelligence of some hidden treasures of his, the product of his robberies on the high road at the old cottage in the lane.

Had Dora possessed this information, she would have seen in a moment all the motives of Surlina's presence at that spot, and she might well have rejoiced at the combination of circumstances which enabled her, with Dottman's assistance, to get as she had done, so that Surlina could have no positive idea that these persons who attacked him on the road looked upon Van Esling's cottage as their place of destination.

Dottman now paused, with his hand still upon the bridle of the horse, drawing the chaise, as though he were giving Dora time for further inquiries.

But she had nothing more to say or to ask; and indeed, the futility of saying or asking anything of a man whose truthfulness she could be no judge of came strongly upon her.

"Let him go—let him go," she said, "It is enough!"

Dottman extricated the chaise and the horse from the deep ditch on the lane side.

"Go!" he said, "but remember your danger, and let us not meet again."

Surlina seemed to have lapsed into a deep melancholy. His expedition had failed—his treasure, which he had sought to make his own was wrested from him, and with a gloomy sort of fatalism, he appeared now sullenly to admit that the force of circumstances was against him, and he could do nothing; without another word he slowly drove towards the high road, but scarcely had the sound of the carriage wheels began to fade away in the distance, when both Dora and Dottman were startled by a strange cry or shout which came upon the night air.

Henry, too, heard that cry, and he emerged from the shadow of the trees, crying out as he did so,

"Dora—Dora, what sound is that? I never heard so strange a mixture of despair and triumph in my life."

Henry Dacres had properly enough described the sound. It was one compounded of despair and triumph—such a sound, indeed, as some one might have uttered in an extremity of evil fortune at the sudden arrival of some unlooked-for succour.

It came from the lips of Surlina; for as evil fortune for Dora, and Dottman, and Henry Dacres would have it, the moment he reached the head of the lane he came upon a strong body of mounted men, some half-dozen of whom were officers of the police, who had been patrolling a road in the neighbourhood of Brentford, where one of the royal family had been stopped and robbed within the last week.

This strange cry, then, which arose from the lips of Surlina was because he saw, or fancied he saw a prospect of the recovery of the bag of gold and jewels which had been taken from him by Dottman.

The shout of exultation brought the horsemen to a standstill, and then, with eager words, the Greek explained to them that he had been robbed both on the road

and in the lane; and what was much more to the purpose, he offered a hundred pounds reward at once for the recovery of what he called his property, which he hastily described as a canvas bag containing gold and jewels.

The officers and horsemen were no less than twelve in number, and they needed no other inducement to proceed at once upon so welcome an expedition.

Almost, then, before they were aware of their danger, the little party by the trees, consisting of Dora, Henry Dacres, and Dottman, heard the rapid clattering approach of this strong party of mounted men coming down the lane.

Dottman felt all the danger of their situation in a moment.

"I see it all," he said. "We should have kept that fellow to ourselves, but we sent him off into the high road, and he has met those who are after us at once."

"Then all is lost!" said Dora.

"No, no! the cottage! Captain Hawk's cottage is the place! if we can get there we are safe."

"But do you think, indeed, Dottman, that will escape search?"

"Perhaps not—but there is a hiding place in it which I fancy they will not find very easily."

"Then we have not a moment to lose."

"Not one. Forward!"

Five minutes more of inaction would have brought this powerful party of horsemen upon them, but they started at as good a pace as they could command towards Captain Hawk's cottage, and as it was much nearer to them than the commencement of the lane by the high road, they reached it before the horsemen could come up with them.

"We must let the horses go," said Dottman, "otherwise there is no chance for us. Our enemies must not be led to believe that we have taken refuge here. Let us start them at once into the meadows."

This was easily accomplished. The three horses were only too well pleased to leave the lane, and make their way into the fields, where the rich, young spring grass was in abundance.

Dottman then searched in a crevice at the bottom of the wall, where he knew he should find a key, and with it he opened the low door by which Dora had made her entrance, faint and weary, on the back of Starlight.

"Come in—come in," he cried, "at once. We may not have a moment to lose."

"Save her—save Dora," said Henry, "and you have my gratitude for a life. I shall yet be strong and well, and able to recompense you."

"Speak not of it," said Dottman, as he closed the door. "Speak not of it—my life for hers. She shall not fall while I can interpose to save her."

There was a large and heavy wooden bar on the inner side of the door, which Dora was surprised Dottman did not avail himself of in order to secure it more effectually; but when she proposed it he negatived the proposition.

"No," he said, "Let us do nothing to lead to the idea that there is anyone in the house, and they will jump at that conclusion at once if any door is fastened on the inner side."

"You are right—you are right! I did not think of that."

"Hush," said Henry, faintly, "They come!"

With a rush the horseman reached the the spot just outside the garden wall. There was evidently some one in command, who felt no doubt of his authority, for he called out in a loud voice, and the others obeyed him.

"Halt!"

CHAPTER XXVIII.

MINA AWAKES HUNGRY, AND FINDS HER-SELF A BREAKFAST—THE FRIENDLESS CHILD.

IT is time that we should return to the little Mina, who, although not left in circumstances of imminent peril, still seemed to be but a waif on the surface of the earth —waiting upon fortune to furnish her with friends and a home, or in its more evil aspect to destroy at once that young and fair existence in which the happiness of Dora was so deeply merged.

But still the little Mina had made an escape, for even the night stars had began to shed their soft influence upon her, and beneath the dews of heaven, her state was infinitely more gracious than as if she had still remained in that home of crime and evil passions which the mistaken kindness of Jack Stacy had consigned her to.

She might suffer hunger and thirst; but she was free from the contaminating influence of Turnbull and his associates.

She slept sweetly and gently, and the morning stole with its soft light imperceptibly over the face of nature, before the child opened her eyes and gazed around, with but a dim perception of where she was, and a still dimmer recollection of what had passed.

The little creature for a few moments was amused at some chickens, which fearlessly hopped about her and pecked at the the hay and straw with which the ground was literally strewn.

But hunger then began to exert its sway, and the child struggled to its feet, and with low, wailing cries begged as if from the bounty of nature for the food, which seemed to be bestowed without care or thought upon all living things but man.

The day was yet but young. In fact, the usual sounds of the commencement even of the labours of the farmyard had not yet begun to make themselves heard, so that Mina had not the chance of awakening the sympathies of anyone.

But the child was rested; the little creature had slept soundly and without any idea of any particular direction in which to tread her steps, Mina crept round the huge haystack, and then made her way through the rails and gates, and commenced wandering in the open fields.

The lowing of cows at some short distance attracted Mina's attention, but she did not associate those sounds with any idea that there might be persons at hand to aid her.

Hunger grew upon her each moment, and the little Mina looked wistfully at the green hedges, in the hope of seeing some wild fruit which might be a substitute for a more civilised breakfast.

But it was too early in the season even for a blackberry or a nut to show itself, and so Mina sat down close to a stile and wept.

She called sadly upon her mother.

Alas! there was no mother there to hear those soft, gentle cries.

But it happened that this stile, close to which the little Mina sat down, adjoined the field where the cows were at pasture, and it happened that those cows belonged to a farm that was some distance off, and that a dairy maid came trudging across the meadows on a milking expedition.

Mina had been terrified at the hovel where she had been left by the honest sailor, and as the recollection of what had been said to her there came more and more to her mind, it might be said that the only fear this poor child had was of human creatures.

This was sad, indeed!

It had the effect, too, when she saw the dairy maid, who probably would have treated her with all kindness, of making Mina shrink almost into the hedge, with a wish to escape her observation.

But Mina could see that the cows were being milked, and she could see a can of the rich, warm, new milk placed close to the stile, near to which she was.

The dairy maid went to a distant part of

MINA RESCUED FROM THE STORM BY THE MILLER.

the field, and the temptation came strongly upon the child to take a draught from the milk can.

It was easily done!

Mina had but to creep through the two lowest rails of the stile, and she reached the full can.

Mina breakfasted.

That draught of milk was as much as the child required.

Wonderfully refreshed by it, she made her way along the hedgerow; and although she went but slowly, and paused many a time to pluck the spring flowers that bloomed in the hedge-row, still by midday Mina had got far into the country.

DORA.—No. 14.

Then sleep came again over the child and she lay down on a bank of daisies, and without a thought of harm or of danger, fell into deep repose.

The sun was deep in the west when Mina again opened her eyes, and a cold wind was scattering the young buds from the tree tops.

A change had taken place in the weather, and there were clouds flitting across the fair face of the sky of a stormy and portentous aspect.

Mina cried out aloud!

There was no one there to hear her.

The sun set in a sea of fire.

The wind blew more fiercely, and a scattering rain began to descend.

The brief twilight passed away, and little Mina was benighted in the open country, amid fields, trees, lanes, and hedgerows.

What would become of her?

Hunger began again to make itself felt, and the child, with wailing cries, staggered onwards over the now drenched meadows.

Stumbling into hollows, which the rain had converted into pools—scratched and torn by the hedges, and still with cries and sobs calling upon that dear mother, who seemed to be for ever parted from her, Mina wandered the greater part of the night.

It was towards two o'clock in the morning that, faint and weary, the little creature reached what she thought was a haven of safety.

It was the garden gate of a little cottage!

Mina sunk down exhausted, and a dog began to bark loudly.

The child could then hear a strange sound in the air, which filled her with fear.

It was the sound of the sails of a windmill, going freely in the night wind.

"Why, wife, what is that?" asked old John Gray of his companion of forty years, who slept by his side on that night of squall and rain. "What be that?"

"John," said Martha Gray, "thee be always a fancying something. Thy conscience be not at rest, John."

The old man laughed.

"My conscience be at rest, wife, though my hair be white, and I am not so strong, mayhap, as in old times."

"And didst thee think, John," said old Mrs. Gray, with a gush of emotion, "that I meant to charge thee with aught? Gracious Providence! the old mill will be down. What a gust was that!"

The wind roared and howled round the mill and mill cottage, and it would seem impossible that any building, fashioned by mortal hands, could withstand the terrible fury of that hurricane.

Then the old man sprung from his bed, as he exclaimed—

"I do hear it—I do hear it again, wife. It is human!"

"What is human—what is human, John? Don't ye frighten a body so."

"It is a human cry, and at our door. Bide thee still, wife, and I will see who it be!"

A low, wailing cry of distress mingled now with the night storm, and the old miller made what haste he could to dress himself and sally out to see who it could be that was abroad on so inclement a night.

"John! John!" cried his wife, "It may be thieves."

"Then we have nought to lose!"

"But John—but John—"

"Bide thee still, dame—bide thee still! I must see who it be, or as thee said, there will be something on the conscience of John Gray!"

The old miller opened the door of the cottage as wide as it would go—or rather, it was opened so wide for him, for no sooner had he taken down the wooden bar that held it close, and lifted the latch, than the full force of the gale, setting in that direction, dashed it open, and the wind roared and blustered so into the cottage home, that for a few seconds it was impossible either to see or hear anything.

"What is it—what is it, John?" cried the wife.

"Naught," said the miller, "I don't see naught."

"Then shut the door."

"Yes I do. Bless us and save us all!"

Looking at first straight out into the night air, honest John Gray had indeed seen nothing, but when he cast his eyes downwards to the threshold close to his feet, he saw something which, in its outlines, resembled a human form.

It was the little Mina!

The child uttered a wailing cry!

Prompt in his humanity and kindness of heart, the old miller lifted her in his arms, and called out aloud—

"Wife—wife, get up at once—here be a child at the door."

"Gipsies!" cried the good wife.

"Gipsies or not gipsies," cried John Gray, "it shall never be said that my door was closed upon a little one like this."

Dame Gray had enunciated her opinion quickly enough that the child belonged to the gipsies; but that had not at all prevented her from rising, and hastily throwing on some clothes; she struck a light, while her husband, having deposited the little Mina upon a chair, by main force closed the door of the cottage.

In a few moments the faint light of a rush candle shone upon the pale and suffering face of the child and its wet and bedraggled garments. A world of compassionate kindness beamed from the eyes of the good old couple; and at least, for the time, until in the whirl of human events, some change shall take place in her condition, the little Mina is safe!

* * * *

It was about the same hour, and while the same storm was raging, that a figure, drenched with rain, and feeble from fatigue and excitement, crawled up the stone steps of the house adjoining the magnificent mansion of the Duke of Kingston.

This was Surlina, the Greek physician and alchemist.

The reader knows something of the expedition he had been upon to Captain Hawk's cottage in the country, and of the disastrous results of that expedition.

Surlina was now returning, overpowered by fatigue, and the unusual exertion he had undertaken, as well as severely bruised in consequence of an accident which had taken place in regard to the chaise, which at all events should have conveyed him with personal safety to London.

He paused for a moment, and held by the handle of the door to save himself from falling, even as Captain Van Esling had done on the occasion of his crawling from the King's Mews Barracks, despite his fearful wound, to seek succour of the Greek.

It was some few moments before Surlina could gather strength enough to take a key from his pocket, and he uttered low groans as he did so.

"I do not think I am hurt seriously," he said, "but I am fearfully shaken, and I have failed—utterly failed in my expedition, which Van Esling will not believe. No, he will not believe it!"

It was as much as Surlina could do to muster strength sufficient to open the door, and then, as he staggered into the passage, he called aloud upon his daughter.

"Neoni—Neoni—Neoni!"

"I am here, father," cried the Greek girl, as, bearing an antique spirit lamp in her hand, she appeared some distance up the principal staircase.

"I am sick in mind and body, my child. Go to the laboratory and decant from the third bottle on the shelf near to the furnaces one ounce of its contents into a graduated glass.

"Father—father, you are hurt."

"Go, I say—go, or I faint."

"You are wounded?"

"Parley not with me, girl, but do my bidding."

The Greek girl disappeared in a moment. She knew enough of her father's art to be well capable of measuring out the quantity he indicated of the medicament in one of the graduated glasses of the laboratory.

Surlina sat on the stairs until her return, and groaned, probably more from vexation of mind than from real agony of body.

The young Greek girl was not gone above two minutes, and when she returned she brought her father some ruby-coloured liquid in a glass.

"Quick—quick!" he cried, as he heard her light footstep approaching.

"I am here, father."

"My good Neoni!"

"But tell me—oh, tell me, father, what has happened?"

"Soon—soon—I shall be better! This is new life!"

Surlina quaffed off the contents of the glass, and then, in less than half a minute, he rose to his feet, with apparently his usual strength and vigour. Not strength and vigour in the full sense of the terms, but that kind of lithe, cat-like action, which he seemed ordinarily to possess.

"I am better," he said, "and rest will quite restore me. "To bed—to bed, child! your looks are wan, and sleep rests upon your eye-lids."

"And you, father? you are unhurt?"

"All is well—away with you! I will see him yet before I sleep."

The Greek muttered these last words to himself, after Neoni, in obedience to his commands, had left him.

"Yes," he said, "I will see Van Esling before I even take rest. Perhaps he may afford some key to the solution of the mysteries and terrors that have beset me to-night."

There was a small chamber at the back of the house, over the door of which there hung a heavy cloth curtain, so that all sounds from within it were deadened, and rendered inaudible, and there it was that the wounded Van Esling lay in a state, so nearly approaching death, that it was doubtful even if the wondrous art of Surlina could save him from the destroyer.

The moment the Greek removed the curtain from the door, he heard the low moans of the wounded man from within.

"Peace!" he said, as he stepped into the chamber "you but aggravate your condition by these complainings."

The chamber was dimly lighted by a small oil lamp, over which there was a shade of green glass. Van Esling uttered a faint scream of satisfaction when he heard the voice of Surlina.

"Hush!" said the Greek.

"You have come—ah, you have come! You have left me to days—weeks of agony!"

"You measure time strangely! I have been about six hours."

"I measure it by pain."

"I left you sleeping!"

"But I awakened to the torments of the condemned. There is a consuming fire in my breast, which is wending its way gradually towards my heart."

"You are fevered," said Surlina, as he laid his hand on the wrist of his patient. "Be still for a few seconds."

Various bottles and vials were on a small table in the apartment, and by the admixture of some portion of several of these,

Surlina concocted a draught, which he presented to the parched lips of Van Esling.

"Drink!" he said.

The wounded man looked in his face, as though he would search his very soul through his eyes.

The Greek smiled scornfully.

"Captain Van Esling," he said, "you always fancy it is poison I am presenting to you. Be assured you are more useful to me alive than dead. Drink!"

"I will trust you, Surlina."

"As you please."

Van Esling partook of the draught, and the aspect of his countenance quickly changed from feverish anxiety and pain, to calmness and ease.

"You will save me, Surlina?" he said, "you will save me, and I will share with you my wealth. Ah! what fearful inroads has this fearful wound made upon my memory! I had forgotten—"

"Forgotten what?" said the Greek, gloomily.

"That I sent you with precise directions to an old cottage I once occupied, called 'the Shadows,' and from beneath a particular portion of the flooring of which you were to bring a canvass bag, containing gold and jewels of price."

"Lost!" said Surlina.

"No, no—not lost! You cannot—dare not say so. Not lost—not lost!"

The Greek spoke in a cold, impassable tone.

"I found the bag with the gold and jewels, and was returning, when I was assailed by ruffians, and robbed of it."

"Shameless liar!" yelled Van Esling.

A deep bronze flush came over the face of the Greek, and then the blood seemed to retreat to his heart, for he turned ghastly pale.

"Captain Van Esling" he said, "when you are well, you shall answer to me for that word."

"Lost, lost!" cried Van Esling. "No, not lost! I might have known—I should have guessed that this would be the tale. It was sure to be—sure to be! sure—sure to be!"

The powerful opiate which the Greek had given to the wounded man, was creeping over his senses. He closed his eyes, and with a deep sigh, lapsed into a profound sleep.

"Rest!" said Surlina, as he slowly left the room. "Rest, while I think—while I think!"

CHAPTER XXIX.

THE PURSUERS FOILED—DOTTMAN'S DISGUISE—THE MYSTERY OF THE HORSE WITHOUT A RIDER.

WE left Dora and her wounded husband, Henry Dacres, with their tried friend, Dottman, under circumstances both of congratulation and peril.

They might congratulate themselves that they had actually, for the moment, escaped the party of men in the woody lane, close to Captain Hawk's cottage, but still that party, although baffled, did not seem inclined to give up the hope of a capture.

Hence the situation of Dora was one of peril and anxiety.

But Dottman had opened the little door in the ivy covered wall of the garden, and they had passed through it, and were in comparative safety.

The halt of the horsemen without was, however, anxious, and full of danger.

"They disappeared somewhere near to this spot," said one of the horsemen.

"No doubt of that," said another. "There is some sort of house or cottage here."

These expressions were more than sufficient to let Dora feel how great was the danger in which they stood.

But Dottman did not seem in any way to share in her alarm.

"All is well," he said. "They may come into the cottage if they will, and search it, but they will only find me."

"You?" cried Dora.

"Yes, captain. It is only right and proper that they should find some one here, or else they will help themselves to the portable property that is lying about; and it would look much more suspicious after all, I think, if they were to find the cottage empty, than some one apparently taking care of it."

"I agree fully with you, Dottman, but how can that be done?"

"You leave it to me, captain, and it will be done well enough; but first let me place you and Mr. Dacres in a safe position, where they will never think to look for you."

"You said there were hiding places in the house."

"Yes, captain, but this is out of the house."

Dora glanced about her in surprise, for she could see nothing but the little garden, with its solid brick wall on the side facing the lane, and in the other direction, a tall fence of rent, oaken planks, such as is commonly called park paling.

"I can see no hiding place," said Dora, "unless you mean us to take the forlorn chance of ascending one of the trees."

"No, no!"

Just as Dottman spoke, the horsemen, who were without. found the handle of an ancient bell, which hung above the door in the wall, and they pulled at it most vigorously.

"Hilloa!" cried one of them. "Hilloa! who lives here? Open the door or a window, and speak to us. We are officers of the police after highwaymen."

"Are you, indeed?" said Dottman, to himself, in a low tone. I don't think that piece of information will be any inducement for me to open the door to you."

"They will force their way in," said Henry, faintly."

"It will take them some few minutes to do that," replied Dottman, "but there is no occasion for any further delay. Follow me."

With considerable curiosity to know what sort of hiding place there could be in the garden, in which any confidence could be placed, Dora, with Henry Dacres leaning on her arm, followed Dottman.

At first, then, Dora thought that he meant them to get over the park railing into the fields beyond, for he stopped abruptly at it.

"Here!" he said.

"Where? where?"

Dottman placed his hand in a peculiar manner on a portion of the paling and on a concealed hinge; a width of it, through which an ordinary sized person might, with some difficulty, make their way sideways, opened.

Dora was surprised that she did not immediately see the open fields through this opening.

"What can this mean?" she said.

"The paling is double at this part of the garden," replied Dottman, "but it is so completely covered with ivy, that it would be impossible for any one to suspect such a contrivance. Between the two palings, there is just space sufficient for any one to stand upright in, and not the sharpest eyes that were ever in existence could see them."

"I understand it all now," said Dora. "Come, Henry, come! I do think, indeed, we shall have a secure hiding place."

"With you, dear Dora," said Henry, "with you, anywhere."

"Ah," said Dottman, "I see now that there is no time to lose, for one of the officers is climbing over the wall."

Dora and Henry made their way at once into the narrow channel between the two palings, and Dottman closed the door upon them, if it might be called such.

He then turned to the cottage, and made his way into it, closing and fastening the front door after him.

At this moment the officer, who had, by the help of his comrades, clambered up on to the wall, leaped down into the garden.

"Hilloa!" he cried, "is any one here?"

All was still.

"Comrades," he said, "I begin to fancy that the cottage is uninhabited. Come over some of you."

This man did not advance a step. There was a something mysterious and alarming about the very silence of the cottage and the garden to him, which kept him to the spot on which he had leaped from the wall.

He was anxious to be joined by some of his companions before he proceeded further.

The others were not slow in getting over the wall. Three of the officers soon made their way into the garden, while the others remained without to look after the horses, as well as to keep a good watch in the lane.

"Come on," said one, "we will make our way into the house at all events."

"Ah, take care," said he who had first leaped into the garden, "that was just what I was about to do."

"You were a long time about it," growled one of the others.

They all three now made their way to the door of the little abode, and when they found it fast, they hammered at its panels with the handles of their hangers.

But no reply was given to the summons for admission.

"The house is empty," said one.

"No, no."

"How do you know?"

"Look through this crevice in the shutter."

"Ah, yes, yes!"

They looked one after the other through a crevice that was in the shutter over the little latticed window close to the door.

The crevice was narrow, but still it was sufficient to allow them to see into the lower room of the cottage.

To their surprise, for they could not understand how, after all the noise they had made, any one could be sitting so quiet and unconcerned, they saw an old woman with a pair of spectacles, reading by the light of a very miserable rush light.

"Why, there is some one!" said the principal officer.

"An old woman!"

"She's alive, too!"

"Alive? I should think so! Hoi! hoi! hoi!"

The officer banged at the shutter with the hilt of his hanger, but the seeming old woman took no more notice than as if she had been a statue.

The officers did not know what to make of this impassive female, who was so utterly careless or oblivious of what was happening so close to her.

After a brief consultation, they resolved to break in the door.

This they set about with a good will that soon accomplished its object.

They made a rush into the little room, where the seeming old woman was seated reading, and then, and not till then, did she seem at all conscious that they were there.

She looked up from her book, and gave a start of alarm.

"Who the deuce are you?" cried one of the officers, "and what do you mean by giving us all this trouble, when you might have got up at once and opened the door?"

The old woman shook her head.

Lying on the table was a slate with a pencil on it, and to the surprise of the officers, she took it up and wrote something in a large scrawling fashion upon it.

"What does all this mean?" cried the principal officer.

The seeming old woman handed him the slate.

He read the words on it, and then uttered an exclamation of impatience.

Those words were—

"_Deaf as a post._"

"She means that she is deaf as a post," said the officer.

The old woman stared at them all with the same vacant countenance that she had exhibited when they looked at her through the crevice in the shutter.

The officer gathered a long breath, and bawled out—

"Who lives in this cottage?"

The old woman took not the slightest notice.

"Gracious powers!" said the officer, "I have met with deaf people, but never one like this!"

"We shall have to write on the slate what we want to say to her," said another.

"I suppose so—I suppose so! Give it to me."

The officer wrote the following words on the slate—

"Whose cottage is this?"

The old woman wrote in reply—

"Don't know."

The officer then wrote—

"You are an old witch, and do know."

The old woman wrote—

"Go to the deuce."

The officer looked vexed. He wrote again—

"Who lives here?"

The reply was—

"Mr. Jones. Why did you not ask that before? It is not his cottage, but the landlord's, stupid."

The other two officers burst into a laugh, which it was not in human nature to prevent.

The principal officer got angry. He wrote in large characters on the slate—

"We are in pursuit of suspicious characters. Have any such been here?"

The old woman replied to this inquiry by writing still larger the one word—

"Yes."

Then the officer wrote again—

"Who were they? where are they?"

The old woman replied—

"Three men. Why don't you go? You know you are suspicious characters, without troubling me to write it on a slate."

This was the end of the conference. The officers searched through the cottage and garden, but finding no one, they left the place, after abusing the old woman heartily.

Then the seeming ancient dame turned to her book again, and it was not until the officers had fairly left the lane that Dottman, for it was he who had played so well the part of an old deaf woman, cast aside his spectacles, and sprung to his feet.

"Well," he said, "I fancy I have got rid of them. It's a capital thing that Captain Hawk stocked the old bureau up stairs with so many disguises. Those men, I don't think, will come here again in a hurry."

Dottman was cautious, however, before he went to Dora and Henry, and he clambered to the top of the wall close to the door and listened intently for full five minutes.

Then when he felt quite sure that the officers had left the lane, he proceeded to the hiding-place that had been so skilfully contrived in the oaken paling, and opened the concealed doorway.

"All is safe now," he said.

"Thank heaven," replied Dora. "Come, Henry, we can now find shelter and refreshment for you."

"Yes," said Dottman, "and plenty of both. There is some of the finest wine that money can purchase hidden in the cellars of this cottage. Captain Hawk was too fond of himself not to have any comfort that money could procure, and now that we feel quite sure he can never come to interrupt us in possession of the place, we may look upon ourselves as his heirs-at-law."

Henry, leaning on the arm of his Dora, was soon conducted to the cottage, and found more comfortable accommodation even than he had been able to command in the lone house in the Savoy.

Dottman knew the place well, and all its resources, so that he was soon able to place some refreshments before Dora and her husband.

And in truth both he and they were in need of food; and perhaps Dora had not made so pleasant a supper for many a long day as on that, her first evening of taking possession of the deeply shadowed cottage of Captain Hawk, *alias* Captain Van Esling.

With all the care and tenderness which her affectionate regard for him dictated, Dora saw that Henry was comfortably sent to rest, and she had just said good night to Dottman, and was on the first stair of the little flight of steps that led to the upper rooms of the cottage, when she saw Dottman place himself in an attitude of listening, with his hand at his ear.

"What is it?" whispered Dora, for she feared to disturb Henry with any further thought of danger.

"I hear the tramp of horses' feet in the lane."

"Ah!"

"Hush, captain! there it is again."

"I, too, hear it."

"It may be nothing."

"Some chance horseman, perhaps, Dottman, who, from caprice or from knowing that it is his nearest way to some point, may have taken this route."

"It may be so!"

"The sounds came more and more distinctly upon their ears, and then they abruptly paused.

Dora and Dottman looked at each other in silence for a few moments.

The cessation of the sound of the horse's feet took place evidently close to the small door in the garden wall of the cottage. They expected each moment to hear some summons from without.

But none came.

"What does it mean? what can this mean?" said Dora, in tones of alarm.

"I cannot guess," replied Dottman; "but I would advise that the light be extinguished."

"Oh, yes, yes—at once."

Dottman blew out the light.

Then in the darkness they both listened again most intently, but all was still.

"Have we been deceived," said Dora, "by any other sound?"

"No, no, captain."

"I thought not."

"No, it was the sound of horses' feet in the lane, and they stopped at the garden door. I cannot make it out, for there was no concealment about the sounds, and yet all is now as still as possible."

"It is very strange."

"I will creep softly out and see what it is!"

"Be careful, Dottman."

"I will, indeed, for all our sakes, captain!"

Dora watched in the dark, and in a state of the most anxious suspense, while Dottman just opened the door of the cottage sufficiently wide to enable him to slip out into the garden on an expedition of discovery into the mystery of the sounds that at one moment had come so clearly on the night air, and then had so abruptly ceased.

CHAPTER XXX.

THE RETURN OF AN OLD AND VALUED FRIEND — UNEXPECTED TREASURES — IMPORTANT CONSULTATIONS — DORA'S RESOLVE.

WHEN Dottman got fairly into the garden, he bent all his energies to the discovery if anyone was on the other side of the wall.

For the space of about two minutes he kept himself in an attitude of intently listening to catch the slightest sound.

Then he heard a horse cough slightly.

Dottman was still more surprised than before.

The sound came from the other side of the small door in the brick wall exactly, but what kind of horseman could it be who had apparently taken up a position there with a determination to preserve it in perfect silence?

Dottman could not but feel the urgent necessity of fully clearing up this mystery.

There was in the garden a light ladder, which Dottman knew where to lay his hands upon in a moment; and now, as noiseless as he possibly could, and taking a long while about it, so that he should not, by any accidental collision of the ladder with anything, give an alarm to the mysterious horseman without, he slowly placed it against the portion of the wall which was close to the right hand side of the door.

Then Dottman paused for a few moments to listen again.

Yes, he heard something.

The sound of a horse's foot upon the moist earth. as it pawed it twice.

A superstitious feeling began to creep over the heart of Dottman.

It was only his fixed determination that no danger should encounter Dora which he could ward off from her, which enabled him to continue his investigations.

Against any mortal danger he would at any time freely expose his life, but Dottman had a dread of the beings of another world.

Slowly Dottman projected his head over the top of the wall, and with such abundant caution that scarce a hair's breadth beneath his eyes was visible, and even that, surrounded as he was by ivy leaves, might well escape observation, except to some very acute observer.

But if Dottman had been greatly surprised before, and greatly alarmed by the singular behaviour of the supposed horseman in the lane, that alarm and surprise certainly by no means abated upon his glancing over the wall and seeing no one whatever.

But Dottman was looking a little too high. He had been so thoroughly possessed with the idea of a mounted man being there, that he looked no lower for a few moments than where he supposed he would be visible.

Glancing downwards lower after the first shock of surprise and consternation had passed away, Dottman understood everything in a moment.

The mystery was solved.

There was a horse without a rider standing by the little door in the garden wall.

"Bravo!" cried Dottman. "That's it, is it? Why, I suppose it's one of our horses from the meadows. Captain—captain, all is well!"

Dora was on the threshold of the cottage, and she knew by the tone in which Dottman spoke that he had made some discovery which put an end at once to all mystery and alarm.

"What is it," she asked. "What is it?"

"A horse without a rider."

"One of those, probably, that we were riding."

"No doubt of it. I'll let the creature in, for there's plenty of provender in the old stable."

Dottman was quite delighted to find that this singular circumstance, which at first had promised to be so perplexing should end so naturally.

With great alacrity he unfastened the door in the brick wall, upon which the horse stepped into the garden as lightly and easily as though it had been its own proper abode.

Then Dottman uttered an exclamation of surprise, which brought Dora to the spot.

"It is Starlight! it is Starlight!" he cried. "Who would have thought of this?"

"Starlight?" said Dora, as she darted forward and placed her arm round the neck of the gallant steed. "Starlight, say you? Can this be possible?"

"It is, indeed, none other," replied Dottman, "and I was going to say I'd almost have given one of my eyes to see this noble creature once again.

Starlight testified in every possible manner his satisfaction at once more finding himself with old friends, and Dora felt as if she could look upon the presence of the sagacious animal as an indication of the return of happier times.

"Dottman," she said, "I will look upon the voluntary return of this creature to our care as a presage of happy fortune."

"It's the greatest piece of luck," said Dottman, "in the world."

It seemed as if Dottman would never leave off caressing Starlight; but the horse was deeply splashed in mud, and one of the stirrups was gone.

"I shouldn't wonder a bit," said Dottman, "but Starlight has had a tussle with the Duke of Kingston, and thrown him."

"It is probable, indeed."

"You may depend that's it, captain, and the creature, finding itself at liberty, has trotted off here with all the sagacity of finding its way of a dog: These Arabian horses always do."

"See to it well," said Dora. "I will now seek some repose, for, in truth, I need it much."

"Yes; but, captain, one word."

"What is it?"

"Don't you think now, captain, that, as Starlight has come back of his own accord, that it seems as if you ought to go on the road again?"

"I will think of it, Dottman."

"Ah, do! what life is there like life on the road?"

"Were I alone I would not hesitate; but since the possibility has presented itself to me of some accident befalling me which will deprive Henry of all my care, I must confess I have hesitated greatly; but in the morning we will speak more of this, and so once more, good night."

"Good night, captain, and happy slumbers attend you. As for me, I shall set up awhile with Starlight."

Dora fully understood that Dottman meant to be the night watch of that lonely cottage; but although she said nothing, her gratitude for his care and devotion was none the less deeply felt in her heart.

No further alarm occurred during the course of that night, or rather the early morning, which had to pass away before another day brought light and animation to that deeply wooded spot.

Henry was still in a deep sleep when Dora made her way to the lower part of the cottage.

Her intention was to insist upon Dottman taking some repose, but he declared he did not want it, for he said he had had one hour's sleep in the stable, and with an alacrity which sufficiently showed that h

DORA STOPPED BY A HIGHWAYMAN.

felt no fatigue, he set about preparing a breakfast as best he could in the cottage.

"Everything is here, captain," he said, "but milk and butter, and both of those I will procure at a farm house about a quarter of a mile off."

Dora made no objection, and Dottman started on his errand. She could not help, however, feeling a slight pang of alarm when entirely alone in that cottage, with her wounded husband.

The very silence of the spot—that intense kind of stillness which surrounds a house standing by itself, far away from neighbours, was calculated to engender imaginary fears, and Dora was well pleased when she

DORA.—15.

heard Dottman whistling a tune as he returned up the garden path.

He was well provided with what he had gone for, and a very respectable breakfast was soon laid at Captain Hawk's cottage.

"I've been thinking," said Dottman, "that we might as well really see what is in the convass bag which we took from that man in the chaise."

"Indeed, I had quite forgotten it," said Dora.

"Oh, I have it here. For when I came into the cottage immediately after you and Mr. Henry had to get into our secret hiding place, I put it on a small shelf that I know of a little way up the chimney. I always felt certain that Captain Hawk had a secret hiding place for money, but as I had no wish to interfere with his gold, I never took the trouble to find it out."

"Then, doubtless,"s said Dora, "that canvass bag contains some portion of his hoard."

"It is like enough, captain—perhaps the whole of it. He was a careful, cautious fellow, and more than once he intimated to me that he was trying to amass a fortune, with which to go to some foreign country, and live like a prince; but there can't be much of a fortune in the bag we took."

"You forget," said Dora, "that the man in the chaise mentioned jewels as forming part of its contents."

"In good truth he did, captain; and that puts me in mind of another thing. Hawk was always hankering about some jewellers' shops in London, and I have no doubt now that I've put this and that together, that he thought that was the best form he could put his money in, in order to carry it away with him easily. Precious stones are of value all the world over; but here's the bag, we shall soon see what's in it."

Dottman cleared a space upon the table, and in a most effectual manner exhibited the contents of the canvass bag, for he took hold of the two corners, and emptied it entirely.

Some six or eight rouleux, evidently of gold, and tightly wrapped in paper, and sealed, came out of the bag.

Along with them, likewise, came forth about twenty small screwed up pieces of paper, containing substances varying perhaps from the size of a pea up to that of a horse bean.

"This is gold," said Dottman, as he broke open one of the rouleux, and showed guineas closely packed together to the extent of about a hundred.

Dora opened one of the screwed up pieces of paper, and there slipped from it a very brilliant white stone of considerable size.

"A diamond, I'll be bound," said Dottman.

"I am no judge," said Dora, "but it seems to me to have the brilliancy of one."

"There is not a doubt of it."

Dora unscrewed another of the little packets, and there could be no mistake about the fact that it contained a magnificent ruby.

"If these are really the treasures they seem," said Dora, "and if we choose to appropriate them, we are rich, indeed!"

"Why, look ye here, captain," said Dottman, "it's the fortune of war. Your uncle, the Duke of Kingston, keeps from you your estates and title, and this rascal,

Van Esling, whom I knew so long as Captain Hawk, assisted him in every way; besides, it was his hand that inflicted upon Mr. Henry that treacherous wound, which has so nearly cost him his life."

"Indeed, and in truth," replied Dora, "such are the facts."

"Then you need have no scruple about it. It's a war, you see, and these are the spoils of the field."

"I do not think I need scruple to possess myself of any wealth which has been acquired by Captain Van Esling, probably a portion of it is the price paid to him by my uncle, the false Duke, for his enmity to me, and his treachery to Henry."

"You may depend upon that," said Dottman.

"If it be so, it comes from what should be my own, for it is only from my estates that he, who calls himself the Duke of Kingston, can obtain a revenue."

"That's it—that's it! only there's one pity about it."

"What is that?"

"You won't see the necessity of going upon the road."

Dora was saved a reply to this remark of Dottman's by a slight knocking in the chamber above, which let them know that Henry was awake.

She found him wonderfully refreshed from his long sleep, and decidedly better and stronger than she had known him since his wound. The excitement that he had undergone, and the exercise appeared to have been beneficial to him. Indeed, he was so much stronger, that Dora felt she could enter into a consultation with him in regard to the singular present posture of their affairs.

Henry, after some consideration, was decidedly of opinion that they ought to keep the cottage for a short time, and then that it would not be difficult, with the ample means at their command, to reside in London, and take some steps for prosecuring Dora's claim to the peerage, and likewise, for annuling and setting aside the criminal charge which had been brought against her by the villanous Duke.

Deep anxiety, too, for the recovery of the little Mina, if, indeed, the flood on the Thames had spared her, mingled with this consultation.

"It will be necessary, dear Dora," said Henry, "that we take into our pay some skilful and honest advocate, who is learned in the law, and who will not be biased by any bribes that may be offered to him by your uncle."

"I know not where to find such an one, Henry. We may light upon the honesty without the skill, or the skill without the honesty. We have suffered so much, that my faith in human nature is shaken; and since we have lost by death, the dear friend upon whom we knew that we could rely, Dr. Langford, I know not who to apply to."

"We will go to some one so eminent, Dora, that character shall be to him of more importance in the path of preferment which his profession opens to him, than any bribes the false Duke of Kingston may offer."

"It shall be done, Henry—it shall be done! And now let us hope that a fairer future is opening before us."

"Dora, you are sure of one thing," said Henry, "tell me that you are sure of that one thing."

"What is it?" asked Dora, with some anxiety.

"Are you certain that the villain, Van Esling, is no more?"

"I am, indeed. No mortal could survive such a wound; and the inquiry Dottman instituted met with the reply that he was dead."

"That removes a load from my heart, while I thus continue in a state of weakness and depression. Were I quite well and able to wield a sword, the thought of whether he were alive or dead would not harrass me, but as it is, I am glad to hear that an enemy so treacherous and unscrupulous is not in the field against us."

The day passed in perfect serenity, and Dora, in looking over some of the contents of numerous packages and boxes which were in the cottage, found quantities of clothing of all sorts and degrees, so that she could find no difficulty, let her decide upon what disguise she might, in proceeding to London without hazard of recognition.

Dora's idea was to make two errands to the metropolis.

The one was to have an interview with some eminent lawyer, and the other was to endeavour to discover, past a doubt, if the seeming precious stones which had been found in the canvass bag were a reality.

By taking one of them with her, and attempting its sale, Dora felt that she should set that question at rest; and with the concurrence of Henry, she resolved to go to London on the second morning of their residence at Captain Hawk's cottage.

CHAPTER XXXI.

PEACE AND SERENITY AT THE COTTAGE—
DORA'S EXPEDITION TO LONDON—AN
ADVENTURE ON THE HIGHWAY, AND
NEWS OF MINA.

DORA was pleased to see, or to fancy she saw, that each hour Henry Dacres remained in peace and serenity at the cottage amid the trees, which had been for so long in the possession of one of their most deadly foes, his health and strength materially mended.

This was, indeed, a consolation to Dora; and when she came to consider the whole of the circumstances that now surrounded her, she could not but feel that she had much to be thankful for.

Her enemies, it is true, had succeeded so far against her that she and the husband she loved so truly were fugitives; but still they had life, youth, and hope left them.

And more than all, the treacherous attempt which had been made against the life of Henry had failed, and there was, indeed, every prospect, not only that he would live, but soon be a protector, as well as a dear companion to Dora.

It was fit that Dora should have some glimpses of sunshine in the midst of all the troubles and difficulties which beset her.

The return of the beautiful and docile Arabian steed, Starlight, seemed to Dora like an assurance of good fortune in the time to come, and without being superstitious, she could not help giving in her thoughts a prominence to that fancy, which it hardly deserved.

It was, then, on the second morning after the arrival at Captain Hawk's cottage that Dora determined to go to London on her double errand.

First, to consult some one in the town concerning the circumstances that surrounded them.

Secondly, to test the real value of one of the seeming jewels that had been taken from Surlina.

Among the costumes at the cottage was one which Dora thought she would be most secure in from recognition, and it was one, likewise, which would not attract any attention in the street.

A plain, dark brown suit of clothes, without any ornament or display about it whatever, made up this complete disguise; and Dora's only difficulty, for a time, was about her hair—that was likely to be rebellious, and to excite some observation.

A further search, however, among the properties of Captain Hawk in the cottage, enabled her to find some exquisitely made wigs, which would defy any ordinary observation; and one of those put an end to all the difficulty about her hair, which she fastened up as flatly as possibly, and then covered with the wig.

The costume which Dora wore, was so purely peaceable, that there was no possible excuse for wearing a sword with it, but there was no difficulty in Dora arming herself with pistols.

Henry Dacres did not absolutely oppose

this expedition to London, although he was somewhat averse to it, from the fact that it might expose Dora to danger.

He felt that while she was abroad he would suffer many anxieties on her account.

Indeed, in his own mind, those anxieties were so great, that it is possible enough, if he had given free utterance to them, Dora would not have been able to persuade herself to leave him.

But Henry was so fearful of adding in any way to Dora's many anxieties, that he would not say one word that was likely to do so.

And Dora, then, equipped herself for the journey by about ten o'clock in the morning.

Dottman brought out Starlight for Dora's use, and somewhat to the surprise of Dora, he brought out of the stable of the cottage another horse ready for his own mounting.

"Why, how is this, Dottman?" said Dora. "I thought that you had set free the horses?"

"So I had, captain. This is another."

"Another?"

"Oh, yes. I thought that as last night was a little cloudy, I might as well turn out, and see what good fortune was in store for me."

Dora shook her head.

"It was running a risk, Dottman, and probably a needless one, for I have no doubt, in my own mind, that the jewels in the canvass bag are real ones, and if so, the value of a horse is of no moment."

"That's all very true, captain; but on the road that goes over Wormholt Scrubs, I met a man riding this horse, and so—and so—"

"You took it?"

"I politely borrowed it of him."

Dora smiled.

"Ride a few paces on to the road," she said, "and take Starlight by the bridle, I will soon join you."

Dora hurried again into the cottage, to take an affectionate farewell of Henry.

"My own dear Dora," he said, as he clasped her to his heart, "be careful of your safety, for my sake."

"Yes, Henry, for your dear sake, I will. Fear nothing—I will seek no danger, and well disguised as I am, it is not at all likely to seek me."

"I hope not—from my heart, my Dora, I hope not."

Dora could not trust herself to say much to Henry on any occasion when she was leaving him, for then her heart was always full.

She managed to let him, however, see that she left the cottage with a smile.

It was by no means her intention to leave Henry alone for any length of time in that lonely cottage; she only meant to take Dottman a three miles' gallop on the road towards London with her, and then he was to take back Starlight, and she, Dora, intended to go on on foot, until she reached the village of Shepherd's Bush, from which she could, no doubt, get some conveyance to London.

But Dottman was of a different opinion in this respect from Dora.

When she joined him on the road and had mounted Starlight, he, Dottman, prepared himself with a speech of remonstrance.

"Look you here, Captain," he said, "I for one should feel a great deal better satisfied if you to take Starlight with you to London."

"Indeed, Dottman!"

"Yes. There are plenty of quiet inn yards, when you might put him up, you see, Captain, while you took a hackney coach and went on the business that takes you to London; and then, only think if you should be hard pressed by pursuit, what a grand thing it would be."

"A grand thing to be pursued, Dottman?"

"No, Captain—oh, no! But if you should be pursued, it would be a capital thing to be able to jump upon the back of Starlight, and laugh at all your foes."

"It would, indeed!"

"There, you see, Captain," added Dottman, with animation "I advise that you ride right into London."

"I will, Dottman!"

"Then my mind is much easier than it would be, and I will go back at once to Mr. Dacres, and tell him that he need have no fears for your safety."

"Do so—do so. Farewell!"

"Good morning, Captain, is all I will say, because I hope you will not be many hours gone."

"As few as possible," replied Dora.

Dottman then trotted back to the cottage, and Dora took her road onwards to London.

She had not ridden very far when she saw a mounted man some short distance before her.

Whether to keep some distance in the rear by riding slower, or to give Starlight an impulse to speed and so pass the chance passenger, Dora debated with herself, but she at length determined upon the latter course, since the former involved delay.

Still she would not, by any show of hurry, awaken suspicions in the mind of the horseman.

Dora patted Starlight on the neck, and the creature got into one of those trots which were almost equal to another horse's gallop.

"Hilloa!" cried the Stranger, as Dora was passing him. "Hilloa, sir, are you inclined for a match on the road, for if so, I am willing."

Dora made no reply to these words, but the stranger put his horse to a gallop, and as Dora had no wish for a race into London, she drew rein, and Starlight subsided into a more ordinary pace.

The stranger was by her side in a moment.

"That is a capital bit of horseflesh," he said, "that you are giving an airing to this morning!"

"Sir," said Dora, "I never make casual acquaintance on the road."

"Oh!"

"Good morning, sir!"

Dora hoped that so curt a reception to his advances would put the stranger on his pride a little, and he would leave her alone.

In this she was mistaken.

The stranger burst into a laugh, and then Dora saw him rise in his stirrup and look carefully about him on all sides.

"Alone," he said.

Dora paused a moment in surprise at these manœuvres, but she was not left for long in a state of suspense as regarded what they meant.

The road was not a very wide one, and the stranger suddenly and adroitly moved his horse in front of Starlight, and cried out—

"Now, young gentleman, your money or your life, or both, if you are inclined to be obstinate."

"A highwayman!" cried Dora.

"Just so—at your service, and at the service of any one who comes down this road with a full purse."

"And do you imagine," added Dora, "that I am going to allow myself to be robbed in the open face of day in this cool fashion?"

"I do!"

"You are mistaken, sir!"

"Very good. You will have it. Now what say you?"

The highwayman drew a pistol from his saddle and pointed it full in Dora's face.

"And so," she said, "for the sake of a few guineas that I may or may not have about me, you would commit a murder?"

"Come, be quick! I don't ride on the road to hold an argument with anyone I meet. We are alone!"

"Not quite," said Dora, as she looked past the head of the highwayman.

"Ah! who is it?" he cried.

Dora gave Starlight a smart pat upon the neck, which she knew would start him at speed, and the Arabian darted past the other horse like a flash of light.

"No," roared the highwayman, "you don't escape me that way."

He fired his pistol after Dora as he spoke.

By this time, however, Dora herself had got one of the pistols which Dottman had carefully loaded for her in her hand, and so soon as she heard the report of the highwayman's pistol, she turned slightly in her saddle fired at him.

He had missed her, but the shot that she had fired was more fortunate.

The highwayman uttered a cry of pain.

"Winged—winged!" he shouted. "Woa —woa, horse, woa! no luck to-day."

Dora checked Starlight, and looked back.

She saw that the highwayman's horse was plunging and kicking, and that the rider was evidently unable to control it.

Compassion urged Dora to return.

She did so, and caught the horse by the bridle, as she said—

"You have brought a hurt upon yourself. I cannot really pity you."

"Ah, I suppose so," he replied. "My arm is broken."

"Are you sure!"

"Yes, only too sure. I'm a fool for my pains. Go on, young gentleman, and leave me to get away as best I can. Turnbull will laugh at me now."

"Turnbull, did you say?"

"Yes; but you cannot know him. He is a pal of mine."

"Was he or is he a man in the service of the Duke of Kingston."

"To be sure he was."

"But—but—he was killed."

"Not he. He was shot by Dora Dacres, who escaped hanging for setting fire to the Duke of Kingston's house some time ago; but he only fell into the Thames, and was picked up by a waterman, and is now at Mother Carey's."

"Where is that?"

"Down by the river side. He wished me bad luck when I came away from the crib, because I wouldn't let any of the gang fire after the child."

"The child! what child?"

"Oh, a little girl who was saved by a sailor from the flood on the river."

Dora uttered now a half scream of surprise and joy.

"Saved—saved!" she exclaimed. "Did you say saved?"

"To be sure I did!"

"How? when? tell me all!"

"I am rather—faint."

"No, no, you must not—shall not faint. Tell me all. You know about that child!"

Dora seized the reins of the horse, and

at the moment she did so several mounted men came at a good trot down the road from London.

"Speak!" said Dora. "Tell me all—all!"

"You have nabbed me now!"

"What do you mean?"

"You will give me up to those men. It is a patrol of officers which, no doubt, you know as well as I do, for I begin to think you were looking for me. Ned Fellowes's career is over now."

"No, no!"

"No, say you? oh, yes, they come!"

"But I will not give you up to them."

"You—you will not?"

"Certainly not. If you can conceal the appearance of having received a hurt, and ride along with me, I will not say a word to them."

"But—but—"

"Trust me—I mean what I say."

Tears for a moment started to the eyes of the highwayman, and he said softly,—

"I have but one arm and hand that I can use, so I cannot ask you to shake hands with me, unless I drop the bridle of my horse."

"Do not attempt it. Come on."

The party of horsemen rapidly approached, and Dora, with the young highwayman by her side, who had so recently attempted her life, proceeded along the road at a walk.

Ned Fellowes was very pale, but Dora made a few gestures as though she was conversing with him on the character of the surrounding scenery.

He did not or could not speak.

"Gentlemen," said one of the patrol of officers, "did you see anyone on the road as you came along?"

"Yes," replied Dora.

"Mounted or on foot?"

"A mounted man. He does not appear to us to be a good character, for he fired a pistol shot at me.

"Ah, indeed!"

"Yes, and I one at him in return."

"Did you hit him, sir?"

"I fancy I did."

"Come on, my comrades," cried the officer, as he spurred past Dora and Ned Fellows. "If he has had a bullet he cannot be very far off."

Dora and the highwayman were quite alone again on the road.

"You saved me," said Ned Fellowes.

"It was easy."

"Yes, easy enough, perhaps, to do, but not easy to make up your mind to do."

"That was easy likewise, and all I want of you in return is to give me the full particulars about the child you spoke of as having been saved from the flood on the Thames."

"That I will do with all my heart. You see, sir, we were about a dozen of us at Mother Carey's, which is a family haunt by the river side not far from Gravesend, and Turnbull was there, where, indeed, he has been ever since his hurt, for there is a bullet in his breast!"

"Will he die?"

"The surgeon says no, provided he lives about another week or so."

"Go on—go on. Tell me all."

"Well, while we were all enjoying ourselves a little, there comes a tap at the door, and a young fellow, a sailor, peeps in, with a little girl in his arms, and says that he is off to sea, and offers some guineas to Mother Carey if she will take care of the little one."

"Yes, yes!"

"Well, at sight of the guineas Mother Carey says yes at once; but when the sailor was gone she makes a laugh of it, and says that the river will be the best place for the little one to go back to."

"Oh, Heaven!"

"Why—why, you—you—"

"No! no!" said Dora.

She clasped both her hands over her face, for she felt that she had, in the agitation of the moment, allowed herself to speak too much in her natural tones to leave much doubt about what she was on the mind of her companion, the highwayman.

"Make no remarks about me," she then said, "and ask no questions. I have done you a service. Let that awaken your gratitude and your desire to oblige me."

Ned Fellowes bowed his head, and at once added—

"Turnbull knew the child, and said it was worth thousands of pounds to some duke."

"Ah, yes! but—"

"Hear me out. The child took fright and ran out of the crib, and I never saw her more."

"Alas! alas!"

Ned Fellowes at this moment sunk down almost on to the neck of his horse, for the pain at his arm made him sick and faint.

"Hold up!" said Dora, "Take courage. We shall soon be in London, where I will get you assistance."

"No, no," he said, faintly. "There—there—that little inn—they know me—the Hay Rick. There—there!"

Dora looked in the direction he indicated, and she saw, some distance down a lane, the swinging sign of a little inn.

"Are you sure," she said, "you can be well treated there?"

"I am!"

"And have you any money?"

"Oh, yes, yes! ride on, and let me go down the lane. The horse will take me safely. Thank you again and again. You might have given me up, and then, before my arm got well, I should have swung at Tyburn."

"Good bye, then," said Dora. "We may meet again, and then you will still remember me."

"I will—I will!"

The highwayman's horse took him down the lane, and Dora galloped on towards London.

CHAPTER XXXII.

DORA DISPOSES OF A DIAMOND—A FIRST LOVE AND ITS MANIFESTATIONS—A MEETING WITH AN ENEMY IN THE OLD TEMPLE.

How strange—how heart-agonising it was to poor Dora that whenever she heard any news of the little Mina, it was but a something that still baffled pursuit.

Once she had seen her in the boat on the Thames, and then had come that fearful flood which had swept her from sight and to apparent death.

Now she had heard of her again, but to be told that she was yet in life on the wide world's surface, without there being added to the intelligence a particle of information where to look for her.

But still Dora resolved that so soon as she had accomplished her errand to London, she would seek out the cabin by the river side, that had been mentioned by the highwayman, and from that endeavour to trace the footsteps of her child.

Starlight carried Dora at good speed to the metropolis, and she took the advice which had been given to her by Dottman, namely, to put up the Arabian steed at some quiet stables, where, no doubt, it would be in perfect safety until she should seek it again.

About the neighbourhood at the top of the Oxford Road, Dora had no difficulty in finding a place of the kind, and she was well pleased to leave Starlight in the charge of an old man who kept a small stable and cow house not far from the corner of the Edgeware Road.

Dora then on foot made her way down the Oxford Road towards Bond Street, which was then the only street of the West end of London which could boast of any jewellers' shops of importance.

Of course it was only in some one of the best of the jewellers establishments in London that Dora could have any hope of fair treatment in the disposal of the diamonds she had brought to London with her.

She was well pleased to notice that she was sufficiently well disguised, that no one turned to take a second glance at her.

And so Dora had made her way about half way down Bond Street before she saw a jeweller's shop, the aspect of which pleased her.

She entered the shop at once.

A respectable gray-headed old man was behind the counter, and to him Dora spoke as she took the diamond out of her pocket and handed it across the counter for his inspection.

"I wish to dispose of this jewel," said Dora.

The old man bowed, and took it in his hand, and then cast a rapid glance at Dora.

Her appearance was so thoroughly respectable, that if at the moment the jeweller had a suspicion that the rare gem he held in his hand had not been come by honestly, he must have dismissed it at once.

"A beautiful diamond!" he said.

Dora was glad to hear this declaration of the genuine character of the gem volunteered, without the awkwardness of a question on her part.

"It is so," she replied.

"And you wish to sell it, sir?"

"I do!"

"May I ask what value you put upon it?"

Dora was now completely at fault, for she had no idea of what might be the real market price of a diamond of such a size, although, of course, she was aware it should be considerable.

"I have hardly made up my mind," she said, "what price to put upon it."

"That will be necessary, however," said the old jeweller, drily, as he held the diamond in various lights, in order to judge of its quality.

"Very well," added Dora, "will you weigh it?"

She had heard that precious stones were of value according to weight.

"And is it possible," said the jeweller, "that you have a diamond of this character, and do not know its weight?"

"Sir," said Dora, "I came into your shop to sell a diamond, and not to answer questions. If you are not disposed to purchase, I will go elsewhere."

"Oh, no, no! by no means! I am disposed to purchase, I assure you. There is a nobleman who wishes to buy some diamonds, and who, in fact, has given me a commission to procure some for him, and if you will leave this I will show it to him."

"No, no!"

"You decline!"

"I do, most assuredly."

"Well, but—but—"

"Sir, I am desirous of selling this jewel. Will you buy it? yea or nay!"

"My good young man, you are terribly hasty. Of course I will buy it. Allow me to consult my partner."

"Very well!"

The old jeweller rung a bell, and another old man in a few second made his appearance in the shop, and they both retired, as they thought, out of earshot, and whispered together about the diamond.

Dora, however, was particularly acute of hearing, and she detected the word "five hundred pounds."

If that were so, those words gave her a valuable hint, which she resolved to act upon.

The old man advanced again to the counter.

"There's a slight flaw in the jewel," he said, "but it is, of course, of value, although that detracts from it. What do you ask for it?"

"Six hundred guineas," said Dora.

"Oh, impossible. Dear, dear! six hundred? oh, oh!"

"Very well. What do you offer?"

"Two hundred."

"No!"

"Yes," said the partner, who had been summoned to the consultation, "Yes, I am sure you will be reasonable, and take two hundred in ready money."

There was at this moment the rattle and dash of a carriage, as it stopped at the jeweller's door, and the first old man that Dora had seen and spoken to in the shop called out with great excitement of manner—

"That is his grace, the Duke!"

"What Duke?" said Dora.

"The Duke of Kingston!"

Dora turned pale and faint for a moment; but then, as she felt all the necessity of presence of mind, unless she would certainly destroy herself, she rallied and recovered, at least, an appearance of composure.

The steps of the carriage were let down, and the false Duke of Kingston, looking pale and out of health, made his way into the shop.

The two old men, who were relations as well as partners in the business, bowed down to the very floor before the Duke.

"I have called," said the Duke of Kingston, "to say that I will very much enlarge my order for precious stones. If you can convert twenty thousand pounds for me into jewels that I may be assured will be of value in any part of Europe, I will take them."

"Yor grace honours us very much," said one of the jewellers; and as he bowed low to the Duke of Kingston, his partner took the opportunity of whispering to Dora.

"Follow me, sir, if you please. We will attend to you in a few moments."

Dora hesitated a moment; and, had she consulted her own inclination, she would gladly have left that shop there and then, but she feared to draw more attention to herself than the one cold, supercilious stare which the Duke had cast upon her.

When those few moments, however, had passed away, one of the shopkeepers came to her.

"My good sir," he said, "hand me your diamond to show to the Duke of Kingston. Who knows but that illustrious nobleman will buy it at once?"

"I will not take less than five hundred pounds," said Dora.

"Well, well! we will see what we can do!"

Dora let him have the diamond, but she repented that she had been so confiding the next moment.

She heard the sound of voices in the shop, and then the door opened and closed, and the rattle of carriage wheels, which was no doubt the Duke of Kingston's carriage—that carriage which ought to have been Dora's, left the spot.

Then one of the old men came into the room in which Dora was staying.

"Well," said Dora, "where is the diamond?"

"My partner," said the old man, "and myself have not the smallest doubt but that you have stolen that diamond, and he has accordingly gone for an officer."

"Ah!" cried Dora, "what treachery!"

"But," added the jeweller, "I am but an old man, and you are a young one, and I am afraid that if you were to push me aside, and run away, and never again show your face in Bond Street, I could not help it!"

Dora felt a great sensation of relief at these words, for they at once opened her eyes to the whole transaction.

The object was simply to frighten her away, and to appropriate the jewel on the chance that she had come by it in some way that would make it inconvenient to raise a public clamour on the subject.

Full of danger as her position was, Dora nerved herself to a courageous course.

"No," she said, "I will not please you by flight. It is you and your precious partner who are robbers, and who would fain come by jewels in anything but an honest fashion."

DORA PARTING WITH THE YOUNG JEWESS.

"I protest—I protest—"

"Peace, sir! Give me the diamond, or the money!"

"Help, Abraham! help!"

The other old man, who, far from going for an officer of police, had been hiding in the shop, now made a rush into the room, and forgetting all the art with which he ordinarily concealed his Jewish tones, he called out—

"Kill him! kill him, Aaron! kill him! Slay the Egyptian!"

Dora darted round a table that was in the room, and made her way into the shop.

The two Jews thought that she would

DORA.—16

only be too glad now to make an escape; but such was far from Dora's intention.

True, she made her way to the shop door, but it was only to fasten it on the inside, which she found it easy to do, for it was loaded with bolts, bars, and locks.

Then Dora turned, and faced the two Jews—she took from a breast pocket one of those pistols which Dottman had so carefully loaded for her, and presented it full at them.

"Now," she said, "my diamond or the price of it."

"Murder!" cried one of the Jews.

"It's a highwayman!" groaned the other.

"Who or what I am," said Dora "is nothing to either of you; but you will find that, be I what I may, I am not one to allow myself to be thus coolly and audaciously robbed by any one."

"My good young man!"

"Sweet young sir!"

"Peace! give me the diamond! I will not deal with men like you."

"We would do so with pleasure, dear, good young sir, but the Duke of Kingston has taken it away with him to get it valued."

"The money, then."

"Two hundred?"

"No—five hundred guineas, and not one farthing less."

Both the Jews groaned.

"Quick!" said Dora, "I am impatient."

She darted forward, and caught one of the Jews by the arm, as she added—

"At least I will take one life."

"No, no—holy Abraham, no! Pay him —pay him, Aaron, and let the wretch go!"

"There! there!" groaned the partner, as he placed before Dora on the counter some bank notes. "There is your money, and if you have any more diamonds to sell, don't let this little past disagreement spoil trade."

"You must be strange people, indeed," said Dora, "if you fancy for a moment that I will ever again cross your threshold; but I will take some precaution against your malice. This is a cupboard, I see."

Dora opened a door in the shop, and saw that it revealed a deep cupboard full of shelves, on which was plate.

"He is going to rob us," said one of the old men.

"No—but I do not choose that you should, either of you, have the power to raise a hue and cry after me when I leave the shop, so I will trouble you both to get into this cupboard."

"We are ruined men!"

"And," added Dora, "I will turn the key on you."

"Murder! help!"

At this moment there came the sound of horses feet and carriage wheels again from the street.

The jeweller had spoken perfectly truly concerning the destination of the diamond. The Duke of Kingston had been desirous of purchasing it, but had insisted upon getting it valued by some other jeweller.

He was now returning at that critical moment when Dora was about disposing of the two old jewellers so effectually.

It was rather from a natural impulse to avoid actually encountering the Duke of Kingston than from any calculation of what she was about, that induced Dora to shrink back from the shop into that small apartment again, where she had before waited the leisure of the Duke.

But Dora was surprised now to find that she was not alone in that apartment.

A young girl, in a very fanciful half oriental costume, occupied it; and when Dora closed the door which communicated with the shop, this young girl seemed, at first, seized with terror, and shrunk back as if to make her escape, but as she did so, she kept her eyes fixed upon Dora, and the result of that earnest gaze seemed to be an entire alteration in her feelings and sentiments.

The look of surprise and alarm gave way to one of pleasure and confidence, and well, indeed, might these feelings be engendered in any one who was prepared to take a romantic view of the beautiful and the interesting, for plainly as she was attired, there was yet a charming grace about Dora, and an exquisite beauty of expression, which no human eyes could look upon with indifference.

Dora was fair, and had the delicate complexion of the northern regions, while this young girl, with her raven hair, and dark flashing eyes, presented a true type of the daughters of the ancient people whose claim to beauty is considerable still in those cases where regularity of features is to be met with.

It was evident that this young Jewess had led a secluded life of orientalism, and that none of the conventionalities of modern existence had any weight with her.

She spoke what she thought as freely as those thoughts came to her mind.

"Ah," she said, "I could not see you through the blinds, but now my eyes tell me you are beautiful. I thought I heard a sound of strife, and calls for help, but I see you, and I am reassured and happy.

Dora's first impression certainly was that there must be something the matter with the wits of this young creature, who addressed a perfect stranger in such extraordinary language.

"There was some disagreement," said Dora, "and I am exceedingly anxious to leave this place. Would it be possible to do so without passing through the shop?"

"Yes—but you will not leave me now, for if you stay here, I will love you, and none but you."

Dora knew not what to answer, and during the slight pause that ensued, she heard the Duke of Kingston's voice from the shop.

"I will stand here," he said. "I have my sword, and no one shall pass out without my permission."

"A thousand thanks, your grace," said one of the jewellers. "The villain happened to come into the shop just before your grace, and hearing some talk about a diamond, pretended it was his, and being young and strong, while we are but old and feeble, he has robbed us of a large sum in bank notes, and would, indeed, have escaped but that your grace reached the door at a happy moment.

"And are you sure that he is in the house?" said the Duke?"

"Quite, your grace. He fled into the back apartment, yonder."

"Then I will assist you so far that he shall not escape."

"What does that mean?" said the young girl to Dora.

"It means that I am in danger."

"You in danger?"

"Yes—and yet I assure you, upon my sacred word, I have done nothing that could provoke it, and am only sought to be injured by the two old men who keep this shop."

"My uncles!"

"Are they, indeed, your uncles?"

"Oh, yes—and money is their idol. They think of nothing—dream of nothing—talk of nothing but money, and yet they have so much that, were they to live to the age of one of our patriarchs, they could not spend it."

"What is your name?"

"Zillah."

"Then, Zillah, if you really love me, you will contrive that I leave this place without the necessity of passing through the shop."

"If I really love you?" exclaimed Zillah. "How can I love any one but you? I shall think of you by day, and dream of you by night; and if you will promise to come to me again, I will show you how to leave the house."

"I will," said Dora. "But it is indiscreet of you, Zillah, to tell a stranger that you love him."

"Oh, yes, it would be to any other stranger; but to you, whom I really love, it cannot be so."

These words were spoken with such an air of simplicity and candour that it was evident the young girl thought them very conclusive in the way of argument, and Dora felt that it was of no use contending the matter.

Zillah was as good as her word, for she now made her way to a French window, and opening it, disclosed a short flight of stone steps which led into what, many years before, had possibly been a garden.

"There is a door," she said, "in yonder wall, of which this is the key. It will lead you into some place where, I believe, horses are kept, for I have heard the sounds of their presence in the still hours of the night. You can, from thence, walk out into the open street. How strange it must be to walk in the streets!"

"Can it be possible," said Dora, "that you have never done so?"

"Never! One of my uncles brought me from Cairo two years ago, and I never go out of this house, except in a coach, to a house and garden somewhere out of the city, which belongs to our people."

"I thank you with all my heart," said Dora, as she stepped out of the room on to the steps. "I have no doubt you have saved me from a great danger, and I shall always think of you with affection."

"And you will come to me again?"

"I will try."

"Nay, you must promise."

"I promise, then."

"And you must tell me a name I must call you when I pray for you."

Dora had her own name on her lips, and only just saved herself from the pronunciation of it; she substituted, then, her husband's name for Dora, saying—

"Think of me as Henry."

"That is your name?"

"Yes, that is the name which I would have you pray for."

"I will do so, and I will put that name in my prayers instead of my two uncles, since you say they have tried to be unkind and unjust towards you. Farewell, dear Henry, you will think of me?"

"Often, Zillah—often! and knowing you now as I do, I feel that the greatest kindness I can do you is to ask you one favour."

"What is that?"

"It is, that if ever you see any other stranger, whose appearance may strike your fancy, you will, for my sake, use no words of affection towards him such as you have used towards me."

"How can I, when I love no one but you?"

"Keep that feeling, then, dear Zillah, as a safe-guard over your ingenuous simplicity, and so, farewell."

The young Jewess maiden had handed to Dora a key, which readily opened a door in a wall at the back of the house—Dora then found herself in a stable yard, with a large carriage entrance into a street running at right angles from Bond Street.

It was Dora's object now, to place as great a distance as possible between herself and that jeweller's shop, where she had encountered so much peril, and where she could not but reflect with regret she had awakened, in her male costume, a flame of love which probably would never be extinguished in the heart of the young Jewess.

But Dora had been successful so far in one part of her mission to London, that she had sold the diamond, and probably had a much fairer price for it than under ordinary circumstances she might have expected.

The next object was one invested with some hazards, since it was to make a confidance—but she could not believe that any professional man of standing would betray a client who came to him with ample means, and with right on her side.

During the anxious career of Dora, since the death of her father, she had found more than once that chance directed her into better channels than the most laborious calculations could possibly have opened to her, and in this case, most especially of seeking out a professional man to interest in the singular circumstances connected with the Kingston peerage, Dora made up her mind to trust to that Providence which, as yet, had not deserted her.

She knew that the Temple, in Fleet Street was a resort and residence of persons in the law, and with but a very ill-defined notion of the difference between counsel and attorneys, Dora made her way to that legal colony, with a resolve to be attracted by a name, rather than make any inquiries whatever in the way of recommendation.

But Dora had no intention of proclaiming who and what she really was—she merely meant to put a supposititious case to some one learned in the law.

With this intention, Dora paced up and down some of the narrow courts and thoroughfares of the ancient abode of the Knights Templars; but as name after name upon the various door posts met her gaze, she became more and more critical with respect to them.

There was a very narrow court, so dark and dismal that Dora had serious doubts of whether it was a thoroughfare or not. She made her way down it very slowly, and paused once or twice with the hope of seeing if it really led anywhere, but it seemed to increase in darkness and in gloom, so that even if she could leave it at its further extremity, Dora did not think it worth while to pursue it, and she turned to retrace her steps.

Scarcely had she done so, when she heard the rapid sound of footsteps approaching from the gloomiest recesses of the court.

A strange fear came over Dora, and yet she knew not why, for nothing could be more improbable than that any one should recognise her in her present disguise.

The footsteps still approached and then Dora, with a natural curiosity, turned to see to whom they belonged.

The moment she did so, the advancing stranger, who was within a few paces of her, uttered an exclamation of surprise and satisfaction.

"One of them—one of them!" he cried, "I have not the faculty of ever remembering a person I have once seen for nothing! My name is Surlina, and you, sir, are one of the party who took from me a bag of gold and jewels in a narrow lane on the Western Road.

CHAPTER XXXIII.

DORA ENCOUNTERS AN ENEMY—THE STUDENT IN THE TEMPLE—THE REFUGE—THE MYSTERIOUS MAN IN GREY.

DORA comprehended all her danger in a moment; at the same moment that Surlina had recognised her, she knew him as the man who had been encountered in the narrow lane leading to Captain Hawk's cottage.

And now these two persons confronted each other with widely different sensations. Surlina was full of exultation and delight at the possibility of recovering his treasure, while at the same time revenge glared from his eyes. Dora, on the contrary, felt that this was a most unexpected and cruel blow of fate, and one from which it would be difficult, indeed, to extricate herself.

"Yes," added Surlina, in a shrieking voice, as he crouched down like some wild animal about to spring upon its prey, "yes, I know you well—I cannot be mistaken! Give me my gold! give me my jewels! I will have them, or your heart's blood shall answer to me."

Dora cast one anxious and bewildered look about her.

"Surely it was possible," she thought, "by flight to escape the deadly enmity of this man!"

But whither was she to fly? From the Temple into the crowded thoroughfare of old Fleet Street, with the desperate and maddened Greek yelling at her heels into the very heart of London, amidst such throngs of people that the hue and cry after her must of necessity ensure her instant capture.

"No! flight was in vain!

Dora drew back a step or two and spoke faintly.

"You mistake—you mistake! I know you not!"

"You know me not!" Shrieked Surlina in still higher tones. "You know me not, when I could swear to you either in heaven above or in the shades below. Give me my gold—give me my jewels!"

" I have them not !"

" Murderer ! robber ! I will raise the city on you. Help ! help ! Robbers ! robbers !"

Dora felt that if anything was to be done to extricate her from this dilemma, it must be done at once ; and on the chance of there being a free passage through that gloomy court in the old Temple, she resolved to make one bold effort to pass Surlina.

" Out of the way," she said, " I will not be stopped by every madman who crosses my path."

The infuriated Greek uttered another cry of rage, and drew from the breast of his apparel a long bladed poignard, which glittered in the daylight as he held it above her head.

" Attempt to pass me at your peril," he said.

" You are mad !"

" No, I am not mad ! If I were, I should sheath this dagger in you heart ; but you must live to tell me where are my gold and jewels. Help—help ! murder and robbery ! Help ! good people all who hear me—citizens with honest hearts and well-filled purses—men of substance who would hold their own, oh, help !"

Dora felt that shouts like these would soon bring about her a mob of assailants in that densely populated district.

There was not a moment to lose, if she would save herself, for Henry's sake and for her own.

Drawing at once, from the breast of her apparel, one of the pistols with which Dottman had furnished her, she presented it full in the face of Surlina.

" Back, maniac !" she cried, " at your peril. A bullet will be swifter than your dagger. Your death be on your own head."

Surlina shrunk from the death-dealing weapon, and Dora seized upon the opportunity to dart past him.

The speed with which she went, premeditated as it was, carried her some twenty yards past Surlina before he could rally his physical energies sufficiently to follow her.

Then at the same moment, as several persons came rushing into the old Temple from Fleet Street, Surlina, with shouts and cries in his own language, and flourishing at the extent of his arm the dagger, darted after Dora.

But our heroine was considerably in advance now of her pursuer. Fleet of foot, and firm of purpose, Dora would soon have left her foes far behind her amid the intricacies of the old Temple.

But alas ! her worse fears were confirmed.

There was no thoroughfare through that gloomy court. Its extreme end was blocked up by one of those irregular shaped houses which, with an open doorway and common staircase, are let out in many suites of chambers.

Dora recognised her situation with a pang of alarm.

What should she do ?

Surlina was raging after her, and quickly following him, attracted by his cries, was the heedless crowd, who always take pleasure in hunting a fellow-creature.

There was no other resource. Dora darted at once into the doorway of the house at the extremity of the court.

A wide old gloomy staircase was before her, and she sprang up with celerity, nor paused until she reached the second floor of the house.

Panting and excited, then, Dora stopped and listened. A confusion of shouts, cries, and imprecations sounded from below, and amid them all the wild excited tones of the Greek rose uppermost.

" Here—here," he cried. " I saw him enter here. Drag him out for me, and your reward shall exceed your fondest hopes. I will keep guard at the door. There seems but this one entrance, and he shall only repass it over my lifeless body."

Then came a confusion of voices and a pattering of feet upon the staircase.

Dora's situation was critical in the extreme.

" Now heaven aid me," she said. " I know not if we be creatures of chance or accident, on if in our actions there be a directing power, but the time has come for me to run a great risk. I must try a fearful experiment upon the quality of the human heart—will it now respond to me ?

There were numerous doors opening from that landing to different sets of chambers ; but there was one in particular, immediately opposite to Dora that looked more old and more massive than any of the others.

The knocker upon it was some fanciful device in dim and faded brass.

Dora knocked at this door sharply

" This way—this way," cried the voices from below. " This way ! he must be still on the staircase."

The moment or two that elapsed before the chamber door was opened made up a period of intense agony to Dora. Her life seemed to hang upon a thread, and she had the knocker again in her hand, when the door was opened, and she was confronted by a tall, pale, slender personage, attired in a faded morning gown, of what had once been brocade of a gay pattern. This personage had in his mouth a pen, and there was a dreamy look about his eyes which betokened great abstraction; but still the expression of the whole countenance was gentle in the extreme. It seemed as if the battle of life, and the war of jarring interests about him had failed to reach the heart of this singular personage.

"Sir," said Dora, "I am pursued."

The pale, studious looking man seemed hardly to comprehend her.

"My enemies," added Dora, "are on the stairs. I crave of your humanity a shelter."

"Ay surely," said the singular inhabitant of the chambers.

He stepped aside, and Dora crossed the threshold.

The voices and footsteps on the stairs came nearer still.

"Save me—save me," she cried, and with her own hands she closed the door and shot a heavy bolt into its socket.

The studious personage rubbed his forehead with his hand and looked perplexed.

"Do not refuse me," added Dora. "It will cost you but a word. When my foes, who are without, appeal to you if anyone has taken refuge here, save a life—more than a life, by a justifiable falsehood."

"That is the point of the whole case," replied the pale student, "the original patents carry the succession in the heirs female."

"Sir—sir," said Dora, "do you not comprehend me?"

"Your servant, sir! what is it you wish?

It was quite evident that, up to this moment, the mysterious man, in his intense state of mental abstraction, had not been at all aware of what Dora had said, and now, as her lips parted to speak to him, there came a heavy knock at the door of the chambers.

"Ah!" said the pale student, "Some one knocks."

Dora clung to his arm.

"Sir, you have not heard me—you have not comprehended me. I am pursued—my life is in danger."

"Your life?"

My more than life—my life and the life of others more dear to me than life itself."

"Ah!"

Bang came a knock again at the outer door of the chambers.

"You hear, sir—you hear! you will be asked if any one has taken refuge here, and you will answer "No!"

The student shook his head.

"My good sir," he said, "How can I answer no, when here you are, taking refuge—"

"But to save me—"

"Excellent friend, I never lie!"

"Cold—heartless!"

"Nay, I will defend you; for if a dog, a cat, or the poorest, meanest thing that crawls were to come to me for refuge, it were granted."

The student stepped back a pace or two, and from a corner of the ancient and dingy looking apartment he lifted a heavy, long, straight-bladed sword, with a cross hilt of exquisite workmanship, which had no doubt been borne bravely in the wars, by some crusader on the plains of Palestine.

"Stand behind me," he said, "I will defend you!"

There was a strange air of enthusiasm about this singular personage, which Dora feared was not untinctured by some wandering of the intellect; but before she could utter a remark there came another heavy appeal at the knocker of the door, and the pale student, without the slightest hesitation, opened it.

A confusion of voices arose from the outside, and among them all could be gathered the words, in different intonations—

"Has a man, sir, taken refuge in these chambers? a slight built, slim young man, in a plain suit."

"My gold and jewels!" yelled Surlina at this moment from below.

It was well for Dora that he did so, since the screaming shout of the half-maddened Greek precluded for a moment the reply of the singular occupant of the chambers to the question which had been put to him.

That moment's pause no doubt saved Dora from much peril.

"Sir—sir!" she whispered. "You will not utter an untruth. They ask you if a man has taken refuge in your chambers—I am a woman."

"Good," said the pale student.

"He made a stride forward to the opening of the door, and the manner in which he cried out "No!" made everybody dart back several paces.

Another instant and he banged the door shut in the faces of his questioners, and Dora, springing forward, again shot the bolt into its socket.

"I owe you my liberty and life," she said.

"Let me see," said the student, "where was I? By the letters patent of Edward the First. Ah, to be sure, that's where I was."

Without taking the remotest notice of Dora, this singular being marched past her and went through a doorway into an inner apartment.

"But, sir," cried Dora, "you will let me thank you; and if I should remain here for a time you will not think my presence an intrusion, or perhaps you will be able to inform me of some other outlet from this house than the door in the court at which I entered."

Dora had followed him quickly, and stood on the threshold of the door of the inner room.

"Yes, certainly," he said in reply. "There are the windows."

A strange noise at this moment sounded apparently in some third apartment of the chambers, and in an instant the student appeared to shake off the abstraction which had been about all his actions and words and to start into new life under the action of some powerful excitement.

A flush of colour came over his pale face, and his eyes flashed with brilliancy.

"Ah!" he cried, "Am I duped so easily? Oh! fool—fool! but you, at least, spy and traitor as you are, will find your errand one of danger and difficulty. You leave not these rooms alive.

"Nay, I harmed you not—I am no traitor and no spy," cried Dora.

"What seek you here, then, but the secret I have sworn to keep even with my life?"

"I know of no secret—I come on no errand but one of personal safety.

"It is false! I am all unused to the world and its ways; but this is evident to my senses, as a plot of the base, cruel, and false Duke."

"Duke!" cried Dora. "What duke?"

The pale student made no answer, but dashing the sword from its scabbard, he strode towards Dora, lifting the ponderous blade above his head.

With a cry of real terror, Dora shrunk before him.

"You wrong me," she cried. "I'll prove to you you wrong me, for see here, your life, even, I have in my hands. These pistols—behold, I lay them at your feet. I cannot fire upon a man who has just saved me. What dupe is it you mention? what mystery lies hidden in your words? there is a something in your face and in your tones which bids me trust you; and know now if it be the false Duke of Kingston of whom you speak—

"It is—it is!"

"I, then, am his much injured niece, Dora the Duchess!"

A concealed door in one of the walls of the chamber was now suddenly dashed open, to the intense surprise of Dora, and there emerged from some apartment of that old suite of chambers, which appeared a perfect place of concealment, the identical figure, cloaked in grey apparel, which had more than once already crossed her path in life, and always with the object of benefitting her, or of lending her some aid at a critical moment of her fortunes.

Now, however, that the light of day shone upon this most mysterious personage, Dora was able to see much more clearly his general appearance and costume.

The suit of clothes he wore fitted so loosely that the folds of the dark grey cloth hung about him like a cloak—grey gloves covered his hands, and he wore horseman's boots reaching nearly to the knee.

But the most remarkable thing about the aspect of this strange man, who came and went ever so like an apparition, was, that he wore over his entire face a grey mask, apparently of cloth, which fitted closely to the features.

At the same time, however, that this mask fitted closely to the face of the mysterious man, nothing could be a more effectual concealment of identity.

Dora was half on one knee, with her hands outspread to ward off or deprecate the threatened blow from the sword of the pale student of the chambers, when the grey apparition made its appearance.

The moment the student saw it he raised a cry of dismay.

"Oh, why," he said, "why do you show yourself? this is some imposter—some spy—"

"No," said the grey man, in a deep and evidently assumed voice. "No! as you love me, Wonnel—as my cause is dear to you, pity, advise, and cherish Dora the Duchess!"

"Ah! say you so? then—"

"Hush—hush! oh, hush!"

"But you know—you identify—"

"I do! this is Dora, the daughter of the Duke of Kingston. She is worthy your utmost care."

The grey man strutted majestically across the floor of the apartment. A deep sigh came from his lips as he passed Dora, and she thought that at the same moment his footsteps lingered, and he shook as if with some sudden emotion. He raised his hands likewise, as though he would stretch them over her head to pronounce a blessing upon her at the time.

Then with another deep sigh he passed on, and made his way out of the apartment through a narrow door that was close to the old chimneypiece.

The pale student dropped the sword.

He spoke in a voice of great sweetness and emotion.

"And so I find that you are indeed that Dora who may lay claim to the Dukedom of Kingston?"

"I am, indeed!"

"Alas! poor child! what chance brought you to this house? was it chance?"

"It seemed like chance," said Dora, "and yet I hesitate to think it such. But if you have any sympathy with me—if you have any kindly feeling for me and all my persecutions, you will tell me who is that mysterious man who just passed like an apparition before my eyes."

The student shook his head.

"I cannot!"

"You surely know him, and if he be of this world or not—for you expressed more alarm than surprise at his appearance."

"I do know him!"

"Ah, then you will dissipate the mystery that surrounds him, and tell me who and what he is!"

"I dare not!"

"Dare not?"

"I have said it? I dare not, nor is it for your good that I should tell you."

"More mystery—more mystery!" sighed Dora. "Alas! when shall I see my way through all the maze of troubles that surrounds me?"

"Providence, surely, not chance," said the student, "has conducted you here. I am a student of the law, and knowing something of your history, I am most anxious to be of service to you."

"This is, indeed, more strange," said Dora, "for my errand into the Temple was to consult some one upon the subject of my claims to the title and estates of Kingston, now withheld from me by the base, cruel, and treacherous Duke, who arrogates to himself the title, which was my father's."

"Your father is no more!"

"No more! no more!"

The tears started to the eyes of Dora as she uttered those sad word.

"But," added the law student, "do you not know one thing, and that is, that if he were alive, there would be an attainder of the title on account of his complicity in a Jacobite plot, and that the estates would be confiscated to the crown!"

I have heard as much.

"It is well. You, then, comprehend that your father's death has kept the Dukedom of Kingston on the roll of peers because an attainder of a title will never take place to the detriment of the next heir, provided he has come into possession by the traitor, so called, before such attainder has been made to take place."

"I comprehend all that," said Dora, sadly.

"You do?"

"I do, indeed, as well as the conclusion you would draw from it."

"That my poor father's death is a direct benefit to his successor.

"Well, it is so !"

"And yet," said Dora with animation, "I would rather that he had lived, and that I, his child, had had to work for him at the poorest occupation that would present itself to me. I would gladly barter titles and wealth for one kind smile from those dear lips, that never parted to speak to me but for the utterance of some tender word of dear affection."

At this moment there came a short, sharp knock at the outer door of the chambers.

CHAPTER XXXIII.

THE DUKE OF KINGSTON CONSULTS A LEGAL ADVISER — STARLIGHT IN DANGER— DORA'S NEW ALLY.

WHEN this sudden and sharp knock came at the door of the gloomy suite of chambers in the old Temple, where Dora had found a refuge, the first feeling, both of herself and the singular occupant of the rooms was that some one or other of those persons who had chased Dora to that place of security had returned.

It might even be Surlina himself.

Probably his suspicions had gathered fresh force that she, Dora, was to be found in those chambers.

"What shall I do?" said Dora. "Can you hide me?"

"Easily—hush!"

"You will save me!"

"I will save you at the sacrifice of my life, if it be necessary so to do. Step this way."

The law student led Dora to the adjoining room, and then advancing to one of the walls, he ran his finger down a rich moulding that surrounded the old wainscot panels.

One of the lower panels then flew open, disclosing beyond it a secret recess between the brick wall of the house and the wainscotting of the room.

"There," he said, "there you will be in perfect safety. The panel closes by a spring. Stand just within it, but do not close it unless you hear me say loudly, 'Those who hide can find.'"

"I will remember."

The knock came at the outer chambers again.

Then the student left Dora close to the open panel, and leaving likewise the door of that inner apartment open, so that she might hear what should take place, he hastened to admit the visitor.

The moment the outer door of the chambers was opened, Dora thought that she must surely be in a dream, for it was the

DORA TAKES THE LETTER FROM THE DUKE OF KINGSTON.

voice of the false Duke of Kingston that came most distinctly upon her ears.

"Are these the chambers," said the voice, "of one Chevan de Wannel?"

"I am he," replied the student.

"That is well," added the Duke of Kingston. "I am told that, although you have never yet appeared as an advocate in any of the courts, your legal knowledge is great."

"Well?"

"And as such is the case, I am desirous to employ it in my service."

"I am busy, sir."

"Nay, I will pay you with a liberality that will far exceed any result from ordinary

DORA.—17.

business. You know not as yet who I am."

"I do not!"

"Then, sir, I will tell you that I am the Duke of Kingston.

The pale student uttered an exclamation of surprise.

You seem astonished," added the Duke; "but when I explain to you the circumstances of the case in which I wish to consult you, your surprise will cease.

"The Duke of Kingston!" exclaimed the student.

"Even so, sir! you repeat my name as though you had some previous knowledge of me."

"What want you with me?"

"I want to show you some documents, and to ask your opinion if they are strong enough, provided they were in the hands of my enemies, or there was such other evidence of this existing as would satisfy the courts, my brother's daughter, or her child or children could ever contest with me my dukedom."

"What document?"

"There is a letter from my late brother to myself, in which he gives an account of his marriage, and states that he has a daughter named Dora."

"Well?"

"You will comprehend that I have always denied that such a marriage took place.

"Give me the letter."

"That is it?"

"A copy?"

"No, it is the original. It states, you will see, at the end, in a sort of catalogue, all the documents and patents by which the dukedom and estates are held.

"I see!"

"Now, what I want to know is, how I can safely proceed to rid myself of all trouble and inconvenience concerning any claim that may be set up by my brother's assumed daughter, a girl named Dora."

"My lord Kingston," said the student, "I am an honest man, I hope."

"I hope so, sir."

"And, therefore, I inform you that I cannot, and will not aid you!"

"Ah!"

"Never, my Lord Kingston! Never will I be the base tool of such a man as you! I scorn to retain this letter, most precious as it would be to those who may contest with you your title."

Not a word of this most interesting dialogue had escaped the ears of Dora.

When, then, she heard the pale student speak in such a fashion, and feel that in the eccentricity of honesty which he possessed, he was about to give back the precious letter to the Duke of Kingston, she could restrain her impatience no longer.

Darting out of the recess in the wall, she passed rapidly through the room in which it was situated, to that outer one where the false Duke, her uncle, and the pale student held this singular conference.

"Hold!" she cried, as she made so unexpected an appearance before the petrified Duke of Kingston. "Hold! I must have that letter!"

"Ah!" said the student.

The Duke of Kingston staggered back a pace or two.

"Help! murder!" he cried.

He thrust the letter half into the breast of his apparel, and drew his sword.

"The letter!" cried Dora, "the letter! I must and will have it!"

"'Tis she!" shouted the Duke. "By Heaven, 'tis she! Dora! Dora!"

"Yes, I am Dora."

"Ah! One lucky thrust, and all is over."

"Dora the Duchess!" she added.

At the moment she spoke the Duke of Kingston made a violent lunge with his sword, and the weapon passed so closely to Dora's heart that its point tore up a shred of her apparel.

There was then a loud clashing sound, and the Duke of Kingston's sword was dashed out of his hand by the pale student, who had caught up that long crusader's sword with which, before he knew her, he had threatened Dora.

Then Dora sprung forward, and with one fortunate snatch, she secured the letter which the false Duke had tried in vain to hide in his breast.

"I have it! I have it!" cried Dora. "Do not kill him! Oh, spare him yet!"

"Fly!" said the student. "Fly, Dora! Seek now some place of safety that will be better than these chambers. I will leave it to your own ingenuity to find a means of again communicating with me."

The outer door of the chambers was open, and Dora dashed out, and descended the stairs quickly.

The thought that Surlina might possibly be still on the watch below came over her mind for a moment, but such was not the case. The Greek had given up the search, and the dull dingy court in the Temple was silent and deserted.

But Dora thought it would be safest to leave the old legal precincts by some other route than that at which she had entered them, so she made her way towards the river, and at the Temple stairs she hired a wherry to Westminster.

By landing at that bridge, she could easily make her way on foot to where she had left her horse, Starlight; for Dora was most anxious now to mount, and get back to Captain Hawk's cottage as soon as possible.

Upon reaching the little stable at which she had put up Starlight, Dora was put somewhat upon her guard by seeing several men who were lounging about, suddenly disappear, as though they did not wish to be seen by her.

That there was danger she suspected in a moment; but what would be its precise character she had no means of ascertaining.

"Oh, you want your horse, sir?" said the stablekeeper. "To be sure! to be sure!" A fine creature it is, too! Why, I feel sure that I know more than one great nobleman who would be only too glad to give you a thousand pounds for it."

"My horse is not for sale," said Dora, coldly.

"No offence, sir—no offence!" said the man. "There, Jim, get out the gentleman's horse, will you?"

"Yes, master."

"Be quick now!"

"Coming, master!"

There was something so like acting in all this, that Dora felt convinced she had not seen the end of it, and that in a few moments something would develope itself that might require all her courage, and skill, and presence of mind to meet.

"Here you are," cried the stable boy, as he brought out a horse.

But it was not Starlight.

"What folly is this?" said Dora. "That is not my horse!"

"Really?" said the stableman. "Are you sure, sir?"

Dora looked the man in the face inquiringly. There was an expression of insolent defiance about him that was quite sufficient to convince her that some foul play was intended.

"Hark you, captain," said the man, "I know you."

"You know me?"

"I do. I have seen the horse before. You are the well-known Captain Hawk, the highwayman."

"Indeed!"

"Oh, yes, I am sure of it. Now, if you want to escape the officers, you will just mount this bay horse that Jim has brought out for you and be off, and ask no questions."

"While you keep my own horse?"

"Just so, captain."

"And if I refuse?"

"Then all I have to do is to raise a shout, and half a dozen officers will be here in a moment."

"Raise that alarm," said Dora, "and it will be your last shout in this world."

As she spoke she dashed one of the pistols so close to the face of the stablekeeper that the barrel rattled among his teeth.

"Utter one word above your breath," added Dora, "and I will scatter your brains over yon wall."

The stableman glared at Dora with eyes that each moment seemed to protrude more and more from their sockets.

"Speak!" she said, "where is my horse?"

At this moment Dora was not a little surprised to see Jim, the stableman, rush past her with a hay fork in his hand, and dash its two prongs against a door of the stable close at hand, and there hold it with all his might and strength."

"You be off, captain," cried Jim. "Don't mind master—you be off! The officers can't get out while I holds on to the fork. You be off."

"My horse," cried Dora, "where is it?"

"Next stable."

Dora entwined her left hand in the cravat of the landlord, and dragged him to the stable indicated by the boy."

There, sure enough, was Starlight.

"Listen to me," said Dora, speaking rapidly to the stablekeeper, "for your life's sake, listen to me!"

"I—I—will—captain! Oh lord!"

"Resist what I am about to do, and I will shoot you as I would a mad dog."

"Oh, oh!"

"Peace, not a word!"

The man seemed to have lost all strength with the abject fear that now possessed him. The rattle of the barrel of the pistol among his teeth seemed completely to have prostrated him.

Dora dragged him into the stall where Starlight was haltered, and removing the halter from the Arabian steed, she placed it round the neck of the stablekeeper, and left him in the stall."

Attempt to move," she said, "until I am fairly off, and I will have your worthless life yet."

"The stablekeeper fell down among the straw in the stall.

Another moment, and Dora was mounted on Starlight, and out into the yard.

The boy, Jim, was still holding the door of the next stable fast shut with the hay fork.

There came a furious knocking on the door from within.

"Hoorah!" cried Jim, when he saw Dora mounted on Starlight.

"I don't know how to thank you," said Dora.

"All right. Be off, captain."

"But what will become of you?"

"I haven't thought of that."

"I ought, however, to think of it. Do you think you can jump up behind me? The horse will carry us both easily."

"To be sure I can."

"Quick, then."

Jim flung down the hay fork, and then, before the officers could dash the stable door open and sally out, he had sprung upon the back of Starlight.

"Off and away!" cried Dora.

Starlight, with a bound, dashed from the stable yard, and was some couple of hundred yards down the road before the officers could recover from their confusion, or keep from jostling each other.

A few pistol shots were discharged at random, but so hastily and without aim, that none of them took effect.

The officers may or may not have had horses, but if they had they must have entertained a perfect conviction of how entirely futile any pursuit would be of Starlight, the beautiful Arabian, with whom speed was but a pleasant walk and pastime.

A mile of road was passed over in an exceedingly short space of time, and then Dora began to breathe more freely, and to review, with something like a feeling of bewilderment and astonishment the startling adventures which had been crowded into the brief space of one morning.

But in the midst of all those adventures and dangers, she had yet succeeded in all she had proposed to herself by her visit to London. She had sold one of Captain Hawk's jewels for no less a sum than five hundred pounds, and she felt that she had made a legal friend of the strange student in the Temple, who, if any human being could aid her in a successful appeal to the laws of the kingdom, was surely the man to do so.

And now Dora felt light-hearted and comparatively happy, for uninjured and even unfollowed, she was making her way back to that cottage amid the deep shadows of the trees, which she felt was entitled to the name of home so long as it was a place of refuge for her wounded husband.

All these thoughts and considerations passed with rapidity through the mind of Dora, and then she turned her attention to the boy who was seated behind her on Starlight.

Dora could not well make up her mind if either Dottman or Henry would approve of the addition to their little household at Captain Hawk's cottage, but still the service the stable boy had rendered her was so great that Dora never for a moment contemplated the idea of casting him off if he were friendless.

It was upon this subject she proceeded to question him.

"I think your name is Jim?" she said.

"Yes, that's it," said the boy, "and you are Captain Hawk, the highwayman?"

Dora evaded giving either an affirmative or a negative reply to this remark.

"You have lost your situation at the stable," she said, "by befriending me."

"It wasn't much of a situation!"

"What was it worth?"

"Victuals and what people chose to give me!"

"Have you any friends?"

"Lor bless you, yes. There's grandfather and grandmother, that keeps the old mill near Crayford; but they haven't much for themselves, so I went out to see what I could do."

"And what will you do, now that through me, you have lost your place?"

Jim was silent for a few moments, and then he said, with some hesitation,—

"Perhaps, captain, you might want a boy to look after your horse?"

"No, I have a man already. But do you think, if I were to put you down here, you could find your way to Crayford?"

"Oh, yes, I could easy do that, because you see, Captain, I came from there to this part of the country."

"Very well, then. I cannot take you with me, or I would gladly do so. Take this bank note—it is for fifty pounds—and go to your grandfather and grandmother at Crayford, and tell them that a person whom you befriended presented it to you."

"I'll tell them it was Captain Hawk, the great highwayman."

"It will be better not to do so; and besides, it would be wrong, for I am not Captain Hawk, the highwayman."

"Not Captain Hawk?"

"Certainly not!"

"Why, all the officers said you were, because they knew your horse."

"They might know my horse, and yet I not be Captain Hawk. Be careful of that bank-note, and ask your grandfather and grandmother to endeavour to lay it out to your advantage. Now we must part. You have done me a great service, and possibly the day may come when we may meet again."

"Well," said Jim the stable-boy, as he leaped from Starlight into the road, "whether you are Captain Hawk or not, I shall always be ready to come to you or do what I can for you, and I dare say, now, I shall stay with grandfather, and help in the mill, and if ever you come that way you'll easily find us. There's two mills close to Crayford. One's called the old and the other the new mill. It's the old mill—that's grandfather's."

"I will remember," said Dora. "I know not what friends I may need in any part of the country, but I will not forget that I have one in the old mill near Crayford. Farewell!"

Dora set Starlight to speed, and in a very few moments Jim the stable boy was left very far behind on the road, gazing with no small admiration after the person whom he still in his heart believed to be Captain Hawk, the highwayman.

Dora gave Starlight the rein, and the gallant Arabian, as if with a perfect knowledge that she was proceeding to that cottage among the trees, the route to which, along the Western Road, it knew so well, needed neither guiding nor urging to make the best of its way to its home.

Several horsemen were passed upon the road, who looked with wonder and envy on the superb animal, which seemed rather to fly through the air than tread the solid earth.

At the top of the lane Dora met Dottman, who was beginning to get exceedingly anxious concerning her protracted absence.

"Thank Heaven!" said Dottman, "there you are, and safe."

"Quite," replied Dora. "How did you leave Henry, or rather, why did you leave him?"

"Oh, Mr. Dacres is quite right, captain, and getting better every hour, but I couldn't help coming to the top of the lane to take a look down the road to see if I could catch a glimpse of Starlight.

"I thank you! but you are on foot, Dottman, and I shall reach the cottage much sooner than you can."

"Take the key, then, captain, of the door in the garden wall; but tell me, was the diamond a real one?"

"Perfectly real, and sold for five hundred pounds."

Dottman whistled a long, shrill note.

"It appears we are rich," he said.

"If all the contents of that canvas bag be as valuable, we are, indeed."

"There's no doubt of it, captain. That diamond was not of the largest. Ah, that's a great pity, because, you see, captain, you won't feel to care now to go on the road.

"The necessity ceasing," said Dora, "surely you would not wish me."

"Well, I don't know that! but I detain you, and I see Starlight, too, is impatient."

Dora waved her hand to Dottman, and then galloped down the lane. A very few minutes sufficing her to reach the door in the garden wall, and soon she was with her Henry, who welcomed her back with a cry of delight.

"All is well," she said, "and I have much news to tell you."

Dora then entered into a statement, which comprised a history of her adventures in London on that eventful morning.

There was so much that was hopeful in all that had occurred, that Henry Dacres seemed to gather new life from the intelligence.

"I cannot help thinking," he said, "that affairs will soon wear a different aspect. Let us go to town, Dora, and there, surely, both you and I can disguise ourselves, having ample means to do so most effectually. It will be well to be upon the spot which contains our enemies; for your sake, Dora, and for that of our child this battle must be fought."

"Alas!" said Dora, "where are we to find our lost one?"

"I will not despair. The feeling has always kept possession of my mind that our little Mina is safe and well, and will be restored to us. These are grievous trials we are passing through. They commenced here, Dora, with this pistol shot in my breast; but each day I feel better and stronger, and soon I shall be able to stand between you and all danger. Oh, happy time! would that it were come!"

Little did Dora imagine that that very old mill at Crayford, which had been mentioned by the stable boy as the residence of his grandfather and grandmother, was the harbour of refuge into which the tide of Fate had drifted the little Mina.

But so it was. By a strange combination of circumstances, Dora had been befriended in a moment of critical danger by one who was soon to be high in the affections of her child as its playmate and companion.

———

CHAPTER XXXIV.

THE DUKE OF KINGSTON COMES TO A RESOLUTION — SURLINA'S DANGER — THE MURDER IN THE PRISON-ROOM — THE GREEK GIRL AND THE LABORATORY.

THE Duke of Kingston sits alone in his splendid town house. He is a successful man so far as having, in the eyes of the world, compassed all his desires.

Is he not a great noble?

Has he not large estates?

What more can he desire for happiness? and how many people must deeply envy the great, grand, noble, rich, Duke of Kingston?

But if ever care sat upon the brow of a human being, it did upon that of this successful schemer and man of many crimes.

He is alone! a loneliness that sets brooding at his very heart is about him.

No human sympathies are his! no human voice addresses him in tones of friendship or affection!

There is no human heart into which he can pour the tale of his sorrows, and from which he can hope or ask for sympathy.

Alone! quite alone!

Various disquieting events have taken place to disturb the serenity of the Duke.

There has arisen an awkward rumour, propagated by a certain pardoned Jacobite, of the name of Pearson, that his brother, the late Duke, is not dead.

That was disquietude number one.

Then the escape of Dora from his machinations, and the disappearance of her child, likewise, possessed him with the idea that, for him the future was full of mischief.

And so he sat alone, wondering what it would be best for him to do.

"There is danger," he said, "for me—much danger, I fear, both in the present and in the time to come, and I must avoid it. I will go abroad for a time, and wait until all these events are forgotten; but I will leave such a reward as a promise to Surlina if he will contrive to rid me of my foes in my absence, that the cupidity of the Greek will make him act just as I would wish him."

The history of the connection of the Duke of Kingston with Surlina would, one have thought, have made him careful how far he trusted the Greek; but it is the misfortune of men like the Duke that they are compelled to dealings with men whose treachery to others they purchase along with the full conviction that they are quite ready to be treacherous to them in turn.

The Duke proceeded to that secret door in the wall of the apartment, which was covered by the portrait of Charles the First.

He touched the spring, and the panel moved back.

All was black darkness beyond.

"Surlina—Surlina!" said the Duke.

There was no reply.

The Duke stepped through the opening in the wall, and closed the panel behind him.

He did not call to Surlina again. A feeling came over him that he would like, if such a thing were possible, to steal upon the privacy of the Greek, and see what he was about.

With this object the Duke of Kingston trod very softly, and made his way along a narrow passage of the house until he came to a steep staircase.

That staircase led to the lower portion of the mansion, where Surlina had his laboratory, and carried on his chemical and alchemical studies and researches.

A strong odour came upon the senses of the Duke as he neared the laboratory.

It was that odour which ether gives forth, and which is so commonly the compound of the atmosphere of laboratories.

Two doors, however, shut in the laboratory from the rest of the house.

The Duke opened one of these doors and then, through a small glass frame in the other he was able to command a view of the interior of the laboratory.

Surlina was there!

Neoni, too, was with him.

A bright, ruddy glow from one of the furnaces was over the whole of the laboratory, and the Greek was busily engaged in watching a crucible, which now and then emitted bright red sparks.

Neoni from time to time went to the shelves of the laboratory and brought various bottles to her father.

From those he poured small portions of their contents into the crucible.

The door closed too well, and was too thick to enable the Duke of Kingston to comprehend what was said.

He could only see by the actions of Surlina, and the motion of his lips that he occasionally spoke to Neoni.

And now, as the Duke looked more and more earnestly at the beautiful Greek girl, with the red glow from the furnace and the crucible upon her face, he thought she had never looked so lovely.

The old passion he had had for her seemed to revive in all its original force.

"She is beautiful!" he said. "She is, indeed, most beautiful, and I will make her a sharer in my politic absence from England."

The Duke tapped at the door.

Surlina, however, was too much engaged in what he was about to heed him.

Neoni had rested her head upon her hands, and was in deep thought.

The Duke then opened the door quietly, and placing his ear to the crevice, he heard the Greek's voice plainly.

"Neoni," he said, "it must be and shall be! I do not comprehend your hesitation!"

"Be merciful!" said Neoni.

"Merciful! Was he merciful to you when he blighted your young life?"

"Alas, no!"

"Then I will show him no mercy."

Neoni sighed.

"Listen to me, my child. You shall yet be the wife of this man, and then comes the retribution."

"You will kill him?"

"No, no!"

"What retribution, then, father?"

The Greek was silent for a few moments, during which, millions of bright sparks sprung up from the crucible.

When he spoke again, it was in tones of deep, concentrated hatred.

"To kill a man is nothing!" he said. "It is but one short pang, and all is over. Nay, it is perhaps a benefit! for who would willingly stay in this world, to endure all its miseries, but that there is a mysterious principle in human nature which makes the preservation of existence a part of the mind?"

Neoni was silent.

"No, I will not kill him, my child, but I will leave him to disgrace, to contumely, and to despair. Ah, the compound is good!"

The Greek had drawn back a little from the crucible as a shower of violet-coloured sparks was suddenly evolved from it.

On his face he had a glass mask, which imparted a hideous aspect to him.

The Duke then knocked so strongly on the panel of the door, that it was impossible the sound could escape either the Greek or his daughter.

"Ah, some one knocks!" said Surlina.

Neoni sprung to her feet.

The Greek took a small vial in his hand, and muttered—

"Shall I kill him now?"

Neoni was half way towards the door of the laboratory, when the Duke pushed it open, saying, in well acted tones of carelessness."

"Surlina, I want to speak with you."

"Ah, noble sir, you are welcome!"

"I know I am. What is that your art is now compounding?"

"A noble elixir. A something which will much advance our search for the rare powder which will convert lead to gold."

"A consummation devoutly to be wished," said the Duke. "But come with me, Surlina, I have something to say to you."

"I come. The crucible can cool."

Surlina lifted the crucible from the furnace, and then turning to his daughter, he said—

"Place everything in order, my child, I shall soon return."

The Greek carefully hid about him the small vial which he had taken so hastily in his hand at the moment of the Duke's entrance to the laboratory.

He followed the Duke to one of the upper rooms of the house.

"Surlina," said Kingston, "I am weary of the life I lead. It is one of too constant apprehension."

"Ah!"

"You seem surprised, but you must know that it is such."

"You will yet triumph."

"I know not. But be that as it may, I have made a resolution."

"What resolution?"

"To go abroad."

"No!"

"No, say you? What power shall hinder me?"

"Abroad! alone?" mused the Greek.

"No. It will be for you to give me a companion. I will take the fair Neoni with me."

"*She* lives!" said the Greek.

As he spoke, he made a gesture with his hand towards that portion of the house in which the unhappy Duchess of Kingston was imprisoned.

The Duke fully comprehended him.

"Yes," he replied, "she lives, but it is for you to put an end to that difficulty."

"And then?"

"Then I will make Neoni my wife. According to the rites of your own faith I will do so."

"And your faith, my Lord Duke?"

"Heed not mine. I will go with Neoni to the fair Isles of Greece."

"Let me think."

Surlina was silent for a few moments, and then he said—

"On condition that I make you a free man, by the murder of the present Duchess of Kingston, you will wed my child, Neoni?"

"I will," said the Duke, in a low voice.

"Be it so. Come!"

"Whither?"

"Come with me, and you will see the deed of kindness and mercy done."

"Kindness and mercy?"

"Yes. Do you think that life, such as it is to the Duchess of Kingston, is worth the having? Ha, ha! death is mercy!"

The Duke shuddered.

"How—how—will you do it?"

Surlina took from the breast of his apparel the small vial, and held it up in the imperfect light which an oil lamp gave to the room.

"You see this?" he said. "If it be broken by being cast at any one, it will liberate a liquid from which will rise a vapour that must be present death."

The Duke shrunk back.

"Can that be so?"

"You will see."

"Then that is the mode by which you will rid me of the Duchess?"

"It is. I have but to open the small panel of the door, and cast this vial into her prison chamber, and she will cease to live in five minutes."

The Duke shuddered.

"Come," added Surlina, "it is time.

"It is time!" said the Duke to himself, in a low voice.

As he spoke, the Duke loosened his sword in the scabbard.

Surlina preceded him, and they ascended to that portion of the house in which the unhappy Duchess was imprisoned.

But on the route there they had to pass the door of the chamber in which lay the wounded Van Esling.

A deep groan came from the suffering wretch at the moment that Surlina and the Duke were passing the door of the chamber.

The Duke started.

"What is that?"

"What mean you?" said Surlina.

"I heard a groan."

"Twas I."

"You?"

"Yes—I was lamenting."

"About what?"

"That when you should reach our ancient Grecian Isles, you would find that time and the barbarous despoilers had robbed them of their glory."

The Duke was far from being satisfied with this answer.

That he had heard a groan, and that such groan proceeded from one in physical pain he was quite convinced.

But he did not press Surlina on the subject, for he had his own mind full of what he intended shortly to do.

The door of the chamber at the top of the house, where the Duchess of Kingston had for so long, as a forlorn prisoner, expiated her sin of indifference to the woes and wrongs of the fair young Greek girl, was reached.

Surlina paused and listened.

The Duke remained a few steps below the head of the narrow stairs.

"She sleeps!" said Surlina.

"I cannot sleep," said the Duke.

"Sufferers sleep—inflictors seldom do," added the Greek, quickly.

"Quick!" said the Duke, "let the tragedy be over!"

"You are impatient, my lord."

"I am—I am!"

Surlina opened the small panel at the upper portion of the door, through which he was in the habit of conveying just sufficient food to the unhappy Duchess as would suffice to prolong existence.

"You sleep," he said. "Let that sleep pass into the sleep of death."

As he spoke, he cast through the narrow opening in the door the little vial.

It was heard, both by the Duke and Surlina, to break on the floor of the apartment.

The Greek closed the panel of the door immediately.

"Is it done?" asked the Duke.

"It is done."

"Come away, then! Oh, come away!"

"Nay, my Lord Duke, if you would verify the work, you have but to wait here some few minutes, and then you can, with perfect safety, enter the chamber."

"No, no! not for worlds!"

"Be it so."

The Greek turned from the door, and descended the stairs.

The Duke of Kingston shrunk up into a narrow space, and let him pass.

"Are you certain now, Surlina," he said, "that death is in that chamber above?"

"As certain as that above that chamber again there are the stars of heaven."

"You have been very useful to me, Surlina, although you have failed in making gold."

"I have."

"And I feel convinced that never again can you be so useful as you have been this night."

"Indeed!"

"Quite convinced."

The Duke had drawn his sword noiselessly and quickly from its scabbard, and as he uttered these last words, he plunged it into the back of the Greek.

Surlina uttered a yell of agony, and fell forwards on his face.

He rolled down the remainder of the stairs, uttering shrieks that echoed through the gloomy house.

The Duke of Kingston sprung after him, and stood upon his prostrate form.

"Peace, villain!" he said. "Peace!"

The Greek was silent.

The Duke trembled in every limb, and he made a most ineffectual attempt to restore his sword to its sheath, but his hand trembled so excessively, that he could not do it.

He stepped over the body of Surlina, and springing towards a door that shut in that narrow staircase from the rest of the house, he hastily closed it upon the dead!

The Duke shot a couple of bolts in this door to their sockets, and he turned the key that was in the lock, and then flung it away into an obscure corner.

"Lie there and rust," he said. "Time may roll on for years before the secrets of this house are revealed to the light."

The Duke then took his way by the same route which the Greek had conducted him to the chamber of the Duchess, for he was anxious again to pass the room from which he felt certain he had heard a groan.

That was the chamber of the wounded Van Esling!

CHAPTER XXXV.

THE DAWN OF HOPE—THE MIDNIGHT ROBBER—FLIGHT—DORA'S LOSS.

THERE was much of congratulation now in the present prospects and position of Dora, and she could not conceal from herself that that mainly arose from the accidental acquisition of so much wealth, that she may be enabled, not only to purchase safety for herself and her husband, but that kind of consideration for her claims which is ever accorded to the possessor of ample means.

A day and a night was passed at Captain Hawk's cottage in perfect peace and security, and in the arrangement of plans for the future.

DORA AND HENRY'S ESCAPE FROM CAPTAIN HAWK'S COTTAGE.

Those plans were materially modified by the evidently rapidly approaching convalescence of Henry Dacres.

It was a great delight both to him and to Dora to imagine that they would soon be able together to engage in the search for the lost little Mina.

But pending this event, Dora determined to ride over to the banks of the Thames in search of that hut which Ned Fellowes, the highwayman, had assured her once, for a brief space, had sheltered her child, and where the villain, Turnbull, might still be lying oppressed by his wound.

One of those calm, delightful evenings of early summer, which are incidental to our

climate fell upon the cottage among the trees, and Dora retired to rest with greater peace of mind than she had done for many a day.

Alas! how fallacious was that peace, and how soon was it to be disturbed by an accident, the like of which it had never entered into her imagination to conceive.

It is midnight.

A deep silence is over the face of the country, and so profoundly still is the night air, that not a leaf stirs upon a tree.

It was at this hour, so serene, so quiet, and so apparently free from danger, that a stealthy figure might have been observed slowly making its way up the lane towards Captain Hawk's cottage.

This figure was attired in a cloak which covered up the actual costume completely from observation.

A low crowned slouched hat concealed his face, and amid the darkness, for no moon on that night shone out from the heavens, this person, as he made his way forward, looked more like a moving shadow than a man.

Ever and anon he muttered to himself disjointed sentences which, however, sufficiently betrayed that he had some design against the cottage among the trees, and its inhabitants.

"I'm sure it's here abouts," he said, "for I dodged him all the way down the lane on the other side of the hedge. I never saw such a creature in my life! I shall get a thousand pounds for it anywhere, and perhaps more. I haven't been brought up all my life among horses not to know what that was! Bless me, I thought I should have fainted away when I saw it. It's a real beauty! and there's not a nobleman in the land that won't give a thousand pounds for it. It's a pity my brother, Ben, was hanged about that colt he took from the common, for he would have been just the fellow to lend a helping hand. Howsome'dever, I must do it by myself."

Creeping on, and muttering in this manner, the horse stealer reached the garden wall of Captain Hawk's cottage, and then he paused, and passed his hand slowly over the door till he felt the keyhole.

"Ah!" he said, "there's a keyhole, and I'd soon find the key if that was all; but I dare say there's bolts and bars inside enough. I wonder now if these people are so disagreeable as to keep dogs."

The horse stealer listened intently with his ear close to the panel of the garden door.

"I don't think they do," he muttered. "How I do hate dogs to be sure! It's quite astonishing the number of nice little pieces of business they spoil of a night, and some of the wretches won't be coaxed no how. I must try, though, for I don't like to get over the wall, and I mean to do the job as sure as my name's Bill the Couper."

Bill then took from his pocket a small paper parcel which contained some pieces of meat duly prepared to be especially attractive to the appetite of a dog.

These temptations he flung over the wall, but as not the slightest sound came upon the night air, he concluded there was no dog on the premises.

"That's a wonder," he muttered; "where there's horses there's generally dogs. Let's see if there's any broken bottles on the wall. I can't think what people mean by being such wretches as to put broken bottles on a wall."

Bill managed rather adroitly to scramble up by the side of the door sufficiently high that he could place his hand on the top of the wall, where there were no broken bottles.

"No," he said, "there's nothing of the sort. Why, these are comfortable, easy-going people, and they don't place obstructions in a fellow's way when he wants to carry out a little idea about a horse."

Silently and cleverly the well practised horse stealer clambered over the wall of the cottage, showing himself as little as possible in the process, just gently rolling over the wall, so that if anyone had been looking from a window, they could scarcely have seen him, and then dropping into the garden as noiselessly as a bird.

All was still in the cottage.

Dottman was sleeping in the lower room, for he had a partiality to sleeping anywhere but in a bed, and he had extemporised a couch by the aid of chairs, upon which he reposed to his perfect satisfaction.

A sense of security had come over Dottman that evening, which perhaps made him sleep sounder than he ordinarily did, but still any unusual sound would quickly have awakened him, and on a table close to him lay a pair of loaded pistols, which he would not have been slow to use.

In his way, however, the horse stealer was an accomplished man, and he crept along under the shadow of the garden wall with all the stealthy and even motion of a cat.

Even in the deep gloom of the night his practised eyes enabled him to see at once in which direction the stable lay, and he soon reached it.

Then he knew he would have no difficulty in effecting an entrance, since the door must be fastened from the outside only.

The lock was a large one, but the horse-stealer was too great an adept in his profession to be without the means of picking it with ease.

Another moment and he glided into the stable, where Starlight was quietly resting through the night.

Both the horses were there, and the practised ears of the horse stealer could detect, even by their breathing, that two horses occupied the stable.

"It won't do to take the wrong one," he murmured. "It's the Arabian I want. The other may be a good horse, but it ain't worth a thousand pounds."

In order, then, to see which horse occupied the respective stalls, a light was indispensable; for, clever as he was, the horse stealer could not see in the dark.

It was only the light of a match, however, for a few moments that he required, and in another moment a faint blue flame lit up the stable.

That was enough. In a moment he saw which stall contained the Arabian, and he extinguished the match.

Great as might be the intelligence and docility of Starlight, it was hardly to be supposed that the creature could have the capacity of discriminating sufficiently among its human masters to greatly prefer one to another.

It was the law of kindness that held good with that instinct almost approaching reason the noble animal possessed.

And no one knew better how to approach a horse in such a manner as to win its confidence than this man, who made a practice of stealing them.

Bill crept into the stall and aroused the Arabian, who permitted him, without resistance, to slip a halter round its neck and turn his head towards the stable door.

"Now," muttered Bill, "you can't get over the wall as I did, so I must unfasten that ugly little door in the brick wall."

Bill thought it would be better to do this before taking the Arabian out of the stable, and he crept back to the door in the garden wall as cautiously as he had made his way from about that spot to the stable.

"Two bolts and a lock," he whispered to himself. "That will do, and now I think, I'll take Ben's plan of giving the people in the house something to do that will amuse them for ever so long, and make them think the horse has only got loose in the row, for there will be a row, or my name's not Bill."

A great portion of the roof of Captain Hawk's cottage was of thatch, and into the midst of this the horse stealer cast various pieces of ignited touch paper, which would continue smouldering for a considerable time, and which even rain would scarcely extinguish.

The thatch was dry, and in some places where the touch paper happened to fall, it was so far protected from the weather, that the slightest approach of anything in the shape of combustion would be sure to set it in a blaze.

"That'll do," said Bill. "And if the crib ain't half burnt down by morning, it ain't my fault. Now, my beauty, the door in the garden wall's open, and out we goes."

The horse-stealer reached the door of the stable, which he had left only lightly closed, and standing on the threshold as he opened it, he reached in his arm to take the halter and fetch out Starlight.

But now he gave a sudden start, for amid the intense darkness of the garden, there came a long radiating gleam of light,

falling fully upon him, and glancing past him into the stable.

The horse started back, and jerked the halter from the hands of the depredator.

Bill turned sharply round in surprise and alarm, and then he saw from whence the light proceeded.

The window of one of the lower rooms of the cottage was half open, and there was Dottman with a lantern in one hand, through the lens of which had streamed the long ray of light, and a pistol in the other.

Bill uttered a cry of alarm.

"Perhaps," said Dottman, "you don't mind saying who you are, and what you want here."

The horse-stealer found that his expedition was a failure, and his personal safety became the only consideration left him.

He made a sudden rush to door in the garden wall, which he congratulated himself now he had left open.

"Good night," he said, derisively, as he reached it. "I'll call again another time."

"Don't trouble yourself," said Dottman.

Bang went the pistol shot as though it were an echo of the words.

The horse-stealer, with a shout of pain, pitched headlong out into the lane; but although hit, he was a man of great nerve and resolution, and he contrived to gather himself up and scramble on for two or three hundred yards.

Then he fell again, and with a deep groan rolled into a ditch by the roadside, where he lay without sense or motion.

The sound of the pistol shot at once aroused Henry Dacres and Dora; but after firing at the midnight depredator, Dottman had jumped out of the window into the garden, and he called out in a loud voice—

"It's all over—it's all over! There was only one of them, and I fancy, from what I saw and heard, it was the horses he was after."

"Are you hurt, Dottman?" said Dora from the window.

"Oh, no. It was I who fired the pistol, and I think I must have winged the fellow."

"I will come down directly."

"Don't you do any such thing, captain. I shall not sleep again to-night, and you may depend upon my keeping a sharp look out, though there is nothing to fear now, for these kind of things are never tried twice in one night."

Dora knew well that she could accept implicitly the assurance from Dottman of safety, and she closed the window, for she was anxious to calm any apprehensions on the part of Henry, since, although he was gaining strength daily, she feared too many excitements might throw him back, and retard his recovery.

If Dottman had remained out in the garden, as he at first intended, all might have been well, but after going into the stable and seeing that all was right there, he felt so certain in his own mind that all was right, that there would be no repetition that night of the attack upon the cottage, that he went into the little parlour again, and contented himself with keeping the window open, so that he could both hear and see if anything unusual occurred.

This was an unfortunate mode of action on the part of Dottman, for his sense of fancied security induced him to drop into a half slumber, and the external air that made its way into the cottage, aided greatly the villanous plan which the horse stealer had had for its destruction.

At about four o'clock in the morning a strong odour of fire pervaded the entire place.

A small flame was curling about in the thatch, and wreaths of blue smoke were making their way from many crevices under the eaves of the roof.

The cottage amid the trees was on fire.

The quiet, peaceful home, so deeply embosomed in vegetation, and so apparently removed from all such a result, would soon be in flames.

As the early morning advanced, a very light wind had began to make itself perceptible, and this fanned the flame, so that in the course of another half hour the whole roof of the cottage was on fire, and the red hot sparks began to fly up into the night air.

Then there came a sudden crash, and the woodwork supporting the thatch, which had been smouldering some hours, gave way, carrying with it a mass of burning embers into the principal room of the cottage.

"Fire!" cried Dottman, as he sprung to his feet from the slight slumber that had come over him.

Dora was fully aroused, and in a few moments a scene of confusion ensued which can only be witnessed amid a night conflagration.

Personal danger there was little or none; but it was something astonishing to see how the flames, when once they attained a certain power, run riot through the cottage.

Roaring, hissing, and swallowing up in their destructive embraces everything within their reach, they threatened in a short time to leave but the charred embers of that little country abode.

It was with difficulty that Dora succeeded in helping Henry down the narrow staircase, and although they had had time to amply attire themselves against the night air; there was no opportunity of saving a single article but what they wore, from the ruins of the cottage.

"It's all over," said Dottman, as he stood in the garden. "And the very best thing we can do is to go to London, for in the course of another few minutes there will be engines from Brentford and the people will be riding in from the farms in the neighbourhood; but as we don't at all want to make acquaintances, or answer questions, I fancy the sooner we are off the better."

"We will go at once," said Dora. "Thank heaven, Henry, that you are well enough to ride. You shall take Starlight."

"No, no!" said Henry. "Dottman has a horse. If anything disastrous should happen it will be pleasant to me to think that you are the best mounted."

Dottman ran to the stable, but it was with considerable reluctance that either of the horses faced the firelight sufficiently to come out into the garden.

"How are you to proceed, Dottman?" said Dora.

"I will come to town on foot, and we shall find some place of meeting."

"No," said Henry, "I am but a light weight, and this horse is strong and powerful, it will carry us both easily for a few miles."

"That it will," said Dottman, "and I must confess I am loth to part company."

The cottage now was a complete blaze, and the heat thrown out by the fire was very great. There was no portion of it that was not enveloped in flames.

They left the garden, and reached the lane.

It was then that Dora clasped her hands, and cried out aloud—

"The money and jewels! the money and jewels! Alas, we have forgotten all in the excitement of this conflagration!"

Henry Dacres uttered a deep sigh.

Dottman looked aghast, and raising himself as high as he could upon the horse, he glanced over the garden wall only to see how utterly hopeless it would be to attempt to recover anything from the fire, which was now blazing like a furnace.

The sound of horses feet now, and the grinding of wheels came rapidly down the lane.

CHAPTER XXXVI.

DORA TAKES REFUGE IN OLD KENSINGTON PALACE—THE SEVEN CONSPIRATORS—A NEW MYSTERY—DOTTMAN'S ADVICE TO DORA.

DORA felt the necessity of soon leaving the spot where, at all events, she had hoped that, until the time arrived when a remove to London could be easily effected, she and her husband would find a shelter.

It would be manifestly imprudent to re-remain by Captain Hawk's cottage until strangers reached it.

"Come," she said, "all is over here. Let us proceed at once."

It was not possible that Dora should utter these words without a deep sigh accompanying them, and she, perhaps for the first time, at that instant estimated how much peace and happiness she had passed in that little lane among the trees.

Henry Dacres, too, sighed.

"Never mind," said Dottman, "the world is still all before us."

"It is—it is!" replied Dora.

"I am not yet strong enough," said Henry Dacres sadly.

"We will fight for you, Mr. Dacres," added Dottman, "until you are."

"And there is one thing that we may yet rejoice at," said Dora.

"What is that, dear Dora? What is that?"

"The return of Starlight."

"Ah, then you mean to take to the road again?"

Henry said this in a tone of great depression, and Dora was anxious to do away with the idea.

She was hardly, perhaps, aware of how much her husband really knew of the many adventures she had already met with in company of the noble Arabian steed.

She had had to keep the knowledge from him, because she thought it would cause him disquietude, but it was a matter of impossibility completely do so.

Both herself and Dottman could not help letting fall a word now and then which sufficiently betrayed the secret.

But there was no time to waste in the discussion of such a question.

A very few moments more would bring the neighbours to the conflagration.

They, therefore, at once, after one more look at the burning cottage, took their course down the lane.

They had not proceeded far when they became aware that some horsemen were rapidly approaching.

"Some danger threatens us!" said Henry.

"Let us hope not," said Dora.

"I will ride on in advance,"' said Dottman, "and see who these people are."

"Do so—do so!"

Dottman's horse was a strong one, and although on this occasion it carried double, the creature made no difficulty about breaking into a trot.

Dora proceeded about twenty yards behind.

Dottman soon saw the horsemen, for the night clouds had become much lighter, and the reflection, too, of the burning cottage came strongly among the trees."

"Halt!" cried a voice.

"Ah!" said Dottman, "I know that voice."

"Whose is it?" asked Henry.

"It is that of an officer of the police, named Shearman."

"Halt!" said the voice again.

"We are lost!" said Henry.

"No, no! where is your hand?"

"Here—here!"

"Take this pistol, and when I say 'fire,' do you at once discharge it among our foes."

"And Dora?"

"That will save her. I have agreed with her that whenever there is danger on the road, I will go on in advance, and she shall play the part of one who has been assailed by a highwayman."

The officers, for such they were, now reached the point of the lane where they could not but see Dottman and Henry Dacres.

Dottman spurred the horse forward.

"Halt! or we will fire at you!" said the man named Shearman.

"Fire!" cried Dottman.

Henry Dacres at once discharged the pistol with which Dottman had furnished him.

Dottman at the same moment spurred the horse forward again, and in the confusion which the officers were thrown into by the pistol shot, he succeeded in passing them.

"Stoop low, Mr. Dacres," he said.

Henry did so, and Dottman himself, likewise, stooped in the saddle.

It was well that they did so, for the sharp report of a pistol let them see that their enemies were disposed to do all the injury they could.

"Safe!" said Dottman, and they galloped onwards.

Dora, in another moment, came face to face with the troop of officers.

"Have you stopped the highwayman?" she asked.

"No," said one of the officers. "What highwayman do you mean?"

"A man on a dark bay horse, who has just gone on in advance, with another behind him."

"Was it a highwayman?"

"Most certainly. They stopped me and robbed me about half a mile down the lane."

"The rascals!"

"So say I. But I am well mounted, and mean to follow them into London."

"Good luck to you," said the chief

officer. "I am only sorry that my duty lies in this direction, or I would go with you."

"Are you, then, on some expedition in this part of the world?"

"I am."

"May I ask what it is?"

"Oh, yes, it is no secret now. We have received private information that a country cottage near here is in the occupation of suspicious persons, and we want to search it."

"Ah, indeed! Does it not strike you that that may be the very cottage which is in flames?"

"No. We thought the fire was at some hay stacks or corn ricks."

"I think you will find it at the cottage you name. Good night!"

"Good night. Come on, my men!"

The officers rode hastily in one direction, and Dora rode hastily still in the other."

Dottman had stopped at the corner of the lane for Dora to come up, and Henry was in an agony of apprehension. His delight at seeing her and still in safety, was very great.

"Ah, Dora," he said, "I shall never be able to ride on again, and leave you to the chances of whatever may befall you."

"I am safe."

"Thank heaven!"

"To London! to London now, at once!" said Dottman. "There is, after all, more rest and safety there than anywhere else, because there is more obscurity."

"It may be so! On—on!"

They galloped forwards now towards town; but it became a matter of very serious consideration, indeed, where they should go to when they got there.

Dora knew that she had given Dottman some money, and as she had, in the hurry of escaping from the fire at Captain Hawk's cottage, left all behind her, she was now anxious to know what means he had at his disposal.

They were really not far from the little village of Kensington Gravel Pits, when Dora asked the question of Dottman.

That district of London was at the period of which we write, much more thinly inhabited than it is now.

Bayswater, Kensington Gravel Pits, and Notting Hill, which now all run the one into the other, forming one immense suburb of the giant city, were then distinct villages.

"Dottman," said Dora, "I fancy we have no money but what you may happen to have about you."

"Eight guineas," said Dottman.

Dora sighed.

"And only a few hours ago," she said, we had reason to think ourselves positively rich, and it was becoming almost a perplexity to know what to do with our money."

"Alas, alas!" said Henry Dacres.

"That was about it," added Dottman. "But never despair, captain."

"I will not despair."

"But what shall we do?" said Henry, "and whither shall we go for shelter?"

"I am thinking," said Dora.

"May I think, too?" said Dottman.

"Oh, yes, yes! and it is more than probable that your thoughts will be the most useful and practical of the two."

"I don't know that; but I will tell you what they are."

"Speak freely, Dottman."

"You may know, captain, and you, Mr. Dacres, or you may not, that old Kensington Palace, since there have been two deaths in the royal family within its walls, has been abandoned as a residence."

"I did not know," remarked Henry.

"Nor I," said Dora.

"Well, such is the fact. I have no doubt in the world but that there is no one in the palace. It may be that in some one or other of the out-offices there is a servant, or perhaps two, but the palace itself is shut up."

"We are close to it, Dottman."

"We are captain."

"Then I can guess what you would say. You think we might find refuge there."

"I do, indeed."

"It is a romantic thought," said Dora, "to be burnt out of a cottage, and then to find refuge in a palace."

"A change for the better," said Dottman.

"What say you, Henry," said Dora, "shall it be so?"

"You shall decide, Dora."

"Then I say yes."

"And a wise decision it is," said Dottman. "The palace can be easily reached so soon as we can make our way into the old wilderness of a garden that surrounds it."

"Ah," said Dora, "there will be the difficulty."

"Not a great one, captain."

"Can you surmount the wall with a horse?"

"No, captain—but towards the north portion of the palace there is a little private garden, and a conservatory. The wall which bounds that garden has a small door in it which goes out into a narrow lane, that winds along to the grounds of Holland House. Follow me, captain, and I fancy it is not a door in a wall that will stop our way."

"Certainly not, if that be all."

Dora followed Dottman, who, being so

well acquainted with the neighbourhood as he was, soon led the way to the narrow lane he had mentioned.

The place was most profoundly still.

They had left all sight and sound of the conflagration of Captain Hawk's cottage some miles in the west behind them.

The hour of the morning was just that one at which the greatest stillness and repose prevails over the whole face of nature.

It was the hour before the first faint rays of the sun of a new day would gleam up from the eastern horizon.

The horses were made to go at so slow a pace that their feet scarcely made the least sound.

The stillness, indeed, was so great, that it began to be offensive.

"Do you think, Dottman," whispered Dora, "that it will be easy to effect an entrance to the palace?"

"Oh, yes. Some door or some window will yield to us. Stop!"

"Yes, yes. Where are we now?"

"Close to the small door in the wall of the little private garden."

Dora looked up, and she saw the palace looking dark and solemn against the night sky.

There came now from old Kensington gardens the gentle murmuring sound of a light morning breeze among the tops of the tall trees.

It was a sound that resembled the faint rushing of the tide of the sea.

Dottman dismounted.

He was well provided with the means of picking any lock which might come in his way; and that of the door before them yielded in a moment.

But the door remained fast.

There was some mode of fastening it from within.

This, however, presented no difficulty, for the wall was not by any means a high one, and from the back of the horse Dottman could easily put his arm over the top of it.

He climbed over the wall, and dropped easily upon the soft mould of the bed on the inner side.

There were two stout bolts to the door, and upon their removal of course it opened in a moment.

Dora and Henry Dacres rode at once into the private garden of Kensington Palace.

"It will be better to dismount," said Dottman, "and lead the horses."

"Far better," replied Dora, as she alighted from Starlight.

Henry too dismounted, and then, preceded by Dottman, they noiselessly made their way along a narrow garden path towards the palace.

There was a range of windows belonging to some saloons upon the ground floor, and it seemed to Dottman that it would probably be easier to get into the palace by one of them than at any doorway.

On approaching one of the windows, Dottman was rather surprised to find that it could easily be raised.

To be sure there were closed shutters within, but if they were only fastened by a bar of iron, Dottman thought he could manage to raise that by inserting the thin blade of a knife.

Dottman was about to do so when, to the surprise and consternation of them all, they heard whispered voices coming from within the room of the palace which that range of windows opened into.

Dottman spoke to Dora in a very low voice indeed.

"Do you hear?" he said.

"Yes."

"What can all this mean?"

"Hush! stand aside."

It was in good time that Dora gave this order, and she and Henry and Dottman only just succeeded in drawing back and hiding themselves and the horses among the shrubbery of the garden, when the shutters of the very window which Dottman had opened, were unclosed.

A very faint light from a hand lantern shone from the room within.

Dora then counted no less than seven men who came out of the palace into the garden.

They each stepped over the window sill with ease and deliberation, and it was quite evident that they had not the least idea that any one was there present but themselves.

Dora was afraid that one of the horses might make some sound which must have had the effect of at once letting these seven men know that other persons were in the private garden.

That, in fact, was the principal danger.

The men all reached the garden, and the last one of the seven pulled the shutters of the window close.

Then one of them spoke.

"It was imprudent, my lord," he said, in a low subdued voice, "to leave the window open."

"I could have sworn I had closed it," replied another.

"It was open."

"Then I must have left it. But we are so completely alone here that our safety is assured."

"Oh, no doubt of that," said another.

"I am rejoiced," added a fourth voice,

"that we have agreed so well to-night in our resolution."

"And I, too," said another.

"Yes, my lords and gentlemen, "a common and complete agreement will have the effect of convincing the Court of Rome that the change in the government and religion of this conntry, which we propose to bring about, will be effectually carried out."

"No doubt—no doubt!" said another. "And now that you have all adopted my opinion, that the death of the king is a much more safe measure than his dethronement, I am sure we shall succeed."

"We must succeed in our plot," said another. "It is success or death!"

So speaking, these seven men made their way through the garden by the very same little narrow path which had been so recently trodden by Dora and Dottman, and Henry Dacres.

In about five minutes, when no sound of the slightest character signified that they could be within hearing, Dora ventured to speak.

"This is, indeed," she said, "a strange piece of fortune. We have, by the merest accident in the world, it appears, become cognisant of a plot against the government."

"Yes," said Dottman, "and a project to assassinate the king."

"What shall we do, Dora?" asked Henry Dacres, in a tone of anxiety.

"What can we do?" replied Dora. "We are ourselves in peril."

"Well," said Dottman, as he pushed open the shutters of the room window by which the conspirators had emerged, "I don't at all see what it matters to us. If the Jacobites can get the upper hand of the Hanoverian faction, why well and good."

"You are a Jacobite, I know, Dottman," said Dora.

"And so, captain, was your honoured father," replied Dottman, as he touched his hat, which ceremony he always went through whenever he mentioned the late Duke of Kingston, Dora's father.

"Alas, yes!" said Dora, "and hence all the calamities which have fallen upon our house."

"It is the right cause for all that!" muttered Dottman.

"We must think over all this," remarked Henry.

"Rather forget it, Mr. Dacres," said Dottman. "But here, you have nothing to do but to step into Kensington Palace."

"The horses?" said Dora.

Dottman struck his forehead with his open hand, as he said—

"How could I be so forgetful? There are stables close at hand—I will soon give them a royal lodging. Wait for me, captain, and I will be with you presently."

The stables of Kensington Palace were not many paces from the private garden, and Dottman soon succeeded in placing Starlight and his own horse in comfortable quarters, with plenty of hay.

Corn he must procure for them, he found, in the morning, as best he could.

He then made his way back to where he had left Dora and Henry Dacres.

———

CHAPTER XXXVII.

DORA'S REFLECTIONS—THE FALSE JEWELS —THE START FROM TYBURN GATE.

THE room of Kensington Palace into which Dora and her husband made their way by the open window, was a very spacious one.

They were in profound darkness as yet in it, but they could judge that it was large by a certain feel that the air had within it.

When Dottman came back, he spoke in a low, cautious tone.

"There is no likelihood at all, captain," he said, "that any one is in the palace, but we may as well ascertain the fact before we make any noise."

"Yes—we cannot be too cautious," remarked Henry Dacres.

"I would fain," said Dora, "see where we really are."

"That you shall soon, captain," added Dottman, as he carefully closed the window and the shutters, and then lit a match, and by its aid ignited a piece of wax candle, which he held high above his head, so that it shed a feeble ray of light for a considerable distance around it.

Dora uttered an exclamation of surprise.

The spacious apartment in which they were was most elegantly and sumptuously furnished and fitted up.

The roof was very finely painted, and the walls very profusely gilded; but the most remarkable piece of ornamentation in the apartment was a very large chimney-piece, a fine exhibition of carving.

In the centre of the saloon was a table, around which were grouped seven chairs, which, no doubt, had been in the occupation of those seven conspirators who had been so fully observed, while they, at the same time, thought themselves so free from observation.

"We shall lodge royally enough here, my Dora," said Henry Dacres, "if we can do so with safety."

DORA AND DOTTMAN AT TYBURN GATE.

"The conspirators will return," said Dora.

"But the palace is large enough," remarked Dottman, "and we may find many a room in which we can lodge without interrupting them. It seems to me a lucky chance which has brought us here, captain."

Dora was silent for a few moments. She could guess very well what was passing in Dottman's mind—he was anxious for the success of those seven men who were conspiring against the government—in all probability he would adopt some means of letting them know how much he sympathised with them.

DORA.—19.

This idea filled Dora with a thousand apprehensions, for she had seen with terror and confusion in her own family the fearful consequences of mingling in Jacobite plots.

Had not her father come to his death, and was she not a penniless fugitive simply on that account?

Dora made up her mind seriously to remonstrate with Dottman on the subject.

She had little doubt that by putting his affection for her in contrast with his political animus, that the former would triumph over the latter.

Dottman's little light by which that large apartment had, for a time, been illuminated, now showed signs of going out; but as it expired, there came through a crevice of the shutters a light of a different kind.

The morning was rapidly approaching, and this light was comprised of its first faint beams.

And now came other serious considerations connected with her sojourn in the old Palace of Kensington.

How were they to procure food?

"Dottman," said Dora, "at whatever danger, you must sally forth, and procure for us the means of sustaining life."

"I'll manage that," said Dottman. "You may depend upon it that we are the only inhabitants of the palace at present. The morning is coming, and I shall soon be able to go out into the village of Kensington for the purchase of provisions; but before I do so I would recommend that we make a tour through the palace, and pitch upon some rooms to stay in that will not be of so public a character as this one."

This advice was too rational to be neglected, and Dora and Henry, with the assistance of Dottman, made a most interesting tour through old Kensington Palace.

They finally pitched upon a suite of four apartments which were on the first floor, and two of which comprised elegant bed chambers.

"So long," said Dora, "as we are permitted to occupy this place, these would be the rooms I should prefer, 'for they command an extensive view of the gardens."

Henry, whose strength was still but inefficient, had suffered a good deal of fatigue on that early morning, although certainly, in consequence of the fire at Captain Hawk's cottage happening late, he could not be said to have been entirely deprived of a night's rest.

Dora was glad to see him, however, sink into a state of profound repose, and then, while Dottman, with abundant caution, made his way to the village of Kensington to procure a store of food, she gave herself up to reflections on the singularity and many perils of their present position.

What was she to do for the future?

That was the question which presented itself to her with startling earnestness.

How strangely had wealth come within her grasp, and then eluded it; and then, in how singular a manner had Starlight, the horse, found his way again into her possession!

Was it fate, destiny, or call it what she might, which seemed to point out for her at present a life on the road as her only means of subsistence?

Then she thought of the singular scene which had taken place in the old Temple;

and she asked herself if it would be prudent ever again to venture within the precincts of those chambers so full of mystery.

There was something melancholy in the profound stillness of Kensington Palace.

The atmosphere seemed to take a different character as it ranged through the suite of those deserted rooms, and it was a great relief to Dora to be able to listen to the quiet breathing of Henry Dacres as he slept in peace in the palatial residence.

She became anxious for the return of Dottman, whose stay she thought was protracted considerably beyond the period she had supposed.

But time lagged slowly in that silent place, and although Dottman was in reality quick about his errand, he appeared to Dora to have been gone a long and anxious time.

Provisions sufficient to last for several days were brought by Dottman, and there was quite a look of gratification upon his face as he said—

"I got into a brief talk with one of the men at the lodge of old Kensington Gardens, and he tells me that he, as well as all the other keepers, is convinced that the palace is haunted; and if that be the case, we are not likely to be interrupted, and if we are, it will not give us a deal of trouble to assist a little in the popular belief. There is one thing, however, captain, that I want to speak to you of."

Dora had left the chamber in which Henry was sleeping, and was conversing with Dottman in another of the suite of apartments.

"It is something that makes you anxious, I can see by your looks," she said.

"It is, indeed."

"Speak freely. I have learnt to bear with equanimity ill tidings."

"Well, it's not so very bad, captain; but I found when I came to look in my pockets that there was but one guinea instead of eight left in them."

"Then we are nearly penniless?"

"Not far off it, captain."

Dora looked sad.

"I feel it," she said, "I know that it is coming. A life on the road again, with all its excitements, and all its perils. Conceal this from my husband! It is sufficient that I encounter danger, without his having the agony and terror to know that I do so while I am absent from him."

The day wore on in the old palace without any evidence of note; but Dora was curious and anxious to know if the conspirators would make another appearance at night for the purpose of further hatching their treasonable designs against the government.

But midnight came and passed away, and

the solitude and silence of the old palace were undisturbed.

Henry had recovered much from his fatigue, and Dora had held another consultation with Dottman, which had resulted in her consent on the next evening to mount Starlight, and seek her fortune once again upon the road and on the heath.

Dora thought there were more difficulties in the way of this proceeding than there really existed, for Dottman had kept in the stable at Captain Hawk's cottage, in a small travelling valise, the whole of the appointments and accoutrements with which she at first sallied forth from the ancient house in the Savoy to try her fortune on the highway.

This valise Dottman had brought away with him from the burning cottage securely strapped to his saddle.

Dora adopted a little deception as regarded Henry, which, however excusable it might be from its motives, she, for a long time, shrunk from perpetrating.

It was this:

She sent Dottman to the village of Kensington, where, at a small lapidary's shop, he purchased, for a few shillings, some mock jewels, which, being of different colours, might well represent to uninstructed eyes, stones of beauty and value.

The plan, then, was that Dottman should inform Henry Dacres that he had succeeded in saving some of Captain Hawk's hoard of precious gems.

Dora, then, whenever she went out on an evening expedition on the highway could merely produce one of them, and affect to be proceeding to London cautiously to sell it.

This was disingenuous, but Dora reconciled herself to it for the sake of the peace of mind she knew it would bring to one so dear to her.

It was nine o'clock on the second evening of Dora's residence at Kensington Palace that, close to the little garden door, at which Dottman had originally effected an entrance, he might have been holding a couple of horses.

Dora was above in the palace, as briefly as possible, making Henry understand that it was necessary she should proceed to London to sell one of Captain Hawk's jewels, since their ready money was exhausted.

Every word came reluctantly from Dora's lips, and Henry could not but perceive that there was considerable agitation in her manner.

"I have thought over this Dora," he said, "since Dottman spoke to me of it; and although I am not strong enough to do battle with our enemies, or to defend you, I am quite capable of proceeding to London on such an errand as this."

"But have you no enemies, Henry?"

"I have but one."

"The Duke of Kingston!"

"Yes, Dora—and that, so to speak, is an enemy but at secondhand. He aims at my life because by doing so, he knows and feels that he aims at your happiness."

"Alas, yes!"

"And should he kill me he feels assured that you would scarcely contract a second union, and he would be safer as ultimate heir-at-law to the dukedom, which your existence, and that of a child of yours, would alone deprive him of."

"Yes, Henry, all that is too true; and yet I implore you to let me go on this errand, for were you, in your present weak condition, to encounter only the same perils that I did on the last occasion, I know not what you could do."

"Do you make it a personal wish, Dora, that you should go?"

"I do, indeed!"

"Then I am conquered, and will say no more."

Dora was well pleased to get rid of so startling a difficulty thus easily, and she retired to another room in the palace, where she quickly arranged herself in that costume in which already the reader, in his mind's eye, has seen her so gallant and so handsome seeking adventures on the highway.

Dora performed her highwayman's toilet rapidly, and then, with hasty steps, made her way across the little private garden of the palace to where she knew Dottman would be anxiously awaiting her.

It was a surprise to Dora to see both the horses.

"What is this, Dottman?" she said. "Are you, too, about to leave the palace?"

"With you, captain."

"With me?" exclaimed Dora in surprise.

"Yes. When I urged you to take to the road you didn't suppose, captain, that I meant you to go out alone? No, let me follow you—I shall be able to assist you in case of need, and in a hundred ways to facilitate your operations. Mr. Dacres is as safe here as he can possibly be, and I do not think you need be under the slightest fear on his account. Let me go with you, or give up your intention, and let me go alone."

Dora considered a moment.

She was reluctant to leave Henry alone in the old palace, and yet that reluctance was not of the same character as it had been when they were inhabiting the house in the Savoy.

Then his state of health was not such as to justify his being left alone.

Now the case was widely different.

He could not be said to be strong, but

he was not suffering, and he required no assistance.

Be it so," said Dora, after the few moments of consideration had passed away. " Be it so—you shall go with me. But it is proper that Henry should know that he is left alone. I shall be back to you quickly."

" The dress, captain," said Dottman.

Dora had forgotten for the moment, and would have surprised Henry by going back to him in the full costume of a knight of the road.

" For the moment I had forgotten," she said. " Be yours the task, then, Dottman, to inform him that you accompany me—I will wait for you here."

Dora took charge of the two horses, while Dottman went on this errand, from which he soon returned to say that Henry was much better pleased to hear that he, Dottman, was to accompany her, than as if she went alone.

The small door in the wall was opened, and Dora led Starlight through it into the little lane beyond.

Another moment, and she had mounted the gallant Arabian.

" Once more," cried Dottman, " we're on the road. Hurrah for the road !"

" It is my fate," said Dora.

" And which road, Captain Arod, would you wish to take to-night?"

" You shall choose, Dottman."

" Any but the western, I should say, for it is all alive and astir with what has happened in and about Captain Hawk's cottage."

" Name some other."

" There's the Edgeware Road, captain, commencing at Tyburn Gate."

" An ominous commencement, Dottman."

" But none the worse on that account. It's a capital road, with eight miles of level riding, and twenty offshoots at different parts in the shape of green lanes, by-ways, and narrow turnings, into any of which you might dash with Starlight, and by leaping a fence or two, effectually puzzle all pursuers."

" Be it so. Let that, then, be the road. Lead the way to it, Dottman."

" It wants no leading, captain. You have but to ride straight on till you come to the gate."

" Tyburn Gate ?"

" Don't mind it's name, captain."

" It has a sad recollection for me, Dottman."

" Banish all sad recollections. Let the past take care of itself—the future is all before us, and believe me there's no life in the world like life on the road !"

CHAPTER XXXVIII.

AN ADVENTURE ON THE ROAD—THE HIGH-WAYMAN IS TRUSTED—DORA GOES IN PURSUIT OF PRISCILLA—THE DRIVE TO-WARDS KILBURN.

THERE was certainly something exhilarating to the spirits of Dora in finding herself once again beneath the bright stars, and mounted on that beautiful Arabian steed, which fate seemed determined to present to her as her own.

If she did not feel absolutely inclined to cry out with Dottman that " there was nothing like life on the road," yet the prospect of adventure that presented itself to her was not without its pleasures.

Dora cantered on until they came to the toll house, at Tyburn Gate.

Some contention was going on at the gate with a lady and gentleman, both of whom were on horseback ; and as Dora approached, she heard the lady say, in a cold, harsh voice—

" It is very strange that you cannot tell who has passed through the gate within the last hour."

" It's no business of mine," said the man, with a certain abruptness of manner, " and besides, it is not the best way, ma'am, to get a man to say what he knows, to call him a ' fellow,' and the other to lay a riding whip over his shoulders."

" There ! there !" exclaimed the gentleman, " you have, as usual, Roxy, spoilt all by your abominable temper, you see."

" Sir John," said the lady, " I will trouble you to mind your own affairs, and to recollect that among strangers I am Lady Lufton, and at home, not Roxy, but Roxalana, if you please."

The gatekeeper laughed.

" Hark you, my good fellow," said the gentleman, " here is a guinea."

" Ah, sir, you know how to speak."

" I will give it to you if you will tell me whether or no a young girl on a cream-coloured pony, has passed through Tyburn Gate within the last hour?"

" No, then, sir," replied the man.

" There is your guinea, then."

The turnpike keeper tossed up the guinea and caught it in his hand again, as he added—

" I don't at all mind telling you, Sir John, that a young lady on a cream-coloured pony did not come through Tyburn Gate, but she went up the Edgeware Road."

" Ah, indeed !"

" Are you sure ?" cried the lady, whose name was Roxalana.

"What will you give, ma'am, if I say I am sure?"

"Come on! come on!" said the gentleman, "come on, Lady Lufton! We shall soon overtake Priscilla, and take her home again, when, I hope, you will look more sharply after her for the future."

They both turned their horses heads in the direction of the Edgeware Road, and galloped off.

"Now, young fellow," cried the turnpikekeeper to Dora, as she was passing with Starlight through the gate, "the toll, if you please."

"Here," said Dottman, as he flung the man a crown, "you can keep the change."

"Thanks your honour."

"You will know us again, and if we should be in a hurry—"

"Ah, I know. You can have the gate opened quick, you mean?"

"That is all right. I understand."

Dottman laughed

"You make friends of the turnpike men, Dottman, I see," said Dora, when they had proceeded a few paces up the Edgeware Road.

"To be sure, captain. It's the very best thing you can do. If you are pursued, through you go like a shot out of a gun, and bang goes shut the gate in the faces of those behind you. Bless you, captain, a clever pikeman, who wants to do you a good turn, can give you a good five minutes start at any time."

"I don't doubt it. How dark the road is!"

"Very. A good job, too!"

"What sounds are those?"

"Carriage wheels, captain. Ah, there are the lights, too! It is a chariot, I fancy."

Dora's heart beat quickly.

"Well, captain," said Dottman, after a slight pause, "do you know that in learning to swim what is one half the battle."

"No. What?"

"The first plunge."

"I think I comprehend you."

"To be sure you do, captain. We are on this road to-night to do the best we possibly can, and the first cry of 'Stand!' that you give, is like the first plunge in swimming—you will think nothing of it after that."

"Then that chariot which is advancing you think I may as well begin with?"

"Just so."

"Be it so, then."

Dora touched Starlight slightly on the neck, and the Arabian bounded forwards.

The chariot was coming down a little rise of the road, at the top of which was a windmill, and by the time it had reached the hollow Dora was close to the horses' heads.

"Stand!" she cried.

"Woa!" said the coachman. "By jingo, it's a highwayman, my lady!"

A scream came from some one within the carriage, and an old lady put her head out in so insolent and reckless a manner that it encountered one of the lamps, and smashed it to pieces.

"Murder! murder! he has killed me at once!" cried the old lady, under a full belief that it was the highwayman who had struck her, or sent a bullet into her brains.

"We are all murdered!" said the coachman.

"If you don't keep your horses still," said Dora, "I will put a brace of bullets in your head."

"Woa! woa! good lord, Mr. Highwayman! don't be obstropolous! Oh, don't!"

Dora was by the side of the chariot in a moment.

"Now, madam! your money, if you please."

"Murder!"

"Very good. If you have a fancy for being murdered, I don't mind."

"You wretch! you artful villain! Cannot a poor lone gentlewoman travel in her own chariot from Kilburn to London without being stopped by a Jackanapes like you?"

"It seems not," said Dora. "My time is rather valuable likewise."

"Is it?"

"I assure you it is, madam. Therefore, if you will be quick with your purse—"

"Oh, you young villain! There, then!"

"A thousand thanks!" said Dora, as she took a tolerably well-filled purse from the old lady. "I am sorry to have incommoded you, madam, and so now good night."

"Stop!"

"What is it?"

"As you have taken my money, perhaps you don't mind answering me a question?"

"Certainly not."

"Did you come up the road from the Oxford Road?"

"I did."

"Then have you seen a young lady— quite a child, indeed, for she is only fourteen years and a half old, on a cream-coloured pony?"

"No, madam."

"Dear me! dear me!"

"Everybody," thought Dora, "seems to-night to be interested about some young lady on a cream-coloured pony. I wonder what it can mean?"

"Poor child! poor child!" said the old lady in the chariot. "Where can she be?"

"Perhaps, madam," added Dora, "I can

give you some other information that may be useful to you."

"What? oh, what?"

"I came through Tyburn Gate from the Western Road, and as I reached it I found a lady and gentleman on horseback questioning the keeper of the turnpike."

"Ah!"

"Yes, madam, and about a young lady on a cream-coloured pony. They wanted particularly to know which way she had gone, and the gentleman gave the turnpike-man a guinea to tell him."

"Oh, my poor, dear, dear Priscilla!"

"That was the name mentioned."

"Alas! alas! What man, can you tell me?"

"The gentleman's name was Sir John, and the lady was called by him, Roxalana."

"Then the dear child is lost!"

The old gentlewoman in the chariot sobbed bitterly.

Dora's sensitive heart was touched.

"Madam," she said, "will you trust me?"

"Trust you? How? how?"

"To help you."

"Alas! I know not how you can help me!".

"Tell me who the young lady on the cream-coloured pony is, and what the lady and gentleman, who are in pursuit of her want with her?"

"I will tell you. Something at my heart seems to whisper to me that I may tell you. The young girl is my godchild, the gentleman is her uncle, and the lady is her aunt, by marriage with Sir John Lufton. She is entitled to a large property if she marries with their consent, or when she comes of age, and they want her to wed with the son of the Lady Roxalana, who is as bad a youth as his mother is a woman."

"And she has fled from them?"

"Yes. The dear young creature has been a prisoner for weeks in their house in Bedford Square, because she would not consent to marry James Brickerton, the son of that terrible woman."

"And the son of Sir John?"

"Oh, no! Her son by some former marriage, if marriage at all."

"I see—I see!"

"Well, poor dear Priscella managed to get a note conveyed to me by a groom boy, who had the care of her pony, and who is much attached to her, and I sent her an answer to say that I would protect her if she could get to me, and so at last it was arranged that by the assistance of Samuel—"

"The groom boy?"

"Yes, yes. By his assistance, she was to start on her pony this night, and meet me here on the Edgeware Road."

"And you have not seen her?"

"Alas, no!"

"Her foes are on the road, too, and by this time must have passed your carriage."

"She is lost! oh, she is lost! They will take her back again, and her situation will be worse than before."

"I will help her," said Dora.

"You will?"

"On my word I will."

"Ah! then how well bestowed is that purse I gave to you, young man."

"Don't say anything of that; I must give it back to you, or else I shall think I am paid to help you. There it is."

"You are not a highwayman, then?" Dora smiled.

"No, I am not exactly a highwayman."

By this time Dottman had become rather alarmed, or if not positively alarmed, certainly a little anxious at the long delay of Dora by the carriage door, and he advanced to the side of the road and blew a silver whistle he had with him.

The old lady uttered a scream of surprise and terror, for she thought that the road was beginning to be alive with highwaymen.

"Oh! who is that? What is that?"

"Only a friend of mine," said Dora. "Oh, Dottman, come this way!"

"Here captain!" said Dottman, as in another moment he was by the side of Dora.

"Will you gallop up the road, Dottman, and see if you can find a young lady, or a cream coloured pony?"

"Do you mean the young lady that was mentioned by the turnpike-keeper, captain?"

"The same. You hear, madam, that I have not deceived you, since my friend here and myself have had no communication for the last few minutes."

"I am perfectly satisfied."

"Holloa!" cried Dottman, "I don't think we shall have to go far, captain, for I can hear the sound of horses' feet upon the road—ay! and loud voices, too; I should not wonder if the young lady is captured after all."

"Save her—oh, save her!" cried the elderly gentlewoman in the carriage. "I will be most grateful to you both if you will save her; but there will be no safety for her if they know where she is—they will take her from me, and I have no one to resist their doing so."

Dora considered for a few moments.

"Madam," she said, "I think if you will be guided by me, this matter may be satisfactorily arranged. It seems to me that you must lend me your chariot for a short time, and let me appear to be the rescuer of the young lady."

"Yes, yes—a most happy thought," cried the old gentlewoman. Neither Sir John Lufton, nor that dreadful wife of his are acquainted with either my carriage or coachman."

"Then, madam, if, for the accomplishment of this object you do not mind getting out and walking up the hill, which you can do without observation under the deep shadow of the hedges on the wayside, my friend and myself will manage this little matter for you."

"Anything! anything!" cried the old lady. "Anything to save the dear girl from those people who would make her wretched for life."

"The sound of approaching horses' feet came nearer still—voices, too, were heard; one in expostulation and grief, and others in loud threatening tones."

There was no time to be lost.

Dora turned to Dottman and spoke to him anxiously and quickly.

"Tie your own horse, Dottman, to some tree or gate-post, and mount Starlight. I am about to get into the carriage, and it will be your duty to rescue, from the lady and gentleman we saw at Tyburn Gate, the young lady on the cream coloured pony who, no doubt from the sounds we hear, is in their power."

Dottman quickly comprehended what was required of him; but he suggested an alteration in the mode of proceeding.

"Let me keep my own horse, captain," he said. You may safely trust to Starlight; he will follow the carriage like a dog, knowing you are inside, and will be quite safe at the same time from any stray shot if a few bullets should happen to fly about in this adventure."

"If you think so, so be it."

"I am certain, captain."

"Very well, then, I leave the rest of the affair in your hands."

"I will manage it."

Dora immediately dismounted, and patting the neck of Starlight, she let go the bridle, looking anxiously for a few moments to see if the creature shewed any alarm or disposition, now that it was free, to make use of its liberty.

But the Arabian steed looked quite calm and contented, seeming, at the the same time, with its sharp intelligent eyes, to be watching the whole proceeding.

"He will follow," said Dottman—"there is not a doubt in the world about it."

"Now then, madam," said Dora to the old gentlewoman, "if you will alight and walk on, I hope that not many minutes will elapse before we shall be able to place the young lady in your charge."

"Heaven bless you both!" cried the old gentlewoman as she alighted from the carriage. "Providence has certainly sent you to the rescue of the innocent and the oppressed this night."

The old lady, notwithstanding all her fears, was a woman of determination; and although the road was in anything but a pleasant state for travelling in on foot, in consequence of the recent rains; and she was probably as unaccustomed as any one could possibly be to such a mode of proceeding, she yet, with much more alacrity and speed than any one could have supposed her capable of, went to the roadside, and under cover of the deep shadow of the bushes, hastened onward.

"It seems to me, captain," said Dottman, "that we have, at all events, set up our carriage."

"No, no!" replied Dora, "let a little adventure like this at times plead to our own minds and consciences as a set-off against more doubtful proceedings."

"I don't see a bit, captain, that so respectable a calling as the road needs any excuses."

"Forward! forward!" said Dora— "there is no time to lose! Stop those people, and rescue that young lady from them."

"It's as good as done!" said Dottman, as he loosened the pistols in the holsters of his saddle, and then giving the rein to his horse, darted forward on the road.

Dora stepped into the chariot and closed the door after her.

She let down the front window, and gave the coachman a pull by the cape of his coat.

"What's your name, my good man?"

"Ebenezer, if you please, Mr. Highwayman; but as I'm much the same as a dead man now, I don't know that I ought to call myself anything."

"What's the matter?"

"Won't murder be the end of it?"

"Nonsense! Turn your horses' heads towards the country, and drive slowly."

"Yes, Mr. Highwayman—anything you please, but spare my life."

"Your life is in no danger—you have but to obey my directions and you will be perfectly safe."

"I only wish I was," muttered the coachman. "There's going to be a fight I'll be bound; and perched up here on the box, they'll all have a shot at me."

"Quick!" said Dora, "I'm not in the habit of having to ask people to do things twice."

"I shouldn't think you *was*," said the coachman, "with a cut-throat pistol in your hand to frighten people out of their lives."

The coachman turned his horses' heads country-ways, and at an easy trot, the carriage was taken towards Kilburn.

CHAPTER XXXIX.

MATRIMONIAL DISPUTES.—THE CREAM-COLOURED PONY—PRISCILLA'S DARING AND COURAGE.—THE COUNT IN SEARCH OF A WIFE.

DOTTMAN was considerably amazed at the whole transaction in regard to the young lady on the cream-coloured pony; and as he had taken a great and sudden aversion to the masculine looking female who was named Roxalana, he began to enter more into the spirit of the adventure than at first he had felt inclined to do.

The road was quiet enough; and owing to the wind blowing from the north, the sound of the approaching horses' feet, and of the remonstrances of the young lady on the cream-coloured pony, and the threatenings and abuse of her captors, by a good space of time, actually preceded the presence of the party.

Dottman, however, soon saw them a little a-head of him, and then he checked his horse's speed until it became first a walk and then he stood perfectly still, like a dark equestrian statue set up in the middle of the road.

"You shall not escape us a second time," he heard Lady Lufton cry in a shrill vicious tone of voice—"you knew perfectly well, you wretched girl, that Sir John Lufton is your guardian, appointed by law; and as I am the wife of Sir John Lufton, my will and pleasure is the only thing you have to look to."

"But I am cruelly treated," replied Priscilla—"you know that I am cruelly treated; and your son, madam, whom I cannot help hating, makes it no secret that it is my fortune you want him to possess."

"Hate my son? You insolent hussy! Hate my son, with every quality on the earth!"

"Oh, Lady Lufton, you know that he is so ugly, and such a bad disposition, that not even a dog will stay with him. I appeal to you, Sir John Lufton, for you are my real uncle— I appeal to you to protect me from your cruel wife and her vicious son."

Lady Roxalina Lufton uttered a yell of rage.

"Wait till I get you home, hussy!" she said, "and I'll teach you to appeal to people who you know dare not call their souls their own in my company—that is to say, I mean, who fully approve of all I do."

"Madam, your first words were the true ones," said Priscilla, with unwonted spirit.

"Hold her a moment, and let me box her ears!" cried Lady Lufton—"hold her, Sir John!"

"My dear Roxalana," said Sir John, "don't you think we had better get home with as little confusion and noise as possible? When you get her to Bedford Square it will be quite another thing."

"Hold your tongue, Sir John, nobody wants your silly remarks!"

"Hold! hold Roxalana! what's that?"

"What's what?"

"In the middle of the road. There! A man on horseback!"

"It's nothing to me if there are fifty men on horseback."

"Halt!" cried Dottman in a loud ringing voice.

"Help! help!" cried Priscilla. "I will call upon any one to help me, for I cannot be more unhappy than I am."

"Stop her mouth!" said Lady Lufton. "Push your gloves into her throat and stop her mouth."

"Halt!" said Dottman again, and then he rode forward until he was face to face with the two horses, and the cream-coloured pony.

Lady Lufton had hold of one side of the bridle of the pony, and Sir John of the other, so that unless Priscilla had voluntarily thrown herself on to the road she was completely a prisoner.

"Halt!" cried Dottman a third time. "Halt I say, on peril of your lives!"

"A highwayman I'll be bound," said Sir John—"the road's infested with them."

"Shoot him at once," said Lady Roxalana.

"My dear, that's very easily said, but to shoot a man you must have pistols, and I have none."

"Then you ought to have."

"That's quite another thing."

"May I ask," said Dottman, assuming a high sarcastic tone of voice, "who has the impertinence to ride upon this road without leave of the count?"

"Leave of the who?" cried Lady Roxalana. The man's mad!"

"What's the age of the young lady?"

"What's that to you, ruffian?"

"And what's your age? And what's the age of the man?"

This singular mode of address so astonished Sir John and Lady Lufton, as well as Priscilla, that they all three gazed at him in silent amazement.

The count is weary of his seventh wife," said Dottman—"and as this is one of the

PRISCILLA AND DORA BECOME ACQUAINTED.

roads upon his little manor, he has come out to look for an eighth. I am his secretary and likewise his treasurer."

"Get out of the way!" said Lady Lufton Some escaped lunatic, I see. Knock him down at once, Sir John!"

"He seems a stout fellow," remarked Sir John.

"He is," said Dottman—"and armed. The first person who attempts to pass me, will have a swift winged bullet in chase."

"But what do you want," said Sir John, faintly.

"Your money, watches, and trinkets for myself."

"I thought he was a highwayman!"
DORA.—20.

"The villain!" cried Lady Roxalana.

Priscilla began to have hope that after all the pretty well declared highwayman, notwithstanding all his eccentricities, might let her escape.

At this moment, however, the chariot was observed slowly approaching the spot, casting, as it came, a broad glare of light upon the bushes from the one lamp that remained to it.

"Ah! there is help," said Sir John. "Now Mr. Highwayman, your best plan is to make your escape as quickly as possible."

"Oh, no," said Dottman, that's the count."

" What count ? " screamed Lady Roxalana.

" My master."

" But his name ? "

" It is so long and intricate that I have never ventured to pronounce it, although I have been some years in his service."

The carriage stopped.

Dora looked out from the window, and in a languid drawling voice, said—

" What is all this ?　What is amiss ? "

" My Lord Count," said Dottman, " I don't think we need go any further.　Here is a young lady on a cream-coloured pony, who will be only too happy to become your eighth countess."

" No, no ! " cried Priscilla, I only ask of you to be so good as to allow me to pass on freely.　You see I am quite a prisoner with these people, and I want to leave them."

" I fancy she will do," said Dora.　" My last countess was too old."

" I always said so," replied Dottman— " and this young lady, who will be only too happy—"

" No, no ! " again cried Priscilla.　" I do not wish to escape one misery to be plunged into another.　This is cruel jesting, but if you will really do me a service, rescue me from these people, who are my relations it is true, and pretend to be my friends, but with whom I am so unhappy, that I would. rather die than remain any longer in their charge."

" Do you hear her voice, count ? " said Dottman.

" I do."

" Does it suit, count ? "

" It does."

" My dear young lady, you have nothing to do now but to place yourself under the care of the count, who, as quickly as possible, will convey you to his *chateau* in the Pyrenees, where you will live the life of a sovereign princess."

Priscilla seemed to be of opinion that, notwithstanding all she had to endure and suffer while in the custody of Sir John and Lady Lufton, it might be no change for the better to be taken possession of by a strange count, and carried off to a *chateau* in the Pyrenees.

But in this moment of confusion and contrary interests on the road, it seemed to her that there was possibly a third alternative.

Sir John and Lady Lufton were so much occupied and alarmed at what was taking place as not to hold their ward in such strict custody as they had done.　Priscilla was a girl of some spirit, and she thought that it might be possible to break away from them, and make her escape in one direction or

another, from both her guardians, and the singular count who came upon the Edgeware Road to look for an eighth wife.

Priscilla retained the little riding whip in her hand, with which she had started from town on the cream-coloured pony.

She now made good use of it.

With the rapidity of thought she gave, first the hand of Sir John and then that of Lady Lufton, so severe a slash with the whip, that they both, involuntarily, let go the bridle of the cream-coloured pony.

Priscilla was free !

A third appeal of the whip to the flanks of the pony made it give a bound forward, and if Dottman had not been exceedingly smart and rapid in his movements, the young girl would have passed him, and in a few seconds would have been half a mile towards London.

But Dottman wheeled his horse suddenly and caught the bridle of the pony before, after its leap forward, it could arrange its limbs for a gallop.

Priscilla uttered a scream of dismay.

" Hush ! " whispered Dottman, " we are friends of your godmother's, and are doing all this to restore you to her with secrecy."

" Ah ! " cried Priscilla, and the cry was one of joy.　" I understand now."

" Hush, then ! "

" I will—I will !　But do not let them approach me again."

" Trust me for that."

All this passed so suddenly, that Sir John and Lady Lufton could not but suppose that Priscilla had merely exchanged their custody for that of the count's secretary.

They both made a movement forward to the rescue, and that movement brought them sufficiently close to Dottman to see that he held in his hand a long bright barrelled pistol he had taken from the holster of his saddle.

" Keep your places," he said, " or I fire ! "

They both paused, and then Sir John called out to Priscilla—

" Home, girl, home !　No one seems to hinder you !　Ride home, and wait for us— we can but be robbed."

" Well," cried Priscilla, " I'm thinking, uncle."

" Thinking ! " cried Lady Roxalana. " How dare you think ? "

" And I am wondering," said Priscella.

" Wondering about what, you wretched girl ? "

" If the count was handsome."

" Decidedly handsome ! " cried Dottman.

" Then I might do worse," said Priscilla.

" It's the end of the world," said Sir

John. "She seems actually willing to go with this perfect stranger."

"And refuses my son!" said Roxalana.

"Come and look at me, my dear," said Dora from the carriage. "Come and look at me, and judge for yourself."

Priscilla urged her pony to the carriage door, and then Dora said gently—

"Be under no apprehension whatever, young lady—this carriage belongs to your godmother, who is waiting for you on foot some distance further down the road. It seems to me necessary, not only that you should escape from the tyranny of your uncle and aunt, but that they should be in complete ignorance of where you have taken refuge."

"Yes," said Priscilla, "or they would soon reclaim me by force."

"No doubt they would try to do so—therefore all this is to baffle them, since your godmother found that they were on the road in pursuit of you."

"I am very much beholden to you, sir."

"And you will trust me?"

"Oh, yes! how could I refuse to trust so very—"

Priscilla was about to utter her mind rather too freely about the personal appearance of Dora, who certainly looked very handsome in her smart highwayman's costume.

Dora smiled, for she recollected at that moment that Dottman had prophesied to her one of the incidents of her career on the road would be that she would make many hearts ache.

But Dora did not feel disposed, just at that moment, to give up her *incognito*.

"Add to the confusion, my dear Priscilla," she said, "of your uncle and aunt by calling out that you have made up your mind to accompany the count."

"With pleasure. Uncle, I've seen him."

"What do you mean, girl?"

"And I like him and mean to go with him, so good-bye! it's no use looking after me any longer!"

Sir John Lufton and his wife were struck dumb with consternation.

"Say," added Dora to Priscilla, "that the count will instruct his legal adviser to look after your property."

"Uncle," cried Priscilla.

"What now, miserable girl?"

"I don't feel miserable in the least; but I merely wish to say that the count's legal adviser will look after my property."

"I should like to wring your neck and the count's too," screamed Lady Roxalana.

"Now, sir," said Dottman, as he clapped the pistol close to the eyes of Sir John Lufton. "Now, sir, I will trouble you for

whatever coin and valuables you have about you."

"Then you are a highwayman?"

"Anything you please, so that you are quick."

Sir John, with a groan, parted with his purse, which seemed tolerably well filled, and he likewise handed to Dottman a handsome gold watch.

Dottman then turned to Lady Roxalana.

"Now, madam," he said, "it is your turn."

"When you rob a gentleman you have already robbed his wife," she said.

"In ordinary cases, yes," replied Dottman; "but you are evidently so much the better half, that I have no doubt that your purse is even more richly lined than Sir John's, so I will trouble you for it."

"You're a mean wretch!"

"You are welcome to your opinion, madam, so that I have the money."

"Take it, and I wish every guinea of it would choke you."

"Thank you, madam; and now, as I have had my fee, I mean to give you a piece of advice. You know advice gratis is seldom good for anything, but mine will be valuble, as I am pretty well paid for it."

"What is your advice?" said Sir John.

"That you make the best of your way to town, and place, as soon as possible, as long a piece of the Edgeware Road as you can between yourselves and the count. He is a very eccentric man, and after a little adventure like this he is sure to fire all his six pistols out of the carriage windows."

"Come on," cried Sir John. "Confound his eccentricity! it's bad enough to be robbed, but to be shot by a madman as well is worse still."

Sir John and Lady Lufton started forward, and as they passed the carriage Lady Roxalana screamed out—

"You infamous hussy, Priscilla! I will take care that you shall not touch one farthing of your fortune."

"Do not reply to her," said Dora. "I suppose you are a ward in chancery!"

"I am, and my uncle has been appointed guardian."

"Your godmother will, no doubt, be legally empowered to take his place, so that you will have nothing to fear from them."

Dottman rode up to the carriage door.

"They are off," he said.

"Are you certain?" asked Dora.

Dottman looked down the road.

"By Jove! no, they've come to a halt, and seem to be considering what to do next. I think, however, I can start them forward a little quicker."

Dottman fired both his pistols in rapid succession.

Sir John and Lady Lufton thought that the eccentric count was beginning the kind of fusilade from the carriage windows which had been promised, and as they were much too near to be pleasant, in case of stray bullets whistling their way through the air, they put their horses to speed, and soon disappeared towards London.

Dora pulled the coachman by the cape again.

"Ebenezer, you will go on."

"Goodness gracious! is it all over."

"Go on, I say!"

"Yes, your worship's honour, I'm going."

The carriage started forward, and Starlight trotted by the side of Dottman, who, with his right hand, held the rein of the cream-coloured pony, of which so much had been heard on that eventful evening.

The elderly gentlewoman was not above a quarter of a mile a-head, and when the carriage reached her, she cried out in great excitement—

"Priscilla—Priscilla! my dear child, are you there?"

"Ah!" cried Priscilla, "that is my dear godmother's voice. Now, indeed, I know, count, that you have been a friend to me, and I shall love you all my life!"

CHAPTER XL.

THE INVITATION REFUSED—THE ROYAL MAIL — DORA'S EXPEDIENT — THE WOUNDED YOUNG LORD—THE ACQUISITION OF BOOTY.

DORA was well pleased with this adventure, inasmuch as it combined both the elements which she would like to see exhibited by her feats on the road.

Profit and moral justice. She had taken something from the wicked, the bad, and the designing, and she had given something, that is to say, peace and serenity to the good, the gentle, and the deserving.

Priscilla's godmother was delighted to see her, and profuse in her thanks to Dora for the efficient aid she had rendered in her rescue.

"And now, dear sir, you must visit us," she said, "the night is wearing on, and I am quite sure that you can have no business which should interfere with the expression of our gratitude at our own house."

Dora smiled and glanced at Dottman.

"Madam," she said, "I regret that real business of importance must keep me in the open air yet awhile. I am only too well pleased to think that I have been of service to you, and hope that we may meet again

under happier auspices than those of to-night."

Dora then cut short the dozen remonstrances on the part of the old gentlewoman by waving her hand in adieu, and then galloping from the spot.

Dottman followed at good speed, and he and Dora soon found themselves alone together on the road.

"That is over, captain," said Dottman.

"But not the adventures of to-night. I would fain yet go through some other trial of my skill as a highwayman."

"If that, indeed, be the case," said Dottman, "I don't think there will be much difficulty, for I hear the sound of horses' feet, and the grinding of coach wheels upon the road."

"I, too, hear those sounds," said Dora, "but I see nothing."

"No, captain, but that is because we are down in a hollow, and the coach or carriage, or whatever it is, is in another, there being a hill between us. There it is!"

Even as Dottman spoke, a four-horse coach appeared on the brow of the hill which was in advance of them.

The horses were snorting and stamping heavily, and a broad gleam of light shone from each side of the coach, as the lamps flitted past the hedges."

"It is a mail coach," said Dora, "and really I should think too much for me."

"Not at all," replied Dottman, "my old master, Captain Hawk, used to say the bigger the vehicle was and the more horses it had the easier it was stopped."

"There may be some truth in that, Dottman, and yet I must confess I shrink from an encounter with a mail coach and four horses."

"Look you here, Captain, then we will do the thing with a little finesse. Suppose we play them a trick!"

"What trick, Dottman?"

"What would you say to being invited to the inside of the coach, and there helping yourself at leisure to the watches and jewellery of its inmates."

"I should say, Dottman, that could hardly be done!"

"I will show you how," said Dottman.

To the surprise of Dora for a few moments, and then to her great amusement, Dottman laid hold of the bridle of Starlight and began to speak in a voice of excitement, as though his feelings were almost too much to permit him command of language—

"Stop, good folks all," he said. "Stop for the love of heaven, if that's one of his majesty's mails, stop at once, for here the young and handsome Lord Nozoo has been stopped by a highwayman on the king's highway, and been badly hurt. If there is only one inside place in the coach, let him in, by all means, and if there's not, he's quite willing to sit on any lady's lap. Oh, dear! oh, dear! he's very bad, indeed."

Dora could not refrain from laughing outright.

"I don't think for a moment, Dottman, that they will be deceived by so shallow a pretext?"

"I don't think it's a shallow pretext at all," said Dottman. "They will certainly stop, and you'll be asked into the coach by acclamation. I will follow, leading Starlight, and as soon as you have astonished the insiders by making them surrender their money, watches, and jewellery, we can stop the coach again, and you can mount and be off with the certainty of escape."

"The way you plan the adventure," said Dora, "promises some amusement, and I will undertake it."

"You couldn't say or do a wiser thing, captain, and here comes the coach!"

The descent from the brow of the hill on which Dottman and Dora had just seen the coach was rather abrupt, so that the driver was careful to keep his horses well in hand, and they came down towards the valley at an easy trot.

"Now is the time," said Dottman. "Lean forward, captain, on your horse's neck as if you were rather hurt and faint."

"I will! Is that the way?"

"Capital!"

The coach was within about fifty paces when Dottman burst out into such a fit of lamentation that it startled Dora for a moment, and made the horses restive.

"Murder! help! fire! robbers! footpads! incendiaries and burglars! stop, good people all. Is that one of his majesty's mails, stop—oh, oh, stop!"

The driver of the mail coach involuntarily drew his reins, and a loud voice from some one among the luggage at the top called out—

"What now? what's all that about? Come, come, this won't do! the king's mail mustn't be stopped."

"Only a moment—only a moment," cried Dottman. "Oh, oh, oh! such a calamity."

"Woa!" cried the coachman, as the leading horses began to rear and plunge.

"Hold hard," added Dottman, "you'll be thankful when you know all."

"Come, come," cried the guard, who had before spoken, "this won't do; we know there are bad characters on the road, but I tell you what, my fine fellows, my blunderbuss has got a quarter of a pound of gunpowder in it, and eighteen tenpenny nails."

"I'm so glad to hear it," said Dottman, "and I do hope before the night's over, they will all be lodged in the stomach of the notorious highwayman who has robbed and nearly murdered my young master, the handsomest and most distinguished nobleman of the court of St. James's, and here he is, nearly doubled up like a foot ball or a broken candle over the neck of his horse, and all I ask, is this one of his majesty's mails?"

"A young nobleman?" cried the coachman.

"A young nobleman?" echoed the guard.

"A handsome young nobleman, and an ornament of the court!" screamed two ladies from the inside.

"Yes," added Dottman, "it's the well-known Lord Nozoo."

"Is it possible?" said the guard.

The two ladies inside uttered two distinct screams, and then they each tried to look from the coach window at the same moment, by which their heads came in violent contact, and they withdrew them again precipitately.

One of the ladies then apostrophised the other as a cat, and the "cat" joined issue by calling her defamer an elderly wretch.

"Groan!" whispered Dottman to Dora. Dora uttered two audible moans.

"That's the young nobleman," cried Dottman, "don't you hear him groaning? is there an inside place?"

"Certainly," cried the two ladies at once; and then, again, as if they had been acted upon by some machinery, they each tried to look from the coach window, and produced a concussion more violent than before.

"You vile woman," cried one, "you did it on purpose."

"Vile yourself, madam," cried the other, "it was easy to see all the way from the White Horse in Piccadilly what a character you were!"

"Ladies! ladies!" said a Quaker who was in a remote corner of the coach. "Yea verily I say unto thee both that one of thee, in withdrawing thy head from the window, struck me on the nose, and it bleedeth."

"Fire and fury, sir!" cried another passenger in an angry, warlike tone. "Fire and fury, sir! I'm glad to hear it, for ever since my ears have drunk in the intelligence that so distinguished a young nobleman as the Lord Nozoo has been robbed and wounded on the highway, my thoughts have all been of blood! blood! blood! sir!"

"Then verily, friend," said the Quaker, "I wish thy nose had been in the way instead of mine."

"You'll make me ill among you all,"

said the fifth occupant of the coach, who was a very crabbed old dame with an enormous basket of provision. "You'll make me ill if you go on talking in that horrid manner, and I shall be compelled to take a small drop of bitter waters."

"Yea, madam," said the Quaker, "I am bound to say that thy bitter waters have a remarkable odour of the spirit called rum."

"Is there an inside place," shouted Dottman, "for the young Lord Nozoo," as if in despair.

"Yea," said the Quaker.

"Fire and fury! yes," said the warlike gentleman.

"To be sure," screamed the two ladies.

"Well, I don't know," said the elderly female, "but I suppose I must take my basket on my lap."

"Goodness gracious!" said the guard, as he leaped into the road. "I never saw such a beautiful horse in all my life as the young nobleman rides."

"Yes," said Dottman, "it was sent over here by the great Mogul."

"The great Mogul?" exclaimed all the insiders in a breath.

"But we can't go back," said the coachman. We carry the mail bags. It isn't as if we were the up mail. We're the down mail, and we shall only be taking his lordship away into the country, miles off from the court and his noble relations."

"It don't matter," said Dottman. "His lordship will get out where you change horses."

"That's at Edgeware."

"That will do—that will do. Now, my lord, be careful—be careful for the sake of his majesty and the royal princesses. I'll take care of the horse. Lean on the guard's arm, my lord."

Dora affected great weakness, and with some sighs and moans allowed herself to be helped into the coach, and when once there she was seized hold of by the two ladies, who almost came to blows upon the question of where the young nobleman was to sit.

The guard closed the door, and clambered upon the outside again.

"All's right, Bill—he's gone inside."

The coachman started his horses, which were fretted and impatient, and off rolled the mail coach, with Dora snugly ensconced as its sixth inside passenger, while Dottman trotted on behind, holding the bridle of the beautiful Arabian, Starlight,

"Dear me! my lord," said one of the ladies, "I do hope your honourable lordship is not seriously hurt."

"And I, too, hope so," said the other lady, "and have been hoping so for ever so long, only I thought it was more delicate not to speak."

"Delicate, ma'am!" cried the other. "How dare you say I'm not delicate? I'm almost too delicate, and have been so from an infant."

"Yea, ladies, I say unto thee," said the Quaker, "that if bawling and screaming be not essential to the recovery of the young man whom the vain call a lord, it will be better to be quiet."

"Mind your own business, Mr. Broadbrim, if you please."

"Verily my name is Jincum—Tobias Jincum. Murder! help!"

"Never mind," said the elderly female, "it's only my basket,"

"Yea, I thought some projectile had entered the coach, and was intent on my destruction."

"My lord," cried the warlike gentleman, "I only wish I had been on the road, I would soon have settled the fellow. It's my special delight to rub out, use up, squash, and extirminate highwaymen!"

"I'm glad to hear it, sir," said Dora. "The villain has robbed me of a thousand pounds."

"A thousand pounds, my lord! that was indeed, a booty."

"Yes, ladies and gentlemen, and he had the audacity to say, after he had taken the money, that there was a mail coach on the road, and that stopping and robbing me was better than any booty he could expect to get from all the beggarly insiders put together."

"Fire and fury!" cried the warlike gentleman.

"Yea, that was uncivil!" said the Quaker.

"The wretch!" exclaimed the two ladies.

"The mangy villain!" said the elderly female, as a curious gurgling sound betokened a return to the bitter waters.

"He meant," added Dora, speaking rather faintly, "that you were all a poor lot; but for my part, as a British nobleman, I am inclined to believe that he was wrong, and that I am with most respectable people, who have money."

"I should think so," exclaimed one of the ladies.

"I have a hundred pounds, all of my own, in a little leather bag. Lady Bellair, who resides in Curzon Street, requested my acceptance of it."

"A discharged waiting-maid, I presume?" said the other lady, "with the plunder from her last situation."

"Fool! baggage, and vixen!"

"Ladies—ladies!" said the Quaker, "I beseech thee to remember that if two persons fight in the inside of a coach, it involveth personal dangers to others. For my own part, I should be sorry if this young nobleman should esteem me otherwise than respectable. Yea, I have two hundred pounds, the which I intend to lay out in Northamptonshire, in fleecy hosiery."

"I have a matter of fifty pounds about me," said the warlike gentleman. "Ha, ha! I should like to see the highwayman on this side of the infernal regions that could take that."

"Well," said the lady who had not yet declared her amount of riches, "since everybody speaks, I don't mind owning to thirty pounds sixteen and fourpence."

"Yea, madam," said the Quaker to the elderly female, "we have all declared the extent of our pecuniary resources but thyself."

"Twenty pounds and some halfpence."

"Then," said Dora, "if that audacious highwayman had ventured upon stopping this mail coach, he would have obtained a good booty."

"Oh, dear no!" cried the fierce gentleman with the fifty pounds. "He would have obtained a bullet, sir—a bullet in his skull."

"Have you pistols, sir."

"Well, I can't say I have exactly at hand."

"Oh!"

"But at home, my Lord, I have a complete stud of arms; and I should have come out upon the road again to-morrow night and hunted the fellow up."

At this moment Dottman blew a shrill note upon the silver whistle he always had with him, and Dora fully understood that he meant to let her know that the time for action had arrived, and that further delay was probably dangerous.

Dora roused herself.

"Ladies and gentlemen," she said, "as a preliminary to what I am about to observe, allow me first of all to state that the first person who gives the slightest alarm, or makes the least outcry, will receive the contents of a double-barrelled pistol in his or her brain, as the case may be."

A suppressed cry arose from every person in the coach.

"Silence!" said Dora abruptly.

By the dim light that came into the interior of the vehicle, they saw that the supposed young nobleman had a long, bright-barrelled pistol in his hand, which he moved slowly from face to face.

The effect was magical.

Everyone seemed unnerved; and as if struck with a very paralysis of fear.

"I may as well now inform you all," added Dora, "that I am the most notorious, unscrupulous, and bloodthirsty highwayman in all England."

"Gracious heavens!" cried one of the ladies.

"I am a lost sinner," said the other.

"Have mercy upon us!" said the warlike gentleman.

"Yea, I have been an ass," said the Quaker.

"Where's my bottle? I've lost my bottle," said the elderly female.

"Now, sir," said Dora, as she clapped the muzzle of the pistol fiercely against the forehead of the warlike gentleman. "Now, sir, I begin with you."

"I—I—upon my life, sir, I've got no money."

"Upon your life? you stake your life upon that?"

"No, no—that is—oh, dear me! I'm only a poor valet, sir, out of place."

"But you have fifty pounds?"

A deep groan responded to this demand, and the fifty pounds were produced.

Dora put the purse coolly in her pocket, and then gave a tap with a barrel of the pistol against the stone bottle, which the old lady had at her mouth, and she said—

"Madam, I will trouble you for your twenty pounds—the halfpence you may keep!"

CHAPTER XLI.

THE OFFER OF MARRIAGE—DORA AND DOTTMAN HAVE REASON TO CONGRATU-LATE THEMSELVES—DOTTMAN'S RUSE—THE PURSUIT—THE RETURN TO KEN-SINGTON PALACE.

THE elder female thus apostrophised by Dora, feeling it to be manifestly unsafe to adopt any aggressive feeling towards the highwayman, revenged herself upon society at large by hitting the Quaker a smart rap on the top of the head with the stone bottle.

"And would you rob a lone woman," she said, "of all she has in the world?"

"Verily, madam, it is not I. Why thumpest thou me upon the head? If thou hittest anybody, let it be this young man with defective morals."

"Come, madam, quick, if you please," said Dora. "I have no time to waste."

The proximity of the pistol barrel made the lady with the stone bottle turn as pale as death, and she handed out the twenty pounds at once."

"Now, sir," said Dora to the Quaker, "it is your turn."

"Needs must," said Tobias Jincum,

"when the—hem! drives. There is the money, friend, and yea, I will not be so unpolite as to say that I will give an extra fourpence to purchase a rope with a noose at the end of it for thy especial behoof."

"Now, ladies," said Dora, as she lent back in the coach, "I have reserved you two to the last, because I wish to make a communication to you."

"To us?"

"Yes, ladies, to you. I am young, and, as you see, not bad looking; I find my life lonesome at times, and have some thoughts of taking a wife."

"Indeed!" cried both the ladies in chorus.

"Yes!" added Dora, with a sigh, "If I could only find some congenial heart that would consent to devote itself to me, and who would be the highwayman's bride."

Both the ladies sighed.

"Indeed, sir!" said one, "if you would promise to be a good husband, I wouldn't mind considering."

"Perhaps, *mem*," said the other, "you'll wait till you're asked—I believe I *squeezed* his hand, which, I believe, is as good as saying "yes" at once."

"The one who loves me best," said Dora, "I am sure will be the first to comply with my little demand of to-night."

There was a terrific rummaging of garments, and two purses were thrust into Dora's hands.

"The acts of devotion were simultaneous," said Dora, "and as bigamy is not permitted in this country, I can have neither of you."

"Neither of us?"

"No—and there is another reason."

"What—oh, what?"

"I forgot I was married already! Such little matters slip one's memory. Ladies and gentlemen, I bid you all good night! and I need not recommend to you that the next time you meet with the Lord Nozoo on the king's highway, it will not be prudent to be quite so ready in declaring what money you have about you."

The passengers in the mail coach might, to the full, appreciate the little piece of advice, but it did not tend to reconcile them any the more to their losses.

Still, although they were so many in number, they did not think it prudent to interfere with the dashing highwayman as they thought Dora, who had played them such a trick.

Thus one pistol overawes a mob.

"Who will sacrifice his own life for the benefit of his creatures?"

"No one!"

Dora leant from the coach window.

"Hilloa!" she cried, "Hilloa!"

"Here, my lord!" said Dottman, as he made his appearance with the horses.

"You can say I am better, and that I will get out here."

"Yes, my lord!"

Dottman rode to the front of the mail coach, and shouted out to the driver.

"Stop, my good fellow, stop! His lordship feels so much better that he will get out and mount his horse again."

The coachman pulled out.

"And he has told me," added Dottman, "to give a guinea to each you and to the guard."

"Ah!" said the coachman, "His lordship is a real gentlemen."

"Quite!" said the guard, "but I saw that as soon as my eyes fell on him. Here's a real gent, says I, who will think no more of giving a guinea to a guard than of saying ' How de do? How de do?'"

Dottman handed up the couple of guineas to the coachman and guard, and then he went again to the coach door, and leaning from his saddle, opened it.

Dora alighted.

"Ladies and gentlemen," she said, "I have the honor of bidding you good night."

A suppressed groan burst from all the occupants of the mail coach.

But a new idea had taken possession of one of the two ladies who had been so willing to share the fortunes of the knight of the road.

The idea was this.

What if, after all, the pretended highwayman was a young nobleman, and the robbery of the mail coach passengers was, after all, only a joke, such as in their opinion a young nobleman who was the idol of the court had a right to perpetrate if he chose so to do.

The moment this extravagant notion found a home in the heart of the lady who thought of it, she looked out of the coach window and called out—

"Mr. Highwayman! Mr. Highwayman!"

"What?" said Dora.

"I am quite willing to accompany you now at once."

"You baggage!" exclaimed the other lady, "he knows that I have been always willing to accompany him."

"But I don't mind a bit whether he has another wife or not."

"And do you think, you shameless wretch, that I mind a bit? No! not even if he has two wives."

"Take that then!"

A hasty slap on the side of the face succeeded these words of the two ladies who were so willing to join their fortunes to those of Dora, highwayman, or nobleman, engaged in a fierce single combat to the great terror of the Quaker.

DORA AND DOTTMAN GIVE THE OLD MAN AT THE COTTAGE AN ALARM.

"Come," said Dora, as she sprung lightly to the back of Starlight. "Let us be off, Dottman."

"All right, captain—off is the word!"

In a very few minutes the mail coach was left far behind them on the Edgeware Road, and both Dora and Dottman were nearing London at a sharp trot.

"Well, captain," said Dottman, "is there any luck?"

"Plenty."

"Ah! a good booty?"

"Excellent."

"Then am I not right when I say that there is nothing like the road?"

"I admit that the life of a highwayman,"

Dora.—21.

replied Dora, "is profitable enough if it could be divested of some of its perils."

"Its perils, captain? Bless you that is one half the fun."

"What's that?" said Dora suddenly.

They both turned round and listened.

The furious galloping of horses feet on the road behind them made them feel assured that they were pursued.

But by whom? That was the question.

"I don't altogether like those sounds," said Dottman.

"Nor I."

"Then, Captain Arod, all we have to do is to get out of their way as soon as possible. You will have no difficulty on Starlight in distancing any mounted riders. Put the Arabian to the gallop and make for Kensington Palace."

"But you Dottman?"

"Oh, I will manage to take care of myself, you may depend.

"No—I would much rather we should keep together. Come on—your horse is by no means a bad one, and those mounted men, who are advancing upon the road, are a good quarter of a mile from us yet."

"No doubt of that."

"On! On then!"

Dora put the Arabian just to so much speed that Dottman's horse at such a gallop might keep up the pace without absolute distress.

The trees and hedges of the Edgeware Road flew past them with rapidity. The village of Cricklewood was soon passed through, and then Kilburn came in sight.

But still they heard the tramp and rattle of the pursuers in the rear.

"Stop!" cried Dottman.

Dora pulled up.

"I don't think," he said "that it is worth while blowing my horse in this fashion. Here is a narrow lane to the left which leads to the village of West End, near to Hampstead, I propose that we turn into it.

"They will surely suspect us if they are in pursuit of us."

"I mean them to do so, captain."

"Indeed."

"Yes—you shall see. May I manage this little affair in my own way?"

"Most certainly."

"Very good."

Dottman paused just at the corner of the narrow lane leading from Kilburn to Hampstead; and raising himself as high as he could in his stirrups, he tapped at the wooden wall of a cottage that stood just at the corner.

Dottman was able to reach high enough with the handle of his riding whip that the raps he made were just under the first and only upper floor window of the cottage.

It was now about half past one o'clock in the morning, and the inhabitants of the cottage—an old couple—were not a little alarmed at such a noise close to their window.

The little casement was flung open in a moment, and a nightcapped head looked out.

"Lord save us! what's the matter?"

"Nothing particular," said Dottman.

"Is it fire?"

"No, thieves!"

"Thieves, say you?"'

"To be sure I do! We are two highwaymen, and want to know if this lane leads to Hampstead."

"It does!"

"All right, old stupid. When those who are pursuing us come, you need not say we have turned into the lane, old dunderhead. Come on, captain!"

Dora and Dottman dashed down the lane.

"Well," said the old man of the cottage, "if that is not the coolest piece of impudence I have met with for a long time. Stupid and dunderhead, indeed! well, I'm sure! I will tell—I will tell! perhaps I might not if they had only been civil, but to call a man a stupid and dunderhead! It's too bad—it's too bad! I will stay at the window on purpose to tell, that I will."

In a few minutes a mounted party of six men rode up, and were rushing onwards, when the old cottager called to them.

"Hoi—hoi—hoi!"

The officers, for such, in truth, they were, drew rein and listened.

"Hoi! hoi! I am here at this window.

"Well, what now, stupid?" cried the principal officer.

"Good gracious!" cried the old man, "is all the world going to call me stupid? I can tell you that if you are after two highwaymen, they have gone up West End Lane."

"Are you sure?"

"Quite—quite!"

"We are after them, for they have robbed, in the most audacious manner, one of his majesty's mails, and gone off with a capital booty."

"They are gallopping, then, up the lane to Hampstead."

"Come on, comrades, come on!"

The six officers turned into the narrow lane, and thinking that the two highwaymen would of course, in consequence of the temporary delay, have a good start of them, they set spurs to their horses and gallopped on with all the speed they could possibly command.

In a few moments, then, Dora and Dottman quietly emerged from a field, into which, at the side of the lane, they had made their way.

"That will do," said Dottman. I think we may now go at an easy trot to Kensington.

Dora laughed.

"You have certainly thrown them off our track, Dottman."

"To be sure I have, captain! I felt quite sure the old man at the cottage was too angry to keep our secret.

"So it seems."

They were in another moment on the high road again, but Dottman could not make up his mind to pass the cottage without taking some notice of the old man.

Raising himself, then, in his stirrups just as he had done before, Dottman tapped with the handle of his riding whip again, exactly on the spot that he had reached on the former occasion.

"Hilloa! hilloa!" he cried.

"Bless me!" said the old man, as he again flung open the casement, "who else is on the road to-night?"

"I say, old stupid," said Dottman, "I hope you did not tell those men we were on the lane to Hampstead!"

"Murder!"

"Did you, eh, old dunderhead? did you?"

The old man, in great trepidation, closed the casement.

"I'll give him a fright," said Dottman.

"How?" asked Dora.

"Oh, only at the expense of one pistol charge. Here goes!"

Dottman fired one of his pistols, and so terrified was the old man in the cottage that he quite forget he had closed the casement, and dashed his head through the glass, calling out—

"Murder—murder—murder!"

"Now, captain, come on," said Dottman; "we shall have all Kilburn in a commotion behind us, no doubt."

They rode on, and in half-an-hour from that time they reached Kensington Palace.

All was profoundly still in and about the palace, and as Dottman opened the little door in the private garden wall, the clock struck the hour of two.

"Well, captain," said Dottman, "you see we are home in good time, and have made a good night's work of it"

"We have, indeed."

"Let me take Starlight's bridle."

"There it is, Dottman."

"Dora—my Dora!" said a voice.

It was the voice of Henry Dacres.

"Ah, Henry, are you here?" said Dora. "Why do you venture out into the night air?"

"Are not you, dear Dora, venturing for my sake into that night air?"

"Nay, but I am well and unhurt, while you, as yet, are far from strong, Henry."

"I hope soon to be strong enough to relieve you, Dora, from all perilous duties and enterprises."

Dora and Henry entered the old palace together, and they held a long and anxious conference with regard to what it would be best to do in the present aspect of their affairs."

Dora was of opinion that they ought to wait for a short time, until, by her exploits on the road, a sufficient sum of money should be got together to enable them to successfully undertake the expenses of a lawsuit against her wicked uncle, the false Duke of Kingston.

To this arrangement Henry Dacres found himself constrained to coincide, but it was not without a hope that before many days had elapsed he might be able himself to undertake the perilous duty which Dora had set herself.

As it was, however, Dora was determined, in her own mind, that the next night should see both herself and Dottman on the road again, seeking such adventures as fortune might throw in their way.

A deep sleep came over Dora, and it was mid-day on the succeeding morning before she awakened, perfectly refreshed from the fatigues of the strange and exciting adventures upon the Edgeware Road.

———

CHAPTER XLII.

THE DEPARTURE—THE HONOURABLE MRS. SPRAGGELL—THE GENEROUS HIGHWAY-MAN—THE DUEL—FRIENDLY ADVICE.

THE hour of six was striking by the old Palace of Kensington when Dora might have been seen in one of the chambers of the palatial residence fully equipped in her highwayman's costume.

Henry was gazing at her with thoughtful and rather sad eyes.

Dottman was waiting by the little door in the garden wall with the two horses.

Dora felt that it was she who must break the silence; for in a few more minutes would she not be placing many miles between herself and her much loved Henry? There was bitterness in the thought; but then she hoped that each adventure would bring that time nearer when she would never more separate herself from him who was so worthy of her heart's best affections.

And then, too, there were times when strange thoughts took possession of the mother's heart, and she asked herself whether it was not possible that in some of these adventures on the road she might fall in with some chance passenger who might be able to give her some clue to her lost Mina.

With these thoughts, then, Dora approached Henry Dacres, and rested her head for a moment upon his breast to hide the tears which had welled up to her eyes at the sight of what would be his loneliness when she had left him.

But not for long did Dora give way to gloomy thoughts and forebodings, and raising her sweet face to his, she smiled as she said—

"Well, my Henry, do you think you

would know me if you were to meet me on the road, thus equipped?".

Henry Dacres returned her smile as he gazed fondly into her lovelit eyes, as he said—

"No, my Dora; but I would fain see you as I always picture you to myself when left alone with my reflections, as the dear girl, so gentle and affectionate, that I can scarcely recognise you even now in the dashing costume of a knight of the road."

"Say no more—say no more, dear Henry; but believe that I am still the same in heart and thought as when you made me your happy bride. But I must not linger—time wears on. Heaven bless and keep you, dearest!"

For one moment Henry Dacres pressed her to his heart, and Dora, as much to conceal her feelings as from a desire to set out on her night's adventures, left the apartment.

Henry Dacres was alone!

"I'm afraid, captain, we shall be late," said Dottman, as Dora made her appearance. "Which road shall we take to-night?"

"That you shall decide, Dottman."

"Well, then, captain, let it be the Western Road."

"Be it so, then," said Dora.

Dora and Dottman now put their horses to a gallop, and soon left the little village of Kensington far behind them.

They had now been walking their horses down the Western Road, when they heard the sound of carriage wheels and the tramp of horses."

— "Do you hear anything, captain?" said Dottman.

"The sound of carriage wheels not far ahead of us, I think," said Dora. "Let us spur onwards."

The vehicle which had attracted the attention of Dora and Dottman was a richly emblazoned and highly fashionable family carriage.

In this fashionable carriage were two persons; and probably no two persons could have been found who presented a more remarkable contrast to each other than these.

The one was a lady of about forty years of age. She was of the large style of feminine humanity, and in her dress and her appointments everything was of that character which seemed to challenge observation.

Her ample robe was covered with large embroidered flowers, and the jewellery, with which she was profusely decorated, was fearfully massive. There was also a kind of blooming expression on the cheeks of this fair dame which suggested just a suspicion of rouge.

Seated, not by her side in this carriage but immediately opposite to her, was a young, fair girl, apparently about eighteen years of age. Small and delicate to a degree, and plainly attired, with no ornament about her save a costly diamond ring, Bella Templeton was a most trying companion for the lady, whose large dimensions seemed to eclipse her entirely.

The beauty both of feature and expression of this young girl consisted a great deal in that winning gentleness which makes the beholder gaze on the possessor as being too fragile and delicately fashioned for the world's harsh usage.

But on this occasion the sensitiveness of the young girl was called more than usually into action, and every particle of colour fled from her face.

The little hands were clenched in the plain grey shawl, and she was looking in the face of the elder occupant of the carriage with such an expression of mental agony upon her fair face, that it ought to have moved to pity even the obdurate heart of the person to whom that look was directed.

On the face of the elder there was a look of scorn, of contempt, mingled with fiery glances of anger.

In order, however, that the reader may be better able to individualise the two persons in the little dialogue that took place between them, we will inform him that the elder lady was the Honourable Mrs. Spraggell, and that the younger, Bella Templeton, was her companion.

Their relative positions were employer and employed.

"You! you!" bawled the elder lady.

"You try to set yourself to make a conquest of my son—you miserable wretch! What do you mean by it? You that are no better—not one bit better than a menial! You fancy because I give you board and lodging, and twenty pounds a-year, that you are going to intrude yourself into such a family as the Spraggells. I am disgusted with you! And if I had not promised your mother, on her deathbed, that I would look after you, I would turn you adrift this very night, and then you would see what your doll's face would do for you."

"Oh, hear me!" began Bella.

"I will not hear anything you have to say. But I will tell you now why I have brought you out alone with me at this time of night—it is because I would not have you sleep under the same roof as myself for all the world—you will now take up your abode with my sister, Lady Allworthy—and Edward will soon forget the intriguing companion of his mother."

"Oh, no, no!"

"What do you mean, girl? Do you suppose that my son ever thought of marrying you?"

"He told me he loved me."

"Oh, did he? And, of course, you believed him."

"With all my heart."

The Honourable Mrs. Spraggell felt strongly inclined at that moment to do something desperate, and probably might have gone to the length of shaking Bella, had not a voice at that instant crying "Halt!" turned all her thoughts into another channel.

"Halt!" again said the clear ringing voice—and at the same time Dora placed her hand upon the door of the carriage.

"Good evening, ladies," said Dora—"I will not detain you many minutes; I merely want whatever money or jewellery you have about you."

"A highwayman!" screamed the extensive lady.

Bella shrunk back in the carriage pale with terror.

"Quick, ladies!" said Dora, "time presses—I will ease you of your watch and chain, if you please, madam!"

"Wretch" cried The Honorable Mrs. Spraggell—"take them—it is all I have about me."

"Pardon me, madam, you have money and other jewellery—I must have all as a gift, or I shall be compelled to take them for myself."

"There then—and there—and there!" said the Honorable Mrs. Spraggell, as she placed in Dora's hands a ruby ring of considerable value, a very handsome brooch' and a well-filled purse. There, now you have everything—go!"

"Not yet!" said Dora. "I have not received anything from your young companion."

Bella ventured to look into the face of Dora, and said in a trembling voice—"I have nothing but a ring, which I value above gold. Oh, must I give you that?"

"Of course you must!" shouted the elder lady, with something like triumph, "Of course you must. I am heartily glad to think you will so soon have to part with your love-token—give it up—Mr. Highwayman, this young woman has a beautiful ring, which ought never to have been hers—she pretends that my son gave it her of his own free will; but I know the arts she has used to make him give it to her. Take it, Mr. Highwayman, and I will forgive you for robbing me."

Dora held out her hand to the young girl, who drew from her finger that ring, which was a pledge of love from one to whom she had given her young heart's best affections.

Dora took the ring, and Bella Templeton, when she thought she had gazed for the last time upon the cherished gift, threw herself back in the carriage, and sobbed as if her heart would break.

"A very pretty ring," said Dora, as if to herself, "and as I never like to separate two loving hearts, but would rather do all in my power to serve them—take back this ring, and when you think of the giver, remember also the highwayman, who could be generous and sympathising."

Bella raised her head at these words, and Dora was amply repaid by the grateful thanks of the fair girl.

"I have the honor to wish you good evening, ladies!" said Dora, as she gracefully raised her plumed hat; and turning to Dottman, who had kept guard at the horses' heads, with the muzzle of a pistol presented full in the face of the terrified coachman, she said—

"That will do, Dottman—let them pass on."

The coachman was nothing loth to avail himself of the permission to continue his journey, and whipping his horses, they gallopped off, and were soon lost to the sight of Dora and Dottman.

"Well, captain," said Dottman, "I fancy you have not made a bad thing of this adventure."

"I am more than satisfied—I have some very valuable jewellery belonging to the old dowager. I seem doomed to come to the rescue of persecuted damsels, do I not—I wonder who they are—or rather who that sweet girl is to whom I returned the ring?"

"Never mind who she is, captain—of one thing you may be quite sure, that you have made a conquest!"

"Oh no! I fancy not," said Dora, smiling, "for she has already given her heart to another. But what are those sounds I hear—surely it is some one calling for help? Forward, Dottman, our adventures for tonight are not over."

Dora and Dottman came to a standstill after a pretty smart trot of some hundred paces, and listened, and then they heard the voices of two men, evidently in anger.

"Draw, my lord," said one, "for one of us shall not leave this spot in life, while Alicia has a brother to revenge her."

"Fool! madman!" replied another voice, "do you think that you have chance with me? Incense me not, or your death be upon your own head!"

"Draw, villain!" cried the first voice, and Dora and Dottman could see from where they had stationed themselves, that a tall figure rushed forward and aimed a terrible thrust at his adversary, which the latter parried, and while the tall slender young man—he was evidently not more than four and twenty—was recovering himself, turned suddenly round and passed his sword through his body.

The young man fell like a dead mass.

"Ha, ha!" yelled, rather than laughed the conqueror, "so perish all who would cross my path."

Having sheathed his sword, this man made his way to a clump of trees not very far distant, to two of which were tied a couple of handsome horses.

He was mounted in an instant, and was about to gallop off, when he was surprised to find that, drawn up on either side of the road, were two mounted men, each presenting a pistol full in his face.

"Stand and deliver!" cried Dora, in a clear ringing voice.

So sudden, so unexpected was this apparition to the eyes of the horseman, that on the impulse of the moment he reined in his steed with such violence, that the animal reared and plunged to such a degree that his rider, skilful horseman that he was, had some difficulty in retaining his seat.

His astonishment, however lasted but for a few moments, for quickly recovering his self-command, he cried out,

"And who dares thus address me?"

"I!" said Dora. "I demand your purse and whatever valuables you may have about you."

The horseman seemed to be debating with himself whether it would be prudent to resist, or comply with this demand, and turning his eyes from the slight form of Dora, who, in her masculine attire looked extremely youthful, he met the stern, almost ferocious expression which sat on the features of Dottman, who appeared at that moment equal to an encounter with at least half a dozen opponents at once.

"Highwaymen, I perceive!" he said.

"Exactly so!" said Dora.

"And you demand my purse and whatever I may have about me? At least we will try, young sir, which is the best swordsman."

Thus saying, the stranger drew his sword, and made a rush towards Dora, who by a sudden swerve of the noble Arabian, escaped what would certainly have been her death wound.

"Coward!" cried Dottman, "is not one murder enough in one night? Take that!" and drawing a pistol from the holster, he fired it, and the bullet did its errand, for the horseman with a shriek of pain, drooped upon the pommel of the saddle.

Dora had remained passive while all this was going on, which took much less time than we have taken to describe it, for to tell the truth she had been somewhat alarmed at the narrow escape she had had herself, and from the few words she had overheard which had passed between this strange man and the youth he had just killed. Then Dora felt a sickening sensation about the heart, which unnerved her arm, and made it impossible for her to enter into this adventure with that spirit which we have seen she always brought to bear upon her nightly exploits upon the road.

Dottman was not backward in pursuing the advantage he had obtained in this skirmish with the stranger, so he trotted his horse up to the wounded man, and began at once to search for anything he could find in the way of booty.

This examination on the part of Dottman, did not last many minutes, and as the stranger remained perfectly still, he met with no obstacle to his operation.

"All right, captain!" he said, "I think I have found sufficient to satisfy us; there is a well filled purse, a sword handsomely mounted, besides a watch and rings, so we will leave him here—even as he has left the young man yonder.

"Oh, do not leave him, Dottman, to die alone, let us gallop forward, and we may meet some one who will put him in the way of getting assistance."

"Never fear, captain, he's only shamming; he found we were too many for him, so he is pretending to be badly hurt; but I took good care how I fired my pistol, and so captain, as we have got all the plunder, suppose we turn our faces towards home."

"Well, be it so," said Dora, sadly, "for this last adventure had not been such as suited the kindly and gentle impulses of Dora's heart, and she would fain have ascertained if the young man who had lost his life in defence of his sister's honour, were really past all relief from human aid; turning to Dottman, then, she said—

"Let us go back, Dottman, and see if that young man be really dead—if he still lives we may be able to be of use to him, for I feel strangely interested in his fate."

"He's dead enough, captain; a fellow can't be run through the body very well, and life still remain in him; however as you wish it, I will go and see if he breathes."

Dora was left alone.

Alone with her own sad thoughts, for as she waited there beneath the silvery rays of the pale moon, her wounded Henry, and all he had suffered, her own escape from a horrible death, the loss of her dearly beloved little Mina, her contest at the barracks in the King's Mews with her arch-enemy, Van Esling, her sudden acquisition of wealth and as sudden loss of that wealth, and now the strange combination of circumstances which seemed to force her as it were to try her fortunes as a knight of the road, all passed in review before her, and she became, so to speak, a spectator of her own actions, thoughts, and impulses.

Oh, how she wished that the battle of life was over, and that she could lie down and be at rest.

But not long could such thoughts occupy such a mind as that of Dora's, for these were after all but selfish longings—had she not yet a husband and child to live for? Could she wish for rest to herself, since that very rest would but bring grief and anguish to her Henry?

"No, no!" she murmured gently, "I must live and hope—yes, hope."

As Dora had given way to these reflections, she had rested her head upon the neck of Starlight, and that beautiful creature seemed to be holding communion with its sweet mistress, for it every now and then gave utterance to a strange kind of sound, which it frequently did, when alone with Dora.

It was now some minutes since Dottman had left Dora, to go and examine the wounded man, whom they both believed to be dead. What then was Dora's surprise to see, slowly approaching, two figures, the one was Dottman, and leaning on his arm was a young man dressed in military costume, and who seemed to have great difficulty in walking, even with the assistance of Dottman.

———

CHAPTER XLIII.

THE WOUNDED MAN—"COMING EVENTS CAST THEIR SHADOWS BEFORE"—MISFORTUNES STILL PURSUE DORA—HENRY IN DANGER—THE MIDNIGHT MEETING.

DORA experienced a feeling of thankfulness when she beheld the young man approaching, although from the frequent pauses, and from the difficulty Dottman had in supporting him, it was evident the young man was badly hurt.

It was Dottman who first spoke.

"I think, captain, if we could find any means of getting this gentleman conveyed to some house, where his wound could be seen to, he'd soon be all right. I think, even now, I hear the distant tramp of horses' feet. What say you, captain?

Before, however, Dora could make any reply, the wounded man made an effort, although he spoke with great difficulty, as he said—

"I cannot be mistaken—I find I am indebted to two highwaymen for my life."

"Such is the case, my friend," said Dora.

"May I ask you, sir, if you answer to the name of Captain Arod?" asked the young man.

Dora started! Did he know her? had they ever met before? Perhaps so, in happier times. Why did Dora feel so interested in his fate? As these thoughts chased each other through her mind, Dora looked more closely at her interrogator than she had done upon his first approach.

The young man's dress was in very good taste, neither too smart nor too plain, well fitted for a journey, yet not unfitted for a drawing room in the morning. There was a look of habitual thoughtfulness, one might call it sadness about the face. He was dark in complexion, and though not a handsome man, yet few would have scrupled to pronounce him good looking. There was also an easy air about him, which generally engages kindly feeling, if it cannot secure much respect.

It took Dora but a few minutes to discover the sort of person with whom she had so strangely been brought into contact, and curiosity induced her to reply to his last question by asking him another.

"Captain Arod," she said, "will be glad to know whom he is addressing before he answers any more questions."

"Then you are he? fly—oh, fly for your life—even now I hear the sound of your pursuer's horses."

"How? what mean you?" said Dora, now thoroughly excited, and somewhat alarmed; for was not her danger Henry's despair?"

The young man sank to the ground exhausted from the effort he had already made; but in a gasping voice he faintly spoke—

"Leave me—here—and save—yourself. I tell you—you are pursued. Perhaps even now it may be too late."

"And leave you here? perhaps to die for want of assistance?" said Dora.

"In a few moments there will be officers on this spot. I shall be properly cared for. Now go!"

"At least tell me your name," said Dora, still strangely excited.

The young man made an effort to raise himself, but sunk down again, and Dora heard not the name he uttered.

The wounded man had fainted.

At this moment Dottman almost dragged Dora from the prostrate figure, saying in a hurried whisper, "we have not a moment to lose, captain, for there are several mounted men on the other side of the hedge who are evidently in pursuit of us."

To crouch down behind the hedge, which was on the other side of the lane, and to draw the two horses through, and afterwards to replace the brushwood so that no visible marks were left, was soon done, and Dora and Dottman had the satisfaction of overhearing all that was said without themselves being perceived.

"They must be hereabouts," said a voice, for his grace could not have been deceived. He said it was by this old elm tree that he had the encounter with the highwaymen, and received the pistol shot."

"It's all very well to say this is the spot, but if it were, we should be able to see them, for they could not go either to the right or to the left," said another.

"And young Hargrave," said another voice? "His grace told us that he believed he was killed in the skirmish. We must look for him first, and the highwaymen afterwards, so let us push onward, gentlemen."

So saying, the mounted men began their search for the young man, who had been drawn by Dottman close under the hedge —a large tree with out-spreading bauches —threw the spot so much into shadow that it had escaped the observation of those who were in search of him.

A deep groan was the first intimation they received of his vicinity, and they hastened to the spot.

Every one seemed anxious now to render whatever assistance was necessary to the wounded man, who was evidently well-known to all of them. One was instantly dispatched for some conveyance, and the rest busied themselves in forming a kind of litter, in order to carry their comrade as easily as possible in the direction from whence they expected the carriage to arrive.

"The murderous villain!" said one. "I only hope we may catch him. I for one shall be glad to see his body swinging at Tyburn!"

"Catch him? catch who?" asked the wounded man.

"Why, the highwayman, to be sure, that first robbed, and afterwards murdered you, as he thought."

"My friends," said the young man, "I have not been robbed, neither have I received this wound, which I believe will be mortal, from a highwayman."

"No?" cried all in chorus.

It was some minutes before the young man could speak again, and then it was to ask for water.

A little rippling brook, upon which the silvery rays of the moon threw a broad gleam of light, ran close by, and one of the horsemen, having satisfied his young companion's demand, asked him if he had not then met with a highwayman.

"Yes—oh, yes," murmured the young man. "and it was he who saved my life, and would have risked his own, had I not urged him to seek safety in flight."

At this moment the sound of wheels was heard rapidly approaching.

It was the carriage which had been procured to convey the wounded man to his home, where he was the hope and joy of a widowed mother, and loving sister.

As soon as the cavalcade had got some distance, Dora turned to Dottman, and said—

"I think, Dottman, we will have no more adventures to-night. Let us return and see how it fares with Henry.

"As you will, captain," said Dottman, and putting spurs to their horses, they made the best of their way towards Kensington.

Dora felt a relief, perhaps, which she had never before experienced, as she found herself nearing the little village of Kensington.

It is such happiness to the pure to love; but oh! such more than happiness to believe in the worth of the one beloved.

There was a yearning in Dora's heart on this night, to see and listen to her Henry, and so much had her mind been occupied with her husband's lonely and helpless situation, that she had not heard Dottman's attempt at conversation until he laid his hand upon the bridle of Starlight to attract his mistress's attention.

"Really, captain," said Dottman, "if you were what you look—I mean a real knight of the road, I should think the young lady, Templeton, had made a conquest, for I never knew you so silent before."

"Indeed?" said Dora, as she started from her reverie. "I know not why, Dottman, but I do feel unusually thoughtful to-night. I should like to know why that young man, who was wounded, wished to save us. I cannot but think he penetrated my disguise. Perhaps he recognised me."

"All fancy, captain. Don't you see, you saved his life. It was but right that he should in return do what he could for you."

"It may be so—it may be so; but let us not tarry, my friend, for Henry will be anxious for our return."

"Oh, he's all safe, captain, and for the matter of that, I told him not to expect us back again till after dawn to-morrow. I left him with some books I happened to have in the stable at Captain Hawk's cottage, for I managed to put them in the valise, in which your costume as a knight of the road was packed so snugly."

Dora was glad to hear that Dottman's thoughtfulness had provided her Henry with something which would make the time pass more pleasantly in their absence, and this thought brought a feeling of serenity and happiness to the heart of Dora.

DOTTMAN ALARMED TO FIND DORA HAS FAINTED.

They came at length to the little door in the garden wall, by which they had at first effected an entrance to the old Palace of Kensington, and Dora's heart beat high in expectation and hopefulness.

They traversed the gardens, after Dottman had secured the two horses, and proceeded to the room where Dora was to surprise her Henry, by returning so much sooner than he had been given to understand he was to expect them.

Dora advanced rapidly to the well-known door of the apartment which contained her Henry, turned the handle, and entered.

A shriek of despair alone reached the ears of Dottman, and rushing forward into the

DORA.—22.

apartment, he beheld Dora lying on the floor insensible.

Dora and Dottman were the only occupants of that apartment.

* * * *

It is necessary that our reader, who has gone thus far with us, should retrace his steps, in order the better to understand what had occurred at the old palace two hours after Dora had left Henry Dacres in that lonely room.

As the clock of a neighbouring church was striking the hour of midnight, Henry Dacres, who had just fallen into a doze, was suddenly aroused by what seemed to be the shutting of a door very close to him.

At first he listened with some alarm, fearing that something had happened to Dora; but hearing nothing more, he believed that it was but a trick of the imagination, and that he had only after all fancied that he had heard a noise.

A very short time, however, sufficed to convince him that such was not the case; for it was quite evident that some one was moving a chair or some other light article of furniture in what must have been an adjoining room.

For some few seconds he listened intently, to discover if there was only one or more persons in such close vicinity, but he only heard a low murmuring sound more like the tones of a person speaking to himself, rather that conversing with another.

"He told me to be here by twelve o'clock," said the voice, "and he would meet me. "What can detain him? he said I was not to have a light, for fear of attracting notice; but it's a queer place to be in without a light."

Henry Dacres listened intently.

"What can they want to come here for? I'm sure it's a ghostly sort of place. I'll just light a match. No one will see it. Besides, he ought to have been here before this."

Henry Dacres could hear the occupant of the next apartment draw a breath of satisfaction.

"Ah, that's a little more cheerful. The shutters are quite close; but for fear of prying eyes, I will let down these heavy curtains over the windows. There, that will do!"

Henry drew near to the partition, which divided the two apartments, in order that he might not lose a word of what passed.

"There goes a quarter past twelve, and he told me he would be here by twelve. Ah, what's that? I thought I heard something. Perhaps it was the wind!"

Henry quietly extinguished the lamp Dottman had taken care to provide him with; but in returning to his station by the wall which separated the two apartments, he stumbled over one of the books he had been reading.

The occupant of the adjoining apartment was silent, evidently listening.

"Well, I never knew him to be so much after his time before; but it's not for me to complain. Ah, he comes!"

Henry Dacres now heard another voice say—

"Jabez Lockwood, are you there?"

"Yes, my lord!"

"Good! I am glad to find you punctual, and I know you may be trusted. See that everything is in readiness for to-morrow night. I will show you the rooms I wish to have prepared. The apartment, however, adjoining this one we cannot get into to-night, as I have not the key; but to-morrow morning you can send Joseph for it, and I shall expect everything to be in readiness by to-morrow night at twelve o'clock."

These words were uttered as the speakers were leaving the room. What more passed he knew not, nor did he understand what those apartments were wanted for; but he had heard enough to convince him that that room was no longer a safe asylum for him and Dora.

Henry, however, still stood in an attitude of listening, and he soon heard the second comer say to the attendant, as he re-entered the room in search of a riding whip he had left on the table.

"On second thoughts, Jabez, it would be as well for you and Joseph to complete the arrangements to-night. There are some hours yet before the dawn. I will send the key I spoke of by Joseph.

What was Henry's consternation as he heard these words?

Where was he to seek refuge? how let Dora and Dottman know his whereabouts?

For some time he leant his head on his hand in deep thought; but he quickly roused himself, for he felt that the time for action had come.

It was quite evident that the speaker, from whom had issued the order to prepare a certain suite of rooms,, was in the habit of frequenting that now deserted palatial residence, and that the man Jabez would not be behindhand in carrying out his instructions. Was it not most probable, therefore, that the apartment in which Henry Dacres and Dora had found a refuge would be soon visited?

Henry Dacres must find some other apartment!

With this intention, having waited until all was still, he glided noiselessly into the corridor.

There were several doors opening from this corridor, and Henry Dacres hesitated for some few moments in doubt as to which would be the safest refuge.

He at length resolved to try to effect an entrance at a door farthest from the apart-which he and Dora had so lately occupied, he turned the handle, and it yielded to his touch.

The apartment which he now entered had scarcely any furniture in it, and Henry Dacres was rather pleased than disappointed to find such to be the case, as in all probability he and Dora might there remain undisturbed.

Having satisfied himself that all was still silent in that part of the old palace, Henry

Dacres wrote hastily on a small piece of paper the following words :—

"All is well! but remain not in the apartment we had selected as an asylum. I am near you still."

Having written these words, Henry Dacres was about to retrace his steps, in order that he might place the paper in a secret recess which had been agreed upon between him and Dottman, in the event of anything inducing him, Henry Dacres, to vacate the apartment during any of Dora's temporary absences from Kensington Palace.

This paper, however, was not destined to reach the hand for which it was intended, for just as Henry Dacres was about to enter the apartment to secrete the paper, he heard unmistakeable footsteps approaching.

He had just time to get back to the unfurnished apartment as two men appeared in the corridor and stopped at the door of the room which Henry Dacres had just left.

"This is the room," said the voice of him whom Henry Dacres had heard named Jabez, "this is the room. I can't think what he wants this one for. He has never used it since the night he brought—

"Hush!" replied another voice. "It's much better not to ask one's self any questions at all when employed on such an errand as this. Let's set to work and get finished. For my part, I don't fancy these old apartments. People do say they're haunted, and I shouldn't much wonder if they are. Hark! did you hear any thing?"

"Nothing but the wind and the rain."

The two men set to work, and in less than two hours seemed to have completed their arrangements to their satisfaction, for Henry Dacres heard Jabez say to his companion—

"Well, now we'll leave the old place to the ghosts and hobgoblins, for I dare say there's plenty of them when there's nobody here to see them."

"Ay, ay," said the other. "I've no wish to stay a minute longer than I'm obliged, so come on."

Henry Dacres heard the two men descend the staircase and was about to proceed to the apartment they had just left, as much from curiosity to see what kind of preparations had been made, as from a wish to place the paper, on which he had written those few words in the spot agreed on by him and Dottman.

Again, however, he was to meet with disappointment, for as he was leaving the room he had fixed upon as a temporary abode, he heard footsteps approaching, and fully believing that they belonged to those who were about to occupy the suite of apartments he had heard so much about, he shrunk back into the room, and closed the door.

Little did Henry Dacres think that the footsteps were those of Dora and Dottman.

* * * *

When Dottman heard the shriek uttered by poor Dora, as she sunk fainting on the floor of the apartment, he rushed forward, and he, no less than Dora, was amazed to find the room so changed in appearance, and Henry Dacres not there.

He tenderly raised Dora, and bathing her face and hands in cold water, she soon recovered consciousness; but oh! how heartbroken was that courageous woman now.

"Oh, Dottman, Dottman!" she cried. "They have robbed me first of my child, my Mina, and now my husband! Oh, God, why do I still live?" and covering her face with her hands she swept bitter tears of anguish.

Dottman strove hard to give the comfort he was far, however, from feeling himself. But his presence of mind did not desert him in this trying hour.

Taking her hand in his, he said gently, as one would speak to a little child—

"We must not stay here—it is quite certain that some one else occupies this room. I suspected that such might be the case, and so I agreed with Mr. Dacres where to leave us a line, if at any time he should be obliged to leave this apartment. I will return to you in a moment."

Dottman left Dora to examine the little recess, but as our reader is aware, found nothing.

Dora clasped her hands over her face and wept convulsively.

CHAPTER XLIV.

THE DUKE OF KINGSTON AND HIS VICTIM—
THE DEATH SHRIEK—NEONI'S COURAGE
—THE ABDUCTION.

THE Duke of Kingston after he had closed the door which shut in the narrow staircase upon the dead body of Surlina, retraced his steps towards that chamber where he felt sure he had heard a deep groan.

At length he reached the door of that apartment in which the Greek had disposed of Van Esling, in the vain hope that by his arts the wounded man might recover health and strength, and be instrumental—he knew not how exactly, in helping him to carry out his vengeance against his patron—the false Duke of Kingston.

It was near the time for the Greek to visit his patient, to whom he had adminstered a powerful opiate, the effects of which were passing away; and Van Esling waited in feverish impatience for his coming—hoping to hear that his gold and jewels were not lost, as Surlina had represented at their last interview.

As time wore on, and Surlina did not make his appearance, Van Esling tried to rise, hoping to drag himself to the door, and by battering upon it, to attract attention.

Then came the recollection of what Surlina had said to his daughter, Neoni, on the night of his arrival at the alchemist's—how that the Duke of Kingston wished for his death, and Van Esling feared to knock lest other ears than those of the Greek should be made aware of his proximity.

What was he to do? Faint and weak from suffering, and that suffering increased tenfold by the thought that all his wealth—that wealth which he had acquired by many an outrage and much personal danger, and in the acquisition of which he had hoped to make himself all powerful.

Another hour passed away, and still the wounded man was left alone—alone with his bitter thoughts.

At length he heard a footstep, and hope again sprung up in his breast—a hope that Surlina was bringing him word that his riches were not all lost. That he relented, and restored them to him—for Van Esling never thought for one moment that the Greek had really had them taken from him as he stated.

The Duke of Kingston paused to listen; for as he had passed that door on his way to the prison-chamber of the unfortunate Duchess of Kingston—bent upon murder, his coward heart had quailed, and although that groan had come upon his ear—yet was he quite unable now to decide from which room the sound had issued.

The Duke of Kingston paused to listen, and now very faintly did he hear a murmur as of some one at a distance, calling to Surlina.

As that name greeted the ears of the murderer, a cold perspiration broke out upon his forehead, and he clutched the balustrade, for he felt sick and giddy.

He had stood by to see the death-dealing liquid thrown into the chamber of his deserted wife, and had felt no remorse—for did she not stand in the way to his gratifying his unholy passion for the beautiful Greek girl—but now that he heard a voice calling upon the name of him whom he had treacherously murdered—after that one had done his behests—he felt the guilty thing he was.

"Surlina! Oh, Surlina! come to me, for pity's sake," said the feeble voice from within the room.

The Duke of Kingston did not recognize that voice, so changed from suffering.

"Who can it be?" he muttered to himself—"and what can he be doing here—I will enter."

The Duke of Kingston laid his hand upon the handle of the door, and at the same time a shriek of joy issued from within the apartment.

The lock, however, yielded not to his touch—the door was locked.

"Oh, be quick, in heaven's name!" again said the wounded man, for at that moment riches, comfort, health—all were forgotten in the longing to look upon a human face.

"I cannot open the door," said the Duke of Kingston. "I must go and seek for the means to force it open."

Van Esling recognized the voice of the Duke of Kingston—the man who wished for his death—and then a feeling of indescribable fear and anguish took possession of him, and he fainted.

The Duke of Kingston was not long in finding the means of forcing open the door, and in a few moments he stood on the threshold of the apartment, and beheld the man who, of all others, he wished to get into his power, lying senseless at his feet.

"Why, surely Fortune smiles upon me," he said with a sardonic laugh. "He has fainted—shall I let him recover, or shall I now and for ever rid myself of one who already knows far too much?"

"Villain that he is! I feel that he did but half do my bidding. Henry Dacres still lives! And did he not tell me he had killed him? Perchance, from some reason he never intended to take his life. But he moves—he moves! I will be patient—he had something to say to me—yes, something to say to me."

The wounded man groaned faintly.

"Some water will restore him," said the duke.

There was a jug upon the table, and the Duke of Kingston poured some of its contents into a glass, and held it to the lips of Van Esling.

"Thanks! Oh, thanks!" murmured Van Esling, without opening his eyes. "Thanks Surlina—you have been long absent, and I know not, but I think I am dying,—dying—dying!"

The Duke of Kingston felt that there was no time to lose if he would hear what Van Esling had to communicate.

"Speak, Van Esling," he said. "It is I—your friend, the Duke of Kingston, who addresses you."

"Oh, heavens!" cried Van Esling—"what want you with me?"

"Nay, it was you who appealed to me," said the duke. I was on my way to the laboratory of Surlina, when I heard you call for help."

The wounded man shuddered.

"Speak, Van Esling—have you aught to tell me of Dora or her child?"

"No, no!" murmured the dying man.

"Die, then!" shrieked the Duke of Kingston, and he buried his sword up to the hilt in the breast of Van Esling.

A cry of agony resounded through that lonely house, and Captain Van Esling had gone to his last account.

* * * *

That cry reached the ears of Neoni, who had been pacing the laboratory to and fro, ever since her father had quitted it.

So appalling had been that cry, that the beautiful Greek girl clasped her hands over her ears to shut out the sound of, perhaps, another. And yet terrified—with eyes dilated, and head thrown back, she listened.

For a moment she seemed, as it were, rooted to the spot—but then came the thought that perhaps her father was in danger, for she knew the treachery of the Duke of Kingston, and quick as lightning, she seized a wax taper, which stood on a table close by, and sped along the narrow passage which led to the staircase.

As she reached the door of the apartment which had been in the occupation of Van Esling, she felt herself clasped in the powerful arms of one who hissed into her ear—

"Mine now—oh! beautiful Neoni—mine at last!

With a sudden bound, however, which he little expected, Neoni freed herself from the grasp of the Duke of Kingston, and with eyes flashing, and arm uplifted, she looked like an avenging spirit calling down judgment upon the head of her betrayer.

"Approach me not, villain, or your death be upon your own head! Think you that the daughter of Surlina is a second time to become your dupe—your plaything?"

So unexpected—so sudden had all this taken place, that the Duke of Kingston, for a moment, lost his presence of mind, but quickly rallying said—

"I can pardon the beautiful Neoni for this exhibition of maidenly reserve, for I am well aware when I tell her that she no longer has a father to control her choice, that she will be too wise to refuse the overtures of one so much her superior in birth and station."

"False man!" cried Neoni. Too well do I know you, and rather than listen to your infamous propositions, I will sheathe this dagger in my breast.

As Neoni spoke, she took from the folds of her apparel, a richly ornamented poignard, and there was so much determination in her tone and manner, that the Duke of Kingston feared that she would indeed plunge it into her heart then and there.

"Rash girl!" he cried as he made a step towards her with the intention of disarming her of so deadly a weapon. "Rash girl! you know not what you say. I offer you honourable marriage—I will, for I can now, make you my duchess."

For a moment, but only for a moment, the unhappy Neoni caught at the hope that peace of mind might at length be hers if she were to become the wife of the betrayer of her innocence, but believing it to be only a vile scheme by which the man hoped to get her again into his power, she exclaimed—

"It is false! Thy wife lives!—and although she once spurned me, I now pity her. Leave me—leave me! I would seek my father!"

Neoni tried to pass the Duke of Kingston, but as she did so, he caught her by the robe.

"Hold, maiden!" he said—and this time he spoke more gently. "I tell thee that thou shalt be Duchess of Kingston—a coronet shall yet encircle that fair brow."

"And thy wife?" asked Neoni.

"Is no more," said the duke, in a low voice.

Neoni buried her face in her hands and was lost in thought, then raising her head, she looked steadfastly into the face of the duke.

"I must see my father—to-morrow I will give you my answer."

The Duke pursued the advantage he perceived he had gained, and his coward heart rejoiced to think that the fair girl had not heard or not understood him when he said she had no longer a father.

"Your father has left the house upon urgent business of mine, Neoni, and will not return until after our nuptials. He bade me give you his blessing, and I was on my way for that purpose when you unexpectedly made your appearance."

"My father left the house—and without seeing me?" said Neoni, incredulously.

"Even so. He left your future husband to make known to you his departure—but full of anticipation for your welfare and happiness."

"Oh, heaven!" ejaculated Neoni, "what am I to think—what am I to believe?"

"Believe!" said the Duke of Kingston, that as my wife you will have nothing left to hope for—but time flies—I must leave England on the morrow—and this night, if you will consent to wed me, you shall be Duchess of Kingston."

It will be remembered that Surlina and Neoni had often conversed together upon this subject, and that the chief desire of both father and daughter was to induce the Duke to make Neoni his wife, in order to repair, as far as might be, the deep wrong which he had done her.

But it was not Neoni's intention to fulfil the duties of a wife to the man who, above all others, she loathed—no—having obtained her object, she was content to die—to sacrifice her young life, and all that made life worth the living for.

Again the Duke addressed her.

"Speak to me, Neoni!" he said. "Will you consent to be in readiness to-night, to accompany me to the house of a friend, where our nuptials may be celebrated this very night."

After a moment's pause Neoni faltered "Yes!" "Now leave me, my lord," she said, "for I would fain be alone."

"Be it so, fair Neoni. This evening, at nine o'clock, I shall be ready to attend you. Farewell."

A few minutes more Neoni was alone in that house which contained so many horrors.

She slowly descended to the apartment which had been converted into a sitting room by Neoni and Surlina, and sinking on to a chair, she buried her face in her hands and thought, and as she thought she wept bitterly.

It seemed as though with those tears the young girl was washing away all her past hopes and wishes—all fond records of love and virtue—all hopes of a happy home, with smiling content as its inmate.

Life too, to her, seemed now so beautiful, that she dared scarcely contemplate death —and death, too, by her own hand—and yet was that not preferable to living a life of misery with him who had caused her so much sorrow.

How the wind whistled and moaned round the house !

Dizzy with strange thoughts, and an idea that some savage relentless destiny was pursuing her, Neoni fell at length into a profound slumber.

Neoni still slept.

The Duke of Kingston, when he left the fair Greek girl, was not long in deciding upon the arrangements he thought best adapted for carrying out his villanous projects with regard to Neoni.

But it was no part of his arrangements to have any eye witness to his enterprise. He therefore intended to convey Neoni in his cab to the old deserted Palace of Ken-

sington, little dreaming that that palatial residence had become a refuge for the persecuted Dora and her husband.

The hour of ten was chiming on the neighbouring church as the Duke of Kingston noiselessly let himself in with the aid of a latch key, with which he was always provided, at the hall door of that apparently deserted mansion.

He lingered a moment in the hall to listen, but no sound met his ear.

Could it be possible that Neoni had evaded him ? Had she fled from that house, and foiled him again ?

" Fool ! fool that I was !" he exclaimed, " to trust a woman's word—why did I not secure her when she was powerless to help herself."

He dashed wildly up the staircase; but then a desire to see how she was employed, if indeed she were still in the mansion, took possession of him, and he glided noiselessly through the apartment which led to that which he knew Surlina and his daughter were in the habit of using for a sitting room.

His heart beat violently as he reached the door of the apartment, for all was still—still as death.

He laid his hand upon the handle of the door—it yielded immediately to his touch.

The sight which met his gaze was one well calculated to give him satisfaction.

Seated on a low chair, her head slightly thrown back, was the beautiful Neoni— more beautiful than ever in that sweet childlike slumber.

A faint smile played upon her lips—and she murmured words in a soft low tone.

The Duke of Kingston bent down to listen.

"Fear not for me, oh, my father," she murmured. "Thy Neoni shrinks not from death—and yet—and yet"—

The Greek girl moved uneasily.

"'Tis better so," muttered the Duke of Kingston to himself, " if I can remove her without awakening her it will save me a world of trouble."

He raised the sleeping girl gently—her raven hair streamed over his shoulders, and her breath fanned his cheek.

The Duke of Kingston strode rapidly down the grand staircase, and through the hall of that deserted mansion, in which lay entombed all that remained of the unfortunate Duchess of Kingston, and the hapless Surlina.

How little did Neoni imagine at that moment, that her arch-enemy was thus separating her for ever from the lifeless remains of her fond father—even as he had placed the barrier of death between them.

The change in the atmosphere from the warm, and what Surlina had made for her, luxurious apartment, roused Neoni, who uttered a cry of dismay and terror, on finding herself clasped in the arms of a man—who seemed to be conveying her from her home

At first the thought occurred to her but half awakened faculties, that it was her father' and raising her head, she tried to gaze into his face.

"Speak to me, my father," she cried, "is it you?" You have come to save your Neoni from that bad man."

There was no answer.

Neoni now seemed endued with superhuman strength, and with one bound succeeded in freeing herself from the grasp which held her as in a vice.

The villanous Duke of Kingston was long in again taking captive the unhappy girl; but clutching her tightly by the wrist, he hissed into her ear, and as he did so, his hot breath seemed to scorch her cheek.

"Now I warn you that if you raise your voice above a low tone, or make any outcry, I will murder you.

The frightful truth that she was so completely in this man's power rushed across the heart of poor Neoni, with a gush that was almost enough to make her swoon, but she did not yield to the deadening impulse.

Again she tried to elude his grasp, but it was in vain. This time he twined his arms about her as he said—

"I have a conveyance at the door, which is to take you to your father, who will then accompany us to the house of the friend of whom I spoke to you. Will you, or will you not consent quietly to submit to my guidance?"

Neoni cast a hurried glance up and down the street; but at the moment, no pedestrian was near to whom she might cry for assistance. There was also a feeling of security in the fact of being under the broad canopy of heaven with this unscrupulous man—instead of being shut up with him in that lonely mansion—so Neoni was silent, and the duke mistook that silence for acquiesence.

A few minutes more and Neoni was seated in the cab of the Duke of Kingston, who, immediately seized the reins, and urged the horse at its utmost speed through a part of the town which was entirely unknown to Neoni.

CHAPTER XLV.

THE SEARCH THROUGH THE PALACE—THE RETURN OF JOY—THE EAVESDROPPER —THE UNEXPECTED MEETING.

DORA's was not a mind to succumb to

grief when there was anything to be done for those she loved, and after a few moments in which she had wept, as though her heart would break, she started up, and approaching Dottman, she said,

"Dottman, dear friend, we must search for Henry. I cannot but think he will find some means of communicating with us. He may not have been able to avail himself of the recess agreed upon between you; but probably we shall find some means of tracing him yet."

"No doubt of it, captain," said Dottman, "and I've been thinking that after all he may still be in the old palace—you see this room, captain, has been almost refurnished since we left it.

"True, true, I had not observed that," said Dora.

"Well, you see captain, somebody has wanted the room, and perhaps it was those gentleman you and Mr. Dacres called conspirators."

"Well?"

"Well, you see, captain, he would then have to turn out, don't you see, and perhaps after all he may not be very far off. What do you say to beginning our search at once?"

"Oh, do so, do so!" said Dora, "for I cannot bear to think of what he may have had to endure during our absence."

Dora and Dottman now left the apartment, and found themselves in that gallery from which opened the door that led to the unfurnished room, now occupied by Henry Dacres.

"It is not likely, captain," said Dottman, "that he is on this floor—you see it would be too near to his former quarters—let us descend the staircase."

Dora obeyed mechanically, for her heart misgave her—she had no hope of finding her Henry in the old palace, and yet she was unwilling to abandon it until she and Dottman had visited every apartment in which they thought it likely he might be concealed.

Having reached the foot of the staircase, Dora paused, for she fancied she heard a door shut in a distant part of the palace.

"Hush, Dottman!" she whispered, "did you hear any thing?"

"I fancy I heard a door shut; but perhaps it was the wind. I've a great mind to blow my whistle—Mr. Dacres knows the sound of that, and if he is in the palace, it will let him know we are here.

Dora stood for a few moments in deep thought—then she said—

"Let us look through these apartments first, Dottman, and then if we don't find Henry, then you can make use of your whistle."

"Very good, captain, now for number one."

Dottman strove by every means in his power to effect a cheerfulness he was far from feeling, in order that Dora might be in some measure re-assured—Dora was not behind hand in perceiving and appreciating to the full his kind intentions.

Dottman now turned the handle of a door against which they had been standing while they held their brief conference as to what it would be most expedient to do, and entered a room which was magnificently furnished.

It was a long room which had been most elaborately fitted up as a library. There were book-cases upon all the walls, extending up three parts of the height, and then terminating for the remainder of the distance in beautiful Gothic carvings. Between each of these book-cases were pedestals with busts from the antique upon them

An immense lamp of bronze depended from the ceiling, in which a solitary candle was lodged in some manner, so that it gave a dreary kind of light over the large room. The carpet felt soft as driven snow, and strewed about the floor were couches and chairs of the most repose-inviting character.

A table covered with a purple velvet, occupied the centre of the floor.

"It's quite evident, captain, that we are not the only occupants of the old palace," said Dottman. "It is quite certain that some one has been here very recently, by the lighted wax candle in the lamp."

"It is very strange," said Dora. "Perhaps some one who, like ourselves, is hiding from those who would hunt them to death. Oh, Henry, where are you?"

"Well, it's quite clear he is not here, captain, and the best thing we can do is to continue our search."

They then quitted this apartment, and closing the door, they entered a room opposite to them.

The furniture and decorations of this apartment had been of the richest description, but everything was faded and worn. The walls had originally been covered with a crimson damask paper, over which still glistened here and there the remains of an intricate, small network of gold, which must have had, when in its beauty, an exquisitely beautiful effect. The ceiling had been lightly tinted, and all the moveable appointments were in perfect keeping with the decorations.

Poor Dora turned away with an expression of deep mental suffering upon her face, and turning to Dottman, she said—

"Let us hasten to complete our search. We know not how soon we may encounter the occupants of the rooms we have already entered, which are without doubt tenanted. My heart tells me that my Henry has had to fly, and alone, too, in his state. Oh, Dottman, I ought not to have left him."

Well, but, captain, you did all for the best, and I feel sure things will come right in the end ; but here we are at the foot of the staircase again. Shall we ascend, and explore the rooms on the floor above "

"Oh, yes, yes, anything—anything that may lead to the discovery of my Henry."

As Dora and Dottman were ascending the staircase, the former laid her hand upon the arm of Dottman, and by a sign bade him listen.

As they did so, there came upon the ear unmistakable sounds of footsteps, gliding noiselessly along the corridor above them.

"Oh, heavens!" cried Dora, "we are watched—we are lost!"

"Hush, captain ! perhaps it is Mr. Dacres himself—let me go first."

Dottman took from the breast of his apparel a small pistol, and thus armed, he advanced towards the approaching footsteps.

To ascend the staircase was the work of a moment, and Dottman pushed open the tall narrow door which was facing him and passed in. All was still, however, and it was evident that the apartment was untenanted.

Dora leant against the balustrade, and a feeling of great anxiety passed over her countenance.

"You are ill," said Dottman.

"Oh, no, no ! but I am so confused. Surely I heard footsteps. I am trying to think. Hark ! did you hear nothing ?"

"What ? speak !" said Dottman, now almost partaking of Dora's fears.

"A footstep ! it is his footstep ! I know it well !"

Dora made a rush forward, and was clasped in the arms of her husband.

"My Dora—my own Dora—look up ! it is I ! do you not know me ? do you not hear my voice ? it is your own Henry who speaks to you."

Dora, with a gush of tears that could not be restrained, looked up into her husband's face.

"And you are safe and unhurt ?" said Dora.

"Quite safe, my Dora, and almost well. Ah, are you there, Dottman ?"

"All right, Mr. Dacres. You gave us both a bit of a fright, for we had begun to give up all thoughts of finding you in the old palace. But tell us how it all came about that we see you turned out of your old quarters."

"Well, Dottman, I did not allow myself to be turned out, but when I overheard

THE MEETING OF DORA AND NEONI.

some one give an order to prepare that apartment we had appropriated for another tenant, I made my way to this room, and finding it had been long disused, I fancied we should be safer here than in one of those which are furnished.

While Henry Dacres was speaking, he led Dora and Dottman into the apartment he had selected, the appearance of which, however, did not seem to meet Dottman's views with regard to what was a fitting habitation for Dora.

"I don't see, Mr. Dacres," he said, "why we should put ourselves off with an unfurnished room, when there are so many only waiting for us to take possession of.

DORA.—23.

What say you, captain? shall we go and secure the one you said had been fitted up as a breakfast room?"

"As you will, Dottman; but I feel fatigued, and if you will keep watch for about two hours, I will in turn keep guard while you sleep.

"All right, captain, and on one of those couches, of which there are so many in the apartment, you will be as snug as possible."

Dora cast herself upon one of the couches, with Henry sitting by her side, and through pure exhaustion, after a time she fell into a disturbed slumber, in the course of which many strange distrustful images presented themselves to her imagination, unchecked by the comparative power of reason.

It was quite a mercy when she awoke, for that was not the sleep that sent refreshment and calm peace and joy into the heart and brain.

"What shall we—what ought we to do now?" she said, taking Henry's hand in hers. "I have a strange presentiment, dearest, that this palace is far from being a safe refuge for us, and where—oh, where can we go?"

As Henry was about to make some reply to this question, a low tap came at the door of the apartment.

"It is Dottman," said Dora.

Henry opened the door, and Dottman entered with his finger upon his lips to indicate silence.

"Speak low," he whispered. "I hear footsteps and voices approaching. In all probability it is the new comer about to take possession of our room."

They all listened intently.

They heard a soft female voice say—

"And is my father here?"

"He will be here shortly," replied a male voice.

The two speakers entered the room which had been occupied by Dora and her husband, and the door was closed with a loud bang, and silence once more reigned in the old palace.

"This is strange," said Henry Dacres. "I made sure that we were to have the seven conspirators for our neighbours. But what can they want here?"

"Perhaps I shall be able to find out," said Dottman; "for there is a kind of cupboard that seems to have been used, at some time, as a lumber room, adjoining the apartment into which the lady and gentleman have entered, and I fancy if I can only get there without being seen, I shall be able to hear all that's going on."

Dora looked at first as if she disapproved of this proceeding, until Dottman said—

"Who knows, we may be called upon to help some one who may need our assistance? It is quite certain the voice belonged to a young lady, and that young lady evidently had been led to believe that she was to have met her father here, so if there is anything underhanded going on, why, you know, captain, we may as well have an adventure in the old palace as upon the road. It certainly has novelty to recommend it."

Dora smiled, and holding out her hand to Henry, she said—

"Be it so, Dottman, and come what may, I feel that I am not alone now that I am near Henry."

Henry pressed her hand to his lips, and assured her that he felt quite capable of defending her against any one assailant.

In the meantime Dottman had made his way to the little lumber room he had mentioned, where he ensconced himself behind the door, in which position he could hear almost every word that passed, although unable to see the speakers.

"And now I will take my leave, fair Neoni," he heard a voice say, "for some hours' repose are necessary to you. The dawn will soon appear. At seven o'clock this evening you may expect me."

"And my father?" asked the female voice.

"No, your future husband will probably be alone."

"Oh Heaven! what mean you? where is my father?" cried the female voice.

"I mean that you are entirely in my power, and that nothing can step between you and my love."

"Love!" almost shrieked the young girl. "Profane not the holy word by letting it pass your lips. Never shall you wed me until I have seen my father, for my heart tells me there has been treachery at work. Oh, why was I so easily duped as to listen to your promise that he should meet me here?"

"Beware, girl!" hissed the man's voice. "I have been forbearing, but one more epithet, and you shall find, to your cost, that it were better to have the Duke of Kingston for a friend rather than for an enemy."

As these last words reached the ears of Dottman, he almost staggered back with surprise, and but that he felt it was now more than ever necessary for him to hear as much as possible, he would have gone at once to Dora and Henry Dacres to apprise them of the close proximity of their deadly foe.

"I fear you not," said the girl. "Fiend! monster! do your worst. I have not left myself without the means of freeing myself from you; and again I say this hand shall never be yours until I hear the tale of the Duchess of Kingston confirmed by the lips of my father."

"Ha, ha!" laughed the man's voice. "I take my leave of you. I leave you but for a few hours to your own reflections, and when I return you will, I hope, receive your husband that is to be with somewhat more affection than you have manifested to-night. Adieu!"

A door swung to with a bang at this moment, and Dottman knew that the apartment was tenanted only by the young girl. He waited some few minutes, in order that he might avoid encountering the Duke of Kingston as he left the room, which he had intended for a prison-house, for the time being, of the beautiful Neoni.

Dottman allowed a full quarter of an hour to elapse before he ventured to leave his hiding-place, and then he walked noiselessly past the room which Dora and Henry Dacres had looked upon as their own, but which was now in the occupation of Neoni, and made his way to Dora.

As Dottman entered the room, Dora and Henry could see at a glance that something unusual had taken place. After closing the door carefully, Dora laid her hand on his arm saying—

"Speak at once, dear friend. I can tell by your looks that you have something of importance to communicate. Are we in danger?"

"I scarcely think that we are in danger, captain, and yet I must say we have been much nearer to the Duke of Kingston within the last half hour than I like to think of your having been.

"The Duke of Kingston!" exclaimed Dora and Henry Dacres simultaneously.

"Even so," said Dottman. He then detailed to Dora and her husband all that he had overheard from his hiding-place.

"And this young girl," said Dora, "who is she? who can she be?"

"That I could not gather, captain, from what they said. It is evident, however, that the false duke has deceived her in some way; but that you must find out."

"I?" said Dora.

"Why, yes, captain, did you not agree with me that an adventure in the old palace would be quite as amusing as one on the road?"

"I did," said Dora; but of what assistance can I be? alas! am I not myself hunted almost to the death?"

"Well, for the matter of that, captain, I think you could go and talk to this young girl, whoever she may be, and if you find that she wishes to elude the Duke of Kingston, what so easy as to bring her here? He will never think of searching for her here, but will suppose that she has made her escape by one of the windows, which I will contrive to leave open to mislead him.

Dora turned to Henry now, as if to seek counsel. She seemed strangely altered since the events of this night, and did not appear to rely so much upon her own judgment as she has lately been in the habit of doing.

Henry understood her, and had no difficulty in persuading her to act in accordance with Dottman's suggestions.

It was finally agreed that Dottman should sally out into the corridor and see that all was quiet, and that then he should return for Dora, whom he was to conduct to the door of the apartment in which was confined Neoni.

All this was quickly accomplished, and Dora and Dottman had made their way to the door of Neoni's apartment.

Dora laid her hand upon the lock of the door. It was fastened.

"Oh! never mind that, captain," said Dottman. "I've my large clasped knife. I'll soon open the door."

The door was soon open, and Dora and Neoni were in each other's presence.

CHAPTER XLVI.

THE UNEXPECTED FRIEND—THE SECRET REVEALED—THE DUKE OF KINGSTON IS FOILED FOR A TIME—DOTTMAN'S ADVENTURE ON THE ROAD.

THESE two girls—for they were still youthful—presented a striking contrast as they stood in that apartment, facing each other. What pen can describe the sweetness of Dora's mouth—the peach-like bloom of her cheeks, the delicate tenderness of the half-closed eyes, the wavy hair parted over a brow full of genius and ingenuousness?

And Neoni, too, was beautiful; but her beauty was of a different character to that of Dora. Neoni was much taller—her hair was black as night, and there was in her countenance a look of stern determination. She looked the person to will a something, and then unflinchingly, like Destiny itself, to carry that something fully out.

For some few moments Dora and Neoni regarded each other in silence.

Neoni was the first to break that silence.

Starting to her feet, the Greek girl exclaimed passionately—

"What intrusion is this? But I suppose his grace, the Duke of Kingston, is in the habit of making promises which he never intends to carry out. I was at least to be allowed some hours of solitude."

Dora was at once struck with the beautiful but melancholy countenance of the Greek girl, and advancing a few paces into the room, she said gently—

"It was to ascertain if I could be of any service in aiding you to avoid the Duke of Kingston that induced me to visit you.

"What is your name? I would fain trust you—and yet what friends has Neoni in this cold land?

It would seem that these few words had conjured up to the mind of the young Greek visions of her own sunny land, for she again sunk into the chair in which she was seated when Dora entered the room, and burying her face in her hands, seemed unconscious of the presence of Dora.

Dora felt that there was no time to lose, and stepping up to her she quietly laid her hand upon the shoulder of the Greek girl, saying in that low, sweet tone, which was peculiar to her—

"Your name is Neoni. Perhaps when I tell you my name you will trust me—I am Dora Dacres."

"Dora Dacres!" exclaimed Neoni. "Dora Dacres! Why are you here? What strange fatality brings us face to face at last?"

"It is too long a story," said Dora, with a sigh, "to tell you now, suffice it to say that I am willing to do all in my power to save you from the vile machinations of that bad man who falsely calls himself the Duke of Kingston."

"And you are Dora the Duchess?" continued the Greek girl, as if speaking to herself rather than addressing Dora.

"I am Dora the Duchess," replied Dora —"that Dora whom the wicked duke has pursued almost to the death—that Dora whose husband he sought to have assassinated—that Dora whose child has been stolen from her—that Dora who now is a—"

"Oh! say no more — say no more!" cried the Greek girl, the fire of indignation kindling in her eyes, from which all gentleness and tenderness had flown. "Say no more, but tell me can I leave this place? Where am I? It looked a large rambling kind of building as we entered in the darkness."

"Is it possible that you know not where you are? This is old Kensington Palace, where I and my husband have found a temporary refuge, for you must know it is now no longer used as a residence."

"Then," replied Neoni, "in all probability there are rooms in which we may secrete ourselves for a time—I would fain see what comes of this."

"There are, there are," said Dora, "but I would introduce you to my Henry. Ah! you are ill."

"No, no," replied the Greek girl, faintly —"it has passed away, but I would gladly rest awhile, and defer my introduction to Mr. Dacres."

Dora was glad to find the colour return to the cheek of Neoni, and hastened to prepare Henry and Dottman to receive this addition to their circle.

As soon as Dora mentioned the name of Neoni, Henry began to question her respecting the appearance of her new found friend.

When Dora told him that she was evidently a Greek—and spoke of her beauty and majestic bearing, Henry exclaimed—

"Then we have met before, my Dora. I was of some assistance to her and her father once when I was on foreign service, and an intimacy sprung up between us which suddenly ceased from some unknown cause. I was soon after this ordered to rejoin my regiment which was about to return to England. Soon after that, my Dora, I had the happiness of becoming acquainted with you—then followed our marriage—afterwards the cloud of adversity burst over our devoted heads, and I had ceased to remember the existence of these friends.

While Henry had been hurriedly making known to Dora his former acquaintance with the Greek girl and her father, Dora recollected the start, and the sudden paleness which had overspread the expressive countenance of the beautiful Greek girl.

"Poor girl—poor girl," murmured Dora, "she is, indeed, to be pitied."

"Yes, my Dora, but we will help her to elude the machinations of the false Duke of Kingston."

"Ah! Henry," said Dora, as she threw her arms about him—I can well understand that having once loved you that love will be lasting, especially in one of her temperament."

"My Dora, you mistake," said Henry, who was really unconscious of the impression he had made upon the heart of Neoni —"you mistake, my Dora, we never loved each other—the intercourse between me and the Greek and his daughter was simply little acts of kindness that I had it in my power to show them as strangers among a strange people."

"As far as you are concerned, my Henry, I have not the slightest doubt in my mind that you were not aware of the influence you exercised over her, and therefore, perhaps, it would have made your course all the easier had I not spoken to you on the subject, but I am in the habit, as you know, Henry, of speaking my thoughts aloud to you—it is your right to expect that I should do so, is it not, dearest?"

"Do so, my own Dora, but I think," added Henry, with a fond smile, "I can remember a certain person donning the costume of the knight of the road without then uttering her thoughts aloud."

It was now Dora's turn to smile, and for the brief space of a few hours, these two loving hearts were happier than they could have supposed it possible for them to be under such adverse circumstances as they now found themselves.

Hour after hour passed away—twice had Dora glided noiselessly to the apartment to which she had conducted Neoni, but each time, from her quiet breathing, she fancied the young Greek girl slept.

Little did Dora imagine the conflicting passions and emotions which had been called into existence in the head and brain of Neoni on hearing that she was beneath the same roof with Henry Dacres, the husband of her who had come forward to proffer her friendship and assistance.

Alas! poor Neoni.

* * * * *

Dora left the young Greek girl, as she supposed, to seek that repose of which she appeared to stand so much in need, and had returned to detail to her husband all that had passed between herself and Neoni.

No sooner, however, did Neoni, find herself alone in that dreary looking apartment then she began to pace it with uneven and agitated steps—ever and anon muttering to herself broken, disjointed sentences.

"And it has come to this," she exclaimed—"that I should be brought a prisoner here beneath the same roof with *him*. Oh! Fate—Fate! how crully hast thou persecuted me! What have I done that I should be thus tortured?"

Covering her face with her hands, she burst into a passion of hysterical weeping, after the subsidence of which she made a resolution, which, dangerous though it was, she thought more prudent than remaining where she now was—that resolution was not only to endeavour to escape the Duke of Kingston, but to fly—she knew not whither—but far away from the dangerous influence Henry Dacres yet had over her heart.

"Yes!" she said, half aloud, "I will fly, better so than that his wife should despise me.'

For a few moments the Greek girl was lost in thought—then she murmured—

"How could he have been ignorant of my love? True, I tried to suppress the beatings of my heart in his presence—stifled my first love, because he did not or would not see how dear he was to me. *I* should have read his heart more truly had our cases been reversed, and why did he not return my love?

Neoni sunk upon the couch upon which Dora had so tenderly placed her, and buried her head in the cushions, and again she murmured—

"Yes she is beautiful; but have I not been called beautiful also? But enough—enough!" she said, as she started to her feet, "I will conquer this love, so unworthy of me. Father! father! oh, why have you deserted your unhappy child? But once let me feel thy breath, like a blessing upon my cheek, and I am content to die and be forgotten.

Neoni once more began pacing the room, but this time it was to examine the apartment to see what means it afforded for her escape.

Alas there was none. The apartment in which Neoni sat, was one which seemed to communicate on three sides with other rooms of which two of the doors were locked, and the third one was that which led immediately to those rooms selected by Dora and her husband for their temporary abode.

The window looked out into a narrow paved court, and was such a height from the ground that Neoni could never hope to reach it in life if she tried to escape in that direction.

Returning then to her seat on the sofa, Neoni sat and thought, and at length dropped into an uneasy slumber.

Sleep gentle Neoni, and may "Nature's sweet restorer," bring peace to that crushed heart.

* * * * *

Half past eight o'clock had chimed by the clock at Kensington Church, and Dora and her husband were listening intently for any noise that might come upon the silent air—Dottman had ensconced himself as we have before stated in the little lumber room, near to the apartment which had served as a prison house for a time to Neoni.

As the last sound was echoing through the deserted palace, a hasty step was heard mounting the stairs, and in another moment the Duke of Kingston had reached the door of the apartment in which he had secured his prey.

Before opening that door, however, he placed his ear close to the panel in order to catch any sound which might proceed from within.

"All quiet," he said to himself, "by this time I have no doubt the lovely Neoni is reduced to submission."

He now abruptly opened the door, and stood upon the threshold.

Neoni was not there.

A pang of alarm shot across the guilty soul of the Duke of Kingston, and it was a moment or two before he could summon courage enough to go into the room—nothing seemed to be displaced, but certainly it was empty.

"Oh, how weak and foolish I have been of late," he said, with a sickly smile, "could I forget that in the inner room she was much more likely to fly for security than in this."

To search that room was the work of an instant, and the Duke pushed open the tall narrow door that led into the apartment that immediately joined the one that might be considered more specially to be the prison of Neoni. So confident was he that he should find her there, that as he pushed open the door he had her name upon his lips.

"Neoni, have you slept well?"

The room was empty.

"Gone!" exclaimed the duke, "escaped! Then I am lost!"

He staggered to a seat, and turning as pale as death itself, he sat down, and for a few moments was incapable of thought. His eyes, however, rapidly traversed the room, and he could perceive nothing to elucidate the mystery. Every thing was in its usual place and position. The window was closed and no one would have supposed it possible that any girl could have escaped from such a place.

"Not from here," cried he, "not from here has she eluded me, but by the door, and upon examining it more closely, he found that the lock had been removed, and replaced. "By the door I find that she had abundant means, no doubt, by which she succeeded in leaving the place. Oh, fool, fool that I was, not to secure her more effectually."

With a feeling of desperation, he again examined what he considered might have served as hiding places to the Greek girl—for the idea, and it was the last one that could give him any consolation, came across him that she must be only hiding from him—but all was in vain. In three minutes more, the duke was not only thoroughly satisfied that Neoni was in neither of the rooms—but he was likewise satisfied that the mode of her leaving them was to him a mystery.

"What is the meaning of all this?" he cried. "Am I mad? did I bring her here at all, or did I dream it?"

He covered his eyes for a moment or two from observation of external objects, and then starting up, he said—

"She must be in the palace—I do not think that she could leave the palace, I will search it! There is no other inmate within its walls, or I could understand how that the door might have been opened from the outside; but that is impossible—she was alone, quite alone in the palace.

Again the duke paused to think.

"Yes!" he muttered again, "without my keys, and I know they were in safe custody until they were delivered up to me only a short time since—she could not leave it, and yet, how dare I say she could not leave the palace, when as if by magic, she has left these rooms where I thougt that she was so secure? I must resolve these doubts!"

With a look of greater anxiety than his face had worn for many a long year, the Duke of Kingston now proceeded to make a hasty kind of search through the apartments contiguous to those in which he had confined the unhappy Neoni.

A quarter of an hour sufficed to convince him that if she was in the palace it would require some more active search to find her than he was just then willing to devote it, and time passing, for at eleven o'clock the duke had promised himself the pleasure of re-visiting the laboratory of Surlina, in order that he might appropriate any valuables belonging to the murdered man.

The reader is aware that our old acquaintance, Dottman, had been a listener to the duke's soliloquy—as soon, therefore, as he believed it safe to leave his hiding place, he made his way noiselessly to the apartment which was occupied by Dora and her husband; Neoni, too, by this time had listened to the persuasions of Dora, and accompanied her back to her apartment.

They were all three then waiting impatiently for any sounds that might indicate the approach of Dottman.

He was not long in putting them in full possession of the state of affiairs—and when he had finished speaking Neoni begged to be allowed to follow the false duke in a disguise that she would borrow of Dora.

"For what purpose," said Henry, "would you expose yourself to danger that must inevitably ensue should the Duke recognize you?"

"I would know where my father is—my heart sorely misgives me, and I fear I know not what."

"Well, captain," said Dottman, addressing Dora, "I fancy you are pretty safe—and I think I should like a bit of an adventure myself, with the false duke—what do you say to me going—who knows it may turn out no such bad enterprise after all; for I may see fit to cry "Stand" to this man—and if so, why, we shall not have lost much time, you see."

It was at length agreed that Dottman should do as he proposed, and with the understanding that he would return to them before noon on the morrow, he took his leave.

Dottman glided quickly and noiselessly down the staircase, and made his way to the stables where he had secured the horses, and taking Starlight from the stall, he led the creature out of the little door in the garden wall, when he mounted and trotted on some hundred paces on the road to London.

He then deemed it expedient to draw rein, and await the coming of the Duke of Kingston.

Dottman had been thus waiting about three quarters of an hour when he heard the tramp of horses' hoofs upon the road, coming from the direction of Kensington.

"It is he!" said Dottman to himself, and concealing himself as much as possible from observation, he still listened intently.

A few minutes more and Dottman emerged from the shadow of the trees, and stationed himself right in the path of the approaching horseman.

The mounted figure was enveloped in an ample cloak, and it was impossible to distinguish friend from foe at that moment, for a heavy cloud had just obscured the moon, that but a moment before was bathing everything in its soft rays, making all objects look black and sombre from the contrast to their previous brightness.

The horseman still advanced, and it was not until his horse reared that he was aware that something or some person was in the centre of the roadway.

"Stand!" cried Dottman, in a clear high voice.

"Out of my way, fellow!" shouted the Duke of Kingston, for it was indeed he— "out of my way, fellow—I am in no mood to be played with to-night."

"Neither am I in any mood to play!" answered Dottman. "Quick, my lord— your money and whatever valuables you may have about you."

"Ah! you know me?" said the Duke.

CHAPTER XLVII.

THE DUKE ENCOUNTERS A HIGHWAYMAN —DOTTMAN VISITS SURLINA'S LABORATORY—THE MASKED FIGURE—DORA'S PARDON.

THE words with which we concluded our last chapter were uttered by the Duke of Kinsgton in a tone of voice which certainly betrayed a hope that the man who molested him might be mistaken, for the duke was not anxious to be recognized on this road at that late hour, and unattended.

"Ay, my lord, I know you for a man steeped in crimes and plots and intrigues— but, beware, false Duke—the wisest schemer that ever lived—the most wily plotter—the most subtle contortor of circumstancs that ever breathed, holds his frail life upon such a tenure, that I wonder you should think it worth your while to commit bloodshed, and—"

"Ah! villain—what say you? Let me pass, or I will sweep you from my path as I would some noisome reptile."

"Not so easy done as said, my lord!" replied Dottman, and raising a double bar-relled pistol to a level with the eyes of the duke, he again repeated 'Stand and deliver.'

This time the duke saw that he was no match for his opponent, for he was quite unarmed, with the exception of a heavily loaded riding whip.

"There's my purse," he cried, "take it —and now let me pass."

"Not just yet, my lord—I must have your watch, and that diamond ring."

"Fiend! take all I have, and now go your way."

"Farewell, my lord—pleasant dreams! ha! ha!" laughed Dottman, as he allowed the Duke of Kingston to pass on his way.

But it was not the intention of Dottman so soon to loose sight of his grace as he pretended, and the duke had not ridden many paces forward when Dottman turned his horse's head, and galloped after him on the soft turf, so that the tramp of his horse's hoofs was not audible to the duke.

As he expected the Duke did not draw rein until he had reached the locality in which was situated Kingston House.

"He is going home!" said Dottman, to himself—"I have had my ride after all for nothing—but I will watch a short time, and see if he comes out again.

Dottman, however, was too precipitate in his opinion, for the duke had no intention of entering Kingston House at that moment, and after taking a hasty survey up and down the street, he drew from his pocket a key, and entered the deserted house adjoining his mansion.

Dottman's curiosity was now thoroughly awakened, and giving his horse into charge of a lad who happened to be passing at the time, he resolved to follow the duke.

Fortune seemed to favour Dottman on that night, for the duke, who had been thoroughly thrown off his balance, first by the disappearance of Neoni, and then by the robbery, that he forgot to remove the key from the lock, shutting it outside as he closed the massive hall door.

Dottman was not slow to perceive the advantage he had over the duke, and only waited a sufficient length of time to enable him to leave the hall before he, Dottman, entered.

Having waited about the space of ten minutes, Dottman noiselessly turned the key in the lock and entered the spacious hall.

All was profoundly dark.

No sound met his ear.

Dottman drew from his pocket a small box containing matches, with which he was always provided, and having lit one, he listened.

He could hear the duke slowly mounting the staircase. Ever and anon he paused, as though uncertain of his way.

At length he opened a door on the right, and was about to enter a room, when he turned suddenly round as though he felt that he was being watched.

Dottman crouched down behind a pillar, and he heard the duke say to himself—

"I must have been mistaken. It could only be fancy, but I thought I heard a footstep."

Again the duke proceeded on his way through a narrow kind of passage, still followed by Dottman, who had been instructed by Neoni to follow him in order to ascertain, if possible, whether her father met him.

The duke paused at the door of what had been Surlina's laboratory, and still holding the door open with one hand, and clutching his sword with the other he seemed to hesitate before entering that apartment.

Of what was his coward heart afraid at that moment? surely it was the dead and not the living that bad man feared to meet?

"Tush!" he said, "this night's adventure seem to have quite unnerved me. Is he not dead—dead! the dead utter no reproaches. I must be quick, for I have much to do before daybreak."

While thus communing with himself, the Duke of Kingston had been divesting himself of the heavy riding cloak which he had worn, and having done so, he commenced an examination of the crucible, which Surlina was in the habit of using for chemical purposes, in the vain hope, perhaps, of discovering at the bottom some of those false diamonds which he had so often promised the duke, and which were to stand the test of real ones.

Little did the duke imagine that Dottman, the faithful friend and servant of Dora the Duchess was a spectator of all his movements, for through a small glazed frame in the door Dottman was enabled to command a full view of the interior of the laboratory.

"Duped!" cried the duke in a voice of passion. "Duped! but that is over. By to-morrow's dawn I shall have left this hated house and all that it contains. Yes, all that it contains," he repeated with a ghastly smile. "But before I do so, I must make myself sure that the pardon is destroyed past all recovery. She will then still be in my power, for were she to lay claim to my titles and estates, I can easily set the myrmidons of the law about her, and I shall yet see her die, and all may yet be well."

The duke rose from the chair on which he had thrown himself, and approached the door at which Dottman had stationed himself, as if to leave the laboratory.

With the rapidity of lightning, Dott-man stepped aside in time to allow the duke to pass out, who, before doing so, however, proceeded to light a small lamp which was suspended from the ceiling.

From this Dottman rightly concluded that the duke intended to return to that apartment. Therefore, after watching and listening for some few minutes to his retreating footsteps, Dottman seized the opportunity of entering the laboratory in the duke's absence, believing that be should be of more use to Neoni, and perhaps, too, to Dora, if he could get nearer to the duke.

As soon as Dottman entered the laboratory, he begun to look hastily about him for some place of concealment, and in doing so his eyes fell upon the glass mask worn by Surlina when engaged in his chemical researches, and a kind of loose robe which the Greek generally wore when employed in the laboratory.

To fix on the mask and throw over him the robe was the work of an instant, and Dottman had just time to secrete himself behind an old cabinet, in which were phials and various utensils used by the Greek, when the Duke of Kingston entered the apartment again, with some papers in his hand.

The light from the lamp was only just sufficient to scatter darkness, and to shed thoughout the apartment a dim radiance that was like a slight reflected dawn.

To eyes accustomed to that light as were those of Dottman's, it was amply sufficient to make everything fully visible.

In a few moments he heard the duke reading, in a low tone, various endorsements which were on the papers he held in his hand.

At length the duke read the following words, which almost took away Dottman's breath, so much did he feel the necessity of possessing himself of that paper.

"The pardon of Dora Dacres," read the duke. "Ha, ha! this must be destroyed at once and for ever. No one suspected that it was I, the Duke of Kingston, who waylaid the king's messenger just in time to prevent him delivering the pardon to the authorities. True, the girl escaped— no one knows the existence of such an interesting document as this but myself, so the sooner it resolves itself into its natural elements the better."

The Duke of Kingston rose from the chair, evidently with the intention of setting fire to the document, the possession of which would be priceless to Dora and all she loved.

With one bound Dottman cleared a considerable space which was between him and the duke, and stood before the guilty man.

DOTTMAN TERRIFIES THE DUKE INTO GIVING UP THE PARDON OF DORA.

With a harsh strange cry, the duke staggered back until he reached the wall of the apartment.

With eyes dilated, and terror depicted on every feature, he fixed his fascinated gaze upon the apparition, as he thought, of the murdered Surlina.

"Back! back!" he cried, holding out his hands before him. "Neoni is safe and well!"

Dottman stood before the Duke of Kingston and regarded him in silence for about the space of a minute—then advancing towards the shrinking man, with arms outstretched, he spoke in a low deep voice—

DORA.—24.

"I know that my Neoni is safe and well—it is given to the spirits of another world to behold those they love in this."

"Oh heaven!" gasped the duke.

"Call not on heaven, murderer!" said Dottman.

"Mercy—mercy!" groaned the duke.

"It is too late! Have you had mercy on your brother's child? Even now are you not plotting her destruction?"

"Alas! alas! what do you require of me?" asked the duke, sinking lower and lower to the floor.

"Restitution!"

"Restitution!"

"Even so."

"I cannot call the dead to life. Oh! have mercy."

"I would protect the living. Give me the document you are trying to conceal beneath your apparel—I must and will have it, or I do not leave this chamber but over your corpse!"

"What document do you speak of?" asked the duke, still hoping that the pardon had escaped the knowledge of his ghastly visitor.

"The pardon of Dora Dacres."

For a moment there was silence, but when the duke again raised his eyes to Dottman, who wore so hideous an aspect beneath that glass mask, he shrunk still further back in terror, and suffered Dottman, who had advanced towards him, to take it without resistance

Having assured himself, by the aid of the little lamp, that he had the long wished for document really in his possession, Dottman strode to the door of the apartment, and waving his arm in the air, disappeared, leaving the Duke of Kingston paralysed with fear.

No sooner had Dottman regained the hall than he made the best of his way out of that house, taking care carefully to secure the precious document which was to bring so much happiness to Dora and to her husband.

Dottman was not long before he had mounted his horse and gallopped furiously, at first, so eager was he to carry the good tidings to those who were so anxiously expecting him.

Suddenly, however, he reined in his horse, for he fancied he saw several mounted men not far a-head of him, and he felt that if he continued to ride at such a rate he might attract attention.

Walking his horse, therefore, he endeavoured to keep the horsemen some distance in advance of him, but they, too, seemed to have slackened their pace, so that Dottman saw clearly that it was intentional, so trotting leisurely forward he soon reached the mounted party.

"A fine night, sir," said one of the horsemen as Dottman passed them.

"Yes," replied Dottman—"but there will be rain before another hour."

"Very likely," replied the first speaker. You must be fond of solitude to ride alone at this hour. Have you far to go?"

Dottman felt that he was being gradually hemmed in by the horsemen, and knew how great was the risk to himself if he attempted flight—so, as was usual with him on great emergencies, he quickly resolved upon a course of action.

"Well, to tell the truth," said Dottman, in reply to his questioner, "I have rather further to go then I cared to go alone—not that I am a nervous man by any means, but I have heard of so many robberies of late on the highway, that I was just asking myself when I came up to you gentlemen, where I could stay for a few hours. Perhaps you can direct me to some inn, and will kindly allow me to travel in your company until we reach it?"

"Right willingly, my fine fellow," said some of the horsemen in chorus—"and if we should happen to fall in with the highwayman of whom we have heard so much lately, why you can share with us the honour of capturing him."

"That will I," said Dottman. "Only the other day I hear the mail was stopped, and all the insides robbed of every thing they possessed."

"Too true—too true!" said one of the horsemen—"My uncle happened to be one of the victims on that occasion"

Dottman was anxious to hear more, but feared to appear too interested lest suspicion should attach to him.

The whole of the party trotted their horses up the hill until they came to a little way-side hostelry, which bore the sign of "White Lion," suspended over the door.

"Halt!" cried one of the party who seemed to be the leader—"let us see if there is accommodation here for man and beast for a few hours"—and knocking with the handle of his riding whip on the door, he called out—

"Holloa there! House—house!"

In a few minutes a man's head, with a night-cap, was thurst out at the window, and a voice demanded, in rather surly accents, what was wanted.

"Accommodation for man and horse, and good pay into the bargain. Make haste, friend, and let us in, and get us some of your best ale."

The landlord of the little inn was not long in arraying himself in befitting garments to receive his unexpected guests, for in an incredibly short space of time he appeared, lantern in hand, to escort his visitors into the sanded parlour, where they soon made themselves at home.

Dottman, however, was ill at ease, for he was most impatient to place in Dora's hands that document, the possession of which would remove a host of anxiety and terror from her gentle heart.

There was a suspicion in Dottman's mind, too, that the men who had arrested him, and who had so willingly consented to his travelling in their company, were not quite so satisfied with his account of himself as they appeared to be—and this thought, if it were correct, was fraught with untold danger.

He determined, however, to play his part, and to continue to feign ignorance should the conversation chance to turn again to the highwayman, which, however, he devoutly hoped would not be the case.

His hopes, however, were doomed to be disappointed, for before many minutes had elapsed, one of the horsemen said, addressing his companion, and as Dottman fancied, looking askance at him, Dottman,

"Well, comrade, if we intend to do anything to-night in the way of capturing this highwayman, we must look sharp, for these folks take their leave of the road at daybreak."

"Have you ever seen him, any of you?" asked another.

"I saw him once," said a young man of the party—"and I must say that what I did see of him makes me inclined to believe a report I have heard, but whether it be true or not it is hard to say."

"What report—what report?" asked eagerly several voices in chorus.

"That the highwayman is nothing more nor less than a beautiful girl."

"A beautiful girl?" shouted a voice, "and making choice of such a life—so full of danger? Nonsense. No woman would thus venture upon the highway, alone, in such a disguise?"

"Oh, but she is not alone," said the first voice, "she is always accompanied, or attended, call it what you like—by a man many years her senior. Now, for my part, comrades, I should prefer capturing the old man rather than this young girl, if she be a young girl."

"Well, so would we all, perhaps. What say you, Mr.—a—a—"

"Jennings," said Dottman, replying to the last speaker.

"Well, what say you, Mr. Jennings?"

"For my part," said Dottman, "I must say I should like to see this lady highwayman very much; so if you will allow me to suggest, we will not lose more time than is just sufficient to finish this excellent ale, and then we'll be off in pursuit of him, or her, as the case may be."

At this juncture a man who had gone out of the room in order to see that the horses were ready to start, returned, and whispered something to the man who appeared to be the leader.

"All right," he said aloud. "Now let us away."

They all rose, and were quickly in the inn yard, where all the horses but Starlight were in readiness.

"But I do not see my horse," said Dottman.

"Oh!" said the innkeeper, "how stupid that boy is! he has forgotten him! Come this way, sir. Jim said something about the horse being unmanageable—he'll know your voice fast enough! This way, sir—this way!"

CHAPTER XLVIII.

THE FRIENDLY INNKEEPER—THE IMPORTANT DOCUMENT—THE STORMY NIGHT—THE CAPTURE.

DOTTMAN followed the innkeeper to that portion of the premises where were situated the stables of the little hostelry, but still with many misgivings in his mind that all was not straightforward.

The innkeeper, who went by the name of big Ben, on account of his gigantic stature, ever and anon turned his head towards that part of the inn yard in which he and Dottman had left the men.

None of them, however, had thought it necessary to follow them, feeling assured, perhaps, of the good principles of "mine host," which it put out of the question that he would allow a highwayman to escape, when they had so good a chance of taking him without resistance.

As soon as Dottman and big Ben had got at a sufficient distance from their companions to render it safe to speak without being overheard, big Ben said, in a hurried whisper—

"Quick! you have not a moment to lose! Those men believe you to be the companion of Captain Arod, the famous highwayman, and are only waiting for you to join them in order to take you prisoner, and lodge you in Newgate."

"Ah, say you so?" said Dottman, placing his hand on his breast coat pocket, where he had so securely hidden the pardon of Dora. "Say you so?"

"Hush! do not speak so loud! I guessed that you were the highwayman, for I knew his horse, and I determined, if possible, to save you. The captain once did me a kind turn, and I thought the time had come for me to pay him back again, so I told Jim not to bring the Arabian round, so that I might put you in the way of getting free."

"Thanks—thanks, friend!" said Dottman.

"I have taken care," continued big Ben, "to give your horse a good feed, and if what I've heard be true, there is not much chance of their overtaking you, when you have once fairly started; so mount, and start out at this gate, turn to the left, and leave me to account to them for your sudden departure."

Dottman was not long in availing himself of the instructions and kindness of the innkeeper; and putting spurs to his horse, Starlight, rather flew than gallopped down the road.

Big Ben stood by the stable door for a few minutes, listening intently to the tramping of the horse's feet, and smiled in a jocund sort of way as that sound became distant and more distant.

"Now that's what I call cleverly managed. How was I to know all these gentlemen wished to leave together? If one wanted to quit the inn by this gate, what was to prevent him doing so I should like to know?"

"Well, I shouldn't wonder if they are beginning to grow impatient," continued big Ben, "so I'll just walk up leisurely, as if nothing had happened."

With this determination, the innkeeper thrust both his hands into his pockets, and whistling furiously, soon made his way to the spot where he had left the mounted men.

"Well," shouted one of them, "where is he? Does the horse refuse to obey his master? Why is he not coming? We are waiting for him."

"Waiting for the gentleman whose horse would not come out of the stable?" asked the innkeeper, with a look of well-feigned innocence.

"Of course, idiot. Who else should we be waiting for, if not for him?"

"Oh," said big Ben, "I didn't know you were waiting for him! Why, he's been gone this ten minutes."

"How? What? What do you mean?" burst from every mouth.

"Why, I mean to say, that as soon as the horse heard its master's voice, it came out in a jiffy, and he mounted in a crack, and away he tore like the wind."

"Which way did he go?"

"Why, he turned to the right; but I fancy there's not much chance in overtaking him at the rate he went."

"Fire and fury!" cried the leader, "it is all your fault, Staines! If it had not been for listening to you we might have secured him before he left the parlour, but you persisted in it that he would be no match for us, so I was persuaded to let him ride with us as far as Newgate before we declared him to be our prisoner."

"Well, gentlemen," said big Ben, "I hope you don't blame me in the matter. If I had only known he was a highwayman, I would have killed him on the spot—indeed I would, gentlemen."

"Oh, we know that very well, good Ben. Just bring us out a jug or two more of your ale, and we will push forward."

"Certainly, gentlemen, certainly," said

big Ben; and then, as he turned aside, he muttered to himself—

"This, after all, has not been such a bad night's work after all! and I've not looked at what the captain put into my hand as he rode away. I dare say it was half-a-guinea. I'll just look before I go any further."

At this point of Ben's soliloquy, he had reached the sanded parlour, through which he had to pass before reaching those regions from whence came the far-famed ale. What was his surprise, then, as he came to a standstill before the fire, which sent up bright serpent-like looking flames, to behold that he was the fortunate possessor of three golden guineas!

More than ever satisfied with his night's work, he proceeded to the cellar and quickly re-appeared with a couple of cans containing the ale.

His guests, having despatched the ale, after wishing mine host good night, turned their horses heads in the direction of London, and were soon lost in the darkness.

Ben immediately retired to his couch, where, in all probability, his dreams were tinctured with visions of golden highwaymen.

It is now time that we return to our old acquaintance, Dottman, who had that night had such a narrow escape.

When he thought he had sufficiently distanced what might properly be called his pursuers, Dottman drew rein, and suffered Starlight to subside into an easy trot.

"So far, so good!" said he to himself. "I wonder now if I shall really get this document placed in Dora's hands—it would be hard to lose it now, after so miraculously getting possession of it—well, there's an end of that trouble, at all events.

Dottman was glad when he saw the little village of Kensington bathed in the morning light—looking calm and tranquil, and although there was no romance in his composition, he could not but be influenced in some degree by the beauty of the scene.

Now if Dora the Duchess—(Dottman always gave Dora her title when communing with himself)—Now if Dora the Duchess were here, she would most likely rein in her steed and say a good deal about light and shade, and all that sort of thing; but for my own part, I can only see that morning is coming, and that it looks very pretty as it creeps over the village.

Dottman reached the little gate by which he and Dora were in the habit of entering the gardens of Kensington, just as the church clocks were striking the hour of five.

"I wonder, now," said he to himself, "if they are all asleep, or expecting my return so early—ah, if Dora did but know that I carried in my pocket her pardon, how anxiously would she be awaiting me!"

Dottman soon secured Starlight in the usual spot, and made his way as silently as possible towards that part of the palace where were situated the apartments in the occupation of Dora and her husband.

He cautiously approached the door and listened, and was both pleased and surprised to hear voices within the apartment. He knocked three short sharp knocks as they had agreed he should on his return, and the door was opened by Dora herself, who held out her hand to him, exclaiming—

"Welcome back, old friend! I was beginning to get anxious about you, and was only just saying to Henry, that if you did not return by noon, as you fully expected to do, I should sally forth in search of you."

"All right, captain, you see no harm has befallen me—but where is the lady you called Neoni?"

"Safe and well," replied Dora. "I have just prevailed upon her to retire to the other room, where I hope by this time she has found some repose—but tell me, Dottman, have you seen or heard aught of her father?"

"I have seen nothing of him," replied Dottman, "but I fear I have heard enough to make me fear some foul play has been used towards him."

"Good Heavens!" cried Dora, "you alarm me—what mean you? speak!"

"I know nothing for certain," replied Dottman, "but I fancy, from the fright the Duke of Kingston had when I personated Neoni's father, that if he had not himself been accessory to his destruction in some way, at least that he knew something respecting him."

"Then you have seen and spoken to the duke?"

"Yes, and what is better still, I made him deliver up to me a certain little document, which he was exceedingly loth to part with, and which he certainly never would have given to me but from the belief that Surlina—whom I feel sure he knows to be dead, demanded it of him."

"A document?"

"Yes, and one which I think concerns you very closely."

"Oh give it me quickly—what is it?"

"Merely a pardon," said Dottman, "for something which you never did; however, as most people believed his falsehoods, it is much better that such a paper should be in your hands rather than in his—so take it."

"How shall I ever be able to repay you, my dear kind friend?" said Dora, holding out her hand to him, "how shall I ever be able to repay you for this? Oh, how have

I longed for this paper—or for the means of proving my innocence. Thanks, thanks, a thousand times!" and Dora gave vent to the pent up feelings of her heart in tears.

These tears, however, were not wholly painful—no there was joy, joy unspeakable, in feeling that she now no longer feared to encounter that hateful man, Turnbull, with the conviction ever on her mind he had the power of at any time carrying her to Newgate as an escaped criminal.

Henry Dacres was no less affected by the sight of the document than had been Dora herself—for had he not passed many lonely and anxious hours—long weary hours picturing to himself all the horrors of his Dora's re-capture."

"Thank Heaven!" he said, after a silence of some minutes, as he watched Dora. "Thank Heaven, my Dora, that you are now free, free as air."

"Yes!" replied Dora, looking up through her tears with a bright smile, "and who knows, Henry, but that I may some day hear of our lost darling, when we least expect it?"

"To be sure," said Dottman, who was well pleased to see Dora smile again, "to be sure—who knows but that the little one is being taken good care of until we can provide a home for her? so you see, captain, there's no time to lose, we must seek the road again, to-night, and when we have sufficient means to retire from business—why, then you know, you can bequeath to me your costume of the knight of the road."

"That will I, Dottman!" replied Dora, "who has so good a claim to that, and anything else I possess, as you, my faithful friend? but you know, Dottman," she continued, when we retire from business, as you say, that implies also that you will have no need, anymore than myself, of going on the road."

"Well, captain, we will talk about that when the time comes; for my part I don't seem to like the idea of saying, good bye to such a life as life on the road."

"We shall see—we shall see, Dottman!" said Dora, and then she added in a lower tone, "if ever our darling Mina returns to us, I shall make her persuade you to remain with us to look after Starlight, for I hope never to part with that beautiful creature again."

"Ah, captain, somehow you understand just what to say to bend me to your wishes. Methinks if I could only see you and Mr. Dacres and the little Mina all happy together, I, too, could settle down into a quiet, sober sort of citizen, and, in time, forget the pleasurable excitement I always feel when galloping over a wild heath, or along a turnpike road in order to make all comers and goers pay toll to the highway-man."

It was now six o'clock, and the morning had risen bright and beautiful, glittering on the water and illuminating the old Palace of Kensington—all was yet in the stillness of the early morning—not a sound was heard save the whistle of some labourer going to his work, or the lowing of the cattle.

Henry Dacres now turned to Dora and begged of her to retire for a few hours and seek repose, in order, as he said, that she might be the better able to encounter the fatigue which her night adventures might expose her to—and Dora, after getting a similar promise from Dottman, retired to seek some repose.

Hour after hour chimed on the different church clocks in the neighbourhood, and still Dora slept—little did she imagine how many weary hours would come and go without sleep again visiting those eyelids—but we must not anticipate.

Ten o'clock was striking by Kensington church just as Dora had taken the plumed hat in her hand, fully equipped as a knight of the road.

The profound slumber which had visited her had served to restore to her all that elasticity of mind and body which was natural to her, and she said, almost cheerfully, to Henry—

"Good bye, dearest! Expect my return in a few hours. To-night, somehow, I have a feeling at my heart that something is about to happen—let us hope it will be something that will enable me to bid adieu once and for ever to the road, with all its dangers, perils, and disappointments. Now wish me good speed, Henry, and let me be off on my gallant Starlight."

Henry, however, seemed lost in thought, and what was most unusual with him, he seemed unable to sympathise with Dora in her bright anticipations. Pressing her in his arms, he said—

"Be careful, oh, be careful, my Dora—may not this feeling which you speak of be a kind of fore-shadowing of evil to you, and therefore to me?"

"Oh, say not so—say not so, Henry," cried Dora, throwing her arms round his neck, "surely there is less danger to-night than there has hitherto been, for do I not now possess that valuable document, without which I was at any moment liable to be arrested?"

Henry saw that it would be useless to try to prevent Dora going on her nightly expedition, and, besides, he could not really imagine that there was more, or, as Dora herself had said, so much danger as upon former occasions—he therefore assumed a cheerfulness he was far from feeling, and kissing her fondly, bid her depart, and return as soon as possible.

"Indeed—indeed I will, dear Henry, and now farewell."

Dora would not trust herself to linger longer, for every moment she felt less and less inclined for the expedition, and she hastened to Dottman, who, as usual, was in readiness with the two horses, as much for the sake of having her courage strengthened as from a desire to bring that night's adventures to an end.

"I began to think, captain, that you meant me to start to-night alone—Starlight is getting impatient, and has been pawing the ground until the gravel flew around me like so much rain."

"Ah!" said Dora, patting the neck of the beautiful Arabian, "I will not keep you longer waiting!" and she sprung lightly into the saddle. "Now forward, Dottman—and let us hope that this night will bring us fair booty."

"All right, captain—I will follow you within call. Let us away!"

Dora and Dottman trotted their horses at a brisk pace, until they had left the village of Kensington far behind them, and turning off into the turnpike road, they drew rein, and held a short consultation as to what was to be done.

"I think, captain,' said Dottman, "that we cannot do better than wait here, and cry 'Stand' to all who pass."

"Be it so'" said Dora, and they accordingly stationed themselves behind a clump of trees, so as to be completely concealed from observation.

The night had become unusually dark—black clouds obscured the face of the moon—the wind howled in fury among the trees, and large drops of rain began to fall thick and fast upon Dora and her companion.

From time to time a keen blue streak of lightning crossed the descending deluge, and for an instant the trees appeared to be great black masses—or like grim spectres of another world—and then the roar of thunder was added to the scream of the blast, seeming to shake the very earth to its foundation.

Dora had some difficulty in maintaining her control over Starlight, who seemed to be irritated by being held in with bit and bridle, and turning to Dottman, she said—

"Surely we shall have no adventure to-night—no one will venture out on such a night who is not compelled by hard necessity. Shall we return?"

"Why, captain, it is on just such a night as this that we may expect to meet with a rich booty—the storm has come on so suddenly that—"

"Hush!" said Dora. "What is that?"

"I heard nothing!" said Dottman.

Scarcely, however, had he uttered these words, when from behind them came the sound of the trampling of horses' feet, and Dottman had just time to seize Starlight by the bridle in a peculiar manner, which was understood by the Arabian to mean that he was to lie down—and to whisper hastily to Dora to remain perfectly still, whatever might happen—when several mounted men leaped the low hedge that divided the fields from the road, and surrounded Dottman, who was but too anxious to concentrate all their attention upon himself, so as, if possible, to give Dora a chance of escape.

The first words Dottman heard were pronounced in a loud but melodious tone, and were as follows—

"Pursue him quickly—there were two of them, and bring him back."

Dottman's heart sunk, not for himself, but for that fair and gentle girl, for she was still but a girl, who was in so dangerous a position! His heart sunk, as, looking up in the direction of the sounds, he beheld a tall, powerful man on horseback some five or ten yards before him, with fifteen or sixteen other gentlemen, some fully armed as was the custom of the day, but others in the garb of peace.

The next words which Dora heard sounded like a death-knell to her heart. They were addressed to Dottman—

"You are our prisoner!"

Dottman was immediately surrounded, and the cavalcade passed on leaving Dora and Starlight alone!

CHAPTER XLIX.

DOTTMAN IN PRISON—AN UNEXPECTED SURPRISE — THE MEETING OF OLD FRIENDS—THE ATTEMPTED ESCAPE.

THOUGHT after thought—all painful—flashed through the brain of Dottman as he found himself being quietly but surely conducted to Newgate. His thoughts were many—innumerable—and ere he could give them any clear or definite order, the gate was thrown open for his entrance, and a few minutes after the low, damp dungeon of a criminal received him.

They left him in solitude and silence in all the bitterness of thought, and then all that was to accrue to Dora, in consequence of his capture presented itself to his mind in full and terrible array.

Oh! how much did he bewail ever having used his arguments to induce her to undertake a life fraught with so much peril and danger! What must now be her feelings? Alone, at that hour, with no arm to shield her from her bitter foes.

"How often," said Dottman to himself, "would she have been content to give up all hopes of future wealth, and have lived a life of retirement in some quiet, peaceful spot, but for me! Oh, would that the past few months might return!"

Vain hopes! the heavy iron door was there, barring from him every active scene of life; but that was not all poor Dottman had to suffer that night.

To the felon's dungeon was to be added the felon's chains.

The door opened, the torchlight flashed in—fetters were placed upon his hands and ancles, and the ring of the chain was fastened to a ring in the wall.

The turnkey withdrew, but left the door a-jar, and a narrow line of light marked the entrance. It grew fainter and fainter as the torches receded, and then a human figure, like a dark shadow, crossed the light as it became broader, while some one entered.

Could it be anyone to bring him comfort? Oh, no! that was not possible in such a place! Well might it have been said that on crossing that threshold hope departed, giving place but to that despair of the soul which can know no sunlight. So associated, too, had Dottman become with Dora and her husband, that it was no small addition to the pangs of imprisonment to be separated from them; were it not that there was one magical word which he kept repeating to himself, he might have succumbed entirely to the perils of his situation.

That one word was Escape!

Little, however, did Dottman imagine that the person who was now approaching his gloomy cell was in any way calculated to assist him in such a project.

A tall man crossed the threshold, and placing at his feet the lantern which lighted him through the dreary passages of Newgate, he looked for a few moments fixedly at Dottman.

"Well comrade," he then said, "it seems that I have grown out of recollection."

"Comrade?" said Dottman, as the voice seemed to come upon his ears with a familiar echo. "What comrade can I have or find within the walls of Newgate?"

The man laughed, and that laugh more than ever convinced Dottman that the seeming rough and brutal turnkey was no stranger to him.

"Speak," he said. "If you've come as a friend, I shall be right glad to know you, but if a foe, I don't see that you could do me any worse harm than is done to me at present by my being cooped up here."

"I'm sent," said the turnkey, "to search you carefully, to see that you have no concealed knife or other weapon about you; but before I begin, I will just ask you one question, and that is if you remember ever to have seen the Duke of Kingston's regiment of horse?"

"Seen it!" cried Dottman—"I served in it for many a good year—alas! the good duke is no more, and evil has fallen upon his house."

"Then it's odd to me," returned the turnkey, "that you don't remember Sergeant Hutchinson."

"By heaven! it is Hutchinson! You here? Why, then fortune has raised me up a friend even from the very stones of Newgate."

"Hush! said the old sergeant, who had become a turnkey of the prison in his latter years. "Hush! none of your nonsense to me—you're a great scoundrel of course, and will swing at Tyburn."

Dottman was surprised at the moment at this sudden change in the tone and manner on the part of his old comrade, but he soon saw a reason for it, since by the dim, slanting light of the lantern which was upon the floor of the cell, he observed a hideous, snarling looking face just projected over the threshold, with a pair of ferret looking eyes, which were glaring at him with glances of spite and hatred.

"Yes, my fine fellow," added the sergeant, "you may make what promises you like, but they are all one to me. Sergeant Hutchinson does his duty and cares for no man—and as I find you've nothing about you by which you may work your way out of old Newgate, why you may go to sleep as soon as you can."

Dottman was fully convinced now of the continued friendly sentiments towards him of the sergeant, and the latter then turning suddenly, pretended for the first time to see the hideous face and ferret-looking eyes of the person who was looking into the cell.

"Oh, Mr. Weevil!" he said. "Is that you?"

"Yes it is me!" said Mr. Weevil, as he now came sufficiently far into the cell that about one half of his body was visible. "It is me—I dare say it's all right—I only came to have a look at the new dick-bird, and to see how he liked his cage. He, he! You can go, Mr. Hutchinson—you can go."

The sergeant, with manifest reluctance, left the cell, and then Mr. Weevil, taking care to keep at a respectful distance from Dottman, said—

"Perhaps you don't know me—I'm the governor's cousin, and there never was such a humane man as I am in the world. When a prisoner comes into Newgate I always visit him to see what I can do for him, and as one good turn deserves another, I'm sure you'll tell me if there's anywhere I can lay my hand on any hidden plunder or swag, for I know you gentlemen are apt to put away till better times a good bag of plate, or a little jewellery—eh? eh?"

"I don't know what you mean?" said Dottman.

"Oh, indeed, Mr. Tunorence, you don't—then I'll explain. If you can make it worth my while, in any way, I'll speak to the governor, and you can have indulgences in Newgate, and, perhaps, a good word said to the recorder who will try you."

"And if I don't? said Dottman, "what then?"

"Why then you're trial shall not go amiss for the want of a little evidence, and you shall swing to a certainty."

"And suppose I say this to the judge when I'm taken into court?"

Mr. Weevil nearly laughed aloud.

"Who'd believe you? Where's your witnesses?

"You're a great rascal," said Dottman, "and I'll have nothing further to say to you."

"Very good,—he, he!—very good. That's the way with some birds when they get into the cage, they scream and knock against the wires, but after a time they say anything one likes."

Mr. Weevil withdrew his head, and banged shut the door of the cell.

Dottman heard the grind of the heavy lock as it was shot into its staple. He was alone in that gloomy receptacle for shattered fortunes and bleeding hearts; and as he turned to pierce with his eyes the gloom that surrounded him, for the lantern had been removed, he felt that if he could only accomplish it, his best plan would be to take the advice of his old comrade, the sergeant, and go to sleep.

The fetters made a dull, clanging sound as Dottman arranged himself in as easy a position as he could, and by resolutely closing his eyes, tried to shut out the thoughts along with the perceptions of the world.

He had gone through much fatigue of late with but little consideration for himself, so that amid the intense silence about him, and that darkness which seemed like something that could be felt, Dottman was not many minutes in actually subsiding into deep repose.

It was impossible for him to tell how long he had slept, for the sleep was undisturbed and dreamless; but he was suddenly aroused by a light flashing across his eyes, and the intense stillness of the cell was broken by the voice of the friendly sergeant,

DOTTMAN'S ESCAPE FROM NEWGATE.

who seemed much afraid that upon immediately awkening, Dottman might utter some exclamation in a louder tone than was prudent.

"Hush, comrade!" he said, "speak low —speak low!"

"Ah!" said Dottman, "it is you! What's o'clock?"

"It is past three. I am on night duty in the corridor adjoining these cells. What did that rascal, Wcevil, say to you?"

"Only that if I could tell him of any concealed booty that he could lay his hands on, I might secure his good services, but if not, most certainly his bad ones."

"He's a great villain, and always attacks

DORA.—25.

prisoners in such a fashion. He and the governor goes shares in what they can get. But I hope soon that you'll be far away, and out of their power. But tell me, is it true, old comrade, that you've gone upon the road?"

"Oh, true as gospel," said Dottman.

"Well, it ain't worse than campaigning, is it?"

"Not near so bad."

"I thought not—I thought not! And now look you here, Dottman, my pension is sevenpence a-day, and I get eighteen shillings for being a night watch in Newgate; but I'm sick of the stone walls, and so I've been thinking that as I know pretty well all the ins and outs of the old crib, you and I might bid good night to it together."

It was now that Dottman found it difficult to suppress a cry of gratification, for all his gloomy feelings were dissipated in a moment in the sudden hope and expectation of release.

"Do not mock me, old comrade," he said, "but tell me again and again that there is a chance of release from these stone walls."

"It is a chance, and but a chance," said the old sergeant. "Of course I could go out in the morning if I pleased, but I don't like to leave an old comrade in limbo; and, therefore, you see, Dottman, I mean to lend you a helping hand; but it'll be a ticklish matter, and has one or two ways of doing it."

"Let's take the one most likely to succeed," said Dottman.

"Then listen to me. There are but three men on duty at the outer lock, and in about half an hour there will come a visitor into the prison. It's an old woman, that brings to the turnkeys some hot purl in a can, and she is let go about the corridors and passages at pleasure, till she has sold all her cargo. Now she'll come down this way to me as I'm night watchman; and what I propose is, that you should borrow the old lady's gown, cap, and bonnet, and walk out of Newgate with the empty can in your hand. That's one plan, you see."

"And what's the other?"

"The other is to break away into a small room at the end of the corridor called the 'Council's Consultation Room,' and from there by a short flight of steps we get into the gallery of the chapel, then out by the roof on to the leads of the governor's house, and so, perhaps, if we're lucky, on to some of the leads in Newgate Street."

"Either way," said Dottman, "is equally pleasant if it succeeded, but there's one little difficulty, what am I to do with my fetters?"

"I've a key that opens them, so that will soon be got rid of; but I tell you, Dottman, that either way the principal person we have to fear is that confounded Mr. Weevil."

"What's that?" said Dottman? suddenly through a small crevice, which was left at the bottom of the cell door, there came a faint stream of wavering light.

The sergeant had a light with him, but he had closed the shade, so that it gave forth no beams whatever. This light, therefore, must come from the passage beyond the cell.

Both the sergeant and Dottman watched it narrowly, and after a few seconds it became stationary, and the sergeant felt confidant of what was indeed the fact, that Mr. Weevil was prowling about the prison as usual, and that one of his ears was placed flat against the cell door to listen.

"Answer me anyhow," said the sergeant, "to what I shall say."

"Yes, yes!"

The sergeant spoke in a loud voice.

"It's all very well to call the night watch and pretend you're ill, but it's my belief you're only shamming. Oh, we're used to the tricks of fellows like you in Newgate."

"Well, you see," said Dottman, "I felt dull and wanted a little company, so I thought even you would be better than nobody."

The sergeant uttered an exclamation of impatience, as though he were very much disgusted with this conduct of the prisoner, and then he dashed out of the cell so quickly, that he succeeded in doing just what he wished, which was to tumble over Mr. Weevil, and deal him sundry hard kicks in the struggle to regain his feet again.

"Confound you!" roared Weevil, "what do you mean, you clumsy brute."

"Dear me, sir, why, are you there? Number four has been shamming ill."

"Purl! purl! purl!" cried a voice at this moment in miserable, cracked, feeble tones. "Here's your fine morning purl. Now, my fine fellows, buy your purl of Betty Widdikin."

"What?" cried Mr. Weevil, "Does that infernal old witch come to Newgate still?"

"It's an old custom, Mr. Weevil," said the sergeant, and I doubt if a single turnkey or night watch would stay in the prison if they didn't get it. It's a great comfort, Mr. Weevil, on a cold morning, and you know when any poor fellow is taking his last ride to Tyburn, Betty Widdikin is always by the side of the cart to give him a dram at starting; and besides, she says she pays you five golden guineas at Christmas time for the privilege."

"Lies! lies! lies!" cried Mr. Weevil. "I won't hear a word you've got to say; but as it is rather cold, I think I'll take a glass of purl myself, Mrs. Widdikin, and I'll owe you the groat for it. Take care, Hutchinson, that you've turned the key in the lock of that cell."

"All's right, Mr. Weevil."

"Here's your fine purl!" cried the old woman, "your beautiful purl! and only fourpence for a good alehouse half-pint measure."

Mr. Weevil now seemed inclined to pursue his perigrinations through the prison, and the old sergeant hastened back to the cell in which was Dottman, and opening the door, whispered hurriedly—

"Quick—quick! now's your time, old comrade, if you mean to escape! The old woman, of whom I spoke, is just outside the door of the cell. She'll do anything for money. Give her a guinea, and no end of promises for more if she will lend you her cloak, gown, and bonnet."

"All right," said Dottman, "but these fetters?"

"Good gracious!" said the sergeant, "I had forgotten all about them!" And stooping down, Dottman had the unspeakable satisfaction of seeing them fall from him one by one.

Dottman rose to his feet, and holding out his hand to his old comrade, said, with some emotion—

"Good bye, and good luck attend you, old comrade! and whether I succeed or not in making my escape, I shall never forget what you have done for me this night."

"Don't mention it—don't mention it, old fellow!" said the sergeant. "But there is no time to lose, for that villain, Weevil, begins to suspect something. I fancy, for he is more than usually on the look out. Stay here, and I will send the 'old witch' to you, as we call Dame Widdikin, and you must make your own terms with her while I keep watch in the corridor."

"All right!" said Dottman.

The old sergeant left the cell, and in a few minutes old Mrs. Widdikin appeared at the cell door.

Dottman immediately seized her in his arms, when the old woman raised a half cry, thinking, probably, that Dottman was about to do her some bodily harm; but when she found he only intended to give her a salute on the cheek, the ancient dame merely said, as she bridled up—

"No liberties, sir, if you please. I never allow gentlemen to kiss me unless I knows 'em."

"I beg your pardon," said Dottman, "but when one sees a pretty girl in a place like this, why it makes him forget himself."

"Lor, what a nice man!" muttered the old woman to herself—then turning to Dottman, she said—

"Mr. Hutchinson said, sir, that you wanted some purl."

"To be sure I do," said Dottman, "but I want you to lend me your bonnet, cloak, and gown."

"Lor, sir!" interrupted the old woman, "what for?"

"Why, you see, I want to have a bit of fun, and frighten the turnkey. Nobody will be a bit the wiser, because I will bring them back to you; and if any one should come and find you here, you might say I took them by force."

"I couldn't do it, sir—indeed I couldn't! it would be more than my life is worth."

"Not if I gave you this?" said Dottman, holding up a guinea.

The old woman's eyes sparkled at the sight of the gold coin, and she said—

"I'm sure you should be welcome to my poor clothes to keep altogether for that money."

"I thought so!" said Dottman. "Now be quick, my dear girl, and let me have them directly."

The old woman was not long disrobing, and Dottman was much less time in getting into her clothes, and snatching up the empty can from the floor of the cell, and bestowing another kiss upon the "dear girl," he strode from the cell rather too hastily for his disguise to be very perfect."

"Hold hard, comrade!" said the sergeant. "You must remember that you are the 'old witch,' and you must hobble along as if you were walking upon hot irons, not go at that rate!"

"All right—all right!" cried Dottman. "I'll remember; but I was too pleased to think of anything but freedom. Now let me out—oh, let me out!"

"This way—this way, then, old fellow! and mind you keep up the hobbling walk as you pass out at the outer gate."

"Trust me for that," said Dottman.

CHAPTER L.

SHEWS HOW DOTTMAN MADE HIS ESCAPE FROM NEWGATE—DORA'S CAPTURE— THE ENCOUNTER WITH AN OLD ENEMY.

THE old sergeant and Dottman pursued their way through the various passages and corridors of Newgate until they came to a kind of ante-room, where were seated three or four of the turnkeys playing at dominoes.

"Ah, Hutchinson!" said one of them, "there you are, doing the amiable to Dame Widdikin! Come, old lady, you might stand treat to-night for once in a way!"

Dottman, in order to avoid giving any reply, began to cough to such an extent, that the pretended old woman was fain to sit down on a stool which happened to be standing in the shadow of the doorway.

"Hilloa, old 'un!" said another, "it seems to me that you are in a bad way, Mother Widdikin!"

"Oh lor! oh lor!" groaned Dottman.

"I think the best thing you can do, Mrs. Widdikin, is to make the best of your way home; you have already stayed longer than I ought to have allowed you, and if Mr. Weevil should happen to come this way, we should both get into a scrape; so clear out as quickly as you can."

"I'm agoin'!" wined the pretended old woman. and Dottman rose to depart.

Hutchinson was but too glad to open the gate for his old friend, who was not slow in making good his exit when he saw that there was nothing between him and the outer world.

Dottman was once more free!

His first thought now was to make his way as quickly as possible to a little court in the Old Bailey, where. at a little shop, he was always sure of a welcome from the proprietor.

On reaching the door, Dottman touched a little bell, and it was immediately opened by Jack Stapleton himself. who. however, did not in the least recognise his old acquaintance in Dame Widdikin's cloak and bonnet.

"Let me in, comrade!" said Dottman, "I'm in a hurry!"

"Bless us and save us! why, I declare, it's Dottman! I suppose you've been up to a little business out of the common line by your dress. But come in—come in! It's many a long day since we met!"

Dottman was but too glad to rid himself of the apparel of Mrs. Widdikin, and having done so, he recounted to Jack Stapleton so much of the night's adventure as he thought prudent, taking care merely to mention himself in the transaction.

Having satisfied the curiosity of his friend, Dottman was anxious to make his way to Kensington with as little delay as possible; and taking leave of his friend, saying at the same time that he made him a present of the female apparel, he hastened from the little shop.

And now that he was once more free, Dottman became painfully anxious to know what had become of Dora. Was it probable that she had reached home in safety? or had she not, perhaps, encountered like dangers as himself? and might she not then be a prisoner, without a friend to turn to?

There was something frightful in the picture which poor Dottman conjured up in his imagination; and it was well for him that the hour was an early one, or his hurried strides, and half uttered expressions must have attracted notice.

As it was, however, Dottman arrived at Kensington without any further obstacle; and it was with a hand trembling with excitement and expectation that he opened the little gate at which he was accustomed to enter the old palace.

It is necessary, however, that we now return to Dora, whom we left in so critical a position when Dottman was captured.

It would be impossible to describe what her feelings were when she found that her faithful follower was, indeed, a prisoner.

Her first impulse had been to endeavour to save him by engaging in a personal contest with his foes; but when Dora found that so large a force had collected round Dottman, she gave up the idea, and resolved not to add to the discomfiture of her friend by any vain attempts at a rescue, which could only result in the capture of both

She thought, too, of Henry, who would be suffering all the pangs of anxiety and suspense if she did not return at the time he expected her, and so she resolved, with true heroism, to be still, when nothing could be done that could bring relief to either herself or Dottman.

Then, too, she had to use all the influence she possessed over her beautiful Arabian, in order to keep the creature still, for Starlight began to grow tired of his unwonted position; but Dora maintained her command over the animal, and was relieved of a load of anxiety when she could no longer hear the tramp of the horses' feet on the road.

As the last sound had died away, Dora rose from her crouching position, and Starlight soon followed her example.

And now Dora asked herself what was next to be done?

It was quite certain that she could be of no assistance to Dottman, and s e determined to return at once to Henry, and make known to him the misfortune which had fallen upon them both by the capture of Dottman.

No sooner, however, was Dora mounted, and about to make her way back to Kensington, when the tramp of horses' feet coming at a swinging gallop along the road, induced her to conceal herself behind a little clump of trees by the roadside.

Scarcely had she so stationed herself, however, when two horsemen rode up to the spot, and from their conversation, Dora soon learnt that she was the very person of whom they were in pursuit.

To find herself thus, for the first time, alone in so critical a position, was, indeed, almost too much for poor Dora; for although, as we have seen, she was not wanting in moral and physical courage, yet there was also in her constitution of mind all that gentle clinging dependance which makes one of the principal charms of the female character.

With every nerve on the stretch, and listening most intently to all the speakers said, Dora scarcely breathed, lest she should make them aware of her close proximity.

"Let us pause a few minutes, Justin," said a voice, "before we proceed any further, for I am quite sure the other did not pass us on the road, which he must have done had he put spurs to his horse."

"I quite agree with you, Reginald," replied another voice, "and I fancy that we have only to beat about the bushes here to find him. What say you, shall we begin?"

"With all my heart," replied the first speaker. "But be careful, for I have heard he is a desperate fellow."

"Never fear—there are two to one! Surely it would be an ignominious defeat if we failed to get the better of this man."

Dora at this moment took one of the pistols from the holster, for she felt that she might have occasion to use it in self-defence, much as she revolted at the idea of taking life.

The two speakers Dora could see had now begun their search in good earnest, and it was quite evident that she could not remain long concealed where she now was.

Seeing, then, how matters stood, she quickly resolved that it would be better at once to brave the danger, and trust to Starlight's speed, and to the good service of her pistols for the preservation of her liberty, and perhaps her life.

And between resolving and acting were crowded more reflections upon the past, present and future than Dora would have thought possible in so short a space of time.

As ever, Henry and her Mina stood out in bold relief, forming something distinct and apart from aught else on earth.

What if that night were to end her career in life? How would her loved Henry reproach himself for ever permitting her to leave him? And Dora herself began to question whether this taking to the road had not been all a mistake.

How was it—as she had once thought to herself—how was it to be the means of giving her tidings of her lost child?

True, it might give her wealth; but at what hazards to all she held dearest? for if she perished, either by a random shot, which was not improbable, or lingered out a life in prison, or worse, expiated what would be called her crimes, on the scaffold, where would be the good of riches to Henry, deprived of her whom he courted his richest treasure?

As these thoughts chased each other through the brain of Dora, she felt the burning tears coursing down her cheeks; but she hastily brushed them away, and murmuring to herself—

"Courage—courage, Dora! Be brave, for the sake of those you love!"

These few words seemed to reanimate her, and giving Starlight a slight tap on the neck, she caused the creature to leap into the middle of the roadway, where she stood out against the night sky like an equestrian statue.

She had scarcely took up this position, when she was immediately perceived by one of the two horsemen whom Dora had heard conversing.

He gallopped up to her within a few paces, and presented a pistol full in her face, as he said—

"Surrender! Our orders are to take you dead or alive."

"If you can catch me!" said Dora; and putting spurs to her horse, she had passed the horseman some dozen paces when the report of a pistol shot, which seemed to have been discharged just above her head, made Starlight rear and plunge so violently, that she had great difficulty in keeping her seat.

With bit and spur Dora still urged on the creature, but all was in vain, and ere another moment had passed, Turnbull dropped from a tree.

Seizing the bridle of her horse with his left hand, he presented a loaded pistol in the right, as he cried—

"At last, my lady—at last we meet again! Ha, ha! do you remember the last time I had the pleasure of seeing you?"

"Alas, alas!" groaned Dora, and has it come to this?"

"Ay, indeed, has it! and you may be sure you shall not escape me this time."

"But you dare not detain me!" said Dora, as she regained somewhat her presence of mind. "The accusation of the Duke of Kingston was a false one, and I am in possession of my pardon, which he basely intercepted."

At this moment Turnbull was joined by the other horseman, who had first accosted Dora, and who seemed to have been cast in a very different mould to that of his companion. Riding up to Dora, he placed his hand on the bridle of Starlight, saying—

"It is of no use to resist—you see we are two to one! and, therefore, your better plan will be to surrender at once."

Turnbull did not seem to approve of the civility displayed by his companion, and said, with a hideous leer, which made Dora shudder—

"Thank you, Glennie! if you just ease my lady of her holster pistols, I think I can manage to take her to Newgate; it is necessary that I receive orders of his grace the Duke of Kingston regarding the prisoner."

The other man reluctantly withdrew, after having removed from the holsters the pistols Dora had counted upon as being the only means of defence she had.

Dora's only hope now was in being able to spur Starlight to her utmost speed, and she then knew she must soon distance the villain, Turnbull, who had mounted his companion's horse, taking care, however, to secure the bridle of Starlight so as to prevent the result which Dora hoped would be yet accomplished.

When they had fairly started, and had left the man, whose horse Turnbull had mounted, far behind them, Turnbull turned towards Dora, and in an ironical tone, asked her where she intended supping, as he had ridden far, and felt inclined for something nice.

Dora disdained to return any answer.

Why, you're not going to sulk with your old friend now, surely! Haven't I been at no end of trouble to get at you to tell you I forgive all past grievances? Come, now, let me hear your voice, for I fancy I'm somewhat of a judge of pretty voices."

Dora, however, rode on in silence, utterly cast down at the turn circumstances had taken; and it was not until they came in sight of some houses, and an exclamation from Turnbull, that she could be said to be conscious of what was really passing around her, so deep was the dejection of mind into which she had lapsed.

"Here we are, my beauty!" he said. "I cannot offer you much accommodation, but such as it is, you are welcome to."

"Oh, heavens! where are you taking me?'

"Only to a little crib that owns me for its master. So now, perhaps, you will dismount without giving any alarm, for if you do, rest assured a bullet will be lodged in your brains."

"Monster! how dare you thus address me?"

"Now, no more nonsense, Dora the Duchess! He, he! Dora the Duchess! That sounds grand! No more nonsense, but do as I tell you!"

At this moment the door of one of the houses was opened, and a horrid-looking old woman, bent almost double, appeared on the threshold.

"Ah, you be there, Mr. Turnbull, be you? I've been a looking for ye never so many times, and I began to think mayhap something had happened to you, but—"

"Silence, hag!" roared Turnbull, "no more of that, but do my bidding. Take this young lady into the room that has the iron bars to the window; and look you here, if she escape your old bones shall feel the weight of this!"

As he spoke, Turnbull raised a heavy riding whip, and gave the old woman a cut across the arm with it; then turning to Dora, he dragged her from the saddle, and carried her into the house.

In vain did Dora shriek and struggle to free herself from his hated grasp; he held her as in a vice, and reaching the room he had indicated as the one with the iron bars at the window, he released her.

"Now, Dora the Duchess, if you make it worth my while, I may set you at liberty, but if not, I know who will gladly purchase my pretty bird! Good bye, Dora the Duchess! He, he! Dora the Duchess!

In another minute Turnbull was gone, taking care to lock the door of the room.

Dora sunk to the floor in an agony of mind too poignant to be described. Her last words were—

"Alas, alas! what will be the feelings of my Henry when hour after hour passes away and neither Dottman nor I return? Oh, unhappy fate—unhappy Dora!"

CHAPTER LI.

MURDER AND ROBBERY—DORA'S DANGER —HER STRATAGEM—SHOWS HOW THAT THERE IS NOT ALWAYS HONOUR AMONG THIEVES.

THIS circumstance, so full of alarms, and so suggestive of every kind of terror, which had befallen Dora, was highly calculated for a time to take such possession of her imagination as to disqualify her from coming to a calm and correct judgment in regard to the chances or perils of her condition.

But with Dora's intellect, such a state of things was not calculated to last long, and she soon began to form a more just estimate of the perils that surrounded her, and tell herself that no situation on earth would be wholly desperate, or without some ray of hope.

It had been a surprise as well as an infliction to her to find that the villanous Turnbull was still in life, since she had every reason to suppose that the pistol shot with which she had favoured him upon a recent occasion, had for ever put an end to him and to his villanies.

The few words he had uttered, too, were significant of the fact that he considered himself in the employment of the false and wicked Duke of Kingston.

What might not Dora have to dread, if he, Turnbull, should sell his captive to one so much interested in her destruction.

But these considerations did not prevent Dora from rousing herself to something like energy, and she commenced an examination of her prison, in the hope, faint and distant though it was, that she might discover some means of escaping from it.

It was but a narrow apartment, some twelve feet in length, by about nine in width, and the only light that in day time could struggle into it, was through the small diamond shaped panes of glass which made up a latticed window.

That window, however, was crossed by bars of iron, and the night that made its way into the room, even accustomed as Dora's eyes were getting to it, was but a faint and gloomy twilight.

One miserable chair and a table, in such a state of delapidation that it seemed to threaten to fall to piecs every time that Dora accidentally touched it, constituted the whole furniture of the apartment.

The ceiling was so low that it was scarcely necessary that Dora should stand on the chair in order to reach the iron bars that crossed the casement. She did so, however, but soon found how utterly futile would be any attempt to escape in that direction, since the bars were thick and strong, and to all appearance, deeply embedded in the walls of the house.

While Dora was making this examination, she suddenly heard a voice in the little rural roadway beyond the house, speaking in tones of apparent lamentation.

In those tones, too, Dora thought she detected the voice of the old hag-like woman to whom Turnbull had committed her, and it seemed to her strange that so sudden a change should have taken place in the mode of speech in one who was an associate of the villain, Turnbull.

"Alas, and alack!" she heard the old woman say. "It's a sad accident! and the poor young creature will surely die! Oh, dear sir, it would be a mortal charity for any good kind gentleman just to look at her for a moment! Alas, alas! what shall I do?

These words were uttered in tones sufficiently wailing and wretched, and yet sufficiently high, that amid the silence of that place, they might be heard a considerable distance.

Mingling with them, then, there came the sound of horses' feet, and that sound again ceased abruptly at the door of the house.

"What's the matter, my good woman?" cried some one in manly tones.

"Alas, and alack, sir! its the dear young creature, who is taken ill all of a sudden! and if you will only step in a moment and look at her, it will be a thousand mercies."

"Very well," said the horseman. "But who'll take care of my horse? Oh, I can tie the bridle to the paling here—that will do nicely. But I'm no doctor, my good woman, if the young person you speak of is ill."

"Never mind that, dear sir, but come in. It will be a human face for her to look upon as well as mine."

In the few brief sentences that Dora had heard pass between this old woman and Turnbull, the style and manner were so entirely different from her present expressions, that she, Dora, could not persuade herself but that the hag was playing some part, and that this horseman, who was accidentally passing the door, was cajoled into the house for some nefarious purpose.

Fain would Dora have called out, and warned him to be upon his guard, at the same time that she might claim his assistance for herself, but the whole affair had passed over so rapidly, and the stranger had tied his horse to the paling of the house, and crossed its threshold so quickly, that Dora had no time for action.

She turned from the window, and then she was near uttering an exclamation of surprise, for a strange, bright pencil of light streamed throught the apartment.

Where this thin ray of illumination came from was to Dora, for a few moments, a matter of great surprise, for it appeared as if it originated in the middle of the floor of the narrow room.

This was a mystery, however, which a few minutes' observation sufficed to solve. The light streamed from below through a narrow crack in the flooring, which, being only of woodwork, permitted the rays of light from some candle or lamp below to faintly stream into that upper apartment.

Along with this discovery, likewise, Dora heard the murmuring sound of voices in the lower part of the house.

She knelt down upon the floor in the hope that some crevice would be sufficiently large to enable her to see what was going on in the room below.

But in this hope she was disappointed for a few moments, until she accidentally placed her hand upon a portion of the floor which felt loose to the touch, and then she found that there was a large knot in the wood, which, owing to it projecting slightly, she found no difficulty in removing.

A gleam of light about the diameter of a shilling now found its way into what might be called Dora's prison, and she was enabled, by stooping down close to it, to obtain a tolerable view of the apartment immediately beneath her, and of the persons who were in it.

The scene that met her eyes was very singular, and one which she would hardly have supposed for a moment could possibly be exhibited in a house where such a man as Turnbull was a visitor.

The apartment was larger than that in the occupation of Dora, and no doubt ran under the ceiling of another room, of equal size to that in which she was imprisoned.

It was gloomily but still tolerably well furnished. A log fire burnt in the grate, and it was lighted by a small oil lamp, which stood upon a bracket at some height above the chimney-piece.

A very massive old-fashioned couch, covered with faded chintz, was drawn close to the fire-place, and on that lay what appeared to be a human form enveloped in a variety of wrappings.

Low moans, as if some one were suffering from great pain, issued from the occupant of the couch, and bending over it, with looks of interest, was the casual traveller, who had dismounted from his horse at the request of the old woman, while the hag herself stood by him, and, really or affectedly, wrung her hands in despair.

"Ah, kind sir," she said, "I'm certain she will die! and she is my own daughter's daughter! But she has something to say, which she will not tell me, so pray do, sir, ask her what it is, and we shall think Heaven has sent you to hear the secret."

"What is it?" said the stranger; "if I can be of any service, I shall be well pleased enough."

There was a sort of commotion now among the wrappings of the sick person on the couch, and a hand was projected and waved about, as if the person to whom it belonged was in great trouble and distress.

"The diet drink, grandmother!" said a faint voice, "give me some of that, and I shall be able to speak to this gentleman, who, from his face, I can perceive has a kind heart."

"Where is her diet drink?" said the stranger.

"Here, here!" said the old woman, with apparent flurry, as she took from the fire-place a small saucepan, and poured some hot liquid into a silver cup. "It is here, good kind sir."

"It is too hot!"

"Oh, no! the good physician said that she was to have it hot."

"But this will burn a sick person, I am sure—it is too hot!"

The stranger, by a natural movement, placed the silver cup to his own lips, and just tasted the contents.

"It is very hot!" he said.

At this moment the envelopes, shawls and bandages, which enveloped the apparently sick person, were cast aside, and there sat, bolt upright upon the couch, a young lad with about as vicious an ex-

pression of countenance as it was possible for the human face divine to wear.

"Ha, ha! granny," he said, "he's taken some of it, and there he goes!"

The stranger dropped the silver cup, and reeled back. He caught at the chimney-piece, and then at a chair for support.

"Help! help! help!" he cried.

He caught at a flimsy window curtain, and it came away in his grasp, then reeling quite to the further end of the room, he fell to the floor, uttering a deep groan, as though in the pangs of death.

"Yes," chuckled the boy, "he's taken it, granny, and enough, too! Now when cousin Turnbull comes, he'll finish him off, and we will see what he's got in his pockets. I'll take the horse to Smithfield, and sell it, so it'll be a good job altogether."

All this had happened so suddenly, that Dora was paralysed with apprehension, and fascinated, so to speak, at her post of observation.

A spell seemed to have come over her feelings, and although a sensation that something was wrong had taken full possession of her mind, and she would gladly have warned the stranger, yet she found it impossible to speak; and it was not until he reeled into the corner, and she had every reason to believe he was a dead man, that she found voice to utter a scream of dismay and warning.

That scream reached not the ears it was intended for, but the old hag and her grandson heard it with echoing cries of alarm. They both sprang to the door of the house so quickly, that but they impeded each other, they would, no doubt, have left it, believing themselves to be in imminent danger.

Then they both seemed to recollect at once that they had a prisoner in the room above, and the idea that she had been a spectatress, in some strange way, of what had been going on, seemed to rouse in a moment all their vengeful feelings.

The vicious-looking lad seized an axe, which was in the corner of the room, while the hag armed herself with a knife, and they both made a rush towards the narrow staircase, which led up to the apartment where Dora was a prisoner.

Our heroine now felt all her danger. She was completely unarmed, and there was nothing in that apartment which she could even convert into a weapon. She felt how completely helpless she was, and that if she could not adopt some mode of dispelling the suspicions of the two persons who were rapidly ascending to her room, her life would certainly be sacrificed.

There was but one hope—but one chance. She crouched down on the floor, covering

NLONI DISCOVERS HER FATHER IN THE OLD HOUSE.

the narrow orifice she had made by the withdrawal of the knot in the wood, and resting her head and arm upon the chair, she assumed the attitude of one who had fallen into a profound sleep.

Another moment and the door of the room was opened to admit the hag and her grandson. The former carried the little oil lamp from the room below, which Dora could but dimly see through her eyelashes.

"Where is she?" cried the lad. "If she has seen anything, our game's up, and we do no more good here."

"She sleeps—she sleeps," said the old woman.

DORA.—26.

"That's a sham," cried the boy.

Dora thought it would be as well that that pretended sleep should not appear to be too profound. If she could impress them with the idea that the cry which had alarmed them had been uttered by her in a dream all might yet be well, since they must be well aware that Turnbull had other views in regard to her than taking her life.

The lad at this moment stepped up to Dora and made a sign to his grandmother to approach with the little oil lamp, which he took from her hand, and flashing it several times before the eyes of Dora, strove by that means to ascertain whether her sleep was feigned or real.

So brightly did the little flame burn, that it was with difficulty that Dora could bear its light, after having passed so long a time in the darkness, but the imminence of her danger endued her with strength and courage.

Still, however, the boy was not satisfied, for, turning to his grandmother, he said in an undertone—

"I'm sure she's shamming."

Dora moved uneasily, and muttered some inarticulate words.

"Don't be a fool, lad! can't ye see she's asleep? she's dreaming. That scream was nought as regards us. Better leave her to Turnbull. You know he said he would settle her. We shall only get into trouble, I tell ye, if we interfere with him."

"Perhaps so," said the lad sulkily; "but remember, the chap downstairs is my property. I shall take whatever he has about him, remember. Do you think he's dead yet?"

"Not yet; but I fancy he took quite enough to kill him. Bide awhile, my boy—bide awhile, and we'll see!"

"I shan't bide no longer, but shall go down stairs and help myself at once, so here goes."

To Dora's great relief, the old woman and her grandson left the apartment. She shuddered as she heard them turn the key in the lock, for the air of that low, dark room began to feel painfully oppressive.

As soon as Dora felt that she might safely do so, she applied her eye to the little opening she had made in the flooring of the chamber, in order to see what took place in the apartment beneath.

She saw now the vicious-looking boy approach the recumbent form of the stranger, who had entered that house in order to be of use to a fellow-creature, whom he was told lay at the point of death. Alas! how little did he imagine that his life would be attempted whilst engaged in his mission of mercy

"Quick, granny—quick! hold the lamp this way. Ah! he's dead, sure enough! well, that's lucky, now, I mean to say," and the boy's eyes glared with a baneful kind of demoniac exultation. "Here's a purse with no end of yellow boys in it, and a watch and seals, and stop! here's a pocket-book, too. Well, I mean to say I played my part of the sick young girl beautifully."

The old hag seemed no less pleased than did her grandson, to see this booty produced before her eyes, which sparkled in the anticipation of sharing in the plunder.

When the boy had rifled the pockets of their victim, he and his grandmother began to ask themselves what would be the best means to adopt in order to deceive Turnbull as to the amount of plunder they had obtained.

"Put the purse back again, my lad," said the old hag, "Turnbull will be sure to think we have taken it; and you know he always likes to have the first pickings! So put the purse back again into the man's pocket—be ruled by your granny."

"Not if I knows it!" said the boy. "I shall keep the purse myself, and—"

"You can keep nearly all the money, boy, of course! but I mean just leave a few guineas in it, so that when Turnbull finds it he may believe us, when we tell him we waited for him to come before we took one of them."

"All right, granny—you know how to do business. Here goes—one, two, three, four—there, that's enough, in all conscience, for any gentleman to be travelling with."

The boy slipped a handfull of guineas into his pocket, and the old woman was forced to be content with the promise that he would divide the spoil with her at some future time.

CHAPTER LI.

SHOWS HOW DORA FOUND A NEW ALLY IN THE PERSON OF THE CAPTAIN HARGRAVE — DOTTMAN AND DORA MEET UNEXPECTEDLY.

No sooner had the boy possessed himself of the money and other valuables belonging to the stranger, than Dora could conjecture, from what she heard, that he was anxious to hide his new found riches in some secure place, out of the reach of his cousin Turnbull.

"Now, granny," said he, "you stay here while I go and hide the plunder—our plunder, you know—for if old Turnbull comes back he will be sure to search us both to see if we have got anything for ourselves; and if he finds it, why, he'll make an end of both of us, I shouldn't wonder in the least."

"Go, my boy," replied the old hag, "I'll wait here till you come back; but don't be long, my lad, for I don't like staying with *him*."

As she said this, the old woman pointed to the apparently lifeless corpse at her feet, and a shudder passed over her as she averted her eyes, even accustomed as they had been to all kinds of crimes.

"All right," said the boy; and turning to leave the house, he stumbled over the lamp which the old woman had placed on the floor, and immediately all was darkness in that room which contained the murdered stranger.

The old woman raised a shriek of terror, and tried to reach the door, but her affectionate grandson swung it shut, and she was left alone with her victim.

For a few minutes Dora could hear her making efforts to reach the door, and at last having found it, she, too, left the house.

Dora was alone in that house with the murdered man !

Oh, how she longed for some instrument with which to force the door, or even raise one of the boards of the flooring, so oppressive was the thought of all the horrors she had witnessed from her prison chamber, and so much did she dread the moment arriving which would bring the villain, Turnbull, to witness her misery, that she fancied at one time her reason would leave her ; and clasping her hands over her eyes, she began to think ; but all her faculties seemed absorbed in the one of listening.

In each sound she recognised the footstep of Turnbull ; and then the thought took possession of her imagination that perhaps the wicked Duke of Kingston might accompany him.

She started to her feet, and again recommenced an examination of her prison.

Again she strove to shake the iron bars that were placed across the window, but in vain, they were far too well secured for her to be able to move them.

But what is it that makes Dora pause in her examination of the window and the walls of the apartment, with breath suspended, and hands outstretched ?

A deep groan came a second time upon her ears, and Dora flew to the small orifice in the flooring of the apartment to look into the chamber beneath.

Alas, all was wrapped in in impenetrable darkness !

She beat upon the floor with her hands in order to attract the attention of the stranger, whom she now believed to be recovering from the effects of the opiate, which had been administered to him by the old hag.

No response of any kind was made to her efforts.

Dora began to think that she must have been mistaken, and a sickening feeling of despair took possession of her ; for the thought of hearing the sound of a human voice, who would speak to her in accents of kindness, had filled her heart with joy.

She was about once more to resume her search, when once again a deep groan, and this time a feeble cry, as of some one calling for assistance, came upon her ear.

Again Dora rapped upon the floor, and this time, placing her mouth close to the little opening, she said—

" Who calls ? Speak—oh, speak ! I am imprisoned here—but we may be able to help each other."

Dora waited some few minutes, but no reply came to her question. She resolved, however, not to leave her post of observation, if such it could be called, seeing that there was no light either in the apartment in which Dora was imprisoned, nor in that in which the stranger was.

In a few minutes, however, Dora had the unspeakable joy of hearing a voice from the chamber below, speaking in a low tone, as if communing with itself rather than addressing another.

She felt that there was no time to be lost, but again beating on the floor with her hands, she said—

" Speak ! speak, I pray you, if you are still in life ! Rouse yourself, for in a few minutes it may be too late to save yourself."

Dora could hear a movement of the occupant of the chamber below, who appeared to be startled somewhat on hearing a voice just above his head.

" Alas !" he said, " I know not what to say, my brain is so confused ! but I fancy I am speaking to a friend ! if so, oh, come come to me ! this darkness, and all that I have gone through is terrible—terrible!"

" Thank Heaven you are not dead !" said Dora ; and the thought that there was at least companionship, and perhaps a prospect of escape from that den of vice and crime, caused her heart to beat almost audibly.

Stooping so low that every word she uttered could be distinctly heard by the occupant of the lower room, she said—

" Can you rise, and find some means of forcing open the door of the room above you ? I am a prisoner here, to serve the vile purposes of the people who inhabit this house."

" Ah, say you so ?" replied the stranger. " I will try to reach you."

Oh, what a moment of anxiety was that for poor Dora, as she thought how much depended on the success of his efforts.

Dora could hear, from where she was, that the stranger had succeeded in struggling to his feet, and appeared, from the sound, to be groping his way towards the staircase which led to her apartment.

Dora closed her eyes, and words of thanksgiving found their way to her lips.

" Quick—oh, quick !" she cried, as the prospect of liberty became more tangible. Oh, quickly, for heaven's sake !"

An exclamation burst from the lips of the gentleman, and then he said—

" Fortune seems to befriend us, for I

have just stumbled over what appears to be a key. Perhaps the old woman, as she fled from the house, thinking me dead and you securely locked in, dropped it in her fright; at all events, I will try if it will open your door."

Another moment, and the door of Dora's prison was open!

But the deliverer and the rescued could not see each other. In the darkness, however, their hands met, and the mutual pressure assured each of the other's sympathy.

The stranger was the first to speak.

"I know not to whom I have had the pleasure of doing this slight service, but I have no doubt I shall meet with rather a different return to that I experienced only a short time ago, when I was anxious to comfort one whom I believed to be dying. But enough of this, we must be quick, and save ourselves. Whither are you bound, Mr.—"

"To London," replied Dora, without appearing to notice the implied desire to ascertain her name. "And you?"

"Why, strange to say, I am going to London also; so if you have no objection, we need not part company yet."

"I shall be only too happy to avail myself of your company; so we will linger no longer in this abode of villany, but proceed at once on our journey."

"I have a horse," replied the stranger, "but we cannot ride double to London— we must be content to ride and walk by turns."

"Not so," replied Dora, "I, too, have a horse, which I believe is somewhere on the premises."

"That is fortunate," replied the stranger. "And now let us lose no more time, for that old hag and her villanous grandson may return, and Heaven only knows what addition they may have made to their party."

Dora and her companion sallied forth into the night air, and found a young moon struggling amid drifting clouds to perform its office, and refining, with its pearly radiance, flower and tree of its big brother, the earth.

Dora hoped that it would still continue too dark for her young companion to observe her too closely, for she had already recognised in him the young officer whose life she had been the means of saving so recently, when he was left for dead by the roadside, on the night of the duel.

Fortunately the clouds gathered more densely over the face of the moon, and at length it seemed as if it had settled into a cavern of precipitous, dim-looking rocks, and all was dark. A wailing sound swept through the air, and borne on its irresistible wings, there came the sound of some clock striking the hour of three.

The young stranger and Dora were quickly mounted, and soon put their horses into a trot.

They trotted on for some distance, each occupied with his or her own thoughts, when the stranger drew up suddenly, and said, in a frank, manly tone—

"I have been thinking that, perhaps, my company may be an intrusion, Mr.—" he paused at a loss for a name by which to address Dora.

"It is quite natural," said Dora, "that you should have a desire to know to whom you have been of such essential service this night; but for reasons, best known to myself, I must trust to your generosity not to press me for an answer. Some other day— at some future time, perhaps—"

The stranger gracefully inclined his head, as he said—

"I perceive I have had the honour of being of some slight service to a gentleman; and if there be reasons why you should not make yourself known to me by name, I will rest content to remain in ignorance upon one condition."

"And that condition?"

"That I may have some name by which I may identify you to my own mind when I remember this night, which was so near proving my last in this world."

Dora thought for a moment. Then raising her plumed hat from her head, and throwing back the ample riding cloak which she had taken care to wrap so carefully about her, she said—

Has Mr. Hargrave never seen me before?"

As Dora spoke the moon struggled from behind a cloud, and its rays fell full upon the sweet face of Dora.

"Ah!" exclaimed the young man. "Is it possible? can it be, indeed, Captain Arod, the highwayman, of whom I have heard so much?"

"What if I am?" replied Dora. "Do you now repent having set me at liberty?"

"Oh, no no—but—but—and yet it cannot be true?"

"What cannot be true?" asked Dora, sadly.

"I have been told," replied the young man, with some hesitation in his tones. I have been told—at least its said that— that—"

"What?"

"That Captain Arod, the highwayman, is a beautiful girl."

Dora laughed a clear, ringing laugh, as she said—

"But my dear sir, you do not believe all

the absurd stories you hear about highway-men. Captain Arod is said to be a very ferocious, bloodthirsty sort of fellow; and from what I know of him, I can deny the charge."

"But you are Captain Arod, then?" added the young horseman, looking interested and excited.

"Nay, I said not that. I merely asked you if you had ever seen me before?"

"Yes, oh, yes," replied the stranger, "on that dreadful night when my bitter foe left me for dead. It was you who saved me from perishing, and my gratitude will last as long as I live."

"It was I who saved you. I saw the cowardly thrust. But did you not render me a service likewise on that night, or do you think that my memory is more treacherous than yours?"

"Oh, what I did was merely an act of gratitude—say no more about it; but tell me, why do you follow this life, so fraught with danger? I would fain have you say it is a mere freak—a whim—a wager—anything rather than a profession."

Dora sighed, for now more than ever she longed for a time the life she was leading would be at end; but still, until she was furnished with the means for maintaining her rights against the claims of her wicked uncle, the false Duke of Kingston, Dora felt that there was no other course opened to her.

"You are silent," continued the young man.

Dora started, for her thoughts had become so concentrated upon those who were dearer to her than life itself, that she might almost be said to have forgotten the existence of her companion.

"I was silent," replied Dora, "from many reasons; but I would fain hope that you will put as good a construction as may be upon my present life and actions. I know not why, but I feel that it would be somewhat of a gratification to think that you remembered me with kindness."

"Of that rest assured," said the young man, holding out his hand to Dora. "Of that rest assured; and if at any time I can be of service to you, belive me nothing will afford me greater pleasure."

Dora took the proffered hand, and then said—

"And now we must part company, for I have business of importance on hand which requires all my attention."

"But stay yet a moment interrupted the young man, "will you not tell me of some address where I may hear of or communicate with you?"

"At present I can give you no address; but you shall one day hear from me. I will send to your chambers, and if ever you choose to renew this acquaintance, most assuredly you shall have the opportunity."

"Be it so, then," replied Hargrave, and once more offering his hand to Dora, they bade each other farewell with as much sincerity in their manner and tones as though they had been friends of long standing."

Young Hargrave took the road to the right, while Dora pursued that which led more directly to Kensington.

"Now for my Henry!" she said. "Oh! what has he not suffered on my account?"

Dora urged her horse to its utmost speed, and was just turning into a lane which led by a nearer route to the village of Kensington, when she became aware that there was another horseman immediately before her, going at a slow pace in the same direction that she was herself travelling.

"So," said Dora to herself, "my adventures for to-night are not yet over. We will ride on, Starlight, and she patted the creature on the neck, and it immediately made that curious noise as if holding converse with its gentle mistress. "We will ride on and see who this may be."

Dora quickened her horse's pace; but the horseman, who was now only a few paces ahead of her, did not seem conscious of the fact that there was anyone behind him, or if he were conscious of the fact, he certainly gave himself no trouble to ascertain who that person was, neither did he appear to think it necessary to quicken his pace.

Dora reached his side and said—

"Good night, sir!"

No sooner, however, were the words spoken, than the horseman exclaimed—

"Heaven be praised, captain! I see you at last safe and well.

"Dottman!"

Dora could say no more. The meeting with her old, faithful follower was too much for her already over-wrought feelings, and she bowed her head upon the neck of Starlight, and burst into tears.

CHAPTER LII.

NEONI RESOLVES TO LEARN THE FATE OF HER FATHER FROM HENRY DACRES—THE VISIT TO THE HOUSE OF SURLINA—THE DYING FATHER.

WHEN Neoni awoke from the deep slumber in which Dora left her on that eventful night which had had for her, Dora, so many terrors, the sun was streaming broadly in at the window.

After some difficulty Neoni succeeded in opening the long disused lattice, and the fresh breeze of morning stole upon her, perfumed with the sweet breath of the clematis, and musical with the numerous voices of the feathered inhabitants of the forest.

Looking out upon a lawn where the long shadows of the trees pointed from east to west in the colourless rays of the morning light, the young girl sighed deeply, and buried her face in her hands.

"Another day has passed away, and my father comes not, and yet he knew where the Duke of Kingston had placed me. Would chance direct him to this room? Perhaps he has already visited what the Duke intended to be my prison—and yet—"

She paused, and for a few moments seemed lost in deep thought. After a few minutes she raised her head, saying—

"Yes, I will seek *him*. I feel convinced that he and his wife know more than they have told me respecting my father. I am brave now. I can talk to him as to an utter stranger. Yes, I will seek him."

Hastily throwing around her a mantle, which she had found in the cab of the Duke of Kingston on that night when he had forced her from what she had so long been in the habit of considering her home, Neoni passed to that apartment which was in the occupation of Henry Dacres and Dora.

When Neoni reached the door of that apartment, she was forced to pause again and take breath, and placed her left hand upon her heart, as if she wished to reassure herself that it had not ceased to beat.

At length she summoned up courage to knock gently at that door.

It was immediately opened by Henry Dacres.

Neoni advanced into the room, and having seated herself on an ottoman which had been indicated to her by Henry Dacres, she commenced speaking; but her breath came short, and at times she was compelled to cease speaking.

Henry appeared not to notice the emotion of Neoni, and endeavoured to turn the conversation upon indifferent subjects.

"Thank you, Mr. Dacres," said the Greek girl, now thoroughly master of her emotions. "Thank you for your kind intentions; but I am not to be deceived. There was a time when you were anxious to prove your friendship. It is to put your sincerity to the proof that I now come to you to have all my doubts solved respecting my father."

"Alas, lady," said Henry. "I fear that the small amount of information I possess will be far from satisfactory to you. All I think I will tell you, if you wish me to do so."

"Speak, and tell me the worst," said the Greek girl, in a tone of suppressed agony.

"I know only," said Henry, speaking gently and kindly; "I know only that our friend, Dottman, has every reason to believe that the false Duke of Kingston appeared to be in the possession of—of a secret which—"

"Which? oh, tell me all!"

"Which led him, Dottman, to believe that your father was dead."

"Dead?" exclaimed Neoni, springing to her feet. "Oh, no, no, not dead! tell me that he is not dead!" and as he uttered those few words, she clasped her hands together, and looked imploring at Henry.

"Let us hope not; but you wished me to tell you what I thought, and now the worst is over. Tell me if I can serve you in any way, and be assured that I am now as ever at your service."

Neoni looked at him for a moment as though she would read his heart, and the manner in which he bore that scrutiny convinced her that, at all events, she possessed a friend."

"Mr. Dacres," replied Neoni, "I have resolved upon my plan of action, and all I ask of your friendship at present is not to try to thwart me in my intentions. Have I your promise?"

"You have—you have! but do nothing until the return of Dora. She will be able to advise and perhaps assist you."

"It is that I may not have to refuse that advice and assistance that I purpose carrying out my intentions immediately."

"Well, be it so," replied Henry; "but let me urge you to well consider your plans before you undertake anything."

Neoni promised not to be too precipitate, and holding out her hand to Henry begged him to make what excuses he thought proper to Dora for her abrupt departure.

As soon as the Greek girl returned to that apartment which had been set apart for her use, she began to make what few preparations were necessary for her departure.

But how was she to leave the palace, clad in the fanciful dress she usually wore, and in which the Duke of Kingston had carried her off from her father's house?

Neoni resolved to commence a search in the different cupboards and cabinets which were in the apartment. For this purpose she approached a kind of armoise which stood in a recess by the side of the fireplace.

There was a key in the lock, which, from its rusty condition, Neoni found **great** difficulty in turning.

At length, however, it yielded to her touch, and the interior exhibited to view a number of shelves, on which were strewn, without any regard to order, a number of papers.

Taking a hasty survey of the contents of the armoise, and feeling persuaded that she should not there find any wearing apparel, she was about to close the door again when her attention was drawn to an inner door, which she had not yet noticed.

This inner door presented no difficulty, for it was secured merely by a small brass button, and Neoni lost no time in examining the inside of this compartment.

With a cry of joy she seized upon an ample red cloak, such as was then worn by old women of the lower order upon festive occasions; and pursuing her inspection still more closely, she soon found a bonnet and other articles of clothing, such as would effectually disguise her.

Hanging to, on the inside of the door of this inner cupboard, was a handsome dirk, or poignard, richly ornamented with gold and precious stones.

"Kind fortune favours me!" said the Greek girl to herself. "With this weapon I can defend myself."

She hastily concealed the dirk, and having dressed herself in the clothes she had found, and concealing the weapon in her apparel, she made her way as rapidly as she could towards the little gate in the garden wall, which Dottman had pointed out to her as the best means of exit from the palace.

A few minutes sufficed to reach the little gate, which Neoni quietly pushed open, and sallied forth, without any interruption, for although the sun was now high in the heavens, at that particular moment, neither pedestrians nor equipages happened to be upon the spot.

And now, Neoni bent her steps from that deserted mansion, whence she had been carried under a promise of seeing her father.

Rapidly the Greek girl pursued her way; and as she turned into the street in which was situated the mansion of the Duke of Kingston, her heart beat almost audibly, for she dreaded a meeting with him, her worst foe, and as she fully believed, her father's murderer.

At length the house was reached, and hastily taking from her bosom a small key, she entered the mansion, and closed the door after her.

And now, as she stood in that gloomy-looking hall, Neoni felt her courage fast forsaking her; for what had she come to seek in that dreary mansion? If, as she began to fear, her father was no more, could she encounter alone the dreadful sight which might be presented to her eyes?

She pressed her hand on her heart to still its beating, then speaking in low tones to herself, she said—

"Ah, yes! I pity her now, the poor deserted wife! He told me she was dead, and that I might now be his duchess. Can this be true? and if so, how did she come by her death? I will seek her chamber, and ascertain for myself."

Neoni now ascended the staircase, holding the dagger which she had found in the *armoire* in Kensington Palace, in her hand.

She had reached the floor on which was situated the laboratory of her father, and was about to enter that apartment, when she heard a noise, as if some person had fallen to the ground.

At first she could not determine in her own mind from which direction the noise had proceeded. Did it come from the room in the occupation of the duchess, or from one of those opening from the same landing as the laboratory?

Neoni listened.

All was still.

She was about to proceed towards the little staircase which led to the prison-chamber of the unhappy Duchess of Kingston, when, to her horror, there came upon her ear a groan so unearthly that every drop of blood in her veins seemed to curdle.

"Oh, Heaven!" cried she, "am I going mad? or was that really a human cry?"

Again she listened.

And now came the sound as if some article of furniture were being dragged to and fro, as if to attract attention.

Neoni had no hesitation in deciding at once whence proceeded the noise this time.

It came from the passage which led from the laboratory to the chamber of the duchess.

She flew to the door which shut in this passage from the rest of the house, and placed her ear close to the panel.

"Neoni—Neoni! my child—my child! where—oh, where are you?"

With a shriek of joy and despair, Neoni beat upon the pannel of the door.

"Father—father! open the door! I am here—I am here! your Neoni!"

No voice responded to her cry.

Despair but added strength to her efforts, and with a crash the lock of the door gave way as she thrust the point of the dagger between it and the lock.

In another moment Neoni had entered the passage; but who shall paint her anguish of soul at the spectacle which there met her eyes?

Lying on the floor, his eyes closed, and the line of death stamped upon every feature, there lay Surlina, the idolised father of Neoni!

With one bound she threw herself on the floor by his side, and clasping her arms about him, gave one wild shriek, and fell senseless by his side.

*   *   *   *

"Neoni! Neoni! Oh, Heaven spare her! My child—my only one!" faintly murmured the dying man. "Dear Neoni, look up—it is I! Do you not know me? do you not hear my voice? It is your father who speaks to you! Oh, my Neoni! blessed—blessed is this meeting! I never thought I should look upon your dear face again!"

The swoon into which Neoni had fallen immediately after beholding her father, was one of those prostrations of the physical and mental energies that baffle for a long time all the resources of art to grapple with.

At length, however, with a thrill, her senses returned to her, and opening her eyes, she looked confusedly around her.

And now she turned her gaze upon her father.

How Neoni looked at him!

"Speak, my Neoni," gasped Surlina.

"Father! father!"

"Yes, yes, your father—but—"

The head of Surlina sunk upon his breast, and now it was that his devoted child made an almost superhuman effort to control her emotions, in order to restore her father to consciousness.

Neoni tottered to the door of the passage, and entering the laboratory, soon returned with some water, which she sprinkled on her father's face.

This presently revived him, and Neoni had the happiness of seeing him once more open his eyes.

He made a sign to her to approach nearer, and then in a faint whisper uttered the one word "violet," holding up, as he did so, three fingers.

Neoni understood that he wished her to give him three drops of a violet-coloured liquid, which was in the laboratory; and this time she was enabled to reach that apartment with greater speed than when she went in search of water.

The violet-coloured liquid was as well-know to Neoni as to her father. She therefore lost no time in possessing herself of it, and taking a crystal cup from the table, she commenced to drop the given quantity into it.

But alas! her hand was unsteady, and at least twenty drops escaped from the vial.

To pour this away was the work of a moment, and again she strove to do her father's bidding.

And again she failed!

"Oh, what shall I do? what shall I do?" murmured the Greek girl. "My father so near to death as he appears to be, may be restored to me, if I can but administer to him this potion. Oh, aid me, Heaven!"

Again Neoni commenced dropping the liquid, and this time her hand was steady, and the three drops of the violet-coloured liquid, after effervescing for an instant, gradually changed the water into which they had been poured to a palish blue colour.

Neoni hastened, as fast as her trembling limbs would permit her, to her father, whom she found still lying on the floor completely prostrated; but his eyes were open.

Throwing herself on her knees by his side, she held the mixture to his lips, which he drank greedily.

"Thank Heaven!" ejaculated Surlina, when he had taken the potion. "I shall soon be a new man! but tell me, my child, why have you stayed away from me so long?"

"Father—father! the wicked Duke of Kingston told me you had gone away on business for him, and that I had your commands to wed him."

"Villain!"

"He took me from this house, and made me a prisoner in Kensington Palace, where I should still have remained until he had matured all his vile projects, had it not been for Dora Dacres, his niece."

"What mean you, child?"

"She, you know, father, has been persecuted by this bad man, and is now obliged to seek refuge wherever she thinks there is a chance of escaping the eyes of those whom he has set as spies upon her movements; this Dora, then, father, by some unhappy accident, had also taken refuge in old Kensington Palace, and happening to overhear a conversation which took place between me and the Duke of Kingston, she discovered, to a certain extent, the plot he had set on foot for my destruction—"

Neoni paused abruptly, for her father was gradually sinking into a profound slumber.

"Alas! what shall I do? father, speak to me—look up—look up! leave me not, now that I have found you. Father! father!"

The words of the young girl fell upon the ears of one who could scarcely be said to have passed the confines of life; but still the look upon the face of her father so resembled death in its cold rigidity, that it was only natural Neoni should mistake that deep sleep for death itself.

"Oh, woe is me!" she cried, "woe is me! Homeless and friendless! what must I do?"

Again she clung to her father, and placed her hand upon his heart.

THE MILLER AND HIS WIFE WATCHING THE SLEEPING MINA.

"He lives! he lives still!" she cried, as she started to her feet." I must seek advice for him! All may yet be well!"

Hastily equipping herself in such garments as the Greek girl thought would attract the least attention, she glided down that gloomy staircase, reached the hall, and passed out at the front door.

And now whither should she direct her steps?

At this moment Neoni remembered to have heard her father speak of a Doctor Lane, who resided not far from where she now was; and taking the nearest route to the house occupied by her father's friend, Neoni soon stood upon its threshold.

Dora.—27.

With a beating heart, Neoni raised the knocker, and the summons for admittance was soon answered by a man in livery, who, in reply to Neoni's question if Doctor Lane was at home, replied.

"Yes, ma'am. If you will walk in I will acquaint master with your request to see him."

"Do so!" said Neoni, "and say at the same time that it is a case of life and death!"

So agitated was Neoni, that the few words she uttered came in strange, gasping accents, and she was obliged to sink into the depths of an easy chair which was near to her, to prevent herself from falling.

Not many minutes elapsed before Doctor Lane made his appearance.

This physician possessed a kind and sensitive heart, and was ever ready, in the gentlest manner, to soften the afflictions of all with whom he came in professional contact.

"Oh, sir!" exclaimed Neoni, as Doctor Lane entered the room.

"Oh, sir, my poor father is dying—has been murdered."

"Indeed! where is he?"

"Oh, come with me! come with me now! Perhaps it may not yet be too late."

In another moment Neoni was seated beside Doctor Lane in his carriage, which happened to be waiting for him just as Neoni knocked at the door.

In less than a quarter of an hour the physician stood beside Surlina.

CHAPTER LIII.

SHEWS THAT THE LITTLE MINA HAS FOUND FRIENDS AT LAST—THE NEW PLAYMATE —THE LAUNCH OF "THE LITTLE MINA."

It is now time that we return to the little Mina, that fair and gentle child, whom we left in wet and draggled garments, being tenderly ministered to by the good miller and his kind-hearted wife.

"Well, dame, the best thing to do will be to get the child to bed," said the honest miller.

"Ay, ay! pretty dear!" returned Dame Gray, "and while I take off her wet clothes, you just light a bit of fire, and warm some milk, it may do her good."

The miller was not long in obeying the behests of his help-mate; and while the little Mina was being divested of her wet clothes, the miller busied himself in preparing the milk as he had been directed.

The little Mina opened her eyes.

A strange, startled expression was in them, as she glanced round that humble but cheerful apartment.

It was evident that the scene at the hut by the river's side, in which the villain, Turnbull, had played so conspicuous a part, was not yet effaced from her remembrance.

The kind-hearted matron said, in a low voice—

"Don't be afraid, dear—I am going to put you to bed, and give you some nice warm milk. Do you like milk?"

There is an unerring instinct in children to recognise either the tone of kindness or that of harshness in those who approach them; and the voice and manner of the kind old woman, to whose care Providence had conducted little Mina, won the child's heart at once.

She held up her little hands, and stroked the old woman's cheek, and whispered something in so low a tone that Dame Gray did not hear that first appeal to her affection; but her heart responded to the touch of that little hand, and the old woman stooped down, and drawing the little hand close to her heart, kissed the beautiful bright hair, and Mina nestled close to her.

When Dame Gray gently raised that little head, it fell forward on her shoulder again.

The child's fears were dispelled, and she slept the deep calm sleep of innocence and childhood.

Just at this moment the miller appeared, carrying in his hand a cup and saucer with smoking milk, into which he had crumbled some bread.

"There it is, little one!" he said, gaily, as he pushed open the door of the room into which his wife had carried the little Mina. "Here it is—" but he was not permitted to utter another word, for Dame Gray held up a finger, while at the same time she pointed to the sleeping child.

The miller placed the bread and milk upon a table which stood by the bedside, then drawing nearer, gazed, with an expression of curiosity at the little sleeper.

"She's no gipsy's child, dame," he whispered, after he had contemplated the child in silence for the space of about a minute.

"Not she!" replied his wife. "See what beautiful hair she has! Who can she be? and how came she to be out alone in such a night as this? Hush, she speaks!"

It was a beautiful sight, to witness those two old people gazing with such interest and affection upon that child whom they seemed to be prepared to love and cherish as a new-found treasure.

"Mamma! mamma! don't let him take me!" murmured Mina in her sleep.

"Pretty dear!" whispered the old woman. "I think she's been stolen."

"Like enough—like enough!" replied her husband. "But yet it seems strange, that if she were stolen, whoever did it did not keep her! and see, dame, she has good clothes—so it's quite certain they did not want her for them."

"Very like not, good man. But I 'dare say the gipsies stole her—and there's no knowing, perhaps she gave them the slip."

The miller and his wife now determined to go to bed again, and wait until the little Mina should awake.

The reader knows more than did the good miller and his wife, how that the child had satisfied the wants of nature by taking a good draught of new milk from the milking pail which the dairymaid had set down close to the rails of the stile.

The child's slumber was deep and undisturbed.

Towards ten o'clock the next morning, however, some hours after the good miller and his wife had been stirring, the little Mina opened her eyes, and the sunbeams, as they entered the little latticed window, fell upon her sunny hair.

She had just risen to a sitting posture in the bed, when Dame Gray entered the room.

The child sm 'ed as the good old woman approached the bedside and stroked her hair as she imprinted a kiss of affection upon her pure brow.

" Well, dear, do you want your breakfast?" asked her new friend.

The child looked inquiringly, but did not speak.

" Will you love me, dear?"

The child looked straight into the old woman's eyes, and then holding up one of her litttle hands, she touched her face.

Dame Gray caught the little hand, and kissed it.

" Do you like milk, dear?"

" Yes," whispered Mina.

" Shall I go and fetch you some?"

The child did not seem to like this arrangement, for she gazed round the room as if looking for some one.

" What's want, dear?"

" Will that man come if you go away?"

As Mina asked the question she trembled in every limb.

" No, no, little lamb! no one shall come to you! but if you like I will dress you first, and we will go together to get the milk."

" Yes, yes!" and this time the tone was joyous and childlike.

The old woman had not been idle while the child slept, for she had washed and smoothed the bedraggled clothes, and they were now clean and comfortable for her to wear.

A few minutes sufficed to dress the child, and it was strange to see that old woman, who probably had not had such an occupation for many a long year, to see how quickly and neatly she performed her unwonted office.

By the time the last ringlet was properly arranged, the little Mina had had ample opportunity of becoming perfectly well acquainted with her new friend. As she took the old woman's hand, she said—

" Where is mamma? You will take me to her?"

" Yes, yes, dear!" said old Mrs. Gray, " some day, I hope. But now, come and have some breakfast."

Fearlessly and caressingly the child placed her hand in that of her friend, and trotted by her side to the little sanded parlour, which was the " best room " of the good old couple.

Never was a meal more enjoyed than was that first one of the little Mina beneath the humble roof of the miller.

Mina had just concluded her repast, when the door of the room was thrown open, and a lad, about the age of fourteen, entered.

" Jim! you here?" exclaimed old Mrs. Gray, as the boy entered. " Art thou not well, lad ?"

" Quite well, dear Granny!" replied the boy, as he gave the old woman rather a noisy kiss on the cheek, " quite well, granny, only, you see, I've come home to help grandfather at the mill."

" What does thee mean, boy? I hope thee has not been doing anything wrong ?"

" No, granny, I've done nothing wrong! and look here—I've brought you and grandfather lots of money."

As the boy spoke, he displayed to the astonished gaze of the old woman, the bank note for fifty pounds which Dora had given him as some return for the service he had rendered her.

" Alas! alas!" answered the good old woman. " Alas, alas! that I should live to see this day! How came thee by that money?"

" Why, quite honestly, granny! Don't take on in that sort of way!" replied Jim, " why, I thought you and grandfather would be ever so glad, and that's why I ran almost all the way, to get here before he went into the mill."

" Tell me how thee got it then ?"

" Why, in this way. A gentleman put up at our stables, and there were some ill-looking fellows came in soon after, and I happened to hear them say that they meant to take him to prison ; but I'm quite sure he'd never done anything to be taken to prison for, so I just managed to get him away before they were any the wiser. I got up behind him on his horse, and when we had ridden a good way, he turned round and asked me what I meant to do, as it would never do to go back again to the old inn."

" And what did thee say?" asked the old woman.

" Why, granny, you must know that he was no other than the great highwayman, Captain Hawk, and so I asked him to take me into his service to look after his horse."

" Alack and a-well-a-day!" cried the good old creature. " Alack and a-well-a-day! to think that your father's son should ever think of entering the service of a highwayman !"

"And why not, granny? he is brave and generous, and I should like nothing better than to follow him on the road. But who have we here, granny?"

These words were spoken in reference to the little Mina, whose large blue eyes had seemed to drink in every word that had been uttered by old Mrs. Gray and her grandson.

"A little girl who, I hope, will soon be friends with you, for I am too old now to amuse a child of her years."

"No fear of us not being friends, granny," replied the boy, and as he spoke he stooped down and kissed her cheek gently.

Mina did not seem to consider this in any way a liberty, and when the boy asked her to come and see him swim his boat in the pond, she put her hand confidingly into his without uttering a word.

"God bless you," murmured the old woman, as the child held her cheek up to her in expectation of receiving a kiss.

"God bless you, little one, and grant that you may some day be restored to the sorrowing hearts of those whose duty and happiness alike it must have been to protect you."

The two playmates left the cottage.

They wandered across some fields with the boat carefully carried under the boy's arm, and as they went Jim said—

"What is your name, little lady?"

For some time the child did not answer his question, and yet there was a look of serene happiness upon her sweet, young face, which had not been there for many a weary day.

The boy sat upon the stump of a tree, which happened to be in their path, and drawing the child gently towards him, he said again—

"Will you not tell me your name, dear? I have not given my boat a name yet, but I will call it after you if you tell me what your name is."

The child's eyes sparkled as she glanced at the trim-looking little vessel, which was to be called by her name, and looking up into the boy's face, she said softly—

"My name is Mina!"

"Mina! oh, what a pretty name! and how pretty you are! have you any brothers or sisters, and have they as pretty names as yours?"

This question seemed to puzzle the little Mina and she shook her head.

"Well, never mind about them now," said the boy. "The pond in which I want to swim my boat "The little Mina," is out there yonder. Will you come with me?"

"Oh, yes!" joyously replied the child, and hand in hand the two flew across the intervening field, nor stopped until they had reached the side of the pond, on the bosom of which was to float, for the first time, "The Little Mina!"

With childlike glee the child clapped her hands as the boy undid the string which was to tow the mimic ship to and fro on the water, and some two or three hours had elapsed before they felt the necessity or the desire of returning home.

Drawing the boat to shore, and drawing it carefully upon the grass, which there grew tall and thick, the two friends then betook themselves to the cottage again.

As they reached the door it was opened by the good miller himself, who welcomed the child back with as much cheerfulness and sincerity as that bestowed by his good old wife.

Then turning to Jim, he said—

"Come hither, my lad, and tell me what you know of Captain Hawk, who gave you this bank note, for I do not like to spend it until I hear more about it."

"Why, grandfandfather, the fact is, the gentleman who gave me that fifty pounds bank note said he was not Captain Hawk at all, but was only riding his horse."

"I am well pleased to hear that, for from all I have heard of Captain Hawk, he is anything but a man to be admired or imitated."

The boy laughed.

"Oh, grandfather, granny has been telling you that I said I should like to follow his example; but I don't mean to do any such thing! but I hope some day I shall have a horse like his, and then I would teach Mina to ride."

"Mina?" exclaimed the old couple together, "then you have succeeded in making her tell you her name?"

"Oh, yes, and I have christened my boat 'The Little Mina.'"

The old man laughed, and srotking the head of the little girl gently, he said—

"Mina what? what is your name?"

"Mina Dacres," replied the child.

"Mina Dacres!" exclaimed the miller. "Thank Heaven! I may now find some clue by which you may be restored to your parents."

The boy did not seem quite satisfied with this arrangement, but the little girl walked up to the knee of her generous protector, and said, with an earnestness of tone and manner surprising in so young a child,—

"And will you take me to my mamma?"

"Most assuredly, little one!"

The child was satisfied, and content to rest in peace and security for that day which would restore her to the almost broken heart of her fond mother.

And thus in calm peacefulness the hours passed away. The child forgot, in the happiness of the present, the many horrors which had already been crowded into her young life.

Little did Dora imagine that her little one—her precious Mina, was so well cared for, and that a few short hours only would be sufficient to place that child in her arms, for which meeting her heart had looked forward to as something too fraught with happiness ever to be realised in this world of suffering.

And now, once more, night had spread its dark mantle over every tree, shrub, and flower. The inmates of the little farmhouse had retired to their beds, some to sleep, some to think. Yes, the good old miller and his wife had much to think about and talk of—plans to settle in order to restore that beautiful child to her lawful guardians, and vain conjectures as to who those guardians were.

The boy thought of the beautiful child and how he would amuse her on the morrow.

And Mina? what shall we say of Mina? Ah! Heaven was good to Mina. She slept!

CHAPTER LIV.

THE DUKE OF KINGSTON RECKONS WITHOUT HIS HOST—THE PLOT AND THE COUNTER-PLOT — DORA POSSESSES TWO UNKNOWN FRIENDS.

IT is necessary, for the right understanding of our story, that we return to that wicked plotter against human happiness, the false Duke of Kingston.

No sooner had Dottman taken his departure, after having possessed himself of that valuable document, the pardon of Dora, than he begun to feel that he had been unnecessarily terrified, and to curse his ill fortune for ever allowing himself to be frightened out of that paper, of whose existence no one was cognisant but himself.

"Fool that I was," he cried, striking his forehead with his hand. "Fool that I was, to allow myself to be taken by surprise. But I will stir heaven and earth now to get her apprehended, and then it will perhaps not be very difficult to get her executed. Yes, yes, I will try! What can be done? when once I am assured of her death and the death of her child, I shall breathe more freely. There will then be no one to dispute with me my titles and estates."

He rose from the chair on which he had thrown himself, and begun, with hasty strides, to pace the laboratory.

"Yes," he continued, half aloud, "yes, if I can but get her into my power. Yes, if I can but get her into my power. Perhaps it would be better myself to become her gaoler. Ah, yes, a happy thought! she may disappear, and she has no friends to make inquiries about her. There's her husband; but he is so far invalided that if I manage well his search will prove ineffectual. I am about to leave England. What so easy as to take this Dora with me? Ah! happy thought!"

The Duke of Kingston smiled a ghastly smile as he thus sketched out his plan of procedure, and seizing a little silver lamp from a side table, he left the laboratory by the passage which led from the house in the occupation of Surlina to his own by means of an opening which could be effected by touching a secret spring.

The Duke was once more in his own luxurious drawing-room.

He drew a chair to the fireside, and rang the bell.

The summons was answered by the valet who had received orders to sit up for him.

The man started when he saw his master seated in the drawing-room, for he knew that he had not been admitted into the house by any of the domestics; but the servants of his lordship were too well accustomed to his proceedings to allow curiosity or surprise ever to be depicted on their features. Bowing low, then, the valet advanced towards him, and handed him a billet.

The Duke took the letter from the salver and proceeded to read it, forgetting at the time that the valet was waiting to be dismissed.

The billet ran as follows—

"My Lord,—You know who I mean by D—— D——, and I think you will not be sorry to hear that the person alluded to is in my power at the present moment. If your lordship has any commands for me, write me a line addressed to the 'Nag's Head,' and I will attend your lordship at any time or place your lordship may appoint.

"I beg to subscribe myself
Your lordship's faithful servant,
S—— T——

The Duke of Kingston had no difficulty in the world in deciding in his own mind that the person referred to in the foregoing billet was none other than his much injured niece, Dora, and that the writer of the billet was the villain Turnbull.

"It is well," he said, speaking to himself, and turning hastily for the first time, he perceived that he was not alone.

"Blockhead!" he said, addressing the valet, "what are you waiting there for?"

"I was awaiting your lordship's orders."

" You may go—yet stay ! bring me those writing materials."

The valet placed before the duke a beautifully inlaid writing case, in which was to be found everything which was necessary for letter writing.

The duke waved his hand in token of dismissal to the valet, who withdrew as quickly as possible.

As the valet made his way to a kind of ante-room which he was in the habit of calling his own, inasmuch as it was there that the duke always wished him to wait, when he considered himself more immediately in attendance on him, he threw himself into a comfortable arm chair by the side of the fire, saying as he did so,—

" He's in one of his black moods to-night. Ah, well, I shall be glad when I can say good bye to this house, for I feel sure there have been some ugly doings in it, and I'm sure it's all a tale about the duchess being sent away into the country because she was ill. Why, don't I know that she was quite well and as beautiful as ever up to the very day she disappeared. Eh ? what was that ?"

This question was responded to by a grating sound just outside the window of the room in which the valet was sitting

Again the grating came, and the valet jumped up and opened the door, admitting, as he did so, a tall figure, enveloped in a cloak.

" Is that you, Fred ?" asked the valet.

" Ay, ay, man—don't you know your own brother now ? of course it's me."

" I began to give you up, you see," said the valet, " for you told me you would be here by ten o'clock to keep me company, and here it is nearly three."

" Better late than never," replied the new comer. " But tell me. Hillyard, has the Duke of Kingston come home ?"

" Well, he is at home ; but how he got into the house is rather a puzzler, for nobody let him in, I'm certain. However, there he is, and looking more frightful than ever."

" Ah ! then he is in one of his gloomy fits, is he ?"

" I believe you. I took a billet, which had been left here by as ill-looking a scoundrel as ever human eyes looked upon, and after he had read it, he turned to me and asked me what I was waiting for in such a voice that I was only too glad to get out of the room."

" Do you know what was in the letter ?"

" How should I—it was sealed. But stop, I did hear him mutter something to himself which I fancy was in the letter."

" What did you hear ?"

" Well, it was only a few words here and there like, but it spoke, I know, of somebody being in the power of the person who wrote the letter—and it went on to say that the writer would be ready to do any villany his lordship wished."

" I understand it better now. I happen to know, Hillyard, who wrote that letter."

" You don't say so."

" But I do say so—it was Turnbull."

" What, that fiend in human form that I did my best to put out of the world the day that sweet young creature, Dora Dacres, was to be executed ?"

" The same," replied the visitor.

" But who was he writing about ?"

" About that same Dora Dacres."

" Good heavens ! you don't mean to say that he has got the poor girl into his clutches again, do you ?"

" It is only too true."

The conference between the two brothers was here interrupted by the violent ringing of a bell, which the valet but too well recognised as his master's.

He started up, and bidding his brother to await his return, hastened to obey the summons.

As soon as he entered the room, the Duke of Kingston held out a small billet to him, bidding him at the same time to take it to the address with all dispatch.

The valet bowed and left the room.

As soon as he rejoined his brother, who had begun to grow impatient, although in reality, scarce five minutes had elapsed since Hillyard had left him to obey his master's summons—he, by the aid of a little lamp which burnt upon the table, read the following address—" To S. Turnbull, The Nag's Head, Edgeware Road."

" Hem !" said the valet when he had perused the superscription—" I would give something to know the contents of this precious epistle."

" Read it then," returned his brother.

" It's all very well to say read it, but how is it to be opened without a chance of discovery ?"

" Why, very easy indeed—give it to me."

The valet hesitated but for a moment, then delivering it to his brother, he said—

" Well, Fred, it seems to me that it can be no harm to find out what those two rogues and villains are about. You must be aware that I have never ceased to take an interest in the fate of my poor late master's daughter, and as we know it is against her they are plotting, why the best thing we can do is to make all the discoveries we can in order, if possible, to be of use to her."

" To be sure—to be sure. Now give it me."

Fred turned the billet over and over in

his hand as if by that process he thought its contents would in some miraculous way ooze out; but finding, at the expiration of some few seconds, that he was no nearer to them than he was on first taking the letter, he looked up at the valet and asked him to lend him a knife.

The valet in a few moments brought him what he required, and he then deliberately held the blade over the candle until it was hot enough to melt the wax without disturbing the impression.

It was a curious sight now to see those two men, each intent upon watching the success of their plan which was to lay bare, at least, part of a plot for the destruction of Dora.

At length the paper gave way, and it was with the greatest ease that Fred opened the sheet of paper, which was so folded as to render it impossible to get at the contents unless the letter had been so opened. It ran as follows—

"You have done well to communicate with me before taking any steps with regard to the person of whom you speak. You may expect me about mid-day tomorrow—when, rest assured, your services shall not go unrewarded—I shall not sign this,"

"Mid-day to-morrow!" repeated the valet.

Fred seemed lost in thought.

After a few moment's pause, he said suddenly—

"We must set her free before mid-day to-morrow!"

"Would that we could—but you know that it will be impossible for me to do anything, as his lordship, of course, cannot dispense with my services, even if I were to frame some excuse for my absenting myself."

"True, true! but I will try, for I have a feeling at my heart for the late Duke of Kingston, under whom I served, which will not allow me to know of a plot for the destruction of his child without lending her a helping hand.

"Thanks—thanks! a thousand thanks!" said the valet, holding out his hand to his brother, "and whatever happens, be sure to let me know."

"All right—but now I must go, as I have much to do before I can be of any service to Dora Dacres."

"We may as well walk together as far as we can," said the valet, "for I have, you know, to take this letter to the 'Nag's Head.'"

"Ah, I had forgotten!" added Fred, "let me secure the billet again."

This was the work only of a few minutes, and then the two brothers sallied out together.

And the Duke of Kingston! of what is he thinking as he sits in that luxurious drawing room, surrounded by every comfort which wealth can procure?

It is worth while to take a long look at his face.

To look upon that pale, haggard countenance, one would suppose, indeed, that years of care and suffering had conspired to give the stamp of the passing agony to it.

The paleness of his face was a kind of special paleness which may not be described.

His eyes seemed to be enlarged, and to have about them a most unnatural lustre. Every moment or two there was a nervous twitching of the muscles of the mouth, as though he intended to say something, and then left the words unspoken from secret dread of them or their consequences.

The slightest sound, too, would act like an alarm bell upon his heart, and he would start up with looks of terror and affright. In person he was thin to the very verge of emaciation.

He held a book in his hand, and appeared to read, but he turned the leaves restlessly, and it was evident that he took not the slightest interest in the meaning of the words.

"She is now in my power!" he muttered between his teeth. "One death more or less is of little consequence!" And as his thoughts reverted to the two ghastly spectacles that were only separated from him by a few yards, he shuddered.

"Yes, the duchess and Surlina," he continued, "have run their race—Dora alone stands in my path. Lionel is dead—must be dead, in spite of what was reported not long since at court—if he still lived, he would have made known his existence to Dora; and it is quite certain he has not done that from what she said the last time we met in the office of the lawyer in the Temple."

The duke rose from his chair, and paced the apartment with hasty, uneven strides, as he continued to talk to himself.

"Yes, my mind is made up. I will take this Dora Dacres to Ostend. Why should not she bear me company, since the fair Neoni has fled? Ah, I had almost forgotten her in the satisfaction of having found Dora! Where could she have hidden? I must search the palace—yes, I must search the palace before I leave England, or she may discover, by some means, that Surlina has been murdered, and then suspicion might attach to me through her means."

He approached the bell, and rang it violently.

His valet answered the summons.

"Well," he said, "did you deliver my note?"

"I did, my lord," said the valet, with a low bow.

"I will retire to my bed chamber now," said the Duke of Kingston, "and remember that I wish to be be awakened at seven o'clock to-morrow morning."

"I will not forget, my lord!" replied the valet; and taking a silver candlestick from one of the side tables, he preceded his master to his bed chamber.

The Duke of Kingston soon dismissed his valet, for there was a something about the man which he specially disliked. Might it not have been caused by the impossibility of two such opposite natures amalgamating, so to speak?

As soon as the door was closed, the duke muttered to himself—

"I must get rid of that man—he knows too much, I fear? Can he have any suspicion of the secrets contained in the next house? Well, well, I will soon rid myself of his presence. But now I must seek some rest, for I am weary."

He threw himself upon the bed, and after a time, fell into a troubled sleep, muttering ever and anon disjointed sentences, which betokened how ill at rest was that man who had spent so many years of his life in plotting and planning for his own aggrandisement, and the destruction of those whom it should have been a sacred duty to protect from the storms of life.

But this man, whose rest was but one troubled dream, how was he the envied of many an unhappy fellow-creature, who could see only the outward glitter which surrounded this false duke.

How very strange and instinctive a thing would it be to be able to peep behind the mask which all men wear to the world, and see the motives and passions that rule them. What a new and strange page in the history of human nature would that investigation open to us!

———

CHAPTER LV.

SHOWS HOW THAT A SUPPOSED ENEMY TURNS OUT TO BE A FRIEND AFTER ALL —HENRY, DORA, AND DOTTMAN BID ADIEU TO KENSINGTON PALACE.

WE must now return to Dora whom we left in company with her faithful servant and follower, Dottman, on the night of her narrow escape from the durance in which the villain, Turnbull, had placed her while waiting the commands and instructions of his patron and employer, the Duke of Kingston.

The torrent of tears which fell from the eyes of our heroine was a great relief to her overcharged heart, and in a few minutes she again raised her head, and holding out her hand to Dottman, she said—

"Do not chide me, dear friend, for these tears. I believe there is as great an admixture of joy as of sorrow in them. It was so fearful a thing to know that I was completely at the mercy of those two unscrupulous men.

Dottman pressed the hand of Dora with so much warmth, that it was not difficult to believe his total silence proceeded from a very different sensation than that arising from a want of sympathy.

The silence spoke volumes to Dora's grateful heart, and she was satisfied.

After they had gone some two hundred paces, however, Dottman turned to Dora, and said—

"To what two men did you refer a little while ago when you spoke of being in the power of those two men?"

"I forgot, dear friend, that you are in ignorance of all that has befallen me since we parted; but I will tell you in a few words. It is best, however, that we defer entering into particulars until we reach a more secure place in which to converse."

"You're right, captain; but I should just like to hear enough to satisfy my curiosity."

"You shall—you shall, my friend!" replied Dora; and then, in as few words as possible, detailed to Dottman all that she had suffered during the last few hours.

When she had finished, Dottman said—

"Well, captain, I'm heartily glad now that you took so much trouble about that young Hargrave, as it is quite certain he is a good sort of fellow. Perhaps some day we may have another chance of doing him a good turn."

At this moment Dora drew close to Dottman's side, and said in a whisper—

"We are observed—there is a man on the other side of the hedge. What shall we do?"

"Why, cry 'Stand!' to be sure, captain!"

"Oh, no, no!" said Dora, imploringly, "I cannot engage in any adventure to-night—do not ask me!"

"Leave it to me, then, captain; I'll soon find out if his business be with us or not!"

"Be cautious—oh, be cautious, Dottman, there may be others behind!" said Dora.

"All right, captain—I'll keep out of danger!"

As Dottman said these words, he called out in a voice sufficiently loud to be heard by the man who appeared to be dogging their movements.

"Hilloa, comrade! methinks the road-

THE RETURN OF DORA AND DOTTMAN TO KENSINGTON PALACE.

way is better travelling than the heavy fields!"

"Ay, ay, comrade," replied the man; "and if I mistake not, it is better travelling in the company of friends than alone on so dark a road.

"Perhaps so! but I should like to know my friend's name before I admit him into my company."

By this time the horseman had leaped the hedge, and coming up to Dottman, held out his hand.

"Why, comrade," he said, "do you not know me? I recognised you immediately by your voice. Do you forget Fred Hill-yard?"

Dora.—28.

"Goodness gracious!" said Dottman, as he grasped the speaker's hand. "Why, who would have thought of meeting you in England?"

"Ah, well! I've a long story to tell you, Dottman; but not now." Then dropping his voice to a whisper, he said—

"Who have you with you? for I have a bit of business on hand to-night in which I wish you to give me your assistance, for I have been disappointed of a fellow upon whose aid I counted. Can you trust your friend; for I take for granted that he is a friend as you were so particular upon that score when you first accosted me."

Dottman laughed as he replied, while he

made a motion with his hand for Dora to come forward.

"Whatever you have to say you may speak unreservedly before this gentleman. I have known him for many years, and you may trust him thoroughly."

"I'm glad to hear that," said Fred Hillyard; "for it will strengthen our party. But first of all tell me if you are willing to engage in the undertaking?"

"I can speak for myself, certainly; but my friend, here, is not well, and we were about to look for the nearest inn, in order that he might rest, when we observed you."

"Very well, we will ride on then, and at the first public house we come to your friend can stop, while we go on to that rascal Turnbull's house."

"Turnbull's house!" exclaimed Dottman—"why, what on earth business can take you there, man? You're surely not one of his men?"

"I hope I don't look much like one," said Fred, with a light laugh—"but notwithstanding, I hope to call upon that gentleman, and to take you with me."

"Well," said Dottman, "it's quite certhain there's something afloat of which I am at present in perfect ignorance, but if after hearing what you're got to say I think I can be of any use to you, why all well and good—I'm your man."

"You remember, then," said Fred, "serving with the late Duke of Kingston?"

The question almost paralysed both Dottman and Dora, but he replied as steadily as he could—

"I should think I do remember—God bless him!"

"So say I, comrade. Well, you must know that my brother is valet to the present duke."

"Ah!"

"Yes—well, there's nothing in that is there? An honest man may be servant to a knave, may he not?"

"Yes, yes—but go on—what do you wish me to do?"

"I'm coming to that part of my story presently. Now, my brother has come to the knowledge—no matter how—of a vile plot that is being concocted by the present Duke of Kingston and that villain Turnbull, for the destruction of our old master's only child.

"Oh Heaven!" ejaculated Dora, no longer able to restrain her emotion.

"Eh! what? do you know anything of the Duke of Kingston," asked Fred, turning round, so that he almost faced Dora; but the darkness was yet too great to enable him to discern her features.

"Oh, yes," replied Dora. "I seem to have known him well from hearing Dottman speak of him, and for that reason I take the greatest interest in his child."

"That's well," said Fred; "then perhaps you will not object to lend a helping hand to Dottman and myself, in order to set that daughter of the late Duke of Kingston at liberty, for she is now a prisoner in Turnbull's house, and the Duke of Kingston has written him, Turnbull, a note to say that he will meet him at his house, where Dora, who should be Duchess of Kingston, is now a prisoner.

As Dora listened to the words of this man, who was a perfect stranger to her, but who had expressed himself so willing to assist her out of respect to the memory of her father—that father who had lavished so much tenderness upon her, but who had been taken from her so suddenly and so unexpectedly, she let her head droop upon the neck of Starlight, and wept.

Fred Hillyard was puzzled.

After a few moments' silence he said to Dottman in a low voice—

"What is the meaning of your friend's distress? Does he know the daughter of our late officer?"

"I should think so," said Dottman; "for it is no other than Dora the Duchess herself who is before you."

"Gracious heavens!" exclaimed Fred, is it possible?" Then turning to Dora, he continued—

"Lady, I will ask no questions. Whatever you may desire to tell me I will listen to; and after what has passed between us this evening you will have no hesitation in trusting me, for you must be fully aware that my intentions are to serve you in any way that I possibly can."

"I do, indeed, trust you!" said Dora, raising her head, "and accept my grateful thanks for your kind intentions. I knew not that I possessed so sincere a friend in all the world, for Dora the fugitive and outcast is no longer remembered by those who used to regard her as a future duchess!"

"Well, let's hope for better days!" said Dottman, cheerfully. "And as we have now one more friend, let us hope that there are others yet behind who may be only waiting a fitting opportunity to testify their willingness to serve you."

"It may be so!" said Dora, sadly, "but I am weary of the life I now lead, and would that all were over, if it were not for Henry and my darling Mina."

Dora and Dottman now consulted with their new friend as to what was best to be done under existing circumstances.

"Well, I should say," replied Fred Hillyard, "you had better return home, wherever that may be, and wait there until

I can bring you intelligence as to what are the movements of the duke, your uncle."

"Be it so," said Dora. "And perhaps by to-morrow evening you will contrive to meet Dottman somewhere in the vicinity of Kensington Palace, and tell him what are your plans."

"Kensington Palace!" said Fred, and he gave a kind of prolonged whistle. "What on earth makes you fix upon the neighbourhood of Kensington Palace of all places in the world? Why, the Duke of Kingston has business of his own there, and we may come into unpleasant contact with his lordship just at a time when we least desire it."

"We know all about that," said Dottman, "and I am happy to say that, through our intervention, the little bit of business his lordship had on hand at the palace has been frustrated. But the fact is, we have taken refuge there, and have been located beneath the roof of the palace for some time now, and intend to remain there until we find a more suitable home."

"It'll never do!" said Fred, shaking his head. "It'll never do! for my brother told me that he heard the Duke of Kingston talking to himself, as is the custom with people who are ill at ease in their consciences, and he said that he intended to search every nook and corner of the palace before he left England."

"Indeed!" exclaimed Dottman and Dora in a breath. "I thought he had given up the search for Neoni!" added Dora.

"You seem to be better informed than myself as to the name of the person of whom he is in search. I fancied he might have heard that you had taken refuge there, and that he intended to seek for Mr. Dacres."

"I know not," said Dora; "but I am anxious, now that I know the duke is likely to visit the palace again, that we hasten to Henry and apprise him of the danger we run in remaining any longer there. What say you, Dottman? Had we not better hasten homewards as quickly as possible, and acquaint Henry with all that we have learnt?"

"I think that will be our wisest plan. And now, where is our friend, Fred Hillyard to hear of us? Let me think."

For a few moments there was a pause, for where could Dora now look for a home? But a thought—a remembrance of another friend, who had assisted her when in great peril, crossed the mind of Dora, and she said—

"I have it—I have it! Do you not remember Jim, the stable boy, who did me such good service? He told me if ever I wanted a friend to go to the old mill, at Crayford, and I should be sure to meet with kindness from his grandfather and grandmother."

"Oh, I know them well," said Fred. "You mean the Grays; as honest an old couple as ever breathed. Let me advise you to seek shelter with them until you hear from me, which, I trust, will be not later than to-morrow night."

"We will—we will!" said Dora; and there was a feeling at her heart, as she contemplated making the acquaintance of old Mr. and Mrs. Gray, for which she could not account.

Who shall say but that in some mysterious way, unaccountable to us, the mother's heart was drawn towards the roof that sheltered her innocent child?

"And now, good bye!" said Fred, extending his hand to Dora and Dottman, "and God speed."

"Farewell!" said Dora; and in a few minutes she and Dottman had ceased to hear the tramp of horses' feet, which bore from them as sincere and noble a heart as ever beat in human breast.

"So far so good!" said Dottman, as he gallopped his horse by the side of Dora. "So far so good! and now for Mr. Dacres."

A short time brought them within sight of Kensington Palace, and with a cry of joy Dora sprung from her horse, and entered, by the little gate, into the palace grounds.

In another five minutes she had reached Henry's apartment, and hastily turning the handle of the door, she entered the room, and was clasped in the arms of her husband, who was pacing the room in an agony of suspense.

"My Dora—my own darling!" he said again and again, as he kissed her pale cheek. "Look up, and speak to me! oh, tell me that you are uninjured!"

Dora had fainted.

Henry applied such restoratives as happened to be at hand, and he soon had the unspeakable satisfaction of seeing Dora open her eyes and look around her.

As her gaze fell upon Henry she clung to his breast, and hiding her eyes upon his shoulder, seemed only too anxious to exclude from them every surrounding object.

"Oh, what a frightful dream!" she said at length. "Oh, Henry, you are with me, and I am safe."

"Yes, yes, darling!" whispered Henry, "quite safe! and look at me, Dora, I am, almost well again, and hope, henceforth, to be ever able to protect you, dear one, from every danger."

Dora looked up, but the dreamy, abstracted look now gave way to one of intense anxiety, as she said—

"What am I doing, Henry? wasting valuable time—it is no dream I have had! but everything has been fearfully real! We must not sleep another night beneath the roof of Kensington Palace."

"Yes, yes, dear!" said Henry, soothingly, "we will leave this place if you wish it! but there is no need to use precipitation."

"But I tell you, Henry, there is! Dottman! oh, where is Dottman? he will tell you that the Duke of Kingston will be here before many hours have passed—perhaps he has already arrived."

"Well, but Dora, you are needlessly alarming yourself, dear! was he not here the night before last, but he did not see us!"

"But he will see us! But here comes Dottman."

Dottman at this moment entered the apartment, saying that soon as Mr. Dacres and Dora were ready to start, he had made all the necessary preparations.

Henry was now made aware of the perilous position of affairs; and when he was acquainted with all that Dora had gone through, and of the risk she still run of falling into the hands of the base and wicked Duke of Kingston, he aided in the arrangements for their departure, and the three friends bade adieu to the old Palace of Kensington to seek refuge among strangers.

"Oh, that the time were come," said Dora, as she took a last look at that palatial residence, which had proved a harbour of refuge to them, "Oh, that the time were come, when we could call even such a poor apartment as that we have just left, our own."

"Come, cheer up, captain!" said Dottman, cheerfully, "better times are coming, I feel certain. I never saw you look so cast down before!"

"There is an oppression at my heart for which I cannot account," said Dora. "It seems to me that coming events are casting their shadows before."

"I've felt just like that myself, captain," when something good was about to happen, so let's hope that will be the case with you."

"Heaven grant that it may be so in my case!" said Dora, with a sigh, as she suffered Henry to lead her to the little court, where Dottman had tied Starlight and the hunter to two trees.

"Mount, captain—and you, Mr. Dacres. You take the hunter, and I will meet you at Crayford soon after you get there."

"I do not like to leave you, dear old friend!" said Dora.

"Don't fear for me, captain, I shall be all right. I will beg, borrow, or steal a horse, and very likely I shall overtake you long before you expect to see me."

"Be it so then," said Dora; and in another moment she had mounted Starlight, dressed no longer as a knight of the road, but as a farmer's daughter might have equipped herself to carry to the neighbouring town such articles as her father's farm might have produced.

In another moment they had ceased to rivet Dottman's attention, for a turn of the road bore them from his sight.

CHAPTER LVI.

DORA AND HENRY SEEK THE OLD MILL AT CRAYFORD—MINA IS NO LONGER AN ORPHAN—A MOTHER'S JOY—THE DREAM OF HAPPINESS.

DORA and Henry pursued their way for some time in silence, each occupied with many painful thoughts.

The scenes of peril and excitement which Dora had lately undergone undermined, as we have seen, that elasticity of spirit which was so peculiarly her own, and she now felt, as she rode through those beautiful lanes, how utterly impossible it was for her to feel anything like pleasure or happiness while she was thus compelled to wander about, and seek for a home among strangers.

Henry broke the silence by saying—

"But, my Dora, how will your *soi-disant* friend know you in this garb? you look so different to what you must have done when he aided your escape."

"I have made up my mind, Henry, what to do. I intend to make myself known to him as the person whom he befriended, and I have no doubt but that he will recognise Starlight in a moment."

"True, true—I had forgotten that he took such a fancy to Starlight! let us hope the boy's grandfather may prove our friend, and at least grant us a refuge for a few days beneath their roof."

"I have no fears on that head!" said Dora, cheerfully, for she was particularly anxious that Henry should not be aware of the depression that had settled upon her spirits.

It was towards four o'clock in the afternoon that Dora and Henry reached Crayford, and they soon perceived the two mills which had been mentioned to Dora by the stable-boy, Jim.

A labourer happened to be passing at this moment, and Dora asked him to direct her to the "old mill."

"Eh?" said the man, as he looked up, more asleep, apparently, than taking any notice of any object in the outer world.

"Can you tell us which is the 'old mill,' my man?" said Henry.

"There be two mills! which on 'em do ye mean?"

"I mean the one which is called the 'old mill.'"

"But they be both old!" persisted the man

Henry made a gesture of impatience; but Dora thought she might have better success if she asked for Mr. Gray's Mill.

"Ye mean old John Gray! he ben't Mister Gray!"

"Yes, yes—John Gray I mean!" said Dora, fearful lest the man should finish his sleep before he answered her question.

"Well, then," he said, "ye see that there mill straight 'afore ye?"

"Yes," said Dora, "thank you—that is John Gray's?"

"No, it ben't—that be Ned Ratbone's."

"Then it is the other. Thank you—thank you, my good man!"

They were about to ride on, when the man called out to them to stop.

Dora and Henry drew up.

"I say, missus, I want to know how you *knowed* that there mill belonged to John Gray before I had time to tell you?"

Dora smiled at the man's simplicity, and she said kindly—

"I knew there were two mills; and when you told me the one straight before us was Ned Ratbone's, I concluded at once that the other must be that of John Gray."

The man scratched his head, and seemed still to think that Dora had come the knowledge by some very mysterious means.

Dora and Henry now quickened their horses' pace, for they were anxious to arrive at the miller's before dusk, thinking that would be surest means of gaining access to their hospitable abode.

They reached the door of the cottage.

Dora knocked with the handle of her whip.

It was soon opened by old Mrs. Gray.

At sight of two mounted figures the good old woman was taken somewhat aback, but looking into the sweet face of Dora, she soon recovered herself.

Have you a grandson, named Jim, my good woman?" asked Dora.

"Yes!" said Mrs. Gray. But she could say no more, for her thoughts reverted instantly to the fifty pound bank note, and she began to think that Henry and Dora had come to demand it.

"I thought we were right," said Dora, not noticing the evident trepidation of the old woman. "Can we see him?"

"He's out now, ma'am," said his grandmother, "but if you can leave any message, I will be sure to deliver it to him when he comes home—he's only gone to gather some blackberries with the little lady."

"Then," said Dora, "if you will allow me, I should like to wait here until he returns."

Poor Mrs. Gray could hold out no longer, but clasping her hands, she said, in an imploring voice—

"Oh, do not injure him! none of it is spent! it is locked up with the old Bible in a chest! He meant no harm, I assure you! he meant no harm when he took it."

"My good woman," said Dora, "what do you mean? On the contrary, we would do anything in our power to help your grandson?"

"But the note—the note!" continued the old woman, "I knew it would bring disgrace upon us!" And she wept as if her heart would break.

"Oh, I know now what you mean, my good friend. You mean a bank note for fifty pounds, which your grandson brought you not long ago."

"Alas, yes! But how did you know about it? he said he had not mentioned it to any one, and—"

"Nor has he!" interrupted Dora; "but when I tell you that I know the person quite well who gave him the note, and that that person has never forgotten the great service Jim rendered on that occasion, perhaps you will not mind allowing me to rest in your house until Jim comes home!"

"You know the person?" exclaimed old Mrs. Gray. "Why, it was Captain Hawk! as bad a man, if all I hear be true, that ever lived!"

"Oh, no!" said Dora, "the person who gave Jim that fifty pound note was a very different person, I hope, to Captain Hawk! Perhaps before I leave I may tell you, and Jim, too, who the person really was whom he mistook for Captain Hawk."

By this time Dora and Henry had dismounted, and had tied the bridles of their horses to the palings.

The old woman, who had seemed greatly reassured since she had heard that Captain Hawk was not the person who had made so munificent a present to her grandson, now bustled about to make her guests as comfortable as possible.

"And where is your husband?" inquired Dora.

Old Mrs. Gray stopped short in the act of giving a finishing touch to some article of furniture, and said, with some hesitation—

"John's out, ma'am; but he'll not be long before he returns."

There was a look of embarrassment about the old woman as she made this answer, which somehow raised Dora's curiosity.

"Does he often leave the mill, then? I should think you must be glad to have your grandson at home again, for it must be dull for you!"

The old woman was saved from replying to this last question, for at this moment the cottage door was flung open, and Jim, carrying in his arms "the little lady," as the miller and his wife always called Mina, entered.

Mina was asleep.

Her hair had fallen over the boy's shoulder, and the little arms were thrown caressingly round his neck.

At the sight of the sleeping child, Dora's heart beat quickly, for she thought of her own darling, and longed, for her sake, to fold the little one in her arms.

Little did Dora imagine that that little one was her own lost Mina.

But now, as she reaches the boy's side, she gives a start and a shriek, and clings to that child as though nought on earth could now separate them.

"My child! my Mina! my darling! Henry, our little one!" was all poor Dora could say.

Her cries awoke Mina, who looked around with her large wondering blue eyes, as if to gather the meaning of that strange cry, and the fond embrace in which she now found herself.

At last the little Mina is thoroughly aroused from that sweet sleep into which she had fallen, having tired herself with play, and raising her little hand, she softly stroked Dora's cheek, saying as she did so—

"Mrs. *Dray* said she would take me to my mamma."

We cannot attempt to describe the scene which followed in the cottage—it is far beyond human cognisance; but there were smiles and tears, laughter and deep sobs, and prayers and thanksgivings to Heaven.

Good Mrs. Gray, as soon as she understood what was the state of affairs, made signs to Jim to follow her into another room of the cottage, for with true delicacy, innate alike in gentle and simple, the old woman thought it would be best to leave the newly-found child alone with her parents for a short time.

"My Mina! my own darling!" again repeated Dora, as she kissed the golden ringlets which lay upon her lap.

"Heaven has saved her for us! Oh, Henry, I feel now as if all our trials were at an end!"

Henry was as much affected by the sudden appearance of Mina as Dora had been, and it was some minutes before he could trust himself to speak.

"Heaven be praised!" at length he ejaculated, "I, too, Dora, feel now that I can do battle with the world for you and this little one! We will hope now, that this, our greatest misfortune, has passed away, and that as we are all united, our future may yet be bright and happy."

"We will hope—we will hope my Henry! But now let us see these good people who have protected our little one, and thank them, as well as we can, for all that they have done for us!"

"Shall I fetch Jim?" asked the little Mina, perfectly unconscious of the emotion experienced by her father and mother.

"I will go with you to fetch him," said Dora. For now the mother's heart began to fill with vague fears that some untoward circumstance might again separate her from her newly found treasure.

"Go, dearest," said Henry, "and I will wait here until you return.

Dora had not to be long absent, for in that humble cottage there were no stately corridors to traverse to reach from one room to another; as she opened the door of the apartment in which they had been seated with their little one, it led them immediately into the room to which Jim and his grandmother had retired.

Dora entered the room, holding her little Mina by the hand, and the child had twined both her little hands around her mother's arm, and was pressing it to her lips.

Old Mrs. Gray rose as they entered the room, for although Dora was clad in humble garments, there was that unmistakable *distingué* air about her which made old Mrs. Gray feel at once that she stood in the presence of a superior.

Dora noticed the action, and springing forward, and taking both the old woman's hands in hers, she said as she knelt at her feet.

"How can I—how can we ever thank you sufficiently, my dear, kind friend, for what you have done for our precious child?"

Mina here drew her mother's attention to Jim, who was evidently in great trouble, for by this time his grandmother had been able to make him understand that henceforth he must not think of little Mina for a playmate.

"Look, mamma!" said Mina, "look at poor Jim! what is he crying about? Speak to him, mamma."

Dora turned towards the boy who was seated by a deal table, his head rested in his hands, and it was quite certain this was his first trial.

As Dora's eyes rested upon the boy, she recollected how much he had also done for her, and laying her hand kindly upon his shoulder, she said—

"Are you sorry, then, Jim, that Mina has found her father and mother?"

"Yes," said the boy through his tears, "because grandmother says I shall never see her again."

At this moment Mina glided from her mother's side, and putting her little arms round the boy's neck—

"Yes, you shall see me again, Jim! Mamma shall take you home with me, and we will always play together, and you shall swim your boat at my home, shan't he, mamma?"

Dora heaved a deep sigh, and again taking old Mrs. Gray by the hand, she said—

"I was about to ask you a favour when I came here to-day, but now that I know how deep an obligation I have already incurred I dare scarcely venture to do so."

"Speak—oh, speak, madam!" said Mrs. Gray. "I am but a poor creature, but I trust my heart is warm towards my fellow-creatures. We love your little one, and would do anything to serve you, if it be in our power."

Dora drew the old woman aside, and then made known to her sufficient of their history to enlist all the kindly sympathies of the noble heart which beat beneath that humble robe.

"You can stay here and welcome!" replied the old woman, when Dora had made her acquainted with their reasons for wishing to be as retired as possible until they were in a position to justify them in taking steps for the recovery of their rights. "You are welcome to stay here, if so be you can put up with such poor accommodation as our poor cottage can afford."

"Thanks—thanks! a thousand thanks!" said Dora, "but I must tell you before-hand, that we are not poor, we shall be able to refund to you whatever you may have kindly laid out for our dear child."

"No, no!" interrupted the old woman. "Not one farthing will I receive of what we have spent upon that sweet child! she has been like an angel in the house ever since the night she entered it."

"Well, well," said Dora, "as you will! provided you will accept this note, as in part payment for our board and lodging so long as we remain here."

"I'll not say no to that, madam, for we are too poor to board a lady and gentleman like you and your husband, so I'll take that and lay it out to the best advantage."

"That I am quite sure you will. And now, Jim," said Dora, "I want you to tell me what you have been doing with yourself since last we met?"

The boy raised his head from his hands, on which it had been resting since his grandmother had explained to him the state of affairs, and staring at Dora, he said—

"I have never seen you before, but I know your horse, it belongs to Captain Hawk."

"But do you not remember saving a gentleman when he was in danger of being captured, on account of some people thinking that, because he happened to be riding his horse, he must needs be Captain Hawk himself?"

"Oh, yes, I remember that gentleman very well! and he gave me a fifty pound note, which I gave to my grandmother, but she won't spend it, because she thinks he did not come by it honestly."

Dora smiled, and then laying her hand on the boy's shoulder, she said—

"I gave you that note, Jim."

"You?" exclaimed the boy. "Then are you not Mina's mamma after all? Hurrah! hurrah! then she will stay with us."

"You mistake me," said Dora; "I am Mina's mamma, but I hope that I am not going to take her away so far but that you may come and see her as often as you like."

The boy sprung to his feet, and testified his joy at the prospect of seeing "the little lady" as often as he liked, by executing a kind of war dance all round the room.

The little Mina now looked perfectly contented and happy as she nestled close by her mother's side.

We will now leave this happy household, and return to those who have been already too long neglected.

CHAPTER LVII.

THE TWO FRIENDS—THE MAN IN GRAY RESOLVES TO SEEK MINA—DORA MEETS WITH A JOYFUL SURPRISE.

IN a magnificent furnished apartment in one of the first hotels at the West End, were seated, one bright afternoon, towards four o'clock, two gentlemen.

The elder of the two friends had thrown himself back into the recesses of a luxurious easy chair, and there was a thoughtful, even sad expression about the eyes, an expression which women, however, would call "beautiful."

His companion, who might have been, perhaps, some few years younger, was, in every respect, the very opposite in disposition and in looks. All about Lionel, formerly Duke of Kingston, but who, from being mixed up in some Jacobite plots, was living as a fugitive in his native land, was rigid and firm—while all about Eustace Pearson, Lord Rutherford, was easy and graceful as a child.

"You were only, then, in jest," said the father of Dora, for it was, indeed, he, "when you said that it would be easy to obtain my pardon, and be reinstated?"

"Far from jesting, my dear friend, I have every hope that the desire of your heart will now soon be accomplished, for I intend, myself, to present a petition to His Majesty, beseeching him to grant your pardon, even as he did mine, and to reinstate you in your former and proper position in society."

"The desire of my heart!" repeated the Duke of Kingston, for by his rightful title will we now designate him, although that title was then wrongfully enjoyed by his brother, the false duke. "The desire of my heart! Alas, my friend! you little know a father's feelings when you talk of the reinstatement to my title and estates as being the desire of my heart! Would that I could disabuse my Dora, my beloved child, of the idea that I am no more!"

"All in good time—all in good time, my friend!" interrupted Lord Rutherford, "it will not be safe for you to make yourself known to any one until after you have obtained the king's pardon, then all will be easy enough."

"But my child!" pursued the duke, "to what perils is she exposed! Each moment my heart trembles to think that, to serve his own vile purposes, my unnatural brother, this false duke, may succeed in accomplishing his plans for her destruction. What would then be wealth and honours to me?"

As the duke uttered these last words, he clasped his hands, and buried his head in the cushions of the chair on which he was seated.

"Courage—courage, my friend!" said Lord Rutherford, "a few days now will suffice to place you in such a condition that you will be enabled to make yourself known, not only to Dora, but to all the world, and surely, as you have so long denied yourself the happiness of making known to her that you are still, as you have ever been, watching over her—surely, I say, you will not mar all by a precipitate declaration now?"

The Duke of Kingston raised his head, and holding out his hand to Lord Rutherford, said—

"I feel, dear friend, the value of your advice, and I will still restrain the yearning of this poor, desolate heart, to press to it my beloved child, because, by so doing, I may be doing what is best for her as well as for myself; but I begin to feel that so long a time has elapsed since these eyes were blessed with a sight of her dear face, that you must forgive what, perhaps, seems to you undue impatience."

"Not at all—not at all!" returned his friend, "and it was to give you some tidings of your daughter's child that I requested you to come to me to-day."

"Tidings of Mina? Oh, heaven be praised! Is she well? I have heard nothing of her since she was abandoned in that boat on the river. Speak—oh, speak!"

"I have every reason to believe," said Lord Rutherford, "that the little Mina is well and happy, and has found refuge in the house of an honest miller and his wife, at Crayford, and that—"

"Oh, let me go to her, and see for myself! I have never ceased to reproach myself for ever having lost sight of her. Oh, say that there will be no danger in my going to ascertain for myself that the child of my Dora is yet alive and well!"

Lord Rutherford thought for a few minutes, and then he said—

"Perhaps I was wrong to have said this much to you! I know not even if it be Mina—but from the description I hoped that it might be her."

"Yes, yes! oh, let me go! No one will recognise in the careworn man, the former Duke of Kingston—the child herself will have forgotten me! But oh, let me seek this miller, and see for myself whether it be *her* child or not."

"Well, be it so!" replied Lord Rutherford. "But promise me to be guarded, or you may ruin all."

"Trust me—oh, trust me!" said the duke. "And now for Crayford!"

"Nay, my friend, it is too late to start to-night! you would get there after the inmates of the quiet little cottage, in which I have every reason to believe your grandchild is domciled, will have retired to rest, so make up your mind to let these be your quarters to-night, and then you shall start as early as you like to-morrow."

"Perhaps it will be best," said the duke, sadly. "But oh, how I long once more to look upon that child's face!"

Lord Rutherford and the Duke of Kingston, now that matters were so far arranged, began to give themselves up to that kind of conversation which was sure to take place between two persons whose minds were so richly stored with every kind of information as were theirs—cemented by a friendship, which all the shafts of adversity had been powerless to sever.

Hour after hour passed, and Lord Rutherford had the satisfaction of seeing the old smile return to the lips of his friend, that was wont to rest upon them in former years, and as they bade each other "good night," there was a look of peaceful serenity upon the countenance of the old Duke of Kingston which rejoiced his friend.

THE MEETING OF DORA AND HER FATHER.

As soon, however, as Lionel, the real Duke of Kingston had retired to the apartment which had been prepared for him, he threw himself upon an ottoman and seemed lost in deep thought—a few words now and then broke from him, more as if he were thinking aloud than if he were conversing.

"Can it be possible that I shall ever be able to raise my head and meet fearlessly the gaze of my fellow men? but, after all, was not Eustace also once a proscribed Jacobite? he has obtained his king's pardon, and may not I hope to do the same? And my child, my Dora, so good and beautiful, will she too, ever be able to take her proper standing in society?"

DORA.—29.

The duke leant his head upon his hands, and seemed to give himself up to some bright vision of fancy, for when he raised it again there was a smile upon his intellectual countenance which lighted it up with an expression which partook of the beauty that had belonged to it before time and care had laid their hand upon that head and changed its raven locks to grey.

He now rose from the chair and sought that repose of which he felt he stood so much in need.

We will leave this good and noble heart now for awhile, and follow his wicked brother, the false Duke of Kingston, who was at that precise moment seeking repose also; but by what different feelings were the two brothers actuated!

Lionel, so good, so noble, and gentle, the companion of children, had never been able to gain the confidence of his younger brother, even in childhood—when they shared alike in the caresses of their parents; and as they grew in years, the gulf seemed rather to widen than decrease between them.

Reginald was ever stern and fitful in temper, silent and reserved to all around him—but his brother, who was a general favourite—perhaps for that very reason—appeared to be his chief aversion.

Behold then, these two brothers, the one hunted and oppressed—yet enjoying a peaceful slumber—the other, surrounded by every luxury which wealth could give—tossing about on a sleepless couch, and longing for the dawn that he might be up and doing deeds of which his conscience upbraided him day and night.

"I can bear this no longer," he said, as he started from his couch, "I can bear this no longer! I wonder what time it is?"

By the light of a little shaded lamp, which stood by the bedside, he could see the time by his watch, and found that it was just four o'clock.

"Three hours yet to wait before Hillyard comes; but I will arrange some of my papers while I am waiting."

Taking a key from a little casket which stood upon a little table, he approached an escrutoire which was in his dressing-room, and opened one of the drawers.

He took from this drawer a handful of letters, and carelessly threw them on one side, saying as he did so—

"They will be better destroyed—*she* is dead now, and it will be better so."

As he uttered these words, he lighted a wax taper, and held the letters one by one over the candle until all were destroyed—letters in which in words of affection the unfortunate Duchess of Kingston had plighted her faith to the faithless man who had been accessory to her death — her murder indeed.

The false duke breathed a sigh of relief when the last of the packet was reduced to ashes.

"It is well," he said. "I will now visit Surlina, for the last time, yes the last time—perhaps he yet lives, and may not keep my secret so well as I could wish if I leave him behind me—yes, I will go and visit him—of what need I be afraid? did I not see him die—die before my eyes?"

Stealthily, like some midnight assassin, did the duke cross the corridor which led to the staircase by which he could reach the drawing-room, and having entered the apartment, he turned quickly and locked the door behind him.

"No prying eye must watch my movements—but I must look upon Surlina again, to assure myself of his death—pshaw! why do I tremble? am I become a poor weak girl that I fear to look upon the face of the dead?"

He advanced towards the painting behind which was the secret spring that opened the panel which led to the house in the occupation of Surlina.

He touched the spring, the panel yielded to his hand.

"It is well," he muttered, "for the last time I enter this house—now for Surlina!"

The duke traversed the passage, and at length arrived at the door of the staircase, at the entrance of which he had left Surlina, pierced with, as he believed and hoped, a mortal wound.

He held his breath as he listened for any sound—any indication that life, instead of death, was on the other side of that door.

All was profoundly still.

He placed his hand upon the handle of the door and gently turned it.

It yielded to his touch.

Lying on his face was the Greek, and so still and immoveable was he that the duke felt that his treacherous weapon had done its work effectually.

"Ha, ha! my friend, you sleep well," came from the lips of the false duke, "it is well, it is well—sleep on, sleep on—now for Neoni!"

It will be remembered that it was just at this juncture that Neoni had fled from the house to seek the assistance of Doctor Lane, and it fortunately happened that the duke had so timed his visit to the Greek, that he did not encounter the heart-broken girl.

As soon as he had satisfied himself that Surlina was no more, he hastily closed the door and returned by the way he came, to his own house, when he lost no time in regaining his dressing room.

At seven o'clock Hillyard knocked at the door of the dressing room, and was somewhat surprised to find that his master had not undressed, for he still wore the same dress he had on the evening before.

"Be ready to start with me at four o'clock, Hillyard," he said. "I am going out this morning, but shall want no attendant—tell Jones he need not go with me as I arranged last night. I shall be back by four."

The valet bowed and retired.

In another hour the false duke was on his way to Turnbull's house, where he hoped to make a capture of Dora—but the reader is already aware of the disappointment which awaited him in that quarter.

And where is Lionel, the rightful owner of those fine estates which have been usurped by his brother?"

Mounted on a horse belonging to Lord Ruterhford, he was making his way towards the old mill in the occupation of miller Gray and his wife, in the hope of seeing the lost Mina. Little did he think that his Dora, his beloved child had found a refuge, too, beneath its humble roof.

The sun was now high in the heavens, as the duke, dressed in the grey cloak which he had lately worn for the purpose of concealment, rode slowly towards the mill.

All was calm and peaceful about the humble cottage—but how fixedly did he regard every window in hopes that at one or other his eyes might be blessed with the sight of a child's face.

He had been thus engaged for some time, when the cottage door opened and Jim, the playmate of the little Mina, came out.

At the sight of the horseman the boy looked up with an inquiring look upon his countenance.

"Holloa! my lad," cried the duke, "can you tell me if Mr. Gray is within?"

"He is at the mill, sir," said the boy—"but I will go and tell him if you wish to see him."

"Do so then— and in the meantime, I will rest in the cottage if I shall not be intruding."

By this time Mrs. Gray appeared on the threshold of the door, and, making a low curtsey, asked the duke to step in and wait while she sent to the mill for her husband.

The duke dismounted, and having tied his horse to the pailing in front of the cottage, entered the neatly furnished parlour.

How rapidly did he gaze about him as he entered the apartment; but no child, nothing to indicate a child having been there met his view.

He heaved a deep sigh, and threw himself into the first chair that presented itself.

"Alas, alas!" he murmured, "my last hope has vanished!"

In another room in that cottage was a lady seated, apparently reading, but if a close observer had regarded her, he would have seen that her eyes were not bent upon the page, but rested upon the beautiful child who was playing at her feet.

As it was not thought prudent for either Henry or Dora to shew themselves, the good miller and his wife always took care to apprise them whenever they saw visitors approaching their cottage.

It was the case in this instance. The old woman had seen the gentleman in grey mounted upon a horse, making his way to the cottage, and had lost no time in acquainting Dora and her husband with the fact—thus it was that no vestige of them remained in the room to which the visitor had been conducted.

Old Mrs. Gray bustled about the room, apparently quite absorbed in the domestic duties, but in reality, taking in at a glance all that met her eye or ear.

"Did you speak, sir?" inquired Mrs. Gray, as the duke made an exclamation expressive of his disappointment.

"I had hoped," he said—"I had hoped to find one here for whom I would peril my life to shelter—a little child—but I have been misled, I have been misled, I ear."

"There was some talk about here a few days ago," replied the old woman, keeping her eyes fixed upon his face, "there was some talk about a child being seen in the meadows hard by, but whether it was true or not—"

"Stop! tell me—was she fair—a little girl, beautiful as an angel? Speak, oh speak—tell me—

So excited had he become that the visitor forgot at the moment all else in his desire to behold the little Mina; and it was not until the alarmed look upon the face of the good old woman recalled him, so to speak, to himself, that the Duke of Kingston was made aware of the strangeness of his behaviour.

But the high excited tones in which he had last spoken had procured for him another listener than the old woman, for at the half open door might now have been seen the slight and graceful form of Dora, her beauty enhanced by the rich, golden tint her hair took in some lights. Her face was one which for expression alone would have pleased a painter, for there was a world of thought and feeling in the deep blue eye, and intellect on the broad, noble brow—that charm about the whole face which immediately attracted.

In another moment she stood before the duke, in whom she only recognized that strange man in grey who had so often befriended her and Henry.

"Dear, kind friend," she said, as she clasped both his hands in hers. "Do we meet again? Oh, let me here thank you for much that I know you have done for me and mine; and I feel, at the same time, that there are many benefits of which we have been recipients which, coming from an unknown hand, must, I know, have been received from you."

The Duke of Kingston did not withdraw his hand, but a feeling of happiness too deep for words, took possession of him, and the brave man, the fearless soldier, felt as he held the hands of his beloved child in his, that it was not in the power of his enemies now to disturb that peace to which he had so long been a stranger.

He threw to the floor the cloak in which he had been enveloped, and removing a wig which had covered his once raven hair, but which was now sprinkled with grey, he held Dora at arm's length, saying—

"And am I, my child, so well disguised that you fail to recognize me? Dora, my child—my Dora! do you not know your father?"

With a wild cry of joy Dora threw herself upon his breast, and kissed his hands, and passed hers caressingly over those whitened locks as she said—

"Dearest father, oh, how is it that we meet again—I believed you dead and lost to me for ever? Oh, why did you not make yourself known to me in the Savoy? My heart yearned to you—oh, surely it was not like you to let me mourn for you as dead, when in reality you were watching over my safety and that of those who are dearer to me than life?"

"Not now, not now, my child!" returned the duke, "can I tell you the motives which actuated me. Suffice it to say that all was meant in kindness—but now tell me of your child—your Mina—it was to seek her I came here, little dreaming I should be so blessed as to find you, my Dora!"

"She is here—she is here, dear father! but so overjoyed was I at finding in my kind benefactor a much dearer relation, I had almost forgotten her—but I will fetch her."

There was no need to fetch the little Mina, for Henry had been anxiously listening to all that had passed between Dora and the duke, and opening the door at this moment, entered the apartment.

CHAPTER LVIII.

NEONI DIES BESIDE HER FATHER'S CORPSE —THE HAPPY REUNION — DOTTMAN'S SUCCESSFUL SEARCH FOR THE LOST JEWELS.

WHEN the kind physician stood with Neoni beside the insensible form of Surlina, the look upon his countenance but too fully justified the fears which had from the first taken possession of his child.

Doctor Lane shook his head, and turning to Neoni, said gently but firmly—

"You were right in supposing it was a case of life and death, my poor child—alas, it is too late—the vital spark has fled!"

Neonia uttered not a word — the lips paled a little, and then she said steadily—

"Do you mean that my father is dead?"

"He has left this world of suffering for a better, I hope," replied the physician, in a low calm voice.

Neoni seemed now fully to realize the heavy affliction which had visited her—yet she spoke not a word—but it might be seen in the deadly pallor of her face, in the lines of suffering which now lightly crossed her brow—in the wan haggard look that should never have been known to one who had scarcely numbered eighteen summers.

At length, holding out her hand to Doctor Lane, she said—

"Thank you—I would now be alone with him!" pointing to her father.

The kind physician took her hand and gently retaining it in his, endeavoured to lead her from the room.

"No, no! do not seek to take me from him now—I am calm—do you not see that I am calm? Fear not for me."

Doctor Lane, clever physician though he was, and skilful in reading the human countenance, as he considered himself to be, yet failed to detect what lay under that cold calm exterior of the young girl, and remembering that his patients would be waiting his coming, he allowed himself to be persuaded to leave the Greek girl alone.

She returned to the passage in which she had discovered her father.

There was a dreamy look about her eyes now, which was not there when talking to Doctor Lane—if it had been, his practised eyes might have feared for her reason.

She glided close up to the inanimate form, and crouched down by its side.

Then she took one of the stiffened hands in hers, and rocking herself to and fro, as one would try to pacify a sick child.

"Hush! hush!" she said, "do not wake him yet—we are going to the sunny isles when he wakes from this slumber."

For some moments she still sat there, looking so lovely, yet so lonely and desolate —her hair had escaped from beneath the fanciful turban which she had put on as she sat there watching by the dead, and it now fell in masses, black as night, forming a natural veil around her.

There was a wistful look about her eyes as she now contemplated her father's face, which she had raised from the floor and laid lovingly in her lap—she bent lower and lower to feel the breath fan her cheek—but in vain—at length, with a shriek, she called upon her father, and with that wild shriek seemed to come to her the full conviction that she was fatherless, and abandoned.

She started to her feet, and dashing aside

the hair which fell across her brow, she hastened from the passage.

On—on she sped, until she reached the laboratory, and then snatching from the shelf the vial which contained the violet-coloured liquid of which she had administered three drops to her father—

"This—this!" she said, holding the bottle up to the light, "this will enable me to rejoin my father on the long journey upon which he has set out—yes, I remember he told me ten drops would be sufficient to rid the world of the false Duke of Kingston—I will take the ten drops, and bless Fate for having put in my power the means of leaving this cold dreary world."

Clasping the vial tight in her left hand, she hurried back to her father.

There was upon the face of the beautiful girl a look of calm despair, and sinking down beside her idolized father, and taking his hand in hers, she pressed it to her lips, saying—

"Soon—soon, dearest father and only friend, your Neoni's spirit will rejoin yours, and in that far-off land where all is joy and peace, we may yet know peace and love and joy."

She raised the vial to her lips, and drank the contents.

In a few minutes her head sunk lower and lower, until it rested upon her father's breast, and then she sunk into a profound slumber.

A slumber that was to know no awaking in this life.

Neoni's spirit had winged its flight to those realms of the Unknown, where she hoped at last to meet with love and joy and peace.

We will not here contemn the lonely orphan for the means to which she had resorted—we will hope that He who reads the heart would be less severe in His judgment than would be frail weak man.

We must now return to a happier picture.

In that same magnificent apartment which had already been the place of meeting between the two friends, Lionel, Duke of Kingston, and Lord Rutherford, might be seen a young and beautiful woman—her fair hair was hanging in ringlets about her shoulders, and the spring light which entered the room through an open window played among her tresses, making them look golden in places.

At her feet was a lovely child, and the likeness which was apparent between them would lead anyone to the conclusion that they stood in the close relationship of mother and child.

Our reader has already divined that these two were none other than Dora and Mina.

There is a look of expectation upon the young mother's face, and ever and anon she turns her head towards the door of the apartment, as if expecting some one to enter.

At last there was a knock at the door, and upon Dora saying "Come in!" our old acquaintance, Dottman, made his appearance.

"Oh, Dottman!" exclaimed Dora, as she seized him by the hand, "where have you been? You know not how anxious we had become about you—you promised to overtake us before we reached Crayford."

"All right, cap—"

Dottman paused, for Dora looked anything but a captain in her present attire—in fact, so feminine did she look that Dottman seemed scarcely to realise the fact that he stood before the handsome Captain Arod.

"Captain no longer!" she said, with a smile, "but I see you look puzzled, my friend, for you know not of the change in our prospects."

"Change in your prospects, cap—Miss Dora—I mean Mrs. Dacres."

"I see that good Mrs. Grey has kept our secret well, and that she has only told you where you might find me."

"Exactly so—but what has happened?"

"I have seen my father, Dottman?"

"Your father?" gasped Dottman, for we have already stated this brave man feared no living man, he yet had a superstitious feeling about the dead, and at the moment he knew not whether Dora had had too many shocks during the last three months, so that her reason was unsettled, or whether she had been visited by a spirit from the other world.

Do not look so alarmed," said Dora, as she perceived the look of amazement which had come over the face of Dottman, "my father is not dead—his wicked brother spread the report, and my father, prosecuted on account of the part he took in some Jacobite plots, was content to let the report spread for a time, until—"

"Then the Duke of Kingston—the rightful Duke of Kingston—my old master—really lives?"

"Even so, Dottman—and is anxious to be able to express to you all he feels for your devotion to his child."

The intelligence was so sudden, so unexpected, that Dottman was obliged to sink into a chair, for although he had ever looked forward to Dora yet taking her proper place in society, his wildest dreams had never pictured to him the possibility of his old master being yet in life.

Dora took this opportunity of going into an inner apartment, and returned in a few minutes, carrying in her arms her long lost Mina.

The child looked wonderingly from her mother to the rough old man, who to her childish imagination appeared to be ill, and as the best remedy that suggested itself to her on the spot, she raised a large doll from the floor, and said—

"There, you may play with that—Mina doesn't want it for a long time."

"Bless your little kind heart!" said the veteran, as he placed his horny hand upon the silken tresses of the beautiful child, "Bless your little heart—I never thought to see this day!" and the old man now fairly wept.

At this moment footsteps were heard approaching along the long corridor, and the 'door was opened to admit Henry Dacres, Lord Rutherford, and the Duke of Kingston.

As soon as the latter perceived Dottman, he held out both his hands to him, and the mute pressure, for his emotion at perceiving one who had so often been the preserver of his Dora was too great for words, testified how great was the obligation incurred.

While this had been passing, Lord Rutherford had taken the opportunity of acquainting Dora with his intention of presenting a petition to His Majesty for the pardon of her father, which petition he hoped to present on the following Thursday.

"But where is my uncle?" asked Dora with some anxiety.

"Have no fears on his account—his power to injure you and yours will soon be at an end, and the time, I hope, is not far distant when you will be able to think over the past as a troubled dream."

"Heaven grant that it may be so," said Dora with a hopeful smile; and turning round, she perceived that Dottman wished to say something.

"Speak, dear friend; I can see by your looks that you have something of importance to communicate."

"Well, it's just this," said Dottman, taking from beneath his apparel a small iron chest.

"What have you got there," said Henry laughing. "You don't mean to say you have been crying 'Stand!' in the broad face of day?"

"Not exactly, Mr. Dacres; but you see somehow I couldn't rest satisfied until I had examined the ruins of Captain Hawk's cottage, for I knew fast enough that if the little chest had not been seen by somebody it must still be in the ruins, so accordingly I made my way there as soon as you had both started, and hiding myself beneath the hedge, I waited until everybody who had come to have a look at the place had taken their departure."

"Nobody supposed there was anything worth taking or looking for even among the ruins, so I fancied I should not have a bad chance of regaining our lost jewels. My search was successful, and here they are, all right.

As Dottman spoke he opened the little chest, and sure enough there lay undisturbed the magnificent jewels and precious stones which Dora had thought was lost to them for ever.

In a few words Lord Rutherford was made acquainted with the history of the jewels which had come into possession of Dora and her husband.

"Why, these are indeed a fortune in themselves," he said, bending over the chest. "Let me congratulate you upon such an accession of riches."

There was a moment's pause, and then Dora said—

"I could at one time have appropriated these jewels and precious stones, but since they came into my possession I have met with one whom I think has a greater right to them than myself."

"You mean Neoni, the Greek girl," said Henry.

"Even so, for it was from her father—whom we have every reason to believe is no more—that I took them, and if she is now left an orphan, she will have more need of these things than I, for have I not you and my Mina?"

"It is like you, my Dora," said Henry, with a fond smile—"and we will take the first opportunity of making known to Neoni her acquisition of wealth.

"Ah! that reminds me," said Dora—"I had forgotten her in the excitement of the last two days. When she left you, Henry, for the purpose of searching for her father, did she tell you where she intended to go?"

"No," replied Henry—"she seemed anxious that I should not question her on the subject, and, therefore, I forbore; but I must confess I am somewhat anxious to know what has become of her."

Dottman here stepped forward saying that if Dora and Henry could dispense with his services for a short time, he thought it would be advisable to go and see if Neoni had returned to the house that was in the occupation of her father."

"And I will go with you, Dottman," said Dora. "I have nothing now to fear from the false duke, my uncle; for have I not the pardon which he endeavoured to destroy, in order that I might be executed, so that he might usurp my father's property without fear of any one disputing with him his right to the title and estates?'

"As you will—but I think it would be much better for me to go alone, rather than that you should expose yourself to any possible disagreeableness that might arise from an encounter with the Duke of Kingston."

"I have no fears," said Dora, turning to Henry, "but that you will not give me your permission."

"Nay, dearest, do as you think best in the matter. I think if Neoni be in any trouble she would like to feel you were near her, and you might afford her great assistance in the way of counsel should it turn out as we fear it may, that her father has come to an untimely end."

"We will go at once," said Dora—"shall we walk or ride?

"Why, I think that we had better walk," said Dottman—"it is but a short distance from here, and we shall be embarrassed to know what to do with the horses."

"True, true," said Dora—"wait for me here and I shall not be long before I rejoin you."

In a few minutes Dora returned equipped for her walk to St. James's Square, where was situated the mansion of the false Duke of Kingston, and adjoining which was that which had formerly been in the occupation of the Greek and his daughter.

Dottman was at no loss to effect an entrance into the apparently deserted house, for he had retained the key which, upon a former occasion, had done him such good service—that key which the false duke had left in the lock, and which he, Dottman, had not been slow in appropriating.

When they reached the house, they paused a moment to observe if they had been followed, but all was quiet, for the hour was early. A single carriage alone passed them—the carriage of Doctor Lane, who had been persuaded by Neoni to leave her alone.

Dottman produced the little latch key and opened the hall door.

Dora and he entered the once handsome hall, but there was now a look of gloom about it, and Dora felt a thrill pass through her frame as she said in a whisper—

"It seems as though we were entering some huge sepulchre, Dottman—does it not strike cold and unearthly?"

"It does, indeed, but let us not waste time. We will make our way to the laboratory at once, for it is there most probably that we shall find the poor girl."

They ascended what had once been called the grand staircase—up and down the stone steps of which had passed the gay, the beautiful, and the happy.

Now all looked sombre and dark, and Dora felt that even now she could have turned and fled from that house, had it not been for the one thought that she

might be of use to the beautiful girl, whom she feared was now indeed an orphan and friendless.

In another moment they had reach the laboratory.

It was tenantless!

Dora breathed more freely.

"I was almost afraid," she said, turning to Dottman, "of what we might encounter in this apartment—it is a positive relief to find it empty."

"Well, now I advise," said Dottman, "that you remain here while I go and have a look in all the rooms, so that we may be sure the Greek girl is not in the house."

"No, no," said Dora—"I will not turn coward now—we will go together, Dottman."

CHAPTER LIX.

DORA IN DANGER—DOTTMAN'S CAPTURE—
THE VALET OF THE FALSE DUKE BE-
FRIENDS DORA.

"TOGETHER!" repeated a harsh, coarse voice. "Yes, fair Dora the Duchess, if you will have it so. Mine, indeed, this time, beyond all hope of escape."

So sudden and unexpected was the encounter with six or eight men who were all masked, that neither Dora or Dottman could for a moment believe in the evidence of their own senses.

Dottman instantly threw himself before Dora, and placed his hand within the breast of his apparel in search of some weapon, which he made a rule of always carrying about him.

A look of deep anguish passed over his face as he withdrew his hand.

He was completely unarmed.

"So, so, my fine fellow!" said the voice that had spoken. "So, so, you did not expect to be received thus, and so you have not come prepared to do battle. It is well! so now you will just do us the favour to descend into a comfortable apartment beneath the foundations of this house, where you will have plenty of time for reflection, before you are coveyed to Newgate.

Dottman saw at once that it would be folly to contend against so overwhelming a majority, he therefore bowed his head in token of acquiescence, keeping, however, one arm around Dora, who was so terrified at the suddenness of the whole proceedings as to render her quite unequal to walking without assistance.

"Lead on!" said Dottman, "we are ready to follow you, whereever you may lead."

They were quickly surrounded by the eight men, and hurried down the grand staircase to the lower regions of the mansion, until they came to a stone passage, having doors on either side opening out of it.

One of the men produced a key with which he unlocked one of the doors, which was thickly studded by nails.

"Now, perhaps you will will do us the pleasure to walk in there—and with a push one of them nearly succeeded in thrusting Dottman in headlong.

But Dottman's greatest fear was of losing sight of Dora, and he grasped her firmly round the waist, fully determined to retain his hold on her as long as possible.

"Loose your hold, fellow!" said another of the men, as he struck Dottman a blow across the hand with a large ponderous key, which he held— "loose your hold! did you suppose for a moment that we considered Dora the Duchess—? ha, ha! that's good! Dora the Duchess, a fit companion for the like of you?

"Oh, let me go with him," said Dora, now thoroughly alarmed at the thought of imprisonment in that house alone.

Our orders were to lodge you as far apart as possible—so if you don't choose to walk of your own accord, young woman, why, we must just find some means to make you, that's all."

Dora turned and looked at Dottman, and she fancied she detected a look upon his face which was meant to advise her to make no resistance.

"Lead on," she cried, "I fear you not—you dare not treat me with disrespect."

In another moment Dottman heard the door of the cellar, for such it was, shut with a loud clang, and the key turned in the lock.

When he felt sure that he was alone, he raised his head, but he was now in darkness; for the light which had entered the cellar, came from small openings in the wall of the corridor, and now that the cellar door was closed all light was excluded.

Another moment, however, Dottman had produced the box of matches he had in the pocket of his coat, and striking a light, he was soon enabled to examine his prison.

It was of large dimensions, but the ground was damp, and it was evidently infested with rats.

"Umph!" said Dottman to himself, "I am glad that dear girl was not forced to share this lonesome place with me; but, perhaps they put her in a similar one—good Heavens! if they do, what will become of her? I must make my escape somehow for her sake."

In the meantime, Dora was made a prisoner in an apartment in the upper part of the house—near to the chamber which had been for so long the prison house of the unfortunate Duchess of Kingston.

The room was scantily furnished—a chair, a table, and a low truckle bedstead was all that it contained.

"There are your quarters, my fair lady, and perhaps you will not object to bestow a smile and a kiss upon Ted Plumtree for not consigning you to the vault below."

Dora shrunk back in alarm as the man advanced a step or two towards her.

"Villain!" shouted another voice, and an elderly man, without a mask, struck her assailant such a blow in the face, that it sent him reeling. "Villain! one more word, and I will beat the very life out of your vile carcase. Begone, and rest assured I will not forget you."

Dora looked up at her champion, but he made a sign for her not to address him, and turning to the other men he said—

"Well, my men, both the prisoners are now well lodged, nothing remains to be done, but to wait for further orders," then turning to Dora, he said—

"You will be treated with all respect, lady, but it is necessary that you should be guarded for the present."

"Who dares to detain me, and for what?" asked Dora.

"Of that I know nothing," returned the old man.

"But who," asked Dora, "gave you orders? the Duke of Kingston?

The old man bowed, but made no awnswer, and again Dora fancied there was a look of interest upon his countenance.

The men now turned to leave the room, the old man being the last to do so, and as he turned to close the door after him, he threw a small slip of paper at the feet of Dora, placing his finger on his lips as he did so to prevent her from uttering any exclamation.

Dora waited until the door was closed, and she could hear the click of the lock which assured her that she was a prisoner, she then hastily raised the slip of paper from the floor, and it may be better imagined than expressed with what feelings he read these few words—

"Be not alarmed at anything that may happen—within these walls you have a friend who will watch over your safety at all hazards."

Dora read and re-read these words, but was utterly at a loss to come to any conclusion as to who could have been the writer, for no one knew of her intention of visiting the house of Surlina but those dear friends who were in total ignorance of her present danger.

DORA A PRISONER OF THE DUKE OF KINGSTON.

Hour after hour passed away, and still Dora was alone.

The darkness, however, which had at first appeared to her so profound, as her eyes grew accustomed to it, was not now so great but that she could perceive the few articles of furniture which the room contained, or, at least, so far as to be able to tell in what position they were placed—so rising from the bed upon which she had thrown herself after reading the paper by the aid of one of the matches, which fortunately they had forgotten to take from the pocket of her dress—she lighted another, in order to make a survey of her prison, and if possible, to find the window.

DORA.—30.

This was soon accomplished, and Dora uttered an exclamation of joy as she saw that the window was quite unprotected, in the way of bars—she perceived that the shutters fastened in the ordinary way, with a bar across them, which she removed without difficulty.

And now it was that Dora held counsel with herself as to what she had better do—what so easy as to call from the window of the room in which she was a prisoner, and thus give an alarm to the passers by?

Then again Dora, ever mindful of others, remembered that it was to the exertions of the old man who had appeared to take so great an interest in her fate, that she owed the good fortune of being placed in that apartment, for she now remembered to have heard some dispute between him and the other men as to which room she was to be taken to.

For some time Dora was lost in thought, and then she opened the window as quietly as possible, and looked out.

She was in an upper room, and Dora could see that with care she could easily get out at the window, and by walking along the roofs of the houses, so contrive to make her escape.

But this was hazardous—what account could she give of herself to any one she might encounter in her way?

"I will trust to my good fortune," and now there was an adventure in view without involving either herself or any one else in very great danger, she resolved to try it.

Cautiously and with as little noise as possible Dora open the window and stepped out on to the leads, which ran along the houses—but she had not proceeded more than two or three paces when she perceived another window belonging to Surlina's house.

She feared at first that this window might be secured from within, but upon using both hands she found it open tolerably easy.

She now resolved to enter this room, and endeavour if possible to leave the house by the hall door, and thus escape the power and malice of her enemies, without encountering any risk.

Another moment and she had leaped into the room.

It was unoccupied, and seemed to have served the purposes of a lumber room, for there were heavy articles of furniture in it, but all thickly covered with dust.

Dora gave but a hasty glance at these details, and made her way to the door.

It yielded to her touch, and she found herself in the upper regions of the house.

For a moment she paused to listen, and then the desise to discover the prison of Dottman became so strong that she could not resist it, and she began to descend the staircase in order to reach the cellars, in one of which she well remembered to have seen her faithful follower securely locked up.

A few moments sufficed for Dora to reach the passage from which opened the doors of the various cellars belonging to that old deserted mansion, and hastening towards the one which she believed contained Dottman, she was about to hammer upon it with her hands, when to her surprise it opened as she touched it, and Dottman was gone.

For a time Dora knew not whether to rejoice or not at the disappearance of her friend, but she felt that if he had made his

escape he would most certainly make some search for her.

With a look of disappointment Dora turned to leave the cellar, when she drew back hastily behind some barrels, for there were voices in the passage.

"She is here, Fred, here in this house I tell you, for some purpose—she and an old man, who I believe is a kind of servant, came here this morning, just as the Duke got here, from his visit to Turnbull. I knew he had some means of entering this house from his own, and so I concealed myself behind a spring, and saw him walk up to a picture that hangs by the side of the fireplace, touch a spring, and it opened like a door into the other house."

"Well!" said another voice, which Dora instantly recognised as that belonging to Fred Hillyard.

"Well, as I was saying, he entered the other door, but returned almost immediately, and rung the bell violently.

"I had come from my hiding place as soon as I had satisfied my curiosity respecting the secret door in the wall, so that I was able to answer the summons, for when he wants me he generally rings twice."

"Well, and what did he say then, when you answered the bell?" asked Fred.

"Why, he told me he was sure all was not right in the next house, for that he had seen a well-known highwayman and a woman enter just before he reached the house, and he ordered me to get all the fellows together; but to disguise our faces so that we should not be recognised, and to go and make them prisoners as best we could."

"Ah, and you did so?

There was no saying no to such an order, and especially as he backed his commands with a handsome present in the shape of a well filled purse."

At this moment Dora was so anxious not to lose a word of what was being said, that she strove to raise herself somewhat from the crouching position in which she was—but in so doing the barrel, behind which she had concealed herself, made a slight grating noise.

"Hush! what's that?" said Fred.

"Oh, I daresay it's the rats."

"Well, go on with your story."

"I soon made known my master's wishes, and we mustered eight strong, and entered the house by the hall door.

"Yes, yes, and you found the highwayman and the young woman?"

"No, but I found an old friend, Fred, who do you think?"

"I can't tell'"

"Dottman!"

"Dottman? how on earth did he get

here? I thought he was safe enough by this time; but who was the young woman?"

"Dora, the daughter of our dear old master."

"Here? in this house? you don't say so?"

"Here in this house, and I have resolved to stand by her, let come what may."

"And where is she?"

"Why, the other fellows wanted to put her in one of those cellars, but I wasn't going to stand by and see her treated like that, so I overruled them, and got her into one of the upper rooms, taking care to let her know that she was not without a friend."

"Well, done! then Dottman is here—let's go and see the old fellow."

"Come on! but we must be quick."

Dora now determined to make her presence known to her two friends; but just as she was about to emerge from her hiding place an exclamation from the man who had been addressed by the name of Hillyard, and whom the reader will recollect was the valet of the false Duke of Kingston, prevented her doing so.

"Hush! what's that?"

Dora was unable to hear the reply to this question, for the two brothers hastened from the spot too quickly for her to make herself known to them.

She had, indeed, gained the passage with the intention of speaking to them, but when she came into the light it only served to shew her their retreating figures.

"What shall I do? Oh! what shall I do! Perhaps if I had remained in my prison chamber I might have received some intelligence from this man whom Providence seems to have risen up as a friend in this my new misfortune. Oh, Henry, where are you? To what anguish of mind will my absence condemn you!"

Dora paused and listened, but all was still within that deserted house.

After some few moment's deliberation she determined to return to her prison chamber, as she now felt convinced that the man Hillyard would befriend her; but if she were to deprive him of the opportunity of serving her, by escaping from her prison, to what new perils might she not soon be exposed?

With Dora, to resolve was to act, and in an incredibly short time she had regained the apartment in which she had been made a prisoner.

———

CHAPTER LX.

SHOWS HOW DOTTMAM MEETS WITH AN OLD FRIEND, WHO PERSUADES HIM TO RETURN TO HIS PRISON—THE DUKE OF KINGSTON PROVES TO BE A GOOD SHOT—DORA'S PERILOUS POSITION.

THE noise which had surprised the valet and his brother, Fred Hillyard, arose from the hard grating of a door at the end of the stone passage. the lock of which had grown rusty—the grating noise was caused by Dottman gently pushing it open, in order to make good his retreat.

The reader must not suppose that Dottman had forgotten that Dora was still a prisoner within those walls; but he thought, and wisely too, that he could aid her escape much more effectually after he had examined the means of egress from his own prison.

Fred Hillyard then, and the valet hastened towards that part of the stone passage from whence they had heard the sounds proceed, and notwithstanding the dexterity with which Dottman crouched down amongst some rubbish that happened to be in one corner of the passage, he was not quick enough to effect his purpose before he was perceived by the two brothers.

"Hilloa!" shouted the valet, "why, I declare it is the man whom I fancied was securely locked in one of the cellars here."

Dottman saw in a moment that it was useless to attempt concealment any longer, he therefore came out and confronted the two men.

The moment, however, that Fred Hillyard caught a nearer view of Dottman, he cried out—

"Ned Dottman, by all that is strange!" Then turning to Hillyard, he said, "why, is this the capture you made this morning?"

As Fred put this question to his brother, the latter came forward—for upon hearing that the prisoner had escaped from the cellar, he had run back to make sure that such was the case—now, however, he came up to his brother and said—

"What are you known to each other, then? It seems almost like a dream to me."

"Known to each other? why to be sure we are. Didn't we both serve together under the old Duke of Kingston? and did we not both love him?"

Dottman and Fred had clasped each other's hands, and the valet looked on with a dubious kind of satisfaction.

"Well, I'm rather sorry to hear all this," at length, he said, "because it will seem, somehow, like acting against a friend; but you know, orders must be obeyed, and seeing, Fred, that he is a friend of your's, why, I'll take care that he has good fare while I have charge of him."

"What? do you mean to say that you would lend a hand—even raise a finger for the detention of our late master's follower? Shame on you, Hillyard—shame on you!" said Fred.

The valet looked exceedingly perplexed; but at length it was agreed between them that Dottman should return to his prison, and there wait for any news that the valet might bring him—in the hope that before long the intentions of the false Duke of Kingston would discover themselves.

And so Dottman consented to return to the cellar in which he had been originally locked up.

Before, however, taking leave of his friend, Fred Hillyard, Dottman begged of him to induce his brother, the valet, to see Dora, and assure her that she was not alone.

"I'll see her at once," said the valet; "but as she has seen you before, Fred, perhaps it would be as well for you to come with me—for in all probability she would think that whatever I might say was merely a *ruse* to entrap her still more to her own destruction."

"True, true!" said Fred, "let us go at once—and now good bye, old friend!" holding out his hand to Dottman, "good bye, and keep up your spirits—we will do our best to circumvent his lordship yet."

The valet and his brother now withdrew, and the former again locking the ponderous door upon Dottman, ascended the stone stairs which led to the upper part of the premises.

Step by step they mounted, pausing ever and anon to listen for any sound which might indicate the return of the Duke of Kingston.

All was still.

The house seemed deserted, and the valet believed that he and his brother, with their two prisoners, made up the inmates of that gloomy abode.

Little did they think that it was a mausoleum for the lifeless bodies of the unfortunate Duchess of Kingston—Captain Van Esling—Surlina, and the beautiful Greek girl.

Little did they dream that it was about to become their own tomb!

At length they reached the door of Dora's apartment, and tapping gently at it at first, the valet produced a key and opened it.

Dora started to her feet as the door opened; but as she immediately recognized in the valet the old man who had defended her from the insults which had been offered her on her capture, she clasped her hands, and said imploringly—

"You have been kind to me, and have given me reason to believe that you are willing to be my friend—oh, tell me that you have come to set me at liberty and the blessing of heaven rest upon you."

The old man was moved to pity. The beautiful face of Dora was pale in the extreme, and it was evident that she had shed many tears in her lonely solitude.

Finding that he did not answer her, she took a step forward, and kneeling at his feet, she said—

"Oh, can I not move your heart to pity? have you no wife or child who clings with fond affection to you, and listens for your approach with joy?"

The old man turned away, and made a sign to Fred to advance.

In another moment he stood before Dora, and she then felt that all was not lost.

"What good fortune," she cried, "is it that sends you to me in this my hour of extremity? Oh, speak to that old man, and tell him who and what I am, and surely he will pity me!"

"I do pity you," said the valet; "but know not exactly how to help you."

"Oh, let me go—let me go! It will be thought that I have made my escape."

"I have thought of that," said Fred; "but I fancy it will be much better for you to remain here until we know what are the intentions of the false Duke of Kingston."

"What mean you by *false* Duke of Kingston? is he not the rightful claimant to the title and estates so long as this lady is unable to claim them?"

"No! a thousand times no!" said Fred —"for the rightful Duke of Kingston— this lady's father and our old master, still lives!"

At this announcement the old valet fairly staggered against the wall of the apartment, so surprised was he to hear that the Duke of Kingston still lived.

"Heaven be praised!" said he raising his eyes to heaven. "Then I may yet see him again."

"Not yet—not yet," returned his brother—"for until he has received the king's pardon for some political intrigues in which he was mixed up, he dare not show himself openly; but that day will surely come, and an evil day, indeed, will it be for him who has falsely usurped his brother's title, and so cruelly persecuted his child."

"Well," said the valet, affairs now seem to have taken a more hopeful turn—let us hope that soon we shall see right done to the innocent; of this rest assured, lady"— and here the old man would have knelt at Dora's feet, but she would not permit him to do so—"that the few remaining days of my life shall be spent in your service; and I will leave no stone unturned that will help to bring to light the atrocities and villanies of your wicked uncle."

At this moment the door of the apartment was flung wide open, and the Duke of Kingston stood before them, a pistol in each hand pointed at the brothers.

"Ha, ha! and so you thought you would compass the destruction of your master, who has been too kind to you, you grey-headed scoundrel, did you? You were mistaken, and thus I put it out of your power to do me any harm."

As he pronounced these words, in a jerking sort of gasping tone—for he was mad with passion—he pulled the triggers of the pistols, and before Dora had time to knock the one nearest to her up in the air the discharge lodged in the brains of the old valet, while the bullet from the other had winged its way to the heart of his brother.

There had been two fearful screams, as the brothers leapt from the ground, and then rolled over and over, grasping the faded carpet with both their hands, and shrieking as they writhed in the deep agony of death.

With one convulsive spasm then, the murdered men turned on their backs, as in death they each sought the hand of the other, and the spirits of the murdered men fled straightway to the foot of that God who has said "Thou shall do no murder."

A much shorter space of time than it has taken us to pourtray the deed of blood, which was to help to weigh down to the earth the guilty soul of the unscrupulous man whom we have had occasion to bring so frequently under the notice of the reader, sufficed to enact the terrible scene of bloodshed; and when the smoke from the fire arms had sufficiently cleared away for Dora to look about her, her two friends lay dead before her.

As she raised her eyes they encountered those of her uncle fixed upon her with a malignancy which made her shudder, and clasp her hands over her eyes to shut out the terrible sight which met her gaze.

With a fiendish smile he clutched her by the wrist, saying—

"One word of alarm and you shall quickly become an object of loathing such as will be those two men whom you had chosen for your friends and associates.

"Remorseless man!" exclaimed Dora, as she shook his grasp from her wrist, "think not because in this, your brief hour of triumph, all seems to favour your designs, that there is not also, in store, a day of vengeance for the false hearted and the murderer."

The Duke of Kingston—for by that title, false though it be, we must continue to call him—bit his lips, which were now white with suppressed rage, and taking two steps towards Dora, he again caught her by the wrist, holding it as if in a vice, as he hissed into her ear, through his clenched teeth—

"Beware! beware how you incense me, girl, for as sure as there is a heaven above us, you shall have cause to repent of every epithet you apply to me. I tell you, girl, you are in my power—wholly in my power; and you shall never quit these walls in life until you have signed a document pledging your word to abandon all claim to these estates—that once done, and you are free."

For a moment the heart of poor Dora beat audibly, for there was the natural longing in that young heart to return to those two loved ones—Henry and Mina—and she was almost tempted to accede to any proposal that her wicked uncle might make to attain such an end.

"You hesitate," he said, with a sneer—"is it possible that your love for your child and for that man whom you call husband is so small that you prefer remaining the rest of your days here to returning to them?"

The mention of Henry and Mina at once decided Dora what course she ought to adopt, and drawing herself up to her full height, she said—

"Never, false man, will I relinquish my claim upon the property you have usurped; and be assured that I have friends without who, when they find I do not return—as they had every reason to expect I should—will soon be on my track, and woe be to you if harm has happened to me."

"Whatever happens to you will be brought upon you by your own folly—but now I will leave you to silence and solitude, and when next I visit you, you will then probably be in a more rational state of mind."

Thus saying he left the room, and was just closing the door when Dora started forward, exclaiming—

"Oh, don't leave me here—don't leave me here! Tell me what you require, and I will"—

The door was slammed shut, and Dora could hear the key turned in the lock.

As she moved from the door, her eyes fell upon the inanimate forms of the men who had lost their lives in her service.

But little light could penetrate that small apartment, but Dora, whose eyes had now become accustomed to the darkness, could see too plainly the awful sight that was contained in that chamber.

With a groan of deep anguish she threw herself upon the bed, and covered her eyes with her hands, in hopes of shutting out the frightful spectacle.

She had lain thus for some time scarcely daring to breathe, so intently was she engaged in listening and deploring her unhappy state in ever returning to that chamber when once she had escaped from it.

But now she starts to her feet, and holds her throbbing brow with both hands, fancying that her reason must be tottering on its throne, for surely it cannot be true that a sound proceeds from one of those two corpses at her feet.

A deep groan, and then another and another smote the ears of Dora, who now felt certain, beyond a doubt, that life still remained in one, at least, of those two men.

We have had occasion to remark many times during our narrative that Dora was ever prompt of action when once convinced that a certain thing was to be done. Her presence of mind in this instance did not fail her, and she quickly made her way to the dark huddled up mass which lay between her and the door of her prison.

Far from feeling a return of that horror which she had at first experienced on finding herself alone with those two dead men, she now felt a species of heroic courage at the thought that perhaps Heaven had so ordained it that she should be the means of saving the life of one, perhaps of both those generous men who had fallen victims to their desire to help her.

Oh, how she now bent over those two brothers, in the hope of catching even the faintest sound from either of their lips.

Another groan, and this time Dora was sure that it came from the lips of the old valet.

With the quickness of thought Dora darted to the little wash-stand which stood in the corner of the room, and returned with some water which she sprinkled upon the old man's face.

She then perceived, more by placing her hands there than from beholding with her eyes, that blood was issuing freely from a wound in the temple, and tearing from some portion of her apparel a long strip for a bandage, soon succeeded in staunching the blood; then pouring a few drops of water into his mouth, she spoke to him in a whisper, but his mind was wandering.

"Save her! Oh, save her! Ah! yes—so, so—down by the window—into the court yard. Hush! he comes—he comes! Fred, let me go! he strikes her—my master's child!"

Dora strove by every means in her power to calm the dying man, for she felt that he could not live long, and the excitement he was now labouring under would, she knew, go far to hasten his death,

"I am here, dear friend," she said gently but firmly and distinctly.

"Raise my head."

A deep groan followed the movement of the head, and it was but too evident that the poor man suffered intensely, notwithstanding the care and tenderness with which Dora performed the kind office.

"There—there," said Dora, soothingly —"you will soon be better now, lean on me."

"Ah, yes, I am better—but so confused. I surely have had a frightful dream," said the valet.

"No dream—no dream, my friend," said Dora—"but a sad reality. But Heaven be praised, the cowardly shot did not execute the dire purpose of your guilty master."

"Then it is true that he came here and shot me—" and the man passed his hand dreamily across his brow. "Ah! I remember all now. But you—you—you still here? Alas! alas! I cannot help you now."

"Fear not for me," said Dora cheerfully, she was now only too pleased to find that the wild excitement caused by fever was gradually leaving the old man, who had become calm and collected.

"Alas! you know not what you have to fear, my poor child! Oh that I could get rid of this dreadful heart sickness, methinks I could yet find means to apprise your friends of your danger. I will try yet to rise."

With the greatest difficulty, and with Dora's assistance, the old man succeeded in struggling to a sitting posture, and then he said faintly—

"Some more water."

In an instant Dora had ran to the little washstand, where was a water bottle, from which she replenished the glass, and returning to the old man's side, held it to his lips.

The water, but still more the bandage which Dora had so skilfully tied round the head of the old man, thereby preventing the blood from flowing, did much to restore him to himself, and resting his head on his hands, he swayed backwards and forwards, apparently lost in thought.

Dora was silent too, for she feared to speak to him, lest a return of that feverish excitement should take place.

In a few minutes the old man became quite still, and Dora bent forward eagerly, for she feared that it was the stillness of death.

As she bent over him, however, she found that he breathed regularly, and only slept. Hope and joy once more sprung up in the heart of Dora.

CHAPTER LXI.

SHOWS HOW THE DUKE OF KINGSTON CONGRATULATES HIMSELF UPON THE DEATH OF HIS VALET — THE INEFFECTUAL SEARCH FOR DORA.

THE false Duke of Kingston was alone.

With a moody and dissatisfied air he paced the magnificent drawing-room—which he reached in an incredibly short space of time, by means of the secret panel concealed in the painting of Charles the Second.

Everything looked the same as usual, yet he felt fidgety and anxious.

It was the dread of how much his valet knew of the secrets of that deserted mansion which had been for so long in the occupation of the Greek and his beautiful daughter, and which had also been converted into first the prison, and afterwards the tomb of the unfortunate duchess, his wife.

Then again he asked himself how much he had revealed to Dora—these were the thoughts that agitated the guilty man.

Truly, Dora's revenge was beginning, even then.

"Curses on him!" muttered he to himself, with bitterness. "Who would have supposed that a quiet hound like that would ever have been able to give one half the uneasiness that I now feel? However, I have put an end to his career, for the bullet entered his brain."

As to any compunction about having taken the life of Hillyard, he had none in the world. Now that it was done, he had as little care about the fact that he had committed such an enormity, as though he had merely taken the life of some obnoxious animal.

He ceased to pace the room as he folded his arms, and looking calmly around him, as though there was no such thing as crime in the world.

"It was sure to come to this, sooner or later," he said; "and now it is over. He might have lived longer; but as it did not suit him to do so, why, he's dead, dead!"

The duke paused for awhile, and rested his chin upon his hand, and appeared to be lost in deep thought.

"The body! the bodies!" he said at length. "Ay, the bodies! that is the question. What shall be done with them?"

There was another pause of thought for a time, and then he said suddenly—

"What does it matter? Nobody will miss them! Van Esling had leave of absence—of course he has gone abroad—and she—nobody will inquire for her—no, no, it is long since she appeared in the world—Surlina never shewed himself—he had no friends. Ah! I had forgotten Neoni! she may yet do me some harm. I must think, I must think!"

He again began to pace the room and muttered to himself—

"And Hillyard! if I do not inquire for him, nobody else will. A few days will settle all my affairs, and then I'm off—off from England for ever, with my wealth—for everything shall be converted into money."

He now proceeded to his private apartment, and took from his pocket a black pocket book, in which he kept his most valuable papers.

It was at this moment that the duke thought he heard a noise just outside the door, and he reeled back, and turned pale.

It was only for a passing moment, however, that he allowed himself to give way to any fear.

"Pshaw, it is nothing!" he said. "Some of the domestics, perhaps; but I will try to find out if they suspect anything."

He rang the bell violently.

A footman in livery appeared to answer the summons.

"Send Hillyard to me!" he said.

The footman withdrew with a low bow.

"He suspects nothing," said the duke to himself, with a self-congratulatory smile.

In a few minutes the footman returned, and making another low bow, said—

"If you please, my lord, I believe Hillyard has gone out, for I have looked for him everywhere, and cannot find him."

"Out?" repeated the duke, with a well acted sign of impatience.

"Send some one to look for him, and bid him come to me as soon as he returns."

"I will, my lord!" said the man as he closed the door of the apartment.

"So far, so good!" said the duke, when he found himself once more alone—"so far, so good! nothing is at present suspected; but I must hasten my arrangements, or inquiries may be set afloat for this dolt."

Let us now take a peep at our old friend Dottman.

After the two brothers had left him, the one promising to see that he fared well so long as he remained a prisoner under his charge, and both promising to go to Dora and give her what comfort they could, under the circumstances, Dottman sta himself upon a barrel, and began to think of making himself as comfortable as he could in his present abode.

But as hour after hour passed by, and he heard nothing, a strange, undefinable fear began to creep over him.

He listened intently.

All was so fearfully still that Dottman was puzzled how to account for the fact that his two friends did not avail themselves of that stillness to bring to him tidings of Dora, about whom they knew he was so anxious.

The very stillness now had something ominous about it, and the deep curiosity which had taken possession of Dottman's mind increased each moment.

Not for many minutes longer could Dottman have endured the state of suspense in which he was; but he little suspected it was to be put an end to in such an awful way as it was.

Suddenly, as if a thunderbolt had fallen upon his head, came those two death shrieks, preceded by the report of fire-arms.

Dottman staggered back in his prison cell, and if the wall had not stopped him, there is no knowing how far he would have gone; but as it was, there he remained, with his arms outstretched before him, his mouth and eyes preternaturally wide open, and his very hair standing almost on end with terror.

What took place after those two frightful screams, Dottman knew not.

The echo of those fearful cries filled up his whole sense of hearing, and it was not until he heard a footstep just outside his cellar door—it was none other than the Duke of Kingston's—that Dottman became at all conscious of his own danger, or that there was anything else to listen to.

That footstep, however, aroused him, and he stepped to the floor, and with difficulty suppressed the utterance of a groan.

He heard the footstep ascend the stone staircase again, after having felt the lock of the cellar door in which he, Dottman, was confined.

He then guessed what had happened. But what had become of Dora? If he could but believe that she had escaped, he would cease to care what became of himself.

Dottman now bethought him of a small flat chisel which his friend, Fred Hillyard, had given him, on condition that he was not to use it unless he had every reason to believe that the valet could not visit him.

Now, therefore, that Dottman had no doubt in his mind as to what had been the fate of Hillyard, he had no compunctions whatever about using the chisel, and doing whatever he could to make his escape, as much for Dora's sake as for his own.

He, therefore, after mature deliberation, determined to make his way out of the house as speedily and noiselessly as possible, and apprise Dora's friends of the iminence of her situation.

Dottman went to work skilfully with his little chisel, and soon had the satisfaction of finding himself once more free.

In a short space of time he had gained an outer door, and as the shadows of evening fell upon the earth Dottman found himself hurrying along the streets towards that hotel where only a few hours before there was such a happy party.

As he entered he was accosted by one of the waiters who inquired his business.

"I wish to see Lord Rutherford immediately," said Dottman, "if he is within."

"His lordship has just returned. Will you give me your name?"

"Tell him that it is the man to whom he gave a commission this morning, and who has something particular to communicate."

The waiter ascended, in a leisurely manner, the handsome staircase, and soon returned with the request that Dottman would follow him.

In a few minutes he stood in the presence of Henry, Lord Rutherford, and the father of Dora.

The latter was the first to speak—advancing quickly, he said—

"Alone? What is the meaning of this? Where is my child, my Dora?"

"It is on her account that I am here—she is now a prisoner of the Duke of Kingston's."

"A prisoner? Dora a prisoner?" said Henry, springing forward—"upon what grounds?"

"I know not—but it is that you may rescue her that I am here. Fain would I have attempted it myself, but I know not exactly in what part of the house she is located, and I feared that I might not succeed, unaided, in setting her at liberty; I therefore determined to effect my own escape, and advise with you what had better be done."

"You have rightly determined, my good man," said Lord Rutherford. "Had you been precipitate, you might have spoilt all. We will now return with you. that is, Mr. Dacres and myself, and demand the restoration of this lady."

The Duke of Kingston here stepped forward, and laying his hand upon the hilt of his sword, said—

"It is I—I alone who must demand my child at my brother's hands—he dare not refuse to deliver her up."

THE DUKE OF KINGSTON VISITS THE TWO SURGEONS.

"What!" exclaimed Lord Rutherford, "would you expose yourself to so much peril when you are on the very eve of demanding of this man a restitution of your rights. Leave the affair in my hands, and believe me all shall be done that can be done, not only for the restoration of Dora, but also for the righteous punishment of your unnatural brother."

The Duke of Kingston bowed his head and said, in a low voice—

"It must be, I suppose, as you say. I will wait as patiently as I can your return."

After some further consultation, it was agreed that they should take with them an officer of the police armed with authority to search the house.

At this moment their attention was turned to Dottman, who had become suddenly of such a death-like paleness that they all thought he was about to faint.

For a moment he seemed to clutch at the air—his eyes wandering round the room with a wild expression, and then with a scream he fell to the floor insensible.

The inopportune illness of Dottman proved almost fatal to the hopes and expectations of those who intended to have taken him as their guide in their search for Dora; and after consulting with the physician, who had been sent for as soon as

Dottman had been seized with his strange and unaccountable malady, they found to their unexpressible grief, that days, weeks, months might elapse before Dottman could be considered out of danger, and the physician went so far as to say that if death did not ensue, he entertained some doubts whether he would ever be of sound mind again.

*   *   *   *   *

The Duke of Kingston was roused from his meditations by a loud knocking at the hall door.

Already his guilty conscience led him to imagine that he beheld an enemy in every face, and something of importance appeared to him to be hidden in the most trivial circumstances.

The knocking which at any other time would have been scarcely noticed by him was, upon this occasion, a source of extreme uneasiness, as was evident by the fact of his starting from his seat, and looking so anxiouly towards the door, muttering, as he did so—

"Pshaw! what a coward have I lately become! Why should I feel so nervous to-day? But I will be calm—calm—for I hear footsteps approaching."

In another minute there was a low rap on the panel of the door, and to the duke's "Come in," a servant entered the apartment There was a look of wonder—terror almost upon the man's face, as he stood with the handle of the door in his hand, and neither spoke nor advanced.

The duke was not liked by any of his domestics—his temper irritable and impatient ever—and, in the present instance, the man's trepidation arose from no kind of sympathy which may and often does exist between master and servant, making the latter take a lively interest in all that concerns the former, but from a feeling that had lately taken root in the minds of all the servanrs, that all was not right in that magnificent mansion.

Seeing the man hesitate, the duke had recourse to some of his usual expletives when addressing his servants.

"Well, blockhead," he cried, "are you struck dumb that you stand there gazing at me as though I were some extraordinary specimen of a new race of beings? Speak, fellow! what would you with me, I ask?"

Thus admonished, the man said with a low bow—

"Lord Rutherford, my lord, is in the library, and wishes to see you instantly."

"Tell his lordship, then," said the Duke of Kingston, "that I am engaged—particularly engaged—and regret that I cannot do myself the pleasure of seeing him just now."

The man still lingered.

"Well," said the duke, "did you not hear what I said? Begone, sirrah, and do my bidding!"

The man made a desperate effort, and then he said—

"If you please, my lord, he is not alone, and he bid me say that if you were too much engaged to attend them, he and Mr. Freckler would proceed to search the house together without troubling you."

The duke's lips turned white, and he felt his limbs shake beneath him, but mustering all his courage to his assistance he said, with an air of offended dignity—

"Search my house? Search my house? What insult is this? Does his lordship suppose that I am a Jacobite in disguise? Ha, ha, ha!"

At this moment the servant was gently pushed aside, and Lord Rutherford entered the room, saying as he did so—

"I will answer the last question in my own person. I do not accuse you of any Jacobite plots or intrigues, false Duke of Kingston, but I do accuse you of retaining in this house, and against her will, your niece, Dora Dacres."

"Dora Dacres in this house?" returned the duke, in a sneering voice. "Ha, ha! well, this is a well acted comedy, my lord. You are perfectly welcome to search my house if that be your intention, and I will gladly accompany you, and afford you every facility for so doing; and after that, my lord, we will have a little private talk upon the subject, for, as a gentleman, I cannot allow this insult to remain unanswered."

Lord Rutherford looked perplexed, but yet he felt quite certain that Dottman, before his seizure with that strange malady, had said distinctly that Dora was a prisoner in the house of the Duke of Kingston.

The reader, however, is aware that the false duke had nothing to fear from a search, as Dora had been captured and confined in a room in the house adjoining that deserted house which had been in the occupation of Surlina and his daughter.

Lord Rutherford turned towards the door and said something in a low voice to Mr. Freckler, who was waiting outside the room.

And now the search began, from cellars to attics, but, as the reader has already guessed, without the remotest light being thrown on the subject.

At length they returned to the library, and there was a look of triumph upon the countenance of the false Duke of Kingston as he said—

"I hope, my lord, and you, Mr. Freckler or Frickster, or whatever your name may be, are satisfied—there are a few boxes in the lumber room in which you forgot to look for your lost damsel—perhaps you will do me the favour to accompany me thither?"

There was a look of calm dignity about the whole bearing of Lord Rutherford, however, which somewhat awed into silence the exultant Duke of Kingston, as he, Lord Rutherford said—

"I am far from satisfied, my lord; but you shall hear from me as soon as I have had time to consult with my friends as to what will be the best means of proceeding in this case."

The Duke of Kingston bowed haughtily, and ringing the bell, ordered Lord Rutherford's carriage.

"Farewell, my lord, when next we meet, it may be my turn to triumph," said Lord Rutherford, as he and Mr. Freckler made their way across the magnificent hall to the carriage.

As the rumble of the wheels sounded in the ears of the Duke of Kingston, a fiendish smile came over his countenance, as he said—

"Now, more than ever, is it necessary that this Dora should be wholly in my power. I will at once see Marshall and Smith. Money can work wonders—yes, money can work wonders; but I will not trust them further than I am obliged. Now, for Dora—Dora the Duchess! ha, ha! Dora the Duchess!"

———

CHAPTER LXII.

THE DUKE OF KINGSTON VISITS MESSRS. MARSHALL AND SMITH TO THEIR MUTUAL SATISFACTION — THE COMPACT CONCLUDED.

AT the time of which we write, it was much easier to append "Surgeon" to one's name than it is in these days of ours. Formerly, any man who had been in a chemist's shop, and had got a smattering of latin could, if he had the means, set up a shop or a surgery, and there was no one to say him nay.

In a quiet, genteel street, of which there are so many in mighty London, might be seen a neat looking house with a brass plate upon the street door, by which the public in general, and the neighbours around— in particular— were made acquainted with the fact that Messrs. Marshall and Smith resided in that house, and that the were by profession, "Surgeons &c."

To this neat looking house then, the Duke of Kingston made his way on foot,

only an hour after the visit which had been made to him by Lord Rutherford and Mr. Freckler.

Knocking then at the door of Messrs. Marshall and Smith, the summons was soon replied to in the person of an elderly female, who answered the purposes of housekeeper and useful companion to the said Messrs. Marshall and Smith.

The Duke of Kingston looked urbane— for it was necessary, he thought, to impress everybody in that house with a high opinion of his philanthropy.

"Is Mr. Marshall at home, my good woman?" asked the duke, in his blandest accents.

"No, sir, he is not," replied the abigail; "but, Mr. Smith, his partner is."

"Will you say then, that the Duke of Kingston wishes to speak to him?"

"Yes, sir, yes, my lord—that is your higness, if you will condescend, your worship, to enter this room, I will be back in no time."

"Thank you, don't hurry. What a cheerful looking room!" This last remark was accompanied by a look of the most condescending affability directed at the elderly female.

The effect was produced which the duke wished, namely, in making the female believe him to be the nicest gentleman she had ever seen in her life; and making her way up close by his side, she said, in a confidential whisper—

"Lor' bless you, your majesty, they're both at home to the likes o' you—it's only to the poor folks as they don't want to be bothered with."

"I'm very glad to hear it, my friend!" said the duke, with another smile, and he turned and busied himself with a book which was lying on the table, in the centre of the room.

The old woman withdrew to apprise her masters of the visit of so distinguished a personage as a duke.

"Well, I never!" she said, when she had closed the door behind her—"well, I never—a real duke, and he took quite a fancy to me, I do believe. What a nice spoken gentleman he is, now! I wonder if he's ill though? he doesn't seem so. Now I wonder what he's come about?"

Before going to acquaint her employers with the fact that they had a visitor, she turned into a little room which she called her "housekeeper's pantry," but for no other purpose did she now visit that little sanctum than for that of beholding her fair visage in a small sized looking glass which hung at a convenient height behind the door.

The survey of her features was evidently

a pleasing one, for she turned from the mirror with a smile, saying—

"I'm not bad looking even now—although there was a time when I was younger—but it's quite certain his majesty, the Duke of Kingston, was well pleased with my appearance, or he would never have looked at me in the way he did, that's quite certain. But now I must go to the *surgins*, as the worshipful duke said as he couldn't wait long."

Kitty Crick, for that was the cognomen by which the elderley female was known among her associates, tripped lightly for one of her years up a flight of stairs and tapped at a door, which opened into what was *par excellence* called the surgery, and where at a table was seated the elder of the two partners, apparently deeply engaged in reading aloud from a ponderous volume.

On the other side of the table was seated the other partner, mixing some ingredients as the other read the recipe from the before mentioned ponderous volume.

So busily were the two engaged, that Kitty having knocked once, and receiving no summons to " come in," took upon herself to use the privilege of old acquaintanceship, and entered unbidden apparently.

With such violence, indeed, did she fling open the door, for Kitty began to be aware that she had lost much valuable time on the way, and so intently were those two men engaged in their present occupation, that they both started, somewhat, on beholding their housekeeper.

"Heigh-day! what's the matter Mrs. Crick?" said Mr. Marshall. " Have I not told you to knock at the door when you wish to speak to us? and here you are rushing in as if you were mad!"

"There, hold your noise, and go and speak to the Duke of Kingston, he's bad—no, no, I don't mean that, he looks beautiful—but he wants to see you both, so go at once!"

"What does she mean?" said Marshall turning to Smith.

"What do I mean?" shrieked Mrs. Crick, now thoroughly in a passion at the bare idea of not being understood. " What do I mean? why, I tell you in plain English that his worshipful highness, the Duke of Kingston wants to speak to you both."

The partners looked at each other for a moment or two; but neither spoke until the silence was again broken by Kitty.

"Well, I shall just go and say that you're too busy to speak to him, that's all!" and she was about to leave the room for the purpose of putting her threat into execution, when Mr. Marshall sprung forward, and seizing her by the arm, said in a voice of suppressed rage—

"Hag! stay where you are—or—no, better still, go to the duke and say that we will have the honour of waiting upon him directly."

A flash of indignation from the black orbs of the beautiful Kitty was all the response she vouchsafed to the command, and sweeping out of the room like a tragedy queen, she reached the room into which she had shown the Duke of Kingston.

The duke was pacing the room to and fro, as she entered, and there was a look of expectation on his face as he turned towards the open door.

"Mr. Marshall will be with you directly, my lord!" announced the old woman.

"Thank you!" said the duke; and it would have been impossible for one of his own domestics to have discovered in the tones of that voice, now so gentle and urbane, those of their imperious master.

Even as he was speaking, the two surgeons made their appearence on the threshold of the apartment, and bowing low, put on a professional look of inquiry.

The elderly female passed out and slammed the door behind her, for she had been vexed at not having had more time to converse with so amiable and high a personage.

The Duke of Kingston was the first to speak.

"I have called upon you, gentlemen, to ask your advice respecting a young woman, who, I fear, is in a very bad state mentally. I am not personally acquainted with you, but I have heard much of your kindness and skilfulness in these cases.

He paused to see the effect his words might have on the partners.

The senior partner now spoke, clearing his throat, and looking much gratified at the compliment which had just been paid to his cleverness.

"Hem! a young woman, you said, I believe, my lord? is she residing with you, my lord?"

"At present she is; but I wish to get her placed in some asylum where she will be kindly treated, and I want you to see her, and if your opinion coincides with mine"— here the duke looked meaningly at his two auditors—" I am of opinion that an asylum would be the best place for her."

The two partners took their cue immediately.

"Exactly so!" said both in a breath. "Exactly! and you wish us to see her, and judge whether she be a fit subject or not for a lunatic asylum?"

"That is what I wish." Then speaking in a low voice, the duke continued—

"Of course I am well aware how valuable your time is, and as I shall have to trouble you to visit the poor thing at my house, I shall not mind a handsome fee, as I wish to secure the best advice it is possible to obtain."

"Then, my lord," said the senior partner, "there is no difficulty in the matter; we will wait upon your lordship when and where your lordship pleases."

"Let it be then this evening at nine o'clock at Kingston House," said the duke.

"We will not fail you, my lord!" said the two surgeons, bowing lower than before, and Mr. Smith stepped forward rather timidly, saying in a meek kind of apprehensive voice.

"Is the—the patient violent, may I ask?"

"At times," said the duke; "but there are days together when she is merely a prey to the strangest delusions in the world."

"Indeed!" said Mr. Smith, and he seemed greatly relieved at the idea of the patient being harmless. "May I ask what form her delusions take, my lord?"

"Oh, at times," replied the duke, "she fancies that she is related to me, and that I am her enemy—then again she talks about somebody whom she fancies is her husband—a young man probably to whom she was going to be married, for she has a wedding ring, and nothing will induce her to part with it."

"I suppose not!" said Mr. Marshall, rubbing his hands one over the other, "I suppose not! these women, when once they get a husband into their head, often get their brains turned in the little affair—ha, ha, ha! But, we'll see her to-night, my lord, and if we find her bad enough to render it necessary to take such a step, your lordship will have no objection to allow us to name an asylum"—

"But where she will be well treated, mind," said the duke, trying to look stern.

"Where she will be treated as one of the family, my lord," said Marshall, placing his hand upon that part of his anatomy where the heart is supposed to be situated.

"Now," said the duke, rising, "I believe then that we understand each other—do we not?"

"Precisely so, my lord! we will bring with us the necessary certificates, which we can fill up at your lordship's house, in case we find the young woman bad enough to remove to some more secure place of keeping."

"Thank you, thank you! I have some feeling of regret in having to resort to such an expedient, and yet, what else can I do?" said the duke.

"Nothing, whatever, my lord!" said timid little Mr Smith, "nothing, whatever; but perhaps the young woman may soon get better, you see, and—and—"

"I am afraid," said Mr. Marshall, coming to the relief of his inexperienced partner, "I'm afraid from what his lordship has already told us of the case, that it will be a work of time—a work of time, eh?"

"I fear so too," said the duke with a hypocritical whine—"I fear so too! it is sad to think of one so young, perhaps ending her days in a lunatic asylum.

"Eh? what? ending her days in an asylum? but I thought she was to go there to be cured?"

"We may hope so," said Marshall with a benevolent smile, "we may hope so; but we can never tell—sometimes these sort of cases are very obstinate."

"Ah, I suppose so, poor thing, poor thing!" sighed good, kind-hearted little Mr. Smith.

The duke by this time had reached the door, but returning to the table in the centre of the room, he took a black pocket book from the breast of his apparel, and holding a bank note for fifty pounds to Mr. Marshall, he said with a smile—

"It is not customary to give a fee before the doctor has seen his patient, but I have been so edified this morning by the sensible remarks which have fallen from your lips, that I must beg of you, as a favour, to receive this as a small instalment of what is to follow when our bargain is concluded.

"Oh, my lord, you are too good!" exclaimed Mr. Marshall, with eyes sparkling greedily, as the duke held out before his astonished gaze the tempting bait. "Oh, my lord, you are too good! believe me, you may command me in all things."

"I do not doubt it, and now, good day for the present."

The senior partner saw his distinguished visitor to the hall door, where the latter paused abruptly, saying—

"Your partner, Mr. Smith, does not seem to possess your discernment and discretion, Mr. Marshall?"

"Oh, leave him to me, my lord, he is completely under me. I find him useful, as he possesses rather an extensive information in some branches of our profession; but as all the money in the concern is mine—of course he knows his position.

"I am glad to hear it," said the duke; "but I began to fear he might be misled by appearances, and fancy that the poor young woman, on whose behalf I have called, was really as sane as she appears to be at times."

"Oh, give yourself no uneasiness, my lord, on that subject; I am used to those kind of patients, who as the immortal bard has it—have ' Method in their madness.' "

"Exactly so!" said the duke, " and I am delighted to think that fortune has directed to me so enlightened a man as yourself.

Nine o'clock then to night, I shall expect to see you and your partner at Kingston House, with the necessary document or certificate—should it be found advisable, after consulting you, to have the poor young woman placed in more secure keeping than my house can afford."

"I will see that all the necessary arrangements are made ; and if your lordship would allow me to suggest a little plan that I think would ultimately save us some trouble— "

"Speak ! what have you to suggest?" interrupted the duke.

"It is this, my lord, that my housekeeper, who had the honour of admitting your lordship, should be in waiting at the corner of the street, to convey the poor young woman to Bigmore Asylum—that is to say, providing the state of her mind justifies us in signing the certificate for her admission."

"Bigmore Asylum!" said the duke musingly, "where is that ?"

"In Yorkshire, my lord."

"Capital ! just the thing ! I mean— that is to say, I fancy it will be better to take her from London, where she seems to have so many painful associations."

"Exactly so, my lord ! I therefore propose that Mrs. Crick should be in readiness to accompany her to the place of destination."

"Can she be trusted ?" asked the duke, with a meaning look.

"In all things, my lord."

"Then be it so!" and in another moment the duke had left the neat locking house, much better satisfied with the whole proceeding than he at first fancied he should be.

"A clever rogue !" muttered the duke to himself, when he had walked a few paces from the house.

"Some villany is going on !" said Mr. Marshall in a low tone, as he closed the door behind his distinguished visitor.

These two unscrupulous men each read the character of the other as plainly as though their hearts had been open books.

Mr. Marshall found his partner standing just where he and the duke had left him— he entered the room, and closing the door behind him, looked very inquiringly at him.

Mr. Smith answered the look in the following words.

"Well? what do you think of this affair ?"

"What do I think of this affair ?" repeated Mr. Marshall, "why I think that we have been fortunate enough to be called in to give our united—mind, I say our united opinion, with regard to the mental condition of a young woman in whom the wealthy Duke of Kingston takes a great interest."

"He certainly seems to take an interest in her so far as to get her put into a lunatic asylum," timidly suggested Mr. Smith.

"And where would you suggest, Mr. Smith, that a mad woman should be placed, but in a lunatic asylum ?" asked Mr. Marshall, with a fierceness that seemed to make little Mr. Smith shrink up into half his original size.

"Oh, if she be mad, of course it is the best place for her, I suppose ; but then, perhaps, after all, she may not be. There is such a thing as getting doctors to sign certificates for people who are as much in their senses as you or I are."

"Silence !" shouted Mr. Marshall, in a voice that seemed to make the very house shake again, "silence man ! do you suppose that because we happen to have been fortunate enough to have been called in in this affair, and paid so handsomely, too, beforehand, that on that account the woman is not mad—what mean you?

"Exactly ! that's just it. It is because we have been feed so handsomely beforehand that makes me think that—that—"

"Confound what you think ! leave it to me, you need not give an opinion—I shall give an outline of the case, and you can just state facts which you know to be true —will that satisfy your tender conscience ?"

"It will, and thank you. As Mr. Smith said these few words, a look, almost of anguish passed across his countenance. His thoughts flew back to the time when his own betrothed had been seized by the fell disease, and had ended her days in an asylum. Since then, poor Mr. Smith had felt a horror at the idea of any young girl being admitted as a patient into one of those institutions which should be a house of cure ; but which too often turned out to be one of detention.

The conference between the two partners was over, and as Mr. Smith moved towards the door of the apartment, Mr. Marshall said—

"Send Mrs. Crick here, I must give her her instructions for to-night."

CHAPTER LXIII.

HUNGER AND GRIEF GAIN THE MASTERY OVER DORA—THE FALSE DUKE OF KINGSTON BECOMES URBANE AND INDULGENT TO HIS DOMESTICS.

THE sleep into which the valet had fallen, and which poor Dora had looked upon as the harbinger of hope had lasted long, and as she sat there, by the old man's side, listening to his breathing, her thoughts wandered from that dark chamber to her beloved husband and child.

Hour after hour passed away, and a faintness began to come over Dora, for it was now long since she had tasted food.

The breathing was becoming quieter and more quiet; but this gave Dora no uneasiness, for she hoped that the longer the sleep, the stronger would the old man be to aid her in her extremity.

But now as she began to feel the craving for food, the thought took possession of her—and it was a terrible one, that perhaps her wicked uncle, fearing that she might continue in the same mind regarding the document he wanted her to sign, might resort to this most cruel mode of ridding himself of her presence—namely, that of starvation.

As soon as the thought took shape in her mind, it became almost unbearable in the atmosphere of that close apartment, and laying the old man's head gently upon the floor, she went towards the door and listened.

Ah! a footstep approaches! joy, joy! I shall not be left to starve; but at this moment she remembered the necessity there was for whoever might be visiting her to suppose that the old valet was dead.

She returned to the old man's side, and was about to raise his head, so as to place it in such a position as to deceive a casual observer, but in doing so her hand encountered one of his.

It was cold! cold as death—for death had visited the old man in that peaceful sleep into which he had fallen

With a groan, Dora clasped her hands over her face, and wept such tears of anguish, that shook her tender frame as with an ague.

"Alone, alone, alone!" she murmured as she swayed to and fro, "alone, now, and in the power of the worst of men. God help me, for man cannot!"

Exhausted nature could do battle no longer with such an overwhelming combination of horrors, and Dora fell back on the floor in a deathlike swoon.

* * * * *

There was a cloud upon the brow of Lord Rutherford as he entered his hotel, after the fruitless search for Dora at Kingston House. He ascended the staircase, and when he reached the door of the apartment in which he had left Henry Dacres and the good Duke of Kingston, the father of Dora, he laid his hand upon the handle, but listened.

"Alas, alas! of what evil tidings am I the bearer; how can I meet the inquiring eyes of those two anxious hearts? but it must be done without delay."

He turned the handle of the door and entered the room.

Henry Dacres was the first to perceive him, and springing towards him with a careworn and haggard face, gasped out—

"My Dora? you are alone—have you not found her? Oh, in pity tell me!"

Lord Rutherford placed his hand upon his arm, and said in his gentlest accents—

"I have not found her yet, but I hope to do so. Have you heard how Dottman is?"

"He is in the same state in which you left him. But tell me, have you heard nothing of my Dora's fate?"

"Nothing, whatever! I feel quite certain that we left no room in Kingston House unsearched."

"It is strange, and yet I have no doubt, in my own mind, but that her uncle knows where she is."

"Of course he does! but he is not likely to tell us, and therefore we must watch the house, and watch his lordship's movements closely."

"And in the meantime," said Dora's father, "my poor child may be exposed to all kinds of indignities! Stay me not, my friend—I must and will show myself to my brother."

"Nay, nay, in two days you will be free—free to show yourself openly in the world—you can then unmask this most unnatural brother, and have more means at your command to enable you to look for your child.

"Our friend speaks truly," said Henry, taking in his the hand of the old duke, "in the meantime I will not be idle, I am strong now, and may mine be the happiness of restoring her to you."

Lord Rutherford held out a hand to each of his friends, saying—

"I must now bid you adieu for a short time," and turning to the Duke of Kingston, he continued—

"When next we meet, I shall be able to tell you of my success at court, for I shall not be able to see you again until after the levee."

"Adieu, and God bless you!" said the old duke; "and God grant that you may obtain a favourable hearing, for now, more than ever, do I long to throw off this disguise; but it is sad, indeed, to think that a brother has done me this wrong."

"It is, indeed, strange and unnatural," replied his friend; "but his crimes, for I feel they are many, must not escape their punishment, any more on that account."

The Duke of Kingston sighed and turned away.

As Lord Rutherford took Henry by the hand, he said, " adieu, then, for the present, I suppose we shall meet at the levee ?"

" I hope to do so, for it is necessary that I present myself before taking the command of the regiment which the commander in chief has kindly placed at my disposal."

" Adieu then ! and who knows but that happy days are in store for all of us ?"

Henry Dacres sighed deeply, and shook his head as he pointed to the little Mina, who was quietly amusing herself with some toys.

" If it were not for that dear child, methinks I should pray for death. My heart misgives me sorely—I feel as if I had looked into my Dora's eyes for the last time."

Lord Rutherford was evidently much affected ; but as he laid his hand upon the sunny curls of the beautiful child, who was again deprived of a mother's care, he said—

" I am rejoiced to think that you have yet this treasure to bind you to life—you must think and live for her sake, now."

" I will, I will, and Heaven aid me !" ejaculated Henry.

Henry drew a chair to the table on which were writing materials, and looking, oh, so mournful, ever and anon at the fair child who was playing at his feet, wrote the following words—

" My dear sister,—Years have passed since last we met—time with you has passed pleasantly enough—with me, the last few years have been only a combination of sorrows and grief. Married to one I love—alas ! I almost fear I must speak of her only in the past tense—I fondly believed that my life would be like one long summer's dream ; fate decreed it otherwise. My wife, my beautiful Dora, has been taken from me, not by death—alas ! *that* would have been preferable ; but by a villain who is plotting for the destruction of herself and even that of her innocent child. It is of this child, fair and beautiful as her mother, that I would write to you, my sister. I am appointed to take the command of a regiment, and may be ordered out upon foreign service—will you take care of this child, and act a mother's part by her until her mother or myself claims her at your hands? The sorrow that is at my heart at the thought of parting from this little one is too great for words ; but I must leave her, and to no one would I confide her so trustingly as to you, dear Agatha. Reply to this at your earliest convenience. Address to the hotel as usual, and

Believe me to be,

Your affectionate brother,

Henry Dacres."

This letter having been written and despatched to his only sister, Henry Dacres felt more fitted to turn all his attention towards the recovery of his Dora.

But whither should he go for information ? True, he and his Dora's father felt convinced, beyond a doubt, that she was somewhere detained, if not by the orders, at least to the knowledge of the Duke of Kingston, and that he had every inducement, which baffled vengeance and ambition—ambition to retain those fine estates to which he would have no right if Dora claimed them—could suggest to wish for her death.

What agony was there in the thought that perhaps at that very moment his beloved wife might then be subjected, not only to anguish of mind, but also to actual suffering.

He paced the room like one bereft of his senses—at the moment he had forgotten that he was not alone ; but that the heartbroken father of his Dora felt to the full all the bitterness of the trial which had fallen upon them.

As Henry turned, his eyes fell upon the old man—for grief and sorrow had sapped the better part of his health and strength. They had changed his dark hair to an iron grey, they had planted furrows in his cheeks, and they had robbed him of all the strength of manhood. At the age of fifty-five, Lionel, the rightful duke of Kingston, was prematurely old. By night and by day he grieved for his beautiful child, and those who were dear to her as her own life—his fair Dora, the darling of his heart—whose image sat brooding with him, darkening the sunlight, and instead of being, as it should have been, the joy of his declining years, becoming by the many doubts and fears it suggested, their agony and their blight, and their desolation.

The old duke rose, and there was a beseeching look upon his countenance which was instantly perceived by Henry.

" Oh !" said the duke, " grieve not as though we had lost all hope, Henry, my son—Heaven is all-merciful, and surely our lost one will yet be given back to our hearts and our arms."

Henry clasped his hands over his brow, and the man wept such tears of anguish that it was enough to break the heart of the beholder.

" I must seek this false duke myself and demand my wife—I must know where she is, if I have to tear his heart out to read there his base secrets ! Seek not to stay me, I must go—go at once !"

Henry took both the duke's hands in his, and wrung them convulsively, and then he rushed from the room.

*   *   *   *

At eight o'clock the false Duke of King-

DORA ON HER WAY TO THE LUNATIC ASYLUM.

ton was seated in his library, and after being some time engaged in deep thought, he rung the bell.

A footman in livery answered the summons.

"There will be two gentleman here," said the duke, "at nine o'clock, show them into my private room, and let it then be understood that I do not wish to be interrupted any more to-night, and should any one call, who wishes to see me, remember that I am particularly engaged, and can see no one—do you understand?"

"I do, my lord!" replied the footman, with a low bow as he withdrew.

The duke rose from his chair, and when DORA.—32.

the sound of the footman's steps had died away, he opened the door of the apartment noiselessly and listened.

"All is still! but I must guard against prying eyes. A thought—yes, they shall enjoy themselves." He rang the bell again.

The same servant made his appearance.

"Tell the butler," said the duke, "that it is the anniversary of my birth, and I wish the servants to drink my health to-night in some of the best wine. In all probability I may visit the servants' hall before I retire to rest, and I hope to see all assembled."

The man looked up in astonishment— for never had the duke expressed any wish for the happiness or enjoyment of his domestics, until that night.

"You look astonished," said the duke with a smile, which he intended to be urbane; "but you will find me a different master to what I have been."

The man bowed.

"Now go," said the duke, "for I have business of importance, and I will ring if I want Hillyard—he need not wait for me as usual."

"If you please, my lord," said the man, "Hillyard has not yet returned, and we are beginning to get uneasy about him."

"Oh, never fear, I have no doubt he will join you, before long."

Once more the wily man was alone.

"Now, for Dora," he said; "but not yet, she must be got here secretly, and she must leave this house when the domestics are at the height of their revelry—ha, ha! what a model master have I become."

Nine o'clock was just striking as Mr. Marshall and Mr. Smith alighted from a hackney coach at the corner of St. James's Square, leaving as its occupant, Mrs. Crick, who had undertaken to accompany the "young woman," as poor Dora had been designated by the false duke, her uncle, to Bigmore Asylum.

In another minute they had announced their presence by a thundering knock at the hall door of Kingston House.

The hall porter was startled, for he had just been indulging in a reverie—wondering what the change in the conduct of their master could portend.

"Hilloa!" he said to himself, "these are the visitors, I suppose, that Blake said were coming on important business."

He opened the door, and Mr. Marshall entered the hall, rubbing one hand over the other, and looking the very personification of amiability.

Little Mr. Smith came a step or two behind his partner, and cast furtive glances around him, as though behind the numerous statuettes and pillars which were in the hall, he expected to see a lunatic concealed.

"Is the Duke of Kingston within?" asked Mr. Marshall, in his blandest accents.

The porter did not answer immediately, for had he not received orders to say that his master was not "at home" to every one but to the two gentleman whom he was awaiting?

"Hem!" said the porter, executing a small cough behind his hand. "What name, gentlemen?"

"Mr. Marshall and Mr. Smith," replied the first named gentleman; we have an appointment with his lordships for nine o'clock to-night."

"All right! I beg your pardon, gentlemen—really—I mean, his lordship is expecting you. Please walk this way—this way, gentlemen."

The two gentlemen followed the man until they came to a room at the end of the hall, which was known to the servants as the duke's private room—he threw open the door and requested them to be seated while he sent to acquaint his lordship of their presence.

It was the same footman who had already received the duke's orders, whom the porter encountered, and who, when he heard that the visitors had arrived, rubbed his hands with delight, saying—

"Nothing like punctuality, old fellow! Come along, do, and let us begin the evening as early as possible, I will go and announce the visitors."

He reached the library, and having received permission to enter, in answer to the gentle tap on the panel of the door, he informed his master that his visitors had arrived, and had been shown, as ordered, into his lordship's private room.

"It is well, it is well!" said the duke, and a look of triumph passed over his countenance, which would at any other time have attracted the notice of the footman; but as it was, he was too much occupied in thinking what Mary Bower, the pretty housemaid, would say to a certain proposition he intended to make to her that night, with regard to sharing her future fortunes with him.

"That will do," said the duke, rousing himself, for he had lapsed into thought, "I will go to them at once; and now I dismiss you, and wish you all a pleasant evening. I hope none of you will be absent when I present myself, to-night, for I have a great desire to see how the hall looks when well filled."

"You may depend upon seeing us all, my lord, for I have already informed your lordship's domestics that it is your wish to do so."

"Very good!"

The duke passed out of the library as the footman held open the door for him, and made his way to the apartment in which were seated the two partners.

They both rose as the duke entered, who, with a look of courteous amiability upon his features, said—

"You are punctual, gentlemen; I am punctual myself, and always entertain a high respect for those who practise it."

"Oh, my lord," said Mr. Marshall, who always acted as spokesman, "oh, my lord, you flatter us; but business is business, you know, and with medical men it behoves us to be puntual when we can—when we can, I repeat; but sometimes our patients take us by surprise—ha, ha, ha! Don't they, Mr. Smith?

Mr. Marshall seemed to think that it was necessary to drag poor, timid, Mr. Smith into the conversation, for unless he had been thus appealed to, it is probable that he would have had no auditor to laugh at the joke he fancied he had perpetrated.

"He, he, he!" echoed Mr. Smith—"take us by surprise—oh, certainly—yes, to be sure, certainly."

"Pray be seated, gentlemen," said the duke, drawing his chair to the table, on which he had ordered to be placed wine, "pray be seated, gentlemen, and pledge me in a glass of this fine old port."

"Willingly, my lord, willingly!" replied Mr. Marshall, and the three quaffed off each a glass of the finest old port that could be procured for money.

In this pleasing occupation the time passed but too quickly, and eleven o'clock had already chimed on the various church clocks, as Mr. Smith, pulling his partner by the sleeve, suggested to him that Mrs. Crick was still waiting in the hackney coach at the corner of the street, and might possibly become impatient.

"All right!" replied his partner, "Mrs. Crick is all right! I took care to give her a certain little stone bottle containing sufficient 'comfort,' to cheer her without rendering her incapable of carrying out the responsible task she will be called upon to perform to-night."

"Oh!" meekly, responded Mr. Smith.

The duke, however, had not lost one word of what had passed, and rising from his chair, he bowed to the visitors, saying—

"I will now leave you, gentlemen, in order to bring our poor patient to you, whom, I trust, you will not find so bad as I have had reason to fear you would.

"Very good, my lord, and here's to her restoration to health, and happiness!" thus saying, Mr. Marshall, who had already paid his respects very frequently to the decanter containing the good old port, raised another bumper to his lips and drained it.

When the two partners were alone, Mr. Smith ventured to suggest mildly, that it would be as well not to take any more wine until after they had given their opinion respecting the patient's state of health.

"What a timid fellow you are Smith," said his worthy partner, "any one would think this is the first patient we have sent to Bigmore. Of course she's as mad as a March hare, or we should not have been called in.

"I hope so! I hope so!" replied Mr. Smith.

"You hope so? ha, ha! Well, you're a funny fellow, Smith—why, I thought all along you had been hoping that she was not insane, and here you are wishing that we may find her as mad as a March hare; but, hush! they come—they come!"

CHAPTER LXIV.

THE DUKE OF KINGSTON SUCCEEDS IN HIS PLAN—THE MEDICAL CERTIFICATE—DORA IS CONVEYED TO A LUNATIC ASYLUM.

IT was the footstep of the false Duke of Kingston which Dora had heard just before awakening to the fearful conviction that the faithful old valet had breathed his last, and that she was now quite alone, and that she was wholly in the power of her unscrupulous uncle, who she knew would not hesitate even to take her life, if no other means presented themselves to rid him for ever of the fear of one day being openly charged with his many crimes.

Dora had, indeed, much to fear from her uncle's vindictiveness, and now too, that she had witnessed the murder of his valet, and that of his brother, Fred Hillyard, she knew, too well, that nothing but a miracle would enable her to escape from the scene which he had laid for her capture.

These were the reflections which presented themselves to the mind of poor Dora as she clasped her hands over her face, and when kind nature, at least for a time, steeped her senses in oblivion, and she fell into that deathlike swoon.

Almost at the same moment that Dora became unconscious, the duke, her uncle, turned the key in the lock and entered the apartment.

At first sight he believed that Dora was only feigning sleep, in order to gain time; but as he continued to gaze upon that form, now so still, a feeling of fear took possession of his coward heart.

But there was no remorse in that guilty man—there was an undefinable fear lest his sins should find him out before he had had time to fully enjoy the wealth and position which he had so wrongfully usurped.

He stooped down and touched her on the shoulder.

There was a slight shudder, even as though that slight touch was pollution.

"Ah!" he muttered to himself, she has fainted. Women faint and recover easily, I will give her some of this water."

He poured from the jug which had already stood Dora in such good stead in the case of the murdered valet, and a look of satisfaction passed over his countenance as he saw that she was returning to consciousness.

Dora held out her hand, but it trembled excessively, and said in a faint weak voice—

"Oh, do not kill me, but let me return to my dear Henry and my child, and all the past shall be forgotten."

"A lucky thought," said the duke to himself, "if she fancies that she is going back to them, there will be no difficulty in getting her to go quietly; but I must be wary, wary."

He advanced a step towards her, saying as he did so—

"Is it possible that you can forget the past?"

"Indeed, indeed I can forget anything, everything, if I may but leave this house, and return to those who are now mourning my absence."

"Well, it is that you might return to them that made me visit you; if you are strong enough, I will conduct you to a hackney coach, which is in waiting."

So guileless was Dora, herself, that wicked as she knew her uncle to be, it never entered into her imagination to doubt for a single instant the sincerity of his words, and after some ineffectual efforts, she at last succeeded in struggling to her feet with her uncle's assistance.

Leaning upon his arm, he was about to lead her from the room, when her eyes fell upon the inanimate form of the poor old valet, and the remembrance of all the fearful consequences of his devotion to herself had brought upon him, smote poor Dora to the heart, and she bowed her head upon her hands and wept bitterly—while indignation at her uncle's conduct again asserted its right in her mind.

She almost flung him from her, as she said—

"Oh that I should forget for one moment the suffering I have brought upon two innocent persons. Have you no remorse for the twofold murder you have committed?"

The duke sprung forward and closed the door of the apartment with a bang, and having locked it, put the key in his pocket.

Dora watched him intently; but now a feeling of fear, lest he should again lock her up, took possession of her, and enabled her to hide her emotions to a certain extent.

She felt faint and weak, and had it not been for the duke's timely assistance Dora would have fell to the floor.

They had reached the passage which led to the room in which was the painting of

Charles the Second, and here the duke paused and listened.

Dora looked up suspiciously.

"For what are we waiting?" she asked.

"I am waiting to know if we are to be friends or enemies?" said the duke.

"Is it possible—is it possible," said Dora, now thoroughly incensed, "that you dare ask me such a question—you a murderer?"

"Take care, my patience will not last much longer, and if ever that word passes your lips again, it shall be your last."

"Monster! let me go—your touch is pollution. Help, oh, help! oh, help!"

It was not that poor Dora thought help was really near at hand, but it was a relief to her to believe in the possibility of help in her present perilous situation.

Her words reached the ears of Messrs. Marshall and Smith.

"Hush! they come—they come!"

In another moment, the duke had touched the secret spring, and Dora found herself in that very drawing room, where she had once, and once only, had an interview with the unfortunate Duchess of Kingston.

The duke seized her by the wrist.

"You know what I have said, that I will send you to your husband, provided your lips are sealed with regard to all that has taken place in this house."

"Heaven help me!" sighed Dora, as she suffered her uncle to lead her out of that drawing-room across a hall, out of which opened the door of the private room, in which were seated the two partners.

At the door he paused again, and hissed in a hoarse whisper, into her ear—

"You will wait in this room while I go and get a hackney coach, and if there be any outcry or alarm given on your part, you will instantly return to that chamber where we have left your two friends.

Thus saying, he opened the door, and Dora discovered that the room was tenanted by two persons.

She darted forward, thinking that her uncle had made some mistake, and clinging to Mr. Smith, begged of him to protect her from her uncle's violence.

This was just as the duke would have had it.

Dora had at once been attracted by the kind face of the junior partner, who, believing Dora to be under the influence of madness, shrunk back as far as possible, turning white to the very lips.

Dora looked from one to the other in surprise and consternation.

"Ah! what means this?" she asked, "why do you all shrink from me? It is that bad man, who has murder on his soul, whom you should shrink from."

"There, there!" said Mr. Marshall, in a

soothing, coaxing kind of tone, " there, there, don't excite yourself—I dare say he is a very bad man."

Dora turned from him, for there was something about him which she did not understand, nor like, and again approaching Mr. Smith, she said—

"Oh, sir, you look gentle and kind, take me to my husband and child, and Heaven will reward you."

The duke gave a meaning look at Mr. Marshall as he said in a low tone, but which, however, reached the ears of Dora, " she is now under the influence of one of her delusions, and just before I got her here there was a violent outburst, and I feared I should not be able to manage her alone."

"She does not seem violent," suggested Mr. Smith, in a timid whisper.

Dora saw at once that there was some sort of understanding between her uncle and Mr. Marshall; but little did she imagine that the very fact of her stating what her real position in that house was only strengthened the Duke's assertion that she was a fit subject for a lunatic asylum.

She made one more effort to enlist the sympathies of Mr. Smith, and again seizing one of his hands, she said—

"If you do not believe, come and see for yourselves. I tell you, gentlemen, that this man, my uncle, is a murderer, and that it is to prevent me from claiming my own that he thus imprisons me in this house."

"Poor thing, poor thing!" said the duke, with a well acted look of sorrow, "it is ever thus, they tell me, with those they most esteem when in health. Just imagine what a wreck her mind must be, when one so gentle as she can believe that only harm when the greatest kindness is intended."

"It is commonly the case," said Mr. Marshall, putting on an air of extreme professional acuteness. It is commonly the case; but we must not suffer ourselves to feel hurt by anything this lady may say, in her present condition."

"And who has brought me to my present condition, but that man, who stands there with guilt written upon every lineament of his countenance? has he not locked me up for hours with the corpses of two men whom he murdered before my face?"

"Hush, hush! don't tell us any more about it now," said Mr. Smith, in his gentle, soothing voice, "it only puts you about, you see."

"Oh, Heaven!" exclaimed Dora, "is it possible that such wickedness can go unpunished? Why, look you, gentlemen, that man's soul is steeped in crime, and yet you stand there gazing at me as though you believed that I was only giving vent to the ravings of madness!"

The duke began to grow impatient, and he bent down and whispered something into Mr. Marshall's ear, to which the latter replied—

"Oh, perfectly satisfied. Have you writing materials at hand, my lord?"

The duke went to a side table, from which he brought all that was required, which would make poor Dora an inmate of a lunatic asylum, so long as it was the good pleasure of her uncle to keep her as such, or until madness really should be vouchsafed to that crushed heart.

Alas! poor Dora!

Mr. Marshall took from his pocket the printed form, which required filling up and signing by two medical practitioners—this certificate would be presented to the authorities of the asylum at Bigmore, and Dora would be indeed lost to her loving husband as effectually as though the grave concealed her from his view.

Mr. Marshall began to write; the purport of his stament was that the patient fancied herself to be related to the Duke of Kingston, for whom she had conceived the greatest aversion, since her attack, (which was supposed to be the first,) at times accusing him of murder, and of a desire to deprive her of her property. That the supposed cause of insanity was a disappointment in marriage, as at times the patient raved about her husband and child.

The statement went on to say that the patient was at times violent, and required much watching, as she had already attempted to commit suicide by poison.

As soon as this precious document was properly filled up, Mr. Marshall appended his christian and surname to it, and passed it on to Mr. Smith to sign his also.

While this was going on, poor Dora had been endeavouring to enlist Mr. Smith's kindly sympathies in her behalf, and it will be seen at once by the reader that the very means Dora took to substantiate her case, only served for an excuse for consigning her to the tender mercies of those employed in a madhouse.

Perhaps, timid Mr. Smith may have had some doubts as to the truth of what the Duke of Kingston had asserted, but it was not for him to dictate to his betters, and he tried to see only in Dora an unfortunate girl, who was subject to certain delusions at times, but he ventured to suggest that it was not exactly, to his thinking, a proper case for an asylum.

"Ah!" said the duke, "you give me great hopes now of her recovery, for it is quite evident that you do not think this unfortunate young person very insane."

This last question the Duke addressed to Mr. Marshall with a meaning look, which the latter was not backward in understanding."

"Well," replied Mr. Marshall, "I must beg to differ from my worthy partner, and I must say, much as I regret to make your lordship uneasy, that I have often found such cases as the present one most difficult to deal with out of an asylum.

"Then you do advise me to send her to Bigmore?"

"Most assuredly, my lord, and let us hope that as the patient is young, and appears to be in tolerably good health, that these sad delusions may soon be eradicated."

"Let us hope so, let us hope so!" replied the duke, who now suggested that Mr. Smith should go for the hackney coach which was in waiting at the corner of the street, and in which was seated, in no very patient mood, Kitty Crick.

Mr. Smith rose to leave the room, but Dora perceiving his intention, darted from the recess in which she had been invoking aid and strength from a higher power than that of man, and begged of him not to leave her, in such touching accents, that poor little Smith's sympathies were all enlisted on her side.

He put her gently from him, and told her that he would quickly return and take her away altogether.

"Take me now, now!" said Dora, "for I am sure you would not deceive me—let me go with you now, and Heaven will reward you."

What a scoundrel Mr. Smith felt at that moment.

"Perhaps it would be as well, Smith, to take the young woman with you," said Mr. Marshall, making a sign for him to do so unperceived by Dora, "go at once, and when you have found a hackney coach, and have told the driver where she wishes to go, you can come back here, and we will go home together."

"Thank you, oh, thank you! I did not think that you could be so considerate and kind; but I was mistaken. Now let us come," and Dora put her hand within Mr. Smith's arm.

"Yes, let us come!" he repeated quite mechanically, for by this time he was so fully impressed with the sense of his own rascality that he seemed to have lost the power of thinking of what he had better do.

At one time he meditated telling Dora of the trap that had been laid for her, then again he allowed his judgment to be blinded, believing that the young woman was really labouring under a number of delusion, one of which was that the Duke of Kingston, who appeared so kind and generous, and who took so great an interest in her, was a murderer.

Was then good Mr. Smith to blame, if after all, he resolved to carry out the instructions of his superiors, and convey Dora to the hackney coach which was to take her to a lunatic asylum, under pretence of seeing her in a fair way of returning to her husband and child, to whom she seemed so bent on seeing again.

Mr. Smith and Dora descended a short flight of stairs, which led from the duke's private room to the hall, and in another minute they stood on the steps of the mansion.

Mr. Smith drew her hand gently beneath his arm, saying—

"This way, we shall stand a better chance of meeting with some conveyance."

The hackney coach was standing not many yards distant from where they were.

"There's a coach," said Mr. Smith, "but I do not fancy he wants a fare, but we will inquire."

"Oh, never mind, never mind, I can walk—I do not wish to ride, let me walk," said Dora, imploringly.

"But you will get home so much sooner, you know, if you ride, so I'll just see you safely to a coach, and then say good bye."

Dora urged no more, for she longed once more to look upon the loved faces of her husband and child.

They reached the coach, and Mrs Crick put her head out of the window, saying, in no very amiable tones

"Oh, you're there, are you? I hope you've kept me waiting long enough!"

Mr. Smith drew Dora aside.

"We have made a mistake, I see, and there is a lady in the coach, how unfortunate! and there is not another to be found, so you must return to Kingston House, and wait there while I go and look for one."

"Oh, no, no, anything but that, I cannot go there again—let me walk, indeed I can."

As Dora finished speaking, she reeled against Mr. Smith, and would have fallen to the ground had he not caught her.

The fresh air, after so long confinement in that dark chamber, all that she had gone through, but most of all the thought that she was free once more, was too much for her tender frame, and she had fainted.

There happened to be no passers by at the time, and Mr. Smith had no difficulty in lifting her into the hackney coach, and giving her into the charge of Kitty Crick, together with the printed certificate which was her passport into Bigmore Asylum.

In a few minutes Dora was disposed of, and the coachman was directed to drive to the nearest inn at which post-horses could be obtained.

The coach rumbled on, while Kitty, by sundry shakes, endeavoured to restore the unhappy Dora to consciousness.

At length she opened her eyes, and they fell upon the ancient female by her side.

"Oh, where am I? where am I?" was all poor Dora could say; but she caught at the check-string, with no defined intention, but it had the effect of making the driver pull up and come to a standstill.

"None of that, mum, if you please," said Kitty, giving her charge a push, which sent her violently against the side of the coach, "none of that, if you please!"

"Oh, tell me where I am going?" said Dora, now thoroughly alarmed.

"Why, where should you be going but home?" said Kitty, with a kind of growl—and then putting her head out of the window nearest to her, she told the driver to proceed.

The horses were lashed into something like a gallop, and the coach soon reached White Horse Cellars.

The coachman alighted from his box, and coming to the coach door, he said—

"Here you are, ladies! White Horse Cellars!"

"White Horse Cellars?" repeated Dora, "why have we come here? I was promised I should go home."

"And so you are a goin' home, if so be as you don't make no disturbance. Here, ostler!

This exclamation was addressed to a stable boy who happened to be loitering about the inn yard, apparently without anything to do.

Thus addressed by the beautiful Kitty the lad came towards the coach, and looking in merely gave utterance to the one expressive word, "Eh?"

"I want to see one of the chambermaids directly—go in and say that a lady wishes to speak with one of the chambermaids."

"A lady?"

"Yes, fool—can't you see I'm a lady?"

"Well, no I can't say as I did—but howsomdever, if so be as you be a lady, why here goes!" and he ducked between the various carts and chaises as only one could do who was well accustomed to that kind of performance.

In the meantime what were the reflections of Dora? That she was again the victim of some well laid plot she could have no doubt—but how could she now escape? If she were to cry out for help there was just the chance of some one being at hand who would listen to her story and help her in her present extremity.

So occupied was Mrs. Crick with the idea of her own importance that for the moment she had quite forgotten Dora, who had so far succeeded as to have opened the door of the coach on her side—but how to lower the steps without attracting the attention of her jaoler—for such she now fully believed Kitty to be, was the difficulty.

But even this difficulty was being overcome, for Dora had quietly succeeded in lowering them so far as to enable her to step from the coach, when she was paralysed with fear upon hearing the old woman say—

"Oh, Mr. Turnbull, I'm so glad to see you—it will save me a world of trouble—will you kindly order a post chaise and horses as quickly as possible for Bigmore Asylum."

"Well, I never!" rejoined Turnbull, "why who would have thought of seeing Kitty Crick here at this time o' night!"

"Mrs. Crick, if you please, Mr. Turnbull!" said that lady, with a look of offended dignity — "Ladies and gentlemen who knows what manners is never calls people by their christian names unless they're authorised so to do!"

"There's no harm where there's no harm meant!" said Mr. Turnbull — "but who have you here, Mrs. Crick?"

"How should I know, except that Mr. Marshall and Mr. Smith are sending her to Bigmore."

"Oh, Heaven!" said Dora, as she clasped her hands.

"Ah! I should know that sweet voice!" said Turnbull—"let me have a look at her."

As he said this he thrust his tall bulky form and bloated visage so far into the vehicle that Dora had to shrink back into the furthest corner in order to prevent him from touching her with his face.

"Ha, ha! we meet again, do we, fair lady—it shall not be my fault if we don't now pay off old scores."

"Well, now, only to think as you should know her, Mr. Turnbull!" said Mrs. Crick, with a smile of satisfaction—"then you will be so good and obliging as to order the post-horses, won't you?"

"Not if I knows it—you don't catch me leaving this ere coach till I have seen her ladyship safely housed at Bigmore—if that's the dodge—but I'll give orders for a conveyance."

Thus saying he shouted to the driver, who had found an old friend in the ostler apparently, to order a conveyance with post-horses, to be ready immediately.

And now all hope had fled from the mind of Dora, for she saw at a glance how matters stood, but she made a last appeal as she was being dragged from the coach by Turnbull and his companion.

"Help! oh, help!" she cried, "will no one help me?"

Two or three people who were going and coming, rushed to the spot, but upon being informed that it was a mad woman who was being conveyed to an asylum for safety, they all shrunk back, and Turnbull had the gratification of placing upon her slender wrists a pair of handcuffs.

He raised her in his strong arms, placed her in the chaise by the side of Mrs. Crick, leaped in himself, and in a few minutes they were going at the rate of ten miles an hour on the road to Bigmore.

Dora shrunk back into the carriage, and clutched convulsively at the cushions, for she feared that her senses might forsake her, and she trembled to think of what might then befall her with two such companions.

CHAPTER LXV.

THE INTERIOR OF A MADHOUSE—DORA MEETS WITH SYMPATHY — NEWS OF DOTTMAN AND THE FATHER OF DORA —MINA IN HER NEW HOME.

THE reader will be so good as to imagine that the world is twelve years older than it was at the conclusion of our last chapter.

Let us glance at the changes of those twelve years as regards the personages we introduced to notice upon that strangely eventful morning when that beautiful girl who had scarcely numbered eighteen summers, was brought out to be executed for a crime of which she was as innocent as an angel.

That beautiful girl has now become the matron of thirty—but there is still lingering on the face that same gentle, dear, kind look we loved so well twelve years ago.

The owner of this dear, kind face is none other than Dora—let us glance at her present surroundings.

She is seated in a long corridor or gallery of Bigmore Asylum, where her gentleness has at length won the hearts of her keepers, and she is allowed as many privileges as are consistent with the "rules and regulations" of the institution.

The task upon which she is employed is that of amusing a poor idiot—who has been won by her gentleness and grace, and who looks at her with her vacant stare, as though she were regarding a being of another sphere.

Let us listen to what Dora is saying—

"Will Nelly try to say ' Mina?' "

The idiot makes an ineffectual attempt to pronounce the name so dear to Dora.

A look of disappointment passes over the face of Dora, as she gives up the hopeless task—and a doll next engages the attention of the unfortunate child.

Dora has sunk back on the sofa—there were sofas in that gallery, and beautiful flowers and singing birds—such as were not in those days to be found in every institution, but which are now commonly to be seen in every asylum—for she feels wearied in heart and body.

The attendants are coming to conduct her to her sleepless, cheerless dormitory.

A young girl, an especial favourite of Dora's, advances towards her, saying, in a kind voice—

"It seems early such a beautiful evening to go to bed, Mrs. Dacres—but it is the rule, you know—it is not my fault."

"I know it is not, my dear girl," said Dora, rising hastily, " but I go willingly— I have ceased to care for birds and flowers now."

The young girl looked lovingly into Dora's face, as she threw her arms around her.

"I cannot think that you ought to be in a place like this—I think so much about you when all is quiet."

"Thank you!" said Dora, gently, "thank you for not classing me with these poor creatures — oh, if I could but leave this place—and yet whither should I go?"

"But I thought," said the young girl, that—that—

"Thought what?" asked Dora.

"That you were married, and that perhaps your husband might be willing to try you at home again."

"Alas! alas!" said Dora, now weeping bitterly, "I know not if I have a husband."

The young warder looked perplexed for a few minutes, and then she said—

"You must not fancy that because he has not been to see you that therefore he must be dead—perhaps he has called, and Doctor Radford has thought that it might be better for him not to see you?"

"Ah!" said Dora, shaking her head mournfully, "I see that you know nothing of my sad history—my dear husband did not place me here—he knows not where I am!"

"Well, well, then let us hope that you will soon go home," said the young nurse, soothingly—for she began to think that although the patient was so gentle and docile, yet that she was still subject to strong delusions.

By this time they had reached Dora's dormitory, which was scrupulously neat and clean, and she threw herself languidly upon the bed.

"You will undress, Mrs. Dacres?" said the nurse, "as I must fetch your clothes before going to supper."

"Yes—oh, yes, my good girl—I will not detain you. Return in five minutes and you shall have them."

MINA AND HER BETROTHED.

In less than ten minutes poor Dora had said "Good night" to the only friend she possessed in that large establishment.

The door was closed, locking of itself by means of a spring at the same time, and our heroine was alone with all her sorrows.

For a time we also say "Good night," dear Dora.

Henry Dacres was also changed since first we introduced him to the reader—twelve years of mental suffering, joined to active service, had done their work on him—and yet perhaps it would not be wrong to say that he looked handsomer now that years had matured his intellect ; but there was a sadness about the face that at once told the beholder that he had known suffering.

For years had he now given up all hopes of finding his beloved Dora, and he had even begun to hope that death had claimed her, for too well did he know that death was far preferable to the state of anxiety and suspense which he was doomed to carry about with him wherever he went.

Dottman, our old friend Dottman, had partially recovered from the paralysis of mind and body into which he had fallen, and was now a quiet, inoffensive old man, the friend and constant companion of the father of Dora, who had retired to a small cottage in Devonshire, where he lived a life of the greatest seclusion—for strange to say, he had never seen his friend, Lord Rutherford, since that day when he promised to return from the levee with the pardon of his friend.

There was a rumour that Lord Rutherford had been found dead by the roadside on the night of the levee; but whether the report were true or not, the Duke of Kingston, for by that title we must sometimes call the father of Dora, had no means of ascertaining.

*   *   *   *   *

In an elegantly furnished drawing-room sat two ladies, the elder was about the middle age, but still looking young, and showed even at that time of life the remains of great personal beauty.

On an ottoman at her feet was a lovely girl about seventeen, with sunny ringlets shaping her marble neck and shoulders, and that sparkling look about the deep blue eye, which is so loveable.

In her hand the younger lady held an open letter, which rested upon the lap of her companion, and there was a look of happiness in that fair young face which was truly enchanting to behold.

"Oh, how I long to see this dear father," said Mina—for it was none other, "oh, how I long to see this dear father, who has suffered so much; but you promised to speak to me of my mother—am I like her, dear aunt?"

"Yes, and no, my child," replied Lady Agatha Poynter, "you are, and you are not like your poor mother. You resemble her, dear one, in form and feature, but in disposition you are different."

"As how?" inquired the young girl, anxiously.

"You have not the courage and energy which she had, my darling, to battle with the world, and should it be your fate to suffer, I should fear for the consequences."

The young girl was thoughtful for a few minutes, then looking up with a bright smile, she said—

"But, dear aunt, I shall not have to battle with the world, for every one is so kind to me, and then—"

"I know what you would say, that Sir Edward Hargrave loves you."

The tell-tale blush spread itself over her brow, and tinged even the delicate ear, for deep, deep, in the recesses of that young heart was hidden an all enduring love for one many years her senior, it is true, but who was well deserving her best affections.

"Oh, yes, aunt! I do not mind telling you, who have been like a mother to me for so many years, that I fear not to engage in the battle of life with him by my side; he is so noble, so good, and loves me so fondly."

"Far be it from me, my dear child, to lessen your faith in the goodness of human nature, but yet, Mina, I must warn you, now that you are with me, not to trust too much to the smiles of friendship."

"But I said love, dear aunt," said Mina, looking up quickly; "who ever loved as I love, and was disappointed? Life to me, with Edward by my side, must ever be bright and happy as one long summer's day."

"Alas, my child, so thought your poor mother!"

"Ah! you were going to tell me of my poor mother; was she not happy in my father's love? tell me of my mother. There are times when I fancy I remember her—did you see her die?"

The last question was put in a low, suppressed whisper.

"No dearest!" replied her aunt, "I did not see her die, and I often think she is not dead."

Mina started to her feet and clasped her hands before her eyes.

"Not dead! my mother—my dear mother not dead? Oh, say it again—shall I ever see her—shall I feel her breath fanning my cheek, and hear her murmur words of love as I speak to her of *him*, and tell her how very dear he is to me? Oh, tell me, dear aunt, that my mother lives."

So sudden had been the excitement into which the few unguarded words of her kind aunt had plunged her, that it took some few minutes before she could make up her mind to say more; but rising from her seat, she advanced towards her and placed her arms around the trembling girl.

Gently then, and tenderly, did Lady Agatha detail to Mina the substance of her mother's sufferings, so far as she knew them herself, adding that all the government could do, all that fortune spent in the pursuit, and a life wasted in wearying researches could do, had been in vain.

If from the moment that she, and all who had been engaged in her abduction had stepped into some newly dug grave, and been covered in and shut out from the world for ever, they could not more utterly and hopelessly have disappeared.

"Is she dead? is she dead?" That was the question which Mina felt she must ask herself by day when she was alone, and in the long lapses of the weary hours of the night she asked in a whisper, "is she dead? is she dead? Oh, if I could but be sure that she were dead—that she did not suffer!"

But no! the consolation of knowing that her gentle mother was in her grave was too great to be vouchsafed to the fair girl who now felt so bereaved.

"Oh, how my dear father must have suffered! Do you know, aunt," said Mina, with a fresh burst of tears, "I now feel as though I were ungrateful for allowing myself to be so happy in his—his love."

"Be ever thus unselfish, my darling," said her aunt, stroking the glossy curls, "and Heaven grant that you may be as happy as you deserve to be."

There was a horseman coming up the noble avenue of elms which led to the house, and Mina and her aunt at once recognised in this horseman Sir Edward Hargrave, the affianced husband of the gentle Mina.

"Sir Edward, my child, must not see those swollen eyes; go to your room, and leave me to entertain him until you return."

"Thanks, dearest aunt!" said Mina, as she tripped out of the room by one door, as Sir Edward entered it by another.

There was a look of anxiety upon the face of Sir Edward as he threw himself upon the nearest chair, after glancing round the apartment to see that he and Lady Agatha were alone.

"I am glad to find you alone, dear Lady Agatha," he said, "for I have heard something which leads me to suppose that our Mina's mother is not dead."

"Thank Heaven!" fervently ejaculated Lady Agatha; "but tell me quickly what you have heard, for I expect Mina to return immediately."

"Be not too sanguine; but, my friend, Harry Rivers, of whom you have frequently heard me speak, and to whom I have communicated as much of the history of Mina's mother as I felt I might do, called upon me yesterday to say that he had reason to believe that she formed the topic of conversation between two low looking men who were seated in a little wayside public-house, where my friend had occasion to stop to bait his horse."

"Is this possible? Oh, would that the information of which you have become possessed might turn out to be correct, for my dear brother, Henry, is now expected home, and we have not been able to succeed in unravelling the mystery of her disappearance any further than we had six years ago."

"The information in his own words was just this: 'When I entered the inn, after having seen to my horse, I called for ale, as my ride had been long and weary, and while I was waiting for the landlord to execute my orders, my attention was attracted by two men engaged in very deep conversation.

'At first I took no notice of them, but presently I fancied I heard the name of the Duke of Kingston mentioned. This induced me to pay some attention to as much of their conversation as I could hear from where I was sitting. I was not mistaken, for I heard one of the men say—

"'I shall not keep his secrets any longer—it was all very well while he paid me well; but now he fancies the affair all blown over, and that her friends have given her up as dead.'

'I felt certain in my own mind that the person who had been given up by her friends could be none other than our Mina's mother—I need not, therefore, tell you how intently I listened to catch more of what they said.'

'The other man who seemed to know but little of the whole affair, or to care but little about it, merely replied—'

"'Well, if I help you to find her friends, of course you will go halves with me in the reward, eh?'

"'To be sure—to be sure! but I forget now the name of the asylum he had her taken to—I know it began with a B, and was somewhere in Yorkshire; but Yorkshire is such a blessed large place to go and hunt up anybody in.'

"'Not at all, Turnbull,' replied his companion, 'there's not so many mad-houses in Yorkshire that we need be long in finding the right one—so let's go at once—what say you?'

"It is Dora, of whom they were speaking," said Lady Agatha, with emotion, "for Henry has often spoken to me of the villain, Turnbull, who was so anxious to recapture her after her escape from that terrible death for the punishment of a crime of which she was as innocent as an angel. But what mean you to do?"

"I intend going into Yorkshire to visit whatever asylums there may be there, and ascertaining for myself whether these men spoke the truth or not."

"But why did you not speak to these men?" asked Lady Agatha.

"For the best of all reasons, my dear friend," replied Sir Edward, "just as I was about to do so"—

At this moment, Mina entered the room. There were traces of tears upon her fair cheeks; but the gentle smile and love light which sparkled in her eyes, told Sir Edward beyond a doubt, that his child-love was his. It was strange to see how eye and lip lighted up as he drew her towards him and imprinted a fervent kiss upon her pure brow—a light which shed a beauty over that young face that was almost more than earthly—it was—

"The light of love, the purity of grace,
The music breathing o'er the face."

CHAPTER LXVI.

MINA HAS REASON TO BELIEVE THAT HER
MOTHER STILL LIVES—SIR EDWARD
HARGRAAE GOES IN SEARCH OF DORA—
THE FALSE DUKE LEAVES ENGLAND.

LADY AGATHA soon formed some excuse
to leave those two loving hearts alone together, and as she softly closed the door
behind her, Sir Edward strained his child-
love passionately to his heart. He drew a
long shivering breath and bowed his head
a little, a very little lower, until his coal
black hair mingled with her sunny curls.

Mina raised her head from his breast
where she had suffered it to rest for a brief
moment, and looking up into his won-
derously beautiful eyes, said gently—

"Tell me, Edward, what makes you look
so sad to-night; there is a mournfulness in
your eyes which I never saw before."

He made her no answer, but dropped a
book which he had been opening and
shutting so nervously, while he was asking
himself how much or little of his intended
expedition to Yorkshire might be told or
witheld from his Mina; as he dropped the
book, he wound that arm about her too, as
if he feared she would fade from his clasp
like a dream or vision.

"Ah, may I not know all?" she asked,
sadly, "you think me a child; but you
know not how long I seem to have lived
within the last hour."

"You! you!" exclaimed Sir Edward
Hargrave, now turning her face so that it
met his, "what has happened, my darling,
to distress you?"

"My aunt has been speaking to me of
my dear mother, and I who have hitherto
been so happy—especially, dear Edward"—
and here her voice was low with emotion,
"since I have known you, that I have
suffered myself to believe my mother was
no more, and was content to think of her
as a disembodied spirit, who was perhaps
permitted to look down from Heaven and
behold her child's felicity."

"Well, my darling, and what has hap-
peded to disturb so sweet and consoling a
belief?"

"My aunt tells me that neither she nor
my dear father have ever been able to
ascertain that she is really dead—on the
contrary, they both believe her to be living
and suffering, while I was allowing myself
to be so happy. Oh, Edward, I feel as
though I had been instrumental almost in
causing her to suffer; but now tell me,
Edward, why you seem so sad?"

"Because, my Mina, I must leave you

for a short time," replied Sir Edward,
drawing her still closer to his heart.

"Leave me? oh, Edward, then I am
indeed, miserable," and the fair young face
sunk lower and lower upon the strong man's
bosom.

"It is to search for this loved mother,
Mina, that I leave you, my darling. I
know nothing for certain, but I hope that I
possess so much information on the subject
that by dint of great perseverance I may
be able to find her, and restore her to you."

Mina raised her tearful face to his, in
which he read such a volume of grateful
tenderness, that he was more than repaid for
the sacrifice he was about to make of leaving her.

Sir Edward Hargreave clasped the slight
form of the young girl to him, whispering—

"My own Mina, my little one, my heart
would be dead, indeed, and my life dark,
without my beautiful Mina."

Long, long, they remained so, neither
speaking, neither moving, her eyes gazing
into the fire, as she rested against him, his
fixed on the grave young face, which lay
with such trusting, confiding love on his
breast, reading the very depths of the
young heart, which knew not itself, but
which had that night unconsciously laid
bare itself to him like an open book,
in which he read all its wealth of a
child's innocent affection, and woman's
trusting pure love, a book in which, as the
Chaldeans of old read the stars of Heaven,
he read her future, his future, that an in-
dissoluble chain bound them together, that
she must be his only in life or death. He
released her presently, saying as he did so—

"And now, dearest, you will promise me
to take every care of yourself during my
absence, and when I return let me find the
rose again in these pale cheeks, and that
dear sparkling look about the eyes I love
so well."

"I will try, Edward," murmured the
young girl, "and you will let me hear soon
of your success?"

"I will, I will, believe me, dear one."

At this moment the door of the apartment
opened, and Lady Agatha entered. There
was a look of inquiry in her face which was
instantly perceived by Mina, who said,
taking her aunt's hand in hers —

"He has told me all, aunt; but although
it must add to my anxiety, yet there is
some comfort in the hope that the day will
come, however distant, when I shall again
behold my precious mother."

"Heaven grant that it may be so, my
child," replied Lady Agatha, as she drew
the fair girl to her bosom, "Heaven grant
that it may be so! But now tell me, Sir
Edward, when do you purpose starting?"

"At once, Lady Agatha! Anything that will bring that time nearer which is to add to the happiness of my Mina, must be done, and at once."

"Be it so, then!" said Lady Agatha, "in the mean time, let me prevail on you to take a cup of coffee, while your horse is being got ready."

The next half hour was spent by the three friends in such dear converse as only such friends can enjoy, and at length the time came for Sir Edward to take his leave.

He took the hand of Lady Agatha in his, and raising it to his lips, said with much emotion—

"Adieu, dear Lady Agatha, I leave in your charge a priceless treasure—be careful of her, for she is my all in this cold, harsh world."

There was a tremulousness about the tones of Lady Agatha's voice as she replied—

"I know and feel how responsible is the trust I have had reposed in me—rest assured that all the care the deepest affection can dictate, shall be lavished upon our dear Mina."

"I know it—I feel it!" added Sir Edward, then turning to Mina, he opened his arms, and for one brief moment he pressed her to his heart, of which she was the pride and the idol.

"Adieu, dearest and best!" he said "Be hopeful, love, who knows, but that I may return with your dear mother?"

Mina was too much overcome to speak; but when she raised her head there was a look of hopeful resignation on her sweet face, which went far to reconcile Sir Edward to this painful parting.

In another moment she was alone with her aunt, and they soon heard the tramp of his horse's feet as he trotted down the noble avenue of limes which led to the house.

Mina sunk upon an ottoman at her aunt's feet, and resting her head in her lap, wept long and sadly.

When the first burst of grief was over, Lady Agatha passed her hand caressingly over the fair hair, and said gently—

"My little Mina must not forget one parent in her anxiety for the other. It is just the hour for the post to arrive—I wonder that we have not heard from your father."

"Oh, how selfish have I grown," cried Mina, starting up, "I had forgotten that we were to receive a letter from him to-day to say when he would arrive."

At this moment a servant entered the room and handed a letter to Lady Agatha on a silver salver.

"It is from him!" exclaimed Mina, her whole soul beaming in her eyes, "read it, read it at once, dear aunt, and let me know, at least, when I may expect to see one parent."

Lady Agatha broke the seal and read the letter hastily, without speaking.

"Well, dear aunt, what does he say?" asked Mina, anxiously.

"He says, dear," said her aunt, fixing her eyes upon the countenance of the young girl with a scrutinizing look, to see how she would bear the disappointment—"he says, dear, that something unforseen will prevent him being with us so soon as he expected."

"Something unforeseen?" repeated Mina, with anxiety—"what could have happened, aunt, to prevent his return? May I read the letter?"

"Read for yourself, my child!" said Lady Agatha, giving the letter into Mina's hand, who read in a low voice the following words—

"My dear sister,—You live a life of such seclusion that you may not have heard—and yet I think it is scarcely possible for the news not to have reached you—that some three years ago the Duke of Kingston, the uncle of my precious Dora, disappeared suddenly, no one knowing where he had gone. He left his mansion in St. James's square, late one night, alone, in a hired post-chaise, and has not since been heard of.

"There were strange rumours among his servants respecting him, and some of them went so far as to say that they believed his old valet had come by his death in some foul way.

"Nothing, however, was proved—advertisements were inserted in various newspapers, both in England and on the Continent, but without throwing any light upon the strange affair.

"The officers of the Crown took possession of the house, sold off most of the furniture, and it was then shut up.

"It is now two years since all this took place, and the affair was almost forgotten, until it was all revived over again by a gentleman appearing who wished to take possession of the house adjoining Kingston House.

"This mansion had been shut up for many years, and it was found necessary that it should undergo thorough repair.

"It was then found that many a deed, dark and terrible, had been committed in that house, for no less than six skeletons were found in it.

"Of this you have heard, but we know not how nearly all this may concern us hereafter.

"Enquiries were immediately set on foot, but no clue could be obtained of the murderer.

"We know more than the rest of the world respecting this apparently deserted house, for Dottman mentioned to us at the time he possessed himself of the document which was to save my Dora from any fear of again undergoing the penalty of a crime of which she was perfectly innocent—that the false Duke of Kingston had some means of reaching his house from that in the the then occupation of Surlina.

"I stated what I knew of the facts of the case to a brother officer, and immediately measures were taken to find the duke—but in vain.

"Yesterday, however, I _saw him_—saw the man whose soul is stained with murder—who has, perhaps, caused the death of my own Dora—my precious wife.

"I am watching — hoping—waiting—to bring him to justice—it is for this reason, dear Agatha, that I must deprive myself of the only happiness yet within my reach—that of again beholding my little Mina—my darling child. And now farewell! Tell my Mina her father sends her many kisses—and will not delay one moment beyond what is necessary returning to her.

"Believe me, your affectionate brother,
                             Henry Dacres."

*   *   *   *   *

It is time that we return to the false Duke of Kingston, who so far had succeeded in the plot for the destruction of Dora's happiness, that she was now in a madhouse.

True, at times, he had misgivings in his mind as to whether or not his brother, whom he had so deeply wronged, might not appear some day, and thus frustrate all his schemes—still, however, he continued to hope that death had rid him of that obstacle to his ambition.

Henry Dacres, he knew, was abroad, serving with his regiment, and for some time he had failed in discovering what had become of Dora's child.

She was now getting of an age to make it very difficult any longer to keep her out of those estates which fairly belonged to her—if her grandfather and mother were dead. To get possession, then, of this young girl, was now his great object in life.

But there were whisperings and meaning glances directed towards him now whenever he appeared at Court, or at any public place of amusement, and the duke begun to think that his better plan would be to leave England, as he had at first intended.

Besides, too, the servants were getting uneasy respecting the continued absence of the old valet, who was a favourite with them all, and he, the duke, was not safe, he thought, so near to the scene of his crimes.

Accordingly, one fine night at the latter end of the autumn a post-chaise might have been seen standing before the hall door of Kingston House, into which the Duke of Kingston leaped, without, however, giving any direction to the driver in the hearing of the footman who was standing in the hall.

This man thought at the time that his master might "be up" to some of his queer doings—but never supposed for a moment that he was leaving his home, probably never to return to it.

Yet such was the intention of the duke. He had converted all the valuables about the house into money, and with this securely hidden he bid adieu to Kingston House.

The post-chaise rattled along the hard roads, and in a few hours the Duke of Kingston had reached the London Docks, where he learned that a vessel was clearing for Lisbon, and would sail at high tide, which would be about the hour of one in the morning.

The vessel took a limited number of passengers, and was a large square-built ship. The duke bargained for a private cabin; he named himself Tomlinson, and promised to be on board at midnight.

His next step was to go to his bankers and draw out all the money he had there.

"That is done!" he said, with a feeling of satisfaction, "that is done. To be sure the ship touches at Havre for some portion of her freight, but the delay will be short, and I shall soon be in the beautiful Tagus. Farewell, then, to England for ever, and all that it contains! Ha! ha! all that it contains! I have given Turnbull instructions with regard to the girl; if I can but get hold of her all may yet be well. He is clever and unscrupulous, and too well paid to turn treacherous—besides, I can hang him at any time, as he knows—but having kept my own counsel, I have nothing to apprehend from him. All goes well—yes, all goes well."

At midnight the duke, who had written the name of Tomlinson upon what luggage he had, stepped into the boat that was waiting to convey him to the ship. The broad river stretched before him like a dusky glass. Not a ripple disturbed its surface, and the winds of Heaven seemed to have crept into some far off cavern and there sheltered themselves to a long sleep, while the world should not be ruffled by their brawling voices.

A preternatural stillness was about all things, and it seemed as though one of those mysterious pauses of nature was taking place, such as strike the listener with an unknown awe, and which makes the heart beat quick with an expectation of we know not what.

"A quiet night!" said the duke, as he stepped into the boat.

"Yes, sir!" said one of the men, "it's too quiet to last—I don't like these here dead calms—it looks as if something was a brewing like."

The boat was pushed off into the glossy stream, which only in huge masses at times gently heaved up as though instinct with a strange vitality, dependant upon those great throbbings, which moved the mass of water languidly.

The lights upon the bank of the river shone clearly in the stream, and through some straggling clouds the young moon was faintly peeping like some wayward child that will and yet will not show its fair face to those it loves, or like some maiden that wishes the world to know that she is beautiful, and yet with a pretty affectation coquettes with the veil that only half conceals her charms.

The men pulled lustily at the oars, and in a very short space of time the London Docks were reached.

"What ship, sir?" said one of the men.

"The Dart!"

"Ship a hoi! the Dart it is!"

"All's right—give us a rope to larboard."

In another minute the wherry scraped against the side of the ship, and the Duke of Kingston was soon upon deck. His first question to the captain was—

"You sail as you intended?"

"Oh, yes—we must—we are off at once. Your cabin is all ready, sir, and you can take possession of it."

"But you can't get out with this dead calm! said the duke.

"Humph! it wants hard on to three hours, sir, to the time of high tide, and we don't know what the wind may say to us by then."

The captain held up his hand as he spoke, and then muttering something, he went aft, and held a whispered consultation with the mate.

A lad showed the Duke into his cabin. It was about the size of what would be considered a very tolerable pantry. A swinging lamp hung from the roof, and a table was secured to the floor, while two or three portable seats and a bench fastened to the side, constituted the rest of its furniture. There was a mysterious looking little shelf that was meant for a bed.

He lay there for some hours tossing about and thinking—thinking of all the crimes he had committed in order to acquire wealth—and now that all his plots and plans had succeeded apparently, there was he flying from his country under an assumed name—for the fear of detection was strong upon him.

He now rose from his recumbent position and looking out, he had the satisfaction of seeing that they had cleared the docks and were going at a good speed.

"Thank goodness!" he ejaculated, "I shall soon be clear of England."

We will leave him now, and return to those personages whom we have so long neglected.

CHAPTER LXVII.

IN WHICH THE READER IS INTRODUCED TO A VERY OLD ACQUAINTANCE—DOTTMAN RESCUES MINA FROM TURNBULL—DORA HAS AN IMPORTANT CONVERSATION WITH EMILY.

AFTER a long and painful illness, from which few thought he would ever recover, we again behold with the eye of our imagination our old acquaintance Dottman.

And yet, notwithstanding that he had suffered much, there is yet a look of vigour about him, which would have led one to suppose almost that time had stood still, so far as he was concerned, during those twelve years.

At the time at which he is again introduced to the reader, Dottman is mounted on a horse, but he had suffered the bridle to drop, his head was bent slightly forward, and he seemed lost in deep meditation. He sat there for full a quarter of an hour—and not a sound had he heard—for the living creatures had sought repose.

"Yes!" he said to himself, "yes, it was here that I last saw her—by this road I led her to her death!" A sigh, which resembled a groan, burst from his lips as he went on. "Oh, would that I could believe her dead—but I fear worse than death is her portion. I cannot rest—I will hunt the world through for that villain, and tear the secret from his base heart!"

He urged his horse forward, for the air of the place seemed oppressive to him in his present excited state of mind—and had gallopped some twenty or thirty paces, perhaps, when he heard cries for help in a female voice.

"What can those cries mean?" he said, aloud, "I fear there is mischief!" and he gallopped on.

The moon by this time had just risen, and Dottman could just see the outline of a carriage, and two figures muffled up in cloaks, with slouched hats, endeavouring to prevent some one from getting out of the vehicle.

"Help—oh, help!" again came upon the ears of Dottman, and there was something about the tones of the voice which made his heart stand still, for in them he fancied he recognised those of Dora.

In a moment he had drawn a pistol from the holster, and fired it at one of the men, who, with a shriek, jumped into the air, and then rolled to the ground, clutching in his agony at the feet of his companion, and dragging him down at the same time.

"Confusion seize you !" shouted the man, "what are you doing ?" and he dealt the dying man a blow with something he held in his hand, which finished the work Dottman had begun.

"Hold, villain !" shouted Dottman, as he sprung from his horse, and knelt upon the breast of the fallen man. "Hold, villain ! at your peril try to rise !"

As he said this Dottman pointed the muzzle of his undischarged pistol right in his face.

The fallen man made an effort to rise, and throw off Dottman, but in doing so he turned his face in such a manner that a ray of moonlight fell upon it, enabling Dottman to recognize in the man he held at his mercy none other than the recreant Turnbull !

"Turnbull !" said Dottman. "Thank heaven, we meet again to settle old accounts."

There was a look of deadly hatred on the face of Dottman as he thus saw before him the man who had so long persecuted Dora, and it is difficult to say at that moment, whether he did not feel justified in dispatching him then and there ; indeed, such doubtless would have been the result, had he not hoped to learn something of the false Duke of Kingston, while this man, who Dottman knew was in his employ, was in his power.

With the quickness of thought Dottman took a thick rope from his pocket, and pinioned the arms of the villain, Turnbull, so firmly that it was impossible for him to use them, then lashing him to the shafts of the carriage, Dottman now turned his attention to the person whom he had heard calling for help, fully believing that he should see Dora.

What then was his disappointment when he saw only a young girl, apparently about the age of sixteen or seventeen, crouched on the floor of the carriage, and weeping as though her heart would break.

"Don't take on so, young lady," said Dottman, speaking as gently as he could— "don't take on so, for I have settled one of these fellows, and the next one will not be long in this world. Tell me who you are, and how it is you fell into the hands of these ruffians.

"Is it possible ?" said the young girl, looking up surprised, "is it possible that I see my dear, kind old friend, Dottman ?"

"Heaven be praised for directing my steps here to-night, my poor little Mina," said Dottman ; "but fear nothing, now ! wait here until I return, for I must speak to the villain who has acted as principal in this affair."

Dottman closed the door of the carriage, and turned to Turnbull, who was kicking and plunging at such a rate that he threatened to break the shaft.

"Hold, villain !" cried Dottman, dealing him at the same time such a blow upon the head that he was nearly stunned. "Tell me by whose orders you were carrying off this lady, or by Heaven I will lay you dead where you now lie grovelling like the hound you are !"

"Help ! murder ! help !" shouted Turnbull.

"Speak while you have yet time !" added Dottman, "speak, and tell me why you have stopped this lady, and by whose orders ?"

As Dottman said this he presented a pistol full in the face of the villain who had so long persecuted the mother of the beautiful girl.

"Take that pistol away and I will tell you all I know," said Turnbull, as a shudder of fear ran through his frame.

"Speak, and at once, or I pull the trigger."

"But are you a murderer, then ?"

"Speak, I say, or I will lodge a bullet in your brains."

Turnbull looked around him, no one was in sight, and there was a look about the eyes of Dottman which convinced him that he would be as good as his word if he refused to give him the desired information.

"The Duke of Kingston ordered me to secure the girl by any means in my power," said Turnbull, in a dogged, sullen voice.

"I thought as much," said Dottman— "now tell me what you know of her mother."

"I know nothing of her," said Turnbull.

"You lie, villain !" cried Dottman, giving him another blow, "You lie, villain ! Tell me what you know of her mother."

"I tell you I have not heard of her for years, man, how then can I tell you where she is ?"

"Then die, wretch !" said Dottman, as he brought the pistol in uncomfortably close proximity to the eyes of Turnbull.

"Help !" he cried, "spare me—spare my life, and I will tell you all—on my soul I will tell you all I know !"

"Quick then !" said Dottman, "for I will tarry no longer with such a villain."

"Listen then," said Turnbull. "He

EMILY SUGGESTING TO DORA A MEANS OF ESCAPE FROM THE ASYLUM.

placed her in a lunatic asylum when he went abroad, and there she still remains."

"Oh, Heaven!" said Dottman, "by this time she may have become insane—where—where is the asylum?"

"In Yorkshire—Bigmore Asylum in Yorkshire."

Dottman stopped not to hear more, but untying Turnbull from the shaft of the carriage, he dragged him along, his arms still pinioned behind him, and bound him to a tree.

"You will be safe there until I am out of your reach, treacherous scoundrel that you are," and with one more well-directed blow, which stunned him completely, Turnbull lay unconscious.

DORA.—34.

Dottman returned to Mina, who was beginning to get anxious as soon as she had ceased to hear the voice of her preserver.

He leapt into the carriage, and finding by this time that the coachman, who had been felled to the ground by a blow over the head, was standing by the side of the carriage, he said—

"Can you drive, my man, do you think?"

"Yes, yes, sir, although I feel fearfully dizzy."

"Then I will take the reins," said Dottman.

He now went to the side of the carriage, and putting his head in at the window, told Mina that he was going to drive, as he feared the coachman had been too seriously hurt to permit him to take charge of the horses.

Mina was rejoiced to hear her old friend had determined not to leave her until he had seen her safe beneath the roof of Lady Agatha, and she sunk back on the cushions of the carriage, full of unknown hopes and fears respecting her beloved mother.

"Oh, that I may see her again!" said Mina, clasping her little hands together— "oh, that I may see her again, and have the happiness of listening once more to the dear tones of her well remembered voice."

The carriage rumbled on, nor paused until it had reached the house of Lady Poynter.

There were bustle and confusion within that house, where all was usually so tranquil and quiet.

Lights were flashing about the grounds, and voices of men calling to each other, were distinctly heard.

"They have missed me!" said Mina, "they have missed me, and my dear aunt has doubtless suffered much during my absence."

"No doubt of it, little one," said Dottman, as he tenderly lifted her to the ground, "but I must now be off—you are safe now, dear, quite safe—I must away, for I have important business to attend to before tomorrow dawns."

"But will you not stay, Dottman, and receive the thanks of my dear aunt for your timely assistance?"

"Not now—not now, Miss Mina—I may return quicker than I expect, and if so, it will be time enough then to receive her thanks!" Then giving her into the charge of the good old coachman, who had been in the family of Lady Agatha for many years, Dottman hurried from "The Cedars," for by that name was the mansion occupied by Lady Agatha designated.

*   *   *   *   *

It was the evening before the eventful occurrences took place which we have detailed above, and we must again transport our reader to that asylum in which Dora had now been an inmate for so many years.

It is a lovely summer's evening, and Dora is seated at one of the open windows, (they could open only about a foot down the centre) looking at the sun, which had just set, and the sky was still full of light, though half way between the horizon— where the deep blue distance cut upon the bright golden expanse of the heavens—and the zenith, where the orange hues melted into rich purple, there hung a dark heavy cloud.

As Dora gazed upon the expanse before her, she suffered her imagination to find an image in the scene.

She thought that the warm golden space below resembled the years of her childhood —that the dark cloud looked like her present life—and that the purple sky above was that far land beyond the grave, in which alone she hoped to meet her loved husband and child.

Dora sighed, but even as she did so the wind moved the heavy cloud slightly to the east, and in the midst of the bright and intense light below burst forth a clear brilliant star, outshining all the splendour that surrounded it.

A faint smile sat upon the lip of Dora, for it seemed to her that inasmuch as she had taken the more sombre view of the lovely scene before her, that she must now also accept the brighter one, which was at that moment presented to her gaze.

She was roused from her reverie by a gentle hand being laid caressingly on her shoulder, and upon turning round she beheld the young girl who was named Emily —and who had already manifested so great an interest in her.

"A penny for your thoughts, Mrs. Dacres?" said she, assuming a cheerfulness which was anything but real, for the young girl was in trouble.

Dora's quick eye at once detected the unusual sadness which sat upon the bright young face, and she said—

"I will tell you my thoughts, provided you also tell me why you look so sad tonight?"

Emily looked around her to make sure that they were alone, and then she said—

"Oh, Mrs. Dacres, you have not seen any of the patients with one of the ward keys, have you? I have lost or mislaid mine, and I must go and report it at once."

Dora put her hand in the pocket of her dress, and to Emily's joy, produced the missing key.

"Oh, how thankful I am!" exclaimed Emily. "But how came you not to use it, since it was in your power to do so, and you have such a desire to leave this place!"

"No one—not even you, Emily, knows how much I desire to leave this place—and no one can ever know the strong temptation it was to me to do so, when I had the means in my power—but another consideration prevented me from taking advantage of the opportunity."

"I am quite curious to know—will you tell me, dear Mrs. Dacres?"

"I will! It was because the only friend who has sympathised with me in all my sorrows ever since I have been an inmate in this dreadful place, would have been accused of aiding in my escape—and rather than bring trouble upon her, I determined to wait and watch for another opportunity."

"Dear kind friend!" said Emily, "how grateful am I for your consideration—it makes me more than ever anxious to see you at liberty, although, if the day should ever come for you to leave this asylum, you will leave at least one sad heart behind you!"

As Emily gave utterance to these words the tears stole down her cheeks.

Dora took her hand, saying—

"Believe me, dear Emily, if the day should ever come, and I am restored to my proper position in society, you, at all events, would not be obliged to continue in this situation—unless you wished to do so—for I would fain ever have you near me, dear Emily."

Emily was moved—but made no answer.

Dora looked up, and she found that one of the other nurses—Emily's superior nurse—was standing beside them.

"I thought I told you, Emily, to lock up all the patients, and here I find you still gossipping with Mrs. Dacres—you know it's against the rules for one patient to sit up later than another!"

"Oh, don't blame her on my account!" said Dora, gently—"I wished so much to watch this beautiful sunset, and Emily was kind enough to allow me to do so."

"Watch the sunset, indeed! replied the head nurse, with a sneer, "one's work would never be done if one was to humour every patient in that way. See the sunset, indeed! perhaps you would like to see the moon rise now, wouldn't you?"

Dora did not deign to reply to this unfeeling speech—and fearing to make the breach wider between Emily and her headnurse, she rose to go to her dormitory.

Emily asked if she should wait and shut Mrs. Dacres' door?

"Of course you will! Do you suppose I am going to do half your work for you—pretty well, I suppose, if I have to look after you, and see you do it, without actually doing it myself?"

With this, Miss Gotch, as she was styled on her letters, swept out of the gallery, leaving Emily and Dora its sole occupants.

Emily was the first to break the silence, saying, in a hesitating voice—

"Mrs. Dacres, I want to speak to you—may I come with you to your room?"

"Certainly—what can you have to say—if you want my advice, you shall have it, provided I can advise you judiciously—it is all I can offer you."

The young girl entered Dora's little dormitory, and seated herself upon the bed.

"Well!" said Dora, "what do you wish to say? Be quick, or we shall be interrupted."

"It is this!" replied Emily, "that I have been thinking I will aid you in escaping from this asylum!"

"You!"

"Yes."

"But, my dear girl, you have often let me amuse myself by reading your "rules and regulations," and in them I find that any attendant who is discovered in aiding in the escape of a patient shall be fined forty shillings, besides his or her name being struck of the roll of asylum warders."

"I know all that—but you do not suppose that I am going to say I helped you to escape, or that I fancy you would compromise me in any way?"

"No, indeed, I would not—but tell me, how can you help me?"

"In this way," replied the young girl; "it is my turn to go out to-morrow evening—I shall not go, but I will take care to go to the laundry or somewhere about the house, so that I may be seen—I will by mistake leave my key in the pocket of my dress, which you will discover—and instead of being so generous as you were to-night, you will really use it—"

"But I shall be discovered and brought back," said Dora, "before I leave the grounds, and then—"

"Of course you would be as Mrs. Dacres—but you must remember that one end of the key opens the wardrobe in my room, from which you may take whatever you please. You will then watch your opportunity—when the nurses are busy putting the patients to bed—to step out, present your key to the porter, and as you do so say as nearly in an imitation of my voice as possible—'I shall be back half an hour earlier than usual—have some roasted potatoes for supper, Mr. Ball.'"

CHAPTER LXVIII.

MINA IS AWAKENED FROM A REVERIE BY A LONG ABSENT FRIEND—MUTUAL CONFIDENCE—HENRY DACRES RETURNS TO MINA.

MINA was worn out and ill; constant wearing sorrow and sickening anxiety had begun, at last, to tell upon her, and she shrunk from anything like society, and yet anything that prevented her from thinking was a relief, so that she was glad when she found herself one evening seated in the old library at the "Cedars" with the grand paintings of the old masters looking down on her.

Oh how many dreary years of silent sorrow had she lived in those short five months since her father had written to say that his arrival was to be delayed for a few days. She never said anything, even to her aunt. She read and wrote, and went on with all the occupations she had been used to since she had become an inmate of her aunt's house, but so quiet and grave that her kind friend, Lady Agatha, read her tearless calmness, and saw that her heart was breaking.

"Mina, my child," said Lady Agatha, one afternoon that they were alone together—"Mina, my child, you make me very anxious about you—you are killing yourself."

"The sooner it is over the better," said Mina, bowing her fair head upon her shoulder.

"My dear child, said Lady Agatha, passing her arm around her, and speaking in her gentle, tender way—"Do I not suffer, too? Have I not enough to bear without the fear of losing you, too?"

She knew well how to reach her heart. The slight tinge of reproach, gentle though it was, touched her to the quick.

"Oh, aunt, forgive me," said Mina—"I can't help it; I don't mean to grieve you."

"But you do," said Lady Agatha. "How do you think I must feel when I see you almost dying, drooping day by day before my eyes? It is dreadful to bear!"

Mina was silent, but her kind aunt felt her slight form quiver in every nerve, and presently she said—"Rouse yourself, my dearest child; surely if I can hope you can hope too? Should we not trust in God, and bow to the stroke of Heaven?"

"I can't bend before the blast and rise again," said Mina, almost passionately—"I must bow to the storm and die!"

"And is that not defying heaven, my darling?"

"Oh aunt, death is all I ask, all I pray for. I might have still hoped to behold my father and my mother—but that Edward should have left me thus, without writing me one line ever since he has been gone is too much—too much!" and the fair head was bowed upon the clenched hands, and tears, such as almost broke the heart of Lady Agatha to witness, streamed through the little fingers.

Now, however, Mina is alone—alone for a long time, so buried in thought—painful, anxious thought, that she did not heed or know how time passed, or notice the sounds which would certainly have, otherwise, attracted her attention.

But as it was she did not even hear a carriage stop, followed by a knock at the hall door, and then voices speaking—then the door opened, and a tall, dark figure,

entered so silently that she did not hear any footfall, but it was rather that indefinite impression that some one was present that made her rise quickly and turn.

"Edward!"

"Mina, my darling—my beautiful!"

She was folded in his arms—close, close to his breast, in a clasp no human power could have loosed, and in that moment all the sorrow they had gone through was forgotten, save as a dark dream that is past.

He did not speak, he could not, until he held her off to gaze into the face so deeply loved

"Mina, Mina, how this dear face has changed; how ill and worn it looks."

"Ah! Edward, if you had written all might have been different," said Mina, touchingly.

He half smiled, and sat down in the seat she had left, and Mina knelt by his side, and laid her head against him, winding her slender fingers round his hand with a tender clinging action.

So for a long time they remained, and then she raised her head, and past her soft hand over his brow, and swept back his rich wavy hair.

"Edward, you too have changed; this grave brow has more lines, and this raven hair is mixed with grey. Five months have changed you, too, dear Edward."

"Look at neither now, my little one," said Sir Edward, gently drawing her head down on his breast again, and tenderly smoothing her fair sunny tresses; my journey has been a fruitless, and very nearly a fatal one—let it be forgotten—a page in my life obliterated."

"It cannot be, Edward! a page once read can never be forgotten, and it is one I have not yet read. Ah, Edward, it has been such a dark dream to your lonely Mina."

"Poor child, poor little one! I know what you must have suffered."

She pressed his hand to her lips as she said—

"Edward, read me your page, and I will tell you mine."

"It is shortly told, Mina. I arrived at the asylum where I believed I should find your mother, my child; but had the grief to learn that I was too late."

"Too late? merciful Heaven!" exclaimed Mina, "had you then found my mother but to gaze upon her corpse?"

"No, no, I said not that, dearest! she had escaped the evening before, and active search was being made for her."

Mina turned dreadfully pale, and then she said with a painful effort at calmness, "Then we shall meet again! thank God we shall meet again!"

"But, dearest, be calm, and I will tell you the worst. Fears are entertained that she may have destroyed herself to prevent being recaptured."

"I fear not that—I fear not that !" cried Mina, " my brave mother will seek her poor little Mina, for I feel convinced that she lives, and that we shall meet again."

"And is this all you wish to know, Mina?" said Sir Edward, " do you not care to inquire why I have been so long absent, and the cause of my silence during that absence ?"

Mina laid her cheek caressingly against his hand, around the fingers of which she had now twined hers with that confiding affection which he so well deserved as she said—

"Forgive me, dearest Edward, but I was unjust to you ; I allowed myself to fancy that perhaps you had found another—not who would love you better, but whom you would imagine so superior to your poor little Mina in intellect, that—"

"Utter not the words, my precious one, my only darling—I will now tell you, Mina, that I met the false Duke of Kingston ; but he was in the disguise of a Spaniard.

"He had joined a band of conspirators, against the government, and was indeed looked upon as their head or chief.

"When I heard this, I too disguised myself and sought the acquaintance of one of the fraternity, who after a time admitted me to some of their secrets, and promised to introduce me to their chief.

"This was all I sought, for I was so well disguised, that I was sure the Duke would not recognize me."

"The long wished for night at length arrived—I had followed him to Spain, and I believed the duke was entirely in my power ; but at that moment, when I thought my plan was about to be crowned with success, I was myself made a prisoner by the police, together with the rest of the conspirators, with the exception of the Duke of Kingston, but he managed to escape.

"He had not recognized me until I spoke, and then I saw him start as he did so.

"Well, I was thrown into prison, and I can tell you, Mina, I can now understand from bitter experience what it is to be deprived of liberty.

"I had no trial—I was brought before no tribunal, and when I stated that I was no Spaniard or conspirator, but an Englishman, and a subject of the king's, with the right to appeal to the English Ambassador, they disbelieved me.

"It is true my dark complexion, and somewhat Spanish appearance told against me, for foreigners seem to think that all English people must be fair.

"Still I could see that they so far thought it possible that my statement of being an Englishman of rank might be true, that they did not venture to execute me as they did the rest, but contented themselves with keeping me a prisoner.

"I offered my jailor bribes to convey a letter to the English Ambassador ; but he said he dared not do it, it was more than his life was worth.

"My child, these five months of captivity have been years of misery.

"But God was gracious, and I escaped at last. Some new governor came, who was quite satisfied to receive a heavy bribe, and so released me.

"Oh, Mina, no one can thoroughly love freedom who has not endured captivity."

She crept closer to him and whispered gently, " Let the dead past bury its dead. Let that dark page be forgotten, save as another link between us."

The stong man bowed his head, and tears fell on her upturned face.

He had never loved her so well as then, for the sorrow they had just gone through had bound them, as he had said, "yet closer if that were possible."

After a moment's pause Mina raised her head, saying—

"But now let us talk of my mother—oh, Edward, perhaps at this moment she is faint and weary, without a friend—oh, God! would that I might seek thee, my own mother!"

Mina sunk down upon a low ottoman from which she had just risen, and gave vent to the overcharged feelings of her heart in bitter sobs.

Sir Edward Hargrave allowed the first burst of anguish to expend itself before he again ventured to address her, but then he said—

"Mina, darling, will you not, for my sake—for your *mother's* sake, strive to control this sorrow ?"

There was a firmness—yet withal, so much tenderness in his voice and manner, that it failed not to produce the effect he wished.

There was one more choking sob, and Mina said in a low voice—

"I will try, I will try ; but it is difficult ! and now tell me, Edward, you have met with my father—what said he ? Have his efforts proved as unavailing as yours ?

"Alas, yes, dearest ! and he bid me say that on the evening after to-morrow he will return to his precious Mina."

"Oh, how I long to see my dear father !" said Mina, clasping her hands together, " did you tell him, Edward, of your—our love ?"

"I did, dear Mina ; and he said his

dearest hopes were now realized with regard to you. He was about to take Devonshire in his way, so as to pay a visit to your mother's father, for he hopes to obtain his pardon from the king to-day when he attends the levee."

"Is it possible that my dear grandfather may yet hope to take possession of his property, of which he has been for so long so unjustly deprived?" asked Mina.

"Even so, my darling. Your grandfather has ceased to take any interest in riches for their own sake, but he still clings to the hope that your dear mother may some day learn that she has a home to go to, so that if ever she becomes a wanderer, as she has been, she may seek the shelter of his roof."

"Would that she were with him! Oh, where can she be? Where can she be?" said Mina again, beginning to give way to a fresh burst of grief.

"Be assured that neither money nor effort will now be spared to find her whereabouts."

"I know, I know all that you would say, Edward," said Mina, "but whither can she have hidden? I dread lest she should be retaken and made to suffer, perhaps, for leaving the asylum."

"I scarcely think that she would be made to suffer by the authorities of the asylum, dearest; because I took care, before I left, to tell the doctor of the institution that she was not insane, but that she had been placed under his care by her wicked and unscrupulous uncle. I said also that she had powerful friends who would not fail soon to discover her, and if should that be the case, that they would instantly demand her discharge."

"It is well," said Mina. "I now feel much more relieved than I did when first we begun to talk about her. But here comes my aunt."

Lady Agatha at this moment entered the room, and was only too glad to witness the good understanding which evidently existed between her beloved niece and Sir Edward Hargrave.

Sir Edward Hargrave now gave Lady Poynter a hurried sketch of all that had befallen him since he left her house in order to commence his search for the mother of his Mina; and the rest of the evening was spent by the three friends in talking over their future plans, and hopes, and fears.

At this moment, however, and just as they were thinking of retiring to rest, there came upon their ears the tramp of horses' feet upon the soft gravel in front of the drawing-room windows, and almost immediately the door of the apartment was thrown hastily open, and a gentleman, in a military uniform, entered the room.

For one moment all were transfixed with surprise; but Lady Agatha rushed forward, and clasping her arms about him, crying—

"Welcome, welcome, Henry!" then breaking away from him, she advanced towards Mina, who was looking on with a puzzled air.

"Come, my child," said her aunt— "come forward, Mina, and help me to welcome your father."

Mina rushed forward.

"Father!"

"Mina! My darling! My only one!"

He strained her to his heart, and kissed the golden ringlets which now hung in disorder about the fair childlike face; then raising her head so that he could gaze into her deep blue eyes, he said gently, but with much emotion—

"How like, how like you are, my precious child, to your dear mother; I can almost fancy that I again behold my Dora as she was years ago. Alas! I know not whether she still lives."

"Oh, father," said Mina, "I am so glad to hear you think I resemble my beloved mother; let us hope that we may yet see her again. God has been too good to me to deprive me of this dear hope."

"We must leave all in His hands, my child," said Henry Dacres, reverently, "and in the meantime we will take what steps we can to bring about our reunion."

At this moment Henry's eyes fell upon Sir Edward Hargrave, who had retired into a recess in one of the windows, for he felt that the meeting between the father and his child was too sacred an one to be intruded upon."

As soon, however, as Henry perceived his dear friend, he held out his hand to him, while an affectionate smile played about his lips, saying—

"And is it to you, Edward, that I am to resign my newly found treasure?

Mina again hid her eyes upon her father's shoulder, for she feared lest he should think her ungrateful to wish to leave him for another's love.

"I ask you not to resign her love, my dear friend, only to let me share it with you."

Henry smiled as he said—

"I doubt whether I should myself be satisfied with such an arrangement were I in your place. But what says my little Mina?" said Henry, drawing her towards him—"is she willing to return your love—speak darling?"

Thus admonished, the fair girl raised her eyes, with a look of deep affection, to the face of Sir Edward Hargrave, and holding out her hand to him, she said, in a low voice—

"If I could only think myself good enough—

"Oh do not speak so, my precious Mina," said her lover, pressing her little hand to his lips—"you are to me so very dear; and all you do seems so entirely well done, that if I accept the boon of your dear love, believe me, it shall be the effort of my life to make you happy."

"I know it—I feel it!" said Mina—then turning to her father, she said, with touching *naivete*—

"And you are not angry, papa?"

"Angry, my darling? Yet stop—yes—I think I ought to be now you remind me of it!" but perceiving the look of sorrow that immediately came into those ingenuous eyes, he added quickly—

"No—no—my child! you have made me very happy in the choice you have made—but now let us retire, for I am faint and weary, and I have much to tell you, but not to-night!"

In another hour repose had fallen upon most of the inmates of that quiet English household.

CHAPTER LXIX.

DORA MAKES HER ESCAPE FROM THE RUINS AT BROCKLEHURST—THE STORM—THE ENCOUNTER WITH AN OLD ENEMY—TIMELY ASSISTANCE.

IT is towards evening of a beautiful day in the month of August that there was an announcement which ran through the wards of the asylum, to the effect that some two dozen of the patients were to be taken by a few of the nurses to some ruins in the vicinity and there to take their tea.

The announcement was hailed by many of them with joy, for it must not be understood that insanity closes the avenues to enjoyments—although the recipients of such kindness as was shewn to the inmates of Bigmore, generally speaking, had not such a keen sense of happiness now as they once might have had.

Mrs. Dacres, as being always "well behaved," was of course one of those selected for this little party of pleasure, and she would probably gratefully have accepted the invitation, had her thoughts not been far more occupied in contriving her means of escape, which she hoped to accomplish through the kind assistance of her friend Emily.

The patients are to be ready by two o'clock in the afternoon—Emily was not going to accompany them, but was to take charge of the ward in the absence of the head nurse.

Dora and Emily had had no opportunity of conversing since the latter had taken her clothes to her in the morning for her to dress—but she had then taken occasion to go back a second time to Dora's room, with some trifling article of dress, and it was then that she said, in a whisper—

"The patients are going out, some of them at least, and you will be among the number selected. Make some excuse for not accompanying them, as I fancy I shall be of more use to you, dear Mrs. Dacres, than perhaps I shall have another chance of being, as several of the nurses will be out."

"But," said Dora, in the same low tone, "are you not going also?"

"No, oh no! I never go anywhere if Mary Ann Beacon says she wishes to go—but I don't mind staying at home one bit, you see!"

"But Emily, dear!" added Dora, "remember, I will not escape—much as I wish to do so, if there is the slightest chance of compromising you in the matter—I have quite made up my mind on that head."

Emily thought deeply—then she said, loooking up quickly into the face of Dora, with her merry loving eyes, "I have it—I have it! The porter will not know which of the nurses are going out, but I will take care to let him think that I am in the van with the patients, for I will ride a little up the road with them, and then return across the little field—I need not be away from the ward ten minutes."

"But your head nurse!" suggested Dora—"she will know that you could not be going if she went."

"But I don't mean to go in the van that takes the patients from our ward—as it is considered the best one, the patients from this ward will ride in the first van."

"Well!" said Dora, somewhat amused, in spite of herself.

"Why, of course they will get in first—as Mary Ann Beacon never allows anybody to go before her, you know. Then I mean to let all the others get into the respective vans, and I will take my place in the last one, with the patients from the laundry—and as we pass out of the gates old Ball will be there, with his good tempered face, to wish us a pleasant afternoon."

"And you will take that opportunity to speak to him?" asked Dora.

"To be sure I will!" said Emily, and he'll believe that I have gone to the ruins."

Dora looked dubious.

At length she said—"Still, Emily, I don't see how your little plan is to aid my escape—for instance, if the porter feels sure that you have gone to the ruins, how am I to get out by personating you?"

Emily laughed merrily, as she said— " Why, by personating no less an individual than the celebrated Mary Ann Beacon herself!"

" But then, Emily," continued Dora, " when it is discovered that I have escaped, and that you were left at home to mind the ward, in the absence of Mary Ann Beacon, you will of course receive all the blame."

This was putting the affair in a new light truly, and Emily looked somewhat puzzled —at length she said—" I know what I'll do—I'll ask the matron to let me go into the laundry this evening, and help them a bit—and then I'll ask her to allow Catherine Wiltshire to take charge of the ward—she's such a stupid thing, you may do anything right before her eyes, and she'll never be a bit the wiser. Besides, she deserves to get into trouble, for she treats the poor creatures shamefully."

" Well, Emily," said Dora, " we will think it all over, and if we come to any better arrangement than that we have already made, all well and good."

" Very well!" said the kind-hearted girl, " but I must be off now, or I shall have *Miss* Beacon after me."

Dora laid her head upon her hand, and thought long and bitterly. She could not but see how very immature was the judgment of her kind friend, Emily, and she dreaded the consequences of a failure.

At length she spoke aloud, but still in too low a tone to be heard by any one not actually in the room—

" What should prevent me from joining this little party of pleasure, and making my escape from the ruins, when I have an opportunity? I am never watched, as no one suspects that I would try to make my escape, for I have never tried to do so— and besides, they all trust me—there have been times when this very Mary Ann Beacon has allowed me to have her keys to shut the windows. It will be much better so— and I shall not compromise that good, well-meaning girl."

At ten o'clock the wards were visited by the different officials of the institution; and when Doctor Radford came where Dora was sitting, engaged upon some needle-work, he said, kindly—

" I hope, Mrs. Dacres, you will go to Brocklehurst to-day?"

Emily happened to be in attendance upon the doctor this morning, for Miss Beacon had gone to the visiting room with one of the patients.

What was Emily's surprise, therefore, when she heard Dora say in her low, sweet voice—

" Thank you, doctor, I shall be glad of a little change—I will go if you will allow me?"

" That's right!" replied Doctor Radford.

" Why Emily," he added, turning to the nurse, " what did you mean by saying that Mrs. Dacres had declined to be of the party?"

" I thought—I understood—that is, I fancied," stammered poor Emily—but Dora interrupted her explanation by coming to her rescue.

" Well, doctor, Emily was quite right, for I did say I should ask to be permitted to stay at home, but an afterthought "—and here she looked meaningly at Emily—" induced me to change my mind, and I now think I should like to go very much."

" I'm very glad to hear it!" said Doctor Radford, and then turning to Emily, he said, kindly—

" And are you going, Emily?"

" No, doctor!"

" How is that?"

" Only because Mary Ann Beacon has ordered me to stay at home and mind—

" The house!" said Doctor Radford, laughing.

" That's just it! She never loses anything but her share in the work, and she takes care not to fatigue herself with that."

" Hush, Emily, said the doctor, smiling. " I'm afraid you are out of temper this morning—am I right, Mrs. Dacres?"

" If she be, it is the first time since I have known her then, doctor!"

" There, Emily, there's a character—I'll go while I am under so good an impression. Good morning, Mrs. Dacres!"

Doctor Redford turned and walked down the gallery, through which Emily attended him until he had passed into another ward, and then she returned to the table where Dora was sitting, and placing her arm around her, looked inquiringly into her face, saying—

And is this sacrifice, dear Mrs. Dacres, for my sake?"

" What sacrifice, dear girl?"

" That you intend to go to Brocklehurst this afternoon, so as to put it out of my power to assist you?"

" I mean to escape this afternoon!"

" Escape this afternoon? impossible!"

" Why impossible, dear Emily?"

" Because you will be watched too closely."

" But I shall try, nevertheless, and you then cannot get into trouble."

" Ah! I see, now, what you mean—you intend to make your escape from the ruins."

" I know not as yet; but I have a feeling at my heart which seems to tell me

DORA RESCUED FROM TURNBULL BY THE BLOODHOUND.

that you and I will never meet again beneath this roof as nurse and patient."

"A bright accession of colour stole over the face of the young nurse, and her eyes filled with tears as she said—

"I cannot bear to think of that, dear Mrs. Dacres, you are the only one I have had to speak to since I came here."

·· "But let us hope, dear Emily, that we may meet again some day under far happier auspices than we have done as yet, and then, believe me, I shall not be backward in testifying, not only my appreciation of your worth, but also the affection which has sprung up in my heart for you."

"Dear, dear Mrs. Dacres! how anxious

DORA.—35.

I shall be for this return, and how happy—yet how sad shall I feel if you do not return with them."

"You must bear always in mind, Emily, that I have no right to be confined here—that I have a husband and child, besides other dear friends, who would give all they possessed in life to know that I am safe and well."

"Yes, yes, I will think of that—I will think of that!" said poor Emily, looking mournfully at Dora; "but now tell me, what do you intend doing? You have no money nor valuables, which may be converted into money—how will you contrive to get to London?"

. "I have thought of that, dear Emily and as you received your wages yesterday, I am going to ask you to lend me three pounds—can you trust me?"

"Oh, so gladly! I had forgotten that I happened to be in the possession of so much money—I will go and fetch it instantly, as we may not have another opportunity of conversing alone."

Emily ran off to the pretty little room she called her own, and soon returned with the whole of her wages, which were wrapped up in a piece of silver paper.

"There, dear friend," she said, as she placed the little packet in Dora's hand, "there! and if you do not find your friends —I mean if you cannot pay me back again, I shall not care one bit."

"Thank you, my dear girl; but there is no fear of my long remaining your debtor, at least so far as money is concerned; but there is the breakfast bell—good bye, and God bless you! we must bid each other farewell now."

Dora passed her arm round her humble friend and gave her the parting kiss.

"Will that be the last time these two noble women will thus testify for each other the affection which binds them together.

We shall see.

All was now hurry and bustle within the asylum. The chosen few were looking forward with no little anticipation to the treat which was in store for them; and Dora had no opportunity of again addressing a word in private to Emily.

Her kind heart was grieved to observe a look of sorrow upon the usually bright and happy face of her kind nurse, but she trusted that as soon as she, Emily, learnt that she, Dora, had fairly escaped, the pleasure which that knowledge would give her would more than outweigh any selfish feeling which she might experience in losing so kind a companion.

Two o'clock has boomed out from the time piece of the asylum, and several covered vans are waiting to take up their passengers.

Now all are accommodated, and crack go the whips of the respective drivers, and the cortége soon vanishes from before the eyes of the less fortunate inmates, who from incapacity or mental disposition were not considered well enough to join the little party of pleasure.

By three o'clock the ruins were reached, much to the delight of all the occupants of those vans.

And now the cake is unpacked, and there is milk, to be distributed, and there are songs sung, and all goes merry as a marriage bell.

And what is Dora doing?

She has joined a little party at a short distance, and is busily engaged in hunting for wild flowers.

She is considered a safe patient, and those who are with her are actually supposed to be entrusted to her care.

There was a look of excitement, of expectation in the face of Dora which a close observer would not have failed to notice; but there happened to be no close observers in that joyous and somewhat noisy little party, and so she had nothing to fear from inquiring eyes.

The happy little party had sat some time enjoying themselves, when it was proposed that some of them, attended by a few of the nurses who had accompanied them, should visit a part of the ruins which went by the name of "Old John."

It was reached only by ascending a very steep hill, and from the summit of "Old John" might be seen many miles round.

To "Old John" accordingly, about twelve of the patients, with three of the nurses, directed their steps, leaving still seated beneath the shadow of the trees a tolerably large party, under the charge of two nurses.

Dora formed one of this party.

For some time the party under the trees watched the retreating forms of their companions, hidden ever and anon by the tall brushwood and gorse which grew so luxuriously in that locality, until not a voice could be heard, and not the flutter of a single garment could be seen; then they turned their attention towards each other, and questions arose as to what they should do to amuse themselves.

Dora, who possessed a very beautiful voice, was urged to sing them one of her pretty little songs with which she was wont so often to beguile the tedious hours, or to soothe the perturbed spirit of those poor afflicted creatures who had lost all interest in life.

Dora, who was ever willing to impart her share towards entertaining her unfortunate companions, immediately complied with their request, and in a sweet but thrilling voice sung the following words—

"I dream of thee at morn,
    When all the earth is gay,
Save I who live a life forlorn,
    And die through a long day.

I dream of thee at noon,
    When the summer sun is high,
And the river sings a sleepy tune,
    And the woods give no reply.

I dream of thee at eve,
    Beneath the fading sun,
When even the winds begin to grieve,
    And I dream till day is done.

"I dream of thee at night,
  When dreams, men say, are free,
Alas! thou dear—most dear delight,
  When dream I *not* of thee?"

The last words had scarcely died away among the trees, when heavy drops of rain were felt, and the distant thunder was heard.

Beneath those noble old trees they might have been securely sheltered from the rain, and they crept closely together for the purpose of taking advantage of their wide-spreading branches.

But now the wind howled and seemed to shake the trees to their roots, and some were frightened and fell to the ground in fear and trembling, while others, on the contrary, took to flight, and it was with difficulty that the warders could restore anything like order.

The lightning now became very vivid, and there is no telling what would have become of those helpless creatures beneath those trees, had it not been for the timely arrival of a man—apparently a labourer—who seeing so large a party congregated, and knowing the dangerous shelter they had chosen, hastened towards them, saying—

"Good gracious! don't be staying here in such a storm as this will be in a few minutes; but hasten as fast as you can across that field, and you will find good shelter in the cottages."

The warders were only too glad to hear such tidings, and they instantly collected their baskets and cans, and hurried across the field towards the cottages.

It was then that Dora resolved to attempt to regain her freedom.

How strong she felt! how courageous!

For some paces she ran with her companions; but in a few minutes she contrived to fall back a pace or two.

She was unobserved! for the rain now came down in torrents, and each one looked to herself.

Dora took a contrary direction—saw a stile, mounted it, and in an instant she was crossing a field, but in an opposite direction to that pursued by her companions.

One field was crossed and then another, and then Dora, drenched through, paused to listen—to think!

She knew nothing of the locality; but fear lent wings to her flight, and still she sped on—on—she knew not where—she cared not.

There was the distant barking of a dog, which was clearly borne upon the wind, and Dora knew not whether to advance or retreat.

She at last determined to advance, for she felt certain that no inquiries would have been set on foot so soon—for she judged rightly, that they had not yet had time to miss her.

There was a little cottage not far distant, and Dora hoped to reach it and there dry her clothes, and be permitted to go her way unquestioned.

The door was reached; but Dora started back in surprise and terror, for instantly she found herself clutched in a pair of strong arms, while a well known and hated voice hissed into her ear—

"Whither away so fast, Dora the Duchess? Ha, ha, ha! It is you who run after me—not I after you, apparently!"

With one bound Dora had sprung from his grasp; but in doing so, her foot caught in a hole just on the threshold of the cottage door, and she fell to the ground with a cry of pain.

"Help, help!" faintly cried Dora; but there was despair in her accents, for she knew not that such efficient help was at hand.

A gentleman leapt the stile, and with him was a beautiful blood-hound.

He had seen all that had taken place, and patting the dog on the head, said—

"Seize him, Leo! seize him!"

In a moment the villain Turnbull was pinned to the ground by the obedient creature, while his master assisted Dora to rise.

CHAPTER LXX.

DORA SEEKS REFUGE IN THE COTTAGE—
WHAT BEFEL HER THERE—THE DEATH
SHRIEK—DORA IN PRISON.

As soon as Dora had risen to her feet, the gentleman who had rendered her such timely assistance, asked her kindly whither she was bound when interrupted by the cowardly Turnbull.

Dora soon regained her presence of mind, and said in as innocent a manner as she could assume.

"I was overtaken by the storm as I was bound on my way to Nickleover, a village only a mile and a half from here, and was about to ask shelter in this cottage, when my steps were arrested by this man."

As Dora said this, she pointed to Turnbull, who was still held to the ground by the blood hound.

He made frightful efforts to speak; but there was an unpleasant sensation in his mind that if he stirred an inch he would be strangled.

The stranger looked up at the clouds, and expressed his opinion that the storm would shortly abate, and advised Dora to carry out her original intention to dry her clothes at the cottage, and then proceed on her way.

Dora looked first at the cottage and then at Turnbull.

"I see what you apprehend," said the stranger, noticing her anxious looks; "but you need fear no more insults from this fellow!" as he spoke he touched him with his foot—"for I will leave Leo to keep watch and ward over him until I send my man, or come myself to release him, so you may make yourself quite easy on that head."

Dora expressed her thanks as well as she was able, for she felt heart-sick and weary, and fearful of being overtaken by some of the officials of the asylum if she lingered much longer where she was.

The door of the cottage was opened at this moment by a woman carrying something in a basket, who, when she beheld the stranger and Dora, and again at a little distance, saw Turnbull pinned to the ground by a dog, exclaimed in a harsh tone—

"Heighday! what have we here? Turn—that is—I mean—what do you all want here? This is a respectable house—we want no tramps here."

Dora shrunk back, for the high shrieking accents of the woman terrified her in her present condition.

The stranger strode forward, and laying no very gentle hand upon the arm of the woman, said—

"This lady is no tramp—but she wishes to dry her clothes by your fire, and then to go on her way. Here is money, to pay you for any slight inconvenience to which you may be put, so take it and hold your peace."

The stranger fancied that it was the money which caused a difference in the woman's manner, but he was mistaken, for it arose from a glance she gave at Turnbull—a glance which he returned, and which said plainly—"Get her into the house!"

"Well, for the matter of that!" added the woman, as she turned the money over in her hand, "for the matter of that, the lady, if so be she is a lady, is quite welcome to any accommodation I can afford her—it is a poor place for the likes o' her, but still a fire's a fire for all that—so come in and dry yourself, and mayhap a draught of milk won't be unwelcome to ye."

By this time Dora had fairly entered the hut, which was one of the dirtiest, perhaps, it had ever been her fate to witness—still there was warmth, and she hoped that a very short time would be sufficient to dry her wet garments, and then she would fly—far away, she cared not whither, so that she might baffle pursuit.

The stranger also crossed the threshold, and as he did so he said in a low voice to Dora, so that it could not reach the ears of the woman, or of a young man, who was apparently so absorbed in mending a net that he did not even look up at the intruders—

"This is, indeed, a poor place—but you do not want accommodation, and the heat of the fire is as good here as anywhere else—but I cannot linger any longer now, for I was on my way to the sick bed of my father when I heard your cries for help."

"Oh! I will not detain you longer!" said Dora—"this good woman will kindly afford me every assistance I require, but—

Here Dora broke off abruptly, for the woman had watched her opportunity to leave the hut, and had found means of communicating with Turnbull.

"Keep her under any pretence," hissed the villain.

He would have added something more, but an uncomfortable reminder from Leo that his throat was in painful proximity to his teeth made him prudent.

The woman understood him, and waved her arms above her head.

At this signal a man's voice from one of the trees might be heard.

"I'll be with you in a minute, old gal—but I am waiting for Jim, who is only in yonder field."

It was just at this time that Dora perceived that the woman had left them, and on going to the door of the hut she saw her, at a short distance, engaged, to all appearance, in picking up sticks.

"Oh there she is!" said Dora—"I did not see her leave the cottage."

"Nor I," said the stranger—"but I see she has gone to gather some dry sticks to throw on the fire, which will certainly be an improvement to it."

The woman now entered, her apron filled with sticks and dry leaves.

"I am sorry to give you so much trouble, my good woman," said Dora, with one of her kind smiles—"but I will soon release you, for I do not feel at all tired; my shoes alone seem wet."

"Why, you're dripping wet!" said the woman. "Your clothes won't be fit to put on for hours. The best way will be for you to lie down there, in that inner room, and leave me to dry your clothes for you."

"I quite agree with you, my good woman," said the stranger—"you are much too wet to risk wearing these clothes even for a short time, so be prevailed upon to rest yourself until your things are in a fit state to put on."

Dora was far from satisfied with the arrangement, not only because she feared every moment seeing a well known face at the cottage door who had been sent from the asylum to capture her, but because there was a something about that loud talking woman, and the silent young man, and the close proximity of Turnbull which alarmed her.

However, she resolved to seem to fall in with the wishes of the stranger who had rendered her such service, and so soon as she could assure herself that he was out of sight, she hoped to find means of escaping from that inner room, of which the woman had spoken.

"I will now bid you adieu! be quite easy as regards that fellow who insulted you—I tell you I intend to leave my dog in charge of him until you are in safety."

Dora longed, yet dared not tell her preserver who that man was; it might lead to questions, and who know's but that he, the stranger, might be in some way connected with the authorities of the asylum, and might think that he was only doing her a kind service by delivering her up to them.

Dora resolved to wait; but it was with a feeling amounting almost to terror, which took possession of her as she saw her protector leave her beneath that roof.

Little did poor Dora know that hut had been long in the use of the villain Turnbull, and that he meditated keeping her there until he could ascertain what were the wishes of the false Duke of Kingston, her uncle.

The stranger, when he left the hut, closed the door behind him, and Dora sunk upon a kind of settle in the chimney corner, and asked herself what was best to be done.

Scarcely, however, had she done so, when she heard the report of fire-arms, and then an unearthly shriek rent the air.

Dora sprung to her feet, and her heart seemed to whisper to her that her unknown protector, was in danger—what she knew not.

She was about to hurry to the door; but the young man who had hitherto not spoken a word—nor taken the slightest notice of anything that had passed, prevented her.

Rising and pushing his chair from him with such violence, that it struck against the opposite wall, he said, as he seized her by the arm—

"Dare to move from this spot and you are a dead woman."

So sudden and unexpected had been his movement towards her, that Dora for the moment stood paralysed with fear; but only for a moment, for a sense also of her own danger took possession of her mind, and lent her courage.

"Unhand me, man! what mean you? Can you sit here and listen to such a scream as that, and not go forth to see what it portends? Coward! at least let me do what I can to help a fellow creature."

"Then it will be in the way of showing your ability in digging graves," said the young man, with a brutal laugh—"for I never heard a shriek like that to come from any one who was likely to be benefited by human assistance."

"Oh, Heaven!" cried Dora, turning towards the door, but she was confronted by the woman, "let me go and see what was the meaning of that awful shriek."

"I'll tell you what it meant, without your taking the trouble to go and see—it means that Sam Turnbull has more friends here than either you or that meddlesome intruder knew of—and that he has met with his just reward for interfering in other people's business.

A cold shudder ran through the frame of Dora as she listened to the words of the woman, for she now felt how hopeless it would be to fancy, for one moment, any assistance from her.

"Ah!" said the woman, with a sneering laugh, "you begin to see the wisdom of keeping a still tongue in your head, do you?"

Dora felt that her position was desperate, and she resolved to act accordingly.

Quick as thought she sprung past the woman, and had succeeded in reaching the door, which was partially open, when she was seized by the young man, who took a pistol from his pocket and presented it full in her face.

Dora knew that her life was not worth a minute's purchase with such a weapon, and in such hands, and she gazed about her with a look of despair.

"Look you here, my fine lady," said the young man, "your life is in no danger so long as you remain quiet and peaceable; but as soon as ever you attempt to raise an alarm, then click goes the trigger, and you're a dead woman."

For a few seconds fear got the better of Dora, and she clung to the wainscot of the room for support.

Just at this moment Turnbull entered the cottage, and with a horrible oath seized Dora by the wrist, saying—

"This is, indeed, a good day's work—so good, in fact, that I can almost find it in my heart to forgive this wound in my throat, caused by the fangs of that brute of a dog; but I have you now—I have you now, and it shall not be my fault if you escape this time, I can tell you!"

"Mercy! mercy!" gasped Dora.

"Mercy, say you? Who ever talked to

Sam Turnbull of mercy, I should like to know? Did you cry mercy when years ago I was thrown against a certain doorway and left for dead? Mercy, indeed, not if I know it!"

Dora knelt at his feet, and wrung her hands.

Turnbull seemed to take a fiendish delight in her despairing gestures, for he laughed his coarse loud laugh as he said—

"It is now your turn to sue to me—ha, ha, ha! Do you remember the pistol shot by the river's brink? you thought you had killed me—but I lived on—lived on for this night!"

Dora sunk to the floor, and for some time she knew nothing of what was passing around her.

She knew not that at the time she had fainted—how that the woman approached at a sign from Turnbull with a lantern in her hand—nor how he, Turnbull, had carried her in his arms into that inner room, which has already been mentioned, and how he again took his way across a little paved yard to a kind of outhouse, of which the young man was holding open the door.

Into that outhouse poor Dora was carried, or rather dragged by the brutal Turnbull, followed closely by the woman with the hand lamp.

But what are they now doing in that outhouse?

The young man having given admission to the party, allowed the door of the outhouse to swing shut, and then he made his way to the further corner of the barn, and by means of a ring opened upwards a trap door.

A flight of some dozen steps was visible, and down these steps Turnbull descended with his fair burden, the woman all the while holding up the lamp in such a position as to enable him to reach the bottom of the flight of steps in safety.

That done, he deposited Dora in a kind of vault, and with a smile of satisfaction he returned up the steps again to his two companions.

"She's safe enough!" he muttered between his clenched teeth—"I'll make her pay off old scores, now, or my name's not Turnbull."

The young man lowered the trap door, and all was still—and Dora was in reality entombed.

"How long do you mean to keep her there?" asked the woman.

"Until she tells me where to find her daughter, Mina."

"Then you will have the trouble of burying her," said the woman.

"We shall see that. But first of all I must find out what she has been doing lately, for I fancied she was in safe custody at the asylum yonder. If she has been regularly discharged it is quite certain the Duke of Kingston has his reasons for consenting to her being at large—and if she has run away, why I must look sharp after her, as there will be inquiries made."

"And then you would have to give her up?" asked the woman.

"Exactly so—and that I don't mean to do so easily, I can tell you. Now then, imp, what are you staring at? Haven't I told you that I would not have you listening to every word that is said by your betters. Take that! and mind what's said to you another time."

The blow which accompanied the above words was quite sufficient to have sent a strong man reeling backwards, much less the little mis-shapen boy, who in addition to a hump between his shoulders, possessed one of the most forbidding countenances it was possible to behold.

The boy staggered and fell to the floor; but in an incredibly short space of time he succeeded in again scrambling to his feet, and assumed a very hostile attitude by doubling his great fists as though about to take aim at his tormentor, Turnbull.

"You'd better mind what you're after," cried the boy, every feature of his face distorted with rage, hatred, and malice—"you'd better mind what you're after, or I'll kill you."

Turnbull laughed his hideous, yelling laugh, and said—

"Go on, young impus—you're getting ripe for the gallows, I can see that!"

"And what's that to you, if I am, I should like to know? I'm not the only one; if everybody got what they deserved, you wouldn't be here.

"Hold your tongue, wretch!" shrieked the woman—"get out of the place, and don't come across me again the whole of the day, or you'll see that I'm not going to stand by and hear Mr. Turnbull talked to in that sort of way."

The boy was about to make good his escape; but in doing so, he came in violent contact with the young man whom we have before spoken of.

"Hilloa! what's the row now?" he cried, placing his back against the door, "can't you leave the boy alone?"

Neither Turnbull nor the woman deigned to make any reply to the question, and the young man said, turning to the dwarf—

"Run away and play, Jack, and don't be so saucy to your superiors."

"I will be saucy, and they're not my superiors—they're paid for keeping me—and I can't get enough to eat sometimes;

but I'll be even with them—I'll be even with them!"

So saying, he made a hideous grimace at Turnbull, snapped his fingers in the face of the woman, and disappeared through the open doorway.

CHAPTER LXXI.

LADY AGATHA POYNTER'S GUESTS—DORA'S FATHER GOES TO TAKE POSSESSION OF KINGSTON HOUSE—THE VEILED FIGURE.

THE morning after the events took place which we have detailed in our last chapter, a small, but not by any means an unhappy party sat in Lady Agatha Poynter's cheerful breakfast room.

First of all, there was the kind hostess of that hospitable mansion, upon whose countenance there still lingered the traces of great beauty, and as her eye rests upon her beloved niece, Mina, there is a look of such deep affection, that few would have believed it possible that such a love existed between aunt and niece—it was more the love of a mother that Lady Agatha felt for the fair girl who was seated by her father's side.

Then there was the venerable Duke of Kingston—the father of Dora, and the rightful possessor of that beautiful property of which he had been for so many years deprived.

He, too, was looking at Mina fondly, while she was gazing up into his face, listening to a recital of what he had gone through since he had last seen her mother.

How he had hoped, even against hope, that he should again behold her in this life, then how the dark conviction took possession of his mind that she was no more.

There, too, was the noble minded and chivalrous Sir Edward Hargrave, who had won the virgin affections of his beloved Mina—he too was engaged in watching her ever changing expression of countenance, and thinking that each expression was more beautiful than its predecessor.

But all unconscious of her exceeding beauty was that fair girl herself as she sat there, talking and listening to those who were so dear to her.

We will listen to what the Duke of Kingston—of course we mean the rightful duke—is saying to Mina at the moment we are introduced to so many of our old acquaintances round the hospitable board of the kind hearted gentlewoman, Lady Agatha Poynter.

It is the duke who is speaking.

"And so, dear Mina, I shall claim you at the hands of your aunt for a few weeks, when I take up my abode in Kingston House; for since, through the kindness of one or two tried friends, I have received my sovereign's pardon, there will be no occasion to hide myself as I have done.

Mina clasped her grandfather's hand, and sought to restrain him from talking too much of the past, for well she knew how deeply he felt her mother's death, or at least, continued absence.

"Oh, yes, my dear, dear grandfather, how gladly will I come and be all to you that a child can be. May I not go, dear papa?" she said, turning to Henry, who was on the other side of her.

"Most willingly, my child, do I give my permission, for it may be some time before I again return to England, for I have resolved to seek this false duke, let him be at the other end of the world, and force him to give me some tidings of your precious mother.

Tears glistened in the eyes of Mina at the mention of her mother, and she said—

"I suppose it must be so, dear papa, but it is so sad to part with you so soon after so long an absence.

"Believe me, my precious child," he said, with great emotion, "that nothing but the task I have now imposed upon myself should induce me to leave my darling; but even you, Mina, would not wish me to decide otherwise under the circumstances"

"Oh! no, no," said Mina. "Never can I be happy until I am convinced, beyond a doubt, that my mother is either dead or in safety. Even the knowledge of her death, painful as it would be, would still be more bearable than this dreadful suspense; and you shall find, dear aunt, that I resemble my beloved mother in courage also, as well as in feature."

Lady Poynter smiled and said—

"I believe you, my child; and think what a reward it will be for all your patience if your father should return accompanied by your mother."

Henry clasped his hands over his face, and his chest heaved—it was evident that he suffered greatly. At length he said—

"I know not why, but something always seems to whisper to my heart that my Dora is still alive and waiting for me somewhere —oh that I may have the happiness of discovering her hiding place.

Sir Edward Hargreave asked Henry if he had received any tidings from Dottman since he had been in Yorkshire.

"No," replied Henry, "and that makes me very sanguine, I must say. I fancy that he must have some clue to her whereabouts, and is therefore waiting until he either succeeds or fails in seeing her, before he communicates with me."

"Perhaps so!" said Sir Edward—then turning to Mina, he said—

"And when next we meet, dearest—which I trust will be the day after to-morrow, you will be the guest of the Duke of Kingston?"

"Oh, Edward," said Mina, "do not call my dear grandfather by that hated title. Never shall I hear it, but I shall remember all that my wicked uncle has made us all suffer. Tell me, dear grandfather," taking his hand in hers, "will you not be called by the name you used to bear, namely, Sir Lionel Danvers, instead of that title which has brought you such misery?"

"I feel as you do, my dear child," replied the duke, "on this subject, and I hope to be able to take the title of Duke of Whitbourne, which became extinct many years ago. It formerly belonged to my family, and I hope that instead of bearing the title of Kingston, to be able to assume that of Whitbourne."

"I am, indeed, glad to hear that," said Henry Dacres, "for I need scarcely say that the former title must ever bring only painful recollections with it."

The Duke of Kingston—for by that title we must continue for a short time to designate the father of Dora—now rose to take his departure for Kingston House, where he said he hoped to have everything in readiness to receive Mina on the day following.

Henry here expressed his intention of accompanying him—having as he said, some curiosity to look at the house which once had been the theme of public talk and speculation.

The two friends therefore now took their departure, leaving Sir Edward and Mina, still the guests of Lady Agatha Poynter.

They trotted their horses along the road, and reached Kingston House just before nightfall.

Their knock at the hall door was answered by a footman in livery—for most of the servants who had formerly been in the service of the father of Dora, as soon as they heard that he had been reinstated in his possessions, made personal application to their beloved master, and were duly reinstated in their respective offices.

The man who opened the door was grey headed, for he had lived many years in the duke's service, and tears came to his eyes as soon as he beheld who the visitors were.

"Welcome—most welcome, my dear master, and you too, Mr. Dacres," said the old man, "I did not expect you so soon, my lord, or the other servants should have been here, also, to express their delight at your return."

"No apologies," said the duke, kindly, "no apologies, Ambrose; I will see and speak to them all before I retire to rest; but I have some business to transact with Colonel Dacres here first, so we will proceed at once to the library."

"Very well, my lord," replied the old servitor, "there is a fire there, for I fancied the rooms felt cold and deathlike."

"It is well!" returned the duke, and he proceeded with Henry towards the library.

There was a bright fire burning in the grate, although the day had been warm and genial; but as Ambrose said, the room had a cold and deathlike feel about it, which nothing but a good fire could have displaced in any degree.

As soon as the duke and Henry Dacres—now Colonel Dacres, were alone, the former said—

"It is this cabinet which I wish to examine in your prescence—for in it, I know, my father kept all his private papers, which of right belonged to me; but owing to my being so unfortunate as to be mixed up with the Jacobites—a price as you know, was set upon my head, and Reginald taking a different view, or pretending to take a different view to myself in politics, stepped into, not only the estates, but also all the family papers and documents."

"I have heard as much," said Colonel Dacres; "but I much fear that your search will prove fruitless after so many years—for it is not likely that your brother, when he left England, left any papers behind which would be of any value to you."

"We shall see—we shall see!" replied the duke; "but it is my belief that Reginald never was aware of a secret drawer which this cabinet contained. It was shewn to me by my father years before his death, and he told me then that no one but myself knew of its existence."

"Then by all means let us at once begin our search," said Henry, and the two friends approached the cabinet, Henry holding in his hand a silver candlestick, which he had taken from the table.

From a bunch of keys which the duke had in his possession, he selected one which quickly opened the cabinet, although the key made a harsh, grating sound, as though the lock were rusty from long disuse.

The cabinet opened in the centre with doors, and when thrown back these displayed to view a number of drawers elegantly inlaid with mother of pearl.

The duke removed one of the drawers, and had placed it on a side table which stood close by, when a shriek so unearthly and deafening rent the air, that both the duke and Henry stood aghast.

Then there came the tramp of many feet,

THE DUKE OF KINGSTON AND HENRY INTERRUPTED BY THE VEILED WOMAN.

and several voices were heard, evidently forbidding some person or persons to approach the library.

"What means this strange commotion?" said Henry, laying his hand upon his sword, "Wait for me here while I go and ascertain the cause of this strange interruption!"

Scarcely, however, had he uttered these words, when the door of the library was dashed open, and a woman enveloped in a long cloak, which she held tightly about her, and a veil, which completely concealed her features, entered the room, followed by several of the domestics, who seemed uncertain what to say or do.

DORA.—36.

"Back! back!" cried the female, holding out her hands, in one of which gleamed in the fire-light a poignard, "Back! back! I say—I have watched for this night for many weary years, and now that it has come at last, would you rob me of my reward?"

Henry took a step forward, with the intention of securing her, but in a moment she guessed his intention, and pointed the dagger towards him.

"Beware I say, beware! for if aught happens to me, who shall guide you to her you call your wife?"

"Ah, Dora! my wife! said you? Speak to me—tell me—know you aught of her?"

Henry took a step towards her with clasped hands, and a look of agonised expectation upon his countenance, which was alarming to behold.

"Ha, ha, ha!" shrieked the female, "Is it possible that such a thing exists as human love? I tell you, man, it is a lie—a base lie—you thought to kill me, but failed—failed—failed! and now I have you in my power."

The Duke of Kingston said, in a kind tone—

"You mistake us for enemies—believe me, you are speaking to those who wish to befriend you—tell us who you are, and what your errand to this house!"

"Ha, ha, ha!" again rang from the lips of the strange visitor, "Is it possible that you dare to pretend you do not know me? I tell you, man, I foiled you when you fancied you had me in your power—the liquid did not do your bidding—the mad woman was cunning—and she caught the phial, so that the contents did not do their foul work. It was murder, nevertheless!"

"Good heavens! what can she mean?" said the duke, turning pale, "there have been rumours afloat which I have discredited —but let us try to learn more—perhaps, if we humour her, she will get more coherent."

"Tell us," he said, in a low tone, "tell us to what you refer—it is evident you have mistaken us for some other people—who committed the foul murder of which you speak?"

The veiled figure had sunk upon a chair, and seemed absorbed in her own thoughts, and did not appear to hear the question which had been put to her, for she said in a voice so touching that it brought tears to the eyes of the two brave hearts, who had suffered so much themselves, that they could well sympathise with another in misfortune.

"So young—so fair and beautiful!" the figure murmured to herself, "that I could not believe her guilty—no—no—Reginald —I tell you she should be Dora the Duchess —I am not the rightful Duchess of Kingston!"

The duke and Henry exchanged glances.

"Fire! fire! Ah, yes, you managed well, Reginald—they believed that she attempted to set fire to the house, but she only concealed herself, in order that she might tell me her claim to the title and estates, and I promised that I would befriend her — poor girl! poor girl! poor girl!"

Henry made a sudden movement, as though he would approach the figure, whose sobs would break the overcharged heart, but the Duke of Kingston laid his hand kindly but firmly on his arm, and held up his finger in the attitude of listening.

Again the veiled figure spoke, but this time the tones were those of entreaty—

"Oh, spare me—spare me, Reginald—I will never mention her name again—I do not believe her—Neoni never had your love —it was mine—ever mine—oh, tell me that it is mine still!"

As she uttered the last words the veiled figure sunk on her knees, and clasped her hands in entreaty.

"Mercy—mercy, Reginald! send me from you—any where, but do not condemn me to a life-long imprisonment—anything but that, and I will yet bless you!"

The figure started to her feet, and with one hasty glance around her fled from the room.

So sudden and unexpected was this movement that the frightened domestics made way for her to pass, instead of impeding her progress.

The duke and Colonel Dacres, however, followed her as quickly as they could, as soon as they perceived what her intentions were.

Along the top of the grand staircase she fled with the speed of lightning, and there they saw her enter the drawing room.

They followed close upon her steps—they reached the drawing room, but it was tenantless!

CHAPTER LXXII.

DORA ESCAPES FROM THE VAULT—THE EXACTED RANSOM—HARDSHIPS ON THE ROAD—DORA DETERMINED TO VISIT CRAYFORD.

"I hate them all! I hate everybody!" These were the words which came from the clenched teeth of the deformed boy, who had just rushed from the presence of Turnbull and the woman. "Yes, I hate them all, and I hate her, too, but I'll let her go, just to spite Turnbull!"

He made his way towards that outhouse to which Dora had been dragged by Turnbull, and standing upon tip-toes he could manage to touch the key which had been left on the outside of the lock—no one suspecting that it would be interfered with by him or anyone else.

"All right!" he muttered to himself, "now I will make my bargain with her, and if she has lots of money, why, I don't mind letting her out, provided she gives it all to me—and then I will go to the "Rising Sun" and have no end of gin, and Master Johnson will call me one of his best customers."

The boy looked stealthily around him,

to make sure that he was not being watched, and then he climbed up the door, and hold-on by a staple which happened to be in the wall, he contrived with some difficulty to turn the key.

He then slid down the door again, and entered the barn.

He made his way directly towards the little trap door, and felt along the ground until he came to the ring which would raise the trap.

"That's it!" he cried, with an exultant laugh, "I wonder if she's dead—I'll speak to her!"

"Hilloa, hilloa, missus! Ain't you afraid of being eaten up by the rats?"

A gasping sob was all the answer that he received.

"Ho! ho! you're alive—*that's* a comfort—for I don't much fancy going down these here steps exactly, to keep company with a dead body—but I wish you'd speak—do you hear?"

A low moan was the only reply.

"Oh, hang it all—why don't you speak? I tell you I'll let you out if you'll pay me well for doing so!"

The boy dropped the trap, for Dora had rushed up two or three of the steps at those words, which had fanned the last spark of hope into a blaze—for he was frightened.

Dora knocked loudly on the trap door, and by this time her feelings found vent in words—

"Speak to me again, I implore!" cried the voice beneath the trap, "I have money—gold—and all shall be yours if you do but set me free."

The boy again approached the trap, and listened, and when he heard the word gold, a light glistened in his small eyes, and a contortion of the features took place which made them still more frightful to behold, but which in reality did the duty of a smile.

"That's good news at all events," said he to himself, "she says she's got gold—now everybody knows, or ought to know that I would do anything for gold; but perhaps it's all a sell, and she is only doing it to try to get me to open the trap—but I'm too wide awake to be taken in by a woman.

"Speak to me again—oh, speak to me again!" said Dora, and there was terror in her tones.

"Eh? what do you say?" shouted the boy.

"Oh, help me, in Heaven's name, to leave this frightful place, and if money will repay you—I have gold, and all shall be yours."

"Well, hand us up the gold then, missus, and I'll try what I can do."

"But you will deceive me!"

Oh, very well, just as you like, if you

want to stay there as long as the man did last summer, why, well and good—nobody shall say I prevented you—so good-night, and pleasant dreams."

With a crash the trap-door was let down again, and Dora was cut off from all communication with the outer world.

"Stay, stay!" again she cried, and beat upon the trap with all the strength she could command—"stay, oh, stay, and I will give you the gold first."

"Ah, now, that's something like business, let's see the colour of your gold first, and then I will give you a hand out of that grave—for it *is* a grave, although you may not think so."

Dora shuddered; but hastily taking from her pocket the little parcel wrapped in silver paper, which her friend Emily had given her—she handed it up to the boy.

"Hilloa! one, two, three yellow boys—well I never! I didn't expect as much as this, I must say—won't I go and enjoy myself now."

Thus saying, he let go the ring of the trap, and it fell with a loud bang. Well was it for Dora that she had not ventured nearer the top of the flight of steps, or most assuredly that would have been her last moment in life.

But with what horror did poor Dora now contemplate her dreadful situation.

Shut up in a living grave—what was to become of her—she began to fear that insanity would, indeed, now take possession of her brain.

Then came also the recollection of what the boy had said about a man having found a grave in that place.

Oh, how she longed to be once more a prisoner in the asylum! for there she had the kind sympathy of Emily—and many privileges—but here? what had she to hope?

Despair lent strength to her efforts, and she ascended the flight of steps, and pushed the trap door upwards.

It yielded not to her touch.

In that moment of dire despair, Dora breathed a prayer to Heaven for assistance, and once more tried to raise the trap.

After several efforts she felt it give way somewhat, and then Hope again sprung up in her breast.

Again and again she tried, and at length she had the unspeakable happiness of finding that she had raised it about a quarter of a yard.

But how was she to keep it open while she emerged through the aperture? She feared to throw it quite back lest the noise which must inevitably ensue should attract attention.

The door was heavy, and Dora feared

that she should not be able to support the weight much longer.

At this moment her foot struck against something on the corner of the flight of steps, and she for a moment loosed her hold of the trap, and it fell shut.

Dora stooped to feel what it was that she had touched with her foot, in hopes that it might be something large enough to insert in the opening to enable her to pass through.

It was a large jagged stone. It was heavy! but life and death—a horrible death was before her, and what may not be accomplished at such a moment?

She raised the stone, and then placed it close to the hinge in such a manner as to prevent the trap from shutting.

Then agile still, she leapt through the opening, and found herself in the outhouse.

Noiselessly she made her way towards the door which fortunately the boy in his haste to go and enjoy himself had forgotten to lock.

A low paling divided the neglected garden from the adjoining field; this Dora had no difficulty, whatever, in clearing, and then she was free—but without money, friendless, cold, and weak.

Alas, poor Dora!

Little did the loving hearts who so fondly cherished your memory imagine all the horrors to which you were exposed on that night!

For a moment a feeling of such utter desolation came over the heart of Dora that she had great difficulty to save herself from fainting, but the strong will gained the mastery, and with the sense of freedom came also that longing for those dear ones from whom she had been so long separated.

Now Dora asked herself whither should she direct her steps—for those long years she had spent within the walls of the asylum had been an effectual barrier between her and the outer world, so that she had not even heard of the flight of her wicked uncle, nor the restoration of her beloved father to court favour.

Her inclination led her towards London, naturally enough, for she concluded that her loved ones would most likely be located there, and thither she resolved to direct her steps.

How bitterly did she regret the dire necessity there had been to bestow upon the deformed boy all her worldly wealth. She was thus deprived of the means of reaching the metropolis excepting on foot, and her heart almost misgave her when she reflected on the weary days and nights which she must spend upon the road.

However, having once made up her mind what was best to be done, Dora hesitated no longer; but drawing tightly around her a large cloak, which she was fortunate enough to have preserved—she crossed the field, making for the road beyond, which she rightly divined was that which led to London.

She hurried onwards, fearing some untoward interruption to her plans; but the night was dark, and from being unacquainted with that part of the country, she was compelled to slacken her pace—hoping to find some shelter in which to rest her weary limbs until the morning.

The sky had been rapidly darkening the last half hour. The wind came wailing with a low moaning sound over the hills.

And now a low sullen rumbling, the herald of the coming storm was heard, and two large heavy drops of rain fell upon Dora's face.

But the storm, as if in pity for that fragile, lonely wanderer, held up a few moments longer, and Dora's eyes brightened as she perceived a kind of barn, attached to some out-buildings belonging to a small farm house.

"Let the storm come now," she said to herself, in a low voice—"at least, here I may be safe"

Safe and sheltered as it was, the little barn nevertheless seemed to shake in the blast.

The rain was falling heavily, and the wind blew so furiously, driving it in her face that for the first moment she shrunk back, and was forced to grasp at a projecting beam to prevent herself from being blown backward. The next moment her dauntless spirit returned, and raising her head, she shook the rain from her dripping locks.

Though burning with feverish impatience to continue her journey, Dora found herself compelled to wait until morning.

The storm seemed steadily increasing—the wind roared wildly, shaking every beam in the old barn, and the booming of the thunder on the hills was deafening.

Perhaps it was the wildly shrieking tempest, the appalling crash of the angry elements, but an unaccountable depression weighed on Dora's spirits, a creeping feeling of horror which no effort could shake off.

She strove to rouse herself, to reason herself out of the superstitious dread that was taking possession of her, but in vain—a nameless terror had clutched her heart, and would not relax its hold.

And so the hours wore on, and midnight approached, and the storm without seemed to have shrieked and roared and worn itself hoarse, and was at last relapsing into sullen silence.

Exhausted and worn out with the excitement which she had endured the last few hours, Dora tried to settle herself to sleep on the straw which was in one corner of the barn, hoping in sleep to lose the strange feeling that was overpowering her.

She lay down but she wooed the drowsy god in vain; sleep would not come at her call; so she tossed from side to side, wishing vaguely, wildly, morning would come, and listening to the wind as it whistled amongst the trees.

A deathlike stillness reigned around, while the storm was still sullenly grumbling.

It was midnight, and Dora lay with her hands still clasped over her forehead when, suddenly, through the silent night, arose the wild, terrific, appalling cry of "Murder!"

Dora placed her hand upon her ears to shut out, if possible, that awful cry, but her next impulse urged her to sally forth to ascertain from whom that cry arose, and if possible to render assistance.

For this purpose she rose, and hastily throwing around her the cloak she had laid aside, she ventured to the door of the outhouse, and looked forth into the night.

Nothing was to be seen but a pale star twinkling here and there.

Dora passed the threshold of the barn door and stood in the open field. The moon at this instant emerged from behind a cloud, and she discovered, at a short distance, a black object lying on the ground.

An undefined feeling of terror at first took possession of Dora, but this she conquered, and made her way towards the huddled up mass.

It was a human figure—that of a woman; the woman who had helped to consign her to that horrible death in the vault belonging to the house in the occupation of the villain Turnbull.

"And has it come to this? Has it come to this?" asked Dora to herself, in a low voice. "Just God! how inscrutible are thy ways! A few short hours and this woman would have killed me had he bidden her; and here I behold her dead at my feet! Alas, what can be the meaning of this? But this neighbourhood is no longer a safe retreat for me, I must away—away, before my pursuers are on my track!"

Dora rose from the kneeling position in which she had thrown herself when she hoped to have been of assistance, but now as she found the woman was quite dead, she turned and left the spot as quickly as possible.

On—on she speed, fear lending her wings, and stopped not until she became aware of a feeling of unwonted langour. A terror run through her frame, her legs refused any longer to do her bidding, and Dora sunk to the ground insensible.

Hour after hour passed by, and still Dora moved not; but about twelve o'clock in the day she became conscious that a hand was laid upon her face.

Dora started, for she still feared to return to the asylum; and the longing to look once again into the face of her Henry was too strong for her to calmly admit the possibility of such a thing.

But there was no cause for alarm to Dora; the hand that touched her cheek so gently was that of a little child who looked wonderingly into her eyes when she heard her exclamation of fear.

Dora now found that she was not far from some cottages in the occupation of labourers, and she hoped to be able to get some food and rest, and then continue her journey.

"What is your name, dear?" she asked the child.

"Eh?"

"What is your name, dear?"

"Dolly."

"Well, will Dolly give me some milk?"

"Oh, yes—I want you to have some of my breakfast—mother sent me."

Dora began to feel more hopeful, but she was grieved to find that she had great difficulty in rising to her feet.

She managed to do so, however, and the child put her hand in hers.

"Which is Dolly's house?" asked Dora.

"That!" said the child, pointing to one which was a very wilderness of flowers.

"Then I will go to Dolly's house, and she will give me some breakfast?"

"Oh, yes – yes—mother always gives to beggars if they're clean."

Dora's pale cheek flushed a little, but she felt glad to find that she might be mistaken for a beggar, for after all what was she? Friendless—houseless—and without a penny piece with which to purchase herself a morsel of bread.

"Oh, if I had but Starlight!" thought Dora to herself, "how cheerfully would I mount him and cry "Stand!" until I was in possession of sufficient funds to get to London more easily than this weary mode of walking. But there is no help for it."

At this moment a voice from one of the cottages called out "Dolly! Dolly!"

"I'm a comin', mother—don't you see I'm bringing the poor woman with me?"

These last few words were addressed to a woman whose physiognomy was anything but prepossessing, and Dora felt inclined to fly rather than enter the cottage, which owned such a woman for mistress.

"Perhaps you'll come in and rest?" asked the woman.

Dora felt that it would be folly to refuse the woman's offered hospitality, for she was faint and weary with over-exertion, anxiety, and want of food.

Dora entered the cottage, and was surprised that hanging against the walls were swords, guns, and several pistols.

The woman perceived her gaze was at once rivetted upon these things, and said carelessly—

"Oh, you needn't be afraid, they won't go off—they're not loaded."

How Dora longed to get possession of one of those pistols! Of what service might it not be to her in her present expedition—but in order to disarm all suspicion, if any existed in the mind of her hostess, Dora said—

"Oh, I'm glad they're not loaded—but I wonder at that, as you must understand fire-arms so well—may I look at these pistols?"

"No!" said the woman, "they are loaded, and women don't understand such things."

This was good news to Dora, and she resolved to possess herself of one or both of them before she left the cottage.

The woman brought her a bowl of milk and a good sized piece of bread. The milk Dora drank, but she saved a large portion of the bread for some future meal.

When she had finished her repast the woman asked her to lie down and rest, and Dora feeling so weary was only too glad to comply with such a request.

There was a small inner room, in which was a hard sofa, covered with faded cotton.

"There, you can sleep there as long as you like!" said the woman, sullenly, as she banged shut the door.

There was something about this woman's manner which puzzled Dora, and she began, instead of seeking repose to try and remember where she had either seen her or somebody else who greatly resembled her.

She had lain upon the sofa, perhaps some half-hour, when she heard voices in the adjoining room talking in a low voice.

"I tell you it is her! Didn't Mary Ann Beacon say that she had got on one of the asylum cloaks?" said a voice which Dora had not heard before.

"Well, we shall soon see," replied the woman, "for I have sent over to the asylum, and they will be here before four hours have come and gone."

"What is she like?" asked the first voice, "I should like to see her, I've never seen a lunatic in my life."

"Don't be a fool! what should she look like? why all scared and wild like, and I've no doubt but that she will break out in one of her mad fits soon, and then there's

no knowing what she may do—for my part I don't half like it.

"You don't say so! Well, I'm off, so good bye; but I'll look in again in the evening, and then you can tell me about it, you know."

"Very well!" replied the woman; "but she's asleep now; I just want to run to Mrs. Warner's for a few minutes, just you wait here till I come back, there's no fear!"

"All right! but don't stay long, because I must be off, mind."

Dora could hear that the woman left the cottage, closing the door behind her.

The thought of being again shut up in the asylum was agonizing, and Dora began to think what she had better do.

She at once resolved to work upon the fears of the person whom the woman had left to keep guard over her, and rising from the sofa she raised a small table which occupied the centre of the room, and dashed it against the door.

A scream rose from the next room.

"I must be quick and follow up my advantage," said Dora to herself, "or I shall be too late."

With this intention she sallied out into the other room, where she perceived a young girl crouched down on the floor in an agony of terror. When she perceived Dora, she made a rush towards the door, but was too late, for Dora placed her arm against it, and presented the two pistols right in the face of the young girl, who had raised another shriek when she saw her removing them from the wall.

"If you don't keep quiet, I'll shoot you," said Dora, "mind that!"

The girl held her breath.

"Go into that room!" said Dora in a commanding tone of voice.

The girl obeyed—for anywhere was better than being face to face with a mad woman with a brace of pistols.

Dora locked the door upon her warder.

"Now for Crayford!" said she to herself, "now for Crayford—with these two friends I may do wonders."

She turned and left the cottage, secreting beneath her dress the two loaded pistols.

CHAPTER LXXIII.

DORA DEFENDS HERSELF AGAINST TURNBULL—RETRIBUTION—DORA IN GREAT DANGER — HER ENCOUNTER WITH A HIGHWAYMAN.

WE must now return to Dora's father, who was at last located in Kingston House.

Mina is seated by the open window, a

book is lying on her lap; but the young girl's thoughts are far away, for Sir Edward Hargrave and her father have been ordered away with their regiments.

"Mina, dear, how long is it since you heard from Sir Edward?"

"A long time," she replied.

Mina's answer was interrupted by the entrance of a servant with letters that had just come by the post. There were one or two for Mina, and a number for her grandfather; but he put them all aside for one large foreign looking one, with the postmark of Marseilles upon it.

"News at last from Edward Dexter," said the duke, for such we must now call the father of Dora. There was a deep silence while he read— "Listen!" he said, "I will read aloud the letter from the detective."

'Sir—I write as you see from Marseilles, where most unfortunately at this moment I am detained. Nothing could be more unfortunate, for I had just discovered positive information of my chase and was on the point of sailing in pursuit. This is the information—he is at Nice disguised as an Italian, and the companion of a gang of men whom I suspect are conspirators against the government—every hour is of importance, and if you, sir, could go yourself to Nice, you might prevent him again slipping through our fingers.

I remain your obedient servant,
Edward Dexter.'"

Mina came forward, and placing her arm round the shoulders of her kind grandfather said, with much emotion—

"You will not go, dear grandfather—he will escape you even as he escaped Edward, and you may share his fate—long and weary imprisonment."

"I know not, my child, what to say, or what to do! Heaven knows how I shrink from bringing this man to justice—would that he were not my brother; but so long as our search for your dear mother is unavailing, I feel that I ought to leave nothing undone that may lead to her discovery. The more I think of it, the more convinced am I that he knows where she is, and since I have heard from Harvey Davis, that his dog rescued her from the clutches of the villain Turnbull, when she had succeeded in making her escape from Bigmore Asylum—I tremble to think to what perils and hardships, and suffering she may be exposed."

Mina sobbed as though her heart would break.

"I know," added the duke, "that this Turnbull is in the employ of my wicked and unnatural brother, therefore one or other of these two unscrupulous men must seek and find, or I shall feel that my poor Dora has been abandoned by her father who loves her so fondly."

Again Mina pleaded, and this time it was not in vain.

"Dear grandfather," she said "will all leave me? Edward suffered imprisonment and almost death; he has again joined a band of disreputable men, and you will have no chance with him—leave him, dear grandfather, in the hands of the police, and let us hope that justice will at length be done."

"Perhaps you are right, dear child," replied the duke with a fond smile—"perhaps you are right. I must confess that I do not feel so well able to battle with the world now as formerly, and I may be of more service here than in a foreign land, so I will write, my darling, to Edward Dexter, giving him instructions to spare no expense so that justice be done."

"Thanks, thanks, dear grandfather," said Mina, a load of care now removed from her heart. "Thanks, dear grandfather, I now feel that we may together, perhaps, be able to think of some plan to facilitate our search for my dear mother. How strange it is that we have not heard from Dottman."

"It is strange," replied the duke, "but his silence makes me suspect that he has some scheme on foot which, perhaps, leaves no time for letter writing. We may, however, be well assured of this, that he is not able."

"Oh no—no, I am sure that he is doing all that he can do to discover my poor mother. Alas! alas! shall I ever look upon her face again?

"We will still hope and trust that such will be our reward for all the sorrow we have endured through so many weary years. But it is now time for you to retire to rest, my child; these eyes are heavy, and these cheeks have lost all their roses within the last few months."

"Oh grandfather," cried the young girl with much emotion, "I cannot bear to think that I ever allowed myself to feel happy while there was any doubt respecting my poor mother's existence."

"Do not reproach yourself, my child; you knew not until very lately that there were any doubts of your dear mother's death, and therefore, at your age it was not to be expected that a vague, uncertainty should rise up in your mind about it."

"You are always kind, dear grandfather," said the weeping Mina. "But come what may I now feel able to do battle with the world for her dear sake."

"Heaven grant that your courage may never be tested, my beloved child," said

the duke, as he kissed the pure brow that
was bent over him.

*   *   *   *   *

Dora still wandered on, and it was
strange to her to feel the comfort and protection she now knew were within her
reach as she grasped a pistol.

True it is that she shrunk from the
thought of taking human life, but still
there was always the possibility of encountering Turnbull; and it was far from
safe, especially as she had again foiled him,
to do so without knowing that she had in
her possession that which would on an
emergency rid her of his hated presence.

Three o'clock had just chimed upon a
village clock which Dora was approaching,
when she became aware that there was the
tramp of horses feet close behind her.

At first she resolved to crouch down and
conceal herself close to the hedge, but
before she had time to carry her determination into practice the horseman was by her
side.

A cold perspiration broke over the face
of Dora, and her limbs refused to support
her as she sunk to the ground, and saw
distinctly the features of her arch enemy,
Turnbull.

"Ha, ha! I am in luck's way, young
woman," said the villain, with a yell which
resembled more the cry of a beast of prey
than the utterance of a human being. "I
am in luck's way, seemingly. Woa, woa,
Ned!" he added, speaking to the animal
he rode, and which was a creature of great
strength and beauty. "Woa, woa! I
must dismount and place Dora the Duchess
beside me. Ha, ha, ha! here's a turn of
fortune."

Dora had soon recovered her presence of
mind, and as Turnbull was engaged in ty-
ing his horse to a tree, she slipped from
beneath her dress where she had hidden
them one of the pistols she was now fortunately provided with.

Turnbull was completely unarmed, but
Dora feared that he might have pistols in
the holsters of his saddle, and in order to
prevent him from having them within
reach she turned, apparently to fly from
him.

The *ruse* succeeded so far as making
Turnbull pursue her, and being light and
active, Dora had no difficulty in placing a
gate between them.

"Oh, that's your dodge, is it, my beauty,"
said Turnbull with a sneer—"you shall
soon see that two can play at that game."

So saying he placed his foot upon the
bottom bar of the gate, and was just about
to throw his leg over it, when Dora presented the pistol full in his face.

"Advance another step, and I pull the
trigger," cried Dora in a clear determined
voice.

"Fiends and fury! What mean you?
How came you by that weapon?"

"It matters not how I became possessed
of it, suffice it for your satisfaction to know
that I can and will use it if you do not
instantly go your way, and allow me to go
mine."

"Nonsense! you wouldn't kill a fellow in
cold blood."

"I certainly intend to shoot you, and
that instantly, if you do not take yourself
off!" coolly replied Dora.

"But you would be killing your best
friend, for look you, I can tell you where
you may find Mina, and—"

At that loved name the mother's heart
beat almost audibly.

"Ah!" added Turnbull, "you see I can
be more useful to you living than dead. Is
it not so?"

"I know not—but you mentioned my
child—what know you of her?"

"Turn the muzzle of that pistol in
another direction then, and I will tell you
all I know."

"Speak!"

"Not while you present that pistol full
in my face—why, the slightest jerk of your
finger and I should be a dead man."

"Which I intend you should be if you
approach a step nearer!"

"She-devil!" shrieked Turnbull, and as
he did so he rushed upon Dora, with the
intention of striking the pistol from her
hand—but she was upon her guard, and
made a sudden step backward, which movement sent Turnbull sprawling on the
ground.

He quickly regained his feet, and it is
certain that the brutal blow he aimed at
that brave but fragile woman would have
been fatal to her, had he not at that moment
lost his footing.

This accident saved Dora's life, and at
the same time gave her ample time to think
as well as to act.

Dora pulled the trigger of the pistol, and
the bullet did its work. Turnbull fell to
the ground a corpse!

Dora clasped both her hands over her
face and wept.

Yes, tears—bitter tears—such as she
had never thought to shed—such as she
would have denied the possibility of her
shedding over Turnbull—forced themselves
from her eyes, and with hysterical sobs and
strange gasping attempts as it seemed to
speak, she swayed to and fro in almost a
delirium of excitement.

"Unhappy man!" she exclaimed, "would
that it had been otherwise—but God knows
I was sorely tried."

TURNBULL SHOT BY DORA.

There was a wild, haggard look about the countenance of Dora that would have startled any beholder.

Often had she looked on death—often had she believed that her last hour had come—often had she played upon the fears of others, when as Captain Arod she had cried "Stand" on the king's highway—but never had she until to-night taken human life, and she felt all the horrors of her situation.

Her first impulse had been to fly from the hideous spectacle—but her natural kindness of heart over-ruled that impulse, and she now knelt by the side of the man who had so long persecuted her—and would

have given worlds—had they been hers to give—for one sign or token that would tell her he lived and breathed again.

She was about to tear open his vest and ascertain if his heart still beat, when she became conscious that the sound of voices was carried on the air, and she felt all the danger of her present position.

"Thank God!" was her first ejaculation —"if there be life in him there is help at hand." And then, with one more shuddering look at the ghastly face before her she succeeded in reaching the hedge, when she passed into the field beyond, taking care to keep within hearing.

In less than five minutes three men,

DORA.—37.

apparently labourers, made their appearance upon the spot.

"Holy saints defend us!" said the one who seemed to be in advance of the rest. "Holy saints defend us! But what have we here, a bleeding man?"

As those words were uttered the three men came up to where Turnbull was lying.

"Merciful Providence! why he's killed hisself," said another voice.

"Killed himself? how could he kill himself with nothing. I tell you I haven't been a soldier for nothing; that's a bullet wound, and he's been murdered."

Poor Dora had great difficulty in suppressing a groan of anguish from her hiding place.

"But where's the murderer?" asked a third voice.

"Murderer!" repeated Dora.

"That's more nor I can tell ye," replied the first voice. "But let us lose no more time, perhaps the poor fellow isn't dead after all. I will feel if his heart beats."

Oh, who shall say with what intense interest Dora listened for this man's opinion —an opinion which would either make her a murderess, or make her once more to behold, without shrinking, the light of day.

There was a silence of some few minutes —minutes which appeared hours—days to Dora, which was at length broken by the first speaker saying—

"It's no go, he's dead enough, that's quite certain."

"Stop a bit," said another voice, "I'm not so certain of that, for I fancy I saw a movement of the mouth just now, or I'm very much mistaken. Let me come and try if I can feel his heart beat."

Another pause of awful suspense for Dora ensued, and then she heard the man who had last spoken, say—

"He's alive—he's alive! help me to bind up his wound, and we will carry him to yon cottages—it's not far; or better still, let us put him on his horse there."

"No, no, better carry him, Fred, it will only shake him—let's leave the horse until we have safely housed him."

"True, true—Fred's alway right. Poor fellow, I wonder now how he came by this ugly wound; perhaps he did it himself, who knows?"

"Not very likely, seeing that there is nothing to be seen with which he could have done it. No, no, comrades, it's a foul piece of work, and the murderer has managed to escape."

"Well, well, let's lose no time; here's a handkerchief, bind it tight round the arm and across the breast if you can, for if this bleeding don't stop he will never live till we reach the cottages."

There was now a busy kind of hurrying to and fro as the men were engaged in binding up the wound, during which Dora remained a close observer of all that passed from her hiding place.

In a short time all their precautions were taken, and the men raised Turnbull in their arms, and carried him as carefully as might be towards the cottages.

"Thank God!" ejaculated our poor Dora, as soon as the men had removed the body. "Thank God! I am not then a murderess; and yet God knows how sorely I was tried. But now, what is best to be done, doubtles a search will be 'made as soon as these men have time to make the affair known."

Dora thought for a moment, and her eyes fell upon the horse which was still tied to the gate.

"Fortune befriends me at last," she cried almost aloud. "I will mount the horse, and then I may hope, not only to arrive at my destination much sooner than I could otherwise have done, but I shall succeed in distancing my pursuers."

Dora sprung into the saddle, and was rejoiced to find that there was another loaded pistol in the holster, as she replaced the discharged one in its place.

"With these," she said, "I may hope yet to make my way to the metropolis, and then I must search for my Henry, and my child."

As these loved ones came to her recollection, a flood of tears fell from her eyes, but she quickly brushed them away, and put the horse, which was a powerful creature, into a gallop; she soon placed many miles between herself and her bitter enemy, Turnbull.

Dora deemed it unsafe to follow in the steps of the men who had borne away Turnbull, therefore she was compelled for a time to return on the track from which she had come.

This course was the only one she thought it wise to adopt, but she knew at the same time that it was also fraught with danger of another description.

Might she not fall in with some of Turnbull's associates, who would not fail to recapture her; or again she was still in fear lest some of the officials from the asylum might encounter her.

"But the latter danger was less terrible to Dora than that of again being in the power of Turnbull, so she continued her route until she came to a lane which branched off to the left.

She had not proceeded many paces down this lane when she was startled by a mounted man leaping the edge, and who seized the bridle of her horse, as he cried—

"Stand!" in a hoarse, coarse voice, which sent the blood curdling through her veins.

"What would you with me? asked Dora, with as much composure as she could command.

"Your money or your life—but as I prefer the money, and you perhaps think life worth the keeping, give me what you have about you that is valuable and you shall proceed on your way."

Dora resolved to try if there was anything to be got by appealing to the man's generosity, and she said—

"Money and jewels I have none; I possess nothing but this horse and these pistols. I have a long journey to make, will you deprive me of the means of accomplishing it?"

There was a something about Dora which at once seemed to convince the highwayman that she was speaking the truth, for he said—

"Before I answer your question I must ask you one. How is it that you are so well mounted, and yet unprovided with money or other valuables?"

"Simply for this reason—I have been robbed of my money."

"But this horse?"

"I took that to make up for my lost money."

The highwayman laughed, and taking from his pocket several guineas, he handed them to Dora, saying—

"Take these—I am not a bad fellow, though some call me such; but at all events you shall not have reason to complain of him who is known by the name of—

At this moment the clatter of horses' feet was heard upon the road, and the stranger raising his hat gracefully, put spurs to his horse, and was soon lost to sight.

Dora drew up, and concealing herself behind a clump of trees, resolved there to wait until the mounted party, who had evidently given some alarm to the highwayman, had passed by.

CHAPTER LXXIV.

THE TWO MASKED HORSEMEN—ZILLAH IS CARRIED OFF—DORA IS AGAIN PURSUED BY TURNBULL — HER ESCAPE— GOOD FORTUNE.

THE mounted party consisted of three men, and the third seemed to act in the capacity of groom, for he remained some dozen paces behind the two horsemen.

They seemed to be talking very earnestly, and Dora crouched low in the saddle, and

was greatly relieved when she found that their conversation had no reference to herself, and yet that conversation, she knew not why, seemed to be invested with a great deal of interest for her.

"They come!" Dora heard one of the horsemen say to his companion. "Thank the fates, it is yet too dark for them to recognize us even if they saw us."

"Saw us!" re-echoed the other. "If they saw us in the noon-day they would fail to know us, disguised as we are. Ha, ha!"

Dora could see from where she was hiding that the two men wore long cloaks and plumed hats, but so arranged as completely to conceal both face and figure.

The one who had first spoken took a mask from his pocket that was made of some elastic material, and with some exertion, after first securing it below his chin, dragged it over the rest of his face and head. There were small orifices for the eyes, and one for the mouth. When his hat was replaced, then the covering was quite secure, and by any light that would have sufficed to show the nature of it, it would have been seen to have been of a pale sea-green colour, and fitting so tightly as it did to the features, it had a very life-like and horrible aspect.

He then disposed his cloak so around him as wonderfully to increase the apparent bulk of the upper part of his person; but he was careful to leave his hands at perfect liberty.

While the one who had first spoken had been thus engaged in putting the finishing stroke to his disguise, his companion had not been idle, but had also assumed a black silk mask.

This done they both listened attentively. All was still.

"I fancy it was only a false alarm, after all," said the first speaker. "What made you fancy, Fitz, that they would be travelling in this direction at this hour?"

"I had it from Zillah's own servant, that she and her uncles would take this route to Salisbury with some valuable jewels which they want to sell."

"I suppose the old men are rich?" said his companion with indifference, which however was only assumed.

"Rich! why I tell you they are as rich as Crœsus."

"And Zillah?"

"Why, she will inherit her uncle's wealth some of these days, and you, my boy, will then be able to do an old friend a good turn."

There was a pause in the conversation, during which Dora asked herself where she had heard the name of Zillah before.

Not long, however, was she in doubt as to whether or not she only fancied that it was familiar to her, for she here recollected that that was the name of the beautiful young Jewess who had aided her in making an escape from the jeweller's back parlour years before, when the Duke of Kingston, her wicked uncle, was negociating the purchase of one of the diamonds she had brought to offer for sale, belonging to those which had come into her possession through Surlina.

The name, coupled as it was with the mention of the word uncle, convinced Dora, beyond a doubt, that it was no other than her Jewess friend, and this conviction made her only anxious to hear more, in order, if possible, to have it in her power to repay Zillah for her kindness and sympathy to herself.

Again the whispered conference commenced.

"I tell you that she evinces the greatest dislike to me—not to me personally, perhaps," said the younger of the two men, with an accent of self-satisfaction—"Not to myself personally ; but in a fit of romantic confidence she told me she would never marry unless she loved."

"Well, man, and what prevents her loving you? Young—many would call you handsome—and with a good name. True, you have no fortune, but then she will have enough for both."

"Oh, I shouldn't have been afraid of failing in my attempts to win her heart were it not for a little secret she told me."

"Secret?"

"Yes."

"And what may this precious secret be, pray?"

"Simply that she loves somebody else."

His companion gave a low whistle, as he said—

"Oh, that's it, is it? Who may the favoured swain be?"

"That she refused to tell me—I only succeeded in learning his christian name, which was Henry."

Dora was no longer in doubt; it was quite evident that the warm hearted, affectionate girl, upon whom she had made so favourable an impression when dressed as a knight of the road, still continued to think of her as the only being she could ever love.

And now Dora would fain hear more, for she feared that mischief was intended to the beautiful girl by these masked and disguised men.

"Well, the only thing for you to do will be to seize her, and carry her off to some place of security, where you can keep her until she promises to become your wife, and then her fortune will be yours."

"I suppose so; but I don't much like the job, I must confess."

"Oh, you're afraid, are you, of a few tears? But perhaps you will be more afraid of becoming acquainted with the inside of Newgate, which you assuredly will as soon as I split about that little forgery."

"For heaven's sake, do not talk so loud! —the very trees may contain eavesdroppers."

"Then don't give me reason to talk about it. If you are such a poor silly coward as to be afraid of carrying off a girl who will some day be rolling in wealth, merely because she doesn't happen to be in love with you—why I've done, and shall just ride back to town, lodge information against you, and then you—"

"Oh, spare me! spare me!" cried the young man, "Heaven knows how bitterly I have repented of my folly—I was maddened by wine—or you should never have prevailed upon me—".

"Silence!" yelled his companion, "I prevailed upon you—what do you mean? It was your own free will and consent that prompted you to sign that little name to the document."

A groan burst from the lips of the young man.

"And now, forsooth!" added his tormentor "you all at once turn virtuous, and tell me that I prevailed upon you!"

"I meant not to reproach you—Heaven knows I blame myself alone for all this misery—would that I could undo the past."

"Poor drivelling fool!" sneered the other, "it is ever thus with cowards."

"Coward! said you?" Incence me no more, or you will find me no coward!" cried the young man, and his hand clutched the hilt of his sword.

"There—there—don't let us quarrel—I meant not to vex you, man, but you are not yourself to-night. Here am I, pointing out the means whereby you may become wealthy, and all the return I get for my good intentions is to be told that I induced you to forge—"

"Hush! oh, hush! for Heaven's sake! do not utter that frightful word again—if I succeed in marrying this young Jewess all may yet be well, and I may yet know peace."

"If you succeed!" asked his tempter— "what is to prevent you doing so?"

"Many things—I cannot be the villain you would make me—I cannot force that girl to marry me against her will."

"And who wants you to marry her against her will, I ask you—if you are ruled by me you will find that she will be only too willing to accept you for her husband, and then with regard to—to the forgery—"

"Enough—enough! oh, God, enough!" almost shrieked the young man.

He was about to say more when the rumble of wheels came plainly upon the ears of Dora and those of the two horsemen.

The man who appeared to have such influence over his companion, exclaimed—

"Here they come—be prudent, and all will go well. Take the girl from the coach—I will lend you a helping hand, and we will convey her to "The Pines," from whence you may, if you like, rescue her in your own proper person—gratitude will soon give place to love, and then your romantic notions will be satisfied."

"It may be as you say—at all events she will fail to recognize in me the Edward Fairfield whom she rejected."

"Why, your own mother, boy, would fail to recognize you!" added his companion —"but now let us conceal ourselves!"

The two horsemen had just time to draw their horses behind a clump of trees when the coach wheels could now be heard rapidly approaching.

Dora was anxious and curious to know what was about to happen, but she felt how futile would be any attempts she could make to save—or even to warn the poor girl of her approaching danger.

There was some comfort, however, in the knowledge that at least one of the two men who were plotting her destruction seemed to possess many conscientious scruples, and that a feeling of honour—notwithstanding the charge of forgery brought against him by his companion—still held a place in his heart.

In a few minutes the bright dancing reflection of the lamps of Mr. Aaron Jones' carriage flashed upon the hedge, as it whirled rapidly past, thus giving that strange metallic colour to the vegetation which artificial light ever imparts to it.

The two horsemen stood still upon the verge of the shadow cast by the clump of trees, to which he and his companion had secured their horses—and when the carriage got to within a dozen yards of the spot, the elder of the two men, with one bound, got to the middle of the road, and seizing the horse which was upon the near side by the rein, he cried out as the animal was forced back upon its haunches by the suddenness of the attack—

"Is this Mr. Aaron Jones's carriage?

The coachman was so astonished at the apparition of a man in the middle of the road, who to all appearance had risen out of the earth and stopped the horses in their progress, that he nearly fell off the coach-box, but he did manage to save himself from such a catastrophe—and then Dora could hear the voice of the old Jew from the inside of the vehicle, calling out loudly to know what was the matter.

The coachman seemed brave enough in his way, and he began to lash with his long whip at the man who so audaciously stopped the horses.

The footman likewise got down from behind, and was rather confused to know what to do, when the man who had attacked them, and who had received a severe cut or two from the coachman's whip, drew a pistol from the breast of his apparel, and with an execration, shot him dead.

At the sound of the report of a pistol the footman fell to the ground, for he made sure that his last hour had come, and then from some unknown agency, although Dora could have said how it was, the horses found themselves suddenly released from the carriage, and being terrified at the pistol shot, they started off at full speed.

All this was the work of a very few moments, during which old Aaron Jones had made unavailing efforts to get out of the carriage.

Something connected with the fastening of the door—it had evidently been tampered with on that side—impeded him.

Zillah had uttered a faint scream at the commencement of the fray, which was borne to the ears of Dora—but she, Dora, could not see the little clasped hands, nor the blanched cheek of the lovely girl on whose account this cowardly attack had been made.

"What is all this?" Dora heard old Aaron cry out, furiously, "Open the door, somebody! Thomas, where are you? Open the door immediately!"

"Try the other one, uncle!" Dora heard Zillah say, in a strangely subdued voice.

Before Aaron, however, could avail himself of his niece's suggestion, the other door was swung open by the man who wore the green mask, and holding one of the carriage lamps just above the level of his face, so that the light fell full upon the hideous green mask.

Zillah uttered a shriek of horror and despair as the man suddenly thrust his disengaged arm into the carriage, and seizing her by the long ringlets that hung in such luxuriance down her neck and shoulders, he had her out in a moment.

Dora, too, at this stage of the proceedings, uttered a shriek, and it was well for her that the man was too busily engaged to take any notice of it, or certain it is that it would have been many a long day before Dora would have been able to say that she was free to go and come as she chose.

She instantly felt the danger to which her imprudence might have exposed her, and it was with no small feeling of relief that she heard old Aaron shout out in a voice of rage—

"Hold, villain! devil!"

Smash went the carriage lamp right in his face, and he fell backwards into the coach.

The light was extinguished, and then a deep hollow voice, cried—

"Ha, ha, ha!"

Half stunned as old Aaron Jones was, however, he rose again and dashed himself out of the carriage into the roadway, shouting—

"Help! murder! thieves! Name your price, villains; but give me back my Zillah. Oh, God! let me hear but one shriek from you, my child, that I may know which way to fly to your rescue."

A bewildering scream rose upon the night air, and then Dora saw approaching from behind some trees, a lumbering, wheezing, odd-looking hackney coach, drawn by a couple of horses that looked coal black in the intense darkness of the road, which was not even pretended to be lighted.

It halted in the deep shadow of those trees behind which the two horsemen had at first concealed themselves.

"Uncle! uncle!" cried a voice.

"Follow us if you dare! ha, ha, ha!" shouted the strange sepulchral tones of the man with the green mask, and then poor Aaron felt sure that it was in the coach that rolled so rapidly away that Zillah was borne from him.

It may be easily imagined with what feelings Dora had been made an unwilling spectatress of that foul deed, and with a choking kind of sob, she said, half aloud—

"God help you now, poor Zillah, for I cannot."

It was with a sensation of relief that Dora now urged her horse on in the opposite direction to that pursued by the men who had acted the part of good samaritans to the villain, Turnbull.

She had galloped some few miles, when she became aware that she was nearing a village.

She now asked herself what course she had better pursue, for now that she was in the possession of several guineas, to which she was indebted to the generous highwayman, she had serious thoughts of endeavouring to procure a masculine costume in order the better to make her way to the metropolis.

With the intention therefore of putting her plans into execution as speedily as possible, she put her horse into a gallop.

Not very far, however, had she proceeded on her way, when she was alike dismayed and surprised to hear the trampling of horses feet fast approaching, and with that conviction also, that somebody was in hot pursuit of her, for now she could distinctly hear shouts in high, coarse accents, of "stop her—stop her!"

At first Dora was in hopes that her ears might have deceived her—that it was her imagination alone which gave to those tones the well known accent which belonged alone to Turnbull; but not long could poor Dora thus hope that she had been deceived, for now clearly and distinctly was borne upon the air the words, "Thief! murderess! convict! A hundred pounds reward for any one who succeeds in taking her dead or alive!"

The creature upon which Dora was mounted was not to be compared to Starlight, either for intelligence or swiftness—nevertheless, it was a strong, powerful animal, and well used to obey the rein.

Dora urged it on to its utmost swiftness, and although she dared not even look back, still she had the satisfaction of knowing that she must be fast distancing her pursuers, for the shouts now only came faintly upon her ears.

"Oh, for some refuge!" she murmured to herself, "oh for some refuge, if it be only for one short hour."

Still she continued to urge on her horse, and at length, to her great joy, she perceived, not far distant, some houses, from the chimneys of several of which the smoke was curling up into the air.

Dora now ventured to look round, and to her great joy she perceived that she was so far a-head of her pursuers that if she could succeed in making a friend of any of the inhabitants in those little cottages, all might yet be well.

For this purpose she thought it best to dismount, and turned her horse into a field, in which there were already cattle grazing.

Dora had too often watched the operations of Dottman not to understand perfectly well how to divest the horse of its saddle and bridle, and in less than a minute she had succeeded in hiding it under the hedge.

"Now," said she to herself, "you will pass muster with the rest, and I shall be able to come and claim your good services again, I hope.

She now sped on towards the first of the cottages, and knocked at the door for admittance. No answer was given to her summons, and Dora pushing it gently, found that the door yielded to her touch, and she entered. The persons in that cottage must have been very deeply engaged, not to have heard either the knock or the intrusion of a stranger.

For a moment Dora stood gazing through the little casement—for from it she commanded a view of the road, and in less than ten minutes she had the satisfaction of seeing several mounted men pass.

They were all talking loudly and gesticulating, and Dora could now and then catch sufficient of their conversation to know that it had reference to herself.

"I tell you she must be hiding under the hedge somewhere, for a woman mounted on a horse is not a thing to be easily overlooked."

"And my horse!" yelled Turnbull—"to think that I should have supplied her with the means of escape; but I'll have her yet—I'll have her yet—and then—then—"

The diabolical expression which came over the bloated features of Turnbull, made him perfectly hideous, and his rage was such that he found it impossible to conclude his sentence; but no doubt it would have been an attempt to say what he would make the hapless Dora suffer as soon as ever she was once more in his power.

Little did he think that his victim was even then watching his gesticulations from the cottage casement—or that he had actually passed his own horse, who was quietly grazing where Dora had left him.

The mounted party seemed to be quite convinced by this time that Dora was no where to be found behind the hedge, and therefore they put spurs to their horses and galloped off down the road at as brisk a pace as they could command, feeling that they must soon overtake her.

We will now leave Turnbull and his men, and look into that little cottage where our Dora had taken refuge.

CHAPTER LXXV.

DORA TAKES REFUGE IN A COTTAGE WHERE SHE MEETS WITH AN OLD ACQUAINTANCE —THE SISTERS' CONFERENCE—DORA'S INTERVIEW WITH THE DUCHESS OF KINGSTON.

As soon as Dora found that she had so far succeeded as to mislead her pursuers, and that at least she was safe for the present, at all events, from the persecutions of her old enemy, Turnbull, she began to turn her attention to the surroundings of the little cottage, where she had unbidden taken up her abode for a short time at least.

The room in which Dora found herself, and which opened immediately on to the lane, was simply furnished, and yet there were some articles here and there which spoke of refinement and education.

There was a guitar, close to which lay a piece of manuscript music—there again was a beautifully inlaid writing case, and upon a table in the centre of the room stood an open work-box.

Dora looked round well pleased so far; and yet these little luxuries seemed to have found their way there from some happy home perhaps, for the rest of the furniture was mean and common enough.

The flowers in an old, broken tumbler, which stood on the window sill, were elegantly arranged, however; but it was evident that they had received no attention from the presiding genius of the place for several days—and there was dust, and a look of neglect about everything which made Dora think at first that she was alone in that cottage.

Not long, however, was she to so think, for from the room above issued the sound of voices.

"You are better now, dearest sister," Dora heard, in a low, sweet voice—evidently belonging to a young girl. "You are better now, dearest sister—you have slept long, and I have never left your side."

"Yes, dear, I am better," was the feeble reply, "I am better—as well as I shall be in this weary world."

"Oh, do not talk so, you will get quite well now that we have found each other, and we will never, never part again."

"No, Stella, I must not suffer you to deceive either yourself or me—I feel that I am dying; but I thank God that He has permitted me to look once more upon your dear face. Do not clasp my hand so, but let me speak to you while I may."

"Yes, yes, dear!" replied the young girl, "you said you had something of importance to communicate to me—something that would make you feel happier after having said it. Tell me now, dear—I will listen, so, with my hand resting on your hand to which my lips are pressed."

Dora could hear a choking sob, and had some thoughts of leaving that cottage, for her feeling of delicacy would not permit her to play the part of listener to a conversation which was evidently intended only for the ears of the young girl.

She had turned to leave the cottage, and was only waiting for the conversation to commence again in order to do so unheard, when the next sentence uttered by the invalid rooted her to the spot, and she felt that she should be justified in listening.

"It is of my husband, dear Stella, that I would speak."

"The Duke of Kingston? yes, go on, dear, I am listening."

"Oh, call him not the Duke of Kingston—he is not such—never should have been!"

"How? what mean you, Laura?"

"I mean that Reginald Hardacre should never have assumed that title."

"But his brother, you know, dear, had forfeited his title and estates through being mixed up with the Jacobites."

"His brother!" said the invalid with a slight tone of impatience.

"Yes, dear! but we will talk no more about that now, it only excites you, and you know the doctor said that the greatest care was necessary."

"But I must speak now, Stella, while I have yet time—I will do a tardy act of justice to one who sought me years ago, and I promised to befriend her—but alas! I had no power to do so."

"Go on, dear!" said the gentle voice again, "I will not interrupt you."

"That is well!"

There was a silence now of some minutes duration, during which Dora could hear her heart beat audibly. What was she about to hear that would probably affect the whole of her future life?—for she could no longer doubt the fact that, by some mysterious over-ruling of Providence, she had been brought beneath the same roof with the hapless Duchess of Kingston, the unhappy wife of her wicked uncle.

At length the silence was broken by the invalid saying—

"I have not time, dear Stella, to tell you what made me the wreck you see now before you—that must ever remain a secret, locked up in my own breast; neither need I detail how, when quite a girl—almost a child, I may say—I gave my heart to Reginald, nor how he crushed and trampled upon those holy affections which should ever be held most sacred; suffice it to say that after I had married him I found, too late, that he cared not for me—nay, rather avoided being in my society a minute longer than the exigencies of society required. It is of other matters that I would speak.

"I was very dear to his father—was present when he died—and in the interview I had with him just before he breathed his last, he made known to me the fact that he had only one son—one legitimate son, namely Lionel."

"Oh, heavens!" exclaimed Stella—what would you say?"

"Merely this, dear, that I had not married a duke as I supposed; but this knowledge made me rather cling the more to him, for I would have sought to make up to him in a happy married life the loss of a paltry title.

"When the duke, his father—for he was his father—made me acquainted with the dreadful fact, he gave into my hands some private papers and documents, which he feared might pass into other keeping, saying as he did so, that he felt sure they would be safe with me, and urging me to do my best, when he was no more, to persuade Reginald to acknowledge his brother's claim to the title and estates, inasmuch as he, the old duke, had taken care to provide amply for all Reginald's wants.

"I need not say, Stella, to you how anxious I was that justice should be done, at least, to his brother's child, Dora; and I pictured to myself the happiness we might yet enjoy, far away from England, in the reflection that we had done what was right.

"Accident soon placed in my hands the means of trying to carry out my project, for one day a servant announced that a young lady wished to speak to me on matters of importance."

"And this young lady," said the young girl, "was Dora."

"Exactly so. I saw her and was at once captivated, I may say, by her beauty and ingenuousness; when she left me it was with the understanding that I would do my best to befriend her.

"Reginald had been dining out, and when he returned in the evening, I saw he was in no mood to be spoken to, so I gave up my intention of doing so until the next day.

"On that next day there was confusion and dismay in Kingston House—a young girl had been seized and accused of attempting to set fire to the house—that young girl was his niece, Dora.

"As soon as I became aware of the fact, I resolved to do my best to save her, and sought Reginald, and made him acquainted with all that his father had told me."

"And he relented?" Dora heard Stella ask.

A deep groan was the reply—and after a minute's pause, the Duchess of Kingston said—

"Far from relenting—he made me a prisoner in one of the turret chambers—where I was delivered over to the care of a Greek, who brought me food and water at stated intervals."

"Alas! alas, my sister!" burst, in sobbing accents, from the lips of the young girl. "But you are ill—tell me—oh, tell me what you wish me to do to avenge you!"

"And is it for the dying to talk of vengeance, Stella? No—no—I would have you seek Dora, that she may lay claim in her own right to the Kingston title and estates. She has suffered much—perhaps

STELLA LYNDHURST, SISTER TO THE DUCHESS OF KINGSTON.

more than I have done—for she was torn from a husband who loved her, while I was in reality alone in the world."

"No—no—not alone, dear—had you not your Stella?"

"Yes, dearest—but I could not communicate with you, and I taught myself to look upon my prison chamber as my grave."

The unhappy Duchess breathed not to that gentle young heart the fact that her husband had in reality stood by while the death-dealing phial was flung into her chamber.

When next the Duchess spoke it was in faint and faltering accents—she said—

"I know not where to tell you, my DORA.—38.

Stella, to seek Dora Dacres—but I can tell you that her father is now in the family mansion, Kingston House. I saw him there not long since, in company with the husband of Dora; I was weak and ill, and scarcely knew what I said or what I did—but my impression now is that they were searching for some of the old duke's private papers. If I had had time I should have pointed out to them a secret drawer, in which they would have found the full particulars regarding Reginald's adoption; but I feared that they would think me mad, so I fled—fled till I reached the drawing room, in which hangs a portrait of Charles the First, and behind which is a secret spring, which being pressed inwards causes the panel to open, and so gives ingress to the next house."

"Of this spring I availed myself, and so escaped. I rested not until I found you, knowing that you would faithfully fulfil my dying wishes to the letter."

"Oh, say not such dreadful words, dear, dear Laury—I cannot lose you so soon after seeing your dear face once again!"

The fiat, dear girl, has gone forth, and perhaps this night my soul may be at rest and peace. But I would fain, now, while I have strength, impress upon you my dying injunction to find Dora, and tell her all that I have communicated to you."

"I will—I will!" replied Stella—"but hush! who knocks here? I will not leave you long, dear—I will return immediately."

It will be necessary to inform the reader that the knock at the cottage door which had interrupted the conference between the Duchess of Kingston and her sister Stella, was given by Dora, who was anxious to soothe as much as might be the dying moments of the duchess. For this purpose she resolved to make her presence known, and also the fact that she had heard the conversation between the sisters which so nearly concerned herself and those dearer to her than life.

Scarcely had the sound died away when a light footstep was heard descending the little staircase which led to the chamber above, and Dora beheld a young girl, about eighteen years of age, whose ingenious countenance was shaded by a wealth of clustering ringlets which took so many different shades, according to the light in which she stood, that it would have been difficult to have defined their precise colour. There was, however, an unmistakable look of sadness—almost melancholy, about the deep blue eyes which at once enlisted all Dora's womanly sympathies in her behalf.

As soon, therefore, as Stella was fairly in the apartment in which Dora found herself, and gently closed behind her the door which led to the flight of stairs, Dora advanced towards her, and holding out her hand, said with one of her kind, gentle smiles—

"You do not know me, that is, by sight; but when I tell you I have been unintentionally a listener to the conversation between you and your sister.—"

"You madam?" said Stella, the rich blood mantling her cheek and brow, " you, madam! I should not have thought, to have looked at you, that you could have played so unworthy a part as to—"

"Listen to a conversation which did not or which should not have interested a stranger, you would say?" interrupted Dora.

"Exactly so," replied Stella.

"But what," said Dora, in a voice broken with emotion—"what would you say to that stranger if she could be the means of bringing some comfort to the crushed and broken heart of her who is now anxiously awaiting your return to her death-bed."

"Oh!" said Stella, clasping her hands, "tell me—tell me who and what you are! Do not raise hopes which can never be realised—can you do aught to soothe her troubled mind, if so, believe me a life-long gratitude shall be yours."

"I can," said Dora gently—"I can tell her where to find this Dora about whom she is so anxious."

"Is it possible? Oh come with me at once to her chamber—you look kind and good, and I will trust you."

"You may do so," said Dora, "for I am that Dora of whom she spoke."

"Oh, Heaven be praised!" said Stella, clasping her hands, while the tears flowed down her cheeks—"at least, one source of uneasiness will be removed."

Stella would have at once led Dora into the presence of her sister, but the latter drew back and told her first to go and prepare her for her visit.

"Yes, yes—thank you; it will be better so. Stay here and I will quickly return."

When Stella entered the sick room, what was her surprise to see her sister seated upright in her bed, and with clasped hands, and eyes fixed on the door.

"Bring her to me—Oh, bring her to me!" she cried. "I heard her voice, and I must see her while there is yet time."

No sooner were the words uttered, than Dora stood on the threshold of that small apartment where lay the dying Duchess of Kingston.

CHAPTER LXXVI.

DEATH OF THE DUCHESS OF KINGSTON— DORA IS CALLED TO HER FATHER'S SIDE —THE WICKED UNCLE MEETS WITH HIS DESERTS—MINA'S MARRIAGE.

DORA could not but feel some degree of curiosity to know why the Duchess of Kingston had so great a desire to see her, but she was not long kept in suspense, for the invalid, no sooner had Dora fairly entered the room and closed the door behind her, clasped her hands imploringly, saying as she did so—

"Oh, say that you will not return evil for evil! Say that you will do your best to save him—my husband—from the penalty of his crimes. Speak, oh speak to

me! Do you not see that I am dying—
—dying—and you will not attend to my last
prayer?"

Dora was terrified—so vehemently, so
frantically did the dying woman throw
her arms above her head as though, by
that means, she would call down the assistance of heaven, either to bless or curse
the injured woman who now stood before
her, according as she should fulfil or not
her last request.

At length Dora spoke gently and firmly.

As far as I and mine are concerned the
past is freely forgiven; and even now,
rather than bring down punishment upon
him—cruel and implacable as he has been
to me and mine—I would fain give up my
claim to these titles and estates; but that
cannot be; he has offended against the laws
of his country, and my influence would be
vain."

"She knows not then—she knows not—"
shrieked the Duchess of Kingston—"that
Reginald no longer possesses the lands belonging to the Kingston estates."

"Does not possess them?" asked Dora,
now deeply interested in her turn.

"No, no, no! Lionel—your father,
girl—has resumed the title, and my Reginald is a wanderer and an outcast!"

"Oh, just Heaven!" burst from the lips
of Dora. "Is my father, then, still in
life?"

The news had come too suddenly upon
Dora after all she had suffered; and she
was obliged to accept the assistance of
Stella to reach a chair which was on the
other side of the fire-place.

"I tell you yes—your father is now Duke
of Kingston, and you will yet be Dora the
Duchess. Can you not, therefore, pity
him, who is nothing now but a scorn and
a bye-word?"

"I do pity him for your sake; and
believe me, if ever I have it in my power
to befriend him, I will not forget the promise I now make to his injured wife."

"It is false—false! He was good, kind
and—

Stella rushed to the bedside, and raised
her sister in her arms—but the dews of
death were gathered upon that brow where
once beauty had set her impress.

"Remember—remember!" was all that
could be heard issuing from the lips of the
still loving, though cruelly neglected wife;
and in another moment all was still—they
stood by the bed of death.

It was some minutes ere Dora succeeded
in disengaging the bereaved Stella from
the inanimate form of her sister, but when
at length she could be made to listen to
the low, sweet tones of Dora's voice, she
was comforted and upheld, and blessed

God that he had sent her such a friend in
her hour of need.

It was Dora now—who totally forgetful
of the change which had taken place in her
own circumstances and fortunes—to comfort the afflicted girl.

And it would seem that even now she
was to meet with her reward for her chari-
table purposes, for scarcely two hours had
elapsed since the death of the duchess,
when another visitor applied for admittance at the cottage door.

The old woman who acted as servant, companion, and humble friend to Stella Lyndhurst, answered the summons.

The aged man had merely asked if the
woman's mistress was at home, when Dora,
from an inner apartment, recognized the
tones of her faithful and valued friend,
Dottman.

She waited not to hear more—she could
not, after so many years of absence; now
to think that, at least, one of her best
friends was so near to her, was joy indeed,
and she rushed, so to speak, and in another
moment had clasped one of Dottman's
hands in both of hers.

"At last—at last!" she cried—"do we
indeed meet at last, dear friend?"

"Ay, ay," said Dottman, as he wiped
a tear which was no disgrace to him, old
soldier that he was. "Ay, ay—but you
have suffered much; but you have not
been alone in suffering, for those whom you
love have sorrowed with you to the full."

"I know it—I feel it! But oh! tell
me—do you know aught of my Henry—of
Mina?"

"Much, much—but it is all good, and
therefore I hope you have shed your last
tears."

By this time Stella had quietly withdrawn
from the apartment from which Dora and
Dottman found themselves—to that chamber which contained all that remained of
her much loved sister.

In a short time Dottman had made Dora
acquainted with all that is known to the reader regarding Henry, her father, and Mina
—and then he told her of how he had gone
to seek her at the asylum, but was too late,
and, finally, how he was fortunate enough
to have an interview with Emily, and how
from what she could tell him of her escape
from the ruins of Brocklehurst, he had
traced her step by step to the cottage.

It was agreed now that Dottman should
hasten with all speed to Kingston House,
and there apprise the duke of the recovery
of his beloved Dora. Henry was expected
to arrive at Kingston House in the beginning of the following week. Mina was
there, as the reader is already aware; and
Sir Edward Hargrave had obtained leave

of absence for a few months, during which it was arranged that Mina was to become his bride.

At nightfall Dottman, pressing his lips affectionately and respectfully on the hand of her who had been so long to him as some vision of another world, took his departure for Kingston House; thither we will precede him.

The Duke of Kingston sat alone in his library; he had that morning found a document which changed the whole current of his feelings towards his unnatural brother—that document, in fact, of which the Duchess of Kingston spoke. In it he found a record of the birth of Reginald, and his father's fondness for the boy, to the exclusion almost of his other son, Lionel.

There was some natural bitterness in the mind of the Duke of Kingston against the injustice which had led his father thus to give the preference to one who should never have been put in competition with his legitimate son; but this feeling soon passed away, for he cared not now for wealth for its own sake—and he had began to realize the fact in his own mind that Dora was no more. What cared he then for titles and estates? Mina was about to contract a wealthy marriage with one who loved her tenderly—then he could die in peace.

It was in the midst of such reflections that a footman announced the return of Dottman.

For a moment there was hope and expectation in the countenance of the duke as Dottman entered the room; but the latter seeing a great change, for the worse, had taken place in the looks of his old friend and master, put a guard upon eye and lip as the duke asked him if he had heard aught of Dora.

For a moment Dottman paused, then saying to himself—"Pshaw! joy never kills!—he detailed to the duke all that had taken place, and how he had really seen and spoken to Dora at the cottage.

"I will go to her! I will go to her!" cried the duke, almost beside himself with joy—but before he could reach the door, he staggered back into the chair he had just left, pressing his hand upon his heart.

Dottman instantly rang for assistance, and despatched a man for medical assistance, who upon regarding his patient some minutes attentively, shook his head and whispered to poor Mina, that there was very little hope that her grandfather would live many days.

The tidings overwhelmed the fair girl with unutterable sorrow, which not even the hope of soon seeing her dear mother could enable her to control.

As soon as Dottman saw that his presence could be dispensed with, he made his way again to that cottage where he had left Dora performing those acts of friendship which she knew so well how to offer to the unhappy Stella.

Dottman had not time to choose his words in making known to Dora the purport of his return, but she instantly guessed that something was amiss, and looking at him earnestly, she said—

"Tell me, dear friend, is aught amiss? Mina—oh, God! she is well?"

"Quite well—but your father—"

"Oh, what of him?"

"Is seriously, dangerously ill; and you must be ready in a very short time to return with me if you would see him alive."

Poor Dora burst into tears.

"Alas—alas!" she cried, "that this deep grief should fall upon me just now. But I will be with you immediately."

There was no difficulty in making Stella see the necessity there was for her friend's speedy departure, and in less than half-an-hour Dora was on her way, with as much speed as two good post-horses were capable of using, to Kingston House.

When the good duke was made aware that Dottman was gone to fetch Dora to his side—at the prospect of again beholding this beloved child—the very memory of his disease vanished. The poor, over-laboured weary heart indeed beat loud, and with many a jerk and spasm. He heeded it not—Nature claimed her own—claimed it in scorn of death.

In that library, now associated with so many painful recollections, he sat dressed with his usual precision—his countenance, however, revealing great emotion—and the sickly flush came and went on the bronzed cheek, and the eye watched the hand of the clock, and the ear lingered for a foot-tread along the corridor. At length the sound was heard—steps—he sprung to his feet and stood on the hearth — beside him stood Mina, breathless with expectation, nervously clasping the arm of her beloved grandfather. Her breast heaved—her colour went and came—her eyes were raised—her lips murmured.

Dottman entered the library first—the duke's eyes rested on him eagerly for a moment, and strained onward across the threshold—Dora came next—involuntarily he opened his arms and clasped that loved one to his heart! For a moment Dora rested her head upon his bosom, then in her turn she opened her arms, and Mina for the first time for many long weary years nestled close to a mother's heart.

The duke's hands wandered in a dreamy kind of fashion to the head of mother and child, and there rested for one brief moment as he bowed his head upon the shoulder of Dora.

When he raised his head all present were struck and appalled at the sudden change that had come over his countenance. There was a film upon the eye—a shadow on the aspect—the words failed his lips—he sunk on the seat beside him. His left hand rested on the table on which were papers and documents, and the fingers played with them, as the bed-ridden, dying sufferer plays with the coverlid he will soon exchange for the winding sheet. But his right hand seemed to feel as though in the dark for the recovered daughter, and having touched what it sought, feebly drew Dora nearer and nearer. Alas! that this happiness so long missed and pined for should slip away from him, as it were, the moment it appeared, hurried away as the circle on the ocean, which is scarce seen ere it vanishes into infinity. Suddenly both hands were still—the head fell back—joy had burst asunder the last ligaments so fretted away in sorrow.

The sounds arising from the busy world without made themselves heard in that still library—but there was one in that room as in the grave, for whom the boom on the wave had no sound, and the march of the deep no tide. Amidst promises of home and union and peace Death strode into the household ring, and seated itself calm and still—looked life-like—warm hearts throbbing round it—lofty hope fluttering upward—Love kneeling at its feet.

* * * * *

Never, perhaps, had the Central Criminal Court been more crowded than on the 4th of August, 18—, and that not merely with the " vulgar herd," but peers and peeresses and M.P.'s had not disdained to shew themselves there.

The length of time elapsing between the murders and the arrest of the accused man—the strange circumstances of the whole thing, and above all the rank and fame of those most nearly concerned—all these things made the trial of Reginald, formerly Duke of Kingston, an exciting one.

Long before it was called on you might have seen in a distant corner, where they see without being noticed, a grey-headed man and two ladies, No one noticed Dottman, Dora, and Mina, and no one guessed who they were.

An eminent criminal law counsel had been retained for the prosecution, and for the prisoner were retained men of equal eminence.

A few more moments of anxious expectation and then the trial was called on, and the next minute Reginald, known as the Duke of Kingston, appeared—his form erect, and his countenance hard and set in all its dark expression, boldly facing them all. A murmur arose, which was instantly repressed—the indictment was read, and the question how the prisoner pleaded asked.

There was a dead silence. The prisoner leaned slightly forward, glanced around, and answered clearly and deliberately " Not Guilty."

As the words passed his lips his eyes met those of Henry Dacres, fixed on him with that watchful, steady gaze he remembered so well, and dreaded even now so much, and he turned aside with a fiercely muttered curse.

The trial lasted many hours, and at length the jury retired, and there was a silence. The prisoner leaned coolly back with apparent carelessness; but in reality, sick and faint with the agony of suspense—so that an hour, that was like years, passed, and then the jury re-appeared. The judge asked the usual question, and you might have heard a pin drop as the foreman spoke, " Guilty !"

A dead fearful silence for a moment, then ensued, and the judge said—" Prisoner at the bar, have you anything to say why sentence of death shall not be passed upon you?"

" If I have, it is useless !" said he recklessly—" no I have nothing to say."

The judge calmly assumed the black cap, and passed sentence of death for the wilful murders of Henry Van Esling, Johan Surlina, and William Hillyard, his valet—concluding in the usual manner, " May God have mercy on your soul."

Then the prisoner turned towards him with all his fiendish passions concentrated in his dark face and black lurid eyes—

" God ?" said the atheist, " there is no God! I answer as one has done before me—after death is nothingness."

Alone now, indeed, alone with his dark atheism—alone with his heavy guilt, and the weight of the fearful defiance he had hurled against Heaven.

There he sat, bending forward, his head resting on his hands, his hair falling over his brow, and his lurid black eyes raised to the barred window with an expression of fierce, reckless defiance. He did not fear death because he could not realize that he was to die—he did not fear death, but he could not face eternity—he dared not acknowledge or believe in a God he had defied in every thought, word, and deed of his life. But with all that he feared the night worst of all; it closed in round him dark, gloomy, and heavy. He had a vague dread of lying down—of sleeping—of the silence.

But with the morning the gloomy shades which to the assassin had filled the night, vanished, and once more the man was the desperate, hardened atheist, fiercely refusing even to see the chaplain, saying, "that he had lived without a priest, and would die without a priest."

But we will now take leave of this unhappy man—suffice it to say, that in due course of time he paid the penalty of his aggravated crimes by suffering death at the hands of his fellow man. Henry Dacres could not consent to Dora's desire to carry out the last wishes of the unhappy Duchess of Kingston—his crimes were too great, and the man himself too hardened in iniquity to make it desirable to let him loose again upon society; and so we will now leave him to that higher tribunal from which there is no appeal.

*   *   *   *   *

It is just one year since the death of Dora's father, that a joyous party is assembled in the state drawing room of Kingston House, for Mina—the Mina whose steps we have followed through so many years, is about to bestow her hand upon him who has so long possessed her heart. Henry Dacres has recovered from the wound which for so many years made him an invalid, and was looking on that day young and handsome; and there is a world of love in his dark eye as he gazes upon his cherished wife, who is holding Mina's hand in her's. A venerable grey-headed old man is there too, and gazes with fond affection at both mother and daughter.

"Dottman," said Mina, with a smile, "years ago you promised to look after Starlight for me—young Mr. Gray, who has now taken the old mill at Crayford, since his grandfather's death, has sent me the beautiful Arabian, and says he has kept it all these years in order to make me a present of it on my wedding day."

There is a confusion at the door—voices—footsteps—the carriages have arrived for the bridal party. Our task is done, and the wedding party go home to Kingston House to breakfast—at the house of the bride's mother—"DORA THE DUCHESS."

THE END.